The man in charge smiled as he surveyed the Group. Draeger told himself that the devil probably smiled the same way every time he opened his front gate.

"We live in interesting times, gentlemen. The country is in the hands of people who insist on knowing everything about everyone except our declared enemies. They have broken the weapons of the intelligence community. You are the point of the new spear. We *must* have information. I will see that it's properly disseminated. If we cannot protect the country, we can assure it's not blind. When the sacrifices threaten to break you, remember, you don't have a task—you have a mission."

DONALD E. McQUINN

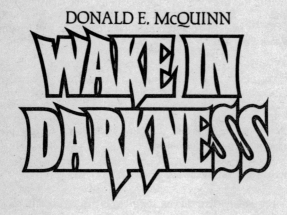

# WAKE IN DARKNESS

A TOM DOHERTY ASSOCIATES BOOK

## ACKNOWLEDGMENTS

I would like to express my appreciation for the many kindnesses extended me by the people of the Philippines. Whatever course their future takes, I hope it brings them the peace and happiness they so richly deserve.

Copyright © 1981 by Donald E. McQuinn

Reprinted by arrangement with Macmillan Publishing Co., Inc.

A TOR Book
Published by Tom Doherty Associates, 8-10 W. 36th St., New York City, N.Y. 10018

First printing, February 1984

ISBN: 0-812-58552-6
ISBN: CAN. ED. 0-812-58553-4

Printed in the United States of America

Distributed by Pinnacle Books, 1430 Broadway, New York, N.Y. 10018

*For my mother,
with love, gratitude,
and in the shared memory
of my father*

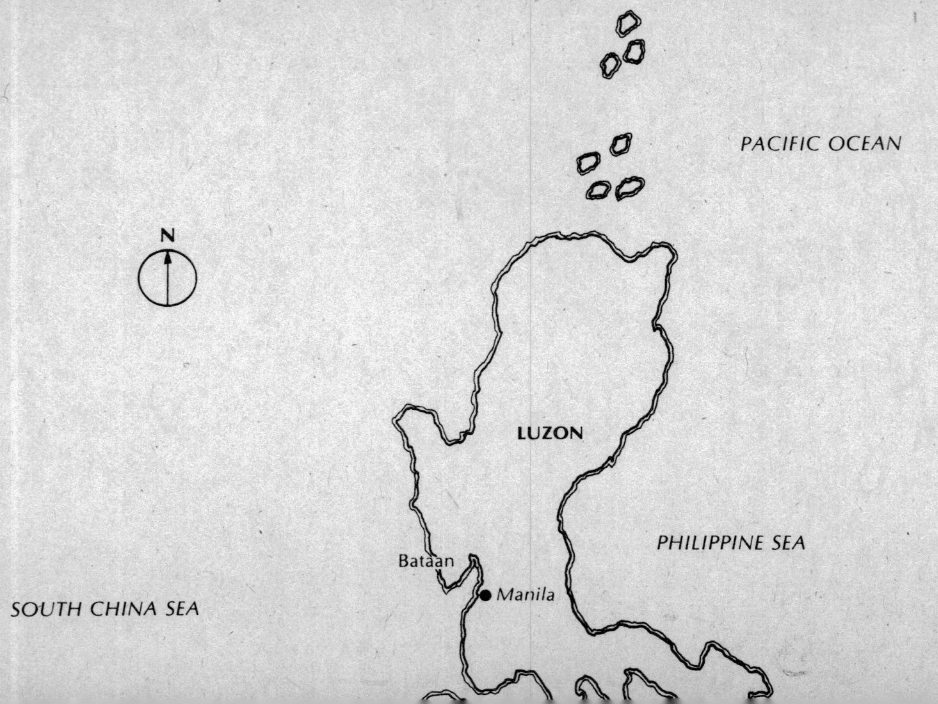
PACIFIC OCEAN
N
LUZON
PHILIPPINE SEA
Bataan
Manila
SOUTH CHINA SEA

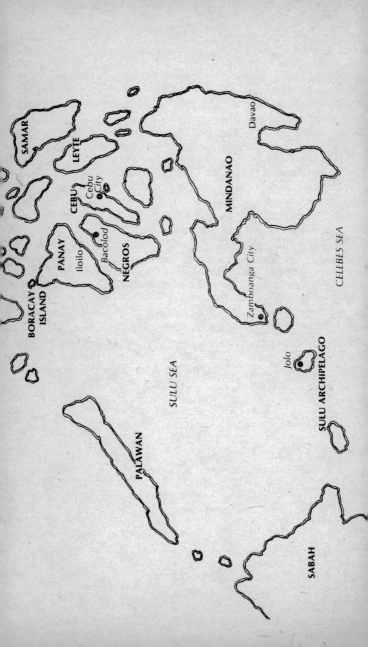

SAMAR

LEYTE

CEBU

Cebu
City

BORACAY
ISLAND

PANAY

Iloilo

Bacolod

NEGROS

MINDANAO

Davao

Zamboanga City

CELEBES SEA

SULU SEA

Jolo

SULU ARCHIPELAGO

PALAWAN

SABAH

The whistle.

It is the shining weld that holds together the pieces of my earliest memory, the mine whistle's wild keening down the valley on the edged wind of a Pennsylvania winter.

The scene is disjointed in my mind, but not unclear. I rode in my mother's arms, too excited to cry, seeing only where I had been and intuitively knowing where we were going. I say intuitively because my mind holds no image of the whistle's increasing volume, as though that first impression saturated my entire listening capacity. It was a wonderful ride, but rough, the cold air forced up under my clothes by the bouncing. Mama's hair billowed out behind us like a cloud. I didn't know she was crying, of course. At that age I was unaware of any tears but my own. Would to God that were still the case.

I remember the gold lettering on the bank window especially well, the blurring glitter as she stumbled, passing it. Another woman helped her. I never saw her, have no idea who she was. She spoke to Mama. The words have been erased by the years, but I remember the message of her voice, full of sympathy and the terrible soft urgency of all women whose men work with danger. Whenever I think back I always wonder whatever happened to that woman.

Forgive me. I was digressing. Old men do that, don't we? Ah, well.

When my mother stopped running, the whistle was very close. In my memory it seems as though I could feel it, a tremor that made my very bones buzz. My mother was holding me very tightly. Her

9

gasping pushed at my chest until I was forced to fill my own lungs in cadence with her, you see. As she inhaled, I exhaled, and vice versa. It was probably the first time in my life I was aware of the act of breathing, and then I was forced to accommodate my needs to someone else's. Isn't it wonderful that we first recognize facts of such nature when we're too young to realize the significance of them?

My reminiscence dims at this juncture. I was probably bored, because it seems to me there was a great deal of standing around and voices, mostly subdued, and a vague tension I wished would go away. There was no more of the whistle, though. I'm sure I'd remember if the whistle had continued.

The next thing I remember clearly is a man. He took me from my mother's shoulder and held me, cradled in one arm. That was very confusing and I was afraid again for a moment. It was so different, you understand. He smelled totally unlike my father, and his hands lacked the hard calluses that should have scraped my forehead when he brushed back my hair. Still, they were strong hands and his smell wasn't unpleasant. One of its major components, I now know, was cigarettes. Almost seventy years that's fascinated me. How on earth did our valley priest, that most circumscribed man, keep his secret vice hidden? What a cunning rogue he must have been!

Another digression. I really am coming apart.

The priest held me, as I said, and I was looking at my mother and I can see her face right now as clearly as I can see yours. More so, now that I think on it. She spoke then. I can't remember her words. Perhaps there weren't any real words. Anguish and dread—they have their own vocabulary.

I can remember the priest's words, however. They came to my consciousness exactly as the whistle had earlier, more of a vibration than a sound. He used our family name. I'm sure I'd heard it before, but it is from that moment that I learned who I am. He pronounced it as I always have, the old way, with the good, round *o* and the broad *ah* sound that makes a person move his mouth.

"I have to tell you the truth, Mrs. Kolar. Anna. I'm sorry, little Anna. Carl's father is dead."

She screamed then. Oddly, I can't recollect the sound. Perhaps I was too preoccupied by her actions, the sudden flight of the fists to her temples and the pressure of the wrists and forearms distorting her face. It seemed to elongate, the circle of the mouth forced into a fleshy crevice, lips blood red from the cold, white teeth gleaming in the pale sun. Her eyes were very bright, positively glasslike. When I was a schoolboy I refused to own a marble that combined blue and white in any manner.

It was several years before I could hear anyone speak of the truth without becoming unreasonably afraid. I never spoke of my apprehension to anyone. I had no idea of the term symbiosis then, naturally, but I was mortally convinced that death created truth and truth generated more death, *ad infinitum*. They were inseparable. Interchangeable.

I learned that I was wrong and congratulated myself on the instinctive wisdom that had kept my mouth shut. The middle years were slipping away from me before I determined I'd been correct in my original theory. Again, I've never discussed my conclusion with anyone else. I would probably be laughed at, as I would have been laughed at before, and I will not tolerate that. Scorn's sting is the same at all ages.

But I was right. Am right.

Life is a continuous riddle, with a different meaning for each of us. People shape their lives in a constant pressure against the grindstone of time, proclaiming eventual wisdom and knowledge. Others, equally industrious, no less intelligent or honorable, curse them for foul liars and deceivers. At the last, it all comes to one irrefutable fact.

There is but one truth in life and that is the ending of it.

# CHAPTER 1

Glen Draeger adjusted his position on his beach towel and aimed his face directly at the tropical sun. Its energy was a sly embrace and his sluggish consciousness warned there could be too much of a good thing.

All power was like that, Draeger told himself. The thought reminded him of the authority held by the man lying on the beach towel next to him, the only other non-Filipino on the beach. A burst of laughter and shouted Pilipino conversation loosened his concentration, and the unformed idea fell away into a lethargic void, leaving the impression it had escaped.

He wondered why the people were called Filipinos and the language was called Pilipino. Someday he would ask someone.

The pressure of the sun forced past his sunglasses and shuttered eyelids to image as a circular glowing coal in the center of each eye. The darkness around the burning disks pulsed with heat.

He let his head loll to the side and runnels of sweat coursed through the new folds in his skin. It tickled and he rubbed at it irritably. The slight sound alerted the man next to him. Bushy light brown eyebrows speckled with gray arched above his sunglasses as he spoke.

"Ready to go back to the house, Glen? Leonila always says she never sees enough of you when you visit."

Draeger said, "I'd rather stay a little longer. I'm sweating off too much San Miguel and not enough exercise."

Munson snorted, the sound rough against the carefree background laughter. "Wait till you're my age, then talk about San Miguel beer and conditioning. How old are you?"

"Twenty-seven." Draeger sat up, looping his arms around drawn-up knees.

"I'm exactly twice your age, you realize that? And you're in better shape than I ever was."

Draeger watched the lean face crack in the familiar smile that always surprised, the way it altered the economical features. It was odd, too, because the smile was always there, as badly hidden as a child behind a bush, if you knew what you were looking for. Nevertheless, the first impression of Roger Munson was of icy distance. Draeger remembered their first meeting in Los Angeles five years earlier, how he'd instantly pegged Munson as an incompetent professor trying to find a way to make a living. With that had come the resentment he always felt when looking up at someone he didn't respect. Munson was at least six-one, almost a head taller than himself.

He laughed inwardly at the memory. Munson's apparently gangling frame was smoothly coordinated, and the mind behind the blue green eyes was usually two moves ahead of everyone.

Continuing to observe him, Draeger grew unpleasantly aware of age's inroads on his body. Penciled shadowing at the edges of major muscles showed lost skin tone. That would grow worse, because Munson's pride would demand he exercise hard. The muscles would turn to straps, ridiculously stout bindings for brittle bones and grating joints.

Draeger shook his head, embarrassed by such morbidity.

Munson said, "You were looking at me." A slight move killed the glare on his sunglasses to reveal open eyes.

Surprised, Draeger could only nod.

"Don't be concerned," Munson said easily. "You're an athlete, always curious about other people's condition. What d'you think?"

"No fat, good muscle definition, good movement. But this sun's going to start killing you pretty soon. You'll get real leathery if you're not careful."

"How very flattering. At least I won't look like you, like some Neapolitan gigolo."

"Well, you asked me."

"I didn't want you to *tell* me. You can be pretty dense sometimes."

"Up yours."

"Never mind sweet talk. It's too late."

They laughed and fell silent. Draeger's thoughts took off on another tangent, still concentrated on Munson.

Ten years on station! It was a miracle. It must have been spooky as hell setting up shop in a place like Cebu, this far south of Manila. The people were no different—a little more easygoing, perhaps, and the city wasn't quite as jammed—but the aloneness of the thing must have been shattering at first. Just building a legitimate business would have been enough to tax a man out of his skull. The Philippine bureaucracy had been born impossible, and every year it aged badly. And the politics Munson had lived through! The Communists, the right-wing feudal lords, the outright bandits and extortionists who claimed to be popular leaders, all had come nosing around one time or another. How could he have displayed an outwardly normal life, pretending to do nothing but diddle test tubes and God-knew-what-all in a cosmetics lab? He did it, and was still able to be Control for five field officers, the best collection net in the Far East. He even did most of his own traveling, dealing with everyone, including the insurgent Moslems south of the last major island, Mindanao.

The older man said, "What's eating you? First you inventory my body and now I catch you staring out to sea with that vacuous grin."

"I was just thinking," Draeger said, and at Munson's continuing quizzical stare, added, "About business."

Munson's eyebrows spiked up from behind the sunglasses again. "You can find humor in that? The least you could do is share it."

"It isn't worth repeating."

Munson's face returned to neutrality. "I was thinking about business too, as it happens."

"I thought you might be. You get that carved-stone look."

"You're getting too damned observant." Munson sighed. "That's a contradiction in terms for us, isn't it?" He paused and Draeger let it run, sensing the question was rhetorical. "I'm sending in my boxtop. I'm getting out."

Draeger blinked. "Out? Out where? Tampa, for the shuffleboard courts? You're good for another forty years. Who the fuck can play shuffleboard for forty years?''

Munson's answer was slow, tentative. "I want to stay right where I am. I think I can manage it. Our people can swing an awful lot of influence, and I've made some friends of my own. The lab's a real business, not just a cover. I've built a good life here in ten years.''

"And Leonila doesn't want to leave here either, right?''

The flash of Munson's eyes penetrated the shielding sunglasses. "My wife goes anywhere I want to go. You, of all people, should know. That wasn't a very nice thing to say. I'm really disappointed.''

Draeger gestured, physical abruptness showing his discomfort more clearly than his words. "I apologize. It was a stupid thing to say, a reaction.''

"I understand.'' Munson got to his feet, clapping a hand on Draeger's shoulders as he did. "Come on, we'll swim the sand off and get home.''

Draeger understood. The decision to resign as Control was made, but Munson was signaling he wanted to talk about it. By dropping the subject, he was giving Draeger time to think.

They stuffed sunglasses inside the trunks as they went, building up speed side by side, kicking spray like oversized children before launching into flat dives and stroking across the aquamarine shallows, headed for the sapphire of deeper waters. They swam east in unison until they were a good quarter mile out.

Munson rolled on his back, pulling long, deep breaths. He said, "Know where you are right now?''

Treading water, Draeger answered, "Still outside a shark, thank God. That's the important thing.''

"You're afloat in the Bohol Strait. You should learn more details of the islands.''

"Forget that. I know all I need. Who can learn about seven thousand islands? I know Manila. That's enough.''

"Point well taken. Manila's the center of the center.''

Draeger floated on his back and smiled into the faultless sky, feeling the crackle of the drying brine enameling his face. Even Munson thought of Manila as the hub. On the north-south axis of the twelve-hundred-mile-long archipelago, Manila was far to the north, a good three hundred fifty miles away. Cebu was much more central, geographically. Still, as with all charismatic entities, Manila oozed power. With the rice granary of the island of Luzon behind her and one of the world's finest bays in front of her, she prospered. Filipinos of every persuasion coveted her. The oligarchs schemed to buy her, the radicals threatened to fit her to their dictates or burn her, and the uncounted poor sheltered in her hard accommodations. Manila boiled constantly. It kept the rest of the islands, places like Cebu, in a steady simmer.

Munson interrupted Draeger's ruminations with a sweeping gesture. Drops like diamonds glinted back into the sea. "The Philippines grow more important every day, Glen. For generations these islands have been mismanaged, when they've been managed at all. They're beginning to come into their own."

"Hell, what's that to us? I mean, we collect information, right? We run our nets the best we can and send the take to you and you do your magic and get it all back to the States and presto! it's intelligence with a capital *I*. We've done all we can do."

"Wrong. What we're *supposed* to do. Because we're exiles. We're two people in one body and neither person leads half a real life. The country we live in wouldn't tolerate us if it knew of us. Some people in our own country would inform on us at the first chance. As a nation we complain about injustice, but look at the regime we're supporting here. We could find good people to back, if we were allowed. We'll end up watching one tyranny replace another, as usual. I'm getting out while I'm still sane enough to enjoy what's available." He flipped onto his stomach and headed for land.

Draeger followed, lifting his head to get a bearing before settling to an automatic rhythm. He forced his mind from the disturbing realization they'd drifted a good distance south of Talisay beach. The effort left him with nothing but the conversation to dwell on. Munson clearly wanted him to think about doing something besides straight out collection. That was absurd, on the face of it. The number of people he had to account for—the agents alone could drive a man off his rocker. Then there were the couriers and the cutouts and the accommodation addresses and the minutiae that made the simplest acts intricate complexities. He remembered the briefings, so long ago in Los Angeles.

The training unit had introduced him to Munson, telling him he would arrange to "meet" his Control when the latter made one of his scheduled trips to Manila.

A new approach, they'd called this collection effort, those tough executive types. They all looked completely different but they sounded alike and used the same jargon repetitiously. Even their gestures and postures were the same. They made Draeger think of expensive one-of-a-kind custom robots.

All pay and allowances were arranged through private industries. He was not to wonder about the bookkeeping games involved. There were eight men in his group. An Induction Group, they were called, setting off the unavoidable rash of bad jokes among themselves. Then had come the psychiatric and psychological exams, far more extensive than anything he'd ever seen, endless hours with strange men who asked questions that sliced ego and self-image away in transparently thin slices. No matter how one twisted and turned, the questions kept coming, and, by and by, the interrogators built up their knowledge of the mind they were dissecting. Eventually the victim was told he'd be contacted later. Two of that Induction Group went back to Washington. They were disappointed, but the blow was softened by the knowledge they were practically assured of successful careers in some other line. Merely to be selected for an interview concerning the new collection effort was high praise. The drop rate was better than fifty percent, even after the exhaustive consideration preceding any man's actually being approached.

The remaining six in the Group were schooled, and although it was intensive, it was hardly unbearable. The real pressure came from the indoctrination. They were cut off from all other contacts and the essential secrecy of their task was hammered at them constantly. It had been put to them bluntly as soon as the two drops were safely packed off to the east. The man in charge had come into the classroom unannounced. He was the only one of the staff who didn't look to have been born and bred to executive status. He was much older, probably in his sixties, silver haired and dignified, and carried a heavy body with ease, testimony that good muscle still worked in the tall frame. Impeccable grooming and clothes failed to disguise hands that appeared bent in physical memory of laborer's tools put aside long ago. There was an unnatural angle in his nose, and when he was relaxed his sharp blue eyes sparkled with a hint of a boisterous youth spiced by carefree violence.

This day he smiled and spoke of a shadow world where men trusted each other implicitly and no one else. Relatives were considered opposition. Wives were potential informants, unwitting or otherwise.

Henceforth the Group would be in a covert status, unknown even to former associates. They would work two jobs. One would provide cover. The other required they initiate and supervise approved collection operations. They would conduct the cover job satisfactorily or be extracted from the program. They would be the best field officers in the business or shuffle papers in Washington eternally.

The man smiled all the while, and Draeger's eyes ignored it because his brain warned him that the devil probably smiled the same way every time he opened his front gate.

Draeger remembered the end of the session.

"We live in interesting times, gentlemen. The country is in the hands of people who insist on knowing everything about everyone except our declared enemies. They have broken the weapons of the intelligence community. You are the point of the new spear. We *must* have information. I will see that it's properly disseminated. If we cannot protect the country, we can assure it's not blind. When the sacrifices threaten to break you, remember, you don't have a task—you have a mission."

The man turned to leave then, and one of the group said, "Thank you, Mr. Kolar."

He turned as if his entire spine were fused. "You're welcome, Mr. Pierce," he said. "I'll remember you thanked me, because in days ahead, you'll curse me."

Taken aback by the sudden steel-coldness, Pierce stammered and Kolar was gone.

The reminiscence ended as Draeger's hand scraped the sandy bottom. The water was barely over his knees when he stood, and he grinned at the laughter in Munson's eyes.

"Really got you thinking, didn't I?" The older man let laughter break free, gusty with tired breathing. "That's what I wanted, you know."

A pair of barefoot boys in tattered shorts sprinted toward them, a blast of churned sand and shouted exuberance. The smaller, pursued one slammed to a stop in front of the Americans and stared with candid curiosity. His pursuer halted as well, maintaining a sporting distance.

"You 'merican?" the small one asked Munson.

"Yes, I am," Munson said gravely.

"You live Cebu?"

Munson's repeated affirmative seemed to disappoint the boy. He looked to Draeger.

"You 'merican, too?"

Draeger nodded and smiled.

"You live Cebu, too, huh?"

"No."

A huge grin slipped across the young face. "Good! Cebu best city in Philippines! *Daan muna kayo!*" he shouted and leaped away in a flurry of brown limbs. The larger boy waved at them and broke after him.

"I'll be damned," Draeger said, chuckling. "The Chamber of Commerce ought to put that one on retainer. 'Visit with us awhile,' for Christ's sake. What can you say about something like that?"

Munson was already moving away. He shrugged, not bothering to look back. "Kids like everyone. What can they know?"

It was a crude response, insensitive, and it caught Draeger up short. There was no reason for Munson to be like that. The job was harsh and it ate at your belief in your fellow man and all that, but you kept a perspective. And there was the necessity for the work. He said, "I know you're feeling down, Roger, but you can't afford to lose your balance, your professionalism."

Munson half-turned, and the prominent Adam's apple moved in convulsive swallowing. Then he smiled. "You're a good man, Glen, and an even better friend. We need our optimism, don't we?"

"Can you imagine this job without it?"

The answering laugh was an unusual dry rustle. "Wouldn't that be a bastard?"

# ■ CHAPTER 2 ■

Every time he visited Munson, Draeger had to search his soul and ask himself if the odd sensation in there was admiration or envy. If he could have expressed his feelings, it probably would have made life easier for him, but he never found the right way to confess to his friend that he couldn't take his eyes off his wife.

Leonila Munson was a beautiful woman. In the Philippines that made her one of many. The genetic pool that combined Malay, Oriental, and Caucasian genes produced a blend that made a commonplace of graceful golden women with hair black and soft as nightfall. Beyond that, however, Leonila enjoyed a personality that intrigued. Her moods were in constant flux, reminding Draeger of the shifting iridescence of oiled water. A man never knew if the visible changes came from internal or external forces.

She lived for Roger Munson. Draeger knew for a fact she was only a year older than himself, that she married Munson when she was little more than a girl. But she was his wife, and never a doubt.

This evening, with a friend in the home, she was very much the manager of her empire, and there was pride in her manner. And her home was right for her, as it was for Munson. It lacked the ostentation of some of the homes in the area, but it was large and airy and comfortable. The view was wonderful, with the lights of the whole of Cebu City stretched out below and the sky full of stars overhead. Night breezes from the sea scoured the land and drifted into the softly lit rooms. The tang of salt air mixed with the smells of plants and earth. The curling grain of tropical hardwood furniture brought out the reality of the edged weapons Munson used as decorative

20

touches. Leonila's taste provided the color combinations that gave the high-ceilinged rooms the benefit of light without heat.

Now they all three sat at the table in the dining room, Leonila across from her guest, gleaming in white blouse and slacks. The men both wore dark trousers and the open-necked embroidered shirt called *barong tagalog*. Munson's was stark white, matching his wife's color choice. Draeger's was a pale blue, the hand-done needlework a touch more obvious.

Leonila's eyes were intent as she watched the maid bring in the dessert, although her lips curled in a soft smile. Draeger understood when he saw she'd arranged for his favorite, the *buco pastelitos*. The maid came to him with the tray, and the aroma made him swallow. Delicate coconut tarts, heartbreakingly delicious, so loaded with calories a man could almost hear his belt stretch with each bite. Leonila took her eyes from the maid to catch his look, and her smile broadened.

"You see, I remembered," she said. "You said you liked the little tarts." Her low voice flowed across the consonants with the softening touch of Pilipino-accented English.

"Leonila!" Munson chided softly. "You promised you wouldn't bring up Glen's bachelor status, and there you go. And so blunt! I'm scandalized."

She colored. "You know I didn't mean that kind of tart!" She burned a look at him and back to Draeger. "But now that you've opened the subject, I won't be rude enough to ignore it. Anyhow he knows I'd never actually pry. Have you found a girl you like, Glen?"

The men laughed, and she waited with unabashed persistence.

Draeger said, "Sorry, Leonila. I'll just have to drown my sorrow in tarts. Unless you want to take me up on Plan A—dump Roger, collect his insurance, and live high forever in Hong Kong."

She put a finger to her cheek, feigning consideration.

During the seconds she posed, Munson's face changed from amusement to staged glower. Finally he said, "I thought you said you weren't going to be rude. What do you call planning to eliminate your husband?"

"I was only wondering. The planning comes after I make up my mind."

"That's not rude, that's brazen." He turned to Draeger. "I can see I'm going to have to keep on your good side. Would an after-dinner drink earn me any sympathy?"

Draeger held up thumb and forefinger about two inches apart. "That much Drambuie'll guarantee you continued good health for at least an hour."

Munson moved to the carved teak bar cabinet. "We'll drink out on the porch."

Leonila rose. "I know that voice. The ladies are expected to withdraw. I'll give you an hour, and then I want to talk to you, Glen Draeger. Something has to be done about the way you live up there alone in that terrible city."

When she reached the door she turned, and the change in her manner made Draeger stare. She said, "Cheer Roger up, Glen. He's been worrying too much. You can help him, I know. A man's understanding, or—oh, I don't know." She made a weak gesture and left.

Munson stepped outside, stiff and silent. Draeger followed and waited, knowing Munson would speak when he was sure of his words. It was an axiom. Munson moved at a pace set by carefully organized facts and considered options. That was how he built a cosmetics business, guided and aided the field officers who provided some of the most treasured information coming out of the Orient. It was how he protected his identity from opposition intelligence and local police, how he protected his legitimate business in a rapacious economy. He was not much given to rash behavior.

The cane chairs creaked at each other as the men sat down. Below on the hill a motorcycle bellowed brute anger. There was a flickering glimpse of the headlight beam swinging stiffly around a curve and, as the commotion faded, Munson talked.

"I'm quitting for a lot of reasons," he said abruptly. "I can live well on my company earnings and my retirement check. But that's a small part of it."

"I knew that. And Leonila does deserve more of your time." Even in the dim light Draeger saw his friend's quick frown, and he gestured his lack of offense. "I'm not saying she's influenced your decision. But we haven't cut nearly to the bone, have we? I know you're proud of your operation, how hard you've worked. They told us about you in L.A., how your team's nicknamed the Bat team because out here bats symbolize good luck. You were one of the first picks for the new collection effort. You're not quitting because you're tired. Don't even try that bullshit.''

Munson's teeth gleamed in a momentary grin. ''You silver-tongued sonofabitch.'' He half-rose in order to turn his chair away from the night, giving him a face-on view of Draeger. ''I *am* tired, you know. Tired as hell. Christ, I wouldn't know how to behave if I wasn't tired all the time.''

He paused and a level of harshness drained from his face. ''When the big boys came to me almost eleven years ago and started talking about the Collection Team concept, it scared hell out of me. I listened, though. Who wouldn't? We were going to be elite!''

''Well, goddamit, we are.''

''Think about that. Are we really elite or simply underground, running agents all over the place with only a handful of people in Washington in on it? Do you actually know any of them?''

Draeger was unimpressed. ''I know who some are, and the information goes where it's supposed to go. We've never had a leak or had to put an operation to bed because someone got nervous. It has to be done our way, or we might as well be in the fucking yellow pages.''

''We're subverting the will of Congress.''

''Like hell. Congressmen and Senators read our stuff every day.''

''People who agree with what we're doing. What about the ones who don't?''

''The ones who think gentlemen don't read other people's mail? The ones who want to reason with the people reaching for our throats?''

Munson spread his hands, a resigned move, and the silence that settled over them was like a break between rounds. It was Draeger who started things again.

''It's not ethics, and it's sure as hell not getting burned. You've been at this stuff too long to go shaky at this late date. I can believe what you said this afternoon about being passive and helping the wrong regimes, but I know damned well you keep hoping someone'll pay attention to what we learn about them. If we quit, no one learns anything. So it's got to be something else. What is it?''

''Fear.'' The word startled Draeger. It came out with difficulty, a flame flickering so erratically it shed no appreciable light. Munson repeated it, louder. "Fear. I'm worried. No, goddamit, I'm afraid. I catch myself doubting every move anyone wants to make. I dread seeing a new op plan because I don't want to have to approve it. A report means questions. Did the field officer debrief his man properly? Were the right objectives assigned? Is our compartmentation still secure?" He reached out a hand to Draeger's arm. "That's when I ask myself about the thanklessness, the hours of strain. And being hated."

Draeger reached for the glass trapped by Munson's grip. When he had it, he drained it, wishing it weren't the thick liqueur. He wanted something that bit and burned. An unease came to crowd the anger from his thoughts. The fears and frustrations were part of the business. They were demons beyond exorcism, creatures that glutted any space left undefended, even momentarily. They were never to be discussed, and Munson had loosed them, was acknowledging them in what could only be a plea for help.

He said, "I won't believe it's nerves," and Munson sighed, physically settling like a man who's heard something hoped for. He took his hand from Draeger's arm. Draeger went on, "You've worked yourself to exhaustion."

Munson agreed eagerly. "That's what I keep telling myself, it really is. When the black mood comes, when I read a field report and start thinking there's something wrong, I sit staring at the goddamn wall and tell myself it's exhaustion. That's the very word." He nodded brisk affirmation, and a paste-up smile slashed his face and fell away to leave it as troubled as ever. "The reports are the worst. You read along and suddenly you're afraid you've seen something that doesn't belong. So you read it again and you think you see something else. Finally you make it all the way through and you do your cross-checks and then you know you've been questioning a man who's unquestionable. It's happened with some of your stuff."

He looked away.

Draeger laughed to cover the sudden grab in his stomach. "That's not important. What's important is, you need a break."

"No! I don't want a break! I want out!" He turned wide eyes on Draeger, then lowered this head to stare at his feet. When he spoke again, he was calm. "I got into this business back in the bad old days, when it was damned near armed combat. I always had a hunch—call it ESP or whatever—before something went nasty back in Europe or Vietnam. Maybe that's where I get the reputation for good luck. I've got that feeling now."

Shrugging, Draeger said, "What can I do about it? Put all my people to bed? Shut down? Shut down half of them? Which half?"

"Use your goddamned head!" Munson's intensity bolted between them like lightning, yet the sound level stayed unchanged. "Warn your people. Tell everyone to review their security and take it slow for a while."

"I will."

Munson spun back, questioning the quick acquiescence, and Draeger smiled easily. "We can afford to be careful. Can't afford not to be. As soon as I get back to Manila, I'll get the word out. Now, how much leave will you take before you get back in harness?"

"No, I'm quitting. I'll sell the business a few years from now, when I've learned how to unwind, and then I'm going to simply enjoy." He pitched forward. "I've lived under a rock because I believed our job needed done. I'm salvaging the time I have left."

"What about control? Who takes over?"

Munson flipped an irritable hand, frowning. "I don't know. If they have to establish a new resident like me, it'll be at least a year."

Tenting his fingers, Draeger leaned back and closed his eyes. He could have been praying. "What a tremendous hole you'll leave. The field guys'll be explaining every move they make for years. Look at Pierce, way the hell down there in Zamboanga."

"What about Pierce?"

The voice was suspicious, and Draeger smiled at the instant protective reaction. He explained.

"Look who he's dealing with. A lot of his people are practically full-time pirates. He knows them and they know him and they've got their *modus vivendi*. Can you imagine some poor nerd coming in here and trying to fit that operation into textbook definitions?"

Munson's answer was cold. "I'd worry about my own area, if I were you. Any new Control is going to recognize a breakdown in compartmentation and roast you. Theoretically, you don't even know Pierce.''

''Theoretically.'' Draeger's tone mocked. ''And speaking of business, next week I'll have a report for you. My man who services the drop in Canton is due.''

Munson nodded, having obvious trouble shifting subjects. ''Good. Maybe he'll have something interesting.''

''He usually does. Egg Roll's well placed.''

''Christ, how I hate that name. I don't know what I was thinking about when I let you code a source with that.''

''SOP. Standard operating procedure says every source has to have a code name.'' Draeger was outwardly smug in his defense; inwardly, he was dismayed by Munson's continuing need to blast away at both their defenses, to forcibly unite them in a battle he alone could see.

Munson waved his arms. ''A spy in the Chinese Ministry of Defense and you've named him Egg Roll. It's absurd.''

''Everything is,'' Draeger said, feeling his smile grow more fixed. Suddenly he tensed. ''Hold it!''

Leonila swept onto the porch. She bent to kiss Draeger's cheek on her way to stand behind Munson, where she framed his face with her hands, pulling his head back against her.

''You two have had your chance to talk. It's my turn.'' Her air of accomplishment was so apparent both men stared as she stepped around her husband to hand Draeger a sheet of notepaper. ''That's the name and address of the godchild of a friend of mine. She's already told the girl you will call on her.''

Munson exploded. ''You can't push her on Glen!''

She refused to face him and locked harried eyes on Draeger's. He said, ''It's OK. Leonila's looking out for me. I appreciate it, honestly.''

She practically skipped back to Munson and bent to rest against the back of his head, looking across him to their guest. Her long hair bracketed his features, enfolding their angularity as if to protect them from whatever might dull the edges. He reached up to stroke that curtain.

At ease again, she continued, ''She's from Iloilo, what we call an Ilonga, and everyone knows about those girls. They have this gentle, singing way of talking, so sweet. But they hold onto a man like steel cables. If you pull too hard, you will cut yourself." She drew a finger across Munson's throat.

Draeger said, "They may have a different speech habit, but they don't treat their men a damned bit different than other Filipinas, seems to me."

Leonila laughed. "We are possessive. There are worse things."

Munson was grinning widely. "There's something in what she says," he said.

Draeger sneered. "You're not being romantic, you're thinking about that finger on your neck."

They continued to laugh as Draeger stuffed the folded notepaper in the pocket of his *barog tagalog,* half-listening to the domestic banter, loosing his mind to pursue its own thoughts.

The word envy crept into his thinking again.

*Envy's a sin, so that's the wrong word. I hope I can be as happy some day. Not a good bet. Munson can schedule his life, even insist field guys adjust to it, but a field man goes where the job says and when. Plan your ass off and the balloon goes up and you go crazy grabbing at everything. What could you tell a wife to cover while you went downtown to hold some hooker's hand while she repeated a trick's pillow talk? How many excuses could I invent for having to be out of the house all night? The government believes the cover, the bullshit about being a prearranged employee with Budley Rubber, because the government doesn't care. Or suspect. But a wife'd care. So would a steady girl friend. Possessive? Milly started to care. Wonder what she's doing now. Dropped her like something on fire.*

*Was that a function of the business or did I look for a business that'd let me live like this? Am I questioning myself because my doubts are troubling me or because Munson's doubts are troubling him or—*

"Glen?" It was Leonila cutting through his preoccupation, puzzled and trying not to be hurt.

His face grew warm. "I'm sorry, Leonila. Come to think of it, it's all your fault. I was wondering what it'd be like to be married."

She laughed forgiveness. "And that's why I nag at you. We care. Roger has other friends here, other Americans who live in the Philippines. They're nice, but you're the one we look for."

Munson left the room, returning in seconds with a guitar in one

hand and the Drambuie in the other. He filled the glasses and said,
"You can't leave Cebu without hearing a Cebuano guitar accompany a beautiful Cebuana's song. First, though, a toast." He hoisted
his glass. "To the dependable one. My friend."

They drank and Munson caressed the guitar, starting an old folk
song. After the first chords Leonila joined in, her eyes singing the
plain words of love to him as clearly as her voice.

The music came from Munson's touch with no conscious effort.
He was unaware of his wife's expression. The dark-shrouded face of
the other man held his entire attention, and he felt a pull inside his
head as though he could draw the younger man's thoughts from his
mind as wire uncoils from a spool. For a moment he allowed himself
to toy with that fantasy, then left it.

*The dependable one. My friend. I never laid a glove on you, did I,
Draeger? You're so goddammed wrapped up in your ideas of camara-
derie and the true faith you never heard what I had to say, did you?
Can you imagine how much I wanted you to hear? Do you think I
want to do what I have to do? If I even had a clue, the tiniest
glimmer of interest from you, we could have been together, could
have said good-bye to all our troubles. How can you stay so blind?
Why won't you see? Why do you make me destroy you?*

■    **CHAPTER 3**    ■

The weary light of pre-sunrise transformed the erratic massed shapes
of the shacks paralleling the railroad tracks into a vision of broken
teeth threatening to sever the dull-gleaming steel. There was no
silence here in the Tondo district, although the noise level was
unusually low. If there was to be a peaceful time of day here, the

few minutes prior to dawn would be it. The whores and thieves would have retired to avoid the unfortunate complications brought by daylight, the cursing wives and husbands would be salvaging what rest they could prior to the next battle, and the day shift of the district's major industry wouldn't go into action until there was enough light to see properly.

The major industry of the Tondo is survival. It is a demanding occupation. Men die in the Tondo because one slips on the slime underfoot and brushes against another. Is this a function of overcrowding, of minds constantly frayed?

Not entirely. It is more a question of surviving without surrendering the *amor proprio*. Literally self-love, it is more accurately thought of as the way one sees one's self.

A man who cannot accept an honest apology is less than human. A man who will accept an affront is nothing whatsoever. And if tempers explode and men will reach for weapons, well, then, the victim was clearly inferior, or he would have won, wouldn't he?

In the Tondo people understand these things.

Why should one form of violent death be any more unexpected or lamentable than another, such as the occasional epidemic that rips through their community like an invisible *amok?* When it comes, the savage joy of victory can be seen to be in no way restricted to armed men. It shows in the ocean-deep eyes of patient, suffering women who wake every morning with a lurch of the heart before assuring themselves that the children have survived the night. They look at their neighbors whose luck has failed, and those eyes are full of pity and condolence and the secret gladness that lives hand-in-hand with guilt, but lives, nevertheless.

There are pits like the Tondo all over the world, places where the denizens measure their state of well-being in terms of greater or lesser pain. The people of the Tondo hurt in the same ways, abuse themselves with the same drugs, kill each other with perhaps a bit more reckless abandon than most similar societies, but generally pass their brief lives in the same hopeless coil as their contemporaries elsewhere.

But there is that difference, that *amor proprio*.

Accuse a man of the Tondo of being poor and he will accept the statement as an unpleasant truth. Tell him he is poor because he is too ignorant to be else and you will have a permanent enemy. Tell him he is ignorant because he is stupid and he will probably kill you. Where you had been merely tactless and impolite in the first instances, the third comment stepped over into that desperately held self view, and there is only one genuinely satisfactory response. There are, however, less lethal outlets for the phenomenon. It can be seen in the dress of the Tondo dandies and in the walk that proclaims their incredible agility and fundamental toughness. It is present in the way a Tondo man attacks a job, when the ones who are willing to work are lucky enough to find it. A Tondo man believes it is as absolute as mathematical fact that, given a handful of rice and the promise of another, he can outdo any other Filipino at anything.

The women are no different. Some drift out of the district in the evening, picking their way through the filth in couples and small groups, laughing and chattering, wrapped in colors rivaling tropical flowers. They are, in fact, suggestive of the lotus, lifting beauty high above the ordure from which it springs. Their beauty is used to snare males to support them. They are damned for it. The alternative is starvation, unnoticed and unmourned by the same society that condemns their manner of survival.

Those women who raise the children are the strongest people in the district, the only ones who live in something besides themselves. Fathers may work themselves to death for their children or die protecting them. The mothers know they must live. To a Filipino, the family is everything, the ultimate security and refuge. The mother knows she is the blood and bone of that arrangement.

The father is the muscle.

Angel Magliba, known now only as Boy Angel to everyone but the police and relatives, was nine years old when his father died. Sometimes he still dreamed about it, seeing it all over again exactly as it happened, as if the whole day were on film and stored on a machine in his mind. A man once told Boy that all dreams last only seconds, and he accepted the statement with an expression of gratitude and marked the man as a total idiot. Didn't his dream cover an entire day, from the time he woke up to dark that night? They had gone all the way to the old walled city of Intramuros, even riding in a jeepney. He could still remember the flowers and scrolls, red and blue and orange, painted on the bus-bodied jeep and how he sat on the front-to-rear bench next to his father and across from his sister and mother. They had all teased each other about which side of the street was most interesting. They walked from Intramuros to a park, and they saw a place where a famous man had been shot. Boy had gotten very excited about that, and his father had said it was a long time ago.

It had been a day of love and joy. When they were back in the Tondo, walking home, a man said something to Boy's mother. It surprised him when his father looked angry, because the other man had spoken very softly and he was still smiling, even when he saw the fierceness in Boy's father's eyes. Boy knew then the other man was very foolish. He had never seen his father look that way, but suddenly his skin felt wet and cold and like it was trying to shrivel up all over him.

Before the other man could change the expression on his face, Boy's father slashed his throat. Boy saw the knife shining on his father's right, a bright movement in the dusk like rain driven horizontally by the wind. When he saw it again it was past the man, to his father's left, and it was dull, stained. It happened so quickly the man continued to stand for the briefest moment, still wearing the insolent smile. It disappeared with the amazing gush of blood and the bubbling attempt to scream. He collapsed in a jerking heap and his friends moved immediately on Boy's father.

Even the Tondo talked of the fight for weeks afterward. Another man died, one lost the use of his left hand, and a third would wear a scar across an empty eye socket for the rest of his life. Boy's father had shown the gang how a man dies, silent, swaying as he stood backed against a wall, his clothes growing heavy and sodden with blood, his own and his enemies'.

Boy himself broke free of his mother at the last, screaming, charging the men when his father finally dropped.

One of the gang slashed at him, more in surprise than anger. The blade opened his skinny chest all the same, skipping downward over the ribs in a tattoo that rumbled like thunder in Boy's stomach. He kicked at that man, and another, more collected member of the gang hit him with a fist, aiming compassionately just behind the small ear. The next thing Boy knew, he was being sick next to his sleeping mat while the neighbors consoled his grieving mother and sister.

The next day they headed north to an uncle's house in the province of Zambales. They rode a bus and Boy's chest translated the least imperfection in the road surface into throbbing pain. There were many imperfections, and by the time they reached the farming community where troubled family could claim them, he was delirious. When he survived the villagers said it was a miracle, granted because they came to the village for sanctuary on its patron saint's day. At the age of thirteen Boy's scar and reputation as an unmanageable terror were the envy of every other young man for miles around, and if his name was ever mentioned in connection with miracles or prayers, it had nothing to do with his survival.

Through some odd jobs, scrupulous saving, and the occasional theft of some small change, he accumulated enough money to take a bus to Olongapo. Once there, he found a corner where he surveyed the American sailors going by until he found one drunk enough and small enough to meet his requirements. Boy wheedled him into an alley with promises of a sister aflame with carnal needs. When they reached the place where Boy had thoughtfully stashed the jackhandle it was a simple matter to club the already groggy sailor and rifle his pockets. There was more than enough to finance the rest of the trip to Manila.

That had been six years ago and Boy could no more have accounted for the number of men he'd rolled since that first one than he could account for the number of stars in the sky. If someone who knew him very, very well had asked him how many men he'd robbed, he might flash his incredibily bright, shy smile and say, "Many." On the other hand, he might have decided the questioner wasn't really that close a friend, after all, and then that individual would be in great trouble. Boy thrived on the rigors of his world, and he'd grown to be rather taller than the average and of slim but muscular build, with an anomalous innocent face. His strength was much admired by his companions. Because of it, and a certain dogged steadfastness of purpose, some of the men Boy robbed died as part of the process. After that happened the first time, Boy calmed himself by assessing his position and acknowledging that if one lived by crime, one of necessity lived by all crime. That decided, he was never disturbed by the problem again. He prided himself on facing such hazards with a cool attitude.

Today, however, he was entering a new phase of his life and he was excited. He wished he could have dressed better, in celebration, but it was necessary to be inconspicuous, so he wore the muted brown-on-beige shirt and plain slacks. His progress along the ties between the tracks was the watchful padding of a cat on unfamiliar ground. It created a misleading image. Boy was graceful and he was exceedingly cautious, but he knew every inch of this place and the prosaic fact of his care was his desire to keep his good shoes clean. The people living in the shacks crowding the rails dumped what little they threw away directly out the front door. Feral dogs and cats, rats, mice, birds, and insects all spent lifetimes sifting through it for anything with food value. What they ate they digested and redeposited, adding to that left by the humans. If one walked carefully, it was usually possible to keep some sort of paper or plastic between one's shoe leather and the fermenting noisome muck.

Turning off the right-of-way onto a cross street, Boy increased his pace. A woman squatted in a shanty doorway, lethargically fanning some coals in a can, preparing to heat the morning meal. She glanced at Boy's legs as he hurried by, not lifting her eyes to identify him any further.

A breeze came up just as the sunlight found its way onto the street, as though the air would clear the way. The light lifted colors from a myriad advertisements and posters. Flaming reds and glistening blues exhorted purchases while the desiccated grays and browns of the buildings glowered. Windows as empty as bullet holes looked out at broadsides extolling the New Society. The breeze clutched at the paper and it danced, fluttering, making a soft chuckling sound where it had worked loose on the drab walls.

Boy was oblivious to those things, but if a form appeared at a window, he was instantly aware. If a person stepped out onto the street, he was noted. Any sign of interest from that person brought Boy's head up until he was sure there was no significance to the gesture. Boy knew nothing of nature's abhorrence of vacuums. He was well aware she had no idea of neutrality.

He was more alert than usual today. After six years as a Sword, he was selected for a special job.

His right hand climbed to scratch at the scar on his chest as he felt a thrill of pride. Boy Angel was unaware of it, but the nervous gesture was part of his persona. The migration of the hand triggered facial responses. As soon as he touched the lower limit of the ridged flesh his eyes hooded as if fearing someone else might read what was in his thoughts. Then his lips curled in the pattern of a smile.

Traffic was increasing on the boulevard called Jose Abad Santos when he reached it, and he swung aboard a jeepney. The ride was a time to relax, and he amused himself by moving his body against the young woman next to him. At first she pretended not to notice. When he moved his thigh against hers she glared at him and crowded further toward the front end of the seating bench. Boy ignored her anger, staring directly ahead as if unaware of anything out of the ordinary until his peripheral vision caught the tiny lines of uncertainty at the corners of her eyes. When his thigh rolled suggestively against hers again, she knew she had not only judged him correctly but had been tricked into worrying about it. A furious exclamation started from her lips before she could bite it back.

It was all Boy could do to keep from laughing at her. He controlled himself, half-turning toward her to release the slow smile. He knew not even his smile would mollify her and was satisfied to see it took a great deal of the fire out of her eyes. He was so pleased by that success he twisted far to his left when she indicated she wanted out, risking soiling or wrinkling his trousers on the bench. He wished he had time to follow her, to play the game just a little longer.

He left the jeepney a short while later, picking the Post Office as an innocuous spot. His instructions had been very clear in that regard. There was to be no attention directed to himself. If he was identified, the Swords could only move him out of Manila and hide him until things cooled off. If he was caught, they would do everything possible to get him out and away from the police.

Boy frowned to himself as he walked, thinking hard. Benjamin himself had said they'd hide him and Benjamin was a good gang leader, a man to respect, but in his six years as a Sword, he'd never heard anyone speak of a hideout in the country. It wasn't pleasant, suspecting Benjamin, but the idea persisted. Boy decided the best way to avoid any problem was to do the job correctly.

A glance at the massive watch that emphasized the thickness of his wrist showed he had a little better than two hours to wait until he could expect to handle his assignment. He walked steadily, paralleling Intramuros, far too preoccupied to remember any other trip there or to be interested in the granite of ancient walls and churches. If he had thought about them at all, he would only have considered that their presence, representing over three centuries of Spanish domination of his country, seemed infinitely more alien to him than the gleaming facades of the first-class hotels spiring upward everywhere he looked. He had been inside the walls of Intramuros many times and never once in one of the hotels, yet this was his Philippines. Here, close to the bay, the area reaching from the Tondo in the north and through the center of the old Manila, and on southward on Roxas Boulevard at the water's edge down to Pasay City. That was the real Manila, where the breath of the sea mingled with the burden of human-smell and engine exhaust. Unconsciously, he drew a deep breath and immediately frowned at the thick aroma of Chinese cooking. If there was anything to be said for the cop-heavy rich man's ground, like Quezon City to the northeast or Makati to the southeast, it was that the damned Chinese didn't own them. Not yet, anyhow.

When he reached P. Burgos Street he followed it all the way to the western end of Rizal Park, the section called the New Luneta. There was nothing between him and the bay here, and he could sit and survey the ships in the harbor with no fear of missing the one called Wadco Trader. Within minutes he saw it, the blue diamond in the white band on the funnel assuring him, even before the ship drew close enough for him to discern the yellow star within the diamond. He waited until he read the name on the bow, then left for the South Harbor dock area.

The man to whom he was assigned came ashore soon. He looked exactly like the pictures Benjamin had given him, square jawed, fat, and slightly bowlegged. He wore khaki trousers and a cheap green shirt and reminded Boy of the store owner where he'd lived with his uncle, a man who had no family and talked all the time. Boy fell in behind him.

They retraced the route Boy had followed in reaching the dock area and were abreast of the austere grandeur of the old Manila Hotel when the man from the ship stumbled. He turned, frowning, to look at the offending crack in the sidewalk and when he raised his eyes, he was looking full at Boy Angel. The contact could not have lasted more than a tenth of a second, yet when the sailor broke it off, each was surfeited with knowledge of the other. Boy had seen the cold glow of fear. The sailor understood what was behind the blandly innocent face.

When he started walking again, the sailor's legs moved at the same pace, but the effort to keep them from running showed in the way they swung forward and pulled to the vertical impatiently, waiting for the body to catch up at each step. His hands were bunched in hard fists. After a few yards he glanced back at the traffic using the move to see if Boy was still with him.

Their eyes met again and the touch of resignation Boy saw this time flooded his body with a joint-weakening satisfaction that was almost a sexual release. The other man hurried, bursting clear of the shade of the palms lining the boulevard. Boy followed, hearing the rustle of the wind in the fronds fade behind him. They whispered that he should hurry, too, and he smiled inwardly because he knew there was no need. Despite the distance between himself and the figure scurrying through the gate into Rizal Park, he could see the wet, black-green sweaty patch on the back of his shirt. He was an overweight little man at the state of near-panic that creates rapid exhaustion. He wouldn't go far.

The dreamlike chase proceeded through the park's trees, past shining fountains. Boy realized the man was almost to the street bisecting the grounds. The man could swing aboard a jeepney, lose himself. Boy cursed Benjamin for promising the man would remain in the park. "To take care of some business," Benjamin said. The man was practically running. What business could that be?

Heat waves shimmered in front of Boy, twisted his vision. Sweat compounded the problem, burned his eyes.

The tension eased some as the man turned, moved along a flowering hedge. Just as Boy told himself all was well again, the stocky figure disappeared. Boy increased his pace, brushing through a group of laughing children. They closed behind him, swirling like colored motes, ignoring his adult irrationality. When he careened around the hedge the sailor was nearly to Kalaw Street, but he turned the corner and made no move to get a ride.

Fool. He meant to run. Even now he was walking up the drive to the National Library building. Boy restrained the urge to break into a run after him again. It wouldn't do to rush into a strange place. Further, he was more determined than ever to attract no attention. The whole matter had become infuriating, insulting.

The guards ignored Boy's entry. He was pleased, because it clearly guaranteed the other man was in no position to look for help. A question flickered in Boy's mind, a sharp bite of greed at the prospect of finding his quarry carrying something valuable. Shaking his head, Boy reminded himself of his instructions and carefully surveyed the area.

Geometrically modern, the lobbylike area immediately inside the door provided no hiding place. Boy moved toward the broad stairs to his left, the twin of those on the other end of the room. They marched up the front of the building and sun streamed through the huge smog-smeared windows, the strength of it muted so that the shadows that should have been edged and crisp were blurred. At the first landing, Boy unaccountably had to stop, seized by a nagging sense of something wrong. He could find nothing and blamed it on the hazy-bright light and the quiet of the place after the traffic outside. He continued upward.

The man waited for him on the landing between the second and third floors with an ingratiating smile. He extended a hand with the palm partially raised, the gesture a compromise between an offer to shake hands and placation. His eyes were soft.

For an instant the pursuer was the pursued, wrenched back to a childhood where his mother took him to the dim church with a roof that was a sky of stone and his every sound was an echoing sin that made him want to scream for forgiveness. There was a man there, too, who smiled and held out a fat hand and made your heart ache with shame because his liquid eyes read the bad thoughts and took them into himself.

Boy Angel had freed himself of those things once and for all, and he smiled back at the man while he rammed the knife home. They both grunted, the sailor in shock and Boy with effort.

He'd aimed well. Perfectly. The strike was right and the wound was a puncture, not a slash. Breathing would be almost impossible and most of the bleeding would be internal and so fast it would be over in a few seconds. Boy was impressed when his victim found enough air to speak. The words fought out of a face already turning to cold pallor.

"I don't have it anymore." The voice accused, scolded. "You didn't have to—" He grabbed Boy's shoulder to stay upright. "I already— I would've—"

The hand clutched convulsively and he choked. A delicate rivulet of blood slipped from the corner of his mouth. He wiped at it with his free hand and looked at Boy and whispered wearily, "Oh, shit."

Boy gently disengaged the hand at his shoulder, simultaneously displaying his smile at an older woman passing by. He turned the sailor so the blotched shirt front was hidden from her view. When he gently leaned the weakening body against the rail by the window, Boy was momentarily distracted before realizing his eye had been caught by a sign across the street. It was the exact green of the sailor's shirt, and it said "United Coconut Planter's Bank." The woman continued on and Boy stepped away. The sailor clasped both hands over the hole in his solar plexus and bent forward at the waist, eyes glazing as he performed a last obeisance only he could appreciate.

Boy was across the street and moving into the Ermita's bars and tourist shops before the feminine scream of discovery came to him. The shrillness grated and made the sound-absorbing mass of humanity around him as welcome as the anonymity it provided.

# ■ CHAPTER 4 ■

The house was the type of single-unit middle-class dwelling built wherever unswerving temperate zone mentality has overwhelmed the tropical's adaptation to its unique conditions. The practical stilts that provide cooling air circulation are discarded in favor of stuffy crawl spaces, carefully enclosed, as if the protection of the vermin living there is a matter of great priority. The best that can be said for the ill-considered construction is that it provides a clapboard-and-stud image of respectability and permanence.

The small front yard was neat, and two hibiscus shrubs like green fountains flanked the porch steps, their scarlet blossoms a proud welcome. The house had an honest look, comfortable in a neighborhood of people who left in the morning and came home after a day spent working for someone else. Wage earners, the quiet ones, hoping for leaders to give them opportunity, growing desperate in their efforts to make the system produce what they'd been assured it would.

Draeger parked and walked to the door. The man who responded to the knock looked like a series of carelessly selected mahogany blocks. He was too broad in all his aspects, as if someone had taken a larger man and compressed him to different dimensions. His eyes were lively and faintly challenging. He said yes? and waited.

Draeger gave his name and said, "Miss Manong is expecting me. I called yesterday." The man continued to stare and for lack of anything else to say, Draeger added, "Mrs. Munson?" making it a hopeful question.

It worked. The square face cracked in a welcoming smile. "You

39

are Mr. Draeger! Ria said you were coming! Please, come in.'' He stepped aside and waved Draeger through, a heavy arm cutting a brief arc. The man ushered his guest to a chair, promised to return immediately, and left.

As soon as he was alone, Draeger got to his feet, the better to inspect the room. It could have passed for an arts and crafts gallery. Where the walls weren't festooned with paintings of all sizes and styles, they were obscured by handwoven fabrics or knotted textile hangings. Every piece of furniture not actually upholstered carried its load of objects, ceramic, metallic, or wooden. He was still inspecting when the blocky man returned.

"Ria is in the back," he said, still smiling. "She told me to ask you to please come there." He turned and led the way, one who obeyed and expected everyone else to do the same. As Draeger caught up they were passing through the small dining room. It was almost filled by a massive, polished table and chairs. He barely had time to admire the design as they hurried into the kitchen and then into the backyard. The man turned as they moved down the stairs to ground level.

"My name is Arturo. My wife is Ruby. I am Ria's cousin. We live here in her house, watch things when she's gone, that sort of thing. You know Mrs. Munson long?"

Draeger nodded. "I know Mr. Munson better." They were already at a shed abutting the garage. Arturo gestured at its dark doorway and stepped aside, grinning. Draeger hesitated only long enough to see the other man's expression edge toward offended hospitality before stepping inside. The interior wasn't as dark as it appeared. There was a double row of fluorescent tubes stretching the length of the ceiling. After the sun outside, they seemed puny. There was a figure working at a bench, standing, head bent forward out of sight. What was visible of the body was draped in a white smock that reached to the floor. The figure moved and there was a loud pop. Draeger stepped back instinctively and his shoulder struck something hard that resisted only momentarily. As he turned, a heavy object hit the cement floor with merciless clangor.

The white-shrouded figure whirled, stopping with an aggressive thrust that pushed a welding mask at him. The muffled voice that erupted from behind it was furious.

"It's bent! I'll never get it fixed in time!" She pushed past him with surprising strength, hoisting an angular composition of welded iron bars and tubes upright. "That piece took me months! Months! It's supposed to be delivered tomorrow and it's ruined!"

Draeger faced the sculpture, unwilling to look any longer at a mask spouting accusation. Being unable to think of anything to say increased his frustration. He blurted the first thing to come to mind.

"How can you tell it's bent?"

In the brittle silence one of the fluorescent tubes buzzed and developed a nervous tic. Draeger decided he had to face the woman or sprint out the door. He resigned himself to the course of honor.

She shoved at the mask's chin, pivoting it to the top of her head, examining the piece with narrowed eyes. After a moment she reached out, tracing the components. The hand was so sure and sensitive it appeared a tactile sense that needed no vision was committing angles and distances to memory.

Draeger only half-noticed her actions while he stared at her and alternately praised Leonila Munson and consigned her to the hottest corner of hell. Ria was lovely. He'd been given the opportunity to see her, and now any chance he'd ever have of knowing her was destroyed. If Leonila had left him alone, none of this would have happened.

She lifted the mask from her head and untied the scarf holding her hair. It tumbled across her shoulders like liquid. Without a glance for him, she extended the torch in his direction and when he grabbed it away, she slipped out of the long cloak, continuing to move around her sculpture. Under the white drapery she was dressed in white shorts and a two-toned blue T-shirt, and her figure was exactly as Draeger had feared, fully as beautiful as her face. He had hoped she would be grossly fat or bone thin—anything to take the sting out of having so instantly disqualified himself.

At last she faced him, still frowning, brows curved to tapering arches. Her tongue slid across her upper lip prior to speaking, and he was so busy admiring the unintentional eroticism of it he almost missed her words.

"I can't believe it," she said, and turned back to the piece. He opened his mouth and snapped it shut, knowing his safest course was silence.

She went on, "Ever since I started sketches on this, I've been worried about that unenclosed space up here. The way it bent restricts the exit. Now it has the cohesion I wanted." She looked at him. "Are you an artist, Mr. Draeger?"

"Miss Manong, I don't know what the hell you're talking about. All I want to do is apologize."

The answering laugh was a soft honest pleasure. She returned her attention to the work, still smiling. "It's not important. Your not being an artist, I mean." She laughed once more, differently, the childlike giggle an unexpected gift. "I'm sorry now. That came out sounding like I'm saying it's OK if you're not an artist but it's OK if you're clumsy. What I meant was, you don't have to be an artist to know art's ninety-nine-point-nine percent a mix of work, inspiration, study, knowledge, and talent. The last tiny bit is luck, and if you don't have that, the rest doesn't mean a thing. The accident was lucky."

"I hope you're not saying that to be nice."

"Nice?" She faced him, the amusement gone. "No way. If you'd damaged it I'd have sued you for every cent it's worth."

"And what would that be?"

She assumed a measuring air and for a cold moment he thought she was going to try a sales pitch. She said, "I couldn't charge you what it's worth. I'd charge you what I'm being paid." Her hand resumed caressing the jutting ironwork. "It's a commission for a construction company. That's what I call it, Construction Feature Alpha. It'll sit in a waiting room where fat businessmen will say stupid things about it and use it for a back-scratcher."

"I hope not." He made a deprecatory gesture. "I can't say much. I just think you shouldn't let people bother you because they don't see what you see."

"I love it!" She clapped her hands together in front of her face and dropped her head so her nose rested on the fingertips. Her eyes peered up at him, pleased and mischievous. Something else circled more warily behind the surface and he probed, seeking to name it. She broke the contact, sweeping past him and out the door. Her voice came over her shoulder. "Come on inside. You've made my day. Lunch is on the house."

He mentally apologized to Leonila for all the unkind things he'd thought earlier.

She seated him at the small table in the kitchen and said, "Tell me something about yourself while I put together a salad. Leonila says you're the greatest catch in the Philippines."

"I must have offended her. She used to say the whole world." He waited to see her reaction. A corner of the full lips rose in a smile and he relaxed, continuing. "She probably mentioned my name. It's Glen. Please. And my job. I'm a market analyst for a rubber company."

"Right. Glen. And she mentioned your work. What's it mean?"

The cover came automatically, so well rehearsed he could recite it when he was only half awake and more than half drunk. Better than that, he *told* it, like an accomplished storyteller, which is what he had to be. He told the cover and he watched as it unrolled, read his audience, played to whatever he saw there. Because it was false, so was he. The sense of satisfaction that others accepted as a matter of course when they spoke of job accomplishments was denied him. The man he claimed to be did only what was necessary to give the illusion of life. The real person that ate, slept, and knew emotions and thoughts lived in the dark and waited, chafing for the infrequent bursts of freedom that fell his way.

Unexpectedly, he was seeing the man named Kolar again, hearing him say, "When you're in the field there are no time outs. If you forget that once, you risk the lives of everyone you know and everyone who works for you. You can relax with us, be yourself with us. Only us."

She glanced at him curiously, puzzled by the pause. He said, "Actually, it's a very interesting job. I travel all over, match our projected rubber needs against the expected crop. I try to stay ahead of grade, price ranges, and so on. On the other side, I help our sales people try to predict a market for finished products here in the Philippines. There's always something going on. I enjoy it."

"It sounds interesting. Do you leave the islands?"

"No, I just work the Philippines. We have other guys in Singapore and Indonesia and so on."

She looked around at him. "The man in Singapore, he's the senior one? The boss analyst, or whatever?"

"I'm the senior one and I'm here because it's where I want to be."

There was a touch of color in her cheeks when she turned back to cutting tomatoes, but she seemed satisfied with the answer. A surge of irritation warmed him. He knew what she was thinking. So many of the Filipinos were convinced no American stayed there because of a liking for the country, but because it was required. Many times he'd asked himself what the root of the problem could be, and the best he ever managed was an amorphous linkage between the long centuries of colonialism and a general anti-foreign attitude. Fortunately, not everyone disliked all foreigners. There was enough animosity around to guarantee that most days provided a reminder, however. Sometimes it was as subtle as this latest attitude check. It could be virulent.

She put a salad in front of him, tomatoes, lettuce, orange and mango slices, all sprinkled with shredded coconut. He refused the dressing offered.

She put the bowl to one side, using none herself, and he hoped he detected an air of approval in her manner and had to squelch a grin at his own behavior.

"How long have you been here?" she asked.

"Around four years. The company's happy to keep a man in place who knows the country and I'm happy here, so it works out fine."

"Where's your home?"

He laughed. "The people in the States think it's Manila. I came from Missouri. Born and raised there."

"St. Louis?" She nibbled the mango, perfect teeth winking into view before disappearing into the gleaming yellow.

"No, not me. I'm a country boy. My father owned a gas station in a little town. Best mechanic for forty miles around. Said he'd break my arm if I didn't graduate from college. I still think he had the best life a man could want."

"He was happy?"

Draeger lifted one shoulder and dropped it. "Who wakes up every morning and sings songs about going to work? He enjoyed most of what he did for a living, had plenty of good friends, loved his family, and we loved him. He had to count every penny he spent, but he never welshed on a debt or cheated anyone. Now that's enough.

What about you? All I know is you're an artist from Iloilo. And your cousin Arturo calls you Ria.''

Her eyes rounded. "I thought Leonila—! Oh, that woman! She sent you here and told you nothing about me?''

He nodded and she made a face. "Well, what can I tell you? The easiest part first, I guess. They call me Ria because when I was little I couldn't say Margarita. There are five children in my family, three girls and two boys. I'm next to last and my brother Julian is the baby.''

Once started, she clearly enjoyed herself, and Draeger saw illustrated once again the importance of family to the people of the Philippines. Her eyes filled with unselfconscious delight as she expanded on names and dates, family episodes and escapades. Despite his desire to absorb all the information possible, Draeger found himself drifting away, caught up in strange speech rhythms, unexpected inflections and unusually emphasized words. As Leonila had warned him, her conversation bordered on singing. Imperceptibly, he stopped concentrating and merely listened.

When it occurred to him she must stop soon, apprehension jarred him.

If she asked for more details of his own family, how was he to answer? What could she understand of a northwest Missouri winter, a wind that slid between naked branches with a sound of steel being edged on stone?

If she hadn't lived through that, how could she know what it was like to stand next to a brother, both shivering as if unclothed before the wind, listening to Mother tell what happened to naughty boys who lied?

What could Ria know of a spring ice storm, the kind that came when the early flowers were in bloom and turned them into convoluted blobs, the colors like crystallized screams crying for the thaw that would let them die?

And never having seen that, how could she comprehend a woman who extended and retracted her affection for her husband and sons, alternating rage and tenderness with shattering and unpredictable caprice?

Ria knew the passions of a family that loved, fought, and loved again. She could never imagine a family where love raced through each day pursued by fear. And sometimes lost dismally.

She said, "You never said how many in your family," and it was a second before he could pull himself up from his memories. He laughed to cover the hesitation.

"There were only two kids, my brother and myself. He's two years older. Like I said, we lived in a small town. Growing up was something that just happened. Nothing to talk about, to tell you the truth."

She was frowning slightly as she picked up the plates and took them to the sink counter, clearly dissatisfied by his answer and unsure how to proceed. Before the silence could extend to an uncomfortable length, Arturo bustled in.

"Ria," he said, with a quick smile for Draeger, "you have an appointment this afternoon, remember? The portrait bust commission."

She made a sharp noise and grabbed Draeger's arm to look at his watch. "Oh, God, I'll never make it," she moaned. "I have to change, get my pad, my sketch kit—"

Draeger rose. "Hurry and get together. I'll take you."

"Oh, thank you. I'll trust your driving. Mine's not that good and when I get rushed—"

Arturo cut her off, speaking to Draeger. "Thank you. Very much." With a nervous look at the glaring Ria, he hurried out of the kitchen.

When Draeger looked away from the retreating back, Ria's face was softer, almost contemplative. A hand moved toward him as if it would touch him, but fell back quickly.

"I wish I could meet your father," she said, talking past his surprise. "He must have been a nice man. You looked—comfortable— when you talked about him."

She trotted out before he could answer. A spot of pain like the end of a lit cigarette touched his temple and he knew he'd have a headache in a few minutes. It was an old nemesis, practically a friend in its familiarity. It would fade slowly unless he was stressed. The body would throw it off then, excusing itself from punishment for a minor problem in order to avoid a greater danger. He'd long since stopped wondering about the psychology of the thing and learned to live with it. The error was the important thing, and this time it was a bad one. He had let himself be seen. Somehow she had understood about his father.

His telling of the facts was flawless, of that he was certain. Nevertheless, she had seen to the heart of his reminiscences.

The realization he should walk away right now was a prelude to an increase in the intensity of the headache. He discarded the idea as quickly as it had surfaced. The pain was unaffected.

He was thinking how unfortunate it could be if she was consistently that perceptive when he heard her coming down the steps. In his pleasure at being assured of her company for a while longer he didn't even notice the headache was completely gone.

# ■ CHAPTER 5 ■

Forbes Park is a suburb of Manila, a residential district south and east of the city. The Manila Polo Club is immediately adjacent, which is not entirely accidental, as any tourist would note. Unfortunately, not many tourists are privileged to make studied conclusions about Forbes Park because it is guarded by men with guns and by fences, walls, road blocks, massive gates, and the best electronic equipment money can buy. Forbes Park is the home of the very rich, and if a place can be said to have a personality, it is a quivering lump of wealth and privilege peeping nervously from behind its various barriers at a world full of ferocity. The human presence within Forbes Park depends on that world, draws its treasure from *out there,* and realizes it is in the unfortunate position of a farmer watching his milk cows metamorphose into tigers.

The capitalist system that created Forbes Park has, in the Philippines, all the classic qualities and flaws to the maximum. For every philanthropic act there is a crooked business deal that destroys innocents. For every dollar invested in schooling to raise a free, enlightened electorate another is spent to suborn a judge or elect a thief. It is a tough-and-tumble economic system, and the people who live in Forbes Park have roughed and tumbled the best of them and should be admired for that, if for nothing else, before they are condemned out of hand.

The homes of Forbes Park are grandiose. That is not to say they're garish and in bad taste, although some certainly are, but that no one looks at them and thinks of them as quaint bungalows and cottages. Poems to the good life, they always look freshly unwrapped and deposited in place with the morning dew, the gift of a moneyed genie. Many have servants' quarters, quaint bungalows, and cottages. If it's not true that the houses speak exclusively of the benefits of honest hard work and perseverance, they unarguably shout the benefits of cash in large quantities.

There are those who are uncomfortable in the face of such luxury.

When Draeger approached the guard post at the entrance to the area, that discomfort was all over Ria's face in a swirling series of responses. On seeing the polelike arm of the gate, she frowned. When Draeger stopped and the guard approached, she smiled for the man, pointedly ignoring the pistol at his hip and his partner, who remained at the guard shack with an automatic rifle pointed at the ground just in front of the car. Both men were crisp and clean, and their eyes were as distant as planets. The one with the pistol absorbed Ria's smile with no visible effect while he explained "an incident" necessitated stricter security than usual. He asked Draeger if he was expected. When Ria explained the nature of their call, he swiveled his head her way and listened with polite chill.

When he returned to the guard shack to verify their welcome his course was carefully roundabout, keeping him out of his partner's line of fire. When he had clearance for them he waved them through. The backup man was already searching the faces in the next car. Ria waved at the man with the pistol, and the gesture was acknowledge and rejected with the same nod.

She sulked. Draeger considered talking to her and changed his mind after a glance at the jut of her chin. After a while she broke her own silence.

"I can't stand a man like that. He works for these snobs so he acts like them."

"He's not being stuck-up. He's paid to be suspicious so the people living here can relax."

"That should tell you something. What kind of people need guards to relax?"

"How'd you like to live in a place with no cops? There's more money and more vulnerability here, so they hire more cops. It's natural."

"It's not natural! What's natural about these people being so rich while so many other Filipinos live in poverty?"

He held up a hand. "Look, I'm not getting into that kind of argument with you. It's your country. Solve your own problems. My country's got enough to keep me busy."

The tone of her voice was grudging acceptance of his attitude. "We've got to find a way to put a stop to the really obscene wealth. It's one thing for people to make money—I like the stuff, myself— but we've got too much poverty and too much obscene wealth."

"I hope somebody gives me a choice someday. I've tried being poor. It'd be fun to be obscene once." He pointed at a mansion up the street. "Look at that place, for instance. How'd you like to live there?"

"I'll let you know. Pull in the driveway."

He braked and looked at her quizzically. She laughed. "That's where I have to go."

He pulled in and slowed more than really necessary, not wanting to miss any of the scene before him. They were on a curving cement strip almost wide enough to be an extension of the street. The arc complimented the curve of the large, shaded porch extending from the front of the sleek contemporary house. It hugged the top of a slight rise, a stark white form relieved by windows that glinted like black ice caves.

The bulk of the space cordoned by the driveway and the street was divided into strict segments of formal garden with a velvet lawn center. Two gardeners edged the grass, heavy knives doing ruthless execution among the more ambitious stolons. Shrubs and brilliantly flowered plants seemed to watch both gardeners and grass with equal disdain. The men looked up and followed the car with their eyes while the knives continued to rise and drop, rise and drop, with a rhythm and precision that suggested the arms had no further connection with the minds.

Once the car was stopped a man in dark trousers and plain white *barong tagalog* strode across the porch to open Ria's door with a flourish. The shirt flared and revealed a .45 automatic in a belt holster. Draeger looked away quickly and stifled an urge to laugh at his punctilio, anxious to avoid being caught staring at a concealed weapon. He knew the weapon could have been hidden far better. That would have been pointless, though. If it couldn't be seen at all, no one would know about it, and the deterrent effect would be lost. The man had probably practiced that door-opening turn persistently.

He smiled a welcome at Ria and ushered them into air-conditioned gentility, showing Draeger to a huge leather chair in a paneled den cluttered with books and magazines. When asked, Draeger chose iced tea over a drink. The butler used the intercom on the desk to order it. Then he led Ria out.

She turned at the door and looked back at Draeger. He hoisted his feet onto the matching hassock and sprawled, grinning. She shook her head, smiling as a teacher accepts minor misbehavior from a favorite.

As soon as they were around the corner Draeger's smile bunched to a frown.

It hadn't troubled him that his man from the Wadco Trader left no drop signal the day the ship tied up. The man had no way to guarantee he'd get ashore the first day. It was unusual for him to miss the second day, however, and anything unusual was bad.

He shook his head to clear the frown just in time to see a maid uniformed in black skirt, white blouse, and cap come into the room carrying a silver tray. Drops of condensed moisture spangled a tall glass on it, and when the woman passed the window they caught the sun and for a moment the ceiling danced with mad dots of pure light. The maid smiled as she lowered the tray to the table next to his chair, the drink accompanied by a silver sugar bowl and spoon, a long silver spoon for stirring, and a fan of lemon slices on a plate. She waited while he thanked her and, when he asked for nothing else, bobbed her head and padded away. She was going through the door before he realized she was wearing black and white tennis shoes.

That discovery made him aware he'd barely noticed his surroundings, and he damned his courier. The room was worth observing. He got out of his chair and strolled with his tea. Pride of place in the room belonged to a desk. It was backed against a wall of books and a seated occupant could observe the entire room. Made of wood, the piece was almost sculptural, a free form resting on a curving pedestal rather than feet. He ran a finger along the fit of the drawers and was impressed that the gap was too small for him to insert a fingernail. The polished surface was completely bare.

The remainder of the furniture was as opulent. He examined the quality of the leather in the chair he'd been using. It was excellent, glossy from years of use, uncracked and supple as it had ever been. He rubbed it on his way by, and his fingers made a scuffing sound. It stopped him, made him catch the animal, tannery smell. He let it carry him back to a time when he was barely school age and his grandfather would walk through the barn with him and stop by the harness hanging next to the stall. The old man's hand was like twisted oak branches held in a bunch with blue twine, all liver spots and trembles. It would rise from his side and settle on the leather straps and the touch would start his mouth working and he would talk about feed and plowing and pulling stumps to a horse named Duchess that had died years before his grandson was born.

One day Draeger's father caught his son listening and smiling and without a word backhanded him across the mouth so hard it split his lip and drove him against the wall. The grandfather had squawked, a bird-cry of utter amazement, nothing Draeger had ever heard from him before, and it frightened him because his ears were ringing and he was sure his hearing had been knocked crazy. He started to cry, and his father swore at him for laughing at the old man, and Draeger said he wasn't laughing at him, he was being happy with him. Then his father had closed his eyes as though he were the one with the split lip, and when he looked at his son again two silver tears rolled down his face. The grandfather started crying, too, and all three of them just stood there until he said, "We must look like three world's champeen horses' asses, standing around bawling our butts off," and then they just stood there and laughed as hard as they'd cried.

The gun-carrying butler spoke from the doorway. "Is there anything I can get for you, sir? Miss Manong will be a few more minutes."

Draeger said, "No, thanks," smiled appropriately, and watched the man leave again. He wondered what a butler did when there was no one to shoot or order tea for.

Continuing his tour, he moved to the window. A swimming pool glared at him, the diamond-edged ripples on the water and the bone-white cement rim hoarding the sun, compounding it within themselves before releasing it in an incandescence. The room felt chill in the shock of that strength. An unwitting process of his mind pointed out the cold was relative, and he retreated into the darkness in order to think without having to ward off the power waiting outside.

He reviewed his major concern. If the courier had been arrested, he would have squealed for help by now. The urge to inquire of the ship pulled at Draeger's mind, as it had since the schedule collapsed, and he continued to resist. The courier had operated this long with absolutely no difficulty because he was unconnected with anyone. A telephone call asking about him would create more interest than the reassurance would be worth.

The options were to either wait or push. Without a drop signal, the only assumptions could be that he hadn't made the drop or that he had made it and couldn't make the signal.

Anger seared Draeger's thoughts.

*Why? Maybe this and maybe that. All the ignorant bastard had to do was make the drop and mark a fucking wall with a pen. Christ! What could be simpler? Oil-based ink. Stain cement for a hundred years, and there wasn't any sign of sandblasting or anything else. The fucker blew it. Something's gone bad. If he'd been picked up after making the drop and before making the signal he'd have spilled his guts on the spot. But maybe not.*

He made a fist and squeezed it in the other hand until a knuckle cracked painfully.

*Cheap. If the cheap bastards running the goddammed government had any balls, we wouldn't be playing with a short deck all the time. If we had one decent rat in the police files here I wouldn't be sweating like a whore.*

When he sat down in the chair again he remained bent forward over the heavy earth-dark rug, his eyes focused on a point below the foundations of the house.

Ria had to call him a second time to get his attention. He practically leaped to his feet.

"I was daydreaming." He gestured weakly. "Seems to me I'm doing a lot of that lately."

Ria smiled, leading him away and patting his arm. "I read tension can do that to a person. People daydream because they always win in their fantasies."

Draeger tried to smile, and her eyes widened. He realized how rough his expression must be and forced a laugh in an attempt to recover. He said, "In my daydreams there's a lot of failure. I guess I'm not good at it."

She laughed with him. The honesty of it tore his mind. "You need more practice," she said.

They reached the door, and he belatedly reached for her sketch pad and kit, making a face over his thoughtlessness. She forgave him with a look, and they walked to the car. The butler helped her in and watched them leave. The gardeners were closer to the driveway and Draeger had the window down while the air conditioner struggled to overcome the stored heat. The scratchy ringing of the blades slashing the earth made his neck hair twitch.

When they were away, he said, "Have you got some free time?"

She nodded with a trace of weariness. "I had to talk pretty hard to get my contract, and I want to relax."

"I thought it was all wrapped up when you went in. You made the deal? Congratulations!"

Her smile carried cynicism. "I hate to sell myself like that. It makes me feel—oh, I don't know."

"You're too sensitive." He turned left onto Epifanio de los Santos, driving west toward the bay.

"I'm not being sensitive." She twisted to face him. "It's not like selling beans, you know. I have to draw sketches and watch people who don't have the least idea what they're doing change them." She puffed out her cheeks and simpered, lifting her voice to a mincing falsetto. "Oh, my dear Ria, you've made me just a *teensy* bit heavy here, don't you think? And I really *can't* be that *severe!* Everyone, simply *everyone,* says I'm always laughing and it just wouldn't be *me* if I didn't have my little smile!"

He laughed. "No wonder you want to relax."

"It's not always that bad. Sometimes it's real fun. What's especially bad is when they turn you down. Rejection. And being an independent woman here isn't all that easy, either."

"It's not easy anywhere. I'm sure it's a lot tougher here. Traditions change slowly, and you're bucking a very old one."

"It's not a Philippine tradition, it's a Western one. Women had more equality when we were a free people, and then you came here and—"

"Hold it!" He held up a peremptory hand. "I've been here four years. I haven't stopped or started one tradition. If you want to badmouth the Spanish or some great-great-great grandkin of mine, go ahead, but don't blame me personally, OK? It makes me feel old."

He looked to see how she'd taken his outburst, and she was smiling at him, the teasing light in her eyes again. She said, "You don't look four hundred years old, now that you mention it."

"You're very kind."

"We're a hospitable people. Polite."

He made a rude sound and she laughed heartily, then, growing serious, "It must be boring, listening to us complain. At least you understand."

He glanced at her again, making up his mind before plunging ahead. "It's not always pleasant, to be honest with you. I do understand, though. In a way, I approve, too. It's a form of patriotism, and I'm one of those people who hasn't given up on that kind of thing."

"I'm glad," she said, and he looked again, sharply, as soon as he was past the lumbering truckload of windblown chickens. She continued to look straight ahead as she added, "I haven't known many Americans. The ones I did meet seemed to believe in nothing. For instance, I'm an Asian, and I'm more attached to the Catholic church than any American I met. It makes me feel suspicious. I mean, they brought it here, right? So why's it more important to me than to them?"

"I never thought of it. I think maybe religion's a more personal thing with Americans. Religious holidays and all that are a lot bigger deal here."

"That's so. But there're other things. Like, I know my country's got lots of problems, but I love it, and I don't want anyone tearing it down. You—oops, almost did it again—*the* Americans don't seem to be happy unless someone's telling them they're no good. For people from the small countries it's too good a chance to pass up."

He merely nodded, and they were both silent while he negotiated the turn onto Roxas Boulevard, headed back toward the city. His answer, when it came, was quiet, almost as if he spoke to himself.

"I wonder about that a lot. I think it's because so many of our people in authority are ambitious and insecure. Groucho Marx had a line that fits. He used to say he didn't want anything to do with a girl who'd go out with a man like him. We've got a lot of politicians and State Department and intellectual types who think that way. They only represent plain old Americans and it galls them, so they fawn on people all over the world to be liked by someone —anyone—else."

Ria made a sound of surprise and added, "You're a little bit deeper than you want people to think, aren't you? You fooled me."

He grinned. "You know what the Asians say about us wily Occidentals."

She sniffed. "I'm sure it's true in your case. Where are we going?"

"Busman's holiday for you. You're the image maker, so I'm going to give you a chance to criticize my efforts. I thought we'd walk around in Rizal Park and I can take some pictures. I've been promising to send some home to my brother."

She protested mightily about being photographed, and they argued happily, cruising the divided boulevard past nightclubs and towering

hotels that stared over vivid green palms to the blue of Manila Bay.
When he found a parking place close to the park he insisted it was a
sign. If she wasn't his intended model the traffic gods would never have
been so kind. He got his camera, and she brought her sketch pad and
kit, and they walked in the park as freely and aimlessly as children
out of school.

When they reached the floral clock he struggled and strained to
get her posed to his satisfaction, and she ended up laughing so hard
she ruined two of his pictures, one by covering her face with her
hands and the other by turning away, amusement bursting free as he
snapped the shutter. When they left the clock they were arm in arm,
and they remained so until they came to a small, fenced tree. A
plaque identified it as planted by Imelda Marcos. When Draeger
suggested she pose in front of it she overruled him, insisting she do
a charcoal sketch of him instead. She posed him in a seated position,
the tree between him and the blaring jeepneys on the street bisecting
the park. When she was done she sprayed the picture with a fixative
and called him to look.

He was honestly impressed. It was a facial study, and she had
used the blunt charcoal stick to vary lines in width and depth with an
artist's deceptively guileless accuracy. The economical strokes had
homed in on his prominent cheekbones and the lock of hair that fell
forward over his forehead. He had been unaware of any facial
tension, but she caught the stress that pulled the brows down in the
center. The effect of the whole drew attention to his eyes. It disturbed
him to see the frigidity in them, knowing it came from a mind
shielding itself behind emptiness.

He studied Ria's face while she examined the sketch and saw no
indication she was aware of what she'd created, just as she'd been
unaware of her insight concerning his father.

He complimented her and tried to express his gratitude.

When he brushed himself off and they prepared to leave he had
never felt so foul in his entire life.

His hand went to his pocket and he fondled the metal object
resting among his keys.

It looked like an ordinary nail. It had a head that unscrewed and a
tiny compartment drilled in the shaft. In an emergency it could be

driven like any other nail. Draeger's courier had placed it exactly as always, punched into the ground at the base of the tree's fencing. There had been plenty of time to check for surveillance, and there was none. Something had gone to hell, but security was still good.

Draeger wanted to believe that. Part of his mind refused. He reminded himself that part of his mind always refused. The resistance was stronger than ever.

Despite that concern, his overriding sensation was of being unclean. Rationality shouted at him that he'd behaved logically, had pursued his mission. The whisper of self-contempt enfolded the argument the way smoke will hide the damage of a fire while inflicting its own poisonous hurt. Ria scrubbed the stubborn charcoal on her hands with a piece of tissue, and he wished what he'd done could be cleaned from his mind so easily.

She turned unexpectedly and smiled at his attention. The expression altered minutely, turned into consideration. It wasn't speculative or calculating. It was one reserved step from shyness. There was curiosity and some attraction and a measure of satisfaction and a willingness to go a little further. Neither of them realized it, but it is a look many had experienced before them. It is a look that demands more of the soul and the emotions than the eyes and for that reason may not exist at all. Nevertheless, it precedes any romance. It demands as it gives. It was far more than Draeger had bargained for and almost more than he could accommodate.

*I used her. There was a need, and I found a cover. As simple as that. If it'd blown up—God Almighty, what's wrong with me?*

Ria knew there was a struggle going on inside him. She saw the lines at the corners of his mouth, the lines she had so carefully avoided recording in the sketch, and the eyes that worked so hard to see without being seen. More, she knew she was at least part of the problem and was at once pleased and flattered and a little frightened. Why couldn't he be Filipino? Why did she have to complicate things by becoming interested in a damned American? Papa would roar like a bull, and Mama would be lighting so many candles the church would be in danger of catching fire. She told herself she would break it off.

He picked that moment to take her arm and start walking back to the car. She stole a look at his profile. He was many things, she decided, and a brief shock raced through her when she thought that some of them might be unpleasant. Another quick look at him, and the urge to comfort him beat down her concern.

There was an unnamed need in him. There was strength. It felt natural to be touching him, to feel his longer stride chopped to match hers.

She would learn more about him. What harm could come of that?

Draeger wanted to go home. He felt grimy, and his thoughts were covered with sand that scraped the inside of his head raw. He wanted a shower. He wanted sleep.

A hundred yards away a man was busily arranging his wife and children for a family picture. It was an odd scene. The family was lower middle class, at best, but the camera was an extremely expensive model. More, it was equipped with a very costly zoom lens of the type that combines great magnification with compact construction. The greatest anomaly of the entire matter, however, was how carefully the man set the zoom for its maximum focal length. Anyone with any knowledge of cameras could have told him his wife and children would be indistinguishable blurs and the only things recognizable in his pictures would be away off in the distance. The young couple—the American and the Filipina girl, smiling at each other as they walked away—they were a good example.

# ■ CHAPTER 6 ■

The lone man on the afterdeck of the large cruiser turned from his seaward vigil and lit a cigarette. He made hard work of it in the swirling wind of the boat's progress and, forward in the cabin, a crewman in a white jacket exchanged glances with the man at the wheel. They smiled, careful to keep their backs to the man.

Their concern appeared normal, the caution of employees. Shortly, however, both managed a second, apprehensive look. Each took as much pain to shield the action from his partner as the man at the stern. Whatever amusement they shared at his expense, the furtive independence of their next action proved neither was prepared to share the outcome of discovery.

The man had returned to his search. He grasped the nylon lifeline with hands browned almost as dark as those of his Filipino crew. At their distance he appeared attentive. On closer view the taut knuckles and active eyes revealed far greater strain.

His name was Anthony Pierce, called Tony by those people who were his friends and many others who merely appeared to be so. He was the part owner and manager of a resort hotel. The gleaming fifty-foot cruiser ostensibly belonged to that enterprise. In truth, it was his toy, justified to the other partners by the cold logic that a luxury resort on its own island, albeit only ten miles from Zamboanga, demanded its own luxury yacht. The partners knew better but agreed since they had practically unlimited access to it on their visits. The crew called their boss Mr. Pierce ashore and Captain at sea. The man at the wheel, bolder than the rest, tried it first, and the crew seized the opportunity to follow suit when they saw Pierce's ill-

59

disguised pleasure. The title had become more than a chance to curry favor, however. It was a requirement, and the one man who had forgotten was accused of letting the starboard engine overheat and dismissed from the crew as soon as the lines were secured that day.

Pierce left the port side and walked across to starboard, scanning the featureless surface long enough to take one hard drag on the cigarette before tossing it overboard. He stepped to the centerline while the boat turned, unconsciously posing against the pitch and roll. Average height for an American, which he was, his glossy black hair contributed to the local suspicion he might be part Filipino, which he wasn't. The eyes under heavy brows were light brown, the nose stubby, a bit small for the heart-shaped face. He wore a gaudy shirt and khaki shorts. The muscles of the bare arms and the calves of the legs were large without being bulky, molded in smooth swimmer's curves. He raised a hand with unusually long fingers to stroke an immaculate black moustache. There was controlled impatience in the quickness of the movement.

The motion stopped abruptly as he bent forward, tensing. A second later he hurried to a cabinet and returned to the starboard lifeline with a pair of binoculars. He swept the horizon, fixed on a point, then made a sound of disgust and moved to a chair. Seated, elbows braced on his knees, he looked again. When he lowered the glasses he was smiling.

"Off there," he shouted at the cabin. His voice was clear and the words precise, but there was a clash of forced heartiness. If the man at the wheel heard a hint of such a false note, he kept it to himself. He was spinning the wheel even as he turned to look for the pointed direction.

Pierce went on. "That'll be Bilongon's man in that prau, sure as hell. Crafty bastards. They knew I'd be expecting him from the west, so he's coming from the south. Juan, send Jesus below. Have him tell Ruiz and Lucian to stay down there. I want him to personally check their rifles and see the goddammed safeties are on and the guns are loaded. Tell him to put them both where they can shoot into the prau, then get his ass back up here. And keep them back from the fucking portholes."

The man at the wheel said, "You heard?"

Jesus said, "Certainly, I hear. Ruiz and Lucian heard. Why doesn't he tell me himself?"

"He is a foreigner. Who can explain? Hurry. I will try to keep our starboard side facing the prau. That Moslem bastard will probably make it difficult. Make sure Ruiz and Lucian know they must keep him in their sights."

Jesus threw him a mock salute. "I understand, my leader." He laughed as he trotted down the steps.

Watching him go, Juan smiled at his back before turning his attention to the small boat. The smile warped to a grimace, and he told himself once more that, for all his high-sounding talk of an independent Moslem state, Bilongon was really nothing but a skulking dog, a pirate. If the government had any sense they would kill the rebellious traitor and every one of his men they could catch.

He struck the wheel at the thought. Every one they could catch, indeed. Dirty savages. Bred like monkeys and hid in the jungle even better than the monkeys.

It was disgraceful to bargain with them. Using an American to do it only made things worse. Still, if the Moro pigs decided to take out anger on someone, it would be the American and God knew there already were too many of them. Especially this one. Big-shot sonofabitch.

Juan eased off to port, thinking how completely the cruiser could grind up the tiny twelve-foot prau. He imagined the look on the Moro's face when he understood he was going under the massive keel.

The boatman was small and intense, dressed only in shorts. There appeared to be no fat on him at all, merely a skin like well-cared-for leather drawn tight over muscles as neatly defined as an anatomy chart. The slim hull of his boat between its outriggers was empty except for himself, a reed food basket, and a water jug.

He let his sail go slack, catching the line Jesus threw him. He didn't bother to tie fast, clearly anxious to be underway. He shouted up at Jesus in his own dialect, and the latter ignored him, smiling with open amusement at the sail with its parallel vertical red and green stripes. A tattooed hand clutched the long-bladed knife at his side, and he yearned up at the insulting Jesus.

The current snugged the prau against the cruiser, the near outrigger squealing when it dragged against the white hull. Pierce gingerly lowered himself over the side, wishing the noise would stop. It sounded like urging. The outrigger was only bobbing a few inches at a time, but it was slippery and narrow. He stepped on it, and the opposite one rose out of the sea as though alarmed. Quickly, he dropped forward, caught himself on one of the spars connecting the outrigger to the hull and flipped his feet directly into the boat, landing so lightly the narrow craft barely bucked. Once sure of his footing, he walked his hands up the spar until he could grasp the gunwale, then moved the food basket and sat down. The Moro looked a bit less reserved, and when Pierce used his own dialect to say, "We go. Now," he nodded almost civilly.

They sheered off smoothly, the sail bellying taut. The boatman brought them up into a hard tack that drove one outrigger into the water while the other stepped clear. The lower one sizzled through the silvered sea, battering into the small waves and exploding them out of the way like a pole driven through melons. Gouts of water sprayed away in chunks that spun in the sunlight, changing shape and color as they fell back into the sea. The raised outrigger was more discreet, satisfied to make fainter music with the wind, trailing an erratic spatter of droplets.

Pierce settled in for the ride, resigning himself to the destruction of his clothes by the hull's encrusted dirt. Each time he visited Bilongon he ruined whatever he wore, and he dutifully billed Colonel Arroyo's expense fund for whatever price he felt possible. Colonel Arroyo equally dutifully haggled him down. It was a game they played.

So was the entire matter of liaison with Bilongon. He supplied information of his Arab connections and superb courier service to Pierce in return for information of government activities. Arroyo knew nothing of Pierce's interest in Bilongon and used him solely because he was skillful at ferreting out details of Bilongon's operations and reported them without charge, asking only the good will of the local government. Further, Pierce was a foreigner and, in the event Arroyo's personal secret machinations concerning Bilongon surfaced, he was a ready-made scapegoat.

The whole thing sounded worse than the actuality. The longer Bilongon remained active, the more money Arroyo could milk out of the government for his counter-guerilla games. As long as Bilongon contented himself with a little pirating and small raids here and there, he was more of an economic asset to the local politicians than a problem. Arroyo, who was far more politician than soldier, would make a career of playing blind man's bluff with him.

If Bilongon would play. He was growing stronger all the time. Once he'd connected with his oil-rich dictator, he'd taken off. Now his men were amply armed and equipped.

They had hospitals with medicines and bandages. When a boat engine gave out they had the money to buy a new one in Singapore. Before, they'd had to steal a car for a replacement. Men had been caught at that, and it was very demoralizing to the warriors. Dying for the faith and independence was glorious. Going to jail for car theft wasn't. Bilongon's navy of high-speed *bancas* and almost-as-fast cargo boats called *kumpits* had been on its last legs when the oil money had come to their rescue.

Some of the money paid for Bilongon's pilgrimage to Mecca. As a *hadji,* his importance skyrocketed.

Pierce shifted in the narrow hull, trying to get comfortable. He half-turned, offering a cigarette, controlling a smile at the conflict on the boatman's hard face. He considered putting it on top of the food in the basket between them. The man could take it whenever he chose and not have to accept it like alms. Pierce discarded the thought, enjoying the man's indecision a few seconds longer before smiling a feigned understanding. He deliberately stuffed the pack back in his pocket. As soon as the scene was played out he chided himself for being so petty.

He squirmed to get his back curved to the shape of the hull, thinking it was too damned bad about the stubborn bastard. They were all that way, so fucking proud they ended up screwing themselves. If there was ever any doubt about pride going before a fall, a quick visit to the goddammed Tau Sug would convince anyone. Even the name—Tau Sug. Five hundred years everyone in the world called them Moros. *They* called themselves Tau Sug, and with this bullshit about a Moslem state stirring them up, there were some who'd as soon lop off your head as smile at you. And some who'd do both at once. Pride. And that's where they were weakest. Everybody had a weakness that could be capitalized on. It was a mistake to let their thickheadedness get to you. Just because they didn't know the difference between practicality and pride was no excuse to make trouble for yourself.

Pierce dropped his cigarette and watched it disappear in the welter from the outrigger. He wrestled about some more and finally found a position where he could doze. It was a studied action. In the first place, he needed some rest. Beyond that, he was impressing the boatman, who would think Pierce confident beyond words to be so relaxed. If he had known to watch his passenger's feet he would have seen the tips of the running shoes moving very gently, and if he had observed the tempo of the movements, he would have noted it was the pace of a heart beating a good bit faster than normal.

For more than two hours they sailed across water that heaved under them as a mother's hand rocks a cradle. They could have been alone on the earth. No other sail, no blaring jet or thrumming engine broke the poetry of the wind in sail and rigging, hull on wave. The men watched each other, the small, dark one determined to catch the white in his brilliant clothes either asleep or faking sleep. Pierce was equally determined to keep the other unsure or wrongly convinced. Most of the time he kept his head lowered, never looking higher than his companion's waist so his brow obscured his eyes. Once in a while he deliberately lolled, keeping his eyes tightly closed when they were visible. The other man pretended complete indifference, but Pierce could tell by the sudden movements of the torso that he was twisting, trying to see under the protecting forehead without actually seeming to do so. On several occasions he changed course drastically, sending his passenger flopping in the cramped space, trying to force open the eyes he could not find by stealth. At those times Pierce let him see the lids flutter partially open before closing again. Once they almost broached, and Pierce bit the inside of his lip to keep from cursing the man for his obstinacy.

And so they passed the time, tormenting each other in unbroken silence until the small boat cut through the waves like a poisoned blade, surrounded by a mist of irrational hate that only seemed to magnify the heat of the sun.

When they stopped Pierce remained still, chin on his chest, rolling easily with the wave-motion. The lines ticked resting signals, and the cloth sail scuffled its folds overhead, the sound of a massive bird grooming feathers. He clenched a fist and told himself he was behaving like an idiot and still refused to move. At last he could stand it no longer and stretched mightily, acting out his waking. When he looked aft the other man was ignoring him studiously, watching the land about fifty yards distant.

There was little beach to speak of, a line of sand perhaps three feet wide, blazing sugar-white, underlining the place where the jungle started. From that point the only view was vertical, and it was all green. In some places the wall of growth exploded outward, protruding at ground level across the thin strand to hang over the sea itself. Pierce stared at it in awe, as he always did. He disliked the jungle. It made him feel caged. No matter where he looked in there, he knew there would be trees everywhere, always blocking escape. He could fit between them, but there were always more, waiting, growing larger and closer every minute. He heard a sound and belatedly identified it as his own wordless disgust.

The other man turned slowly and smiled, an intimate, knowing leer.

Pierce was wondering if it would be possible to push him over the side before the knife came out when they both heard the other sound. It came just once, shrill as a bird call. They searched for its source and found only the silent judgment of the forest looking down on them.

Then the whistle was repeated, twice in rapid succession. The small man adjusted his sail. They got underway, making directly for one of the overhanging clumps of growth, and just as they seemed about to crash, a canoe slid out of it. There were two men, one forward and one aft, and they sped to the side of the vessel. Without waiting for instructions, Pierce scrambled across the outrigger and boarded. When he looked back, the prau had come about and was already skimming away. The man at its stern never looked back before the canoe was slipping through the brush again, headed back the way it had come. Pierce threw up his arms to protect his face and ducked. When branches quit slashing at him he cautiously lowered his guard and peered at his surroundings.

What had looked like scrub growth at the water's edge was the top of a tree, tumbled by some storm, still defiantly alive. The branches had twisted to reach toward the sun, transforming the luxuriant crown into a grotesque lattice of right angles. It hid the mouth of a muddy jungle creek. The forest's canopy screened aerial observation, and the light penetrating to the ground was pale, its rare bright splashes tremulous. The very atmosphere seemed to carry a delicate green cast that should have been soothing, but to Pierce it had the sheen of spoiled meat and he loathed it. The clinging humidity added to his revulsion. The air in the tunnel created by the creek's meandering was still, too burdened by heat to move. The sun at sea had been a searing trial that could occasionally be held at bay by the sail and eased by the wind and water. Here the sun was an infrequently glimpsed fury overhead, but its presence was unyielding, inescapable.

None of that prevented the chill that slid across Pierce's skin and raised his body hair.

This was vastly different behavior for Bilongon. Normally they met in one of the coastal villages, the clusters of huts on pilings that always made Pierce think of wading birds. An inland base, even on one of these small islands, had to be one of Bilongon's more important positions. It made Pierce unhappy to be included in the number who knew of it. Resentment stirred in him, and he reflected on Bilongon's lack of consideration. After all, he had his own secrets. He didn't need all of Bilongon's as well.

Just the ones that helped, he thought wryly, and a smile touched the corner of his mouth.

The trip up the creek was short, no more than thirty minutes. When the boat slipped alongside the bank a moment of genuine fear stung Pierce. He saw no reason to stop at that point, and the man in the bow turned to face him after having resolutely looked straight ahead until that minute. He was openly hostile. A shout from back in the trees sounded like a reprieve, and Pierce looked for it eagerly.

A man he recognized as one of Bilongon's lieutenants named Abdul came toward them and Pierce finally saw the long, barracks-like buildings in the distance. He scrambled out of the canoe and hurried toward the man, relieved by the welcoming smile. They shook hands briefly, and Abdul led the way toward the camp, practicing his English with a review of a movie he'd seen in Singapore. The thought almost brought laughter from Pierce. Abdul lived in a nipa shack in the jungle on an island too small to be considered a decent county, warred with the established government, practiced piracy as a hereditary trade, smuggled anything as a matter of course, and spoke of going to the movies across twenty degrees of longitude as if it involved catching a bus at the corner.

By now Pierce saw there were six of the buildings, built like the long-houses of old and arranged two by two, precise as the spots on a domino. A few men worked around them, watching Abdul and Pierce with careful unconcern. Unexpected music tumbled from one of the buildings on the left. A guitar tentatively chorded settled to a steady beat and the melody followed, a plaint in a minor key. A drum joined in, a small one, with a high, snarling tone. Between them they sang of a loneliness dangerously full of repressed passions and frustration.

When they passed between the first pair of buildings Pierce noted the cleanliness of the grounds, even the space under the structures where they stood on their eight-foot posts. Bilongon had learned the virtues of sanitation, as he had learned of tactics, evasion, and dispersed ammunition dumps. It was unfortunately easy for the characteristic Malay easygoing attitude to slip over into slovenliness, and Bilongon clearly fought it on all fronts. He apparently intended that his men die for the cause, not for something as democratic as disease.

They were idle thoughts in Pierce's mind, familiar ground covered over a span of years. They were shunted aside instantly when he realized what Abdul was actually saying. The movie he described was a new one, only now showing in major cities. Abdul had been in Singapore recently, then perhaps within the week. It was a realization at once exciting and worrisome. It could mean that too many things were happening at once.

They climbed the narrow steps of the left-center longhouse onto the porch and entered. Puddles of light collected under the windows, too weak to push back the gloom further. The music was coming from the far end of the building, and it dropped in volume at

Pierce's appearance. He had the uncomfortable feeling an unseen presence had found him intolerable and retreated to avoid him. The song increased tempo.

Bilongon sat at a crude table directly across from the door, his silhouette recognizable by the rigid set of the body. Pierce moved forward, and Bilongon rose to shake his hand. The oiled-wood handle and scabbard of the heavy knife at his side caught the light and glowed with candle-flame warmth. Pierce avoided looking at it, and when Bilongon offered a cold soft drink he accepted it quickly, suddenly aware of his thirst.

He searched Bilongon's face for some clue, some indication of excitement that might tie in with Abdul's revelation. It was an interesting face, unusual in its construction, and there was no information in it now. The cheekbones were sharp and flaring, the forehead prominent. His chin was sharp, belligerently projected, and the face narrowed toward it and the sharp nose. The effect was of a ship seen face on, and the quick eyes made it clear the mind behind it all was determined in its course.

"I have news," Bilongon said, his English an odd mix of Pilipino, American, and British accents. "It is important news. If you can tell me something of that pig-Colonel's intentions, I will share it with you." He gestured, and a boy appeared from the darkness to deliver a dish of pineapple slices, each with its bamboo skewer. He rolled his eyes once at Pierce and faded back where he'd come from. Bilongon took one of the slices and gestured for Pierce to help himself. The aroma caught him while his mind was racing through the optional tidbits of information he could use for bargaining, and he swallowed noisily. Bilongon smiled at the sound, and Pierce grabbed one of the slices. Juice spurted in his mouth as his teeth cut through the pulp with a sound like meat tearing. It pleased him to hear it, gave him a safe way to vent some of the aggression building in him.

Dealing with Bilongon was a trial. The man was clearly intelligent and reasonably well educated. Cultured wasn't too strong a word to use. Yet he kept himself off in the jungles, always fighting, always running and hiding, living a constant chase. He had nothing but his beliefs and his ragged followers, and still he carried himself with an air of self-assurance that bordered on egomania. Pierce knew himself well enough to know that was only one of the reasons why he resented the man.

He decided what to bargain with. He said, "Arroyo has his operations staff putting together a strategic hamlet plan."

Bilongon scoffed, and Pierce realized he'd have to tell him the entire plan. "You know the government's promising land to rebels who surrender. Arroyo wants to declare the land of anyone who helps the guerillas the property of the state. That'll be given to a man who's surrendered in some other part of the country, but only when there are enough like him, with their families, to form an effective village. The newly located people will have no reason to help you and a lot of reasons to resist you."

Bilongon's face grew steadily darker as he listened. "This has been approved by the Manila government?"

"It's only an idea, so far. He can be fought. If the plan reached international newspapers, pointing out the inhumanity of uprooting families and dumping new ones in their place, the government would deny knowledge, and Arroyo would burn his rough drafts the same day."

"It would take me weeks to get this story to my friends. And the Western press would sniff at it like dogs at a stranger, because it would come from Arabs and be about oppressed Moslems."

"I am not without friends literate enough to write letters."

"You would help? Why?"

"The same reason as ever, mutual advantage."

Laughter pushed between the thin lips before they curled in amusement. "You are a pleasure to deal with, Tony. I can trust you—when I am sure you're doing something on your own behalf."

Pierce forced himself to smile.

*You bloodless prick, you can't begin to imagine what you're into. When your buddies realize you're only another raghead with a bunch of pirates you call your army they'll dump you before you know what hit you.*

"—returned from Singapore," Bilongon was saying, and Pierce jerked his mind back to the conversation, reaching inside his subconscious just in time to understand Bilongon meant Abdul. "I sent him there to make arrangements for a smuggling operation."

He paused, letting Pierce anticipate. The guitar sighed a last few notes, deserted by the drum.

Bilongon said, "We are transporting four men from Singapore to here."

Pierce leaned forward, and Bilongon smiled again, rising from his chair and indicating Pierce should come with him. There was no more said until they were outside, down the stairs and moving away on the packed earth street running between the structures. The sounds of an instructor lecturing came from one and another class was in session to the right, the men sitting on the benches of a primitive outdoor theatre. In a few more yards it was apparent to Pierce they were going to a small outbuilding. A man squatted in front of it, knees splayed wide, rump hanging inches from the ground. He rested his back against the wall, forearms on his knees. His fingers were laced in front of him, cuddling the blue steel barrel of an automatic rifle while its butt end sat on the ground between his legs. The only part of him that moved was his head. It swiveled to watch them come.

Bilongon said, "Your cruiser was stopped by a *banca* on the way to your island. Your men were told to report that you would be returning tomorrow."

Pierce stopped. "That's impossible. I have a hotel to run, goddamit. We have some very special guests flying into Zamboanga tonight. I have to meet them. Arroyo'll be there. If he gets nervous he may come looking for me."

Bilongon had stopped, too. "He's been looking for me for years. He hasn't found me yet. What makes you think he'll find me this time?" For a long breath neither spoke or moved, and the struggle of wills between them was almost visible, like the sibilant blur of whips.

Pierce said, "I was thinking of what would happen to one of your people if a searching plane saw my transfer at sea. They'll bomb him out of the water."

Nodding, Bilongon resumed the walk. "I have prepared this building for the men from Singapore. I want you to see it."

The guard watched them go in. The single room was small, friendly with the woodsy smell of the new nipa walls and roof.

There was a table, as rough as Bilongon's in the other building, but considerably larger. Benches paralleled its long axis. Two double-decked bunks stood against the far wall, and there was a clean, unused cooking pit to the right of the door.

Bilongon watched Pierce circle the room. "It is crude, but it will do for our guests for the few days they will be with us." When Pierce looked at him, Bilongon grew thoughtful. "I know you Tony. I can't trust you, but I can make you dependent on me. I have arranged for you to stay tonight because the men arrive this evening, you comprehend? And they will tell me of their plans, here at this table. And you will listen, there, outside that wall. You will pass that information along to whoever you work for. They will then insist that you assist me and protect me with all your cleverness and connections."

Pierce shook his head. "Bilongon, you have no reason to distrust me, and I've told you a dozen—Lord, a hundred dozen—times, I don't work for anyone, I'm part owner of a hotel—"

"Don't!" The command was like a pistol shot. The words that followed were eerily soft. "Don't insult me, Tony. It is very offensive when you lie badly, because you do it so well when you try. When you do it badly I have to believe it's because you think I am stupid. I know about your expensive playground. I also know you are more than the blackmarket dabbler or influence peddler you claim to be. No, there is something else. I cannot be sure what organization you work for because you have no cause I can discover. But you *do* work for someone, Tony. We all do. We owe money, time, allegiance. Our souls. After tonight, you will be in debt to me."

During Bilongon's speech Pierce feverishly arranged an argument. Bilongon's voice never rose, droning monotonously. Alerted, Pierce looked into his eyes and what he saw there turned the careful debate phrases to dust in his throat. Bilongon was on a swaying line between normalcy and madness. Stories of *amok* drummed in Pierce's mind, and he stared at the hand, clenched like a bird's claws on the knife handle. He froze, afraid to breathe while the sparks of insanity spiraled behind the blank glass that had replaced Bilongon's usual attentive vision. Mechanically, as if responding to distant commands,

the rigid body turned to the door awkwardly and made its way
outside. Pierce hurried behind. Bilongon shivered and his hand slid
off the knife.

The guard looked at him and slipped around the corner of the
building without rising from his crouch. Pierce heard him crash
through the brush and swallowed screaming curses and envy. He had
never seen Bilongon so overwrought, so delicately balanced. He
asked himself how in God's name he ever got involved in this mess
and how he could get out.

Another shiver, and Bilongon looked at him as though surprised
to find either of them standing outside the hut. Without a word, he
led off, stride and manner perfectly unaffected. Pierce could only go
along.

They did not go directly back to the longhouse. Bilongon took
them down a different path, angling away, hardly visible it received
so little use. Suddenly, silently, he stepped to the side. Not expecting
such a move, Pierce was already off-balance and totally unprepared
for the hands that grabbed his shirt, first pulling, then pushing him
ahead and around a bend.

There was a cage there. It was a rough thing of bamboo, lashed at
its joints with wiry vines. A man clung to the bars, no more than
five feet away. Pierce made an involuntary sound deep in his chest
and thrust himself back against Bilongon's hand, the force of his
reaction making them both stumble.

Horrified, Pierce felt disembodied, divorced from what he was
seeing. Part of his mind told him he should refuse to accept any of
this while another part avidly examined everything and registered the
minutest detail.

The man was entirely naked, covered with sores from insect bites
and scratches. His eyes were shut, the lids sealed down with thick,
gummy matter. For a moment there was utter silence. It was broken
by Pierce's repeated internal animallike complaint that threatened to
bring up the contents of his stomach, and then by the flies that
buzzed angrily airborne at the intrusion, lifting heavily from the
corruption on the ground under the raised bars of the cage deck.
Their flight coincided with the shock of the first inhalation, and
Pierce felt himself ignore his own voice.

Matted hair clung to the man's skull like a greasy cap, and the sparser hairs of his beard had an encrusted, heavy look, each one extending stiffly from the skin as if avoiding contact with its neighbors. There was a vestigial bruise in the middle of his chest, a shadow of the dark flesh, and the skin in the middle was torn. The clinical view recorded the inverted U-shape of the tear and focused closer, noting the cross-hatching within the area, and Pierce knew the man had been pounded with the butt of a rifle.

The man's face twisted and worked, and his eyes came open, seeing Pierce's out-of-place paleness. He stared with increasing wonder until he finally let go of the bars and flung his hands outward, turning his head to extend his grasp one more desperate inch. He mashed his face into a cartoon profile against the wood, the eye facing Pierce churning in its socket with almost effervescent activity. He moaned in his search for words, finally producing sounds approximating speech. It was gabble to Pierce.

Behind him, Bilongon shifted his grip to Pierce's shoulder, holding him firmly in place. "He has no English. He's asking you to help him." There was an overtone in the explanation Pierce had trouble identifying. He was startled to realize it was sorrow.

The filthy hands scrabbled at the air, and Pierce tried to step back. Bilongon checked him, saying, "He is police. From Basilan. Two weeks ago we made a recruiting effort there. This one took our bribe to look the other way and then secretly informed the Army. Two of my men were killed. We have questioned him. He is brave. He tells us nothing and says he is innocent. Tomorrow we will have a trial and execute him."

Pierce concentrated on the hands in front of him, seeing how Bilongon's matter-of-fact voice drained the hope from them. He was reminded of plants assaulted by flames. The fingers were affected first, slowing in their clutching. As they weakened, the hand sagged until it drooped at the end of the wrist. The fingers were barely twitching when the elbows bent, allowing the forearms to sag. When the shoulders slumped everything was over, and the arms fell limp and flaccid against the yellow bamboo. The man moaned softly, transcending language in his misery.

Bilongon moved the stumbling, unresisting Pierce onto the other branch of the trail, and they headed for the buildings again.

In the distance a hen cackled hysterics at the appearance of an egg while a hoarse crow from one of the half-wild cocks boasted accomplishment.

The prisoner's voice rose behind them, and a man hurried past in that direction. A few seconds later the cries stopped abruptly, the silence as specific to the ear as a vision of a cut string.

Pierce was ashamed of how glad he felt to have the cries stopped. He also felt a great and unique appreciation for the jungle. It enforced his sanity. In any other environment he would have run by now, bolted like a rabbit. But that was crazy. No matter how dangerous the situation with Bilongon, he could exercise his mind, outthink this crowd.

Bilongon said, "I wish you did not have to see that. I wish we did not have to do it. They treat us no differently when they capture us. Now we will both rest. Maybe in a little while we will talk. First we will rest. Yes."

They walked up the steps and into the building where the dimness welcomed them. Pierce felt better for it. It restricted his vision, and he was tired of seeing. It also screened his eyes and the expressions he feared were marching across his face. And there were walls, solid walls that shut away the things outside, like the memory of the day he took the boatload of hotel guests to see the Moslem village. He was the one who recognized Bilongon's people. He was the one who listened to the old men bragging for the pink and white German girls of fighting and killing. He listened when the old men scornfully predicted few recruits would come from the placid farmers of Basilan.

Pierce knew who told Colonel Arroyo of Bilongon's recruiting team.

# ■ CHAPTER 7 ■

Pierce could never make up his mind what time of day made the jungle most frightening. No matter what cold logic he applied, as soon as he was exposed to that patient savagery, his reason crumbled to dread.

He looked upward at the roof of leaves and branches, at the general lowering of light intensity as dusk came to the island. Already the topmost vegetation was indistinct, its color bleeding away to gray-green that would be black in a few minutes. This time was, in some ways, worse than total darkness. A fire would hold darkness away, and Pierce looked forward to the heavy honesty of nightfall, when he could huddle close to the flame and lose himself in its careless dancing. The dusk moved in with a grim inevitability. There was no sunset here, no glory to day's end, only the cries of birds flocking to their roosts and the infrequent scuffle of some creature seeking safety from the eaters that would come soon.

Staring out the window of the longhouse, Pierce was unaware of Bilongon's increasing tension until the guerrilla spoke. "The praus bringing my guests will arrive soon."

Pierce turned. Bilongon had lit a kerosene lamp, and the soft glow barely stretched to where he sat. Instead of softening his features, it lost itself in the depth of his eye sockets, and the hollows under the pronounced cheekbones. It made him look cadaverous.

Pierce said, "From Singapore in an open outrigger canoe? God-damn, Bilongon—I know they're fast and—"

Bilongon shook his head. "No. They will transfer from a larger ship and make a high speed dash here. The praus can outrun anything the government navy has, but we use darkness, nevertheless.''

"I don't understand all this," Pierce complained. "Why carry these people all over the South Pacific? Why don't they just fake passports and fly out?''

Bilongon smiled. "Believe me, this way is safer for them.''

"Where are they coming from? And what are they supposed to be getting away from?" Pierce tried to sound demanding and failed, sliding off to petulance.

"You will learn when it is necessary. I don't want to talk about it." Bilongon looked away.

"You could at least give me some idea.''

"We will eat now." Bilongon stood and moved toward the door. "It is my custom to eat with my men. Come.''

The combination kitchen and dining area was no more than posts and beams supporting a roof. There were no walls, and Pierce had estimated there were about forty men seated on benches at the long tables and yet another dozen still in the line when he realized he was being made aware of another of Bilongon's secrets, this one as unwelcome as all the rest.

Bilongon waited until the last man was fed before approaching the large pot. A pockmarked, grinning cook scooped a generous portion onto metal plates for his leader and the guest. Drops of sweat bounced from his forearm and wrist when he banged the scoop against the rim of the vessel. The combination of the sight and the mess slopping into his dish nearly undid Pierce. Nausea wadded in his throat, a perverse weight that struggled to rise, rather than sink. He forced down a few bites, resisting the impulse to guess at the identity of the chunks. For once, Bilongon's tendency to drift away to glacial disinterest was welcome. The Filipino ate with mechanical timing, became a device that fueled itself while its other components idled. The dark eyes were aimed at the food, but focused on infinity. Pierce took advantage of that preoccupation to stroll to the dishwashing cauldron. The cook frowned at the amount of food Pierce was throwing away, but said nothing.

On his way back to rejoin Bilongon, Pierce thought of the similarity of this event and one he'd almost forgotten. It was a Thanksgiving dinner, and Aunt Marge had cooked the turkey. Even then—Christ, he couldn't have been more than twelve—he knew Aunt Marge had the taste of a chimpanzee. The dressing was a soggy, sage-laden mass, strong enough to make your eyes water. He could still see the shocked expressions around the table when he spat the first repulsive mouthful out onto his plate. His mother had twittered, as usual, and his father had roared apologies to Aunt Marge and shouted about rudeness and disgusting behavior and ordered him to leave the room. As he ducked under the roof of the eating shelter he was smiling wryly, remembering how, later, in the kitchen, he'd seen his father's plate with the napkin carefully draped over the dressing and a barely nibbled drumstick.

Sitting down again, a murmur of hurried conversation interrupted his thoughts, and he turned toward Bilongon and the excited youngster jabbering at him in a dialect Pierce recognized but couldn't understand. There were a great many sibilants and hard consonants, and in the young man's haste they whirred like small missiles. Despite his hurry, the newcomer shuttled his eyes from Bilongon to the strange white man. Pierce didn't know whether to be relieved or offended when Bilongon intercepted one of the glances and snapped at the messenger. At once the eyes swept back to Bilongon and remained, until the rest of the message was delivered. Bilongon dismissed him with a nod and turned to Pierce.

"They come," he said simply, getting to his feet. He walked to the dishwashing area where the cook insisted on taking the plate from his hand. A look at the remaining men showed they were aware of the increased tension in their leader. Several looked to Pierce with expressions that clearly hoped he could be blamed for the disturbance.

Bilongon stopped in front of Pierce and stared down at him with such metallic determination the latter felt physically compromised. Resentment crackled in his bowels. Unthinking, he rose, gaze locked with Bilongon's, until he was looking down on the shorter man. The troops around them grew completely silent, even the splash and clatter of the kitchen clean-up stopped.

Bilongon looked away. "I did not realize I was staring at you," he said. He gestured for Pierce to follow and turned away. The noise of the camp resumed.

The Filipino continued as they moved on. "I was reconsidering my decision for the last time." He half turned, looking at Pierce from the corner of an eye. "It gives me no great pleasure to do this thing, you understand."

Pierce said, "I'm in love with the idea, myself."

The single eyebrow visible to Pierce shifted, and he knew Bilongon was frowning. In a moment he nodded. Pierce was relieved to see the frown disappear. Bilongon said, "You Americans like to make jokes of things, say yes in a way that means a very strong no. Why is that?"

"Do you mind?" Pierce made no effort to hide his exasperation. "I've got more on my mind than speech habits."

"As you wish, although I see no difficulty ahead for you. You have no decisions to make. You simply sit outside the building and spy on the conversation inside." He paused for a moment. "I do not think it is such a very unusual matter for you."

"That's true. I've listened to many conversations that I wasn't supposed to hear. But I never arranged for someone to spy on my guests, did I?"

Bilongon's shoulders jerked.

They reached the hut in continuing silence. There were two guards now. Bilongon avoided looking at Pierce while he spoke to them. One led Pierce to the rear of the building and behind a large tree. Gesturing, he positioned Pierce before melting into the growth.

For the space of a couple of heartbeats, Pierce was simply amazed at the efficiency of his abandonment. When it came to him that he was utterly alone, his lungs heaved as though the jungle had clutched him and was squeezing his life away. Inhaling through slack lips he backed against the tree, eager to feel its bulk protecting against what he could not see, needing its substance to lend strength to knees that wanted only to unhinge. Even as he told himself he was only yards from the shack and the guards, he heard his own voice.

"Bilongon!" The word mewed, angering him, and when he repeated it, the sound was coarse. "Bilongon! Where the fuck are you?"

Something made a noise in the brush. It came from the direction of the camp, and Pierce pushed harder against the tree, terrified that his cry had brought something other than help.

The guard pushed close enough to Pierce to almost touch noses.

His breath was moist and foul and the night was so thick his eyes were merely multiplied darknesses in the dim oval of his face. Pierce couldn't see his lips move, although he could feel the gusts of breath accompanying the words. When an occasional point of moisture touched his skin he told himself it was either imagination or the effect of the other's breath on droplets of his own sweat. The guard held a long-bladed knife for Pierce to look at, then significantly covered his mouth and shook his head. Pierce nodded. The guard did the same, managing to make a disgusted mockery of the move. Then he sat down, leaning against the tree.

In a few minutes they heard the approaching voices. The language was English, and Pierce realized he'd never considered it might not be. *Bilongon knew. The sonofabitch has been laughing at me because I never thought to bring it up. I owe him for that, too.*

One voice was dominant, besides Bilongon's. It was harsh, heavily accented. Pierce strained to hear it better, leaning away from the tree. The guard looked up curiously, then resumed staring into the night. Pierce knew he should recognize the accent, but the identification kept slipping away.

Then there was another language, not like any of the local dialects. It was crisp, almost staccato. When he recognized it as Japanese he was so surprised he made an involuntary sound in his throat, and the guard rapped him sharply on the leg. Absently, Pierce pulled away and continued to listen. The identification of the accent aided understanding.

"You are sure the government does not know of this camp?" The voice mingled suspicion and arrogance. Pierce consciously resisted imagining a face for it.

Bilongon's answer was so smooth it sounded apologetic. "I am very sure. If the government knew, we would not be here. Was there anything wrong with the arrangements between here and Singapore?"

"Everything went well. The boat uncomfortable."

The conversation died there. They moved away.

Once the movement stopped, the guard rose, tugging on Pierce's shirt. At the back wall of the nipa building the guard positioned him and left. The darkness failed to hide his pleasure in being rid of such an awkward burden.

Pierce wished he could identify him. He slowly adjusted his

position, setting himself for a long session. Bits of firelight from the direction of the mess area knifed through the intervening brush, red and yellow eyes that sought erratically. He found them comforting. In fact, if anyone had touched him on the shoulder and reminded him of the jungle looming a few feet away, he would have been horrified to realize he'd completely forgotten it.

Bilongon glanced once at where he knew Pierce was hiding and returned to the chore of smiling from the head of the small table at the four Japanese arranged two on each side. The gas lantern that was the only light had been carefully placed at the corner of the shack's front, putting it behind Bilongon's right shoulder. His face would be in shadow, less revealing. The whirl of insects fluttering around it distracted him for a second. He jerked irritably, reminding himself he must be alert and look pleasant. It was very difficult to smile while his throat worked so convulsively, but the continuous swallowing was unavoidable, dictated by a clogging taste of blood in his mouth. It made his tongue feel constricted, and the thought of stammering or tripping over words in front of these people made his head throb. He steeled himself and spoke to the apparent leader. He hoped he had the right one. It was bad enough they dressed in identical plain white shirts and black trousers, but all Japanese looked alike at best.

"Now that you have rehearsed the entire operation, do you have any suggestions?"

He had guessed right. The one with the rounder face was the leader. He stared insolently at Bilongon, as though considering if the question deserved an answer. Bilongon willed himself to calmness, forced himself to examine the physical creature before him in order to avoid thinking of its mind.

The moon face was a lie. The neck holding it up was as muscular as a python. The eyes were cold enough to fit the image. Their blackness reflected the light of the hissing lantern unreceptive of any warmth. Bilongon glanced quickly at the man's hand wrapped around his coffee mug and saw what he expected, the callused knuckles of the karate fighter.

Unconsciously, he gestured with his own right hand. They were so foolish, these men, exactly like their counterparts in the Middle

East. Their skills were extraordinary, but so idiotically limited. They were like guns, not only useless when there was nothing to kill, but dangerous to have lying about. Still, it was a time for guns, and no one could deny it. The important thing to remember was that these were guns that could think.

Finally, the Japanese spoke. "I cannot think else we need. You are sure diversion plan will delay police?"

In answer, Bilongon turned around and spoke into the darkness beyond the door. One of his men stepped in with a folded paper, and Bilongon spread it on the table. He waited until the Japanese were in position before pointing.

"This is the house where the conference will take place. I have been told that you will come from the sea." From the corner of his eye he saw a frown slice across the smooth brow and repressed most of a satisfied smile. "Up to that point, we have no part in the operation. Now, when we hear your signal that you are ashore, my men will destroy this bridge and this bridge." He jabbed at the map. "That leaves only this road as access to the house. Nevertheless, you will leave toward the destroyed bridge. You will be met at this point and guided around the damage to come out here. We will have a van waiting, with clothing and papers."

"Ammunition. Extra weapons." The Japanese interrupted.

Bilongon shook his head. "Your weapons will be left in the house. A second vehicle will follow the van. A man and a woman. If there are any roadblocks and you have difficulty, they will assist you."

The Japanese muttered to himself, then spoke rapidly to his group. They nodded agreement and all faced Bilongon. "We have decided be weapons for us in the van. What can you provide? We must have submachine guns."

Bilongon sat back down. "The escape plan is my responsibility, a service I have *volunteered* to the man who hired you."

"We not doing this for money! We do it to fight for masses, punish men who betray them!"

"And we are all in your debt. But we all have our duty. I will do mine, and so will my people. We will protect you."

The full thrust of Bilongon's response took a moment to register. When it did, the Japanese flushed, and the corners of his mouth drew down in a grimace that was almost pain. The others tensed perceptibly. Bilongon wondered if they would be foolish enough to attack him and almost wished they would.

It was an exciting thought, and it brought the strange music to his mind, the silver bells, so like the dancing music of his people, but so much finer. Each note settled on the surface of his consciousness and seeped through, and he could watch them the way he'd watched dyers soaking their intricate patterns into what had been ordinary cloth. The melody changed him, carried him away from the unending problems. He knew that, but he had no idea how he reacted when in the grip of the music because when it left, it was as though he was waking from a deep sleep. The possibility of madness picked at him and he shunned it. There was too much to be done.

His gaze caught the expression of the rigid Japanese, whose confusion was obvious. Bilongon wanted to laugh at him. How puzzled the moon-faced fool must be, first to be insulted and then to see the person who insulted him so completely detached and unaffected by the resulting anger!

Bilongon closed his eyes and fisted his hands until it felt as though the skin would split across the knuckles. The pain muffled the chiming bells.

When the Japanese spoke, it was with a voice that told of fury redoubled by his realization that he could do nothing.

"We not need protection. Not concerned about lives."

Bilongon nodded, using the time to get his eyes back into focus. "We realize that and admire you. If the Singapore police are foolish enough to try to arrest you, we know you will fight, if you have the means. Inevitably, they will kill you. This way, if you are suspected, the people protecting you will be able to surprise the police. If they are killed and you are arrested, we will find a way to free you. The man we both help in this matter is very anxious that your lives and your courage not be wasted."

The Japanese looked relieved at the hinted apology. "We are fighting men, not accustomed to plan escape, retreat. Accept your judgment in this."

A gentle tingling of the bells teased Bilongon. He gestured sharply to ward it off, pretending to hit at one of the fluttering insects. "Then all is right. The passports you used to get into Singapore are being smuggled out now, with all proper stamps and so forth. They will be returned to you in Japan, that you can use them to get in again. Tomorrow you will leave here in one of my people's boats and transfer to a ship.''

"What plan if something go wrong with meeting at sea, if we miss ship?''

''Nothing will go wrong,'' Bilongon rose and walked to the door, turning in the opening. "As you said, we are accustomed to such plans.'' He walked a few steps until he was certain he was out of earshot of the building and stopped, waiting. Within seconds one of his men came down the path, leading Pierce. "You heard?'' he asked the American.

"Enough to confuse me,'' Pierce grated. "Who are those people?''

Bilongon grinned. "Come,'' he said, leading the way.

When they were once again seated at his desk, Bilongon felt more relaxed, felt the poison of the insults dissipating. He was still irritable enough to let Pierce squirm before explaining.

"The Japanese are Red Army. They are going to Singapore on a mission for the man who supplies arms and equipment for our own struggle against the oppressions of the Manila government.''

"And you're to get them out of Singapore and bring them here. I got that. Who are they after?''

"The entire attendance at a conference between representatives of the Vietnamese and Chinese governments.''

"Who? Jesus! How many people? And what kind of conference? The Chinese and Viets are practically at war!''

Bilongon nodded. "My Arab friend is much indebted to the Soviets. It is not in the best interest of that government to see peaceful relationships between Vietnam and China. False evidence left behind will prove the raid was conducted by a militant faction of the Peking government. Chinese divisions will remain pinned to the Vietnamese border, Soviet influence in Vietnam will soar, and China will appear divided at a time when the Soviets most fear an impressive Chinese presence.''

"Wheels within wheels,'' Pierce muttered, then, "OK, so I know about the deal. Why me? You want something.''

Bilongon smiled. "You will see that the Japanese are caught and forced to reveal the entire plan.''

Pierce was stunned. "What? What'd you say?"

Suddenly, Bilongon was leaning on the desk, a fist practically under Pierce's nose. "My revolution is Moslem! We are people of Islam! This man who pays these hired killers puts his politics before his religion! The men he supports deny Allah! They have attacked our brothers! They will not use me, my religion, my men! I will deliver them to the judgment of Allah!"

Pierce instinctively leaned back. "You'll be delivering those Japs up to some people who aren't as merciful as Allah, Bilongon."

The naïveté of the answer startled Bilongon, and he laughed. He failed to see the instant fear in Pierce's eyes, and answered as if talking to a child.

"You are so completely American, Tony. You will never really understand. Of course, there is more than my contempt for people who would use me. There is more than my disgust for the unclean atheists. There is even more than my personal dislike for the manners of that fat-faced Japanese." He leaned back and closed his eyes, taking a breath large enough to stretch his ribs, savoring the rich smells, the human-habitation familiarity of the building and the smoking fires, the humid mystery of the air from the forest, even the nose-prickling sharpness of the pineapple somewhere in the area. He spoke with his eyes still closed, remembering.

"There were Japanese here before, you know. Before we were born, you and I, and because of that, it means nothing to you. What they did to us never happened to America, so you forgive it without another thought. It did happen to us, and we won't forgive so easily."

"You should. What happened is over, has been for a generation."

Bilongon repeated the last word, enjoying a secret humor. "A generation. Exactly." He opened his eyes and leaned forward, the casual sway betrayed by the grating voice. "They killed two of my uncles, guerrillas." He laughed. "Everyone in my family is a guerrilla. They brought them home to kill them. The younger was sixteen, more of a man than most men already. And they brought a pig. The old people tell how the one in charge had it hung by its hind legs from a tree, just where the road enters the village. Then he had my uncles tied up and made to kneel. He drew his sword and cut off the pig's head. With the blood of that unclean animal dripping from the

blade, he beheaded the older brother. Then he cut the pig in half.
Then he beheaded the younger brother. The last thing he did was
have his men load my uncles and the pig in a wagon. All was taken
to my grandfather's house and thrown in a heap in the middle of the
room, mixed together like garbage in a pit. My grandmother never
spoke again, from that day to her death, many years later.''

He stared directly into Pierce's eyes, wishing he could transfer the
memory to them of a small boy sitting on Grandfather's lap while he
told the story and Grandmother puttered about with her continual
smile, humming wordless lullabies to her dead sons.

The thought was barely born before he cast it aside. Maybe some
Americans would understand, but not this one. He knew only of win
or lose. If he won at something he would accept it as one step
toward greater acquisition. If he lost he would run until caught and,
if caught, make the best deal he could.

Why had he even bothered to try to explain? At least the Japanese
had a purpose. And now they would serve a purpose, even as he
arranged their deaths.

The thought made him feel better.


# ■ CHAPTER 8 ■


Draeger's apartment shouted its concerned bachelorhood, with its
overdone neatness and its furniture shoved into functional patterns of
convenient asymmetry. The front door opened directly onto the
living room, and the first impression was of color: the upholstery of
the conversational group of overstuffed chairs and sofa a cool mix of
blues and greens. The white ceramic lamps on rich-grained end
tables were exceptionally tall. Long, slim shades threw a comfort-

ing glow that held back the darkness outside the picture window. The other appointments tended to soothing earth colors and neutrals with the exception of a large framed batik hung next to the bedroom door on the wall to the left. The print was a mass of interlocking green-and-yellow on black angular lines that tricked the eyes and made the eventual discovery of the disguised flowing snake-figure a pleasing surprise.

The kitchen was enclosed in the far right corner, leaving the other half of that area for an intended small dining room. It had been transformed into an office, with a desk, files, and the other paraphernalia of business. Draeger was hunched forward over the desk, his head barely outside the harsh light cone falling from a lamp fixed to a wall bookshelf. The apparatus was a black, gangling thing, and it hovered as though poised to peck at the unprotected skull. Mounted above the lamp, oddly innocuous in contrast to that crooked metal structure, a rifle gleamed in softer light. It was a beautiful weapon, the sleek stock curving away from the deceptively soft-looking blue steel of the metal. There was a scope perched on it. The wooden rack holding the piece was studded with shooting badges and pins. Many an evening Draeger had wondered at the significance of his one, well-used, modern weapon hanging in a bachelor's pad while Munson was happily married and owned a collection of knives and spears that were only touched to be cleaned. No answer had ever come to him, and tonight the question would certainly never occur.

Draeger was twisting the head of the nail from Rizal Park, murmuring obscenities about the technician who'd demanded such fine tolerances, never thinking how someday those delicate threads would have a field man on the edge of madness. The lab man never anticipated that Egg Roll would place the nail in damp ground nor did he expect the courier to die without making a placement signal, sentencing it to yet another moist day.

The top lifted free at last, revealing the tightly rolled paper inside. When Draeger tapped the shaft on the desk to dislodge the message, bits of rust like dried blood speckled the wood. Draeger brushed them away with abrupt slaps that continued long after the stuff was gone. With the other hand he flattened the paper, the sight of the gibberish five-lettered blocks on the yellowish material reacting on him like a tranquilizer. The irritable brushing stopped. His movements took on a workmanlike precision. He examined the number at the upper left corner of the paper while he smoothed it with his fingers, caressing, the obvious gratification suggesting he needed to verify physically what his eyes told him. He reached into the desk for matches and put them next to the ashtray. Then he pulled the chair over to the door between the living room and the kitchen and stood on it. From that height he looked down at a fine line where the plywood door face joined the wooden frame of the door itself. A little pressure from his fingertips widened the gap. By bending and twisting, he was able to get his fingers inside the crack and clutch the monofilament line attached to the underside of the frame and lift it. There was a muffled sliding noise within the hollow door. He had to bend the plywood to its limit before a towel-wrapped book emerged. He flipped it open, tore out the single page that matched the number on the message, and carefully replaced the bundle, pressing the plywood home along its entire length several times before grunting his satisfaction and getting down to put back the chair. Seated once again, he spread the sheet next to the message, got out paper and pencil, and began the tedious business of changing the hodgepodge five-letter groups to something with meaning.

The sheet was one page of a device called a one-time pad, and Draeger liked the system. The man sending the message used a numbered sheet from his pad to encrypt, substituting letters as that individual chart indicated. When finished, he included the number of his sheet. To decrypt the message, a partner needed only the matching sheet. It was simplicity itself. As long as one had the sheet number. Without it, breaking into the cipher could mean trying substitutions practically forever. If one was lucky enough to hit the right combination, or had access to a few years' worth of computer time, the message could be compromised, by which time it would be so untimely as to be useless, and the process could start all over again, if there was a second message. It was a comforting knowledge. Even more comforting was the fact that there were no actual words in whatever Egg Roll sent.

When Draeger was finished, he had another series of apparently unrelated letters forming gibberish.

He folded the page from the one-time pad in length-wise creases, stood it on end and lit it. The paper flared sharply, it's burning swift enough to create a sound much like stifled astonishment. The chemical treatment that speeded its burning left a prickling, unusual smell.

He was frowning as he reached for the squat brown book sandwiched among its taller, more elegant mates. The worn binding said *Chinese-Tagalog Dictionary*. Consulting the letters, he flipped open the book, and it was immediately obvious that the decrypted text of the message from Egg Roll was nothing but a new cipher, the simplest kind, with *A* equaling "One," and so on through J/Zero. The letter *X* indicated breaks. The number combinations gave Draeger a guide to page, column, and word-pair in the Chinese section of the dictionary. He carefully wrote out the indicated Tagalog translations. Then he reached for the taller but equally well-thumbed copy of the *English-Tagalog Dictionary*, thus translating the word to his own language.

The first was familiar, and he had no need to translate. Egg Roll started with the conventional ideograph for "I" or "me." The second word brought Draeger erect in the chair with an exclamation. He counted down the column in the first book again, insuring accuracy.

A feeling like cold mist on his back harassed him while he hurried to determine the rest of the words, not sure if Egg Roll was saying, "I am suspect," or "I do suspect."

The finished message eliminated any doubt. It said, "I suspect. Escape my plan. Will communicate."

*The best score in the entire Bat Team structure burned. A courier missing. No placement signal. Egg Roll abandoning the escape plan. A bullshit escape plan, like always, but it sounded good, and it had a chance. Now he's alone. Poor bastard. Practically recruited himself. Trying to help China survive the Soviets. When his government tries him he'll stand there with his face as blank as a brick, and the hope and apprehension I saw in his eyes will be ashes. But where's the fucking courier? He worked for nothing but money. If he's been arrested for something, he should have called the lawyer, and I'd already know about that. It's not reasonable.*

*I think I would have liked Egg Roll, if I'd known him in a different world. He's going to die because he worked for me, and he was a pleasant, nice guy, and I don't have the faintest idea what I can do to help.*

Draeger folded the written message as he'd folded the one-time sheet. It burned normally, and he stared through the small fire, his eyes so unseeing the only sign of life in them was the false one of the reflected flame. After it burned out, he continued to stare for a full minute before carefully replacing the dictionaries. The ashes went into the toilet to be flushed away, and the ash tray was replaced exactly. He frowned at the matches, still on the table, and scooped them up and threw them back into the drawer. That single gesture, aside from a slightly quickened pace as he left the apartment, was the sole indication of any internal disturbance.

At street level he walked directly to the nearby hotel and its bank of pay phones. The police sergeant who answered the call unquestioningly accepted his claim to be an official of the courier's shipping company. Within minutes the carefully honed language of bureaucracy was detailing the physical facts of the courier's death, a murder reduced to crisp terminology that eliminated possibly unpleasant intimations of humanity.

Rage and frustration boiled at the back of Draeger's throat, and he hung up with a violence that threatened to snap the disconnect hook. His return to his apartment was a controlled walk, but a close observer would have noticed how the heels dug at the sidewalk and the chin seemed to be cleaving a way for the body to follow.

He placed a call to Munson, taking some pleasure in the fact of not fidgeting while he waited for it to go through. When the connection was made, he said, "Hello! Roger?" and Munson's surprised response came across through the background interference. "That you, Glen? How're things?"

"Fine, fine." Draeger wondered how he sounded to Munson, wondered if his tension sounded as metallic in Munson's ear as it felt in his own mouth. "The office tells me I have to head down south again. I expected to be going east, but my trip's run into serious complications. It's been canceled for the third time."

He fought the words, telling himself he was doing everything exactly right, spelling out his emergency signal as smoothly as if he'd done it daily, rather than never.

Munson himself had thought up this one. A trip could be canceled any time, and the mention of it would mean nothing out of the ordinary to anyone. A man could speak of it being canceled for the third time with justifiable emphasis. An emergency signal needed something to account for any untoward vocal behavior, and Munson had supplied it with practiced ease.

"All I need to know is when to meet you. You'll be traveling alone, won't you?"

It took the barest fraction of a second for Draeger to realize Munson wanted to know if he thought he was being tailed. The pause was a mere flicker in the conversation, but he forced a laugh to cover it and formed his answer. "I'll call you from here before I leave. I hope I'll be traveling with a friend. Tell Leonila she's come up with a winner and I'm trying to talk Ria into taking a day off to fly down there with me. Sort of make a holiday of the trip.

"Ria?"

"It's a nickname. It's a long story. I'll fill you in when I see you."

The background hiss rose and fell in a sealike surge before Munson said, "I'll meet your plane. I expect Leonila'll be with me. She won't want to miss the chance to gloat because you like the girl she found for you."

"I hope she won't be too disappointed if Ria can't come."

"She'll be glad to see you, in any case. See you tomorrow."

Draeger hung up without looking, ignoring the plastic chatter of the clumsily seated hand set.

He'd involved Ria. Again. Despite the qualms he'd felt in the park after using her as part of his cover, he'd done it again. This time it was practically a reflex, and even though the same conscience had struck at him instantly, the commitment was made before any conscious deliberation was possible.

He rose from the desk and walked to the window, staring into the night. The city blazed beneath him, hectic color and motion. The view misted in his mind, turned into an internal surrealism, still moving, and although street sounds never carried up to his fifteenth floor, on this occasion the silence was an eerie quality.

*A man died. I recruited him. I recruited Egg Roll. They were necessary. I've involved a woman who thinks espionage and spies and murders happen somewhere else.*

The scene below him fragmented, became individual lights, cars, buses.

*If there's any unreality in this situation, it comes from within me, and it is a weakness to be destroyed. Unreality doesn't come from a mysterious external force. What I do, I do for a reason. Wanting to be with Ria is natural, normal, unconnected with whatever else I do.*

He left the window and dropped into the easy chair facing the opposite wall, where he squirmed for a moment before lurching to his feet and moving to the small kitchen. He poured himself a drink and, back in the chair, swallowed half of it in two gulps. When he put the glass on the end table he continued to stare at it until the bobbing ice stilled. As soon as there was no more action in the liquid, his head lolled back and he closed his eyes.

*It's not all that important. I'm not using her to actually do anything. Even if I was being watched, she wouldn't be involved. She's part of the scenery. I don't even have to ask her to go. No, the hell with that. I want her to come along.*

He lifted the drink and condensation gathered and dripped onto his shirt. Each drop was a shock and he enjoyed it, as if his body wanted to hoard the chill against the heat of the next day. He debated if he really wanted any more of the whiskey. His restless glance swept across the framed batik.

*Ria would like that.*

The thought rose from his subconscious in a reluctant mass. He saw her image and the hard facts of his situation simultaneously, each eye laboring to bring him one picture to the exclusion of the other.

He stepped to the window again. Suddenly he was looking at his reflection, and the sight was like a blow. With no deliberate effort, he'd positioned himself at an angle behind the drape, protected from any but the most oblique view. Self-concern oozed from the image, glinted in the night-chilled eyes. Draeger moved stiffly as he readied for bed.

Roger Munson was also looking out over a city, the difference being that he was making no effort to hide behind anything, nor was he disturbed.

He took another drag on his cigar. The coal glowed more brightly and he studied it, watching the way the light and dark areas moved with the minute inner changes of temperature. It was almost as if a heart suffused the tobacco with blood. Inhaling deeply, he savored the smell and the weight in his chest brought by the arrival of the residual smoke from his mouth.

He delighted in those sensations and even more in the feeling that something almost incandescent was spreading through his veins, displacing workaday blood with pure life. There was a throbbing in his temples, a not-unpleasant rhythm, so much vitality in him it wanted to burst free. The skin across his shoulders and down his arms, his thighs and calves, all felt taut with energy.

Nothing mattered if it carried no chance of danger, he told himself, and felt a drug-thrill pluck at his spine.

There had been danger before. The night of the knives in the alley in Kowloon. The men who had come for him in Laos. There had been the Vietnam years when the deceit and treachery of normal intelligence collection was expanded to insane proportions by the heat of genuine combat.

He shivered, the sudden tremor alien to the sultry climate, a response to a chill born in his guts.

That was what had done it. First, the not-knowing, the suspecting. Then came the revelation that some leaders you'd damned near killed yourself for not only didn't care, but cursed you for your efforts.

Thunder rumbled ominously in the north. He drew on the cigar. When he exhaled, the breeze stretched the jet of smoke away in a horizontal smudge.

Leonila appeared at his elbow. "Something's bothering you. Is something wrong with Glen?" She took his chin in her hand and forced him to look at her. He smiled easily.

"Glen's fine. I'm just enjoying the cool evening."

Her answering smile held more sadness than amusement. "I know when you're troubled just by the way you stand. You can't fool me."

Laughing, he bent to kiss her. "Can you tell what I'm thinking when I sit down, or is—"

She jabbed him in the ribs and the teasing died in a yelp. He put an arm around her shoulder and pulled her to his side, looking back out over the city once more. She continued to look up at his face.

"It's the old trouble, isn't it?" she asked, and when a few silent seconds passed, repeated the question, more as a statement, adding, "It's been so long since you've thought of that, let it bother you. I'd begun to hope you'd forgotten."

Twisting violently, he looked down at her. When he spoke she felt the breath of the words, and it was as if he was throwing them at her. "Forgotten? Goddamit, Leonila, a man doesn't forget seeing his people butchered!"

Thrusting herself between him and the porch rail, she reached up to link her hands behind his neck. "Roger! Roger, please! I didn't mean it! I hoped you'd pushed it out of your mind. It's over, Roger, it's been over for years now, and there's nothing you can do except destroy yourself."

He refused to look at her. "I wouldn't care if I destroyed myself. I've told you that before. But that wouldn't answer the problem."

They stood that way for a few moments. It was Leonila who broke the silence in a voice that barely carried to his ears. He cocked his head automatically, an unaltered expression clear proof he listened with the fraction of his mind demanded by tact.

"You've never told me, you know." He blinked rapidly, and she seized that as a good sign, pressing ahead onto ground she'd never dared test. "As often as you've spoken of 'something' happening to you and your men, I've never known exactly what it was. You've said things about men being killed—"

His eyes drew away from the night long enough to probe into hers, and the unfinished sentence caught in her throat. Even in the dark she saw the pain in his gaze, a pain so complete it poured direct into her mind from his. After a moment she was able to tell him, "They say it helps sometimes to talk about those things. It's like letting the sun heal a cut, or a priest driving out a devil."

He continued to stare outward, and she added a lame postscript. "Sometimes it's easier if someone shares with you."

Extended silence convinced her the subject had again evaded her, burrowed back into her man beyond her reach. A moment later she felt the movement of his arm when he pitched the cigar away. He embraced her and cleared his throat, her ear pressed to his chest hearing the sound as a minor variation on the distant thunder.

"Vietnam," he said, and the word was an exorcism. "Before I

ever met you." He looked down at her, and she turned her face up to receive the hurt in his voice, to share it with him. What she saw shocked her so badly she gasped. His mouth was drawn down at the corners in a cruel grimace, and his eyes struck at her. It was nothing she could identify until he spoke again, and suddenly she knew it was scorn.

"What do you know about being betrayed? Even if you'd been there, you'd forgive and forget. Let bygones be bygones."

Confused and shaken, she turned away and immediately his arms tightened around her, and she felt his lips brush her hair.

"Oh, God, Leonila," he said, practically murmuring. "I don't know why I did that to you. There's no reason to be angry at you. But the anger boils out sometimes."

"I know about you and your moods." She forced a light tone. When Munson's arms tightened around her she misinterpreted the movement as returning anger, unable to see his sharp features twist in remorse. She hurried on. "I don't care what happened. I only want us to be happy, to make you happy."

He said, "Don't worry, honey. I'm going to take care of things. It's not easy living with my temper, and I want to make it up to you."

"There's nothing to make up. We have everything we could want. All that's left is for you to enjoy it."

"No." The correction was gentle, introspective. "There's more to the world than us. Whatever I am now, they made me. It's a debt I won't carry any longer. They owe me, and I owe them."

Leonila stepped back to search his face. " 'They?' Who? We owe no one."

He reached for her again and she made no move to avoid him, but there was a resistance that warned him she would not be pulled forward. He hesitated before dropping his arms to his sides. "It doesn't have anything to do with you."

She raised her chin. "If it involves you, it does."

In the semi-dark of the porch his frown looked like a ridged wound. "We won't argue about it. It's business."

"Oh." Disbelief inflated the word. She walked away.

Silently, he watched her. Only when she disappeared into the living room did he realize he'd raised his arms and stood with them outstretched. She turned out the lights, and his palms shone in the intensified dark. Oddly, he was reminded of the mad-white faces of mimes, and he wadded them into fists and spun to face the night again.

The brilliantly illuminated mass of the Taoist temple hovered in the blackness down on the mountainside. The lights transformed the roof into a jewellike cap of glowing jade, the ornamented walls thrusting it upward. The beauty failed to penetrate his thoughts at first.

*The first thing the do-good bastards in the government'll do is tell everyone I did it for the money. Screw 'em. Undeserving. Living on the backs of better men. Once I'm dug in and under cover I'll tell everyone what I did and why. That's why I have to live through this. It's too important to be stopped, and I'm the only one who can explain. I wish to God I could put that weight on someone else.*

He rubbed his brow with his fingertips, listening to the faint crackle of the coarse eyebrows, letting it override the insistent inner whispers. He leaned on the porch rail, staring out past the temple and the multiple lights of the city to Mactan Island where Draeger and the woman would be landing the next morning.

The temple demanded his attention. *Tao. The Way. The path. So simple. No mocking god to goad a man into traps. No promises of reciprocal honor. You led a good life and that put the universe on center.*

Uninterrupted staring made his eyes water and a kind of vertigo staggered him, and he shook his head.

*Plenty of damned fools believed that shit. You didn't have to be Chinese. Believed it myself once, a thousand years ago. Didn't know anything about Tao. Draeger still believes it. What will he think when his sun explodes, and he sees his path is really hell's own road?*

# ■ CHAPTER 9 ■

The fact that she was actually catching the morning plane south to Cebu sat heavily on Ria's entire expression and manner. She said nothing about it, having exhausted her complaints about getting up at three A.M. Her conversation was minimal in any event, a combination of sleepiness and surprise at her decision to go.

Draeger saw her frown turn to a wince as she stepped from the taxi. "Are you OK?" he asked.

A withering stare came with the answer. "I can't be. Anyone who'd do what I'm doing is crazy."

He laughed. "It's good for you to be up early."

She started a retort and clamped her teeth on the words, moving toward the terminal instead, her steps too heavy with interrupted sleep to afford any impression of dignified anger. Draeger followed, smiling, handling the two bags over to one of the porters who'd descended on them when the taxi stopped.

There was always a crowd at the airport, as if watching passengers arrive and leave was a spectator sport. Four A.M. was little discouragement, and when the international flights came in later the gathering would not only be far larger but as festive as any market crowd. Draeger was the lone non-Filipino this morning, and the eyes of aficionados settled on him with grateful appreciation while he paid the man in charge of the baggage handlers. He fumbled for the money, wondering where the practice of a single collector for all the porters originated. It had the advantage of standardizing fees, at least. The fat man behind the desk took Draeger's offering with immense disinterest.

Once inside, he felt less like a display item. Not that the terminal was a pleasant place to be. More than peeling paint or windows grimed to translucence, the very atmosphere was thick with the smell of sweat, abandoned food scraps, and burning fuel blended into a stew of bureaucratic seediness. The workers moved through it in a paradoxical neatness, their minds untapped by the managers, each one looking at conditions with the functionary's stare that says "not my responsibility" in any language.

Ria led the way to where their suitcases were hefted onto the counter. A stocky woman tagged them without a glance for the owners and gestured toward the security guards to the right.

They stepped into their separate booths, and he was relieved the frisk was run with impersonal skill and attention. Being pawed by an embarrassed amateur made him feel strangely demeaned, in the first place, and further, he had an above-average interest in not being hijacked into certain areas.

He joined Ria in the waiting room. It hadn't changed. The molded plastic seats perched in multicolored rows on their pipe bases. They were solid primary colors—red, yellow, blue. The color distribution was random, but the spacing was centimeter-precise, as if the designers had been forced to concede one irregularity and triumphantly outflanked it with more regimentation. Once carnival-bright, the seats were faded and bore the dull patina of having been chafed by unnumbered patient backsides. There were more people than Draeger expected, territories staked out, turning the mathematical geography of the seats into a tribal map of families, couples, and solitaries. He took Ria's arm and steered her toward the small snack bar in the far corner.

"Coffee," he said. "We'll be here for another thirty minutes before we can board, and you won't make it without a cup of coffee."

They walked to the counter, and Draeger ordered for them. The waitress was a surprise, quick and cheerful. It occurred to him she was the first person he'd seen smile.

Handing Ria the styrofoam cup gave him a chance to savor her appearance. She wore what was practically national dress in the islands, a printed T-shirt and jeans. Her only jewelry was her watch and a thin, flat gold neck-chain. The simple, figure-hugging clothes suited her perfectly. Suited him, too, he mused, feasting on curves shifting gracefully under the material when she moved.

They settled into the contoured seats that molded flesh into proper attitudes with the uncompromising zeal of Marine drill sergeants shaping up recruits. After a few seconds of pointless squirming they resigned themselves to the posture demanded of them and tried to make the best of it.

"I guess I should be glad you talked me into this trip," Ria said. "I haven't seen Leonila for years."

"I had the feeling she was anxious for us to meet, but she seemed troubled, too. Sort of uncomfortable."

"It's not easy for her." Ria smiled, contemplative, studying the distant wall. "Leonila knows I'm determined to be my own person. Women like me are making new rules. A few years ago she'd have schemed a way for a relative to introduce us and then planned for us to 'bump into' each other at another relative's house, and so on. Everyone in my family would have had a chance to inspect you and discuss your points, like one of Arturo's fighting cocks. Now the best she can do is throw us together and watch." Turning quickly to look at him, she added, "She must like you quite a bit. It's very daring of her to simply leave us alone."

Draeger nodded, half-smiling. "I'm glad she's getting modernized. I owe her a favor."

She smiled back at him and moved her hand, the gesture turning to a touch that could have been an accidental contact or caress. The fact that he couldn't be sure was pleasing and somehow increased the interest of the thing. There was a stirring in his insides that was massively out of proportion and comically inappropriate for the time and place. The response smoothed out to a delicious sense of anticipation.

Ria went on, "The changes women like me are creating are really harder on the women like Leonila, you know? She agrees with almost everything we say or do, but she's so afraid we'll be hurt. In my letters, I keep telling her a person learning to walk can expect to fall down a few times."

"You're both right. The old system was wrong, but you owe it to yourself to be careful how you change it."

Her hand closed on his forearm. "You can't imagine how exciting it is, Glen. I don't think any man can. Your whole history is different from women's."

"Different?" Draeger interrupted, amused. "I thought we were all in this thing together."

She twisted in the seat, which immediately pitched her forward to teeter on the leading edge. The fastenings squeaked outrage at violated regulations. "You know what I mean! Your role has always been the exciting one; you were encouraged to prove yourself, to try different things. Women were locked up!"

"Don't blame me! Do anything you damned well choose. I'm not saying you shouldn't."

"You don't have to say anything. You're one of the ones who think being uncommitted is the same as being fair."

Draeger blinked. "You mean I have to take a side?"

"Absolutely." Intensity twisted her face, and he was amazed at its hardness. There was more to see than he could assimilate so quickly. Even as the features ebbed to normal, he realized there had been much more that had merely swept across his consciousness. She was still talking. "The world won't tolerate spectators any more."

"It'll have to," he said, and it was her turn to be surprised. He added, "Look, I was taught long ago that if you take care of the details, the big things fall into place automatically. People are the details. I can't define the difference between communism and fascism, for instance, especially the way I see them around me today. You want me to take sides in your battle. Well, I'll help *you* any way I can, but I won't help something called 'women.' I don't know what that is."

She let herself slide back into the embrace of the plastic, studying him curiously. "Don't you believe in anything? No cause, no standards?"

He felt heat across his face, down the back of his neck. "My friends and my country—is that enough for you?"

"It's not me I'm worried about."

The opportunity to back away from the discussion came like spring water, and he seized it gladly. The comment about caring for his country was the kind of outburst that could destroy him. "How'd this get started?" he asked. "All I meant to say was that I don't want to interfere with your women's lib. I don't want to get mixed up with a lot of theory. I only deal with people."

Accepting the truce, she fired one last shot. "You were laughing at me."

"I tried to make a small joke. It's not like we were discussing religion."

"Almost." She smiled, but the word was a warning. He heard it and understood, carefully steering the conversation to what they could do together when they returned from Cebu. Ria seemed equally ready to get to another subject, and he was once again off-balance, this time unsure if her eagerness to discuss future time together was a function of avoiding a potentially destructive subject or an indication she looked forward to his company. Ruefully, he admitted he was behaving like an introspective adolescent.

Like something from ambush, the thought of Egg Roll leaped to mind, and he wondered if he was trying to get out by air. Visions of the man rolled across his imagination. He saw him clutching his documents, the paper sodden with sweat, limp as old lettuce. No one warned him to leave his papers in his pocket until they were necessary, to handle them as little as possible. No customs official would overlook such a blatant signal of concern. Security people sensed fear with the certainty of dogs. They attacked with the same instincts.

"That's our plane, Glen." The asperity from Ria got him moving, knowing he'd missed at least one earlier cue. A young couple in airline uniforms moved to the door by the Cebu departure sign, and elements of the crowd fragmented from the larger mass, formed its own surge. Ticketholders thrust boarding passes at the couple and pressed on. Draeger watched one younger man moving with an aloofness that divorced him from the rest. He ignored the buffeting. His arms angled out and forward at a shallow angle. Bodies struck those projections, bent them, were repelled. There was no apparent shoving. The smoothly muscled arms simply tensed, and the crowding body was diverted to a path of less resistance. Draeger was behind him, to his left. The young man turned that way, took in the American and the Filipino girl in swift appraisal and checked his own progress, allowing them to flow past. Draeger smiled thanks across the intervening heads at the man, whose height approximated his own, and turned to concentrate on Ria. He did not actually see the other man's answering smile and was left with an impression of startling brightness.

Past the door the crowd elongated, continuing with a pointless speed that was a reflection of the pressure behind it. The loading ramp hung down from the tail of their plane. In the sketchy light of predawn it looked like a fantastic wasp determined to plant its eggs in the taxiway. The line collapsed on itself and trooped up the ladder. Eventually, uneventfully, the crew got everyone seated and briefed. The takeoff was remarkable only for the standard sanctified silence among the passengers that always amused Draeger, as if the wrong word would bring the plane tumbling back to earth.

Draeger took the newspaper offered by the smiling stewardess, watched Ria search for a comfortable position, and closed his eyes. He was sound asleep before the "no smoking" sign blinked out.

The change in his breathing opened Ria's eyes, and even though there was no physical contact between them, the fact that she was next to this sleeping man dredged up emotional responses as discomforting as they were intriguing. She berated herself for those feelings, reminding herself she was no blushing virgin to be reduced to trembling at the presence of masculinity. While she did, her hands moved to lift the hair from the back of her neck where sweat was beginning to tickle. The tress fell forward, a soft weight against the skin where throat and shoulder met. She thought how his hand would feel in the same place. Would he use it to tilt her head, kiss her? Would it drop from there, follow the weight-line of her hair and drift toward the breasts growing warm and heavy at the thought?

She spun in the seat, coming bolt upright in a flurry that generated a groan from Draeger. His eyelids fluttered, but he continued to sleep. Ria opened her paper, determined to read.

It was only minutes before it drooped, forgotten, and she half-turned to look at him. He dressed well. The light colors of the shirt and darker trousers made him appear a bit darker. Almost *kayumangi*. She smiled, wondering about his reaction if she told him he was nearly *kayumangi*—a healthy tan.

The plane lurched through minor turbulance in a series of sealike rhythms that pressed her into the seat and then left her buoyant, almost weightless. Her hand sought his wrist where it propped his chin. The action subsided quickly, the muted engines steady as ever. Untroubled, Draeger's lips parted, and Ria let herself enjoy the sensation of the even breath flowing across her hand. The earlier tightness in her stomach altered to muscles enjoying their own strength. She resumed studying Draeger.

He could be any American his age—or Canadian or Australian— and yet being near him there were times when there was an inescapable feeling of touching things forbidden. There was something beneath the surface, some unexplainable excitement and demand in his eyes that had no counterpart in his voice. His touch never grabbed at her, never underscored a point with the suggestive lingering fingertips other men thought was a unique secret message. Still, when his hand was on her she felt the need of the entire man pulling at her. She remembered the afternoon in Rizal Park, how he'd helped her pose and she'd had to look—*had* to—where he'd adjusted her arm because she was certain he'd left an imprint on the flesh. Intensity sang in the air around him then, as invisible and as undeniable as electricity.

As soon as they left the house in Forbes Park there had been that strange sense of inner, secret activity. At first it repelled her, but that quickly turned to curiosity and the desire to be involved. Not just wanting to know, but wanting to be a part of the excitement. And yet he never gave an outward sign there was anything to be involved with.

There had to be, though. The last thing they'd done in the park was his sketch, and as soon as it was finished, he was different. There was only one thing she knew of that changed a man in that way, and it sent a chill through her to think about it. The eyes betrayed him. Deep inside them was the fracture, the breached wall a woman learns to look for and knows she can only hope to see through into the soul beyond when a man is completely satisfied.

Whatever lifted him to that terrible urgency created a need and a desire that challanged the effect she, as a woman, had on him. Worse, whatever aroused him carried over in his desire for her, so that the unknown thing was inextricably entwined with her. It was a mutuality she loathed. To shed it, she must first identify it.

She turned in the seat, worked to find a sleeping position, came to a truce with her speculations. It was more difficult to deal with the oily smear in the back of her mind that laughed and hid and wouldn't be identified.

# ■ CHAPTER 10 ■

Leonila burst from the small group greeting the plane. She wore a yellow blouse and skirt, and in the predawn darkness her embrace for Draeger came like an unscheduled sun. Rolling his eyes for Munson's benefit, he managed to work loose and hold her at arm's length.

"Nobody can be that excited at this time of day," he said, trying to sound displeased. "It won't be light for—for—" He stopped, unsure.

Munson was unsmiling, the spare figure tense, moving in erratic starts that never developed into definable gestures. "If you had to work as hard as some of us, you'd know. It'll be light in about an hour."

Leonila shouldered past Draeger to put an arm around Ria, repeating the younger woman's name in a litany of embarrassment. "How could I be so rude? I was so happy to see Glen, and then I let these silly men distract me!" She glared at them. "And you, Glen, you never even introduced her, not that I wouldn't know her, even if it has been years since I saw her."

"If you'll listen to yourself, you'll know why I never introduced her." He bowed formally. "Margarita Manong this is my friend, Roger Munson, and his wife—"

"We'll have to pick up your bags," Munson interrupted. The tone was sharp enough to pull everyone's eyes his way. Draeger jerked upright, catching the last of Munson's curt nod. He was already turning, moving toward the baggage reception area. Ria wore a flat mask of uncertainty, watching him. Leonila looked at Draeger with apology before launching into a rushed, gossipy dialogue with Ria.

The suitcases came through quickly, and Munson directed the handler outside. He made no move to pay at the counter, leaving it to Draeger with the air of a man ignoring a menial task for a subordinate. When his driver proved to be just arriving, rather than there and waiting, he said nothing, but a deepening frown left no room for imagining his dissatisfaction. He assigned seats in the back to Leonila, Ria, and Draeger, settling in beside the driver with a finality that had the new arrivals glancing questions at each other. Leonila's manner with Ria moved subtly from deft attention to guarded anxiety.

The trip on the long boulevard from Mactan Island's airfield into the city was unremarkable, save for the faint light of dawn washing the east-facing mountaintops behind the sprawl of Cebu. Draeger saw little to alter his dislike of the place. Past experience in Cebu had convinced him it was a poor substitute for Manila, with all the same problems and few of the advantages. Now, as they crossed the bridge linking the major island of Cebu (and its like-named capital city) with its satellite, Mactan, the first brush of dawn seemed to poise, the heat and light of day working itself into a preassault fury. The city was a dark sprawl punctuated by multicolored lights. A trick of the advancing dawn emphasized the taller buildings, making Draeger think of shattered spears in a stricken animal. It wasn't a fancy that pleased him, and he wondered how Cebu always brought out his morbid streak.

The working section of the city was already throbbing with life, the transition immediately apparent where the boulevard ended and the streets began. Munson's driver maneuvered into the traffic, and they were submerged in the spasmodic job-flood. The scene would be repeated in all the barrios, the neighborhoods where the people slept in their thousands, surrounding the city. The barrios sheltered them in the night and on their holidays, gave them rest, pleasure, a sense of belonging. Workdays, the barrios were multiple hearts pumping out life that made the businesses and factories and markets into functional entities. This was a workday, and people of all sizes mounted buses, jeepneys, cars, and motorcycles altered to passenger-carrying tricycles. The air labored with the stink of fuel and oil, penetrated infrequently by a startling, wonderful shard of food-smell eddying from one of the houses crowding the street.

As the light increased it allowed the exuberant color of the Philippines to assert itself. The jeepneys changed from bulky machines to artworks, rocket-bursts of primary colors in extravagant patterns, side panels illuminated by paintings ranging from idyllic jungle waterfalls to cartoon characters. They all seemed to be as full as they could possibly be, and all took on more passengers at any opportunity. Munson's car stopped at an intersection. Draeger watched the traffic rumble across their front. One jeepney, predominantly fire-engine red, took his eye. It was full of school girls and all that was visible of them was the brilliant whiteness of their blouses, filling the open gap between canopy roof and the body of the machine. He was suddenly overwhelmed by a crushing nostalgia so powerful it was a physical ache in his chest. The jeepney conjured a wildly decorated strawberry glace on wheels, a Rose Parade float. The hubbub around him was a Pasadena crowd, cheering and laughing, happy.

The vigor of the image eased slowly, leaving him with a vague unease, as if a well-known name or fact had retreated to an inaccesible cranny of his memory. He was at the point of mentioning it to Munson, hoping to brighten his friend and at the same time exorcise his demon, when the light changed and they moved ahead. Instead of accepting his reaction to the red jeepney, he questioned it. Thoughts of the dead courier and Egg Roll's message tried to surface, and he resisted, determined to confine that part of his life to its proper place. A fleeting image of the Chinese refused to be dismissed, the earnest ascetic eyes begging for firm assurances. Draeger concentrated on Ria, staring at the thigh pressed against his own. He was rewarded by a surge in his loins, and Egg Roll's expression washed away. So did Draeger's ability to think with any continuity. Thoughts of her—romantic, erotic; fantasy and logic—fell through his mind like a shower of polished stones, beautiful, exciting, so disorganized it frustrated instead of pleasing.

He'd been stupid to suggest she come along. The anticipation of Munson's comments was dismal. Irritability still held him rigid in the front seat. Draeger was sure it was her presence that formed that anger, rather than the potential collapse of their best operation. It was a degrading realization, and he argued with himself, knowing he was rehearsing what he would tell Munson and feeling further cheapened by the admission.

By the time they were in Munson's home, Draeger was ready to argue his case. So was Munson, who led him away over the protests of Leonila, who wanted them to remain "at least until after breakfast." A silence ringing with confused disappointment followed them, and some of the embarrassment Draeger felt for his own actions transferred off to Munson. The older man opened the door to what he called his home office. Draeger knew then there would be no preliminary discussion. Munson's work was done in his office. Not the work of the cosmetics plant, although there were ledgers and stationery and all the other trappings in abundance. The home office dealt with home. Draeger took it in with one sweeping glance.

The desk was an antique, blackened to a patina like an old cast-iron stove, even its few dents and scratches gleaming with the subdued sheen of ruffled velvet. It was against the far wall. The only thing on it was a large dictionary on which, in turn, rested a rectantular humidor of carved *kamagong*, one of the beautiful woods used locally to produce superb guitars. The remaining walls were lined with four-drawer-high filing cabinets, and the space above them to the ceiling was solid bookshelves. There was a safe in the far left corner. That's where the idol lives, Draeger thought, the idol Control tells our secrets to, the idol that passes all things to the gods for judgment. What kind of men give their life's service to a machine that compresses an hour's report, the result of agonized months, into a few bursts of high-speed, coded gibberish that can only be compared to static? And what sort of idol lurks in constant darkness behind armor steel and a combination lock, festooned with thermite grenades, dedicated to immolation before compromise? Does it laugh, in its darkness, knowing us to be its slaves?

He shook away the fantasy, returning to his inspection. There was barely space between the door and the desk for the old cane-bottomed rocking chair, its attendant side table, and the jarringly out-of-place art nouveau brass floor lamp. The arrogant ugliness of the thing affected him several ways. A long-repressed psychological input invariably reacted to the shade, in particular, and it summoned an image of a single sere breast, flaccid with age. The pendant tassels along its edge swayed at the slightest air current, the beckoning of a burned-out whore suggesting delights more obscene for their falsity than anything else. He hated it and was happy in the room only when he occupied the rocking chair and didn't have to see it.

Avoiding the lamp would be no benefit today, he realized. Munson's fury grew more evident each moment. He dropped into the chair behind the desk with a loud thump. For a moment he stirred the papers on his desk, and when he finally looked up his expression suggested Draeger was to blame for there being no solution there, either. Contracted muscles strained his speech.

"Tell me exactly what's happened. Leave out nothing. Don't offer any opinions or interpretations."

Holding his words to the monotone buzzing of a disinterested third party, Draeger recounted his activities in complete detail. Munson took notes, and each time he looked down at his pad, Draeger wanted to cheer. The older man had to look away to mark his pad, which relieved him of the pressure of his eyes. They stared, harder than the glasses in front of them, and when they moved they darted. Draeger struggled to avoid thinking of them as caged creatures, full of malice and eager to escape. He could not. The face surrounding them was expressionless as a glacier. Unconsciously, Draeger used each of the note-taking respites to release his grip on the arms of the chair and wipe his hands on his trousers.

When Munson's head raised again, Draeger's speech rate increased perceptibly before leveling off, and his hands fastened to the arms of the chair as if anticipating a launch into space.

None of this escaped Munson's evaluation. He took the notes as a matter of course, knowing he would make Draeger repeat the entire story, and that it would be almost impossible to find any contradictory statements in the first run-through. During the second, however, there might be a slip. By the time Draeger repeated it a third time, he would be wondering if he was adding or subtracting anything of substance from the previous tellings. He'd lose surety and become tentative here and there. Munson anticipated it with the steadfastness of an owl listening for the scuffle of a mouse in straw. He saw himself move from a darkness of surprise swooping on a mumbled phrase or incorrectly stated address or suddenly remembered passerby. His arms throbbed as he pictured himself plunging talons of doubt into Draeger's mind. He knew it had to happen, and revulsion stabbed at his throat for an unguarded moment. It would happen because Draeger was doing what he should do, telling the truth and cooperating. Those were the things that would destroy him. Munson caught himself drifting away from the narrative and snapped himself back to it, reminding himself that men were invariably damaged for causes, that the best soldiers died because they were brave and committed. If those were flaws, all men should pray for the same.

Draeger had anticipated an interrogation. The harsher the better, he repeated to himself as the questions came faster. Munson openly sneered at an answer for the second time, and Draeger pushed against the floor so hard an ankle cracked. He ignored it, telling himself what was happening was for the best, it was correct. It was like probing for a bullet, painful but the only alternative to seeing the entire organism infected.

Nevertheless, resentment grew. At first a mere spark, unable to do anything but glow and call attention to its tiny circle of irritation. Munson's questions turned hostile. The difference between the chill voice and the burning sensation in Draeger's breast grew accordingly, heat drawing strength from the opposite force.

At the end of an hour Draeger held up a hand. "No more. You've heard it all a dozen times."

"Wrong!" Munson hammered the desk, and the humidor bounded and settled like an old cat disturbed in her slumber. "In the last run-through you mentioned a man who got on the plane with you in Manila, a young man. You never mentioned him before."

"He gave us a little slack in the crowd. I never saw him again."

"You never saw him again. Shit. Why didn't you tell me about him before?"

"I only mentioned him because you're pushing me to talk about everything I saw. I'm telling you what I can remember. Who the fuck cares if someone holds up a line for you for a minute? It's not important.''

"You've blown our best collection effort, and you're deciding what's important about investigating the source of the leak?''

"Leak?'' Draeger came out of the chair in a wavelike flow, bending over the desk. "There was no leak.''

The glasses reflected the lampshade, the trembling yellow light hiding the eyes. "There was a leak, you know there was. The courier was killed because he was a courier, not for any other reason. Your asset is uncovered, doesn't trust his escape plan. All we can do is assume he's told them everything he knows and start repairs.''

"He doesn't know anything.'' Draeger slid back into the chair. "We only had a few days. You remember. He hinted around, and we decided I should cold-pitch him. He was so ready he went for it right there. He doesn't even know I'm American.''

Munson said, "He's guessed. And now every American in the Philippines gets checked out. Picture the countermeasures in their own country. We'll be lucky if we can get back in business in a year!''

For a moment Draeger thought the pain in his head would erupt through his lips. That mental image made him bite the inside of his cheek until the brass-and-salt taste allowed him to think. He had anticipated catharsis, perhaps even penance, but there was no cleansing suggested in what was happening. His anger surprised him. Not that it was there, but the stillness of it, like a sleeping bat suspended in his guts, waiting to project itself. It was an unsettling vision. There was hate and there was no one to hate, only misfortune.

"You better get hold of the front office.'' The words came more easily than he'd expected. "My operation's been clean and tight. If there's been a leak, it was something Egg Roll did, not something I did, nothing I'll take the responsibility for. I've said all I want to say.''

"You want a lawyer?'' It was said almost lightly enough to disguise the edge.

Draeger put his hands to his temples and dropped them quickly. "Don't try to fuck around in my mind. Don't think about trying. I don't know what went wrong, but it wasn't me. I don't want to see you and me get into a bind. Get the front office. Let someone else check it out.''

"I've already done that. I don't have the resources to handle something like this. They'll send someone.''

"It's going to be hard to explain—three non-Filipinos checking out everyone we can find.''

"There'll be more than three people, but you won't be involved.'' He rose from his chair and studied the books at his new eye level over Draeger's right shoulder. "I've recommended that you be suspended from this team and any other activities until culpability is confirmed or disproven.''

Draeger had to repeat the words. "Confirmed? *Disproven*?''

Munson looked at him, facial planes drawn to shapes like the exotic blades displayed in the next room. He raised an arm and pointed. The hand was no more than a foot from Draeger's eyes, and in his state of near shock it took on unique importance. He focused on the tip of the pointed finger, mildly surprised to see the nail was frayed, the clear translucence cloudy where teeth had worried it. Pores contoured toward the hand, whorls and curves unique to this one man who had been a friend. Munson said, "Personally, I'd send you home now.''

"You're too fucking good to me.''

"I was.'' The hand drifted to his side. "A few days ago I told you I was planning to retire. Maybe you've pissed that away, maybe you haven't. I could handle it, either way, but you've jeopardized our whole collection effort and everyone in it. That's unforgivable.''

They stood facing each other in silence, Draeger fighting back words, knowing no explanation would register.

At Munson's first sound, both men drew back almost imperceptibly. "We'll have to act as normal as possible until we get instructions. I'll tell Leonila I have to go down to the office. That way we won't have to be near each other, at least today. I want you out of here on the evening plane to Manila. I'll make your reservations at the PhilAirlines office on my way. Get back to your place and sit until you're contacted. And, for Christ's sake, be professional. You look like a Boy Scout with shit on his merit badge.'' He waited for Draeger to open the door before coming around the desk to follow him out.

When they reached the dining room, Leonila was smiling. "I knew you two would be talking like a couple of old women. I told the cook to hold everything until you were ready." She called to the kitchen, and the cook's voice floated back. Pots and pans rattled, and the maid grinned her way among them with hot coffee.

Ria said, "Leonila was telling me about your cosmetics business, Roger. It sounds fascinating. I had no idea."

"Women always seem to be interested," he said drily and smiled back at her. "What I like best about it is the experimentation, trying to find colors and scents that accentuate the best features of Asian women. I don't think most Western cosmetics do them justice."

The conversation rolled easily. Draeger listened with a growing alienation that drove him from the others, deeper into his own thoughts. As he had been surprised by the silent weight of his anger earlier, now he was surprised by a thirst for vengeance. He no longer wanted to be cleared. He wanted that clearing to damn Munson. The more he thought about it, the more he remembered the questions thrown at him, heard the inflections and innuendo. It became impossible for him to sit at the same table any longer. He mumbled an excuse and left.

Warmth coursed through Munson at the sight, soothing. It must be a chemical thing, the logical half of his brain was telling him, while the emotional part shouted triumph. And yet there was sadness. He thought back to his analogy of the soldier dying, and imagined himself as a commander sending a trooper into combat, knowing he must die in an attack on an unimportant objective. He would occupy the enemy long enough for the real objective to be taken. There was no cruelty in not confiding in him. If anything, it was merciful. The young man would resent his dying whether he understood the entire plan or not, and he could only hurt the more for knowing his was a mere sideshow. The success of the operation was paramount, worth even the life of the commander, should that become necessary. Obviously that couldn't happen prematurely, or the entire operation would collapse. There could be no substitute commanders. Not this time. There'd been enough of them, the second-guessers, the backbiters, the ambitious bastards shadowing you around and waiting to strangle you with your first mistake. Worse, if you trusted one with a task, sure as hell, that was the one the operation ended up stumbling over because it never got done right. No, the commander had to make this one work to the end. If all went well, the trooper might even survive, too, although simple logic dictated against it.

A cause demanded sacrifices, had to have them, if it was to be legitimate. Without them there were no examples for others to follow, nothing to inspire the victories so desperately needed now. And the ones that would have to follow, to consolidate the new positions.

That was not his problem, he reminded himself sternly. All he could hope to do was send history down the right path. Other better qualified men would take command once he'd indicated the route. He prided himself on this lack of vanity, choosing to be merely a pathfinder. The thought of politics put his teeth on edge. Espionage had little of the clean definition of combat—especially the way the old ladies in Washington insisted the game be played nowadays—but politics was even worse. Nothing was ever accomplished by politics.

That was the one possible flaw in his program. If the politicians were too blind to see the golden opportunity he was providing them. It didn't bear considering. They'd curse his name, at first, but when the really thinking ones grasped his concept, they'd pin medals all over him.

Leonila's return with Draeger interrupted his reverie, and he chanced a quick look at Ria. Her watching stare directed at him was feline, as unembarrassed as it was unrevealing. When he smiled at her, she blinked, but that was all. He said, "I was a million miles away. That's what happens when you let business get the best of you."

She nodded, half-smiling, before turning her attention to Draeger. Munson complimented his own outward serenity and repressed a sigh at Draeger's dull grimness. A real professional wouldn't be so transparent.

The maid rolled out the trolley with their breakfast, and he gestured it to Ria, smiling at her. This time she returned it, almost as if anticipating it.

The meal went smoothly, with Draeger becoming more civil as it went on, largely in response to Leonila's mothering. Munson was pleased to see that, and told himself how lucky he was that she loved him. It was a continuing amazement and pleasure to him, an entire geography of happiness. The program he had in mind would test her sorely, but only her patience. Not her love. That was proof against anything. She was the unconquerable bastion, the final defense.

He finished the last bite of *longaniza* with gusto, remembering how he'd longed for the breakfast sausage of his boyhood until Leonila had mixed ingredients and perfected this, a combination of American and Filipino recipes. It was still primarily *longaniza*, cooked down to crispy-skinned fat fingers, a little less sweet and a shade more peppery. Bending to kiss her forehead, lying about the necessity to spend the day in the office, he reflected that it was those little things she did for him that were more a measure of love than anything else.

The women decided they could enjoy the day more if they went shopping, leaving Draeger no choice but to go along. He envied their carefree conversation and the way an inconsequential blouse or vase could provide them amusement. His own mood permitted minimal flashes of genuine interest that died as they were born. He worked at the facade, smiling when called on and feigning participation.

He made it through the morning, even managing to enjoy the quiet little shop on Pelaez where they had lunch. They each ordered *halo-halo*, the women giggling like school girls and teasing each other about gaining weight from the multiple scoops of ice cream and the lacing of fruits and syrups swirled around and through them. A second wave of memories swept him, threatening to further separate him from the women. Vanilla, pineapple, the cloying sugar—so many boyhood smells. And the laughter, uncomplicated and shared freely. He was about to go adrift when Ria's hand covered his. When he looked at her there was concern clouding the happiness in her eyes. He willed himself back to her presence and smiled. Leonila said something. It was enough. Ria was content again, looking to her new friend to continue what he had almost ended.

Pain clutched his head, unlike the headaches he feared. This surged from his eyes to the back of his neck. He dipped the last spoonful of the melted confection from the glass and told himself wryly it was a hell of a world where a man couldn't enjoy a familiar headache.

They were back at the house, waiting for Munson, when the phone rang and Draeger was so sure the call would be for himself, he was already moving when Leonila called his name and turned. Munson said, "I didn't make reservations for you. We're going to have to talk. Something's come up."

Hoping Munson would understand he was talking about Ria, Draeger said, "There are other people involved. It's not just business."

"Yes it is. Business, and nothing else. If there's something else on your mind, it's your problem."

Draeger felt the heat on his face and turned from the women. "I'll think of something."

"That'll be good practice." Munson's professorial tone was slick with sarcasm. "It'll be a change, for sure." He paused to let the barb set before continuing. "You'll have to come down here. I'll get rid of the guard personnel. Be here at nine-thirty. You got that?"

"I understand."

The sound of the connection being broken was Munson's only good-bye. It was a full three seconds before the full import of the dead phone registered on Draeger. He replaced the handset carefully, then went directly to the bar and poured himself a heavy bourbon. Ria made an unconscious gesture that caught his eye as he lifted the glass. There was worried disapproval in her expression, and the interrupted gesturing hand hung limp with self-consciousness. He slugged back the drink and immediately poured another. "I've decided to stay overnight," he said harshly. "Business. Roger's having a client come by around nine-thirty. I have to be there. I'm sorry." Without waiting for reaction, he turned and walked back to the porch.

The women watched him go, only looking at each other when he was around the corner.

"What can it be?" Leonila's question was a plea. "They're such good friends. What can have happened?"

Ria shook her head. "I don't know. It might be best if I left. There seems to be—your husband—" She shrugged, the silence of the unfinished sentence grating on their ears. For a moment neither spoke. Their hands moved, ineffectual gestures, the tentative move-

ments of small animals that would know each other but are too timid
to step forward.

"Never mind Roger." Leonila's hand finally made contact, fingertips on the back of Ria's clenched fist in her lap. "Our Glen—
you like him quite a bit?"

Ria smiled in spite of herself, hearing the "our Glen" that made
him family and someone who could be discussed within normal
rules.

Leonila went on. "You don't have to answer. I get too nosy."

"No, you don't. I want to talk to you. I'm confused."

"Because he's not a Filipino?"

"That doesn't mean a thing to me! I mean, I don't care about it. I
don't understand why he does things, that's all. And I don't know if
it's him that attracts me or if it's just the fact that he *is* different. I
don't know what to think!"

"You can't believe you're the first woman who's felt that way."
Leonila's bantering included sympathy. Ria opened her fist to enfold
the touching hand. Leonila said, "Why trouble yourself with 'why
this?' and 'why that?' Be patient, see if you truly care for him.
Understanding will come in time."

"Is that the way it was with you and Roger?"

She laughed. "The first time I saw him I thought he was so
ugly!" She leaned forward to rest her head on Ria's shoulder before
sitting up again. Through some trick of muscle control she pulled
her chin down, lengthening her face, and accentuated that by forcing
her lips into a drooping curve. Tilting her head, she looked at Ria
down a far-too-short nose, but when she spoke in an affected, husky
voice, the burlesque of her husband was complete. " 'It's a beautiful evening, Leonila. Would you care to sit over here, away from
the others, and talk for a while?' "

Ria laughed with her, then, "They're really not that much different,
are they? American men, I mean. Like your Roger—he belongs here
now, doesn't he? Just like us."

"No, that's not really true, dear. The longer he lives here the
better he understands us and behaves like us, but he wears the
change. It's as if every day he puts on another bit of clothing that
makes him look and act more like a Filipino. I see him naked,
though. I know there is an American under it all." She stopped, and

her point of vision slipped past Ria and aimed at something far beyond the room. There was a movement in her eyes, a scalpel's probe of Ria's before she spoke again. "Even I can't see past his skin, however, and I know there is something he hides inside that I will never be allowed to see."

Ria pitched forward. "It's the same with Glen! It's one of the things that interests me most! What is it?"

"I don't know." The answer was sad, and Leonila lifted her head instantly, fixing a bright smile. "And I shouldn't care. It's exciting, and how many women can say their husbands are truly exciting?"

"I envy you."

"Pooh! You'll find one you want, Glen or someone else. You're too pretty. I'm not going to worry about you. Just don't you dare make eyes at my Roger."

"As if he'd notice. Anyhow, one American to worry about is enough for anyone."

"And that's true of all men."

Ria made a face. "You can say that again. Like this trouble between them. Women would scream and argue and either patch things up or be enemies. Two Filipinos would either avoid each other, or one would have killed the other by now. But Americans! They put their heads together and growl like dogs over a bone and go on and on and on. It's a wonder they don't all have ulcers."

"Maybe they do. Maybe that's why they get angry so easy in the first place."

They both laughed at that, stopping to watch Draeger come in and put down his glass. Ria smiled, the approval turning to a fixed, social mask when he bent to the refrigerator and took out a beer. His return expression was as false as her own. As soon as he was out of sight again, Leonila mimed his shoulder-rolling, stiff-necked posture with the same accuracy she'd used on her husband. Ria erupted in more laughter in spite of herself, and Leonila said, "Come on, let's go out in the kitchen and make something sweet and yummy and fattening. If these men are going to make such fools of themselves, why should we worry about staying pretty and skinny?"

She took Ria's arm and led the way.

At six o'clock the women ate alone. Draeger refused to join them, distant civility harsher than any words. Leonila comforted Ria, who couldn't seem to decide if she was angry, hurt, or confused. Draeger continued his regular trips to the bar refrigerator, draining Sam Miguel beer bottles with metronomic regularity. The women finished dinner quickly and adjourned to the television set.

There was no sunset because of a developing cloud cover. The rain started shortly after dark, a spattering tattoo in the night that filled the air with a tropical-urban aromatic mix of steaming cement and burgeoning plants.

It was shortly after eight when Leonila excused herself and several minutes after that before Ria wondered why she was taking so long. She wandered through the house, her curiosity giving way to bemusement and finally a concern that was evidenced in her questioning calling of Leonila's name. The maid and cook appeared at the dining room entry just as Draeger stepped in from the porch. The maid stared quietly while the plump cook wadded her long white apron as if kneading bread. They all looked at Ria expectantly. All she could say was, "I can't find Leonila."

Draeger frowned. The cook and maid glanced at each other and sidled backward. Ria gestured sharply. "Wait. Where is she?"

The maid, young and unsure of herself, looked to the older cook. The latter shrugged, and Ria faced her full on. "You better tell me," she said, and the cook's courage fled. She spoke rapidly in Tagalog, hands whipping in gestures descriptive enough to let Draeger know that Leonila had left the house and the maid was equally implicated in the cover-up. The girl stared at him, wide-eyed.

"Find out where she went," Draeger said, and Ria translated instantly.

"She had them get her driver. She gave the cook a note. You're not supposed to see it until eight-thirty."

"The hell with that. Tell her I want it right now."

The cook needed no translation. She reached in the pocket of her apron and brought out a folded piece of paper. There was a grease stain on it and noticing it created a coldness in the glowing puddle of alcohol in Draeger's stomach. Why would he notice something so insignificant? Things like that were remembered tomorrow.

The note said: *I don't want you and Roger to argue any more, Glen. If you go see him tonight, the way you are both behaving, I am afraid of trouble. I have taken my car (Don't worry, I'm not driving. My driver is our yard man who lives here.), and I will come home with Roger after I have talked some sense into him. I depend on you, Ria, to do the same for Glen. Silly men! What would they do without us? Love, Leonila.*

"Goddamit!" Draeger drove his fist into his palm. "She shouldn't have done that!" He glared at the cook and the now completely terrified maid. "I need a car! Quickly!"

The cook held an imploring hand to Ria and spewed Tagalog. Tears boiled up in her eyes. Ria made comforting sounds at her before turning to Draeger. "There is no other car. Roger took his own, and now Leonila has taken hers."

The maid managed a few words in a voice not much more than a whisper.

Ria said, "She says there's a motorcycle, the yard man's, in the garage. The keys are on the board in the kitchen."

Draeger moved immediately, snatching the keys and running for the garage. By the time he had the door open Ria was standing by the machine, waiting for him. "You've been drinking. If you have to go after her, call a taxi, Glen, please."

He straddled the machine. "I'm not that drunk, and it'd take too long. I'm not trying to catch her, anyhow. All I want to do is get there and send her home."

She leaped on the back, knowing better than to try to continue the argument on foot. "It's her husband." The engine roared and she leaned forward, yelling in his ear. "It's her husband. You're the one who'll be interfering. She's right. You shouldn't be talking to him, not after all that beer."

He whirled on her so quickly he almost butted her. "I don't give a goddam if I ever see him again. She doesn't understand what's going on, and I don't want her getting mixed up in it."

"Mixed up in what?"

She stared open-mouthed at the sudden change in his expression, from half-drunk ferocity to tenderness. There was a depth to it that spoke of sadness for a future known and found wanting. It was gone as quickly as it had come. He looked past her, walking the motorcycle backwards out the door. She circled him in her arms as he sped through the gate, savoring the contradictory hard maleness while remembering that fleeting tenderness she'd seen in him. Her thoughts leaped to the even quicker contact that had preceded Leonila's wistful comment about feeling closed off from an unknown part of her husband's life.

*There was a spark when our eyes met, like the arcing heat that joins the pieces of metal. It's too bright to really be seen, but anyone ever exposed to it will swear they can define it. The brightness, magic, joining in fire, the new link stronger than either of the old sections. But the welding rod, the agent of the joining—it's destroyed. Electricity explodes away in a profuse blue energy that changes the rod into something no one would recognize if they didn't care enough to learn all the facts.*

The motorcycle complained at the speed of a corner, and she grabbed Draeger's shirt convulsively, dropping the wadded note in the struggle for a better grip.

Leonila stepped out of the car slowly, feeling for good footing while her eyes remained fixed on the darkened building. It was isolated from its neighbors. The drizzle of rain on its cement walls caught the light from the high lamp in the parking lot that stretched between the locked driveway gate and the parked car. The pedestrian entry swung open invitingly. The illumination that should have made the building look brighter gave it a greasy pallor that looked as if it might stick to a hand that touched it. The silence of the scene was accentuated by thin, distant music from a loud radio, music and words melded in an aural blur.

The driver hurried around beside Leonila. "I think Mr. Munson is gone. He would not leave his building with no guard."

She pressed ahead. "He told his friend he would meet him here. He must be inside. I'm sure there's a reason the building is dark."

The driver grunted, unconvinced, and moved quickly to precede her and led the way across the parking area, shifting impatiently while she unlocked the building door. He crowded past her to enter first. There was a faint light in the office space, a luminescence reflecting from the ceiling where clerestory windows faced outward. The inward-swinging door banged a chair and sent it clattering back. Leonila started, grabbing the door jamb. As she drew breath to call out, a voice called from off to the right.

"I'm here, in the office."

"Roger? It's me, Leonila. I came instead, because—"

"I turned the lights out so we could have some privacy." The interruption startled Leonila, and then the incongruity of the statement impressed her more than the rude interruption. She told herself to be calm, that he was there so there could be no danger. The pounding of her heart mocked her, and she shivered.

"It's not Glen, Roger, it's me." She raised her voice. "I left him a—"

Munson talked over her explanation again. "You know where the light switch is—right there in the hall. Be careful you don't stumble over the junk stacked up there."

Leonila glanced at the young driver. His posture suggested his embarrassment. She was grateful for the dim light shielding her expression and wished she'd left him in the car. Her guarding hand extending to the front, she hurried between desks across the office space until she was at the hall door. Munson's office was only a few yards down, a place that kept him out of the routine offices and immediately adjacent to his lab and warehouse complex. The light switch became a goal pulling her forward. She knew how foolish she would look in the harsh glare, could feel her eyes wide and straining. Her mouth was open and her breathing made a wet, snuffling noise. She didn't care. Anything would be better than the unnamed fear. Just then she ran into something at knee level around the corner and against the hall wall. Whatever it was, it didn't belong there and it hurt. She cried out, anger and fear twinning in the wordless exclamation. Her husband's voice said, "There are people watching the building for uninvited guests. Turn on the lights, or they'll be in here like fucking commandos."

It stunned her. All she could think to say was "What?" and she was repeating it foolishly when her hand found the light switch. The change from dark to light made her squint, but she saw the thing that had hurt her knee. It was round in cross section, quite long and such a bright white it glared after the semidarkness of before. There was another one down the hall, just outside her husband's office. There was a humming sound from the closest one, and she stepped back to see what it could be. A small electric motor on the floor was busily reeling in a cord. The other end of it was attached to a jury-rigged reel that turned a handle on the white object. Leonila recognized the white thing as a propane gas tank at the same time the rush of acrid gas whistled free to engulf her. She had time to wrinkle her face and say "Roger?" It was a plaintive croak, and although she was gagging on terror and fumes, a small voice told her it would be an absolutely ridiculous way to be remembered.

She saw the spark that ignited the gas cloud as one sees the first budding leaf on a tree, the leaf itself growing and expanding and other leaves following until the entire forest, the mountains and valleys, the world as far as one can imagine, is nothing but leaves.

The yard man tried to scream and managed a squealing yip that died with him as the burning maul of gas smashed him.

Leonila died while half-shaped thoughts and images scrambled together in her head. She was thrown against the dying driver hard enough to break his bones before their bodies struck the cement block end wall and broke some more, including his skull and her spine. By that time her lungs were evacuated, the fire having pulled the air from them in lust for its own life. It was enough. That alone would have killed her, without the insult of a body broken in all its parts. There was no need for the cruel indignity of exposed skin so charred it lifted from the flesh underneath in ragged, blackened patches. Her dress was torn and scorched, its yellow disfigured by the red of blood, anticipating the fire already hurrying to cleanse the hallway of the horror Leonila and the young man had become.

The ignition of the second propane tank a few moments later was extravagantly excessive, then, from the point of view of causing death. It had a different purpose.

Prior to that explosion, Munson's sound-actuated tape recorder was tied to the side of his desk, and the desk had been shoved up against the wall separating it from the gas container in the hall. The filing cabinets had then been placed against the other side of the desk. The combined mass provided excellent tamping, so that when the tank blew there was an initial resistance, and the cement block driven into the tape recorder was checked while the energy literally piled up behind it before driving it inexorably away from its source. The effect was to turn the recorder into a mess of metallic and plastic confetti, most of it remaining inside the building. The inferno resulting from the burning tons of solvents, oils, greases, powders, papers, and furniture would further cloud any possible identification of the parts, should anyone even consider such an effort.

Some of the pieces escaped by riding the shock wave through the exterior wall. One of them, a jagged chip of what had been the carrying handle, fell to earth at Draeger's feet while he was still staggering from the shock of the explosion. He never heard its whirring flight or tingling landing. His senses were canceled by dread. Beside him Ria wept in shocked hysteria that is unaware of anything around it. Her eyes were round and fixed, tears pouring from the corners in a stream, rather than isolated drops. Instead of a neat channel down her face, there were random paths, the result of sobs that shook her body and implosive breathing that jerked her face into constantly changing patterns. Her hands were wadded in fists, clenched at breast height, prepared to piston outward against any advance by the evil flaming in front of her.

They were completely unaware of the gathering crowd or the increasingly loud howl of approaching sirens.

Boy Angel drifted in with the spectators, as he'd been instructed. It was fun at first, watching the cops run around screaming orders that everyone ignored and watching the firemen pour water into the building while it roared like laughter. When the white guy ran out of the crowd and started yelling at one of the cops, the whole thing wasn't fun anymore.

After a few moments of arm waving and yelling, he said something the cop understood. Boy Angel knew the cop understood because he reached up and grabbed the white guy by the elbow and, in Boy Angel's experience, the only way a cop could communicate was through physical contact of one kind or another. The fact that he didn't belt the white guy had to mean he'd said something that made the cop believe he was too important to belt. Either way, the cop led him off, only slowing down a little bit to watch the good-looking woman who hurried to join them.

At first Boy Angel thought about following them. He decided against it. There wasn't much chance the man could recognize him from the plane ride, but there wasn't any need to take any chances at all, and that was the best way to go, always. Anyhow, he didn't owe anybody anything. Not after the stink over the little fat guy in

Manila. Nobody told him a damned thing about watching the guy to see if he tried to hide something, but when it came time for somebody to be blamed because no one knew if the sonofabitch had hid anything or not, Benjamin was quick enough to blame Boy Angel.

He started to walk away and a young man bumped him. Boy Angel stared him down and felt better right away.

Scratching his chest, he told himself no one could blame him for tonight's screw-up. In fact, this one made him look pretty good. After all, even if he had messed up and not killed the fat guy quick enough, he'd never killed the wrong person, sure as hell never killed the wrong *two* people.

The beautiful smile brightened the night as he thought about that.

# ■ CHAPTER 11 ■

Draeger woke up in the strange bed in Munson's upstairs guest room so totally disoriented he stumbled when he leaped to his feet. He caught himself with both hands on the dresser, an effort that threw him into direct confrontation with the naked image in the mirror. The face answering his stare masked any sign of emotion. It assured him the horror of the previous night was no dream.

The knock on the door was so soft it nearly escaped him. His questioning, "Ria?" was tentative.

"I heard noise. Are you all right?"

"Yeah, fine. Wait a minute." He wrapped up in a towel from the adjoining bathroom. "Come on in. I just woke."

She was still dressed in the T-shirt and jeans, incongruous in this changed atmosphere. Strain added dimension to her features. She stammered, "You—you—the way you acted last night." Her hands moved awkwardly, wanting to convey what her words would not.

He nodded. "I know. The police questions. I had to be calm."

"But you were so—*cold*—about everything."

He extended a hand and she took it. "In my culture we're expected to hold back our feelings at times like that."

She shuddered. "I don't like it. You looked terrible."

He produced a weak smile.

She lifted his hand and held it to her cheek. "There's more, but I don't care. I don't want to know." His expression remained unchanged, but he seemed to press closer to her and her thoughts pounded.

*I don't want to have to trust him. I want to be near him, and I'm afraid. He answered the police and they thought they saw him, heard him speak. The real man never appeared. But it's the real one, the one that only lets me see him for a second, that's the man I want.*

"—breakfast?" he was saying, and she realized he'd been talking.

"I'm sorry. I was thinking." She retrieved her hand.

"I said, have you had breakfast?"

Another shiver raced through her. "I've been waiting for you. There's no staff today, and eating alone in—"

He covered the broken sentence. "I want to shower. Be right with you."

She nodded and left without looking back, allowing him the luxury of an honest frown. She was intuitive. The less she had to work with, the better. Not wanting "to know" was a lie. Everyone wanted to know, but it was stonewall time, and the only one around to build it was himself. He thought of Munson's safe, a malignancy squatting in its corner, full of secrets.

*Where the hell is he? What's going on?*

And there was Ria, watching him the way a jaded child watches a magician, ignoring the performance, only wanting to catch the coin in the disguising palm. Still, she'd put up with a lot. He conceded his delight that she'd stayed with him. Following that he paused, waiting for the pang that would chide him for wanting to share his situation with her when he knew it was impossible.

It didn't materialize. There was relief, instead. He didn't want to share that much with her, and he felt no guilt for it.

There was nothing he could do about any of it. Munson was missing. Egg Roll was blown, the courier dead. Leonila was dead.

He moved to the bathroom in a preoccupied shuffle, gazing at the lapped pattern of the woven floor mat. A few short hours ago he'd been full of anger toward Munson, practically hated him. Before that he'd thought of him as a cherished friend. Now the man was dead, and the anguish still carried the stink of enmity.

Who could have forced him to make that last phone call? Could he have guessed it was meant to lure a friend to his death? With luck, he died not knowing it was Leonila, the compassionate, loving Leonila, who set off the trap.

Leonila. Her death was causing more pain than any other issue. That was a failing. A sense of purpose was necessary. Leonila could be mourned when time allowed. The net had to be preserved, foremost. If the net went, everything went, and who'd mourn for her then?

Hot water burned his hand, snapped him out of his thoughts.

Downstairs later, Ria set a plate of scrambled eggs and rice in front of him. The meal passed in silence, but Draeger felt it wasn't sad or uncomfortable. In fact, whenever their eyes met there was an exchange of strengths and reassurances. By the time a second cup of coffee was finished they were both relaxed enough to talk.

Draeger started. "You heard the police say they'd contact Leonila's family. I don't know what we're going to do about Munson, but I can't possibly stay here. He's got family in the States, and the cops'll contact them, too. They're treating him as a missing person until they—you know, check the building."

She shivered. "I'm certainly not sleeping alone here."

Deliberately misinterpreting her, he affected great surprise, then grinned. She colored, which made him laugh. It sounded good even as part of him fought the concept of laughter, and he let it flow, enjoying it. Ria hesitated, her own thoughts written on her face, and then she was laughing, too. They reveled in the amusement of the moment, in the denial it contained, the acceptance it confessed, the mutuality of the understanding it expressed. They stopped at the same time, looking full into each other's eyes. When the phone rang

Draeger had to drive himself to answer it. The voice on the other end was distant and marred in transmission but still imparted heavy unctuousness.

"Is this Mr. Roger Munson's residence?"

"Yes, it is. Who's this, please?"

"My name is Johnson, Carl Johnson. I'm the President of Chittenden Industries, here in Torrance—a suburb of L.A., you know? We've been notified by the Philippine authorities that Mr. Munson is missing. To whom am I speaking, please?"

"My name's Draeger, Mr. Johnson. I'm a friend of Roger's, his house guest. If you'll leave a number, I'll ask that you be contacted as soon as there's something to report."

"I'm sure Mr. Munson will be in touch as soon as he's able. Meanwhile, please express our deepest condolences at the first opportunity."

"I'll see to it, Mr. Johnson. Is there any other message?"

"No, thanks. One of our people will be out there in the near future. This is no time to concern Mr. Munson with business. Thanks for your help."

"Don't mention it." Draeger hung up and smiled for Ria. "Business. They'll keep till Roger gets himself together."

"You're sure he's all right, then? You don't think he was—was in the building?"

He walked up to her and put his hands on her shoulders. "I'm sure we'd have heard by now. He's out there, probably in shock. As soon as he's found, everything'll be all right. Now, is there some way we can arrange for someone to live here until he turns up? We have to get back to Manila, and I'd like to catch the evening plane."

Administering to the needs of the house was a tonic for her. She attached herself to the phone, contacting relatives, making arrangements for guards and maintenance. Draeger busied himself in a complete search of house and grounds. There was nothing to indicate the place was more than a businessman's home. The codes, the radio, all the potentially incriminating material was in the safe. When he was certain of that, Draeger felt almost euphoric relief, a sense of escape. He was stretching racked muscles when the pool caught his attention. Calling to Ria, he gestured when she came from the living room.

"I'm going for a swim."

Her curiosity fled, replaced by disapproval. "You have no suit." The implication he might be willing to use one of Munson's was apparent.

"I've got one I leave here. It stays in the garage."

"I'll get us something to eat and be right back." She moved quickly, as if anxious to change the morning's activity, force a different direction.

By the time he was changed she had sandwiches and soft drinks waiting on the umbrella-shaded table. The walled yard, accessible from either the kitchen or through glass doors off the living room, afforded complete privacy, discounting the distant mountains. The gray-green ridge loomed beyond the malice-bright glass shards on top of the wall. He ate quickly, the pool beckoning. In a few minutes he was splashing through laps. He stopped to hang on the lip and look up at Ria.

"I was thinking," he said. "There's a clothes dryer in the kitchen, and they keep a terrycloth robe in the guest rooms. Just dive in and when you get out, you can wear one of the robes while your clothes dry."

"You're crazy!"

"Why? Pretend you're your grandmother, wearing one of those old 'covers everything' suits."

She threw back her head and laughed. "My grandmother? If you suggested she wear anything like a bathing suit when she was my age, she'd have fainted dead away."

"Well, then, pretend you're my grandmother. She was a racy old lady, I understand."

Still laughing, Ria looked at the pool, its surface roughened by his activity, a multitude of wavelets applauding themselves against the sides of the pool. Large drops collected where the sleek black cap of his hair lay against the skin.

"You're crazy," she repeated.

"Doesn't mean I can't have a good idea from time to time." He pushed away from the pool wall, reaching behind to create a sweeping stroke with both hands that pulled him upright and halfway out of the water. Two great cords strained outward in his neck and muscles ridged across his stomach like huge fingers. When he

submerged the water closed over him in a curtain of translucent
distortion.

Without further thought, Ria stepped out of her shoes and dove in.
He was waiting for her when she surfaced. They looked at each
other and essayed shy amusement that begged for more than
acceptance, hoped for reinforcement. Something like resolve sounded
in their first, exploratory laughter, and as they washed away inhibit-
ing memory, firm chords of amusement replaced the one-note minor
tones of tension. They were breathing hard when Draeger got out,
returning with a pair of air mattresses, and they laughed more in the
struggle to board them.

After much thrashing and shouting of instructions, they were
afloat, arms and feet trailing under the surface. Draeger found her
hand and held it. They drifted with the faint breeze.

When he rolled his head to look at her she appeared to be sound
asleep. Her hair fanned in the water, a sinuous mist. The wet T-shirt
glared against her golden skin at upper arm and throat, curiously
muted beyond those points, the flesh asserting itself through the
cloth. Her brassiere was a strict white demarcation line that rose and
fell in slow rhythm. A move startled him, but she was merely
drawing one leg upward, bent at the knee. The material darkened
where it was stressed, and friction of the rubbing cloth made a
hoarse whisper. The motion affected the mattress's centerline. The
delicate shift rolled her head on langourous muscles to face him. Her
full lips parted, a razored line showing white teeth. Where her skin
had dried she glowed, and Draeger could only wonder at the inner
warmth that would defy such a raging sun and match it, keeping the
body smooth and supple without allowing the sheen of sweat he felt
himself. It was more than an adaptation, it was utilization. The heat
was part of her, and she was its child, at ease in it. It was no more a
mere environmental item to her than water is merely important to a
fish. Draeger looked at her and understood that she was something
he would never be, that she was an integer of self and surroundings.

And what was he? There was no embarrassment in him for what
he did. On the contrary, there was intense pride, all the more
precious for its privacy, its unshared life. Yet he would never know
her unquestioning knowledge of existence. He would be what he had

to be, not what he wanted to be. Not even what he was, truly, in himself.

That point curled through his thoughts, trying to bind them all together in some recognizable whole, but it, too, proved to be another loose strand. If there was any question that buttressed the other questions, held them up to be examined on their vertical face, it was the one that asked, who would I be if I chose to be me?

It was a mental exercise he'd run through so often he thought of it as his personal catechism.

*Who are you?*

The person necessary to carry out my assignment.

*Do you deny your self?*

My true self is constantly reaffirmed by the act of safeguarding my country against its enemies.

*Do you claim any virtues?*

Truthfulness always with friends, hostility always for enemies, strike only to kill.

*Are you willing to kill?*

Decisions made without data are not valid.

*Are you willing to die?*

No.

*Your existence is denied, your person is unknown, your thoughts are unspoken. To what end do you persist?*

To gain one more day for what I believe.

*And for yourself?*

To live long enough to forget to care so much that I am willing to do what I do.

He closed his eyes and opened them again to look directly overhead at a cloud drifting past. It was a confused mass and it shifted imperceptibly, deceiving the eye into believing one face became another without going through any intermediate stages.

If it could only be that easy, he thought, and small pains danced on sun-cracked lips at his rueful smile. He remembered the classes on customs and diet and distances and all the other myriad fragments of operational data he'd been burdened with before he left the States. And he'd made it work. His net had been good. Been great, by God, the best.

Ria stirred beside him, trying to roll over in her sleep. He reached for her and, half-awake, she recoiled. It was enough to overweigh the clumsy mattress, and she squalled lustily when it flowed out from under her. Her flailing splashed Draeger, and he rolled off to be standing beside her when she surfaced. Instead of laughter, she came up with a throat full of water, choking violently. He grabbed her, towing her to shallower water where she could stand, and she leaned against him, racking through the last seizures of clearing her system. He had his arms around her without thinking about it until she stopped.

Her own awareness came simultaneously, and she pulled back. Still unthinking, he tightened his grip, only long enough for her to look into his eyes. The salient thing he recognized was fear. There was more, but she averted her head, and he was so disappointed to find such a thing in her he didn't want to identify it. He made his own backward move, holding her arm to guide her to the shallow-end steps.

She became more animated as they walked to the table, laughing about the accident, holding onto his arm and leaning against him. As much as he enjoyed it, he could not forget the fear. Still, she was no different than she had been, and he enjoyed her company. They decided it was time to change and went inside. She returned from her first-floor guestroom in a swirling robe of navy blue with red sleeves and triangular side panels. Pirouetting to show it off to the appreciative Draeger, she announced her clothes would dry as well in the sun as in the machine and took them out to the poolside and draped them over chairs. Draeger was waiting in the living room when she returned.

She stepped through the glass door from the pool area and stopped, silhouetted against the outer glare. The nubby material interfered with the light behind her, creating an aureole. Her hair hung heavy down her back on her right side, but the left wing fell across her ear and coursed downward to the level of her breast. It was barely long enough to conform to the upward curve under the robe, an ebony waterfall, caught in a last outbound leap.

Draeger said, "I wish—" and killed the sentence with a quick shake of his head.

Ria held his eyes. The fear caught the light once again, only to dissolve to an impenetrable glow. He took a step toward her and she lifted her chin. When he was immediately in front of her he stopped, and they remained motionless. Laughter had worked for them before, and the secret messages of glances and minute gestures, but those are clues that one accepts or rejects by other subtle, painless mannerisms. This was ultimatum, a demand for commitment.

He encircled her immobility in arms that trembled, and her eyes never left his. When he pulled her to him her back arched, the thrown-back head rigid in its lack of concession. Not until his lips were on hers and their tongues were seeking each other did he begin to believe she wanted him at all, much less as much as he wanted her. He reached to cup her breast and she leaned back, watching, her downcast face shielded. As he parted the top of the robe she looked up at him. Her face was almost puffy, as though she had cried recently. The animation he had come to accept as a constant part of her was replaced by a somnolence that made him think of liquid, a river, dammed.

"Don't ever lie to me," she said, sighing the words, and yet they checked Draeger instantly. When he said nothing, she leaned forward and kissed the back of his hand holding the lapel, and he continued to open the robe, then pulled it back off her shoulders. She stood naked and unashamed while he fondled her breasts, lifting her own hands to unbutton his shirt. When he took the nipples between his fingers and stroked them she made tiny sounds deep in her chest. The effort to unclasp his belt taxed her, and she wrestled clumsily until it released and she could force his trousers down. He stepped out of them and shrugged off the shirt. Naked as she, he scooped her into his arms and carried her to the downstairs guest room where he lowered her to the bed, kissing her eyes, her shoulders, her breasts. She pulled him to her and arched against his thrust, crying out wordlessly once then and, later, several times, the sounds mingling with his.

When he was beside her they were quiet, each content to hold onto what they had shared, unsure where this new direction might take them. In the present the contact and scent of the other was enough. The future was a cold blade only wanting to cut through the warmth they'd discovered.

He looked at her, reached to stroke the marvelous skin, his thick hand sliding from the darkness between her thighs to the earth-red of already gorged nipples. She stretched to bite gently at his neck.

"Don't ever lie to me," she said again. There was submission in it, and iron.

"I won't. Ever," he said.

He knew he already had, even as the thought shattered itself against the sensations of entering her.

Pierce stood looking down at the figure on the bed, steeling himself to watching the injection. He tried to convince himself it was only the impending shot making him ill, but knew it wasn't so. There was far more. He took his eyes from the prone figure and scanned the room. His hotel, a luxury hideout. Filipino-modern, a blend of the best handcrafts and modern design—for what? Hospital to an idiot!

Boy Angel came out of the small bathroom with the hypodermic between two fingers of his left hand, like a farmer with a glass-and-metal cigar. He held a ball of cotton with thumb and forefinger of the same hand and carried a bottle of alcohol in the other. Apologizing to Pierce, he pressed him aside and pulled the body over on its back. Munson's sharp face, slack now in stupor, stared up at him. An uncoordinated arm jerked out from under the sheet and thrashed weakly. Boy Angel dabbed alcohol on the closer arm. He jabbed with the needle and Pierce's breath whistled.

"Jesus Christ, you're supposed to be giving him a fucking shot, not amputating!"

Boy Angel pushed the plunger home and extracted the needle. When he looked up, Pierce was staring through the slim gap between the heavy cream drapes. The blue of the sea and the old-gold sand were duplicated by the room's appointments, bringing the environment inside, controlled, modified to air-conditioned perfection. When Boy Angel spoke, the sharp Tondo accent was so blatantly out of place it made Pierce wince.

"Benjamin told me to help you with him. If I was not in Cebu to see what went wrong, the police have him already. He was like drunk. Cry, make noise, fall down. *I* get him on boat, bring him here. You want take care him? I go home?"

"No, no. We'll be needing you until he gets back on his feet. I don't want anyone except you and me in the room, not for any reason.''

"I am not a houseboy."

"No one said you were." Pierce made soothing gestures as he headed for the door. "You're a guard, and damned important one."

"You got plenty guards. Why you got Moro guards and Christian, too? They don't like each other. I see."

"Never mind the guard force, all right? That's my concern." The door slammed after him. Boy Angel scratched at his chest until the figure on the bed moaned and distracted him. He reached over and flipped the unresisting body on its side and resumed scratching.

He had a bad feeling about things. Nothing seemed to be working the way it was supposed to. There was going to be trouble, sure as hell. And Pierce would get his share.

Munson groaned again, and Boy Angel dipped a washcloth in cool water and swabbed the sweating brow.

Draeger held the door for Ria. When she was part way down the walk toward the waiting cab she realized he wasn't with her and looked back at him in silent query.

"I've got to take one last look through the house," he apologized. "I've got this dumb feeling I've forgotten something." She opened her mouth to comment, and he talked over the attempt. "I'll only be a couple of minutes, and I'll go nuts if I don't do it. Just wait in the cab, OK?" He grinned sheepishly, and she shook her head in mock aggravation before doing as he asked.

Locking the door behind him, he hurried to Munson's office and went immediately to the safe. Carefully wrapping the combination dial with his shirt tail, he turned it until he heard a faint pop inside. A moment later there was a sizzling noise. It grew rapidly to a hoarse rumble, and smoke boiled out the seam around the door. Draeger flicked the air-conditioner on "high" and "exhaust," watching the acrid, gray haze whirl across the desk and disappear into the grill-work maw. By the time the guards were on station there wouldn't be a smell left. The firebrick interior would not only insure complete combustion of everything in the black hulk, it would guarantee the incendiary devices didn't eat clear through the bottom and light off the house.

He closed the door behind him as he left. The thought of Control's equipment and that incredible little radio being reduced to dust filled him with regret, but it had to be. The man calling himself Johnson had been explicit. Any reference to Chittenden Industries meant all operations went to dead stop. Maybe they'd be pissed off because he burned up the safe. So let them. There was no chance Munson's material could be compromised now.

He ran to the waiting cab. Ria snuggled up against him as they wound down the hill. "Did you find what you thought you forgot?"

"It was just my imagination. We didn't bring enough to be able to forget anything."

There was no reaction from Ria, and he decided it was tension that gave the statement a sinister ring in his ears. He closed his eyes. Instead of merely picturing the safe, his mind reached back to the earlier fantasy of the thing as idol. While he looked, it transformed to an altar, with an ancient, emaciated starveling standing on it, all bone and hate. The altar was on fire. So was the man.

# ■  CHAPTER 12  ■

For three days Drager went through the motions of normal life. At first he was philosophical and considered himself lucky that there was no new material scheduled to be dropped by any of his people for a while. He spent most of his time in his office, looking at books and telling himself he was reading, trying to drive out the constantly interchanging images of the frightened Chinese civil servant and the warm deliciousness of Ria. Before the first day was out he wondered how long it would be until he went mad.

Ria called him on the morning of the second day, and he knew the madness was on him already, because he heard his own voice tell her he had to work late.

There was something more than disappointment in her answer, a vocal trick done the way a painter lays one color over another to confuse the eye and demand extra attention. He could have sworn excitement tinted her forgiveness. That uneasy sensation regenerated the concern over the trapped agent.

By the morning of the third day his stomach was upset and he was constantly hurrying down the hall to the men's room. His route took him past the secretary pool, where the young women formed the committee decision that, like the other Americans, he had no stomach for anything that didn't come out of a can, and one shipped from the States, at that. The lone dissenter was accused of less than clinical objectivity and reduced to blushes and giggles.

That evening in his apartment he poured himself a full three ounces of bourbon, sloughed off his shoes and shirt, and stretched out on the sofa. When that drink was gone he measured another, slightly smaller, before dialing Ria's number. Arturo answered, and when he realized who was calling the noncommital voice shifted to a wary neutrality.

"Ria is not here. She asked me to tell you she would be home later this evening."

Draeger thanked him and prepared to hang up, but Arturo went on. "How long have you been in the Philippines, Glen?" He stressed the name, and Draeger cursed himself for not knowing the culture well enough to grasp exactly what message Arturo was including. He answered the question.

Arturo asked, "Are you a sports fan?"

"Yes, I am."

"Ah, good. Perhaps we could get together for one of the events some evening. We have many good fighters, you know, and our professional basketball is exciting. Not the same quality as your National Basketball Association."

"I'd like that. We'll plan something."

"Yes. I've wondered how Americans feel about sports here in the Philippines. If we go together I can ask you questions and get the American view."

"And I can get the Philippine view."

Arturo loosened up appreciably.

"I did not think of that. We will have our own—oh, what do they call it?—information exchange. That's it. An information exchange. OK?"

"I'll look forward to it. What time do you expect Ria?"

"She did not say. Just later, that's all."

"OK. Thanks."

They exchanged good-byes and Draeger hung up, leaving his hand on the phone. There was more to the conversation, he knew, and a man didn't have to be from the islands to know Arturo was concerned about his cousin. He shrugged. What he and Ria did was their own business. When he lifted the glass to his lips he was startled to see nothing in it but ice cubes and lurched forward to study the rug, thinking it must have spilled. There was nothing there, and it came to him that the pain in his throat was curiously at ease for the first time. In fact, he decided, he felt quite relaxed, and if it was the effect of two good belts on an empty stomach, why not? He rolled over on his side and lowered the glass to the carpet. An ice cube dislodged from the top of the stack and pinged to rest.

*The washrag was in his mouth, the taste and smell of the soap overpowering. He struggled in his mother's grip and gagged.*

*"Bring it up, if you want to!" The words were hoarse grunts jarred free by the force of her efforts. "I'll wash the filth out of your mouth one way or another!" He opened his eyes and was looking directly into hers, blazing green the way the sun looked when he'd lay on his back in the pond and look up at it through the water. When he turned away from that his nose was against the bar of soap, shiny and set on the sink counter. It was the same yellow-brown of the foul droppings sputtering out of the sick calf in the barn, and he heaved in earnest. Pressure forced the stuff out his nose onto his mother's hand, and she jumped back screaming. His father came in and said, "What the hell—?"*

*She yelled louder. "He did that on purpose! He was in the barn with that Kiefer kid, and he was talking filth!"*

*"Just the one word, Pa! It was a accident! I'm sorry! The calf, Pa! It's sick, and when it went on the fresh hay I said a bad word! I didn't mean to!"*

*She grabbed him by the hair turning his face up, her eyes burning his.* "*Liar! A dirty mouth and now lies. No one'll ever soap the filth out of your mind, will they?*"

"*Godalmighty, he said he's sorry.*"

*She whirled, discarding the boy.* "*See? The Lord's name in vain! He gets it from you! And the lies!*" *She faced her son again.* "*I could have forgiven you before. Accident! You said the word, and that can't happen by accident. What if I talked that way?* She thrust her face down to his level.* "*Shit!*" *He grimaced until his eyes were closed.* "*Shit! Shit!*" *Then she was facing her husband again.* "*All men lie. Not all men teach their children filth.*" *She walked out, stiff-backed, proof against her son's shouts.* "*I never learned it from Pa! Honest! I never learned it from him!*"

*His father almost smiled.* "*Clean off your face. And the sink and floor. Use lots of that soap.*"

*The only way he finished without puking again was to hold his nose with one hand and slosh the soapy water around with the other. He listened to the mumble of the fight upstairs while he scrubbed, praying his father wouldn't use that terrible word so she'd never guess her husband used it outside the house all the time.*

He answered the phone with a sense of moving in slow motion, and the sight of the handset rising gently in his grasp was extremely funny. There was no reason for it to be that funny, which made the whole thing truly hilarious.

"Mr. Draeger?"

"That's affirmative." A giggle clawed fiercely at his throat.

"Mr. Glen Draeger?"

"Totally affirmative."

There was a heavy silence, the compressed sound of a telephone with a hand pressed against the mouthpiece. The edge of Draeger's humor dulled against it, and he straightened, waiting. Whoever was on the other end hung up. Draeger said, "Hello?" a few times into the dead instrument before replacing it. Amusement gave way to apprehension. Could Egg Roll have given someone a lead? Could it be Munson? The police?

His head hurt, worse than usual, as bad as anything he could remember. He used the arm of the sofa to lever himself to his feet. Unsteady legs carried him to the kitchen where he dumped the dregs and melt water. Refilling the glass with cold juice he drank it down like medicine. For a moment he thought it would bounce, finally understanding how tension, tiredness, and alcohol on an empty stomach were combining to undermine him. The head savaged more, but the stomach eased.

At the harsh rasp of the door buzzer he hurried to the intercom and barked into it. The guard responded with nervous dignity. "There is a message for you, sir."

"You mean someone to see me?"

"No, sir. A message. In a white envelope. From a taxi driver. It has your name, sir, and he said it was for you. I can have it brought up."

"I'll be right there."

He was opening the door before he realized he still had on no shoes or shirt. Fumbling, he corrected that and left at a trot. In the lobby one of the uniformed guards handed over the plain envelope, and Draeger carefully walked away from him before opening it. The message was brief. It said, "Intercontinental Boulevardier. 8:30."

Checking his watch, Draeger couldn't believe it was already seven-thirty. The bad taste in his mouth reminded him of the two fast drinks earlier.

Someone was coming to investigate the Egg Roll-Munson mess. He cursed the whole situation with a sluggish lack of verve duplicated by the elevator's upward crawl.

In his room he jerked his desk chair free and dropped into it. His eyes closed, and his head dropped forward. Moments later he appeared to be in a deep sleep. His mind sought the areas of muscular tension and probed at them, easing combating muscles. Two minutes. Five minutes, the seconds ticked by, then slowed to leaden beats. Finally the brain heard each measure of time in Doppler effect, an impatient rising note that peaked and then descended as it left. The sounds bathed him in a continuum. The mind, no longer encumbered by antagonisms in the body, knifed from subject to subject, associating, comparing, evaluating. When it was satisfied its past performance was acceptable, it cast forward, pressing against the shielding curtain of the future, then drew back to deal with present. A warning went to Draeger's operative thinking: there is nothing but new country ahead and there is no way back.

It was a message he didn't like, and the relaxed muscles shifted imperceptibly, anticipating. He opened his eyes and headed for the shower. He felt refreshed, ready, drawn a bit tighter than he'd prefer, but prepared.

At exactly twenty-eight minutes after eight he hipped himself onto a barstool of the Boulevardier Room and within another minute had his first sip of foaming San Miguel. It would be a long time before he took another. There was no way of knowing when the contact would decide it was safe to make a move. One of the faces around him was watching. The muscular man down the bar—did he always metronome his way through the complementary peanuts or was he being too casual? And the older man, alone at a table—was it an accident he was able to see the entrance without appearing to observe? And why was he so distracted? Was he waiting for someone special, or merely hopeful?

Draeger watched the two bartenders. It wouldn't be unheard of for one of them to be the lookout, the man who insured the area was surveillance-free before a meeting would be attempted. Whoever was coming would be tough, a pro from the top. The choice of a bar stool was Draeger's concession to the other man's task. When he decided to introduce himself he could sit down with no preamble. Trying that at a table would be at least awkward and possibly disastrous. Mistaken identity was a constant horror, and Draeger quickly hoisted the beer to chase away the welling stories of colossal gaffes.

Nine-thirty came and went, the minutes claiming most of the customers who'd been present when Draeger entered. Two men sat beside him during the hour. The first drank with a morose determination that promised forgetful drunkenness and a rueful hangover. He left as Draeger ordered his second beer. The next man was more talkative, an oil field worker from Oklahoma. He had pictures of his wife and children and was anxious to go home.

At ten-fifteen Draeger scanned the back of the room as much to avoid the increasingly disapproving scowl of the bartender as anything else. When he faced forward again there was a face staring at him from the mirror behind the bar.

Kolar said, "It's been a long time, Glen." The rough features were split by a friendly smile that forced the flesh into heavy folds that almost hid the dark eyes. He wore a quietly elegant *barong tagalog* and dark trousers. Topped by the immaculate helmet of silver-gray hair, he looked every inch the substantial executive.

"Yes," Draeger said. "Years, in fact. You look just the same, though."

"Kind of you to say so. You've been nursing that beer for quite a while. Would you care for another?"

Draeger shook his head. "I think I'll have a drink." The bartender hurried over with surprised pleasure and positively beamed at the order to pour two doubles of Chivas Regal. When they came, Draeger raised his. "To seeing old friends again."

Kolar smiled bleakly, tasted the whisky. "I consider this situation potentially catastrophic. Do you have any idea what's happened to our mutual friend?"

Draeger shook his head. "His wife and the driver. Nothing more."

Heavy lids shuttered and when they opened, it was like seeing quenched steel steam to the surface. "I need all the facts. I need more. I need your thinking."

Draeger felt his face warm. "There's a chance he went into shock."

"I don't want to talk here. We'll go outside and walk through that shopping mall across the street."

Kolar set the pace, an easy stroll, two men getting some easy exercise. "There's a connection between this panic with our asset in China and Munson's disappearance. Do you have any ideas about that?"

Still stinging, Draeger said, "There can't be. My operation was airtight. Whatever's scared Egg Roll originated on the scene. He's screwed up somehow and he's running."

Kolar's step checked, then continued smoothly. "You say he's running? You know that?"

"No. I know he means to. I don't think he's actually started."

"What would you do in his place?"

"Steal a plane." The answer was instant. Draeger had given it much thought. "His original escape plan was a serial thing—you've read it, I'm sure. Papers, rendezvous, recognition signals. All very precise and time-consuming. If he's ditching all that, he'll be moving in a hurry, likely. I think hijacking a plane's the safest, fastest thing he can do."

"I prefer the word exfiltrate. Exfiltration plan, not escape plan."

Draeger stopped, and Kolar faced him, expressionless. Draeger said, "Look, are we going to try to salvage something from this mess, or are we going to fuck around correcting each other's professional jargon? Jesus Christ!"

Kolar resumed walking, entering the sprawling mall through one of its multiple doors. This one was adjacent to a bookstore, and Draeger distractedly glanced that way and shied from a window display of massed espionage novels.

Picking up the conversation again, Kolar said, "My first priority must be to determine the reason for Munson's disappearance. Did you know someone tried to open his safe?"

"No one tried to open it. I worked the dial to set off the charges inside." He started. "How'd you know that?"

"Part of the warning system. The radio sent a signal when the grenades were armed. Why did you set them off?"

"When I got the shut-down message, I decided all of his papers ought to be destroyed."

Kolar looked away, admiring an antique shop's offering. A porcelain vase, its graceful column a mass of entwined flowers, caught the muted light of the mall's tunnellike passage. Draeger used the opportunity to get a better impression of Kolar and decided it was fitting that the hard features soften at the sight of the vase. For all the purpose in the thrusting chin and the questing eyes, there was a hinted complexity of character. Even when those eyes drilled at a person, there was intelligence in them, an attempt to understand, as well as to know. Draeger was pleased. Knowledge of another man's thoughts is a weapon to be used against him, but with understanding one can work for cooperation, even alliance. Kolar would create allies.

Draeger wondered if anyone ever made an ally of Kolar.

Wordlessly, they continued their walk. After they passed a few more shops, Kolar said, "For the present I think it's best you maintain the lowest profile possible. Continue your cover occupation. I'll go to Cebu with my assistant. That cosmetics business of Munson's was actually funded by us through a dummy corporation. I'm officially here as Roger's uncle as well as an officer of that corporation, and the pragmatic truth is, we can't afford to let that much money simply melt away.''

When Draeger allowed his surprise to show, the older man continued, ''I've reread all the pertinent reports, naturally. I know how much Munson respected your work. And you.''

He paused for an answer, and when Draeger merely nodded he patted the younger man's shoulder. The self-consciousness of the gesture said more about the man than the act. Kolar cleared his throat and said, ''You may be right that his disappearance is unconnected to the trouble in your operation. Nevertheless, we must find him. It's the only way we can be sure we know what he knows, if you'll pardon a tortured expression. As it is, I've decided we have to use your established friendship with him. I dislike that. It violates all security procedures, but I see no other alternative. If nothing breaks soon, we must assume he's one of three things—deceased, defected, or detained. The simple fact is if we don't find Roger and ameliorate the damage inherent in your asset's flight, we're all up the creek without a paddle.''

Draeger's head snapped around at the unexpected phrasing, and Kolar was waiting for him, wearing an expression he hadn't shown before. He was grinning. Draeger caught himself grinning back, felt an excitement that half-frightened him in its uniqueness. He thought of himself as a cerebral man, intellectually rather than physically oriented, yet there was challenge in the face before him, and he was welcoming it. He was being included in a fight, one Kolar welcomed gladly.

A war-horse, Draeger told himself, a god-damn alley-fighter. Look at him. My old man would've said he's grinning like a mule eating briars. I ought to be scared to death the old bastard'll get us dumped in the slammer, and here I stand, anxious to get it on. I must be crazy.

''You're not a violent man, by nature, are you, Glen?'' Kolar continued to grin.

Draeger said, ''Not particularly. I had my fights as a kid and so on, but I'm no brawler.''

''This may be a time of testing for you, then. I anticipate trouble. You might as well know it right now, I love it. The challenge is as much mental as physical, but I lust after the sense of being in conflict. It's hardly food and drink to me, but it most certainly is salt and spices.''

They walked further, Kolar leading back to the hotel. He said, ''This is probably my last year in this business. I want to find Roger Munson alive and well, I want to get your Chinese asset out free and clear, I want to clean up the people responsible for the death of your courier. I'll put complete faith in no one until I have all the questions answered to my satisfaction. I feel our collection effort is becoming the nation's best defense, and it is at jeopardy. I intend to make a terrible, terrible fight of this, and I intend to win.'' They were out of the building now, caught in crosscurrents of neon that slashed colors across his face. A frown turned accumulated wrinkles into canyons and crags, a desert landscape unashamed of its forbidding appearance.

''We'll handle it.'' The response sounded very strange in his ears, but Draeger went on. ''Your life's work's been longer than mine, but it's no more important to you than mine to me. Roger Munson was my friend since I got here. That's especially important.''

''Good. I was sure you'd help, of course, and I'm particularly pleased to find you enthusiastic. Now I suggest we separate, me for my hotel and you for home. Call on me for breakfast in the morning, around seven-thirty, I think. I'm using my own name. And we can be open about things from now on. We're established as being acquainted.''

Instead of leaving immediately, Draeger watched Kolar make his way across the intersection. The late crowd from the movie was making its move homeward, as well, and the bulky figure drifted with it, the head glacial above the darker-haired mass. When he turned up the steps leading to the front of the hotel and disappeared into the tunnellike elbow, Draeger unconsciously leaned out from the wall, holding that pose until Kolar was walking across the front of the building. Only when he was in the lobby did Draeger head off in his own direction, feeling foolish and stubbornly satisfied.

It was a short distance to his apartment building, not much beyond the massive parking lot that serviced the shopping center. There was still enough traffic to make crossing Ayala Avenue a major event, but he successfully avoided everything once more and laughed to himself from the safety of the sidewalk, remembering Kolar's observation that he wasn't a violent man. Anyone who lived with Manila's traffic might not be violent, but you could well depend on him as a survivor.

He shut out the sound of the vehicles as best he could on the last leg of his stroll homeward, enjoying the feel of the night breeze. A small bat wrapped itself into impossible maneuvers around a light fixture mounted on the side of an apartment building. The glare would discourage all but the most determined thieves, which, in Manila, meant very few. In the meantime, the bat harvested an unexpected bounty.

The guard nodded and smiled at Draeger, leaning against the back wall of the lobby, his shotgun cradled in his arms. The standard armament had been an unobtrusive pistol until a year before, when thieves had burst in and overwhelmed the guard before he could unholster the thing. When the episode was over, the tenants and the guard were unanimous in their agreement that protection should be stepped up, and the shotgun was present every night now. The guard still wore a scar on his temple where he'd been pistol-whipped with his own weapon, and a hopeful smile that invariably faded when he recognized late arrivals as nonrobbers.

Draeger stepped into his apartment and flipped the light switch. Nothing happened. He looked at it in the dim glow from the hall. Because he bent forward to see it clearly, the first blow from the intruder was a glancing one. Nevertheless, it was enough to drive his head into the wall with a demoralizing crack.

The clarity and variety of thoughts lancing through his mind astonished him. It was as if the surprise of the attack freed part of his rational mechanism, and it was uninvolved except to register data and evaluate it. Struggling to regain his balance, he wondered if a neighbor had heard the sound of his head bouncing off the wall and would come to investigate. He pushed off with both hands, keeping his head down, pivoting, trying to land a good body blow. The swing, slowed by his dazed condition, only served to pull him off balance. The punch he received was handled more expertly, landing just behind and below the ear.

There was no pain connected with it, nor did it add to his stunned condition. On the contrary, he continued to marvel at the incredible efficiency of his mind and the heretofore neglect of fear. It came now, eating his strength. As he fell, the mind urged him to get his arms under himself and to land rolling in order to lessen the shock. The body failed, and he pitched forward on his face with his hands at his sides and his knees on the carpet. His mind acknowledged a right to be terrified then, but perversely insisted he know how ludicrous he must look with his ass sticking up in the air like the hump on a camel. A foot drove into his stomach. Suddenly the brain had nothing to report, and there was only agony searing outward from a locus that hurt so much he felt he should be able to grab it. It was enough to give impetus to his arms, and they flopped in spasms, trying to lift him. The foot drove into his stomach again, and the new pain reinforced the old. The brain warned that when the flood of pain reached his head, he was going to pass out.

A voice full of disgust said, "Fuck!" It was his own. The pain reached his head, and he toppled sideways against the wall.

The brain did him one last favor. It made him open one eye as consciousness drained away. The kitchen door was open. The light from the hall showed the panel hiding the one-time pad was undisturbed. Burning darkness draped itself around him.

# ■ CHAPTER 13 ■

The small waves slapped at the sand, silver cat's-paws rising from the turquoise shallows. At the limit of their strength they paused before tumbling back to the sea, tripping the next wave in their hasty retreat.

Pierce hunched over the small table in the shade of the bushy tree, staring across the beach to the distant swimming figure. He had no eyes for playful waves or golden beaches. His thoughts were of the madness in the sea. Too often it stroked the land one day and on the next slashed it to shreds with breakers and rain-torrents that clawed like steel. He'd seen it and respected it. It always gave warning. Not much, perhaps, but if one paid attention, the sea spoke of its passions in furtive whispers and winks. Pierce prided himself on his ability to read those messages.

A frown pulled his squint tighter as he thought how much more difficult it was to read the signals men sent. The sea spoke no man's words but communicated with all men. Men's words and actions were no more indicative of anything than the twittering of the coursing swallows in the palms behind him.

The swimming figure turned, stroked in the other direction, still paralleling the beach. Pierce almost wished a dorsal fin would break the surface near him.

How long had it been? Ten days? It seemed a great deal more. At least now Munson was relatively rational. It was a wonder he hadn't formed an addiction to the tranquilizers, but he was working his way out from under the dosage, sliding back into the real world. His jabber of revenge and all that was less rabid, at least.

Pierce tilted his head forward and let the sweat drip off the tip of his nose. The three drops made tiny plops, forming a cloverleaf pattern. He stirred it around to a lopsided circle, wondering if it might not be wiser to simply eliminate Munson. There was the problem of Boy Angel. That could be dealt off to Bilongon. It would be stretching a point to say Boy Angel was a Christian, but Bilongon wouldn't be too fussy.

Patience, he counseled himself. There was no need to consider anything that drastic, not at this point. Everything was at a standstill after the shut-down message, and there was no need to get excited. If Bilongon's terrorists scheduled their operation during the shut-down period, so much the better. Running a net and cooperating with Bilongon would have been a ballbreaker. Now things were looking up. It wasn't necessary for Munson to talk about why he wanted to disappear. All in good time.

Munson headed in. Pierce told himself he shouldn't allow himself to hope that this was the day Munson would start talking about his plans. For the past week Munson swam like this in the morning, and every morning he walked out of the water, dried himself without a word, then turned to Pierce and said, "A sound mind in a strong body." Pierce had learned to despise the whole thing.

The idea of turning Munson in plucked at that feeling, and a small voice laughed. It was quite impossible.

Munson had some plans, something cooking in his mind. There'd been hints. Not as clean and honest as what the sea sent. Obtuse suggestions, significant silences.

He walked out of the water, squinting against the rising sun. Pierce thought, God, how he's aged. I'd swear he's grayer, but that's imagination. There's no imagining the way he walks or the way he looks at people, though. There's an engine in him, and it's burning pure hate, like we all should have died with his wife. For a couple of days I really thought he was going to let go, but he's sure as hell over that. Now we get hints about "reasons to live" and "reasons to die." But nothing *concrete*.

Munson walked up to the table and began toweling. Pierce waited, afraid to put any credence in the increasing sensation that Munson looked different, had a new air about him. He told himself it was a false alarm. Again.

"A sound mind in a strong body." He draped the towel across his shoulders, and Pierce swallowed a curse.

They walked toward the hotel, angling through the palm grove that buffered the building from the direct glare of the sand and water. The gray tree trunks threw sharply angled black shadows that slanted across the other trunks and each other, creating a monochrome grid against the soft off-white of the walls. To the side of that view, on the right of the building, was the plastic blue of the pool, garish in contrast to the honest vitality of the sea. Further to the right grew a prim hedge of bougainvillea screening the pool and its outside dining area from the approach road. Purple-red blossoms and heavy green leaves vibrated in alternating sun and shade compressed to the precise geometry and repressed energy of a cell block wanting to blow up. A waiter in the doorway from the interior dining room saw the two men coming from the beach and swiftly retreated for the kitchen. By the time they arrived at the outside tables, he beckoned, already placing fruit juice and sliced papaya.

Munson took his seat and smiled at the hovering waiter. "What if I wanted mango instead of papaya?"

The waiter blinked, unperturbed. "Every day you eat papaya. You change your mind, I understand." He reached for the plate. "I change now."

"No, no." Munson laughed easily. "I just wanted to make sure I didn't *have* to eat it."

Pierce said, "Not here. Not if you don't want to."

A peculiar expression shifted Munson's features, too quick to be caught. Pierce's curiosity was poorly hidden, and Munson addressed it. "I appreciate that. Friends, loyalties—I've come to understand a great deal about those things."

"There's no need to talk about it."

Munson stared at him with the predatory glare he'd developed since deciding to live. Pierce turned off his mind to meet it. He fixed his own gaze on a point halfway through Munson's skull. After a moment, the thin face moved, and Pierce focused his eyes. Munson was ordering his meal, and Pierce simply nodded, the waiter leaving to bring him his usual.

Munson spoke again. "I will never stop thinking about the past. It gives meaning to my present, and I intend to influence the future because of it."

"Well, sure, Roger, but I meant you shouldn't brood."

"I know exactly what you meant, but you have no idea what *I* mean, and you must. You're part of it, if you want to be."

"Part of what? Your future? Sure, I'd like to work with you again. First, we've got to get serious about what's happened, and why you haven't contacted any of our people."

Munson chuckled, continuing to smile in silence until the waiter dealt eggs and bacon and cleared off the other dishes. Then he said, "Tony, you fascinate me, you really do. The minute you decided to keep me hidden here, you threw in every card you had but one, and I'm it. You're a born conspirator. You can't even articulate a concept of truth, much less live up to it." At Pierce's open mouth, Munson gestured sharply, thin fingers flicking. "Don't try one of your mind-fucks on me. You know damned well I've gone over the fence. You knew it when I got here, and it was locked when you heard my wife died in my factory. You think I killed her."

Again, Pierce tried to protest and Munson stopped him with the same irritable gesture. "Goddamit, Tony, *listen*. You've got two choices now, that's all. Either you dump me and tell the brass balls back in L.A. you were keeping me under wraps so I couldn't blow things up, or you stay with me.''

"We're going to bare our souls, are we?'' Pierce paused to chew and swallow. "Good. If you have a program I can't support, you leave and we're clear. You never came here. I got the shutdown message, and I've been sitting here, waiting for instructions."

Munson nodded slowly. "Fair enough. I intend to make us rich. If I pull this off, we'll be on every hit list in the world. Understand that.''

"What do you intend to steal?''

"A foreign policy. Several, in fact.''

"I'm listening.''

Leaning forward, Munson lowered his voice although they were alone on the patio. "One of our assets has reported a meeting going down, China and Vietnam. The Russians don't know about it.''

Pierce smiled inwardly, enjoying being in on something so big without Munson's knowledge. He said "What do we do about it? The Soviets'll pay for the info, but not that much.''

"Nothing so direct as a sale. I've had a plan working ever since I heard about the meeting. The Viets are exhausted, Tony. They can't control areas in their own country, much less Laos and Cambodia. They need peace. If the Chinese stir things up, Vietnam'll fall apart. And if the Russians find out the Viets are doing a deal with the Chinese, they'll be back in the country overnight.''

Pierce leaned back, thinking. Munson sipped his coffee and waited.

It was pleasant, Pierce decided, being in the driver's seat. No one got ahead of Munson often. It should be possible to play along with both Bilongon and Munson. The important thing would be to keep clear at all times and to see that any money that changed hands did so before the Red Army people could make a grab. Once those butchers did their thing, the only people showing a profit would be undertakers.

It was dangerous as hell. So many things could go wrong. If he was quick, though, who'd be able to prove anything? After all, he was taking his orders direct from his control officer, and if things came apart that would have to be because Munson lied. Something would have to happen to him, but he was the one talking about snuffing people. But did the stakes warrant the game?

"What makes you think there's so much money in it? If the word gets out, it'll embarrass a few people, but that won't last long."

"Because we're dealing with prestige. If these talks work out, China moves right back into the Big Daddy spot for all of Southeast Asia, and the Sovs are out on their ass."

"And you think the Chinese'll pay?"

"Goddam right. Beats a war. And if they play their cards right, they'll get the money from the U.S., anyhow." He glared. "What's so fucking funny?"

"Us. We're talking about holding up the Chinese while they stick the Russians in the back over who gets to boss the Vietnamese, and the money comes out of our taxes."

Munson glowered. "I can see the irony of it, but it doesn't make me laugh."

Pierce was understanding. "You've put in a lot of thought on this thing. And you know I'll do anything I can to make it work. We've always made a good team."

"The only thing I don't have locked down is transportation. You're in tight with this Bilongon, south of here. We'll arrange something with him."

The hair on Pierce's neck twitched. "I don't think so. He's undependable. As soon as he learns what we're up to—"

"He'll learn what I want him to learn. I want to be smuggled into Singapore and back out again, that's all. My reasons don't have to be any part of the bargain."

"You don't know Bilongon. He'll—" Pierce stopped abruptly, eyes widening. "You want *what*?"

Grinning, Munson said, "I thought that might get to you eventually. Who do you think can handle that kind of negotiation?"

"I don't like it. It's too dangerous."

Munson laughed. "Now's the time to think about that. Once this ball starts rolling there's no backing out."

Pierce rubbed his chin, stared out to sea. Munson watched him. What a difference between him and Draeger! And how much better if some hybrid of Pierce and Draeger existed! The joy of it, to have the imbecile loyalty of Draeger to rely on. Pierce would swear he was in all the way, but he'd never commit himself totally, whatever he said. Ruefully, Munson admitted it was a constant in their relationship. They lied, to the point that some of them had such a ring of integrity they could overwhelm truth.

He pondered, asking himself if there was some deep insight in that. He decided it was inane.

The original awareness of Pierce's untruthfulness hurt horribly. For years he told himself daily he'd do something about it. The searing truth was he allowed Pierce to go his way because he anticipated needing a venal man, and Pierce would be there to be used.

There was a difference, though. Pierce lied because he was looking out for himself. Munson felt his pulse quicken when he reminded himself he was working for a cause. Even if what he was doing was tainted because it involved being untruthful with one of his own, that one was deviant, had turned his back on his own kind long ago. And it was all going to work out for the best in the end. That's what counted.

Looking at Pierce, Munson wanted to damn himself. When you really looked at the man you saw the things that should have marked him. The eyes themselves were stable enough, but the man blinked as though he were staring into a hail storm. And his hands were never still. Odd fingers, thick as stumps at the base, tapering to slender tips, so that each one had a pyramidal look. The four fingers on the left hand stroked a cheekbone now, the chin resting on the ball of a heavy thumb. There was something vulgarly sensual in the slow movement. It was an erratic progress, the fingers stopping as though that point was too pleasant to merely slide over. The fingers reminded Munson of a cat's twisting and posturing, presenting first the top of its head and then the side, or an ear, demanding a certain spot be petted to satiety.

He didn't like cats.

Pierce looked at him. "I want in."

Munson said, "You have a way of contacting Bilongon? Something quick?"

"Some of his people work here. They've got fast boats."

Munson rose from the table. "Send him a message. Tell him we want to meet with him. We'll use your boat and arrange a rendezvous off some point or something before daylight tomorrow. You know how to set it up. Let me know. I'll be in my room."

Pierce got to his feet, hands wobbling through the air. "He may not want a meeting! And what about the Navy's patrols? And that Tondo thug alone here? He's too unpopular."

Turning slowly, Munson could have been discussing the weather. "Boy Angel goes to Manila for me on the morning plane. He'll be back in a couple of days. As for Bilongon, if he doesn't want a meeting, he won't show up at the rendezvous. The Navy? You know damned well the patrols don't have enough fuel and only go out on the basis of information received. If no one tells them we're pissing around out there, they'll never know, will they?" Without waiting for an answer, he continued his stiff-legged progress.

It was evening when the helicopter came, clacking through the sunset-riddled clouds to the north, then unaccountably heading out over the water. The customers and staff all gathered at watching sites, some around the pool, some at the beach, and a few peering from the balconies of their rooms. The chopper stopped, throbbing a monstrous heartbeat in the distance. It was impossible to fix on it because it was masked in the glare from the horizon. The pitch and volume of the engine increased dramatically as it roared toward the beach. The watchers at the hotel exchanged nervous glances. The noise increased. The machine loomed out of the fiery path smeared on the sea, a wavering black object thrashing the air with strokes powerful enough to blast up spray. Once over the land, the sound of the blades changed, triggering a vibration that drove into the physical consciousness of the watchers. A woman stepped back and sprawled awkwardly into the pool, screaming. The lifeguard raced in after her while her transfixed husband watched the machine. Faces disappeared from windows, and two of the help bolted. Coolly professional, Munson noted how automatically they both shed their white coats and chose a route perpendicular to the helicopter's run and remembered Pierce's comment about having Bilongon's men on his staff. The two had dodged strafing passes before.

At the last possible moment the aircraft whipped up and over the trees between the beach and the hotel and settled onto the rooftop helipad. The rocking motion as it settled and the droning decline of the engine were the flurrying feathers and crow of a rooster.

Two men hopped out of the machine, bent over until clear of the blades, then trotted down the outside stairs on the inland side of the main building. By the time they reached the poolside tables the guests and attendants were almost back to normal. There were nervous, irritated glances for the two figures in their green field uniforms. The woman who had fallen into the pool was leaving, and she held her husband's arm, quietly flaying him with invective. She found time to glare at the two Army officers. One of them, the smaller and younger of the two, caught the look and turned quickly, embarrassed.

Munson watched them come toward his table, knowing he was seeing Colonel Arroyo for the first time after hearing so much about him from Pierce. The second man was a captain, and unknown. The Colonel swept past, dropping into a seat at Pierce's table. The Captain, forgotten, pulled up a chair and sat with a discretion that practically rendered him invisible.

"What you think of that pass?" Arroyo said, a fat hand imitating the helicopter, almost knocking over the wine. "That's one heluva pilot, you know? I had to pull every damn string in the Philippines to get him. He flew in that movie they made up north, the real big one. He's great. Really crazy. I tell him to, he'll fly that damn thing anywhere."

Pierce listened with a fixed smile that could have been paint. Munson was more interested in the Captain, and was very glad he had warned Pierce against appearing too friendly with his ailing "guest." Where the Colonel was transparent bluster and heartiness, the Captain was quietly observant. The Captain would learn things and report, and the Colonel would crush whatever was indicated. The Colonel would fatuously believe the Captain was loyal to him until he exposed a vulnerable area. The Captain would destroy a man like the Colonel eventually, Munson knew, having instantly identified the seeking in the Captain's eyes. Both men were dangerous, but the Colonel was a mindless natural force—a typhoon, a flood, an earthquake. Men like him were visited on the world by a God determined to see that no one lost sight of hell. The Captain would be one of those who saw himself operating as God's weapon.

Pierce said, "It was spectacular, Colonel, but you scared the shit out of my customers."

Arroyo's laugh boomed. "Bullshit, Tony. Maybe they act pissed, but they loved it. Look at them." As his excitement died down, his accent smoothed over and the hard "t'em" became "them." He looked over his shoulder at the Captain and spoke rapidly in Tagalog. The Captain rose and leaned forward, extending a hand to Pierce. They shook as Arroyo said, "This is my new 2, my Intelligence Coordinator, Captain Cruz. He used to live on Basilan. Knows the Moros, knows their dialect."

Cruz murmured, and Arroyo waved an annoyed hand. "He knows you don't speak all the dialects. He knows what I meant."

Pierce gave the Captain his name and gestured for a ready waiter. He hurried up carrying a tall Scotch-and-water for Arroyo, who took it off the tray with arrogant assurance. The Captain ordered a beer.

Once more, Arroyo looked behind him, this time assessing Munson. The American had expected it and was deep in study of his menu. From the corner of his eye he watched Arroyo's suspicious scrutiny, knowing he would outlast that inspection easily.

He wanted to turn and meet those eyes, stare down the pompous pig, but that would be self-defeating. There were things to learn and after satisfying himself Munson either couldn't hear or wouldn't care, he would say anything that came to his mind. In fact, if he continued to pound at the Scotch the way he'd started, he'd soon be racing to spill everything he could think of. Munson sighed. Fools like that took all the sport out of the business.

The waiter brought Cruz's beer, and the Captain asked how much he owed. Munson couldn't understand everything said, but easily recognized the local Chavacano dialect with its abundant Spanish words. It was aggravating. One heard enough Spanish to almost understand, but the rest was Tagalog, and the result was harder to grasp than either language would have been by itself. The waiter looked to Pierce for an answer, and he smiled at the Captain, shaking his head.

"I will pay," the Captain said. When Arroyo glared at him Cruz took it without flinching. Arroyo shrugged and made a face for Pierce's benefit. The waiter said "Three pesos, sir," and Cruz counted them out of his wallet and turned them over to the man wordlessly. The waiter smiled thanks and left.

Arroyo pressed closer to Pierce. "We are having some trouble with a bunch of bandits up north. I told Captain Cruz you might know a couple of people up there who could help us."

Pierce blanched. "I don't think—"

Arroyo put a hand on his arm. "Hey, don't worry about a thing. Cruz is like my right hand, you know? He works for me."

Pierce's eyes darted from Arroyo's face to the Captain's flat stoicism and then to the hand on his arm. He wondered if Arroyo himself realized the significance of that artificial clamp of friendship.

The Captain was clearly aware of it. He rose from his chair to light the table candle. Munson knew it was done to give him a better view of Pierce's reactions, and he mentally applauded the Filipino's professionalism. At the same time he noticed the drops of sweat at Pierce's temple, topaz-colored with reflected candlelight.

It was Pierce's only sign of nervousness. He said, "I don't have any dealings with anyone from up that way. I know some people. None who'd be interested in being a bandit."

Cruz acknowledged the minor defiance with a nod.

When he spoke it disappointed Munson. The voice was pleasant enough, but it carried entirely too well. He mentally deducted from the Captain's earlier high score. Cruz said, "They really are bandits, Mr. Pierce. There is nothing political about them. They attack the workers and steal from them, alive or dead. They spread no propaganda. These are not communists or any other kind of political terrorist."

"Can you be sure they're not connected with the Moslem trouble to the south?"

Cruz was shaking his head, and Pierce dropped the theory. Cruz said, "It isn't political. To be honest with you, if I thought it was, I wouldn't discuss it with a foreigner."

Arroyo looked shocked. "Tony? Good God, Cruz, Tony's helped us more times than I can remember!"

Cruz winced at the rising voice, and Arroyo lowered it to a comic whisper. "He deals with Bilongon for us! I told you that!"

Munson dropped his eyes to his table immediately and was gratified to see Cruz's swift check in his direction. When the Captain spoke again strain showed in his words. "I know Mr. Pierce is a trusted friend. Perhaps I am too sensitive about our country's problems. Some of them are very—" He floundered, unable to find a word he wanted.

"Frustrating," Pierce supplied, and Cruz made a smile with no amusement in it.

Arroyo looked at his watch. "Hey, it's late. Come on, Captain. Flying with that crazy man's no fun when he gets impatient." Cruz shook hands and said good-bye. Arroyo waved him along, shifting from foot to foot until the younger man was out of earshot. He spoke quickly to Pierce. "I need to get a message to Bilongon." Pierce nodded, smiling as if at a private joke, and Arroyo rushed along. "We've been told he killed the man who disappeared on Basilan a while ago. They found his body, you know. Tortured. I've got to put out some kind of investigation, but I've got a buyer for some logs, so we'll have to put something together."

Pierce said, "I'll leave as soon as I can. Are there any patrols I ought to look out for?"

Arroyo frowned. "I don't have a schedule."

"That's OK. I'll just have to be careful. But if I'm picked up, you've got to front for me."

The Colonel pinched his lips between thumb and forefinger. A diamond ring batted candlelight into the dark. "If you get caught, don't tell anyone anything. Tell them I said it was OK. I'll think of something if we need it."

With that flimsy assurance, he hurried off to his helicopter. He ran with a peculiar rolling motion, Munson noticed. It wasn't clumsy. There was something of the bear in it, a visible strength that needed no grace to impress. The Captain waited for him and trotted effortlessly after. For an instant Munson thought he'd caught the Captain staring at him, but when the smaller man never looked back he put it down to professional worrying. The helicopter engine worked itself up to a hysterical scream a few moments later and, lights flashing, thrashed off into the night. When the sound had died, Pierce showed Munson a surreptitious roll of the eyes before leaving.

Munson decided to skip dinner, consciously assuring himself it was a precaution against the upcoming boat trip and not nerves brought on by the addition of Cruz to the equation. The impression left by the Captain hovered in his thoughts as he walked to his room, nevertheless. Cruz was the sort of opponent to be feared. There would be no politics in his makeup, other than a monolithic love of his country. His loyalty would brook anything but betrayal by his leaders, and his vengeance in that case would be uncompromising.

For the first time since Leonila's death, Munson felt his body respond with genuine anticipation. The prospect of dealing with the Captain was exciting. That was wrong, a foolish thing. There were enough problems without intelligent opposition. But the excitement was there, the desire—no, the need—to measure skills against someone of value. The Colonel might catch a man from time to time, but it would usually be an accident. Cruz would hunt.

Thinking about Cruz, Munson unexpectedly drifted back to Draeger. A wave of hate rolled up from his bowels, and he was glad he'd not eaten because he knew he'd have lost it then.

Accident.

Draeger would learn about accidents. By God, he would! Leonila was dead because of him. He'd been an unfortunate part of the plan before, and it had caused genuine sorrow to think about risking him, possibly even sacrificing him. But Leonila's death was purposeless, a *mistake*. Munson mixed a gin and tonic at the small bar. He smiled to himself, a bitter thing that carried as much pain as amusement. The carbonation sizzled, continuous explosions flinging pungency into the air. He watched the pinpoints and told himself that was what the search for him must be like, a million fits and starts ending in collapse. He sipped the drink, enjoying the taste and image.

He wondered who'd come out from Los Angeles to coordinate the search. Someone pretty good, for sure. Excitement clutched at his throat, then faded. Whoever it was didn't have a chance. He'd only be able to call on Draeger locally. That wouldn't last long.

He turned out the lights in the room and stepped out onto the dark balcony. Music and laughter from the pool area grated on his mood, and he shut them out. There was an off-shore breeze, heavy-laden by hot sand, the sea, the sweet redolence of coconut oil and lotions.

*Leonila*.

A litany of rage and loss poured out of him, wedging past

clenched teeth. There were no distinguishable words, had there been anyone to listen. The sound alone fouled the night.

The turning of the key in the lock woke him. He moved with speed and surety that belied the lanky body, ending up on the floor against a side wall away from the opening door. The automatic in his hands was rock-steady, braced by both elbows planted on the carpet.

Even in the subdued light from the hall, Pierce's reaction to looking down the pistol barrel was clear. His hands rose and he said, "It's me!" in an urgent whisper. Munson was already getting to his feet. He wore a long-sleeved khaki shirt, battered jeans, and old shoes. Without speaking, he picked up the cloth overnight bag by the side of his bed and followed Pierce. The younger man looked back once to see Munson no longer carried the pistol in his hand. A relieved smile got no response and drifted away in the face of Munson's unapproving scowl. Pierce wished he'd worn older clothes, especially something other than the white jogging shoes.

They made their way cautiously to the hotel's man-made harbor and dock facility. By the time they reached it, Munson was aware that at least two of the hotel staff of roving armed guards had seen them, and there was another on the dock itself, off in the shadows. He grabbed Pierce's arm and demanded an explanation.

"They're Bilongon's people," he said, pulling free. "They're his insurance for my behavior." His smile in the darkness was a nervous flicker of white against the tanned skin.

"I don't like so many people in on this," Munson complained.

"There isn't much we can do. He makes a lot of the rules around here."

Munson said nothing, moving for the white bulk of the cruiser. Pierce checked him with a touch, then led the way to the end of the dock. Munson stopped beside him, goggling at the narrow length of the prau in disbelief. "What the fuck is this?"

"Bilongon again." Pierce sounded almost smug. "He won't have anything to do with our boat. Says it attracts too much attention, and he's right. We'll ride this."

"We don't have time!"

"If we take the cruiser we can hit between eighteen and twenty knots and cruise around twelve. This'll click off better than forty. We'll cruise at about half that.''

Munson swallowed noisily. "Forty?"

"There are faster ones. This'll do for us." Pierce lowered himself into the boat, and Munson winced at the way the bladelike hull skittered. He handed down his bag and stepped in, grabbing for the freeboard. The outrigger bindings squealed laughter at his wobbling progress to his seat. As soon as they squatted down, the boatman started the engine and Munson wondered if anyone within twenty miles could sleep soundly enough to escape that unmuffled bellow. When Pierce leaned toward him and cupped hands over his ear, he was mildly surprised a human voice could carry over such a racket.

"Don't worry," Pierce yelled, "boats come and go all the time. No one'll pay any attention. Here, put this on." He produced a battered straw hat and cupped the ear again. "The sun'll be up in a little while, and it's best you look your part."

Within minutes they were offshore, the hotel island an indistinct smudge against the larger darkness of Mindanao. The engine drummed as the boatman increased speed. The sea was reasonably calm, but each wave jarred the narrow hull and it twisted alarmingly, the wood actually flexing with the stress. Reason told Munson it was best that the hull not be so rigid it tore itself apart, but no logic could stand up to the sight of the bow working up, down, sideways, and sometimes in combination. He took his eyes off it long enough to focus on Pierce, and the sight of the tense back and stark white knuckles on the gunwhale made him feel better. He faced the boatman and gave him a broad smile and a thumbs-up. The Filipino grinned back. He nodded happily and with his free hand patted the engine and pointed east. In further pantomime he indicated a rising sun, then patted the engine again and rotated a finger faster and faster.

Munson turned forward, the smile suddenly painful.

The captain was as good as his word. His speed increased in direct ratio to the breaking of dawn. When the full, red sun broke the horizon Munson estimated he was little short of wide open. The noise was deafening, the spray like pellets, and the battering ride was straining muscles the years had wrapped in flab and forgotten. He knew tomorrow and the next day would be miserable.

The last word fell among his thoughts like a burr, twisting everything around itself. Bilongon wasn't above torture. That was a terrifying thought. Not that such a thing could happen, but that he was putting himself in a position where it could happen to him. He would have to be very much at his best. Bilongon must be extremely clever to have survived, he warned himself, thinking it was a psych, but necessary.

The trip settled to a steady repetition of lurches and leaps with no discernible pattern. Munson held on, simply waiting for it to end.

When it did, it came with an abruptness that caught him completely off-guard. They were headed directly for an island. He attached no significance to that fact because it had already happened on two other occasions. This time, though, one instant everything was as it had been all morning and the next there was the most incredible silence he could imagine. The prau settled into the water with the drawn-out exhalation of an exhausted beast. Waves lapped at the sides and outriggers and, as Munson's hearing adjusted, those gentle touches came to him as applause for self-control. When he turned to the boatman, the dark brown face greeted him with a grin of sheer joy and a gleeful shake of the head. He pointed at the island ahead, stroking with his paddle. Munson faced forward again, and Pierce was looking back at him.

"I was here once before. We'll push right through that clump of brush there, those branches, and there's a stream on the other side. Bilongon's got a war camp upstream."

"Your friend with the chopper would like to know that."

Pierce grimaced. "Hope he never finds out. I'm the only white who's ever been here. You'll be the second. Who do you think'll be the suspects if it's ever hit?"

"I know what's good for me. I don't even see the island."

Pierce had time to laugh and say, "Good thinking," and they were struggling into the canoe that would take them in. The prau went on ahead this time, to be hauled under the overhanging cover.

In minutes the canoe was forging through the greenery. The branches slashed at Munson, crushed their leaves on his flesh, his clothes. He flung up his arms and dodged.

*The door had bamboo carved on it, a bowing clump of perhaps a dozen stalks that swept from floor level up the left side and across the top. Small branches draped downward, the leaves shining in*

*relief against darker wood, cameo-like. A foot rose in front of it, an*
*ugly, dirty green-and-black boot. The movement was slow, too slow.*
*Was it stealth or shame that checked it? It shattered the door,*
*exploded it inward. The ornate lock plate spun away onto the tiled*
*floor, clanging shrilly. The man in the doorway, standing on frag-*
*ments of beautiful bas-relief bamboo, heard it with a fraction of his*
*mind and thought of a small animal shrieking metallically in terror.*
*The other man in the room shrieked, too. He dropped the mouth-*
*piece of the bubble pipe and screamed at the eyes looking at him.*

*The man in the doorway raised a submachinegun and fired. The*
*weapon was old, and the ammunition was .45 caliber, huge, slug-*
*gish lumps. The screaming man was hit at least once in every burst*
*of two-or-three rounds. There were ten such bursts, and the man*
*absorbed the first three before the pounding energy pitched him*
*somewhere where he could finally fall on his face. The remaining*
*rounds went into his back and shoulders. He bounced in a parody of*
*lovemaking. A third man, dressed in the same mottled loose-fitting*
*clothes and green-and-black boots came in and pulled his partner*
*away. He said, "C'mon, Munson, for Christ's sake! You've killed*
*the fucker as dead as he'll ever get!" The killer was disappointed.*
*He wanted to see the fear in the other man's eyes again.*

*And again.*

"You all right?"

Munson snapped out of his semi-trance, half out of the canoe
already. "I'm fine, fine." He tried to keep the embarrassed anger
out of his voice. What in God's name could've happened to him, to
let his mind drift off like that? Criminally stupid. It left him with no
recollection of the trip upstream. He looked back and took some
solace in the realization he'd never find his way through that mess in
any case. It was as classic a jungle as he'd ever seen, a green war.
For an instant, like a picture flashed on and off, he saw the sweaty
face of the drug peddler again. It was an unsatisfactory view, with
the eyes merely white pools, empty, and when it was gone, there
wasn't even a memory.

"This Abdul," Pierce was saying. There was a tightness around
his eyes. "I told you about Abdul. He's the big movie fan."

Abdul grinned, and Munson was shocked at how young it made
him look. He studied the boatman and the spectators. They all

looked like children. Lethal children, standing around in ragged clothes, holding automatic weapons so clean their oiled surfaces looked soft to the touch. He faced Abdul and pushed the others from his mind. "You like movies, do you?"

"Oh, yes. They are much help in learning English." He led off, talking over his shoulder. "A man has to be careful, because they are full of bad women and impure thoughts. If a man can—can—" He made a fist, trying to squeeze out the right word.

"If a man can resist?" Munson suggested.

"That's it! If a man can resist the temptations, he can learn the very best English, just the way the Americans talk."

"That's important?"

"Oh, very important. We must have good relations with America. We will need aid and credit from the World Bank and assistance from the U.N. There are many benefits."

"When do you think you'll need this help?"

"Soon. The progressive states and the true Islamic governments are helping us in our struggle for freedom, and we have world opinion on our side."

"Why don't they give you the aid you'll need?" The sweat was pouring out of him now, and Munson was remembering the first time his mother read *Alice in Wonderland* aloud to him and how it scared the living hell out of him, with all its crap about crazy people and crazy arguments and logic that acknowledged no difference between reason and fancy. He hadn't understood what frightened him then, and he wasn't afraid now, but the dissonances of Wonderland clattered in his ears.

"They are supporting us now," Abdul said. "After we have destroyed the armies of the oppressors, it will be America's responsibility to keep us free."

"You don't even like America."

"Of course not. They are exploiters. They will only be giving back what they have taken from us."

"And if America can't, if she runs out of money, or collapses?"

"Then it will be poor like us and can become a socialist state, and we can be brothers, even if they are Christians."

Munson swabbed at his neck, unable to find a way to continue the discussion. His head felt as if the prau engine was running behind him again. When Abdul gestured them up the steps to the central building he saw it as a pardon and hurried, discounting the new rush of perspiration.

Bilongon waited for them at his table. He rose as the Americans entered, offering them chairs with a manner Munson could only think of as regal. The concept of nobility was ludicrous if you only saw the outer man. His trousers were cheap brown cotton, clean, but so often laundered the knees and cuffs gleamed lighter. The shirt was the blue workshirt favored by the U.S. Navy. His sandals were tattered, worn.

It was the face that intrigued Munson. It was more than proud, less than arrogant, complex in other ways. The uttermost characteristic was confidence. Bilongon would refuse a task his judgment dictated against. If he undertook one, it would be with total conviction of accomplishment. He would never defeat his enemies. He would destroy them.

Munson extended his hand. Pierce looked nervous, and Bilongon paused to consider before accepting. They shook in a single brisk pump. Bilongon clapped his hands. A boy padded out of the gloom with Coca-Cola and a plate of cakes. Munson took a drink eagerly and one of the cakes to be polite. When he'd tasted it he wished the boy had put the plate beside him. He took another drink and gave himself a few seconds to settle his mind and examine his surroundings. The long building was darker than he expected. Sunlight broke through glassless windows only to be trapped by numerous cloths hung as privacy curtains. What light that existed had the ambiguous quality of moonlight.

He faced Bilongon. "I have waited a long time to meet you."

"You are here for a reason."

"I am. I want to work with you. You wish to see a group of Japanese terrorists destroyed after their raid on a Chinese-Vietnamese conference in Singapore. So do I. I can arrange to have them captured or killed, whichever you prefer. Obviously, I can only guarantee an honest effort to capture them. If they kill themselves or put up too much resistance—" He made a face.

Bilongon looked to Pierce in a barely controlled rage. "We spoke in confidence."

Munson's controlled answer rolled over Pierce's frightened stammer.

"Pierce told me nothing. He has betrayed me, not you. I am the man he should have told. I will discuss that with him later. I know about your feeling for the Japanese because it is my business to know. I knew of the conference long ago. I knew of the Red Army contacting you within days of the fact. It is my profession to know what many important men do, and I mean no flattery when I include you. Unimportant men are my tools, tell me what I must know. I have come here because I believe you are a man of wisdom and purpose. I am gambling on that. I can only say one other thing, a question—if I know of your plan, can you be sure no one else is aware of it?"

Bilongon's face was blank, the eyes hooded by lids that appeared heavy with sleep. Pierce wanted terribly to find some sign of emotion there. Munson looked the same way. They were both so cold, he thought. So cold.

Quietly, Bilongon asked, "Can I be sure you have told no one else?"

"You can be sure I have."

Bilongon's right shoulder dipped as the hand caressed the handle of the knife on his hip. Munson continued calmly. "There is a chance you would be so angry at my news that you may be rash. I am not ready to die. If I must, I must, however. Even a Christian can accept the will of God as it comes to him." He paused, and Bilongon's head tilted a bit, interested. Munson said, "If I die without returning to my friends, the messages I have received and the identities of those who supplied them will go immediately to several parties who hold an interest in such things."

Blood suffused Bilongon's cheeks, and the whites of his eyes beaconed his anger. He whispered a single word. "Blackmail?"

"My arrangements are not a bargaining point. I must remain in good health in order to achieve your goals or mine."

" 'Remain in good health.' " Bilongon tasted the words individually, judging, and then he smiled like a man acknowledging a deal that gets him less than he'd hoped for. "You have an easy attitude toward death. Are you a fatalist?"

"No one avoids it. When it comes for me, I intend to be a very difficult customer."

The smile broadened. "I'm sure of it. I think you will probably take others with you."

They smiled at each other, and Pierce repressed a shudder. Sooner or later they'd talk about his life in the same arithmetic, dealing in subtractions and additions with facile phrases and lips that clipped up and down through lives like bright scissors.

They were not terrifying, they incorporated terror. It covered them like skin. In the half-light of the building they were at ease with each other now, had found a communications system. Lending credence to the image, the smoke from Bilongon's cigarette writhed across the table to snake around Munson's head, linking them.

Pierce gripped his thighs, squeezing rolls of flesh painfully. Life was too sweet, too rich to be surrendered, and he must think, must find a way out. A combination of pity and pain threatened to pressure tears, and he relaxed the grip on his leg. Memories of the prisoner in the bamboo cage came to him, impressions out of sequence, so that a recollection of a facial expression transformed itself into a view of the hands holding onto the bars. In an attempt to dislodge the pictures Pierce fastened his vision on Munson, concentrating on that ragged profile. The smile had faded and he'd moved, shifting his buttocks forward on the chair, leaning toward Bilongon. There was aggression in the posture. Pierce was appalled that Munson was pushing.

Bilongon seemed to recognize the fact, as well, and to Pierce's amazement, looked approving.

Munson was saying, "I'm a patriot, Bilongon. My country has become self-indulgent, weak. Something must be done to show them what their capabilities truly are. Today they believe they can only react. If I inform my superiors of this meeting in Singapore, what do you think they'll tell me to do?"

"I would instruct you to influence the meeting to my benefit. If you could not and it appeared the results of the meeting could harm my interests, I would instruct you to expose it."

"Exactly. But they'd tell me to keep them informed. That's all. I intend to use this meeting to remind the American people they can determine world events, not simply drown in them."

"And what is your plan?"

"Much the same as yours." Munson paused and Bilongon noted it, swung his head toward Pierce.

The roar in Pierce's ears almost smothered Munson's response. "It's all right if Tony hears. I think he knows he'd be dead now if I didn't believe he's one of us."

Bilongon nodded. Pierce considered smiling and didn't, the Filipino's dark, dispassionate eyes making it clear he no longer considered it germane if Pierce smiled or screamed.

Munson said, "I'll contact the person doing liaison for the Red Army in Singapore. They'll think they can buy silence for a price. I'll let them know that if the price isn't good enough, I'll alert the Chinese as well as the Soviets."

Bilongon leaned back from the table. "That is patriotic?"

Munson rose, excitement driving him to movement. He threw his arms, his upper body, into his explanation. "They'll come up with the money. That's number one. You need it and I want it. I'm not going to interfere with their raid. What the hell do I care if they kill each other off? If they pay me off, they can do anything they want, that's what I'll tell them. But —*but*—after the terrorists are here, you deliver them to a ship, only it's going to be one I've chartered. We make it look like a mistake, naturally."

"Wait!" The command cracked. "Why do you pick up these terrorists?"

"To use them. We condition them. They tell us of their organization, their links with others. That information's valuable to me. Then, when we're ready, I'll make films of them condemning the apostate government that tricked them."

"What if this liaison man says they won't pay?"

"They'll pay. If they don't, though, nothing changes. The raid comes off. This time, however, we keep the terrorists until we're paid for their release. I share the money with you, the terrorists still make their movie debut, and everything's just fine."

Insect noises intensified in the quiet following Munson's speech. A huge wasp flew across the sun shaft coming through the window behind Bilongon, its wings a filmy golden violin note that sang into the gloom and was lost. Outside in the trees something buzzed querulously. Pierce wished he could shoot it.

Bilongon said, "This arrangement would embarrass people I despise and cause great loss of face for the Japanese. What do you intend to do with the terrorists after you film them?"

"I don't think it would be wise to allow them to identify anything or anyone."

"Exactly." Bilongon fixed a scrutinizing look on Munson, letting him know his next answer would be very important. "I see no great benefit to your country in this. I confess I would expect you to side with the Chinese."

"I'll side with whoever my country backs. My purpose is to force them to back someone."

The Filipino clearly wanted to think that over. He went on, "This plan is dangerous. You know that. Your country will not be grateful, not at first. Where will you hide?"

Munson grinned at him and, not bothering to answer, drained the last of his soft drink. Bilongon laughed quietly before speaking in dialect, a blur of syllables. The boy came running with another drink. Munson sipped before answering.

"We know we can't discuss that. We also know you're wondering if you can trust me to keep your part of this thing secret. There are limits beyond which we can't trust each other. However, to establish my credibility with you, I'll tell you right now the name of the man in your organization who's supplied me with information."

Bilongon cut him off, a hand hacking at the air. "You will tell me that, regardless. You have my promise."

Munson's face twisted in a wry smile. "I'll give you the name of the liaison man in Singapore. I can give you the names of two men in Manila who'll help your cause, cooperate with you. Lastly, I offer you a third of the million dollars I'll demand from the liaison man."

"I should be offended by this offer of names. Because you deal with this scum, you assume I wish to."

Munson dropped back into the chair, pitched onto his elbows on the table, hands upraised as fists. His face, reddened by the windburn and sun of the boat ride, drew in on itself.

He pointed his hand at Bilongon, all the fingers extended, an odd gesture that made Pierce think of a cat-o-nine tails. "*You* offended? I spent my life learning about 'this scum' in order to turn them to some good use, the same as a farmer uses manure for crops. I've driven myself, sacrificed the one happiness I knew. When I offer to help you, you presume to criticize the weapons?'' He ripped the pen from his shirt pocket and scrawled across one of the papers on the table. ''There's your traitor. I've paid for my release.''

Folding the paper, Bilongon rose. Pierce forced his gaze from the impassive face and looked to see if Bilongon was touching the knife handle. He wasn't, and Pierce was so elated he gave an involuntary gasp of relief. Then he heard the sounds in the background, the agitated mumble of concerned voices and the shuffle of bare feet advancing.

Bilongon spoke sharply, continuing to match stares with Munson. At last he said, ''You are under too much strain. English is a language that gives me trouble. There are times when I use the wrong word.''

The anger slowly ebbed from Munson's taut features. ''I overreacted. Too many things have happened to me.''

''I understand. Now you can relax. You are an honored guest. We will have a special meal tonight and music of our people. Later, I will show you the camp and we will plan in more detail.'' Bilongon stepped around the desk, and Munson fell in beside him. They walked out to the porch and down the steps like old friends.

Pierce sat alone, knowing that the men who owned the voices and the pattering feet he'd heard were watching him. He turned quickly, in time to see heads jerked back behind curtains. A single foot, left in the open, was dragged slowly back behind a woven mat. A scratching noise pulled his attention the opposite way, and far down the length of the building a disk of light from a match illuminated a camouflaged poncho from behind, turning the variegate leaves into fiery blotches until it went out.

A guitar came to life, and he wondered if it was the one he heard on his last trip. The music was different, light and lively. He was glad for that.

There's no time for depression, he told himself, trying to be stern instead of desperate. The effort failed, and his next thought was a fear-raddled determination that Munson and Bilongon were both raving maniacs. He gripped the rolls of flesh at his thighs again. There was only one answer.

Escape. He had to reach a Philippine haven and turn himself in. Either Bilongon or Munson would kill him, eventually.

Munson! The treacherous sonofabitch! Had his own source in Bilongon's movement and let one of his own people risk his life in ignorance!

Pain from the thighs made him groan.

*If I'd known about him before, he'd be singing a different tune now. Look pretty fucking important tucked away in that bamboo cage, wouldn't he?*

*Oh, Jesus, maybe that's what they'll do to me!*

*Not unless they do it right away. Night. That's the time. Tonight. That fucking racket they call music. Gongs and drums and shit.*

*I never heard the prau leave. It's still there. I'll steal it.*

*Tonight. Tonight.*


■ **CHAPTER 14** ■


The scrutiny would have been amusing if it had not been so determined. Bilongon had told the two guards to make sure he didn't get away, and they were only too eager to prove their merit. The smaller one, spare as a bird, was practically licking his lips. Pierce estimated he'd been cradling his Kalashnikov in the same position for a good three hours, holding it with one finger on the trigger. By now his best elbow should be locked tight and the trigger finger completely immobilized. It would be worth the excitement to break around the corner of a building and pop back to watch the little bastard shit himself when he found out he couldn't straighten his arm. The problem was the fat, sleepy-eyed one acting as if he was having trouble staying awake. Behind droopy lids the eyes flicked constantly. He moved just enough to stay loose and comfortable. Probably a star performer on ambush, Pierce thought, and spat.

Backstabbers. All of them. And that included Munson. Most especially Mister Control Munson.

Moving slowly, trailing Fat and Skinny behind him, Pierce strolled over to the mess area for the fourth time. He could see his shadows would rather he simply stayed in one place. Or made a run for it. They shuffled along at their fifteen-pace distance that never changed.

From the mess hall Pierce could see the prau. Better yet, he could sit with his back against one particular tree and his escort invariably took position on benches at the tables. They could see him perfectly, but had no idea he was memorizing the appearance of the creek in the area of the prau. When he made his move, he knew he would have but one chance. Crashing around in the brush would be suicide, and an unarmed sprint down the trail would be the same thing, only quieter. Bilongon would have guards at all routes leading to his camp. With a prisoner loose in the area, they'd all be as hopeful as Fat and Skinny.

It was no pleasure thinking of himself as a trophy. The irony of the thing was dizzying. All his life he'd disliked guns and felt only contempt for people who shot animals and made them into tacky objects around the house. Now he was one of the animals. Anyone who shot him would be a hero.

God-*damn* Munson!

Unthinking, he'd driven a fist into the ground, and the inhalation behind him snapped his head around. Skinny was leaning forward, on point with the frantic joy of a terrier expecting a rat. Fat was a little more erect than normal.

Pierce turned back to his study of the terrain.

The trick would be to head upstream, away from the intended escape route. For that to work, they'd have to think he was coming apart, not thinking clearly. Only a panic-stricken fool would try to run and hide from Bilongon's pack, especially on their own ground. He would have to convince them he meant to do just that. Once they were after him, he'd have to make it to the stream and drift down to the prau.

He got to his feet and wandered, apparently aimlessly, until he was within easy view of the camp theatre and one of the interminable classes. Taking a deep breath, he rounded on Fat and Skinny.

"Get away from me!" he shouted, waving his arms. "Stop following me, you little bastards! Leave me alone!"

The bored authority of the instructor stopped in mid-phrase. Heads popped out of the closest longhouse. The class pivoted as one man, took in the red-faced American and his two startled escorts and exploded in laughter. Pierce had planned on that reaction and didn't bother to turn toward it. The only uncertainty in his plan was the reaction of Fat and Skinny, and that could be very dangerous. For a sickening instant he was afraid it had gone past dangerous to deadly. Skinny's tight smile drew thinner until it was a grotesque of no certain meaning, and his eyes blinked at an incredible rate. The arm cradling the gun jerked violently. Pierce was certain the man would fire it if he regained his muscular control before his composure.

Fat reached over and put a hand on the barrel of the weapon. He said something to Skinny and repeated it sharply a second time. The thinner youth nodded, and the discordant non-smile eased.

Air flooded into starved lungs, and Pierce savored it while relief flowed through his body. It would be safe to continue baiting the guards. The surprised embarrassment had come and gone, and as long as he made a fool of himself without embarrassing them further, they would not only tolerate his action, but enjoy it along with the rest of the men. Testing that belief, Pierce shouted some more and waved his arms again. The laughter from the class was general, but more constrained. Fat and Skinny looked at them with a certain pride, as if they were entrusted with the care of a particularly amusing circus attraction. Feigning continuing anger, Pierce turned and walked some more, scowling over his shoulder frequently. Fat and Skinny loved it. They called to friends to watch the fun.

The early dusk of the deep forest was settling before Pierce was satisfied. There was a path to a latrine leading away from the dining area/amphitheatre complex. If he followed it, he could strike out to the right and intersect the creek somewhere inland. From the latrine, looking toward the creek, there were three huge trees in a line. There was only a distance of perhaps twenty yards separating the flaring, buttressed trunk of one from the next. If the creek made no extreme course change, the last tree should be within fifty to seventy-five yards of the bank. He would at least have landmarks for the first part of his trip, maybe for half of it if he was lucky.

He tried to imagine crawling through seventy-five yards of jungle in the dark. Sweat cascaded down his face, soaked his clothes. But what alternative was there? Better to die running, trying to *do* something, than to be shoved into a cage and tormented to death. If Munson was willing to do anything, it'd probably be a half-hearted recommendation for a quick end.

*The sadistic sonofabitch! All those years!*

The theatre was abandoned now, and Pierce settled on one of the benches and consciously diluted his fury by examining the ingenuity of the construction. The seating, planks nailed to posts, curved through the trees in rough arcs. The spacing was good. Everyone would have a good view of the stage. The trees left standing were pillars to hold a leafed roof that would defeat any optical camera. The stage itself was quite large. It fronted a small attached building, undoubtedly storage rooms, possible dressing rooms, as well.

It was all very clever. The people here were at home in this place. They understood. They knew.

The enormity of the odds he faced nearly overwhelmed him. Tears scalded his eyes, his throat constricted. He forced his head up, breathed deeply and steadily, counted to twenty-five. With that touch of self-discipline came a view of himself, of his past. It was like turning a picture around and finding the subject exposed from another view, one never considered before. He felt no need to revile Munson any longer. On the contrary, he felt a glimmer of understanding for the other man's position. The novelty of it fascinated him, and he let the matter run free in his mind.

Munson must have realized he was cutting corners. Bullshit, Tony-boy, he told himself. You cheated everyone you could. You sold Arroyo to Bilongon and vice versa. You covered Bilongon's smuggling and Arroyo's timber rustling. You fabricated reports for Munson to send back to the states when you couldn't recruit agents worth a shit, and you padded every expense account you ever got your hands on. You carried your mistress as a source. For every bit of honest information you produced—and so what if there was enough to justify some pride?—you cheated your own people out of something. If these assholes do kill you, they sure aren't getting much, and the truth is, you asked for it.

A completely different attitude shoved that view aside. He thought, hell, if Munson knew I was cheating, why didn't he stop me? Because he figured some day I'd come in handy. He knew what was going on. He used me, the sonofabitch, and now he talks about his fucking mission and his patriotism, and he's teaming up with that murderous bastard to get rid of me. *He* doesn't trust *me*! He's no better than I am! Shit, he's worse! I'm not letting anyone kill one of my own people; he is! Fuck him!

Again, his agitation aroused the hopes of Fat and Skinny. They shifted from foot to foot uncomfortably, not liking the increasing darkness. They muttered to each other and came closer. Pierce pretended not to notice. That could be the key to his escape. Just as the judo instructors insisted you use the opponent's strength against him, he might be able to make an asset of his guards' eagerness.

Munson called his name. When Pierce turned in that direction, the tall American was just walking away from Bilongon. He joined Pierce on his bench, smiling easily. He cut his eyes at the guards.

"I'm sorry about the escort. Bilongon insists. He's got a high opinion of your deviousness quotient."

"I'm supposed to laugh?"

"It wouldn't hurt. The word's all over camp you're so keyed up you might make a run for it."

Pierce said nothing, and Munson apparently saw something he didn't like. "Don't be a fool. I'll get us out of this if you don't blow it."

"You put me in it, you sonofabitch!"

Munson clamped his wrist in a grip that stopped the outburst in a hiss of pain. "Listen to me. And smile, or I'll break this fucking arm! Smile!" He twisted until he was satisfied with Pierce's expression. "Have you seen Bilongon's bamboo slammer over there? The man who *was* my informant is in it. You want to know what they did to him?"

Pierce shook his head.

"OK. The only reason I'm not in there is because Bilongon believes I bought the information when it was offered to me. If he thought for a second I'd deliberately set out to penetrate his outfit—" He shook his head. "I've been doing some fast talking all day. Bilongon doesn't think too quickly, but he thinks a lot. He comes up with the hard questions eventually."

"Three fucking cheers. What about me?" Pierce couldn't hold back the urge to look at Munson. He wasn't exactly ready to beg yet. It sickened him to realize he would if he thought it would do any good.

"Don't rock the boat, and we'll coast out of here. I gave Bilongon his bad egg. He'll think he's doing the same by turning you over to me. It's agreed. He's mightily pissed at you, my man, but he's not demented. Remember, we're providing him a service."

"You're sure? You wouldn't shit me? I'm too scared, Roger, I mean it." He grabbed Munson's hand.

*It wasn't really begging. Telling the truth wasn't begging.*

Munson gently pulled free.

The sun was setting now, not simply hiding behind trees. There was an opaque quality in the air, a heavier light that squeezed the life from colors. The men drifting into the dining area lost some martial appearance. The groups, two to ten strong, were masses of carefree activity that defied the lowering darkness and rejected the encroaching jungle. It made Pierce afraid and ashamed, simultaneously, to look around and recognize trees his eyes insisted had advanced toward him.

"I'm not lying to you. Hell, Tony, I'm not that bad." Munson rose. They stepped outside the shelter, and he lit a cigarette. Pierce said, "I was so goddam scared! It's a good thing you came around, 'cause I was going to take off during this show later."

The glow from the heavily drawn cigarette accentuated Munson's arched eyebrows, and Pierce went on. "I really was. That's how sure I was I was a dead man. I figured I'd rather get shot than get what the poor bastard in the cage'll get. I was going to throw my ass in that prau and head north until I saw a Philippine flag and then run right up under it."

"I know you were rattled. Keep on acting that way. Half the problem is convincing Bilongon you're in for as much trouble as his man, don't forget that."

"That'll be easy. I won't be able to breathe right until I'm back in Zamboanga." His right hand hovered upward in a tentative move toward Munson, finally gripping him at the shoulder. "If I don't tell you this now, I probably won't ever find the nerve again. I want to tell you I know I was wrong a lot in the past. You may not want to believe me, but I've learned a lot about myself today. You could have let them kill me for what I did, the way that other guy's going to die, and you got me out of it. Whatever else happened, or happens, I won't forget that."

The cigarette fell to the ground, the coal gyrating like an eccentric lightning bug. Munson ground it out. "We're not out of the woods yet." He paused, chuckled. "Let's forget I said that, OK?" He clapped a hand on Pierce's, then moved out from under the contact. "We'll be out of here in the morning and in good shape, if we just keep cool. Now, you go ahead and eat. I'm going to find our host."

Darkness claimed him within a few steps, only a bobbing silhouette visible against the sparse light from the block of longhouses. Pierce decided he wasn't hungry, but Fat and Skinny had no such notion. They were already at one of the tables, digging in with equal vigor. Looking around, he found the men who'd relieved them. They lounged close by, propped on their rifles, hip-shot. Pierce remembered photographs in history books, in magazines, on television. Boys at Fredericksburg, Guadalcanal, Khe Sanh. Some smiled as these did, immortal in their youthfulness. Others held themselves remote, their eyes a match for the cold lens of the camera. They were the ones Pierce shunned, the ones with true knowledge and the ice-blue river of fear in their bowels.

When Pierce angled off toward the theatre his new escort fell in behind. They were more professional in their manner. One remained a few paces further back and off to one side. Both maneuvered to keep Pierce between them and whatever light source was brightest. He permitted himself a smile, thinking how upset he would have been just an hour earlier to find the ambitions of Fat and Skinny replaced by the easy competence of these two. Now he had no worries about any of them. Munson had never really jeopardized him. Knowing the level of danger had been less than he believed at the time had the curious effect of diminishing the memory of the hours of anxiety. When he thought of it now, it was the tang of excitement he breathed, not the stench of despair.

Turning to the guards, he made signs to indicate he would sit here to watch the program. They smiled at him, smiled at each other, nodded, smiled at him again, and everyone sat down. The guards were on the last bench, two rows back. Figures moved in, out, and around the stage area. Men busied themselves placing equipment. They used turned-down kerosene lamps that gave only enough light to suit their purposes, so Pierce couldn't identify anything with certainty. He wished they'd use the brighter gasoline lanterns like the ones in the dining hall, even though they made noise.

The night was cooler, marked by a sigh of breeze. The smells of cooking and kerosene lamps mingled with earth-aromas. Conversation bubbled, frequently boiling over in a welter of laughter or a yelp of triumph scored in some competition. Pierce turned from watching the stage crew to survey the crowd, ignoring the guards. Most of the socializing was done in the dining area where the lamps up in the eaves poured out sheets of light that limned the building knife-sharp against the darkness. Tobacco smoke misted up to the thatch and as it cooled, dropped to curl from under the eaves. The breeze streamed the coils away into the night. Pierce shifted his view to the block of longhouses. Light glowed there, too, softer rectangles of orange-red marking the windows.

He tried to relate it all to something in his experience, nights at camp, evenings in the park waiting for the entertainment to start, gatherings of any kind. There was nothing. Nowhere in his experience was the world so far away that men routinely made their own entertainment. The smells of the food here were rich and interesting. And alien. There was nothing here that contacted his inner self, no sensory or emotional handhold to help him pull up from his singularity.

Murmured conversation distracted him, and he looked to see Fat and Skinny taking over the guard duty again. It was mildly disturbing. The other two had a solidity Fat and Skinny lacked, a point driven home eloquently by the clatter of a round jacked into the chamber of Skinny's weapon.

When he turned away from them, Pierce noticed the increased light on the stage and the number of men filtering into the seating area. He was surprised to see women and children, having seen or heard no indication of them before. The women chattered among themselves, and individual men drifted over to greet some of them and pair off. They made an attractive scene, the women in their long skirts and the bright-eyed excited children matching up with husbands and fathers. There were only two girls that appeared to be unmarried. Pierce guessed their status by the sudden eruption of young male punching and shoving in the dining area and the surge from there to the theatre.

Bilongon's voice came over his shoulder. "I will not be seen talking to him. He is yours. I will wait for you at our seats, in the front row."

Pierce kept his eyes in the same direction until Munson's voice replaced the chill left by Bilongon.

"Everything under control?"

"Fine, if you like being a leper."

Munson sat on the bench in front, facing back toward Pierce. "Don't let it get to you. A few more hours and it's over." He gestured, changing the subject. "Did you know about the families? Bilongon's people have a village farther back in the forest. The bachelors all live here. The women aren't allowed in the camp except when there's entertainment, like tonight."

"Great social planning."

"Yeah. Well, I'm going up with Bilongon. You like the music?" It was one last try at a cheerful note, and Pierce stepped on it.

"It sounds like somebody wrecking a kitchen. Enjoy."

Munson nodded shortly and left. He smiled when he lowered to the bench next to Bilongon. A few moments later the entertainment started. An older man stepped onto the stage, a man Pierce didn't know. He wore loose trousers and shirt and the white skull cap of the *hadji*, the ones who have made their pilgrimage to Mecca. He waited until the audiences quieted, stared over their heads. Unspeaking, unmoving, he waited. Soon the only sound was the distant hiss of the gasoline lanterns and the night song of the leaves, married in a continuous sigh. Fat leaned forward, bringing his head close to Pierce's.

The old man's voice, amazingly sonorous from such a frail body, ripped the tension. He cried one word, waiting, and the audience repeated it in a low chorus, as if fearing the power of it.

Pierce looked his question at Fat. The youth looked at him with eyes a thought away from trance. "Freedom," he said, nodding at the speaker. Pierce was too impressed by the scene to think about Fat's sudden exercise of English. The old man spoke again, and the audience chanted back at him.

Fat said, "Faith."

Then the old man said, "Bilongon!" and the only response from the audience was a long exhalation of such compound emotion it raised flesh on Pierce's arm in goosebumps.

The short speech that followed was too much for Fat's language skills, and he listened, absorbed. Pierce watched him, essaying a peek at Skinny. He was as engrossed as Fat. If he still wanted to escape this would have been the time. Even Skinny's hands were slack, his weapon lying on the bench next to him. Pierce was suddenly aware that this camp was the only place he could remember that wasn't saturated with the Philippine craze for rock music.

Musicians filed onto the stage as the speaker left, and, without introduction, the entertainment was underway. A man lifted his hands and snapped small mallets at a bamboo xylophone, a quiet melody of few notes. The tone was clear, each note a brief entity. Another man stirred, caressing the brass bowl-looking objects that made up the instrument called a *kulintangan*. Its notes were a muted sound providing simultaneous harmony and disharmony in myriad overtones. Then another man struck fiercely at another gong, and the crash created a start throughout the entire audience. Satisfied smiles followed, pleased at the expected eruption. Knowing what was coming in no way detracted from the blood-pulse that grew from it, a rhythm immediately seized on by entering drums.

The women appeared from the right of the stage as if by magic. The soft light of the lanterns imbued them with further mystery. All three wore splendid batik skirts and blouses. The central woman was the taller by a few inches and the only one dressed in a cool color, wearing black with a blue and green design. The others wore the same black background, but where one had a predominantly bright orange pattern, the other featured dark red. They moved around the stage, bending and swaying, arms seemingly light enough to hover at their sides. They were at once erotic, innocent, enticing, distant.

Fat punched Pierce's arm and pointed at the stage. "Jolo," he said, "Home me. Live Jolo."

Pierce nodded. "Lucky you," he said, more to himself. The women were abreast now, the one in the center magnificent. The beat was much faster, and his heart worked to match it. The xylophone and drums teamed, melodic notes coming in the same rhythm as the demanding percussion. As the women swayed, the background movement of the musicians and the gleam of the instruments was a living curtain of visual counterpoint.

The sharp break, marked by a series of clacking sounds, came just as it seemed the pace must stumble over itself. A moth chose that moment to batter itself against Pierce's ear, distracting him. He brushed it away. In doing so, he took his eyes from the stage, and when he looked back, Bilongon and Munson were speaking to each other, ignoring the program. Bilongon was agitated, and when he spoke to Munson his head bobbed with the vehemence of the words. Munson responded by jabbing a thumb toward the rear of the theater, and Bilongon scanned the audience in one sweep. Then he turned to the man on his left and spoke briefly, his hands in angular gestures. The man rushed away, bent over to avoid blocking the view of those behind.

Pierce concentrated on the dancers again. The women moved with impassioned energy now, the earlier languorousness abandoned. The central blue and green figure arched and curved between the hotter colors, a tree beset by flame.

The moth returned, brushing Pierce's face, and he cursed, swinging at it. It fluttered away a mere foot, hanging in midair. He poised to kill it and saw a man detach himself from the crowd and move toward the latrine. He swung at the moth and something told him to stop, to look at the man again. He caught him as he passed a tree-hung lantern, providing an excellent three-quarter view. It was one of the men who'd relieved Fat and Skinny, and he had his rifle with him. Not even here did a man travel armed to the toilet, Pierce realized, and when the man moved beyond that point and simply melded into the darkness, it was no surprise. In fact, although a sensation of mute acceptance struck him physically immobile, Pierce's mind raged. The music increased in volume, and the hammered metal of the *kulintangan* moaned behind the other instruments, a flame of sound that seared across Pierce's brain, refusing to be ignored. He pressed his fists to his temples, creating pain to re-create reason.

Munson had told Bilongon of his escape plan! It was inconceivable! Why? *Why?*

And why did Bilongon post guards on the route?

Because Munson didn't say the plan had been abandoned. And

that meant Bilongon had no intention of letting him escape. Munson hadn't believed him and had informed Bilongon! They were never going to let him off this island. They *were* going to kill him, cage him in the jungle and kill him.

The women swirled on the stage. The flames surrounded the green of life, the green of the hated jungle that was his only hope.

The music spoke to him, unequivocal.

Go or be killed. *Go* or be killed.

Faster, faster, faster.

For Pierce, it was catharsis. He knew what he must do, and a confidence so immense enveloped him his only fear was that his guards would notice a change.

The men in the crowd stirred, tightened and drew themselves into harder lines, the way rigging defines itself in a freshening breeze.

Fat gave him no more than a blink when he rose. Skinny was entranced, uninterested in anything but the music. Pierce stepped over their bench, prepared to point at the latrine and smile if they looked at him. It was imperative to get behind them.

They ignored him.

The edged hand Pierce drove into Skinny's neck created a shock that half-lifted the small man and paralyzed him. Before Skinny started his sideways slump, Pierce had the Kalashnikov in his hands and was whipping the butt upward at Fat. It caught him behind the chin. Blood and teeth geysered between his lips, and he tumbled to the ground. The two of them ended up side by side between the benches, curled up like puppies.

Leveling the automatic rifle at the crowd, Pierce realized no one knew what had happened. The music had their total attention.

He ran for the creek and the prau that meant survival. Expecting the crack of gunfire, he sobbed aloud when a booming eruption behind him turned out to be nothing more than an exuberance from the largest gong. He threw himself along the path, away from the theater. Branches slashed at him when he strayed too far to the right and when he overcompensated, other, low-growing branches on the left clutched at his ankles and tripped him. He continued forward, more in falling than flight, oblivious to the noise he created, the music behind him, oblivious to everything but the single, shining thought that he had to get away or die.

When the man stepped out of the growth he was too close for Pierce to bring the Kalashnikov to bear. He shouted at the man, an atavistic blend of fear and rage from deep in his guts, and lowered his head to bowl him over. There was an amazing burst of light behind his eyes, and he was certain he had been run down from behind and the back of his head was gone, admitting the lamplight from the camp. He fell into a bush that bent under his weight and sprang back upward, rejecting him. He landed in the path on his face, setting off another burst of the infernally bright light in his head. It would be better for him, he decided, to be on his back.

He rolled over and faces were looking down at him, dark faces full of gleaming eyes and champing mouths that worked without intelligible sound, like horses worrying bits.

Waving hands held torches and flashlights over him, but he didn't care. With the back of his head to the ground the light could only enter when he opened his eyes and trickle through his skull. It wasn't nearly as bad as the other way around, but it was bad, and he closed his eyes.

He knew Munson had arrived only because he heard his voice. The words didn't register, and that was maddening, but they flittered around beyond his reach. Just like the moth, he decided, and damned it for starting all this trouble.

Balling his fists in anticipation of the pain, he opened his eyes. It nearly blinded him, but he saw through it, discovering that Munson was very angry. His face was twisted with it until the roughness of it looked like the flanged trunk of one of the jungle trees.

Munson *was* the jungle! It was stupid not to have seen that all along.

Still, Munson should be human enough to see that a man was dying at his feet, surviving only by a miracle. It was necessary to make him see himself as he actually was.

Pierce raised a hand, every nerve in him screaming with the effort. "I know the truth about you. You didn't have to do this to me. You knew I'd be afraid. We were partners."

This time Munson's words were perfectly clear. He said, "You crazy sonofabitch!" and kicked him directly under the ribs.

The light exploded again, a sheer, hot white, so fiery it sucked the air out of his body in a hoarse whistle.

Then it was marvelously dark.

# ■ CHAPTER 15 ■

Pierce slowly raised a tentative hand toward his head. No recollection of any party surfaced, and he puzzled over such a violent hangover with no memories. When he touched his temple, pain whined through every cell in his body.

Footsteps pattered away. He opened his eyes, rolling them just far enough to see a white-jacketed Filipino run from his room. He tried to shout after the man, managing a cracked squawk and another blast of pain. Staring at the ceiling, he tried to remember. How had he gotten to his room? He tried to picture himself on the path leading to his cottage. Other thoughts, other recollections spun across his mind. They hurt, made him groan aloud.

The din of the prau's engine. The feeling of being beaten viciously, not knowing where the next blow would come from. Someone was holding him, trying to protect him. No. Not from blows. Rolling around, being thrown.

*Why?*

Certainly—the prau. High speed, bouncing. Someone—yes, Munson—pulling him up so his arms hung over the sides and his torso was between the long legs, buffered against the pounding. Pain, everywhere, mostly in his head, trying to claw its way out.

Munson spoke in the present. "Tired of lying around, are you? We thought you'd make it a lifework."

Pierce said, "Wa'er," and Munson filled a glass from the carafe next to the bed, holding it up for him. Some slopped past his lips and dripped off his chin onto his neck. He couldn't make up his mind which stream felt better, the one inside or the one outside, and groaned in sheer delight.

Munson continued. "You've been out of it a couple of days. You tried to run over one of Bilongon's guards. I imagine you remember that. What you may not know is there was one on each side of the trail. When you went for one, the other teed off on you. You're goddamned lucky he only clubbed you. A minor concussion, no break in the skin to get infected. And we're both lucky Bilongon decided you'd probably die on the trip back here."

"You sold out. Told Bilongon."

"Told him what?"

"About me. Escape. Past latrine."

A confused frown etched Munson's features. "I didn't— You saw him send the guard up to the latrine! You poor idiot. That had nothing to do with you. He's such a bluenose I was ribbing him about the girls and the men sneaking off into the brush, and he had to show me he wouldn't allow it. Nobody even mentioned you."

Pierce refused to believe it. "You told. Kicked me, too."

"Goddam right I kicked you. I'd do it again. With both feet. You nearly got us both killed. Anyhow, I thought you were running out on me."

"Almos' killed?"

"Think about it. Bilongon doesn't survive because he trusts people, Tony. When he sees something he doesn't understand, it's fight or flight. He's not too likely to run away from that camp if the alternative is some little thing like killing a couple of white guys he doesn't like all that much."

"So wha's deal?"

"No change. I'll have to let him know you're alive and recovering and the operation's a go."

"An'thing else?"

"Boy Angel." Munson crushed the half-smoked cigarette in the ashtray. "He's not back. It's worrying me."

Pierce essayed a minute gesture, barely enough to disturb the sheet covering the hand. "Shacked up. Drunk. Can' trus' him."

"I don't. But I have to depend on him to get me information. He and the others in his gang are the only contacts I can call on in

Manila now. I can't understand why no one from L.A.'s been down here nosing around.''

Grimacing with a different pain, Pierce said, "They will. Too soon.''

"Right. And we need you up and around. Let's get some food into you. I need you strong.''

Pierce closed his eyes as Munson shambled out of the room. Strong. Had he ever been strong? Not really. But now the effort might be worthwhile. Death. The jungle. Panic. All of them had roosted on his shoulders and screamed in his ears. And he was still here. Hurting like a bastard, but still here. Life was sweet.

Painful memories coupled with the more recent terror of Bilongon's camp, and he experienced an exhilaration he had never considered possible. There was a progression to life! A man learned to use the fear. When that was understood, it was a stimulant.

Hunger snarled from his stomach and he smiled at it.

Boy Angel couldn't believe his good luck. Things were going too well, as though strange powers were arranging his life in a huge joke, ready to laugh when they let him drop. Why else would he be assigned to follow a beautiful woman around? And given a car to do it? A *car!* Hardly dented at all and in first-class running condition. Even the inside was pretty clean. He looked around at it for the hundredth time and, thinking about the woman, turned up the radio volume. If Benjamin wanted him to spend his days watching her, that was fine.

The problem was Munson. Benjamin's problem, not his, Boy Angel amended hastily. Of course, it would be him that heard the first ass-chewing, but it was Benjamin who decided he needed Boy Angel in Manila. It was one of the few times he'd ever been defensive about a decision, and it still troubled Boy Angel to remember.

"He sends you here to tell me we have to watch this guy Draeger and everyone he has regular contact with twenty-four hours a day, and he knows how many people that takes and how many I've got. What the hell's he want from me? You'll watch his chick. You don't do nothing else, just watch the chick. At least that way I got an extra man on them when they're together. If she'd just move in the

fucking apartment with him, it'd make things easier for everybody.
Them, too.''

Everyone laughed at that. Especially Boy Angel. He might not be
getting any of what the American was getting, but it was still a
pleasure to keep an eye on that girl. She was bold, driving her own
car around town, sometimes pretty damned late at night. A lot of
things could happen to a car at night.

Ria leaned back against Draeger on the sofa, turning her head to
look up at him, pouting. "Is this the way you're going to treat me
all the time? Here I hurry over here so we can go out to dinner, and
you want to watch basketball.''

Without taking his eyes from the set, he put an arm around her
and squeezed her shoulder. "I'm building up an excitement level.
Get all worked up about the basketball game and then get excited
about the meal, then a few drinks to loosen up my inhibitions, and
when we get back here later, you'll get the benefit of all that. I'm
always thinking of your best interests.''

She pinched the flesh on his ribs, pleased it was tight enough to
make the job difficult, more pleased at his yell and leap.

"Damn!'' He rubbed the welt ruefully. "That'll be an interesting
color tomorrow. I just get rid of some bruises, and you give me
more.''

"That'll teach you to trifle with me. Filipinas don't take that sort
of thing anymore.''

Draeger stepped over to the TV and switched it off, and Ria,
without his support, slid down and onto her side. When he turned
around she patted the sofa next to her and he sat down. She smiled
at him and lifted the shirt, rubbing her tongue across the angry flesh.
Inarticulate pleasure rumbled deep in his chest.

"You could cheat yourself out of a good dinner,'' he said, and
reached for the top of her blouse. She held him off.

"No way. I'm only trying to show you we can get along without
basketball if it's excitement you want.''

He grinned at her. "What a thoroughly naughty lady you turned
out to be. I'm going to change this shirt. If we're going out, we
better do it in the next ten minutes.'' She made a face at him, and he
strode out of the room.

She continued to stare at the bedroom door after him, her normally mobile features pensive.

Uncontrolled.

That wasn't the right word, but she wasn't sure there was a right word for how she felt. When he was out of sight it was as if the most important part of her was withering away unseen, a plant dying in its roots while its leaves continued to yearn lightward. And she didn't love him.

That was where the pain lived, in that one negative.

In his arms, feeling him pressed to her, the unknown energy that drove him bound them in one unit. She had to be with him, had to possess him, totally. Then, when they were lying next to each other and her thoughts coasted on the easy rhythm of his breathing, sometimes she imagined him looking down at a child, a baby, and she shivered at the thought that it might be hers. Those were the times she wept, dreading the sound that might wake him and bring questions.

He was her lover. He could never be her love. And she could find no reason for that paradox and wanted to love him with a desperation she feared would destroy her. Now, when her skin warmed in anticipation of his touch, when she could hear him moving around only a room away, she told herself she must love him to want him so shamelessly.

It was like that terrible telephone call, the morning after he'd been so horribly beaten. After those three days of agony and humiliation, to hear his voice, so raw with pain. That was one of the times of tears, wanting him, afraid for him, and all the while an evil gladness chanted in her heart that his pain was punishment for her suffering.

She had dropped the phone and rushed to him. She blushed, remembering her wantonness, but it had been right. He had forgotten his pain, and she had forgotten hers. If their making love solved no problems, it was a time when there was nothing else in the world.

Draeger came out in his fresh *barong*. "I thought we'd go to Galing-Galing, in the Ermita, then maybe over to the Cowrie Bar in the Manila Hotel."

Before Ria could answer there was a knock at the door. Draeger moved toward the unexpected interruption. When he opened it, he visibly started.

Kolar said, "We should have called before we came over. We just got in—" He stepped into the room and cut off the sentence as soon as he saw Ria, then smiled. "You have company! I'd apologize for interrupting, but she's far too lovely. I'm delighted we found her here."

Ria smiled at the blatant flattery, and the man spoke over his shoulder. "Cindy! Come in so I can introduce you and learn this lovely lady's name!"

Ria shifted her attention past the man and to the door. A blond woman swept past dumbfounded Draeger with easy grace, her smile a tribute to knowledge that she was welcome wherever she went. Bowing with mock formality Kolar said, "Carl Kolar, at your service. This young woman is Cindy Anderson, my administrative assistant. As clever as she is beautiful, you have my word. And you are—?"

Draeger said, "Miss Manong, Ria Manong."

It was an odd tableau. Kolar accepted Draeger's information without turning his head. Draeger himself stood immobile, the open door half-hiding him. The two women smiled without letting it affect their eyes and touched hands. The plain gesture had a stealthy quality, the darker and lighter fingers scanning, sensitive, delicate, probing for a revealing insight through the flesh.

Ria's throat ached with shame. The newcomer made her think of herself as threatened. It was absurd. Although the woman was beautiful, as tall and blond and slender as the American television programs said women must be, that didn't mean she'd be interested in Glen.

A depressing truth added to her discomfort. She was judging everyone and everything in terms of this new thing in her life. If the relationship with Glen was to be more than some physical reflex, it must withstand a passing nod from any American steel-and-chrome mannequin.

Kolar said, "Glen didn't mention you when we spoke." He turned to flash an in-joke smile at him. The act was enough to get Draeger moving again, and he shut the door before hurrying to Ria's side as Kolar added, "On the other hand, he wasn't saying much of anything. Not with his face looking like a battlefield."

Ria said, "I got here just after you left."

Kolar smiled again, the grandfather blue eyes twinkling. "Ah, to tend the fallen? If I had known, I would have faked my own injury, something nonincapacitating but demanding of attention."

Ria laughed with him, enjoying the easy way he made contact. There was a confidence in him that she was sure would put him comfortably into any environment. Peculiarly, she caught herself thinking he'd just as smoothly work his way out of any environment. His naturalness flowed through his words, glossed his face when he spoke. She felt if she looked away, he would image in her mind like a man captured on movie film, visible in all aspects, but ever so slightly out of focus. And in that, he finally reminded her of Draeger.

Draeger said, "I told Ria a friend had been here and left. I can't remember if I told her who. I certainly didn't mention Ms. Anderson. You never said your assistant was a woman."

"I know." Kolar looked rueful for all of them. "I hate to bring it up. People either leer or want to put me on a pedestal for my liberated attitude. The facts are I pick the smartest help I can find. That's Cindy."

The blond offered her hand to Draeger, the contact a millisecond longer than the one that passed between the two women. Ria timed it in the pit of her stomach.

"Call me Cindy," the woman said. Her voice went with her clothes, bold reds and stark whites, colors that told the world the wearer enjoyed life, all of it. She turned to Ria. "I've never been to the Philippines, but your name—Manong—I've read it." She frowned, concentrating. "The in-flight magazine. Art, wasn't it?"

"I'm a sculptor." As always, the statement brought Ria pride. This time it brought something else, something truly surprising. It made her feel closer to Cindy. Perhaps it was the genuine respect in the blue-green eyes or the straightforward way she put her question, admitting she had been interested but not overwhelmed. Most people would have hinted around until they had a few more answers, then gushed.

Ria turned to Draeger. "I think they'd enjoy Galing-Galing."

"You're right. Have you eaten?"

"Just got in and washed up and came over here," Kolar said.

"We were going to ask you to join us, as a matter of fact. What's this thing Ria mentioned?

Draeger explained about Galing-Galing as they rode down in the elevator, telling them how the name itself meant "very good." The food and decor represented the Philippines of the turn of the century.

Draeger drove, mixing with the early evening traffic in a practiced ease that first pleased Ria and then caused her irritation when she saw how little the Americans appreciated it. They should try it, she thought, and inwardly shouted at herself to stop being so bitchy.

Kolar, riding in front with Draeger, waved at the skyscrapers lining Ayala Avenue. "The first time I was here was back in the fifties. This was a village. Now look at it. Miles of business buildings. You can't look at it and not admire the industry of these people."

Cindy broke her long silence. "It's too bad the social progress hasn't kept up with the economics." She touched Ria's arm. "That's a rude thing to say, Ria, but economics is my specialty—business management, actually—and I see so much money concentrated in so few hands it drives me crazy. I haven't seen anyone starving, but there are incredible accumulations of wealth and so much naked poverty. I hate to sound critical, I really do. This is such a beautiful country, and that's such a dangerous situation. It's frightening."

Ria nodded, painfully aware that these were all strangers. "We are new to self-government." In her effort to be very precise her accent thickened. "Our traditions are not yours. We have regained our independence for only one generation. Worse, our traditions for the past five centuries have not been our traditions. We want a government that allows us freedom. We want an economic system that does not crush the poor. We live under the constant threat of martial law, of radical violence, of terrorism. Still, we live. We are trying to build a happy, free society. We fight by working. We make mistakes. Compared to the government we had before the martial law, we are in much, much better shape." She stopped and the others waited, knowing she wasn't finished. "You must understand. We will find our own way. Interfere, and those you help will fear you and repudiate you in order to retain the good will of the people. Those you do not help will hate you for helping someone else."

Kolar pivoted to face her. Ria covered her mouth with her hand and giggled. The eyes challenged him. "Do I sound like a politician?"

He reached to pat her hand. "Lord, no. You wouldn't last ten minutes. You're a statesman." He twisted his face. "Statesperson? Statesthingummy? Dammit, Cindy, help me out of this mess. You're the liberated female."

"Liberated enough to let you simmer in your own juice, you chauvinist old reprobate."

"I'm offended. I'm not old."

Ria giggled again, and Cindy laughed with her, a deeper, heartier expression. It was companionable. Ria appreciated the underlying significance, yet the very tone of their laughter further emphasized their differences. It said that Cindy was used to being included in men's talk, had been considered "one of the boys." Ria only knew such a concept existed. Somewhere.

They ate in the central area of the restaurant, a room within a room, that had the effect of a gazebo. The service was instant, solicitous. Ria plotted the meal with the waitress, refusing to discuss decisions. "Just wait," she insisted. "You'll like it."

Kolar and Cindy greeted each course with question, and Ria made them try to determine what was involved. It made a delicious meal an event. Draeger identified the first course as *sinanpalo kong manok*, a lemon-flavored chicken soup. The entree of *sariwang lumpia*, a delicate dough wrapper around fresh vegetables, quick fried and covered with thick sauce, was no problem. For a main course, Ria took no chances, ordering two. One was a beautifully served whole *bangus*, a commercially raised saltwater fish greatly admired for delicate flavor and texture. It was done with a vinegar sauce that sharpened the palate and the flavor, simultaneously. The meat course was called *humba*, and after much discussion, Ria exploded in laughter and confessed even she didn't know what the sauce was because it was a house secret. For dessert they had a mousse of *nangka*, Tagalog for jackfruit.

Through it all, music flooded the restaurant, lilting strings and piano tunes, gentler music of a past era. Several times, when the women would get involved in matters of tablespoons of this and half-cups of that, Draeger took the opportunity to watch Kolar listen to the music. He lost himself in it, blunt chin resting on the palm of an upturned hand, eyes focused on a distance only he could define. His expression puzzled Draeger. There was sadness that approached melancholy and a touch of a smile. It was as though the man mourned in the midst of gratitude.

With the dessert finished and its components analyzed to the molecule, the women excused themselves. Kolar stood, a courtesy Draeger matched. The older man beamed satisfaction. When they were reseated he changed dramatically, became a demanding overseer.

"When we leave here I want to see you tonight. We have things to discuss."

"I can't just take her home and dump her."

Kolar bit off the words. "I have to see you tonight."

Draeger angled forward over the table. "Don't push. I won't take it."

Kolar was unimpressed. "I've got your signature on papers. You'll do as you're told."

"Probably. But on my terms. Munson gave me a lot of abuse. Then you show up and I get the shit pounded out of me and my room gets tossed. Makes a man wonder, Kolar. Then you take off for Cebu. You think I don't know you're checking on me, right along with Munson?"

The reappearance of the women stopped Kolar's retort. He was on his feet again, gracious and affable. The conversation with Draeger might never have happened. Ria knew better. Her first look at Draeger confirmed that and told her it was unpleasant. She reached for his hand under the table. He returned the pressure with a distracted squeeze, a perfunctory answer she knew was as much a rejection as an acknowledgment. He was away from her again, deep in the heart of his life where she could never go. And Kolar had put him there, had taken the warmth of this man she wanted and driven him to that cold place where everything was unknown and unknowing.

# CHAPTER 16

"There's a tail on you."

The words were a blow. Draeger still had his hand on the doorknob, hadn't had time to turn on the light. For a moment he was paralyzed, bound by the memory of the beating in this same dark room. Another beating would have been more welcome than a repeat of those words. They came, merciless.

"There's a tail on you."

It was Kolar. Despite the darkness, Draeger knew exactly where the man was sitting. The voice came at him with the linearity of a thrown rock. He knew when he hit the light switch the leonine head was going to be at the far end of the sofa. It was an act of will to prove it. The end table lamp burnished Kolar's silver hair from behind, not illuminating the face. His eyes gleamed at Draeger from sockets drawn to slits, holding Draeger's so demandingly he barely acknowledged the presence of Cindy Anderson in the chair facing Kolar. She said nothing.

Moving with an ease he feared was transparently nonchalant, Draeger took the chair next to Cindy. She watched him until he was seated, then turned her full attention to Kolar. It was a forthright indication of where the authority in the room rested, but it infuriated Draeger.

They weren't guests in any sense. He was looking at a tribunal. Kolar and the woman would investigate and determine what other action was required. He chanced a look away from the man, examining the woman. She was as unrevealing as Kolar, a perfect profile against the black slab of windowed night.

Kolar said, "I thought I burned one man when I came in, but I couldn't be sure, and in this traffic a good man could follow you in a tank and you'd never know. Especially if you weren't looking. And you weren't."

"I had no reason to look. My cover's good."

"Your cover's torn to bits. With Munson flown, we're all hanging out in the open."

"Flown?"

Kolar's hands were clasped on his kneecap, and he pointed at Cindy by raising an index finger from the bundle. It was an indolent gesture, the solitary finger moving as if of its own will. She didn't even notice it, watching his face. He said, "Cindy's a business analyst. We pay her a great deal to keep our finances neat and tidy. She's with me because I don't believe Munson's dead and I do believe his disappearance was engineered."

"By whom? Why?"

"I can't find out. Not yet. But he had dealings with people we didn't know about."

Bristling, Draeger said, "We all do. We're not obliged to account for everyone we speak to."

"The hell you're not." The correction had the sound of bits of broken glass in collision. The smile that followed was apologetic, disavowed by a new, avuncular personality. The marvel wasn't the magnitude of the change but the believability of it. Kolar continued. "There's really no need for us to discuss technicalities, is there? After all, we're working toward the same goal. I know I have your cooperation. The problem is, we have some irregularities in Munson's accounts. Payments to people we can't place."

"He's dealt with hundreds of people, some of them from way back in the weeds. Gatherers, traders, you name it."

"Gangs." At Draeger's widened eyes, Kolar nodded sadly. "He paid someone here considerable money to conduct business for him over the years. It was Cindy who realized there were too many chores for any single person, although only one collected money. That means an organization."

"What kind of chores?" There was a rancid taste in Draeger's mouth. The question made it worse.

"We don't really know. There's a suggestion of a surveillance operation because some of the paperwork indicates three-man teams are being paid for. That would, of course, suggest routine ABC teams. Unfortunately, the account books give us no good insight into what he was doing."

Cindy said, "Not entirely," and Kolar's eyes glinted. He continued to watch Draeger.

"She's right," he agreed, and smiled again, this time with some eagerness. "Roger Munson has a source, a Chinese source, on his books. We learned of him only through Cindy's persistence. I should explain that he slipped his extracurricular activities into his business books. I imagine you've already deduced that. Those accounts worked through a series of kickbacks from other accounts. The kickback money paid for his personal maneuverings and was used to establish a defector's fund for the Chinese's eventual bailout. Cindy tracked him down in that jungle of numbers. Masterful."

The woman glowed with the praise, although Kolar continued to look at Draeger. He watched, looking for signs of any reaction. When Cindy moved and distracted him, the head pivoted, dragging the vision, a camera accommodating whatever intruded on the angle of sight. Draeger had seen him do that once before. There had been a lecture, and a man walked in unannounced. Kolar was the lecturer. Suddenly Draeger remembered the subject and almost blurted a remark. His self-control was wasted. Kolar saw something.

"You were about to speak?" he suggested.

Draeger decided to get it over with. "I was remembering your discussion of final responsibility. I think that's what you're working around to, isn't it?"

"Yes." The aureole created by the lamp reflected a myriad lights as Kolar bobbed his head in slow agreement. "Someone is onto us, as they say. Your courier was killed quite professionally. I've no doubt the explosion that killed Mrs. Munson was the work of an expert. You were supposed to meet Munson, not his wife. I find myself forced to consider two primary probabilities. First, Munson meant to kill you, and his wife blundered into the situation. Second, a party or parties unknown meant to kill you both, and Munson was killed in an unanticipated manner, leading to the disappearance of his body."

"Bullshit." Draeger leaned back, curiously relaxed. "There are other possibilities. Maybe I tried to kill him. Or maybe I killed her, too, to make it look real. Or maybe Munson and I have something going and I'm covering his disappearance. You've considered all of those. You still are, aren't you?''

Kolar got to his feet and walked to the kitchen, leaving Draeger alone with Cindy. She adjusted her position and waited. He took the opportunity to look closely at her. Her physical beauty was so undeniable he accepted it as an entity, not troubling to catalog. The three-quarter view of her profile revealed an unexpected aspect, however. She was afraid, with the slightly widened eyes and white nostrils of evasion.

The discovery was mere confirmation. What was lacking was an idea of the thing that made her evasive.

They waited in silence for Kolar. When he stepped out of the kitchen he carried drinks for all of them, whiskey and water. They toasted each other with silently raised glasses.

Kolar took up the conversation. ''I deal in facts. You deal in truth. 'Ah-hah,' you say, 'the senility comes forth like sunrise.' No. Facts and truth are vastly different. You believe in the marrow of your bones that all men are created equal and have the right to the pursuit of happiness. Our country and the Soviet Union may well destroy the world over interpretations of those truths. Our nations supposedly destroyed Nazi Germany because they held the Jews to be less than human. Today's Soviet Jews don't go to Dachau, but they're certainly not created equal, are they?''

''Fine, fine.'' Draeger slashed at the argument with his hand. ''What's all this got to do with me, the tail, or anything else?''

Kolar rolled his shoulders, and the voice turned brisk. ''What I was trying to explain is that I don't have the facts to warrant a concern over final responsibility now. When I have the facts, you can be sure I'll practice what I preach.''

Cindy made a small noise, and Kolar looked at her as if she'd done something unforgivably rude. ''You knew it before you came,'' he said. ''It was explained to you.''

Draeger laughed, clipped sounds. ''I've never been part of a termination either, Cindy. Sometimes the old-timers call it 'putting someone in a bag.' They say it comes from the bags they put bodies in during a war. I've never been to one of those, either. Wouldn't it be funny if Mr. Kolar picks my number? Did he give you the quote? 'Any organism has the final responsibility to protect itself, or it has no right to exist.' That's right, isn't it, Kolar? Live or die, right?''

"You reduce the concept to an absurd oversimplification," he protested mildly, "but it's close. Those things unworthy of preservation must be swept away, as dead cells are disposed of by a healthy body."

"And you decide which cell dies."

"If the system is to be allowed to develop, it goes without saying it must live. It protects itself."

"Would you have me die if I interfered with your view of proper development?"

Cindy's voice cut across the argument. "Stop it! Both of you! You're pushing each other to say things you don't mean!"

Kolar flashed her a hard smile. Draeger refused to be distracted. When the smile died it carried away all expression. He might have been born with the earth itself. Immune to the coldness, Cindy matched his stare. At last, he looked to Draeger, answering her while he did.

"You're right, Cindy. What we're doing is potentially destructive, but he has to understand the imperatives. I'm afraid the leap from abstract to factual has tripped him."

Dryly, Draeger said, "It's my life you're discussing."

Kolar shook his head. A growing weariness showed in the heavy movement. "No. You've cast yourself in the role of victim and inferred it's I who'll do the killing. I don't consider it necessarily revealing, but there's some fascinating psychology involved."

"That's unfair, Carl." Cindy's voice was precise, "and it's inaccurate, which is worse. For you to infer guilt because he thinks of himself as an underdog is too flawed to discuss." She suddenly leaned forward. "He's been completely forthcoming. What more can you ask?"

Kolar remained adamant. "Facts. I must have facts. I must know why the courier was killed, why Munson's factory blew up, where Munson is, and why he's not here."

Draeger said, "Have you checked with the other people in our team? He could be with one of them."

"Without me knowing it? That means one of our people covering for him."

"Not necessarily. Everyone got the shutdown order. Was anything sent out telling people to look for him? If he's hiding out with one of our people, couldn't he simply explain he was ordered to, or just say he needs to be out of circulation a while?"

"Who'd believe that?"

"Who'd doubt it, for Christ's sake? He's the man in charge. We trusted him."

Cindy snapped at the phrase. "Trusted? Past tense?"

Draeger shifted uncomfortably. "I was in a beef with him. He accused me of creating the situation that makes Egg Roll want out."

The silence started as a simple nonspeaking. It grew to a sodden presence. The ice in Kolar's drink slipped, a shrill cacophony that jerked Cindy's eyes wide. She started and caught herself in the new, unplanned position. It looked uncomfortable, and, once more, Draeger saw her as desperate to remain unobserved but unable to leave the excitement.

Kolar said, "You created?"

Draeger's lungs emptied. Kolar didn't know of Munson's accusations. It was impossible. There had been time for Munson to send off a partial report. It wasn't like him to be lax about something like that. Kolar must be running a test. The only choice was the truth.

"Munson said I must have broken security."

"When did this happen?"

"The next day, when I reported the message. That's why I went down there. I considered it an emergency."

Kolar ignored the implied excuse. "With the woman?"

"It was cover. Leonila arranged for me to meet her; I brought her along to see Leonila. I thought it all added up." The explanation came easily and still sounded wooden. Kolar's tight gaze momentarily slipped away, troubled by the poverty of the thing, then locked on Draeger again.

"We'll come back to that. I want to know every word of your talk with Munson, what notes he took, why he never informed us of his evaluation."

Draeger took them back further, starting with the courier's failure to make his drop signal. He told them of the scene with Munson and omitted none of his own feelings. Kolar and Cindy listened, stolid, until Draeger half-believed he could see suspicion emanating from them, waiting to engulf him. When he had to stop, he added a postscript. "I've been honest with you, and I was honest with Munson. I don't want to find myself depending on your mercy, Kolar, because I don't think you have any. I'm as good at this business as you, understand? And I'm honest!"

Kolar drained his glass. "I'll find out if you're honest, whatever the hell that means. Don't think you're as good as I am, though. You're an excellent technician, but you've never had to do what infantry does, so you can't know if you're as good as I am. Frankly, I doubt it."

Cindy said, "Carl, you're doing it again. Why attack him? We have no reason to doubt him."

"We have reason to doubt everyone. His best source, one of the best in Asia, believes himself compromised and refuses to use a preplanned escape route. His Control suspects him and disappears, leaving his wife dead in a suspicious accident. I'll get to the bottom of it, maybe prove he is innocent. But if he expects to survive in this business, he better learn about protecting himself more positively."

Cindy looked to Draeger, and he was ready, caught her movement. For a moment he saw only the shock in her expression but under that her facial muscles built microalterations that revealed fear, then determination, and finally a marble polish that denied further access.

He wondered if that last act wasn't more of a confession than all that had gone before. She would persevere. In spite of his own situation, he asked himself if she committed herself so completely to Kolar's program because of political or sociological orientation or if success alone was enough to pull her along.

He veered away from that, wondering more deeply about himself. What had she been able to observe in him? Fear? Oddly, there was little of that, although he had no doubt Kolar would ruthlessly strike down anyone who jeopardized his operation. He hoped they'd seen the equivalent of Cindy's determination. That was what he felt most, and it surprised him. He was no stranger to anger, nor was he inclined to accept a threat with equanimity. Presently a cold objectivity held him aloof from other feelings, and he realized what he wanted most was to prove he was right. Not merely innocent of any charges, but right. And he wanted to prove it because he wanted to face Kolar with it and use it like a club. And that went for the woman, as well. No matter she'd spoken up for him, she was Kolar's creature.

He looked at her, still curious to know if she would always migrate into the orbit of the powerful. It didn't seem likely. There was an air of self about her, an immense psychic strength.

Kolar was rising slowly, painfully, a man lifting years and cares. Cindy watched him with concern, and when the older man noticed, he frowned and came erect swiftly. Draeger moved toward the door. They followed, stopping abreast of him.

Kolar said, "Right now you can't make up your mind if you hate me or despise me. Probably both. I can't afford the luxury of caring. There've been times when I didn't like myself very much, and that makes it hard to be terribly concerned about someone else's views. I'm going to find out why you're being followed and why this net and its assets are so dangerously jeopardized. Then I'll eliminate the problem. That's my function, Glen, to keep the unit operational. Only that."

"Saves you a lot of thinking, I guess."

Cindy was scandalized. "How can you say a thing like that? Don't you know him? Haven't you understood anything he's said? He suffers the torments of hell."

Kolar patted her shoulder and made soothing sounds, drowning out her protest.

"I think a great deal," he said, one side of his mouth lifted in a half-smile. "A great deal, indeed. Right now I'm thinking we're a very disparate group to be off on such a hunt, but I believe it'll work out. I don't hate you at all, you see, and that means we can function."

"Another of the luxuries you can't afford? Hating?"

Kolar's laugh boomed from deep within, erasing much of his weariness. "Wonderful! What I hoped you'd understand. I didn't think you'd be hard-nosed enough to make a point of it. Glad you did."

He took Cindy by the arm and escorted her down the hall, brisk pace matched by a continuing chuckle. As soon as the elevator doors closed behind them he winked at her, but it wasn't until they were on the street outside that he finally spoke.

"He is a good man, you know." He squeezed her elbow.

"I didn't overdo, did I?"

"You were excellent. Came to his rescue exactly on cue. You'll be as good an actress as you are an accountant."

"I wasn't acting all the time. The hardest part was keeping my mouth shut at all. You were pretty rough. After all, he's the one who told us about the friction with Munson."

"He's also the one who thought I knew it already. He's the one who fired the safe. He's very clever, Cindy. Tougher than he lets on, possibly tougher than even he knows." Kolar coughed, changed the subject. "I hope you appreciate the seriousness of this situation. I can't call for the Justice Department or Big Brother's counterintelligence people to break this open for us. Those are the rules. They don't know us. Not at all."

Cindy shivered despite the leaden heat of the night. "All those years wasted."

"Not so bad as all that. We're not dead yet. Which is probably a good thing, speaking for the man following us. *Don't!*" His hand vised on her elbow hard enough to make her gasp, but it stopped her from turning around. In a conversational tone, Kolar said, "We have to cross the street up ahead. You'll see him when we check for traffic. Actually, I'm rather pleased he's there. It's late to be walking these streets, even if this is a nice area."

She stared at him uncomprehendingly, and he said, "Well, he certainly can't mean us any harm or he'd be a great deal closer, wouldn't he? And if he means us no harm, I'm sure he's not going to relinquish us to someone who does. You have to learn to take what blessings you find along the way, my dear. Any obstacle can be an asset."

Still stunned, she said, "You really are mad. Do you know who he is? Or why he's there?"

"Unfortunately, no and no. But it'll all fall into place."

They were at the corner, and he smiled crookedly at her hurried glance down the street and the way she immediately leaned against him while they crossed. "I saw him," she whispered. "Right back there!"

Kolar directed her to the next curb, preparing to cross Ayala. There was a burr of distraction in his voice. "Of course he's right back there. He has to keep contact with us, after all. Poor devil's obviously alone on the job. Good to know the opposition's undermanned, too. Here we go! Before that bus coming gets up to speed! Quick!"

The man following was forgotten as she was propelled into the street. Kolar clamped her arm to his side, keeping himself between the vehicles and her. She pulled against the grip in an automatic resentment. As she did, a jeepney, horn blaring, flashed its lights and swerved around them. She decided it was wise to keep Kolar where he was.

At the dividing strip in the four-laned boulevard, Kolar changed sides, punctilious about who should be run over first. They launched themselves again. A decrepit truck shuddered past, its diesel exhaust aimed directly at waist level. The driver shifted gears, and the gush of greasy hot soot made her reel. She was still coughing when she half-stumbled over the curb to the safety of the sidewalk.

Kolar cleared his throat before speaking. "I try hard not to judge other people's customs, but I'll never understand why idiocy on a public thoroughfare has to be considered an inalienable right. And that damned truck was murderous, absolutely murderous."

Cindy dabbed at her eyes with a handkerchief. "I expect to be paid extra for all this," she said, and Kolar laughed.

"No combat pay in this outfit," he said. "Incidentally, our man is watching from the other side. He's betting we're headed directly for the hotel. We'll discolor his evening."

Before them stretched the several-acre parking lot of the Makati Commercial Center. The modernized bazaar, dozens of small shops enclosed in a wandering modern brick complex, was directly on the other side of the massed cars. Rustan's department store rose to the right, with its enamellike facade of black and turquoise. Crowds streamed through its bright, yawning entrances. Looming over the square from the left stood the Intercontinental Hotel, its position on a small hill a conscious supremacy. It gleamed assurance from its multiple windows and the porticoed entry.

There was a building in the center of the parking lot, open to the night. It reminded Cindy of a suburban bus stop, except this place was illuminated. A group of men lounged around and in it. Several of them were already aware of her approach, enjoying the proximity of such blond beauty. Their admiration was more than open, it was conjectural, and she was suddenly more aware of them than the lone man behind her. A noise from inside interrupted some of the staring, and she saw that an old man on one of the benches was becoming the center of attraction. He sat like a cellist, with an obviously homemade musical instrument resting on the ground in front of him. It was long and thin, a stringed instrument, and she was amazed to see that the strings led across a fat pink balloon. The old man stroked a bow across the thing and made music. The tone was an eerie effect that sliced through the rumble of vehicles with insectlike insistence. When she turned from the scene, her gaze was pulled to the hotel. The windows, each precisely the same size, suddenly made her think of the multiple lenses of a fly's eye. The portico contributed to the impression, became a jutting mouth, the doors mandibles ingesting bits of food and rejecting others.

Kolar said, "We've given our man enough to talk about. He'll go back and report we stood in the middle of a parking lot and listened to an old man play a weird musical instrument and then walked directly into the hotel. I wish I could be there for that."

Cindy turned to him, glad to have a reason to stop looking at the building. "What's that mean?"

"His story sounds rather strained, don't you think? He'll spend a very unpleasant hour or so explaining he didn't make it all up."

"I'm surprised. After almost five years I learn you've got a real mean streak."

He considered it. "Yes, I do. Occasionally. I want to make trouble for this man, enough to get him chewed out. It'll nick his morale, and that's good for our side. But your observation really reflects back to Draeger."

She opened her mouth to protest, but he was already leading the way across the street between the hotel and the parking lot. She wasn't so sure of her agility she felt free to debate and dodge simultaneously. On the sidewalk leading up the ramp to the doors he gave her no chance to interrupt.

"I'm leaning on Draeger, yes. He's about the best we have at what he does. And I'll be leaning on you, too, as this goes on. You'll come out with a different view of yourself, believe me. If that's mean, so be it. I find out what breaks and what doesn't."

A shift of wind brought a wisp of the old man's music, a rising skirl that struck and died in less than two steps. It was enough to send her forward so quickly the doorman was hard-pressed to do his job and get out of the way.

# ■  CHAPTER 17  ■

Draeger watched Cindy hurry inside and wondered what Kolar could have said to make her spurt ahead that way. He had no time to dwell on it, because the man following them was moving again. Trailing him had been easy, almost too easy. He was either very amateur or extremely confident. Not once had he checked to see if anyone was, in turn, following him. The failure to do so still worried Draeger, and he looked around nervously to be certain he was alone. He permitted himself a small smile as he thought that dealing with amateurs in this business was on the order of dealing with drunks. One never knew what the hell they might do next, and it was nerve-racking.

The man in the parking lot made his way back to Ayala and threaded his way through the vehicles with the skill of a *naturale*, a genuine Manilan. By the time one acquired that combination of confidence and gymnastic skill, the home in the provinces was a thing of the past. Either that, or one grew up in the city and exercised those qualities as a birthright.

This one hurried past Draeger with his shoulders hunched. After a decent interval, Draeger fell in behind him, convinced he could lead, if he felt like gambling a little bit. The man was as obvious as a candle in the night. He'd watched Kolar and Cindy, put them to bed, was headed home for his own well-deserved rest, and nothing was going to stop him. On arriving at Draeger's building, he positioned himself to check the window. His quarry, meanwhile, examined his watch and complimented himself on his foresight. In ten minutes the timer in the living room would turn out the lights there, and the bedroom light would come on. In five minutes more, that would go out.

Fifteen minutes later the man on station stepped out of his shadowed spot and stretched luxuriously. He passed within fifteen feet of Draeger on his way back to Ayala Boulevard. Draeger followed. At the curb the man immediately flagged a passing jeepney. Draeger saw a taxi making its way toward him, mentally crossed his fingers, and trotted out of hiding. He could only hope the headlights and the tail's own carelessness would provide the cover he needed. As soon as he was inside, he leaned across the back of the seat and pointed at the jeepney.

"You see that jeepney—the one that says 'Pasay City Playboy' on the mudflap?"

The driver slowed, turning to stare at Draeger. "Who are you?"

Draeger showed him a sheaf of twenty-peso notes. "Hey, I'm not interested in trouble, man. All I want to do is find out where he's going. No problem."

The taxi picked up a little speed, and the driver moved his eyes to the front again. "You sure? Nobody's watching you while you watch him, nothing like that?" He lurched forward to catch a light, insuring the jeepney didn't escape. Draeger thought of the carelessness of the man in the jeepney and was glad the taxi driver wasn't in the surveillance business.

Draeger answered, "I won't even be getting out of the taxi."

A thick-fingered hand bent back over the seat. Draeger dropped the money in it, and the man said, "Why you after him?"

"Personal matter. Family."

Immediately, the taxi slowed, and the man dug in the pocket where the money had gone. "I don't get in no family stuff," he said, and Draeger had to lean forward to push away the hand.

"I told you, no problem. I see where he goes, and you bring me back to the Makati parking lot."

"OK. But that's it, right?"

"Right."

Secure in his knowledge of the rules, the driver threw himself into his job. He jockied and jostled at the traffic lights to insure a maximum two-car distance between himself and the jeepney. At one point a man swung out of the vehicle, and he pointed excitedly, caught up in the hunt. Draeger assured him it was the wrong man and identified the one he was interested in. The driver nodded sagely.

"Not a good-looking man. He a thief?"

"I think so." The driver's eyebrows went up, and Draeger added, "He's a bad man. I think he's a thief, but I don't know for sure. Listen, you have a family?"

The driver nodded, knifing between two other taxis and tolerating the angry horn behind him with the condescension of a bishop. Draeger gulped and continued. "You have any sisters?"

Another nod.

"She have any kids?"

The arc of the nod increased, became more than agreement, moved into approbation. He understood, lectured. Today's kids, they had no values. While he embroidered his theme, Draeger watched the jeepney. When it slowed to stop by a Mobil station everyone got out. The taxi swept by before Draeger could give the driver instructions. They proved unnecessary.

"That jeepney, he has to stop here," the driver explained. "The riders, they catch another one if they go on. I got our man in the mirror." He frowned at the reflection. "I bet I know where he goes. That fellow's a Tondo man, I think so."

"He might be," Draeger agreed. "I told you he was bad."

The driver gestured. "Tondo's not so bad as before. Still plenty bad, but not like before. Uh! There he goes!" The taxi leaped away from the curb, the tassels around the windshield bouncing hysterically. Underway again, the driver returned to his dissection of modern youth.

A few minutes later he half-turned to grin at his passenger. "I told you. Tondo." He thrust his chin at the vehicle. "Stopping now. Our man getting off. You watch, he crosses street here, goes off there somewhere.''

Draeger watched the man do as predicted, but he was met before he could leave the main street. The taxi stopped at the curb across from them, and the driver winked, saying, ''No parking here, but don't worry. I got a bad engine.'' He was under the hood in a moment, leaving Draeger to watch the meeting out the back window. The two men who'd intercepted the new arrival stood apart, not quite flanking the man. It was a position that made it impossible for him to attack both at once, and Draeger wished he knew if it was environmental or hereditary. They spoke first, and then the surveillance man answered at length. When he was done the other two exchanged looks, spoke again. The head and arm gestures suggested they were less than satisfied with what they'd heard.

The man spoke earnestly, and when he finished, one of the listeners turned abruptly and left. The surveillance man went next, and the third brought up the rear. They entered an alley, disappearing in the narrow gap the way sea creatures slip into coral interstices that seem to have no dimension until the body of the animal lends it credence by utilizing it. Draeger kept his eyes on the place, full of the irrational notion that if he looked away he'd lose it. The driver managed a U-turn and slowed as they passed it. A scrawny chicken on a string looked up at Draeger, the startled round eye curiously appropriate. Beyond the bird, up the alley, children scurried back and forth in a darkness split into a haphazard patchwork by lights from windows and doors. A shallow stream meandered down the center. The night failed to eliminate the noisome stink of it, but the lights turned it into a freeform channel of silver that sparkled cheerfully when the children shattered its surface. A baby complained somewhere, and a dog concurred until his efforts ended in a sharp yelp. The three men were not to be seen.

Draeger was satisfied. He, too, had been certain his man would head for the Tondo. Munson had been funneling money to an organization, and Kolar had guessed it was a gang. Tracing the man to the Tondo added evidence, strengthened the possibility.

Munson. The thought of him made Draeger ache. He surrendered himself to the motion of the taxi.

*The fight had been building for weeks, probably months, without*

*either of them being aware of it, the way animals react to spring
when there's still snow on the ground. And then it happened. Mrs.
Crefeld yelling at Jimmy for talking in class and his own choking
inability to hold back the laughter at Jimmy's scarlet blush. The
pushing and shoving in the hall. When school was out, meeting
across the street in front of the candy store. Scared. Trying to
apologize without looking afraid. Jimmy wasn't too bright but he
knew fear when he saw it, and he banked on that and the first good
punch to win his fight. Damn near made it, by God. Never'd been
knocked down like that before. Didn't feel nothin', just sat there
tryin' to understand why I was on my ass. Thought I'd never get up.
Did, though. Pain started then, blood comin' out o' the goddam lip
like piss out of a horse in the mornin'. And ol' Jimmy's face when I
put up my hands. Best moment o' high school, I reckon. Put paid to
that sonofabitch, that's a fact. Good ol' boy, Jimmy.*

"Mister?" The driver was worried.

Draeger pulled himself out of his slouch. "Sorry. Thinking." He
got out. The driver continued to look concerned as he accepted the
fare and tip. He asked, "Mister, you American?"

Draeger nodded, then quickly, "My sister's married to a Filipino."

"I hope she's happy."

Draeger lied into that good will, hating to do it. "I'm sure she
is."

"We like Americans." The man was twisting the knife. "Like
you, worrying about family. We like to see that. Maybe not good
Christian way to be, but lots of Americans, they think like we
do—know how to get even. Good luck to you."

Draeger stared after the taxi until it was lost.

The jet lumbered overhead, silver and white, the tail decorated
with the twin sails of Philippine Airlines. It ran into wisps of cloud
as it gained altitude, and its vast bulk seemed to be moving so
slowly there was a suggestion of menace in the way the flimsy
tentacles clutched at the wings. The howl of the engines denied any
argument, however, and the plane moved away with the deceptive
speed that never failed to intrigue Draeger.

He shifted his position on the bench, and a huge pigeon coming in
for a landing in front of him shied, flaring its wings in a braking

fan. The maneuver dropped it far short of its intended site, and it cocked its head to study him with gentle accusation. When it was satisfied the disturbance was truly accidental it walked toward the feeding area, turning once to utter a rumbling coo. The sound amused Draeger. It was by far the deepest pigeon call he'd ever heard, which was as it should be, because the pigeon was the size of a large duck. The coo was the *basso profundo* of all pigeon-dom.

Cindy approached from the right, following the gravel path. He was hidden from view and studied her while she walked. She wore brown, slacks darker than the nearly beige blouse, a single diamond on a neckchain the only jewelry accent. Like the coloration of some of the birds in the huge aviary, she was obvious when moving and tended to blend in with the background when she stopped.

He smiled at that thought. She would never really blend into the background. She was uncommonly beautiful. It puzzled him that she had found her way into the intelligence business and how far she'd progressed. The thought registered as highly discriminatory even as it took form. He watched her more closely, driven now by curiosity and a nagging sense of guilt.

The walk alone should have told him she was different. She moved with a deliberate grace, each step as firmly placed as the period at the end of a sentence. When she saw a thing of interest, she looked at it. There was a concentration and intensity that marks people who make their own judgments. Whole areas of the aviary were scanned and specific points selected for closer inspection. He imagined her reviewing his reports. It was a sobering thought.

A string of customers approached from an intersecting path. She noticed them, made room for them. It was a very normal action and, combined with her manner as the situation developed, revealed more to him than all his other observations. The strangers passed close enough to brush her, and he thought at first she reacted as if they were invisible. He corrected that, however. It was as if she were invisible, as if a person could touch her and never be sure it actually happened. Nor would she ever acknowledge the contact unless by deliberate choice.

It was a social mechanism common to many Oriental societies but rare in the West and almost unheard of for an American. Even when evidenced as clearly as Cindy's behavior, it differed from its Eastern counterpart. The packed populations of that part of the world learned centuries ago how to enforce an air of privacy around themselves. It is perhaps the ultimate adaptation by man to his normally catastrophic need to mass with his fellows.

The Western variant is forming, and Cindy was exhibiting an aspect of it as she covered the last few yards before she would see Draeger. Her grace, her assurance, her unique gestures—all those things so clearly visible identified her as herself. She was individual and would be, no matter the numbers around her. In an Oriental culture that is accepted, and each individual contributes to the separative power of each other individual. The West has yet to learn that. As a result, Westerners project an enforced individuality, an intense loneliness generated from within. There are those who refine the capability beyond normal limits. They create an unseen force that repels, creates more distance than separation. It is outward rejection as opposed to inward removal.

Her greeting smile was pure pleasure. "What a wonderful place to meet! It's enchanting! How many birds are in here?" She waved at the overhead netting as she sat beside him. The pigeon poised to take off, eying her warily. The movement drew her attention. "What's that one?"

Draeger pointed at a picture in the brochure. "I think it's him, a Nutmeg Imperial Pigeon. Either that, or it's a moose with feathers. I can't be sure."

She laughed, relaxed, a tourist enjoying company and sights. Still smiling, she said, "We got your message this morning. Carl says to congratulate you on the countersurveillance. He spotted the tail, but he never saw you. He was quite pleased about that. You shook your man this morning?"

"I'd hardly be here otherwise. Where is Carl?" It came out harsher than he meant.

"We have other assets he wants to check with." One eyebrow moved a fraction, a signal that the subject was sensitive. He nodded, and she relented enough to add, "He wants to learn what he can about the gangs, see if he can get a handle on Munson's dealing with them.

"And you?"

She looked at him quizzically. Beyond that, though, he saw her defenses going up. The chin tilted, the eyes narrowed. Changes he couldn't categorize altered her entire manner, cloaking the initial openness. Without knowing how it happened, he was faced with a change. He bulled into it.

"Where do you fit in? Are you supposed to keep me out of trouble?"

"I'm supposed to give you a message. I've done that. I'm also supposed to debrief you on your relationship with Egg Roll from the first contact through your last discussion with Munson."

"Who the hell are you? Why should I tell you anything? What's Kolar think he's doing?"

"He's running the best collection effort in the country. And you'll talk to me because he wants it that way." She pushed toward him. The humid air of the miniature forest condensed the scent of her, the cosmetics, the soap, the femininity. He waved at it irritably. She misinterpreted the gesture. "I'm not going anywhere until I've done my job. You're not the first man to doubt my qualifications, and you won't be the last. I went through the same training you did, and I was the best. I was operational in South America, good enough to get moved up in the organization. I work for Carl because I'm good. If you can't handle that, too goddammed bad about you."

He got to his feet, and the pigeon despaired of his constantly interrupted meal, lunging into the air with thudding wingbeats. From his perch he boomed another chiding coo. The diversion gave Draeger a chance to organize himself.

"I'll cooperate. Of course. It's more than the collection effort for me, you know. I've done all the right things, played by the rules. Now I'm suspected of everything in the book."

"You're not a suspect. No one thinks any of this is your fault, really."

He tried to smile at her and it hurt. It pulled muscles usually ignored, and his view of Cindy was restricted by eyes drawn narrow in a manner he was unused to. When he saw her reaction he was glad he was unable to see himself. He turned away, walking slowly. She caught up, and he started talking about Egg Roll, careful to look at the foliage, the ground, the birds—anything but her and the chance that the pain and pity might still be in her eyes.

They strolled and talked for hours, breaking for lunch at a restaurant close by. Draeger expected the meal to be a matter of cold neutrality, a truce in the constant probing questions. The questions did stop, but she surprised him by extending herself, obviously trying to help him unwind. His first instinct was to put the effort down as an attempt to soften him up, expose some flaw in his review. Slowly, reluctantly, he conceded his error. As determined as she was to guarantee his truthfulness, she was able to relate to him as a human being. The realization was a sunburst of relief.

They returned to the aviary. The break had come when he thought he'd go crazy if he had to repeat one more message text, remember any more conversation, think of anything dealing with that part of his life. Now he was refreshed, eager to go over it again, unafraid of the questions because he knew his answers were being treated fairly. It amused him to think that if she really did mean to put him off guard, she'd succeeded completely. He wanted to tell her that, and he turned to face her. Their eyes met, and he swallowed the comment, telling himself it could be misunderstood, could make her think he'd actually distrusted her. He didn't want that. The rapport between them was still fragile.

It was late afternoon when Cindy wearily lowered herself to yet another bench. She massaged her temples. "I think I've got it all now." She smiled up at him, rueful. "God, I hope I do."

"What'll you do now?"

Her eyes lost their tiredness, drilled directly at his. "I'll sleep on it. Literally. Sort of put it all on the back burner and let it simmer. There's too much to handle consciously, but the subconscious will keep turning it around and around, looking at everything you've said. Dates, times, places. It's all in there, matching up, disassembling, matching up again. If there's a bad connection somewhere, the alarm goes off."

"What if you make a mistake? What if the old subconscious slips?"

She tossed her head, and her hair shimmered when a narrow beam of sunlight struck above her ear. It made Draeger think of a spinning gold coin. She said, "It happens. I forget something or I remember things in the wrong sequence. Then I check it out again. The secret is to remember everything. Everything. Expressions, gestures, emphasis. Everything."

"It must be like watching a movie over and over."

"Right. At least with you it won't be all that painful."

He gave a wry smile and a mock bow. She laughed. "That didn't come out the way I meant. See, when you're trying to remember something, you squint one eye, the left, and you move that jaw forward. It gives you a lopsided look, but it's not as bad as someone who chews his nails. The worst was the man in São Paulo. He'd lie with a perfectly angelic smile, and he really had me coming unglued until I noticed he had a gesture, too. When the lies got really heavy he'd put his hand in his pocket and— Well, I think you get the picture."

He laughed with her; then, "I'm glad you think I'm an improvement. You do this a lot, do you?"

She got to her feet, headed toward the gate. "Whenever something breaks down, or when we think we've got a double or a fabricator. My primary function is business management of the firms we operate, but Carl uses me for—" As if she heard the expression on his face, she turned and took his hand in hers. "Oh, Glen, that came out wrong, too! What is the matter with me? I've said everything all wrong! I didn't mean to put you in with those other people! Please believe that!"

He said, "Don't let it bother you. Sleep on it, and it'll all clear itself up." He passed her, leaning out beyond the neat edge of the pathway.

"I didn't accuse you!" Her eyes blazed, and the gentling hand tightened on his forearm. He stopped and stared at it until she let go.

He said, "See that you don't accuse me. It's not your privilege." He paused, then, "I'm the one who should be apologizing. None of this would have happened if I hadn't thought of you as a woman for a few minutes."

Her hand flew up to slap him, and he grabbed it. For a moment they were frozen, held at distance by the force of the emotions between them. When his strength began to tell she let her arm go limp and settle. He released the wrist. Her eyes still smoldered, and she spoke in a subdued sibilance. "You miserable son of a bitch."

He pursed his lips, burlesque consideration. "I'm learning, Cindy. And while you watch, remember I'm learning from the best."

When he turned to leave she stopped him with her voice. He

turned to look back, and she instinctively brushed at strands of hair clinging to the dampness at jaw and neck. It was done before she could stop it, sickened that she might have given him any reason to think she cared how she looked to him. She said, "There's one more message for you. Carl says for you to arrange to get out of town for a while. He said you're drawing a crowd, and he doesn't want to have to worry about a team on him everywhere he goes."

"Am I being sent home?"

"No. And check with us—with Carl—before you leave."

He nodded without looking at her, holding open the door to the aviary so she could follow. There was barely time for her to slip through before he released it. She gritted her teeth and said nothing. Turning right, he moved to the small shops and interested himself in the orchids they sold. She swept past him.

Walking back across the Commercial Center her angry, long stride generated some whistles and constant admiring stares. Normally that didn't trouble her. This time it was painful.

Why was it so wrong to be a woman? Why was a woman supposed to be demeaned; why was an honest woman a bitch? If a man said something and it was an honest mistake, he could apologize and everything was OK. Let a woman do the same thing and she was a castrating harpy. That was the irony of it. The men yelling about castration, and they always went right for the crotch, blamed the woman's for all the trouble in the world. And when they weren't blaming it they were whistling at it like goddammed birds.

She glared at a particularly insinuating corner creep who continued to smile, but looked away. She wanted to spit.

Look at him, she thought. Gutless bastard. And Draeger's no better. Wounded pride! What's he know about wounds? Who gives a damn about his stupid macho pride? He never thought about mine.

She elbowed past a fat tourist, leaving the doorman to make apologies behind her. The crisp air-conditioned atmosphere plastered sweat-dampend clothes to her body. It was a clammy embrace, and she hurried to the elevator. Alone in the protective confinement she slumped against the wall and wished she had the strength to go ahead and cry and not care about it.

# ■ CHAPTER 18 ■

Pierce watched the hands shuffling the cards, thinking how hard they looked, not much more than bones. The unkempt grizzled beard added no bulk to the face, either. Munson grew thinner every day. He seemed to lose no strength. Indeed, he projected greater danger. The force in him was eccentric, however. It constantly failed to focus, reminding Pierce of a magnifying glass wavering to and from a point where it could hope to concentrate burning energy.

He could have accepted that, by itself, with no trouble. Unfortunately, when Munson did find a point of focus, it was Draeger. Then he lost touch with reality. Discussing the forthcoming Singapore move, he was smooth as ice. When he spoke of Draeger, he seethed.

Turning from the solitaire layout, Pierce looked out the window of his small house at the sea. It was reassuring, the waves soothing in their constancy. There was fine weather due. He wished he could say the same about Munson.

He murmured, and Pierce said, "What?"

"Talking to myself. Missed a play."

"Not a good sign." Pierce smiled.

Munson looked up from the game, hands poised on the table. They rested on the fingertips like spiders arched over cold ground. He closed his eyes in an abnormally long blink and opened them slowly. Without warning, he bared his teeth in a hungry smile. "I'm not crazy. Fanatical, yes, but not crazy."

Pierce shrugged, knowing a response was required. Munson accepted it.

"Hitler was crazy. Stalin was a fanatic. The difference is

uncalculated risk versus calculated risk. You know what Malraux said?' 'A break in the established order is never the work of chance. It is the outcome of a man's resolve to turn life to account.' That's what we are, Tony, men turning life to account. The sound of it! Poetry!''

"Danger," Pierce added dryly.

"We're equipped to deal with that. It's our strength!"

"Letting you eavesdrop on my conversation with that little bastard Cruz will be danger enough for me for this morning, thanks."

The subject soured Munson's mood. "I don't like the idea of his coming here the same morning Boy Angel gets back from Manila." He dealt more cards.

"You missed another play." Pierce pointed. "The red nine on the black ten'll uncover these down cards."

Munson swept up the game and shuffled. "I've got more on my mind than fucking cards, Tony. I'm not just playing games, you know."

"No shit." Pierce flopped onto one of the wicker chairs. "I've only got to run a hotel, come up with an excuse for not setting up Colonel Arroyo's log deal, stall his fucking terrier, Cruz, and hide you and your pet killer. And it wasn't me that suggested you sit here and screw around with the cards, was it?"

"Testy, testy." Munson laid out the new game. His grin was wider, and he raised his eyebrows in mock surprise. The gaunt face rejected the inner attempt to lighten the atmosphere, branded it a lie. "You're tense."

"Damned right. You saw this Cruz. He's tough."

"So are you, so are you. You'll handle him. He may even turn out to be an asset to us. He's like me, a fanatic."

The phone rang and Pierce answered, then, "Send him over." He hung up, turned to Munson. "He's on his way."

The taller man rose from the sofa, craning himself upright. He scooped up the cards, pushed magazines around to eliminate the large cleared space. Standing still, he pivoted his head, searching. When he was certain there was no sign of his presence, he moved quickly into the bedroom and closed the door behind him. Pierce stood by the front door, waiting. In a few minutes he opened it and looked down the path toward the hotel, frowning. Cruz was just coming into view, moving at a pace that should have had him at the door long since. Pierce, caught outside, could only wave and fidget, wondering what caused the delay.

Cruz told him as soon as he was close enough. "I hope I didn't keep you waiting. I looked around the building before I came over. Wanted to see your pool and the bar and so on. You've got a fine place here. Doing good business, too."

Pierce stepped aside and Cruz entered, stopping just past the door. "Ah, this is the way to live!" He was animated, in constant movement. "I've always liked rattan furniture. When I was in the States I used to see it and get terribly homesick."

Unprepared for such volubility, Pierce covered surprise by silently waving Cruz to a chair. Only after he was seated did he think to agree. "The same thing's happened to me. Some detail reminds you of a whole section of your life."

"That's it. Strange, the mind. Full of tricks and mysteries."

"Which is it that brings you out here to look us over, Captain? Tricks or mysteries?"

Cruz was startled, then laughed hugely. "That's the trouble with being in my business. If I was Colonel Arroyo's Supply Officer, you wouldn't give my visit a thought. Let the Intelligence Officer come around, though, and everyone smells trouble."

"You're just another tourist today?"

"That's me. Of course, you know I'll file away everything I see or hear. Hell, that's my job. But I'm not out here to try to catch you smuggling or anything. Should I be?"

Pierce knew the line of his cheekbones was glowing. Cruz laughed again, enjoying himself. "Oh, Mr. Pierce, you'd be a terrible criminal. Your face would give you away every time." Then, like mercury slipping away, the laughter was gone and the quick features were apologetic. "But you're not offended, are you? I certainly wouldn't want that. I've made a very bad joke?" He ended the sentence on a rising note, making it a question.

"Not at all. None of us is so honest we're not guilty of having something to do with smuggling around here. I've got some batik I know came from Indonesia and some old brass from down around the Sulus that I don't think I'm supposed to have. That kind of thing."

Cruz winked. "I've got some of that batik myself. And now we're on the subject, I'd appreciate it if you'd keep your eyes open for anyone who looks suspicious. People like you can be a big help to us."

"Me?"

"Oh, absolutely. The men who deal with the rebels and bandits move in the very best circles, Mr. Pierce. They talk about the poor working people and improving the standard of living for the masses, but they do their business from hotels like yours. There are people who believe them, and there are people like me. We fight and kill each other in alleys and forests and swamps. The people who sell the guns live next to air-conditioners and push-button televisions. Did you know there is much timber cutting going on just a little south of us, right now?"

"How can that be? There's a lot of rebel action there."

"That's the trouble. The rebel bands cut the trees. They damage the young growth, too. Then the peasants come and burn what's left. We call them *kaingineros* because the cut-and-burn agriculture is *kaingin*. So the rebels have money for guns and the peasants have farm land. The land will raise two, maybe three, crops, and it's useless. Then the peasant has no land. The nation has no forest. The rebel still has his gun. Pretty soon men like me will be fighting other men like me only because we don't know how to stop. God knows there will be nothing left to fight for."

"It sounds very bad."

Cruz looked past Pierce, out at the sea, while he pulled a cigarette from the pack in his shirt and lit it. There was no ashtray, and he held up the match like a display item, smiling. Pierce hurried to get one. A tightness was settling in at the back of his neck. Cruz had been the soul of propriety until now. There was a suggestion in his manner, a tentative advancement of authority. With the match disposed of, he continued speaking. "We are a rich, beautiful nation, destroying itself, being destroyed by others. Do you know any Moslems?"

Pierce started. "Yes. I know a few. We have some working here."

"I couldn't be sure you'd know them that well. Sometimes people don't know as much about their employees as they might. I should have known you're not that kind. That's not my style either, but with me it's a fault, not a virtue, you know?''

"I understand what you mean.''

"I thought you would. How many Moslems?''

"Six, I think. Yes, six.''

"All guards?''

"Yes. Why, is it important?''

Cruz flashed the white teeth. "We have some Moslems making trouble a few miles from here. Any of them with a weapon is important. Do you have many foreigners here?''

- This time Pierce was better prepared for the shift in direction. "Most of our guests are foreign. Captain. What's on your mind? You think they're armed too?''

Laughing at the small joke, Cruz looked away too slowly to hide the flame of anger that danced in his eyes. He butted the cigarette, and the ashtray rattled from the force. He said, "An American has disappeared, up in Cebu. Everyone's been asked to look for him. I thought you might have heard some rumor, some gossip. His name was Munson. Lived in the Philippines a long time, longer than you, even. His wife and driver were killed, and he's disappeared.''

"An automobile accident?''

"Oh, no. An explosion. You've heard nothing?''

"I'd remember, I'm sure.''

"Yes.'' Cruz contemplative. "Yes, you would. You remember Colonel Arroyo's visit, when we met?''

"Yes.''

"I don't like him, and he keeps telling me what a wonderful friend you are. I'm glad the Colonel brought me with him because now I know you. I can dislike you and not have to wonder if it's my job influencing me.''

Pierce was too startled to be anything but defensive. "Dislike me? I haven't done anything—''

"Someone told Colonel Arroyo I was sent to his staff because of the corruption in this area. He didn't ask if it was true. He went direct to Manila by phone to get me transferred. It embarrassed him a lot when they said I'm to stay.''

"What's that have to do with me?''

"I have to ask myself why he trusts you and doesn't trust me.

You see what I mean.'' Cruz had an affection for making questions of statements and vice versa, Pierce noted. It was a marginal observation. Primarily, he was enjoying the rush of excitement and elated because a tinge of fear only charged it. It was a heady wine, and he overreacted.

''You know I'll tell him about this conversation. I won't be bullied by some pumped-up snoop.''

''You really don't understand him, do you?'' Cruz's amusement was inward-looking, as though he felt his smile was invisible to anyone else. ''Arroyo fears me now, and he should. I'll fight the terrorists and rebels. I'll go after him if I have a reason.''

Pierce was more interested in his own reactions than the exact points the Captain was making. Instead of numbing dread, he felt a wariness, an intensification of senses and instincts. A thing as insignificant as the scent of the Captain's hair dressing had an intense clarity. The peculiar hand gesture, the balling of the fist before suddenly releasing a finger to indicate an emphasized item was burned into him for permanent retention.

''I'm sorry you think the Colonel and me need watching. When you realize your mistake, there'll be no hard feelings on my part.''

Cruz's hesitation was as good as a fanfare for Pierce. The answer wasn't what he'd expected. Cruz knew of the other Pierce, the one who'd have blustered and denied and protested. This one stroked his moustache and watched, contained.

''Can I do anything else for you, Captain?''

Cruz shook his head. Pierce tactfully moved to open the cottage door. The smaller man recovered fully by the time he reached it. ''Oh, I almost forgot. Colonel Arroyo asked if you'd have dinner with him this evening. He'll be here around eight.''

''Fine. You'll join us, won't you?''

''Not this evening, thanks. I'll be around from time to time.'' He saluted and Pierce waved easily. Cruz never looked back.

Munson came out of the bedroom wearing a speculative frown. ''You handled the bastard pretty well. Almost blew it threatening him with Arroyo. You should've known he'd have Arroyo wrapped up before he'd mess with his friends.''

''He aggravated me.''

"I noticed." Munson's jaw worked, forming words he held back. Finally he asked, "What've you and this Colonel been up to?"

"Bits and pieces. Nothing to interfere with your plans."

"I'll be the judge of that."

"I don't think so. We're in this as equals now. You call the operational shots. But you're not Control. And I'm not a flunky. Never again."

Munson stared so hard Pierce bit his lip to avoid looking away. There was a feeling of delicate fracture between his teeth and then the sweet-salt taste of blood.

It's my blood, he told himself, and I know what's best for it. No more small-time black market. What was the old gag? Never steal anything small. All those years of stealing small and being scared. Now I have control, the knowledge that whenever something goes wrong I'll handle it. Bilongon was responsible for that. Someday I'll tell him what a favor he did me. Then I'll shoot the motherfucker right through the belly button.

Munson interrupted. "You're right. We have to cooperate, or we blow ourselves right out of the fucking tub. As for Arroyo, we'll forget whatever went on before. Still, you know he'll dump on you the first chance he gets. He's going to be scared shitless with that little ferret, Cruz, after him."

"Arroyo's a bigmouth, but he can back it up. He's tough."

"He's a type, a brawler, a bully. Cruz can outthink him before breakfast, and Arroyo knows it. Right now he's afraid. In a few weeks he'll panic. If there's any way he can screw us up, we ought to deal with him right now."

Pierce flinched. "Kill him? There's someone around him all the time."

"Not always."

"You talk like it'd be easy."

"Easy or difficult, if it needs done, we do it. If we have to take him out, let me know. Remember Kolar's bullshit about our final responsibility."

He laughed softly, and silence poured in behind it, thick with sober realization for Pierce.

He started the conversation again. "Cruz can't suspect I'm here. The thing about the disappeared American was a blind shot to rattle you. Still, the people from Los Angeles will be working their way down here to talk to you pretty soon, and we won't be able to hide from them. They're going to have to learn how I died, and soon.''

"Draeger."

Munson erupted from the chair. "What did you say? *Why did you say that?*"

Shamming unconcern at the twisted fury, Pierce held up a palm. "You need a patsy. He was around when you went underground. Who else could you set up?"

For a space of several heartbeats Munson didn't move. His breath pumped in and out in sharp puffs. When he sat back down it appeared to cause him pain. The creak of the rattan could have been his muscles. "I'm not setting him up." The protest was incredibly mild, contrasted with what had gone before. "I'm capable of being hard, even ruthless, but I'd never set up one of our own people. No matter what. This is a war, Tony, and I've been there. I'm sending him into a bad deal. But he'll have a chance. I'm not doing it out of malice. A soldier understands."

Very carefully, Pierce said, "When it's over, I know he'll understand the necessity," and wanted to snatch back the words at the instant change in Munson. He went from patient explanation to rage again, the thin lips stretching under the beard in a snarl, eyes blazing. Then, as quickly as the reaction had come, it was gone. He said, "Be sure of that."

Pierce was anxious to get the whole scene over with. "What do you propose?"

"Make the investigators think Draeger killed me."

"How?"

"I've got some papers, things I've written down. You go to Manila and find out who's running the investigation. Draeger'll know. You tell them I called you to Cebu about a year ago. I gave you an envelope and told you if anything happened to me it was to be delivered to our investigators. They'll ask you why it took so long to get there with the stuff, and you tell them you've been waiting for them to come to you. I don't know why the hell they haven't checked you out already, but it's a break for us and we'll use it."

"Sounds good. What if they want to come down here anyhow?"

"We'll have a problem warning me beforehand."

Pierce thought a minute, then, "Boy Angel can fly up with me. If it looks like anyone's coming down here, I'll get the word to him, and he can come on ahead. If you have to skip, head for Bilongon's camp."

"If that happens, Cruz'll notice I'm not around, and he'll be asking questions."

Pierce rolled exasperated eyes, the heavy brows arching dramatically. "You said it's a war, remember? Everyone gets to take chances."

Munson pursed his lips, massaging them between thumb and forefinger. The wet flesh and hair reminded Pierce of the torn prisoner in the bamboo cage, and he looked away. Munson, unaware, continued to consider for a few seconds longer. "It'll have to do," he decided, and slapped his hands together in a prayerlike attitude as he rose. "I hate this impromptu stuff. These goddammed cowboy jobs want to come apart with a bang. It's like falling down stairs. You keep thinking you'll catch yourself on the next bump."

"When do I leave?"

"The morning plane tomorrow. We'll spend today brushing up your story."

Pierce delighted himself with his own sureness. "Let's go get 'em."

# ■ **CHAPTER 19** ■

The two men stroked at the night-black water in unison, the paddles practically noiseless. An occasional wave caught the hull at an angle, and the slap drew reproving glances from the men, the way one stares reproof at a toe that has carelessly hooked the carpet.

They maintained an effortless rhythm that moved the slim vessel quickly, bits of phosphorescence marking each stroke, crazing the wake with a boil of eerie green dots that died in moments. Steadfast stars contrasted with the hard power of a distant fishing boat's glaring lamps. The prau was far too distant to be seen by anyone on the other boat. The paddlers hunched lower, nevertheless, bare torsos pressed forward over shorts-clad legs like jockeys whipping a lagging horse.

There was a single flame-colored light ahead of them, and only from the corner of the eye could the island be distinguished against the night. Cruz amused himself with that phenomenon, turning his head from side to side, looking with one eye, then the other. Preoccupied, he grew clumsy. The haft of his paddle rapped the gunwale. The noise was minor, but the man in the stern spat like an angry cat.

Cruz knew Ali had been waiting for just such an excuse. It would have been a shame to deny him such a simple pleasure. They had never been close, even as boys, and now they were on opposite sides of a civil war. He was as wild-eyed as his leader, Cruz reminded himself. It was dangerous to think of him as a boy.

The light was closer now. Cruz shifted his weight, eager to get out of the prau and dreading the return paddle back to the village where he'd left his clothes. And his weapon.

He pulled hard against the weight of the sea, feeling the tendons and ligaments of his back strain. Strength boiled in his blood, surged into his loins with a pressure that reminded him he was a man, full of living. The fragile light of the stars let him see the flexing wedge of muscle along his forearm. Beyond his arm the outrigger skimmed the waves, the sound a crackling hiss exactly like a knife splitting a gourd. He inhaled, stretching the act over four reaching, pulling strokes until his ribs threatened to crack. When he exhaled he was careful to do it silently and paid for his caution with a jolt of dizziness that almost made him bump the hull again.

Behind him, Ali sensed something out of the ordinary and made his spitting noise again. Cruz answered it with a sharp grunt.

Such an unpleasant man! And to no purpose whatever. A pawn. All men were pawns, one way or another, but it was especially maddening to see the good ones so badly used. And as a man, Ali was admirable. He was loyal, brave, honest—all the virtuous things.

He was also cruel and wrong. Would it be easier to think well of him if he were cruel and right? After all, there were things done in the name of every good cause that shriveled souls.

A new rhythm interrupted his meanderings. They were close enough to the island to feel the echoing mutter of the waves. It is not so much a sound as it is an awareness, a subliminal intensification of existing, identified sounds. Men who grow up in small boats, who know the sea as farmers know their furrows, will speak willingly of their ability to identify that awareness, but if asked to describe it, they will produce disorganized words and stare past the questioner. It is not rudeness, nor is it actual ignorance. It is understanding that they are being asked to sum up a lifetime, perhaps hundreds of ancestral lifetimes, in a few measured phrases. It is the sort of question they cherish and dread, because it marks them as water men and different.

They are men who comprehend aloneness as no others, and when questioned about things they will not or cannot answer, they retreat to that piece of the sea that is in their minds at all times, gently rocking, peaceful, a womb open to the sky.

Cruz was angry with himself because he had forgotten those things. He had been away too long, spent too much time in rooms where machines battered the air into cold submission and robbed it of its meanings. There had been too many class-hours, fat with the cataloging of men's sins and frailties, too little time learning to balance those things against other characteristics. If you knew a man, you decided to like him or hate him. If you only knew about a man, he was nothing.

No, that wasn't true. He was something. He was prey. When a man like himself set out to learn about another man, it was because that man must be caught.

Their paddling pulled them close to the island, the light from the lamp was brighter, the color stronger. Cruz could see the mat shields that kept it invisible from the flanks. As they watched, the light blinked out. The arrangement had been clear. The beacon would be visible only from a certain direction and only for a certain length of time. Cruz eased his bent legs, determined to avoid stumbling when he got out of the prau. It was one thing to provide Ali with an occasion to exert his authority but providing two such occasions was unthinkable. Cruz slipped over the side an instant before the bow hit bottom, using the bouyant rebound of the boat to advantage, pulling it up onto the beach in an uninterrupted skid. The waves were mere inches high, and the grating of the wood on the sand overrode their whisper. Cruz heard the splash of Ali's legs as he helped propel the prau the last few feet necessary to bring it completely out of the water. Men advanced on them, indistinct figures drifting soundlessly across the sand. When they were closer their identity proclaimed itself first in the metallic clatter of weapons and then in the pungency of oiled metal. They lowered their rifles into the hull and helped with the carry to the tree line.

One of the figures tapped Cruz on the shoulder and said, "This way," leading off through the coconut palms. The new-pewter gray of the trunks was reassuring in the almost total darkness, unfailingly visible. Lesser plants reached out of the blackness to snare him, their swishing disturbingly like laughter.

The sight of a small building ahead, dim light marking the line of closed doors and windows, stirred in his guts. This was, after all, a confrontation with one of his country's most wanted rebels.

The guide pushed aside the mat over the door and spoke too softly for Cruz to hear, then turned and beckoned the visitor inside.

Bilongon, shirtless, looked at Cruz and smiled, coming forward. They clasped hands. Cruz said, "It has been a long, long time, my friend."

"Many years," Bilongon agreed, finally releasing Cruz's hand. He moved to a low table, sat on the floor and gestured for Cruz to join him. A boy brought a tray with two glasses on it, iced fruit juice. Bilongon gestured, and the boy served Cruz.

"It is only *kalimansi* juice. Not what you are used to, I think, living in the cities, becoming an important man." Bilongon's apology was bantering, and Cruz answered in kind. "After so many years away from my people, I expected something better than fruit juice to celebrate my return."

"We prepared it especially for you. The fruit was picked by the prettiest girls on the island."

Cruz smacked his lips appreciatively. "That makes a difference. Now I can drink it and be happy." They smiled steadily, two old friends. Cruz asked, "And how is the family? Your parents? Abdul?"

Bilongon's smile lost a trace of its warmth. "My father is dead. An accident. Abdul was with him. He was injured, but he is better now." '

Cruz dreaded his next question. "A fishing accident?"

"A bomb. Government aircraft. Your government."

"I am sorry. Abdul was like my own brother, as well as yours. Your father was good to me."

"We have learned to expect such things."

"It need not be so."

Bilongon's stony composure shattered.

"You think not? Our homes are destroyed, our people are murdered, everything we own is stolen from us. Why should it not be so? We are Moslems, children of Islam, less than human!"

"Have I ever said that? Have I given you any reason to distrust me?"

Bilongon breathed deeply, regained his control. "Never. You are a friend of my childhood. You are not like the others."

"And that is why I came here, to talk to you, to tell you that there are others like me. We do not hate you, we do not hate Islam. The places being destroyed, the people who die, they are ours as much as they are yours."

"You are a Filipino. I am not. I will never be. We must be independent. Free."

Cruz nodded. "They told me you were like this. You know the government has promised autonomy to this whole region. Many of your friends have joined the government's effort."

"The weak have fallen from the true path. I will show them the way if I must fight alone."

"And if you win? What will you have? A tiny nation spread over dozens of islands, resources almost gone. The poachers have nearly destroyed the turtle harvest, even the forests are disappearing, sold to Japanese and Chinese merchants who practically steal them from you."

"We will not be enslaved any longer!"

"Those days are gone. There are Moslems in the government now, in important positions."

"There are many important men in the central government. One of them dropped the bomb that killed my father and almost killed the man you used to call your brother. Does that mean so little to you?"

Cruz damned himself for becoming angry. "That is a rude question. I will ignore it."

Bilongon rose, put his hands on Cruz's shoulders. "Forgive me. There has been much hurt." He sat down again, staring at the backs of his hands. The index finger of the right one trembled, the flutter of a blade of grass. "Believe me, my friend, many times I have wished I could stop fighting. Many nights I waken, blind in the darkness with the knowledge that I, too, have killed many fathers, many brothers. Life becomes very bitter, those nights. A man waits for the light of day the way a lover awaits his woman."

"I understand." Cruz sipped his drink, careful to make no noise to disturb Bilongon's thoughts. It would be important for him to think his way clear to the next subject himself. Cruz wanted desperately to suggest something else to talk about, but knew Bilongon would resent it as a condescension. He must fight back his own devils.

"What of you?" he finally asked. "What do you do now?"

It was time to speak very carefully, Cruz reminded himself, and sipped his drink once more to alleviate the sudden dryness of his mouth.

"You know I am in the Army?"

Something in his manner alerted Bilongon. His eyes grew wary, and the hands on the table moved delicately, coming to rest with the thumbs clamped to the underside. What had been a relaxed position was now defensive, the table held as shield or weapon.

Cruz continued, "I am on the staff of Colonel Arroyo."

Bilongon nodded slowly. "I had been told. I have been told you help supply information to him."

"People supply me information." It was out now, bright and stinking between them, fish guts on the sand. "I am responsible for all information in this area. People report to me and I report to the Colonel."

"You will tell Arroyo you spoke to me?"

"No. Not this time. I am here as your friend, not as a man in the Army."

" 'Not this time.' " Bilongon smiled. There was anticipation in it and cruelty. It reminded Cruz of the curve of a shark's mouth, waiting under jewel eyes that pinned a man against the sea's black depth.

Outside someone coughed, and a muffled conversation flared and died. The words were indistinguishable, but the tension was message enough.

Bilongon ignored it. "You have forgotten the most important information we have, that Manila itself was under the rule of a Sultan when the infidel Spanish came. You have taken all but this corner of that rule. We will have it for our own or die."

"The government offers you everything you need."

"Damn the government! They offer to let me live according to their rules on land that is ours!"

"They will fight you."

"Speak the truth! *You* will fight me."

Sadness threatened to overwhelm Cruz, and he had to push the words up from his soul. "I will. Not just me. Hundreds. Thousands. They will fight you with guns and bombs and ships. But I am the one who will beat you. I will find the traitor among your fighters and buy him. I will bring teachers to reestablish the old crafts and teach new ones so the people can work in honor and dignity. My teachers will make your children understand that neither God nor Allah wants them to die in His name. You will have to kill me or I will defeat you."

Beads of sweat dotted Bilongon's upper lip, a condensation of the misted hurt in his eyes. "I have never known if you were courageous or obstinate," he managed. Bravado creaked in his voice, and he paused, gathering strength. "I always felt stronger when you fought beside me, because I knew you never quit. The times we lost—ah, what beatings we took, because I was too wild to feel the pain and you were too stubborn to admit it! And when we won! What victories! When I decided to fight the government, I used your mind. I would ask myself how you would do a thing, and I would try to combine your thinking and my love of the battle. And now you're different. Perhaps you have out-thought me once more."

"We see the world differently. We have listened to other voices." Bilongon's eyebrows curved, and Cruz added, "You hear men who preach of your Islamic state, see it as the answer to all problems. I see them, and they don't seem very heavenly to me. And then I look at what so-called democracy has done for us, and I am sickened. Now I concern myself that the country is not divided up into separate kingdoms."

"It will fall into the laps of pigs like Arroyo."

"Colonel Arroyo." Cruz caressed the words. "Arroyo is an enemy to you. We both understand enemies. But I am not sure you understand about me and Arroyo. I am determined he will die."

Bilongon looked away, not wanting to see those eyes in a friend's face. "When you leave here you will be my enemy and I yours, but I cannot imagine one of us feeling this way about the other. It is—not normal."

Cruz said, "We speak of making war on each other, and you reprimand me for wanting to kill a common enemy. And I cannot disagree with your reprimand. Surely God, by any of His names, is mocking us."

Shadows of expression moved across Bilongon's face as he tried to decide if the observation was sacrilegious or accurate. He concluded it was both and asked forgiveness. The lamp flickered at his confused sigh. The two men fell silent. A moth danced too close to a lizard on the ceiling and was snatched from the air. Its struggles pulled the lizard's forelegs free of the thatch. The animal hung on grimly, the clenched back toes yielding in infinitesimal slippage. Mindlessly, the moth changed its thrust, pulling toward the ceiling. The lizard reacted with a speed that defied the eye, clamping its forefeet onto the thatch and simultaneously improving its bite. The flailing right wing was folded back across its thorax, rotated out of its socket and broken. Daggering teeth broke through the delicate webbing and penetrated the body underneath. The moth expired in a series of spasmodic tremors. The tiny crunch failed to disturb the thoughts of the two men below, and miniscule flecks of color fell toward them, dislodged scales from the battered wings. The mad ballet of the motes in the convection heat of the lamp was a cruel impropriety, as unnoticed as the death sounds had been.

Bilongon said, "There is the possibility we could be of some help to each other. I would not suggest we could solve our problems by cooperation. We have both gone too far for that. There is at least one point where we are in agreement, however."

"Now who is talking in circles? You are suggesting I betray Arroyo. You know better. When I destroy him, it will be with honor."

Half-smiling, Bilongon said, "Honor I leave to you. I will share in the gladness when he is gone."

Cruz lifted his eyes, watched Bilongon. "What do you know of the foreigner who owns the luxury hotel on the island, the one called Pierce?"

"Arroyo uses him for errands."

"What kind of errands?"

Bilongon shrugged. "I have enough to do worrying about where Arroyo sends his troops. I have no idea what he does with his messengers."

"Some of your people work for Pierce."

"No. They are Moslem, and they were part of my organization at one time. Now they are not. This life did not agree with them. They still know how to use weapons. They are guards."

Cruz grinned. "They must be very unusual men. They have no wives. They have no friends among the other staff. They never go into the city. I would think this life would be easier, in some ways."

Stiffly, Bilongon said, "I know nothing of that. I would welcome them back, but your lies have turned their heads.'

"Better turned than blown off."

"Stay out of our islands. No one will be hurt."

Cruz held up his hands, surrendering. "No more. A few more words, and we will be arguing again. We will talk of other things, better things. For a few hours, let us forget who we are and speak of who we were and who we hope to be, once there is peace."

Bilongon laughed. "We will find our peace in the grave. But we can pretend. We were very good at that, when we were young." He rose, gesturing at the door. "Come, eat. There are others here you will remember."

"Speaking of remembering, do you remember the time we pretended to go to class and went to town instead?"

"The time we met my father there? Could I forget? I hurt still!"

They stood together outside the hut, looking through the canopy of leaves to the greater, majestic canopy of stars above that. There was no moon and the closed door of the hut eliminated any light from that source, so the darkness suffered no stay in its claim.

Neither man spoke his thoughts while they waited patiently for their eyes to adjust fully to the night. They shared the companionship of savored experiences. Layered over that was the joint knowledge that the future offered no promise of anything to be treasured. One would have to know them as soldiers as well as friends to understand why, in the midst of so much love for what had gone before, they instinctively faced the east while specks of starlight picked up the desperation in their eyes.

■ **CHAPTER 20** ■

Morning infiltrated the camp with benign insistence, spurring increased activity. Voices hushed in the predawn darkness now rose in confident banter and joking. It was still a quiet camp because these were men who had learned long ago to be wary. The troops who occasionally pursued them through the forest were good, and the general attitude of alertness spiking the air was a grudging respect for that proficiency. Bilongon swept an arm in a proud gesture encompassing all of them.

"There they are, the best fighters in the Philippines. On equal terms, they are anyone's match."

"The government will never meet you on even terms. They will send more men, always more men. And worse, they will send machines. Machines don't bleed, they don't scream, they don't leave women and children to weep for them. Why let those things happen to these men?"

"We must. Islam demands it."

Cruz started to speak, and instead waved to Ali. He was reaching for Bilongon's hand to say good-bye when the entire camp stilled. One word leaped among the men like a spark.

"Helicopter."

Men trotted seaward and busied themselves with a prau. Others set about tasks, squatting to mend nets, pretending to work on one of the huts, and one brave soul climbed up on a roof and acted as if he was repairing the thatch. The largest percentage of the group simply faded into the forest.

The helicopter chuffed lazily past, keeping well out to sea. Bilongon stood on the ground, secure the fake village scene was sufficient camouflage. He said as much to Cruz.

"Do not make any unusual moves, and he will go on with his patrol. They always make me think of wasps. Nasty, self-important insects. They leave us alone if we give them no reason to sting."

"They come here often?"

Bilongon looked at him sharply. When he was satisfied the question wasn't an attempt to collect information for later use, he said, "The patrols are irregular and frequent. They have caught us by surprise a few times," he added bleakly.

As if on cue, the helicopter swung to its left and came back. The new observation was slower, close enough for them to distinguish the helmeted pilot. The sound of the blades muted when the machine was obscured by the trees. When it increased again, it was a different note yet, and Cruz realized it was coming at them from farther inland, intending to pass directly overhead. Bilongon looked worried.

"He has seen something," he muttered.

Cruz scanned the faces around him, remembering the talk around the fires the night before. That man there, puttering with the lashing on the outrigger. They had fished from the same boat, many times. And Abdulgani, always laughing, even now, as he leaned against a cart he was supposed to be pushing. Where was Salahuddin? There, acting as if he were cutting out copra. How many times had Salahuddin recited the life stories of his four young sons last night? At least once per son. And the helicopter was looking for them.

Cruz taught the class only a week or so before. He heard himself. "When we strike at the villages we make enemies of the people.

Imagine someone shooting at your own families. We must find and destroy the fighting forces. If they are living outside the villages they will have their own camps. How will you recognize them, tell them from the other villages?''

There had been no answer, and Cruz had despaired of people who rode machines through the air to make war. He looked at them and reminded himself he was afraid of flying, but these men flew and fought at the same time. He swallowed his anger.

"There will be no women and there will be very few, if any, children. If they are very cunning in the camps, they may even dress some men to look like women. It is impossible to make a grown man look like a child. If you don't see children, look again. And again. Never, *never* fire until you are certain you have a rebel camp.'' Men had exchanged looks at that point, and Cruz had swallowed yet more anger. Because he was from those islands, they thought he was being over-concerned. That was stupid. It was the way anyone of intelligence fought rebels.

It came over high, inland, banking slightly to give the pilot a better look, and continued on. The alerting sound of the blades repeated itself. The men looked to Bilongon, concern and confusion more apparent. The driving rhythm of the blades approached again. Breaking past the line where the camp ended and the forest started, it commenced a lazy circling pattern. Bilongon followed it, turning, shading his eyes.

"We have been very careful here," he said. "No one has ever fired at one of the helicopters. We have never conducted a raid near here, avoided foot patrols we could have destroyed. What has he seen? *What?*''

Cruz's throat ached. The rocket pods on the sides of the helicopter seemed to be aimed directly at him every time the pilot wavered in his slow circle. When he finally started to gain altitude again, he wanted to cheer. Pulling his eyes from the machine, he saw the same feelings on the faces of everyone else. He was smiling back to Abdulgani when the change in pitch came to him, the thudding impact of the increased blade speed an unmistakable threat. Those who had been looking up ran immediately. Those who had deluded themselves that the worst was over were forced to look up once more before doing the same. Gunfire snarled from the forest even as the chopper dove to the attack. The whoosh of the answering rockets seemed to last a long time before the first explosions lifted one of the huts in the air and slammed it back down on its side. Something dropped on the ground in front of Cruz as he ran for the cover of the forest. It was an arm, severed at mid-bicep and wrist. The flesh at the smaller end had curled back away from the bone in strips, all remarkably similar in width and length, forming an almost perfect flower. The obscene curiosity of it fascinated Cruz as he carefully adjusted his stride to pass over it. The rushing-water roar of another rocket strike failed to distract him, and he wondered what sort of blast would create such an unusual effect.

The helicopter made three more passes, each one setting another hut or two to hysteric shakes before inevitable collapse and flame. After the blast of each rocket salvo the bandsaw whine of fragments filled the air. Following that, the screams of wounded men flew between the sounds of burning huts and wildly firing small arms, the shrillness swooping and gliding with the fitful agility of swallows hawking mosquitoes.

On the fifth pass the helicopter slowed, clearly surveying the wreckage on the ground. A man hurried out of the forest, moving with a ridiculously preoccupied air over and through burning detritus. He skipped and changed feet like a skittish mare until he was clear of obstructions, and only then looked up at the helicopter. Cruz could only guess that he was obscured from the helicopter's vision. In any case, he raised his M-16 to his shoulder and took careful aim. It occasionally happens on a battlefield that one action attracts the attention of all the participants, and so it was with the man aiming from his exposed location. He squeezed off rounds methodically, one at a time. The crack of the weapon was almost overridden by the roar of the engine, which was exactly what he aimed for, as if incensed by its raucous blather. An infrequent pop from the forest merely underlined his lonesome attack.

Suddenly the engine screamed, a sound that raised the hair on Cruz's neck. His arms prickled. The helicopter was staggering in the air. Nose down, it flew seaward. About fifty yards from shore it mustered enough strength to flare briefly, settling with a battering splash. Before the pilot was clear, Ali was racing toward the beach. He called over his shoulder, and a second man pounded after him.

They had the prau launched in moments, throwing down their rifles, churning into the sea, vaulting aboard. Many survivors hurried to the water's edge to watch the prau's progress toward the struggling pilot. He waved his hands. Ali, from his position in the bow, waved back, shouting instructions to the man paddling in the stern. When they were a few yards away from the pilot, Ali stood and braced himself. The men on the beach made a sighing sound.

Ali brandished a kris, the waved blade like a steel flame. The pilot's screams drifted to them on the soft breeze. He turned on his stomach and thrashed at the water, making little or no progress because of the bulk of his clothing. Cruz remembered dreams. His calf muscles tried to cramp, and he bounced clumsily to limber them.

The aft paddler put Ali in perfect position, to the left and slightly behind the pilot, a helmsman positioning the harpooner. Ali dropped to his knees, the weapon aloft, bright as an offering. The pilot raised one hand in a useless defense. His last scream rose to a screech before it stopped abruptly. There was a moment of silence and later Cruz would half believe it lasted long enough for every heart on the beach to meld in a single, droning boom, like the great gong in the gamelan. Then the men cheered. An echo from behind was the shout from the wounded and those tending them.

Ali lifted the pilot's body by the hair. The knife slashed at the exposed throat. At each blow the watchers grunted in chorus, the power surging in their arms as surely as in Ali's. With the head dangling from one hand, he sat down and grabbed the body by the belt and they paddled for shore.

Cruz turned away and found himself face to face with Bilongon. The latter grinned. "He will trouble us no more. When he fails to return, his friends will be less anxious to come look for us."

"Perhaps. Do you really think it was necessary to kill him?"

"Ask your Colonel about the village that was 'searched' just two months ago. Ask him to show you the graves of the women and children who were the only people there when the troops arrived."

"I will stop those things. Will you stop this?" He pointed where Ali had thrown the pilot's head in the sand. One of the men walked up to it and spat. Bilongon spoke sharply and they backed away.

"Get him into the forest," Bilongon ordered. "We must leave here.

Others will be here very soon. Hurry!'' He turned to Cruz. "You can come with us or try your luck out there."

"I'll leave," Cruz said. "Is there another prau? This one has a great deal of blood on it."

"It is the only one I can let you have. What is a little blood? I thought you were a soldier, an officer." Bilongon drew out the last word.

Cruz answered patiently. "I have no papers. If I am stopped by government people in a bloody boat, there will be no argument."

"I have my men to concern myself about. Do what you choose. I must see to the moving of our wounded."

"I go, then. God be with you, old friend."

"May Allah protect you."

Cruz pushed the prau into the water and hurriedly sluiced some water into it to dissipate the clotting mess on its sides. A pinkish gray residue sloshed in the bottom. Gritting his teeth, he got the boat moving and jumped aboard. Bilongon watched him go, silhouetted against the blazing buildings. A column of dirty smoke boiled up behind him. Cruz waved once and waited. Bilongon turned on his heel and headed toward the forest.

A harsh shout pulled Cruz's head back to the beach. Ali was squatting in the water, washing his kris. Cruz turned his back and bent to the lines, raising the sail. It was more visible than a paddled prau, but anyone seeing him underway without a sail would be especially curious to know why. It would be safer to be seen. He settled back to steer, feet uncomfortably up on the sides, wishing the ugly puddle would dry.

The first inspection took place within a half hour of his departure. A coursing helicopter swerved from its route to hover and stare at him. It was a very helpless feeling. Cruz looked at the rockets in their pods, like wasps poking out of a hive, the blade-wind staggering his small craft. He glared at the pilot, pointed at his slatting sail. The pilot waved, spun his machine on its axis and resumed his patrol.

Cruz sucked air into starved lungs and continued on. Other helicopters scuttled along the shoreline of the island falling astern, an angry flock of five. A few minutes later the distant growl of machine gun fire and the crump of rockets ripped the quiet. Cruz pulled the sail a bit tighter, squeezing out as much speed as possible.

The island was long out of sight when Cruz experienced his second inspection. The plane wasn't a helicopter, but rather a semi-antique, propeller driven and slow. It came up from behind with an old dog's steady grumble. It appeared to Cruz it was adjusting its course to head directly over him. He watched more carefully for a few seconds, but it continued steadily, and he returned to the matter of steering the boat.

The engine noise grew decidely sharper. Cruz looked over his shoulder, and his mouth dried at the sight of the plane's nose-down attitude. Shaking fingers fumbled the halyard free to let the sail go slack before he slipped into the water. At that time the aircraft hadn't opened fire. He was only yards outside the beaten zone of the hail of bullets when it did.

The small prau squatted under the impact of hits, bucked like a living thing. Cruz stopped swimming, treading water with as little movement as possible. The second pass would concentrate on the man or the boat, and he wanted desperately for it to be the boat.

To his amazement, there was no second pass. The aircraft gained altitude and bumbled on its way. The old dog had not bared its teeth at a stranger, it had pissed on an insignificant bush.

The enormity of it enraged Cruz. He forced himself out of the water to the limit of his strength, screaming incoherent curses at the departing shape. He beat the water with his fists, the very unresistance of it a further frustration. At last, blinking back tears, he swam to catch up to the drifting prau.

She had weathered the storm in reasonable shape. There was only one hole of particular concern in the hull. He noted with grim interest that it was exactly where he would have been sitting. The mast had some nicks in it, and the gunwale up forward had a nasty chop out of it where a round had clipped it at an angle. A few minutes work with a rag eliminated any danger from the hole in the bottom, and a few tentative tacks proved the mast was still in working order. The new holes in the sail were no asset, but they didn't seem to be hurting much, either. He looked over his shoulder to check his bearing from the island, nervously scanning for any more planes before getting comfortable.

Within minutes he was calmed down. He attributed it to the soothing effect of the sea, then wondered if the importance of the fact might not lie in the calming itself, rather than the speed of it. So much violence, such senseless killing, and to what gain? Was Bilongon's intermix of religion and independence worth fighting against? Was he so evil he deserved to be destroyed, or were these scattered little islands so valuable that men had to die to control them? And not only men, but the very principles that govern men? Ali beheaded a man and a pilot strafed an unidentified figure in a boat. Acts of savagery. Which was worse? Did it matter?

He tried to think of something else, and Colonel Arroyo's features stuck in his mental vision. And the American, Pierce. There was the ultimate savagery. They were above the genuine killing, the walking with death. But they capitalized on it, ordered it done. Ordered it done. As if there was an unnavigable sea between men born to say, "Kill me that man," and the man who did the killing.

He spat over the side. The American and Arroyo probably saw this whole thing as an intricate, unpredictable game. If people died, that was unfortunate.

The more Cruz thought about it the angrier he became. He berated himself, talking into the emptiness.

"You fool. A man tries to kill you, and you get over it in no time. Now you sit here in your holey boat and get worked up over an American simply because he's a greedy whore's spawn. You really are going crazy."

The prau bobbed solemn agreement.

Hours later, Cruz was at peace with himself. The sea had claimed him again, enfolded him in the benevolence only the sea can conceive. He needed no eyes for the boat now. His body told him what it was doing, as it would tell him if he walked with a limp or if his stomach was upset. The sail pulled comfortably, and the boat conversed with the sea in comfortable sounds of rigging and wood against wood. At polite intervals the sea responded, hissing agreement or with the emphatic comment of a wave slapping the surface. Less frequently it made an audible chuckle that ran the length of the hull, sly, an elbow in the ribs. For the most part, he ignored the dialogue, half-hearing it like so much party conversation.

He reveled in what he saw. Where there were clouds, their

whiteness seemed to draw the contrasting blues of the sky and water to a competitive luminescence.

There was only one trouble with the sea. If it enfolded a man with its loving embrace, it could as easily and carelessly absorb him as it absorbed the rain. It was an insatiable affection, one a man must always surrender to in the end.

A movement to the right caught his eye. It was a bird, a small tern, white as hope. It soared along on the same general course as the boat, slipping aside on investigative forays, occasionally splashing into the water to rise with a tiny fish. One time it was close enough for Cruz to see the prey in the bird's beak, shining and twisting like trapped light. The bird juggled it until it was head-first and swallowed it.

They moved together for hours, man, boat, and the bird. The sun moved directly overhead and slanted to the west. Cruz took to complimenting the bird on especially graceful maneuvers and wondered if they might be seeking the same landfall. It was then he heard the thin cry. The boat and the sea continued their comfortable chat, undisturbed, but Cruz was troubled. He swept the vast space around him, seeking. It was another tern, and his companion answered.

Both birds approached each other confidently, then planed over the sea in loose tandem, separating, closing, separating again in a visual harmony, white bodies against multiples of blue.

Cruz was aware of the beauty and unsettled by it. He busied himself with improving the trim of his sail, forcing the boat to hurry its conversation, giving it almost an argumentative tone. Leaning into the rudder altered his course a few points and introduced a regular beat from quartering waves. When he looked up, the birds were gone.

He had known they would be.

The sea is a place of being alone, and because it is, men learn to value companionship. They learn that words do not mean companionship, any more than prayers mean conversion. Even so, there must be life. As close as a man can become in his relationship with his boat or the sea, they aren't living things. They cannot be companions.

The bird breathed, saw, knew pain and satisfaction. But it was a bird. And when another bird came, the man was different. The man would be alone.

Cruz wasted no time looking for the terns.

# ■ CHAPTER 21 ■

The sun beat down on the luxurious pool and the scattered bodies stretched out on lounges around it. A pair of towheaded children provided the only action in the spacious courtyard. Obviously brother and sister, they leaped in and out of the water with the universal abandon of children, shrieking and jabbering. The language was good, solid German, and it made Draeger smile, more at himself than the children. He couldn't fit German with palms, bougainvillea, cannas, and a sun that tried to burn the brains out of your skull. The full, rich vowels and the granite consonants called for meadows and dark forests and castles. The hotel might qualify as a castle, and one could sprawl on the wiry grass and think meadow. The palms and bougainvilleas could never conjure up forest. They even smelled wrong, a gift of the blazing sun that sucked moisture from them until they smelled half cooked.

One of the hotel staff assigned to the pool misinterpreted Draeger's smile. "You know the children, sir?"

He shook his head. "No. I was enjoying watching them."

The other attendant peered around his companion from inside the booth they occupied by the door to the hotel. "They are the only ones you *can* watch, sir. The rest of these people, I think maybe they're dead."

They laughed together, and Draeger wondered which one of the oiled, sweating bodies might be on a payroll, might be as anxious to hear him speak as he was anxious to avoid being heard. He took a towel from one of the young men, signing Kolar's name, and walked to the rack of lounges, waving off the attendant's assistance.

He pulled one onto the chipped grass, centering it as far from everyone else as possible. His arrival was greeted with reactions ranging from one bleary eye opening to a covert inventory from a stringy middle-aged female in an electric blue Speedo suit. Traffic noise crawled over the high wall, lost itself among the lush trees. It was there, ignored, rejected by the straightforward power of opulence.

Through eyes slitted against the sun, he watched Cindy toy with a drink at one of the small bar tables across the pool. She had a book propped open against the base of the umbrella in its center. Her long blond hair was swept up inside a wide-brimmed straw hat, and oversized dark glasses masked her face. She wore a red bathing suit. Despite the trappings, she was on duty.

Draeger let his eyes fall closed. It would be twenty minutes before she would signal he was unobserved. The floor attendant would know he had changed into his bathing suit in Kolar's room, and he would know when Kolar left in his own bathing suit that he was going to the pool. But there would be no connection with Cindy, who had already been at her post an hour.

The floor attendant was the weak link. There was one on every floor of every hotel, and they watched everything. They were security, information, and assistant in all things. For someone involved in a covert operation, they were a colossal pain in the ass. Draeger peered up at Kolar's window. The privacy drape was drawn. Nevertheless, those eyes were watching, too. Draeger imagined them as searchlights, sweeping the area. It wasn't hard to go a step further and imagine a person caught, transfixed, hands up in surrender.

Looking at Cindy was far more—what? Invigorating. That was a good word. He thought of Ria, not sure if such conscious balancing of one person against another was quite ethical. The comparison was inevitable, he realized, but the notion of an impersonal weighing was callous, somehow. He told himself if he didn't keep his mind occupied, the sun would force him to close his eyes and the squalls of the children would force him to seek refuge in sleep.

There was a hint of red in Cindy's tan, sunburn held at bay. It gave her skin an inner glow. Ria's color was richer, an exuberant adaptation. Cindy's tan was an arrangement, not at all artificial, but something accomplished.

The sun forced minute passages between the shading leaves,

angling past her umbrella in pencil-wide stripes. Where they touched a surface they formed a skittering golden circle smaller than a dime. When they slid over Cindy's arms, the hairs glinted like golden silk threads. With Ria there would have been no such reflection and the warm tone of her skin would have absorbed the energy, taken it into herself as part of her being.

It was a stupid game. He closed his eyes on it. Ria was as much woman as he could want, and matching her off against any other woman, especially one like Cindy, was pointless. Trying to get next to her would be a war.

One of the children mustered a particularly loud yell, and he opened one eye. The boy, although the smaller of the two, had the girl by the throat and was industriously endeavoring to bend her backwards under the water. A woman lifted her head from one of the lounge chairs and spoke sharply. The boy turned to look at her, careful to retain his grip, obviously waiting for the woman to lose interest. The girl understood the rules and took the opportunity to poke him in the eye. He dropped her to clutch at it, issuing another scream like the first. The girl swam away laughing.

Draeger cut his gaze back to Cindy, wondering what significance her liberation-attuned mind might attach to the children's byplay. He was just in time to see her close the book and put it in the bag at her feet. She replaced it with a paperback, outwardly oblivious to any activity around her.

Getting to his feet, Draeger adjusted the towel on his chair and lay back down on his right side, facing the hotel doorway.

Five minutes went by before Kolar came out, chatted with the pool attendants and, like Draeger, declined their offered assistance. He arranged a chair next to Draeger.

"I wanted to speak to you before you leave Manila. Cindy tells me your meeting went well professionally and was a disaster, otherwise."

Draeger drawled, "That's right."

Kolar ignored the attitude. "It seems the surveillance on you is gang personnel. I can't believe any of the regular opposition would use them. I'm getting very perturbed by so much information that tells me nothing. When you're away, be careful. Take no chances."

"Neither of you are followed?"

"Not since leaving your apartment. Curiouser and curiouser."

"It'll stop once I'm out of town. If it's all right with you, I'll leave Monday. Day after tomorrow."

"The sooner the better, then. Perhaps we can shake something loose."

Draeger rose to a sitting position, facing the wall. "What's that supposed to mean?"

"I told you to take no chances. I wouldn't say such a thing lightly. People have died, Glen."

"And you think me leaving town may generate a response, probably a violent response."

Kolar's chest rose and fell in a massive sigh. "Yes."

"I can't accept that. If Egg Roll's been compromised, the only link to me would be the courier, and he's dead. He didn't know anything, hasn't even *seen* me for at least a year. The tail on me has to have some connection with Munson's death. It's got to be the cops."

"My sources insist that's not the case."

"And they probably got it direct from the Philippine Constabulary." Draeger made a hawking noise. "You know how anxious they're going to be to cooperate with us on a criminal matter. We don't even have an extradition treaty with this government. You think they're going to take a chance on a suspect learning he's under investigation?"

"You believe they suspect you?"

"I just said I believed it, but I didn't do anything! If I had, I sure as hell wouldn't have killed Leonila!"

Kolar's eyes slid open so slowly the lids trembled. "That was a very selective comment, Glen."

Dreager stood up. "I want out of here for a while."

Kolar said, "Leave my key at the desk, please."

"My pleasure. I'll call and let you know where I decided to go. Or would you rather have me followed, make a fucking parade out of it?"

Kolar grunted and half-smiled. Draeger was too worked up to notice the deep etching around the older man's eyes or the way the vein in his neck swelled and ebbed, almost fluttering.

*     *     *

Draeger winced at the burst of blue flame from Ria's welding torch. Metal cracked and spattered to the floor in red hot fragments. He wished she'd quit hiding inside the helmet-like mask. It was impossible to argue with the metal hood and its square central eye. When she turned it toward him, he could see nothing but his own reflection. For a change, that didn't bother him. Not now, because he was finally giving her a break.

"I don't think you really have to go anywhere." Her voice reverberated. "I think you just want to get away from here for a while."

"I told you, Ria, I have to talk to some people."

"I heard what you told me. I don't believe you. Who are you going to see? Where?"

He wanted to shout at her, vent his frustrations and confusion by telling her exactly why he had to leave. That would only mire her further, and that was exactly what he wanted to avoid. She pulled up the mask, the motion lifting her breasts until they seemed to aim at him. Her expression was pure misery.

"You haven't answered me."

"I don't know where I'm going. I hurried over here as soon as I heard I had to leave. I wanted to explain, not get in an argument."

"You knew I'd ask. You could at least have told me a believable lie. It's insulting to be treated this way."

Draeger reached for her shoulder, and she pulled back. He dropped the hand slowly, moving to sit on a corner of a workbench. "We have a good relationship. I don't want to wreck that. All I'm doing is leaving town for a few days, not even a week."

She leaned against the piece under construction, an interwoven complex of tubing that twisted upward through a central steel plate. An inverted pyramid, the tubes burst through the unifying center only to dissipate themselves on convolutions. Draeger kept his eyes away from it. She said, "We have a relationship. I hate that word! We have never spoken of love, do you realize that? We've never spoken of *affection!*"

"Ria, I won't tell you I love you because I don't know if I love you. But affection? You can't be serious. You know how I feel about you."

"I don't! Neither do you!"

It was a terminal wound, unarguable. He was sure he didn't love her, but he wanted her every minute. Could he love her? Could he love anyone?

She spun away, attacked the welding. The energy exploded from the rod, overpowered the humming fluorescents overhead and threw manic, skittering shadows on the walls. Draeger watched the torch's point for a few seconds. When he looked away there were red-violet planets orbiting through his vision and the shadows in the background were auras, blues, and greens that interchanged and separated in casual madness. The acrid smell of the tortured steel grew overpowering, threatened to choke him. He grabbed Ria's arm and pulled the rod back from the surface.

"Goddammit, listen to me! I'm trying to do the right thing for both of us, Ria. Try to believe me. All I'm doing is leaving town for a few days."

She took the helmet completely off, let her hair fall in a cascade. A knowing smile pulled at her lips. "And then you forget to call for a few days more. And when you do call, you're too busy to come over right now, but you'll see me as soon as things slow down. Only they never do, right?"

"I don't believe this. It's a soap opera. What kind of understanding can we have if I can't leave town to take care of business? What sort of relationship is that?"

"There's that word again! You get what you want and that's a 'relationship.' If I want something it's a soap opera."

"That's not fair, Ria. You're throwing old standards at me, dead rules."

"They aren't dead. You don't understand. We have our own cultural requirements."

"You're the one who talked about liberation, about making your own way as a woman."

"What's that have to do with sleeping with you?"

When she turned away from him this time he saw she'd eased her posture. She was softer, rounder, as if muscles deep in her body had been pulling the visible flesh into harsh planes. Her eyes were still hard when she looked at him again.

"I think it's time for us to be honest with each other," she said, and instinct told him that more than their man-woman situation was involved.

Ria continued, "You may be everything you say you are. You are more, though. Maybe a criminal. Maybe with the CIA. Maybe you are employed by the government to do something. I don't know. But you are different. I dream about you, you know." She ducked her head and smiled, an embarrassed girl for that one instant. Then her eyes were probing again, hunting the man who eluded her. He stared back, secure she could never see behind the perfected defenses. She continued. "In my dreams we make love. It is wonderful, as long as I keep my eyes closed. When I open them, I have you in my arms, but there is another you, who stands right over there." Her hand twitched in a pointing move. "He doesn't frighten me, or even embarrass me, because he doesn't see us. He waits for you to finish, to be done with whatever has taken you from him."

He tried to smile, disturbed that it took such concentration to make the muscles work correctly. "There's only one me."

"Don't laugh, Glen. I'm not being amusing. I don't ask you who the other man is because you would lie to me and I would have to pretend to believe you, and it would all be very nasty. But I will not be loved by half a man, and I am not afraid to fight for what I want. Do you believe that?"

"Yes, I do."

"If this trip is genuine, I am going with you. If it is not, I can help you. Either way, we will be together. When we come back here, I will have both of my men. Or you will have no woman. I cannot live this way. It is destroying me."

Carefully, very carefully, he said, "There's no reason—" and she cut him off imperiously.

"I can't argue with you. The other man is here now. I know. I'm telling both of you. We do it my way, or I will go to the police. Oh, I know they will find nothing. Not at first. They will always look again, though. And again. And eventually they will find something because there is something."

"That's too crazy to even talk about."

"I'm going crazy, as it is. What do I care if the police think I already have? The question is, how will you feel, having them look into whatever you do?"

He stood, furious. "You'll get me fired, for Christ's sake! What'll the company say when some overwrought woman tells them their sales analyst is a goddam CIA man? I'll be on the street in five minutes!"

"Not you. If I'm wrong about you, you'll make a joke of it and be better off for it."

Draeger massaged his temples. "This whole thing started because I have to leave town for a few days. Jesus, Ria, it's not worth all this."

"Then take me with you." The easier attitude was changing again, and he could see the hardness coming back into her, as indefinable and as certain as watching crystallization.

"You're determined to force this thing?"

She nodded, looking away at the ground. Her chin trembled.

"I'll see what I can do. I'll tell them I'm sick, need some time off." He walked to her, turned her face upward with a hand under her chin and kissed her tenderly, lingering. "I can't be angry with you. You're blackmailing me, and I can't be angry. There's something wrong with me. I only hope this is the right thing to do, 'cause you're in for a terrible disappointment. There's only me, Ria, just plain me. That me's looking forward to one hell of a time, but I don't believe I can handle double billing."

The weak humor brought a faint smile. She shook her head, refusing to speak.

He walked through the house alone, dodging the clutter automatically. Arturo watched from the landing of the stairs to the upper floor. He almost spoke to Draeger, but a second look at the preoccupied frown dissuaded him. It was a welcome situation. It gave him a chance to study the American, if only fleetingly. What he saw was unpleasant. The head was pitched forward aggressively, the body inclined from the waist. He looked like a man who wanted trouble, and Arturo wanted nothing like that for Ria. And he had just come from her. There must have been a quarrel, he decided, and that was good. Let them fight and go their own ways. They would both be better off for it.

Draeger never knew Arturo was in the room, would have ignored him if he had. His options were disappearing, one by one, but with the speed of dominoes tumbling. The feeling of closeness was so real he caught himself hurrying through the front door, anxious to reach the street. Even there the other buildings closed on him, wanted to cut off his escape. At the first corner he stopped and put his hand to a light pole, not steadying himself, merely wanting the substance of it under hand.

As he continued on, a sense of purpose replaced his concern. He thought of the trust he'd lavished on the organization over the years and asked why he was seeing none of it now. He'd been respected for his skills, but an operation had broken down and he was a suspect. A boulevard loomed in front of him, a torrent of machinery. He checked, tottering on the curb. A small boy stopped his bicycle to watch the strange American, staring with total absorption. When Draeger turned to look down at him, he smiled up at the drawn features. When the dark eyes fastened on his own the boy's shy smile disappeared like something ripped from a wall. He leaped on his bicycle and fled, risking a crash to look back and assure he wasn't being pursued.

Draeger was practically unaware of the scene. Kolar wanted him out of town? Good. He'd go. Ria wanted to go with him? Even better. He'd take her. Kolar'd be furious. Too fucking bad. There was more to life than doing the right thing. Getting Munson would hardly qualify as doing the right thing. Marking time with Ria while Kolar made up his mind how to run his hunt wasn't doing the right thing. Who had it in their mind to do the right thing for Glen Draeger?

When he returned to Ria's house the following morning he found Arturo home alone. "The women are in church," he said, frowning. "Ria was very interested to go. She is very troubled."

Arturo spoke English slowly and with difficulty, his mouth working to form the words. It was a manner of speech that suited him. The sentences were ponderous, their slow development contributing to an aura of plain sense well spoken.

"We had a quarrel yesterday, Arturo. A small thing. I imagine you had a few with your wife."

"Many. You are talking of marriage, you and our Ria?"

"No."

"I am sorry. To see her so unhappy, you do not talk of marriage, it makes me wonder what you do talk about."

"It might be best if you ask Ria. I will argue with her, Arturo. I will not talk about her."

He half-turned, looking back at Draeger. There was some admiration in the look. Draeger saw it and scorned himself for being pleased.

"We have some time before they return. Will you have some coffee?"

Draeger thanked him and Arturo left, a moment later returning with a pair of mugs and the inevitable jar of instant. Arturo said, "Ria mentioned a trip. Are you going somewhere? Business?"

"I was. Things have changed."

"Changed? I do not understand. What do you mean?" Arturo shifted in his chair, uncomfortable.

"I have to talk to Ria about it," Draeger said. His hands were clammy. Arturo was right to suspect him, right to want to protect his family. He was a good man.

Voices brought him alert, and the women came through the door, the rapid Tagalog spinning from their lips in gusts of shared laughter. Draeger rose automatically. Ria had never looked more beautiful. Ruby took one look at Draeger, smiled with her greeting, and was gone before he could say more than hello. Arturo followed her. Despite the multiple tensions of the moment, Draeger was aware that this was the first time he'd seen or heard the elusive Ruby.

Ria said, "Is everything all right? Your face is red."

"Everything's worked out. I've got ten days off."

The conversation moved heavily. He would remember it as strained. Patches of dialogue, individual gestures imprinted on his memory. There was no coherent recollection of what led to the final selection of Iloilo as the place to visit. There was something about her family background and his never having seen the place. Ria moved to him, stood directly before him, practically under his chin. "We can be happy, Glen. You think I'm behaving very badly, but it's all I can do. And I'll make you happy."

"You already make me happy." He took her hands in his. They were warm and soft, and he felt the apprehension in them, the way the young rabbits used to lie there when he was a boy, refusing to look at the unimaginable creature holding them. He could think of nothing else for a moment, remembering the averted eyes and the minute hearts pulsing so rapidly the bodies vibrated. He leaned forward to kiss her forehead. "I don't know what else a man could ask for, Ria. I don't know why you put up with me. I wish we hadn't quarreled."

The words burned his throat, and he cursed himself. They were the truth. He'd said nothing that was remotely a lie. And still there was the rasp of nerves through his body.

Ria hugged him impulsively, looking to see if Arturo or Ruby had seen, smirking like a schoolgirl. When she turned her face back to Draeger, it was with the eyes of a woman. "You didn't hurt me, Glen. You frightened me. I want things to be right for us. I want us to be happy, and I want us to respect each other. It's not easy for me to fight. I didn't know what else to do. You were leaving me."

He ran a finger along a cheekbone, tracing the pocket holding the luminous eye. She reached to press the hand to her cheek, and she said, "No more talk. There's been too much seriousness. We're going to enjoy ourselves."

"Oh, yes." She stepped back, glowing. He had never seen her so beautiful, so consummately desirable. He smiled at her, and it was full of admiration and a wanting he had the wit to leave unsaid because he knew his words would fall short. The smile said the male things a man should say to a woman. It sent a lover's songs and promises. It was the ultimate lie.

# ■ CHAPTER 22 ■

Arturo's reentry caught them unaware. When his presence finally penetrated their consciousness, they involuntarily stepped back another pace although they were in no contact whatever. Arturo saw, and his disapproval burned across his face. The smile that replaced it carried a gloss of determination.

"What have you decided?" he asked.

Ria ran to him. "We are going to Iloilo! I will show him where we used to live and where I went to school. It will be wonderful!"

Arturo spoke shortly in Tagalog. Ria's quick glance at Draeger apologized for the rudeness, and she answered in English. "Time changes things, Arturo. There is nothing wrong with us going to the same place to see the same things together. We are talking about my life, Arturo, to live as I choose."

Arturo's feelings were as visible as his efforts to control them, and finally he was able to speak. He looked at Draeger. "It's very easy to misunderstand a thing like this. I am old-fashioned. Mr. Draeger knows how I feel."

"I do, Arturo. I will never harm her."

The chunky man nodded again, slower, thoughtfully. "Thank you," he said, and when he turned to Ria, he smiled. It was tense, but it lacked the hard edge of his previous effort. He said, "I would like to borrow this American of yours for the afternoon. We should be better acquainted."

Ria frowned, and Draeger spoke first. "It's a good idea. You'll need the time to pack. Arturo and I can talk."

"About me, I suppose?"

Arturo said, "No, not about you. About the *pintakasi*."

Draeger blinked at the Tagalog, and Ria explained. "*Pintakasi* means cockfight. Arturo is mad about them."

He slapped himself on the chest. "I am what we call *sabungero,* a man who never misses a cockfight."

"I know about them. I've never seen one."

Arturo looked to Ria. "How can that be?" He flung his hands wide as he turned back to Draeger. "You must see the fights. It is more to us than your football or basketball, more than the Spanish bullfights. If you do not understand the cockfights, you can never begin to understand us."

In a matter of minutes, they were in the car, waving good-bye to the women. After a burst of excitement, Arturo was quiet, almost preoccupied. At first Draeger tried to make conversation, but when even his questions about the upcoming event were met with blunt monosyllables, he dropped the effort. There was that about them that discouraged even the intersection peddlers, selling cigarettes or matches or feather dusters, or anything they hoped someone would buy, at the major junctions. They were young men or boys, engaged in an occupation where agility was as important as sight. Draeger wondered how they managed. There couldn't be much of a living in selling one cigarette at a time. They operated in groups, an easy competition among them to reach customers first. He had never seen more than an occasional sign of friction, never anything to suggest a fight as if they were all agreed that life was far too heavily burdened for them to create trouble for each other. When the traffic light changed, cars, trucks, buses surged to a stop in a grinding wave. The peddlers sallied among them from the sidewalks, bending to search car windows, craning upward at the taller vehicles, flirting down each lane with the brittle bobbing action of sandpipers scouring a beach. Draeger watched them, wondering what dreams soared behind those questing eyes. Did the man selling two cigarettes to the truck driver and his partner see himself driving a truck one day? Or selling cigarettes by the shipload? And the man with the dozen magazines fanned across his chest—was he to be a star in the entertainment world, with his own picture smiling out between the fingers of a thousand peddlers for the delight of ten thousand commuters? How many of them looked at the metal-and-wheels of the New Society and imagined old solutions to a world they considered hopeless? Would they exchange their paltry stock one day, dealing bullets instead of cigarettes, dangling clustered grenades instead of the bunched flowers of the fragrant sampaguita?

Arturo murmured directions, his voice barely audible above the racket outside. When he said, "You can park right here," it came as a surprise.

From the outside the building could have passed as any warehouse. The overhang of the roof left an open space at the top of the walls for ventilation. There was an entryway and a ticket counter. Arturo insisted he would pay and, as they crossed the street, pointed out the red flag hanging from the sign, explaining it meant there would be fights this day.

"Only on Sunday and holidays," he said. "The sport is too popular, otherwise. Too many men do nothing but watch or fight their birds, so it is regulated. Like everything."

He led the way inside, through a tunnellike arrangement of fencing where a man stamped their hands so they could come and go. Draeger stopped to examine his surroundings, and Arturo stood quietly, approvingly, the way a man might watch another examine art.

A mass of men squatted to the right, most of them holding birds. Draeger had seen illustrations of fighting cocks. They were sleek birds, the brighter-colored feathers like living flames and the dark colors as iridescent as oil on a pond. He was unprepared for the speckled birds and the occasional pure white that looked as out of place as he did.

In front of them a wall rose almost to the roof. It was pierced by an open doorway, with stairs leading upward. Arturo led the way into this inner sanctum, and, at the top of the stairs, Draeger looked down into the fighting pit and a maelstrom of activity. The noise from inside was directed upward, emanating from the regular admission customers who crowded around the squared pit. A set of steel bars, jail bars, kept them back from the actual fighting area. They crowded against each other, pressing forward, and the tension building among them was more substantial than the sound of their murmuring. Arturo led Draeger to the right, and they seated themselves just as the first man entered the pit with a bird under his arm.

Another man came into view from under the balconylike upper level. He had been backed against the bars and Draeger had missed him. Still, when the man stepped forward to meet the incoming fighter, Draeger knew exactly what purpose the bird under his arm would serve. It was an eerie feeling, knowing the hidden man carried a Judas bird, a creature that would serve only to provoke the one that would do the actual fighting. True to Draeger's premonition, the bird of no merit was allowed to peck and nip the new arrival. Outside, other birds began to crow, sensing the drama unfolding in the pit. Under the harsh glare of the overhead light the fighting bird struggled against its handler. It was a rich one, vibrant in its reds and russets, an ember of a bird. It wore a single spur, sheathed in bamboo. At each peck the tiny scabbard jerked and struck the air.

The noise level increased. The animal smell of the building thickened.

The second bird was brought in and subjected to the same excitement. It was white, black-speckled, and where the red bird sat in its handler's grasp and watched what was happening between the Judas bird and the speckled one, the latter twisted and turned to duck blows and watch the crowd at the same time.

The pecking bird was withdrawn from the pit, and the noise level went up instantly, became a surf of shouts and bellows. Three men occupied a small runway below Draeger and Arturo, an area on the left side of the pit. They stood with arms akimbo, gesturing with fingers, nodding. Strain disfigured their faces.

"*Kristos*," Arturo explained, seeing Draeger's interest. "From the word Christ, because they stand with arms out, like crucified." Draeger looked again, and before he could ask, Arturo laughed and went on. "It is all in the head. Every bet. See that one, with two fingers pointing to the ground? He is saying he has a bet on the favorite of two hundred pesos."

"What odds?"

"*Sampu apat*. You would call it more than two against one. You bet ten, another man bets four."

"Which is the favorite?"

Arturo leaned closer, shouting to make himself heard clearly.

"The white one with black—we call that kind *talisain*—is favorite. The odds should be more good for the *pula*, the red."

Draeger said, "I'll take the odds. Four hundred pesos on the red bird. It'll kill the speckle."

Arturo grinned. "You want to lose four hundred?"

"I want to win a thousand."

"OK. It is not my money." Arturo rose and put a hand over his mouth. When he shouted his bet he pulled the hand away in a sweep, as if throwing the words out. The *kristos'* normal calculating look was momentarily battered to surprise. Arturo smiled thinly, repeated his shout and gesture, this time inclining his head toward Draeger. An offbeat murmur ran through the crowd, the addition of a new instrument to the orchestra. It was quickly silent once the bet was taken.

The handlers removed the scabbards, lowering the birds to the packed earth surface of the pit. The spurs gleamed, curves of steel that defined lethality at a glance. The handlers were very circumspect about them. They moved the birds close enough to peck each other one last time, then drew them back to their own side of the pit and released.

The speckled bird moved forward quickly, head jerking back and forth with the imbecilic stop-and-go motion of any barnyard chicken. The red was far more tentative, its advance crablike, quartering forward. Arturo watched it with a smirk.

"He is not too anxious, the *pula*. Who can blame him? The *talisain* already has three victories."

An atavistic excitement pulsed in Draeger, and he ignored the other man, bending outward over the pit. The thing in him that cried out for blood shut out the noise, the light, the rest of the world. It was a centripetal force that drew him in an ever-decreasing circle of consciousness until he was no longer spectator or bettor. He was a presence in that pit, involved. The fingers of his right hand hurt, and he took his eyes from the circling birds in a quick look before it occurred to him to release the fist causing the problem. When he looked back it was just in time to see the speckle fly up and forward in a great flurry. The spur slashed mightily where the red should have been, but it pressed to the ground, mashing itself so flat it seemed it must splay outward like real mud. Its legs had barely enough room to function, and they drove it forward in an amazingly quick scuttle. The speckle cut nothing but air, landing in a spinning turn that had it ready to press the attack again. The red was waiting, however, and the speckle settled for stalking. The red tried to move in, and the speckle flew upward from its thighs, throwing the spur out front in a sweep, up and down. Both strokes whistled past the red, and it stumbled in its hurried retreat.

The speckle struck at that failing, leaping high once again. The red rolled on its back and the speckle struck, the blow too quick for the eye to see, but blood trickled off the red's breast as he regained his feet.

They paused, facing each other, heads down and extended forward. Blood continued to drip from the red, and Draeger timed it, feeling foolish, not knowing how long it took a bird to bleed to death at six drops every five seconds. Unprocessed information. Raw data.

Arturo put his hand to his ear as a funnel and shouted to him. "The *talisain* knows. He has seen blood before. He waits."

Draeger looked at him, and Arturo's eyebrows lifted in dark crescents. He slid carefully on the rough bench, opening a gap between his hip and Draeger's. The American was back over the railing and missed the movement. He licked his lips and said, "Get him now, Red. Kill the spotted sonofabitch. *Git* him!" The last came as a shout, demanding.

The red cock answered, erupting in a thrashing leap that turned him into a climbing flame. The speckle rose an instant later, hacking with its spur, grabbing with its beak. It caught the red right where the throat joined the breast, pushing forward. The move turned the birds into a pinwheel of feathers and blood, and they tumbled to the dirt in a confused heap. The speckle disengaged itself, tugging at the spur buried in the red's side. It tottered as it walked, but it moved, while the red lay on the ground. Its head was still up, the eyes wild and fixed, but it was unmoving. The speckle flapped its wings, and a roar broke from the crowd, only to stop as if severed when the black and white body staggered sideways, righted itself, and then pitched forward on its breast.

The red was struggling during all this, and it advanced on the floundering speckle. The bird on the ground cocked its head to peck and defend itself and writhed, attempting to regain its feet. The red walked right through the halfhearted peck and drove its spur into its downed enemy. The speckle shuddered its life away in rustling spasms. All the while, during the execution and the reflexive jerks, the red stared out into the crowd with disoriented preoccupation, as if searching for one friendly face that would comprehend the genuine significance of what it was watching.

With the death of the speckle, the pent-up roar that had eluded the dead bird was granted the survivor. His handler raced to scoop him up and carry him from the ring. Blood continued to drain off the formerly sleek feathers, now matted and fouled. Nevertheless, he looked better than his opponent, being carried away by the feet. "It is too bad the loser must die," Arturo said. "It would be nice if the loser could live in peace, as the winner lives in glory, but that is not the way of things. Even if a man dies gloriously, he is still dead."

Draeger stared at the pit where an attendant scuffed soil over the jewels of blood. Words formed in his mouth, alive of themselves, no more a part of anything he recognized than the compulsion to watch the cocks fight to the death. He said, "The dying will come, regardless. If a man has a chance to do the thing in a creditable manner, he should be glad his luck is strong."

A wad of money flew up to them, thrown by the man who'd lost the bet. Arturo picked it up and handed it to Draeger. The American unfolded it, flattening it on the bench boards beside him with great deliberation, smoothing out each wrinkle and crease. He looked to Arturo. "I never bet on a life before. I'm not sure how I feel about it."

Arturo's frown was more concerned than disapproving.

The babble of the crowd increased. Draeger was drawn back to the pit and the intensity of the humanity pressing against the screen. The judge moved the overhead marker that indicated which bird was the favorite. A young man, not much more than a boy, stepped through the doorway into the pit, nodding at the stern judge so vigorously he was nearly bowing from the waist. The judge accepted it calmly, examining the bird, then waved the boy to the right. The Judas bird was brought out. Behind the crowd a rooster crowed reedy arrogance. Draeger saw the pit entry door open again. The next bird was brought in, greeted with a roar.

They watched eight fights, and Draeger was drained. They descended the stairs to the main floor slowly, Arturo deep in thought,

Draeger holding the rail and watching his feet. On ground level, he turned to the Filipino.

"When the birds are hurt, who takes care of them? They're not just allowed to die, surely?"

Arturo gestured. "I will show you. Over here."

They made their way through a throng still arguing about matching their birds, men whose hands could judge a fraction of an ounce difference in weight and, more importantly, tell where that weight was located and if it was a benefit or hindrance to a bird. They broke off their quiet, tense discussions to watch the American pass, then resumed.

The hospital area was beyond the crowd, up against the wall of the building. The only light came from the air space at the overhung roof, and it was badly degraded by smoke and the position of the sun. The circumstances had no effect on the doctors. There were two, and they sat with their kits of knives and needles and esoteric paraphernalia, each working on a wounded bird. The kitboxes were about the size of a standard briefcase. The tools were neatly arranged, an effect spoiled by the dried blood on them and veneered on the bottom of the case's interior. One of the men held a white bird between his knees, the head pillowed on his belt buckle, the open abdomen exposed. A ragged gash smiled bloodily at the crowd, the toothless rictus of an addled old man. Stretching, Draeger looked directly down at the wound. The doctor quit stitching momentarily, taking his hands away, revealing the organs inside. The stomach churned away at whatever it held and other glistening multi-colored things squirmed or pumped or simply lay inert, performing their function in stoic immobility. The doctor returned to his work, jerking at the flesh until the edges were joined and tacking them together with tailoring deftness. The cock refused to watch, keeping its head turned toward the pit, occasionally slipping the nictating membrane across its eye in a manner that invariably suggested the surgery was too late. Each time, however, the eye popped open again, scanned the crowd to see if the joke was appreciated, then returned to the direction of the obscured pit. Draeger was sure the bird knew exactly what it was looking for.

A movement distracted him, and he looked beyond the rudimentary operating area to see a man approaching from the area behind the pit and its seats. He carried a naked, scarred corpse in one hand, a former fighting cock, now a dinner on its way to the pot.

Arturo saw him looking. "It is not our way to waste things. We even have a special way to cook the fighting cocks."

"As tough as they must be? I'll bet you boil them for a week."

"Not quite so long. The ones in the family who don't care about the bird, they will be happy to see him come home this way. Remember, this one has been fed on a very special diet and exercised. He will be very rich, taste very good."

The bird was passing now, old scars and new wounds crosshatched on the body. Feathers drifted off the man's clothing. They were mottled, black and white. The winnings in Draeger's pocket were suddenly heavy.

"The bird you bet against first," Arturo said, pointing. "That one surprised me. You saw something? You have never been to the *pintakasi* in the States?"

"Never. I was lucky."

Stubbornly, Arturo shook his head. "There was something."

A touch of smile moved Draeger's lips. "The red one was paying attention to business. He knew he was in trouble, and he wasn't letting anything interfere with his concentration. The black and white one wanted to be part of everything going on. The red one wanted to win the fight."

Arturo was satisfied, and he led the way to the exit.

Draeger stopped when they reached the door, turning to look back. It was late in the afternoon, the sun's rays striking from a lower angle. The more direct entry picked out the smoke and dust more clearly, turning each entering shaft into a whirlpool of motes and shifting clouds. Flies dashed among them, silvered bullets. The crowd noise announced another pair of entries. The air throbbed with the smell of excited humanity, excrement, blood. Draeger inhaled again, telling himself it was conceit to imagine he could smell death.

"It is not a very special place," Arturo said, apologizing.

The words seemed prescient to Draeger, appropriate beyond

coincidence. "It's a very special place, Arturo, a place of passion and fury, and the ignominy of the stewpot. A bad place to die."

Arturo crackled laughter, hard sounds. "If you know a good place, take care of it. You said it yourself, it will get us all, no matter."

They were silent until they had driven almost halfway to the house. Arturo's intention to speak was telegraphed by his abrupt turn to face Draeger. He leaned his broad back againt the car door.

"It is not our way to speak of things as Americans do. I must tell you what I feel, however, and there is little time. I do not approve of Ria going away with you. I am asking you not to do this thing."

Draeger gestured shortly. "We're not going to—"

"What you want to do or not do is not important. It is the principle, the idea of it. People will believe the worst, no matter what you say."

"Who gives a goddamn what people believe?"

"Me. And Ruby, and Ria. She talks about her new ideas and new way of life, but it is talk. She is still Margarita Manong, a Filipina girl. Her roots are here, not in a country that talks of a new faith every year, every month. We believe in the things we have always believed in, and when people offend those things, they suffer."

"You know I would never hurt her."

"You will. You don't want to think so, but if you go on this way, you will hurt each other. I cannot allow Ria to be hurt."

"Can't allow?"

"I know I can't stop you from this trip."

Meaning beyond the basic words filled the interior of the car, an instant pressure. Draeger deliberately slowed, insuring the changing traffic light would stop them. The move touched off a storm of frustrated horn-blowing from the truck behind. The men in the car ignored it. Draeger's saturnine features were drawn tight and his chin was elevated. The effect was one of pride backed as far as it could go.

He said, "Ria's a free person. What she does is her business. I understand your concern, but you can't live her life for her. She's free."

Arturo met the hard stare for a few more moments, then looked to the front. His expression softened, turned thoughtful. "And what do we pay for what we call freedom? I am very confused. I know what I must do sometimes, anyway. And I must protect Ria's reputation.''

Draeger started the car with a jerk. His lips pulled thinner, tucked downward. "Be clear, Arturo. If I damage Ria's reputation, then what? Will you shoot me?"

"I do not know. A gun, a knife—something." He shrugged his indifference for technique.

"Over gossip? For something that is truly not your concern?"

"You can't understand, can you?" Arturo tried to be calm. "We are *family*. What happens to one happens to all. And I would never kill you because you caused gossip about her, only if you cause her pain. If she leaves us to live with you, marry you, she can come back to us. We will always love her. You are not family."

"You call it family. I call it imprisonment."

"Who is free? You? I don't think so. When I first met you, I thought maybe. You change. Twice. You were afraid for a while. Now there is more. Still afraid, now more. I don't know what. Maybe anger. Want fight, that I know, for sure." His grammatical structure faded as he strained to organize his observations.

Draeger maneuvered between a belching diesel truck and one of the multitude of buses. This one was baby blue, part of the fleet called Love buses. Inanely, the name tugged at his concentration. Tucked between the two machines, he cut his eyes at Arturo. The mahogany face was pale, responded to Draeger's glance.

"These are not things to be talked about," he said, scarcely audible over the rumble flanking them. "If you were like us, you would know these things, would understand. It is hard for me to speak them. I feel sick."

Draeger asked if he wanted to stop, and Arturo moved a hand. "No. I want to go home, be in my house. But you understand what I say? You see? You have to know. I can not allow Ria hurt. It is honor."

Reaching to touch the other man's shoulder, Draeger said, "We have some similar thoughts in my country, Arturo, believe me. People like me, like Ria, we're trying to figure out where we are. I mean her no harm."

"I hope so. If you embarrass her, it make no difference." He swallowed hard, turning to the window. "Please, no more talk of this, OK?"

Draeger put his hand back on the wheel. "OK. No problem."

It was weird. That was the only word for it. The man could sit there and talk about killing someone, and what disturbed him was the talking about it. And if push came to shove, he'd do exactly what he said he'd do. Maybe it was watching all those cockfights.

He swung out and around a bus, this one far more gaudy and individualistic. The rear windows were painted over with a white daub, and on that was emblazoned a *cri de coeur*, "My Life Is Rock and Roll," in blood red letters. The message was accentuated by individual drops that trailed from each letter.

The Philippines *was* blood. There was the intermingling from all over southeast Asia that produced the people themselves. Draeger searched his memory and could think of no single incident where a Filipino had spoken to him of any "genetic pool." In any conversation that dealt with cultural attributes, people spoke of racial differences and ethnic qualities—and Chinese blood or American blood, or whatever was held responsible. The choice of words had nothing to do with a lack of knowledge. There was as much education about biology and heredity and related subjects in the Philippines as anywhere in the world. It was a matter of habit. Draeger wondered if it was more, a preoccupation with blood that extended beyond education, beyond consciousness, a concept that saw blood as a visible life force, a talisman for good and evil. Violence was as abhorrent to the average Filipino as to any member of any culture. Still, there was a quirk there, an adjustment to a fact of life. Men like Arturo didn't see occasional violence as an unfortunate part of man's existence, they saw it as an unfortunate necessity. And because it had to be there, the entire reality of it was skewed. What Draeger would see as something to be avoided, Arturo would approach with genuine sorrow.

"You are falling in love with our Ria?" Arturo kept his eyes locked to the motorcycle in front of them. His jaw jutted forward.

"I don't know," Draeger said. "I can't be sure."

"Then my question's answer is no. You will go on this trip with her?"

"I have to, Arturo." An inspiration came to him. "There is a need. I have to find out about myself. There is a fire in the blood, and I must control it, or it will control me.''

The heavy features settled to thoughtfulness, and Arturo nodded a slow rhythm. It was an answer he understood completely.

# ■ CHAPTER 23 ■

Draeger slipped the car into the parking stall of his apartment complex and knew he was being watched as soon as his feet hit the cement.

He felt a bit foolish as he reopened the car door, pretending he'd left something behind. Whoever was watching hadn't picked him up at Ria's. He was sure of that, and relieved.

At first he saw nothing. The movement in the distance that eventually did draw his attention was at car-window height and could have been no more than a cloud reflection on glass. Draeger rose, careful to show no interest in the suspect vehicle, and started walking toward the Makati Commercial Center. It was nearly time for him to talk to Kolar, and it'd be worth a little walking to burn the surveillance and let Kolar know what the man looked like in the daytime.

The tail hung back. Even so, there was enough about him that was familiar to make Draeger want a better look. At the first opportunity, he headed for Rustan's, the huge department store.

The tail read the intent and hurried to catch up. Draeger smiled to himself. The other man was in a terrible bind. If his mark got into a place like Rustan's with any kind of a lead, he could disappear in a second. On the other hand, if the mark wasn't headed for Rustan's, closing the gap on him was the best way in the world to get burned.

Draeger could practically smell sweat. He stepped up his pace. Sweeping into the store, he had plenty of time to hurry to the side.

When Tony Pierce stepped through the door Draeger's knees literally wobbled. Pierce looked his way, and Draeger automatically ducked behind a display, reflex taking over. When he stepped out again, Pierce was up the aisle, searching the crowd. Draeger held his position, guaranteeing Pierce was alone, then followed. He was looking directly at the back of Pierce's head when the shorter man turned around and their eyes met across the intervening customers. Undisguised relief flooded Pierce's heart-shaped face. It made him look years younger, almost boyish. A flicker of embarrassment fought for life in Draeger's conscience, and he snuffed it mercilessly.

He turned around and strolled back toward the door, knowing Pierce would follow. He led the way to a small restaurant and was in a booth sipping a glass of beer when Pierce joined him.

Draeger said, "What the hell are you doing here?"

Pierce smiled thinly. "It's good to see you again, too. I'm here because I was told to come. A couple of years ago Munson gave me some papers. He said if anything happened to him, I was to turn the papers over to anyone investigating the deal. I waited until I was sure he's really gone. Now I want to get rid of the stuff. I don't like holding onto it."

"The investigator would have been in Zambo in a little while."

"Who's running it?"

"Kolar. Himself. With one assistant."

Paling, Pierce rubbed his chin with his knuckles. "Shit. The big cheese itself, huh?" He tried for a confident sound and fell short. "Well, let him look. If we had a couple of small security flaws, Munson knew about all of them. He was control, right?"

It was the same reaction as Draeger's, and having it in common with Pierce was an unpleasant realization. He moved the conversation ahead. "I was on my way to meet Kolar. Wait here for ten minutes after I leave, then go to the Intercontinental. The downstairs bar is the Boulevardier. If Kolar wants you to come to his room, he'll have Mr. Barker paged, Mr. Thomas Barker."

Pierce nodded. "I'll wait about ten minutes and then come up. What room number? Is the floor man ours?"

"No. Everything's working under cover." It seemed only good

sense to neglect to mention the beating in his room and the known surveillance. Pierce would take normal precautions, in any case, and if Kolar wanted him to know the total screw-up that was coming down, that was up to him.

An hour later Pierce was in the room with Kolar and Cindy. He asked, "Where's Draeger?"

Kolar continued pouring drinks. "He was leaving town. It was convenient to let him get going. What's this about some mysterious papers?"

"He left them with me with instructions to see that any investigators who came around, if he turned up missing, should get them."

Kolar distributed the drinks and sat down. "That doesn't strike you as odd? A man arranging a voice from the past? Have you made similar arrangements? I assure you I haven't. Where are the documents?"

"I didn't bring them. I took a room and had them locked in the safe."

"Good. Get them and bring them here."

Cindy gave him a slight smile as he left. With the click of the door she banged her drink down on the table hard enough to create a small spill.

"You treated him like he was a proven liar!"

The fatherly eyes swept to her, turned cold. "It might be a good idea to send you home. You're losing your distance, your objectivity."

"Glen and Pierce trust you! They're helping you look for the truth!"

"Truth?" The word lashed. "What do you know of the truth in this matter? I'm trying to teach you to search for facts."

"Truth is truth. You can't argue with that."

"I can. I do. More harm is done in the name of truth than all the evils in the world. A typhoon may blow onto this island and kill people. To the survivors the typhoon is a curse. That's a truth. For an inland farmer whose crops are drying up, the rain will save him and his family, and the storm is a blessing. That's a truth. What's truth to Draeger? Pierce? I trust facts!"

She was trembling as if he'd shouted her down. Not once had he raised his voice much above a whisper.

Ironically, she didn't especially like Pierce, the very foursquare, bright smile and the lively eyes. He had a habit of saying something to one person and watching another from the corner of his eye, checking to see if there was any reaction. Expressions slid across the undeniably intriguing features like chips at a roulette table. Her gaze went to Kolar. He stood with his back to her, staring out at the darkening city.

He had never spoken to her like that before. Oddly, she took some consolation in that fact, telling herself he was extremely upset and it was a mark of confidence that she was the one he felt safe with. She took a deep breath, calming, telling herself there would be more outbursts and it was her responsibility to field them.

For a moment that troubled her. There was a traditional woman's role hinted in the thrust of the situation, and resentment warmed her throat for a minute, the surge of anger she'd learned to control. Objectively, she considered if a man would have exercised the same function she was being asked to perform. A wry smile twisted her lips as she thought Kolar would certainly prefer a man's company in the circumstances. He insisted on treating her like a daughter fresh home from finishing school, and she could hear unspoken profanity dancing on his tongue in his anger. But he could hurt without swearing.

She remembered reading somewhere that it was desirable in combat to wound, rather than kill outright, because wounded men required care. The men caring for wounded were unavailable to fight. Was there some dark psychology in his attack? Did he see her as wounded and therefore forced out of a coming struggle? She set her jaw and glared at the back of his neck. It wasn't going to happen that way.

Kolar turned on the television set. The twist of the knob threatened to break it. When he threw himself down in a chair it groaned at the shock.

Cindy thought of Draeger, deciding it would be especially horrible if he were involved in Munson's disappearance. There was a reluctance in Kolar's manner when he spoke of him, as though he knew, or suspected something he didn't want to talk about. He spoke of Draeger as though there was something missing. What was it he'd said? Yes, he'd described him as not being "hard-nosed." How could he be less than hard-nosed, whatever that might mean, and still be suspected of being a killer? And that's what Kolar was thinking out.

She didn't need words from Kolar to know that, and she admonished herself for thinking in terms of intuition. There was a wariness in Kolar's manner, a ferality. His speech patterns were normal, and there were no unusual gestures or postures she could define. Perhaps everything he was doing was so exact, so precisely in tune because he was determined to give no sign of being different. His studied casualness reminded her of a dog on strange territory. There was the same camouflaged alertness, the unconcerned stride that saw each foot coming down in precisely the right place, ready to coil and spring if need be.

Draeger was more obvious. He was hurt and angry. And, as with Kolar, the eyes hid more activity than they revealed. No one would call him handsome, she decided, especially the way he looked now. Other qualities made up for that. There was an intensity that wasn't always visible, came with a taste of surprise. She thought of summer evenings, too hot to do much but relax in the long shadows when heat lightning made a glowing ballet of the thunderheads. There was awesome power in that beauty, yet the muttering rumble was soothing.

Perhaps that was why she found his voice pleasant. He spoke slowly, particularly when deep in thought, and he had that habit of pulling back his chin. He withdrew when he did that, pulled into himself and dragged the listener closer. It was almost an entrapment.

A line sliced across her forehead, a preliminary sketch of a frown. The Filipina woman, Ria, knew about his attraction. She watched him with the feminine attention that mixes people and passion with a peculiar ownership that distrusts its own strength.

Cindy shifted irritably. Thinking of Ria led to the quick grab in the stomach that convinces a person they are leaving the house and forgetting something. She turned to Kolar.

"What do we know of that girl, Ria?"

The still-rumpled features turned slowly. "Nothing, save your fortunate linking of her name to that magazine article. Why?"

"She's very much involved with Draeger."

"Lucky him." Kolar snorted before continuing. "They make a good-looking pair, but he's on some very thin ice. Terrible choice of images. Thin ice'd be a delight here. With luck, you'd fall through."

"He may already have done so."

"What's that mean?"

"Today, for instance. We know Draeger's being tailed, but we don't know why or by whom. He wasn't tailed when he was with the woman or her cousin. He expected surveillance when he left his apartment, or he wouldn't have spotted Pierce so easily. Maybe, subconsciously, he expects surveillance when he's not with her, and maybe he's right, maybe there's no reason for surveillance when he's with her."

Kolar's eyebrows arched. "God, you really do have a devious mind."

Cindy recognized the tone and manner, knew she was being teased, and couldn't accept the light humor. It angered her. "At least I'm thinking about the problem instead of watching television and waiting for something to happen!"

"I see. And you're right, of course. I can't seem to get a grip on this thing."

"You'll find out. I know you will." There was contrition as well as confidence in her answer, and it left a dry taste on her tongue because it was totally inadequate and she wasn't sure she believed it. Kolar looked at her in a way that said he was aware of all those things.

"I'll certainly try." He sighed and turned off the television set. "It's hell, this outlaw thing. If we had the support of our big brother we'd throw men and money at the problem until we simply overwhelmed it. We sacrificed all that in order to be entirely covert. Now, for the first time, we're being forced to abide by that covert status under stress conditions. It may be the last time. There are people who suspect the organization exists and who need only to hear of a fiasco such as this to begin their investigations."

It was a subject they all discussed. Cindy was unable to resist it this time any more than she had any other. "It's not right! What we do isn't a question of right or wrong, it's a question of dead or alive. My God, we're not hurting the United States!"

"Cindy, why get so excited? I'm on the same side, remember? Gently, dear, gently. Dispassionate. The people we oppose outside our country don't worry about niceties, so we must try to avoid becoming as savage as they are. Those who oppose us in our country would preside over a debate concerning how they should be exterminated, so we try to avoid being that foolish. You know all that. Why do we bother to discuss it?''

She walked to him and put a hand on his shoulder. ''You already said why. Because everything's coming apart. Now.''

He closed his eyes. ''I've got a bad feeling about this situation. I told myself bringing you was necessary, that you had to be exposed to the harshness. Things may get worse than I anticipated. I'm seriously considering sending you home.''

''No!'' Pitch and volume soared beyond intended limits, and she stepped away from him, reestablished control. ''I've earned my position. I was promised opportunity commensurate with my ability. You can't throw me off the job because it might get unpleasant.''

''I'm not talking about unpleasantness; I'm talking about killing.'' He tented his fingers, creating a prayerlike vision that disturbed her. ''A reasonable man can accept a reasonable amount of coincidence. A man—pardon me, a person—in this business never completely trusts any coincidence. There are too many coincidences here and too many unexplained matters. I need my facts, Cindy.''

''And I expect to help you get them, but I don't want to hear any more talk of killing. It won't be necessary, I'm sure.''

''And if it is?'' His eyes held her.

''I couldn't do it except to save my life, or someone else's. If you're talking about an execution, then you're right. I can't do what's required of me. Could you? And even if you could, that's still no reason to take me off this operation. I can still help.''

''Indeed you could. My thought was to put you in a position where you could be spared being involved in whatever hard job might come up.''

''Such as?''

''Draeger's the key to this whole thing, and I believe he's in great danger. Frankly, I'm more afraid of his being kidnapped than killed. It occurs to me that every day he spends in this country he becomes more of a liability. If I send him home, I'd want you to accompany him.''

''I'm not a baby-sitter, Carl, and I'm certainly not a cop. Escorting prisoners isn't my specialty. And how fair is that, anyhow? You don't have any reason to suspect Glen of anything.''

"Because he *is* a suspect. So is Pierce. Everyone is. I've got to shake some trees, get something moving. When I do, Draeger's life becomes even more tenuous."

"He deserves a chance to clear himself, to at least help."

He closed his eyes again, retreating to the earlier meditative attitude. Sharp words to break that pose jammed at the back of her throat, giving him the chance to speak first. "You persist with terms like 'deserve' and 'fair.' Please try to avoid them. No one enjoys seeing his poverty flaunted."

She took the chair that faced outside, where the failing sunlight grudgingly pulled back from the city. He needed someone around who thought of words like "deserve" and "fair," and he knew it. It was a matter of balances. She could never be as ruthless as he could, nor could he be as compassionate as she could. The silence carried that message, an unspoken agreement on parameters. If the same ground ever had to be covered again, the mental geography was known.

They were able to enjoy the silence for perhaps ten minutes before Pierce knocked on the door. Cindy answered it. He went directly to Kolar.

"This is the stuff." He handed the large manila envelope to the older man as though ridding himself of an especially unpleasant burden.

"Not even sealed. Have you checked it out?"

Pierce looked uncomfortable, shooting a sidelong glance at Cindy. "I sure as hell wanted to, but I didn't. I couldn't make up my mind if I wanted to know what was in there or not, so I took the coward's way out."

The phrase jangled in Kolar's ears. There was a time when the phrase would have been appropriate and because of that, Pierce would never have used it. Now he used it, and it was a jest.

It was a disquieting prospect, and Kolar fumbled with the clasp, deliberately clumsy, giving himself some grace to mull over the new concepts.

The papers inside the envelope were handwritten. After the first few lines, Kolar concentrated on his reading with the fervor of a missionary exposed to heresy. Pierce tried a smile on Cindy, and she responded with a patently false attempt before returning to her watch over Kolar. He stopped reading to rub his eyes, and when he looked to Cindy they were red-rimmed and older than anything she'd ever seen. He turned from her to speak to Pierce. "Go back to your station. Be prepared to terminate within four hours. You'll be contacted. Clear?"

Pierce's jaw bobbed with unspoken questions. In the end, he said only "Clear" and left.

Cindy moved to Kolar's side. He replaced the papers in the envelope, and she pointed at it. "Are your facts in there?"

He sagged under the words. "I can't be sure. I'm going to study it in privacy. You'll excuse me, I know."

She murmured sympathy and patted his shoulder and turned to go. Her hand was on the doorknob when his voice stopped her. "I don't want to take a chance on contacting Draeger before he leaves. You'll have to go to Iloilo after him and warn him. Tell him to stay out of Manila until I contact him. He's to trust no one." He paused, then, "I was thinking about sending him home because he might be in danger. Now I have a better idea of exactly how much danger, and I can't send him home. I feel greasy."

She started back to him, and he held up a hand. "Make reservations for me to get back to L.A. as soon as possible. Make arrangements to go to Iloilo, meet Draeger, come back here, and follow me. I want your meeting with him as covert as possible."

"I'll have the airlines people call you."

He nodded, pulling the papers from the envelope, closing her from his mind before the door closed her from the room.

The crabbed handwriting made him think of the insect tracings left in the muck of pond-bottoms. The same revulsion now roiled his stomach that he used to feel looking at lacelike algae and impossible creatures. Once he'd told a teacher of his reaction, and the man undertook to show young Carl the error of his ways. The heretofore invisible creatures conjured by a microscope were even worse than the things his eyes revealed. Magnification of the visible creatures through the wonders of photography reveled in his nightmares for months.

And now he had a different nightmare. No poisoned darts would imbed in his flesh and draw him to waiting fangs. What was on this paper was no honest predation, no attempt at survival. The papers described suspicions, things of darkness and deception. Kolar broke from his reading to pour a drink, neglecting ice or water, enjoying the bite of the alcohol and the sting of the fumes. He had hoped the semi-irritation and stimulation would jar his sensibilities, provide perspective on the material. It merely made him more alert, and that brought a clearer picture of what he was reading.

Munson's papers pointed out that Draeger's operation with Egg Roll was suspect. Munson's evaluation of the reports received indicated falsified reports, common-knowledge data fobbed off as timely information. When questioned, the papers stated, Draeger had been very defensive, not only about the agent, but his own efforts. Evasive was not too strong a word. Munson suggested a parallel operation to test Egg Roll. Draeger resisted the idea violently. Munson's papers had further suggestions, complete with a Grand Cayman corporation identity.

Kolar carefully replaced the cheap notepaper in the envelope, bent the eared clasp outward to secure the flap, and threw the thing from him. He spat obscenities after it, so that the whirling twisting object hurtled across the room in a barrage of filth. It slapped against the wall and dropped to the floor. Kolar continued to watch it, unmoving, daring it to stir.

A lifetime. An entire lifetime. Careers. God Almighty, more than careers, lives. Men had died in this tiny, quiet little war. Some had bought it in alleys or bars, one under a subway in New York, two—no, by God, three—in the Golden Triangle, and two more in Africa. And now it was all up for grabs, and for money. All the integrity among members, all the pain and triumph of a small, elite group challenging the strength of world powers, the dedication to the survival of a nation—all of that was hanging by a thread. A golden thread. The whole thing, endangered by simple, blind greed.

But who was beyond greed?

Not Carl Kolar.

He dropped his head into waiting hands, massaged his temples.

What had created this unit, if not greed? The lust for power, the need to influence decisions and the people who made them? Wasn't that the intelligence operative's meat and drink? What man in his right mind devoted himself to such infernal work, if not to be a source of power in his own right? And what was Carl Kolar? He was the power. When his shadow fell on a man, that man moved, and, by God, it was a good feeling.

And still there was nothing he would not do to stop what was happening before him. The power, the authority, were adjuncts to the backbreaking responsibility. If this unit was exposed, it would die. The country's most closely held clandestine collection effort would wither in the sun like the slashed jungles of these very islands.

It was a satire written by the gods. He would investigate every allegation, suggestion, and innuendo in the papers. They would be proven or disproven beyond the proverbial shadow of a doubt.

When that was done, Carl Kolar, who had built an empire and protected a democracy for his entire life by insisting on unarguable facts, would condemn a fellow member of that democracy to death in the name of that great truth, freedom.

For hours he sat unmoving in the chair, head slumped forward, full of things that taxed the bull-like neck beyond endurance. When sleep finally came it struck like a blow, sending a jerk through his body that was frightening. As it was, Kolar was unaware, and the tense frame slid toward relaxation with a kind of self-conscious hesitance. In a few minutes he sighed hugely, mind and body surrendering. The last move he made was to haul the dangling right hand laboriously up to the arm of the chair. It wadded into a massive, broken-knuckled fist.

# CHAPTER 24

The reservation clerk at Draeger's hotel in Iloilo was delighted to be able to tell Cindy that Draeger was in residence. She was sorry she couldn't be of more help, but Mr. Draeger and his companion had hired a car and gone for the day. Was there a message?

Cindy looked directly into the young woman's eyes, then away quickly, simulating a nervous search for eavesdroppers. "I have a note. In an envelope. It's very personal. You understand?"

The clerk stiffened, but on closer inspection of Cindy's sad demeanor, decided she meant no trouble. And if she did, it was a clerk's responsibility to take messages for the guests, wasn't it?

"Give me your envelope," she said, sliding an arm out onto the counter. Cindy would have sworn the girl was a licensed magician. The envelope was gone before she could blink. Thanking the girl profusely, she hurried back to the taxi. The ride to her own hotel was a matter of a couple of blocks. She directed the driver to cruise through the town, hoping to build some little cover as a tourist.

Going directly to Draeger's hotel was a choice of evils. If she'd hired someone to deliver the message, that would arouse curiosity and the need to talk it over with someone. Trying to establish personal contact with Draeger would almost certainly entail running into Ria, and Cindy had seen enough of her to know how to predict that scene. A telephone call would have been faceless, unidentifiable— except it would be of possible interest to the switchboard in one or both hotels. Cindy had decided the safest bet was to make an ally of the go-between. With luck, the woman at the desk would assume that Ria and Draeger were involved in some sort of triangle. It

274

would please her to play some small part in the drama, and the odds were she'd keep her mouth shut, either in hopes of following the play to its end, or in the interest of self-preservation. And the phone call was inevitable, so better one than two.

It was one hell of a way to run a railroad.

Furthermore, there wasn't even a television in the room. There was a radio. She turned it on and an incredibly amateur rock group belched forth. Whirling the tuning knob brought in nothing relaxing until she discovered the soft string harmonies of the old music, remembered from the restaurant in Manila. She slipped out of her traveling slacks and blouse and stretched luxuriously on the bed. It would be fun to be a real tourist in this place, she decided. Being stuck alone in this room was a drag. Having to work was a drag, period. Life would be much nicer if the money just came in the mail every month. There were so many things to see, to do. Glen probably knew most of them. He was the sort of man who'd be fun to explore with. It would be interesting to see if Ria was aware of that. In fact, it'd be interesting to find out just exactly what she was aware of.

The next thing Cindy knew, the phone was ringing and she was having trouble reaching it. She stopped thrashing long enough to get oriented, then snatched the instrument from its cradle. Her hello was brisk, denying eyes still batting heavy lids.

"I got your message."

"Good."

"Have you seen anything of the town yet?"

"No. I've been sitting tight."

"Fine. Tomorrow, thirteen-thirty. There's a museum on General Luna Street, right by the Provincial Capitol. Any taxi can show you where it is."

"You'll be alone?"

Exasperation tinted the flat voice. "Exactly. Thirteen-thirty."

Cindy continued to hold the phone to her ear after the grating click, hanging up slowly, preoccupied. She felt heavy-limbed, exhausted. Her watch said it was seven-thirty, and she had to look outside to be sure it was evening. It might easily have been morning. The view from her window was of the cement security wall enclosing the building. The top of the wall was just mid-window high, and the

barbed wire crown was aureoled with a salmon glow from the
sinking sun. Swallows flew between distant trees, rocketed skyward
to become hurtling black darts against the clouds. A breeze was up,
the wind that would bring the fishermen home. Palm trees moved
lazily with it, mop-headed adolescents hearing their own music.

She showered and dressed to go to dinner, consulting the Ministry
of Tourism brochure called a Situation Report for a restaurant.
Leafing through it reinforced her wish that she had time and opportunity to actually see the area. Eventually she decided where she'd eat.

The odd lethargy was still troubling her when she walked into the
lobby, and she returned the smiles of the staff with an effort. When
she stepped outside, the full strength of the heat stored in the cement
drive and portico threatened to pull the breath from her lungs, and
she quickly put a hand to the doorjamb. Steadying herself, she
watched a car approach. It was a relic, a junkyard escapee. Gouts of
exhaust boiled behind the thing, pitchlike in the increasing darkness.
With a look of leering drunkenness, it suddenly flashed its lights at
her. Only then did she realize it was a taxi and the driver had spotted
her, expected her to hire him. When he opened the door, she looked
inside at the grimy back seat and checked. She stepped back,
dumbfounded by the rotted-out six-inch square hole in the floor. It
opened directly to the ground.

Embarrassed, angry, she turned and fled. It was a dignified
retreat, accomplished with a straight back and a firm step. Psychologi-
cally, it was a complete route, and when she had flung herself back
on her bed, she bit a lip to hold back tears that smoldered at the
corners of her eyes.

By morning she was reasonably recovered, a bit ashamed of her
performance at the door. When she stepped into the lobby the faces
of the staff were controlled, watchful. She looked at the girl behind
the desk and smiled her brightest. "I don't know what happened to
me last night. I just felt ill. I hope the driver wasn't too upset?"

The clerk smiled back, her relief evident. "No worry, Miss
Anderson. Everybody explained to him. He understands, I think. No
worry."

Cindy thanked her, nodding and smiling for the now-friendly
people around her and made her way to the coffee shop. A waiter
hovered until she chose a table, then swooped. The menu offered

several breakfasts, including a variety of "Filipino Breakfasts" under a separate heading. They were essentially the same as the American, but featured rice instead of potatoes and offered fish or local sausage instead of bacon or ham. She elected the more exotic choice, balking at fish, and settled for the sausage called *longaniza* to go with scrambled eggs and fried rice. The waiter repeated the order uncertainly.

Cindy said, "I want you to tell me how everything is made, too. I've never had fried rice for breakfast and I've never had *longaniza*. I want to know what's in it and how it's cooked."

The waiter was too surprised to return her smile. "You want to speak to the cook?"

She laughed. "No, no—not the cook. Just ask him what's in things, then you tell me, OK?"

The young man shook his head and agreed, scribbling furiously in his order pad as he left. A moment later he returned with the standard tray—coffee cup, creamer, sugar, hot water, clean spoon and jar of instant coffee. He served it with discreet swiftness, obviously afraid of any more weird questions.

Cindy was halfway through the first cup of coffee when the waiter appeared again, this time with help. A man in white, complete with short chef's cap accompanied him. Dealing the meal like a Reno houseman, the waiter did his job and was gone. The chef remained, staunch.

OK, wise guy, Cindy told herself, smiling widely enough to hurt the corners of her mouth, you got yourself into this, let's see how you get out.

She gestured at the chair across from her "Sit down, please. I can't talk and eat while you're standing like that."

Natural courtesy warred with accepted behavior for a moment before he settled into a seat. It seemed to help him relax. When Cindy asked his technique for making fried rice, he loosened up a shade further. When she asked about making *longaniza,* and appeared to understand the finer points, he gestured for the waiter to refill her coffee and bring him a cup, as well. The waiter did, and remained for the conversation. Before the meal was over, Cindy also knew how to select the best mangos, the woman from behind the desk had come out to tell her where to buy the best material in

Iloilo, and the waiter was constantly interrupting for more details about America's rock stars. When Cindy told him she'd never, ever heard a harsh word about either Donny or Marie Osmond, he was literally euphoric.

Cindy was among friends. She knew their names, ages, and the size of their families. What they knew of her was the cover. A school teacher on vacation. Her new friends were impressed. So young, so pretty—lucky students! The chef essayed a hopeful smile that wilted to sheepishness at a sharp sentence from the woman at the desk.

It was a cue to move along. In her room she thought of Draeger and Pierce and Munson, living among such friendly people, telling the same lie over and over. It had to erode the soul as well as the grasp on reality. Each repetition must inevitably carry away a piece of the truth that is the framework of a mind. Could enough lies dissolve the entire structure?

Of course, Pierce lived in a well-insulated situation. He was accepted as a hotel manager because that's exactly what he was doing when people met him. Munson had his home and his work so well built he literally lived his cover at all times. But Draeger traveled. It was no wonder he was more quiet, more introspective. And more cautious. Or was he simply controlled? There was a tension about him, the impression he was constantly ready to move quickly. Suddenly she was quite certain he would never move until he was ready. The violence would be considered, machined. If there was violence in him and it broke out it would be more ferocious for its repression.

She pushed the idea aside, and busied herself with arrangements to catch the evening flight to Manila.

It was almost eleven by the time she had her reservation in order. She returned to the lobby, casually looking to see if there was a satisfactory taxi available. To her relief, the junker was absent and a sleek Toyota waited. Her request to "Just drive around Iloilo" without a specific destination created a burst of argument in Visayan dialect between the bellhop and the driver. A three-way discussion ironed out the difficulty.

For a few blocks the left side was mansions, walled off from the plebian world by cement and ornate ironwork gates. Some of the old homes were relics, run down. Others were freshly painted and well maintained. All were multistoried, the top floors peering over their protective walls through a dazzle of broken glass set in the cement. A few, even more security conscious, sported rolls of barbed wire perched on top of the glass. Whatever wealth, or former wealth, dwelt behind those barriers carried an unending penalty.

More hope-filled buildings appeared along the way, the University of San Augustin on the right and a girl's school on the left. They reached the end of General Luna, where it runs into the Provincial Capitol. Cindy marked the location of the low-slung modern Museo Iloilo and checked her watch. It was a few minutes after eleven. The lingering impression of General Luna was whitewash, the painted trees, wall, and boulevard dividers. That was reinforced by the plump white fountain in front of the capitol building. The taxi turned right, heading into the city.

Cindy was delighted with it. The sole unfortunate aspects were the number of vehicles, which was suddenly almost Manila-like, and the abuse of the wonderful old business buildings. They were straight out of Conrad. There were several of them, pompous two-storied brick and cement temples of commerce, lording it over the lesser constructions of this tropical town. They huddled close to each other, besmirched by years of grime and garish advertising. Still the buildings held their positions, come what may, potbellied fronts held up by arches that formed shaded sidewalks. The scalloped roof fronts, architectural raised eyebrows, made eloquent comment on the changes of their decades.

Cindy wanted to leap from the taxi and tear down the demeaning signboards, scrape away the accumulations of paint and dirt. She wondered if the government would do anything to preserve them before neglect finished them off.

That was one of the paradoxes of the Philippines. Here she was, hoping an executive fiat would come down from Manila and save the charm of some old building, and didn't that imply at least tacit approval of a government that could issue such a decree? The Philippines was a dictatorship, and it was gospel in the United States that dictatorships were evil. But the neglect had gone on through three full decades of democracy, regardless of what you called the years that preceded them. Was one man's judgment inevitably less fallible, less civilized than the judgment of the masses? It would be very difficult to defend that viewpoint by pointing out the more recent voting record of Americans on racial or sexual equality not to mention busing.

They were long past the buildings that initiated her train of thought by the time she was snapped out of it. She looked forward— they were on the waterfront, paralleling the river—just as a man lurched into view from behind a truck. He was crossing in front of them, and the driver stood on the brake. The man couldn't have looked back at them if he'd wanted to. He had two sacks balanced on his shoulder, so heavy each step threatened to topple him. Sweat coursed his body, accentuating the writhing, straining musculature. His face was hidden, and she hoped he wouldn't turn. There had to be pain there, and she dreaded the hopelessness that might live in him and admitted to herself she wanted no exposure to it. Looking away, she noticed the sugar sacks were piled high immediately beside them. Each was marked sixty kilos. The man had been carrying two, a little over two hundred and sixty pounds. The man probably weighed little more than half that. She kept her view on the mountain of sugar, inhaling the cloyed air, more than ever unwilling to look into the carrier's eyes.

The rest of the tour was uneventful. She arrived back at the end of General Luna in time to have a soft drink in a small cafe. It gave her a full view of the museum and the park in front of it. At exactly thirteen-twenty-one she made her way across the street, certain Draeger was watching from a location nearby. She was looking at a Japanese World War II machine gun when Draeger came in. He moved toward her, slowly, observing the material in the cases. He had been in the building perhaps three minutes when the commotion erupted at the front door, and Cindy thought her heart had stopped.

Girls thronged into the museum, none of them loud, but all of them giggling and whispering at once.

Draeger stepped beside her. "If the opposition's good enough to come in with any sort of cover, we're bombed out, so we might as well get that over with, right?" He was half-laughing as he spoke, eyes flicking from the girls to Cindy. "What's going down? We have trouble?"

"No, just a message. He thought it was important enough to send me with it. You're to stay out of Manila until you get the word to come back.''

An older woman appeared to give the girls a guided tour. The group threaded its way between the display cases, the girls in dark skirts with suspenderlike straps and white blouses. When Cindy realized she was looking at them with envy, it puzzled her, picked at a corner of her mind. Draeger spoke again. ''Does he realize I'm not here alone? Didn't he give any indication how long he might expect this situation to last?''

Cindy breathed easier, relieved he wasn't going to fight the orders. ''He only said for you to stay here. I'll be leaving on the evening plane for Manila and then join him back in the States. We'll be back whenever he thinks the time's right.'' Even as she wondered why she was troubling to give him further details, he was gesturing widely. A couple of the girls stole glances at them.

''Home? What the hell for? What's going on?''

''I don't have a need to know.'' The rebuff was sharp, honed by the mutual knowledge of the lie. Draeger knew the envelope from Pierce was the reason. He also knew Cindy must deny any further knowledge. The question was a rudeness.

He lounged against the case. The very casualness of his posture was a warning, and she was prepared for the acid tone. ''Who're you putting on me to see I don't skip?''

Her face warmed and she damned it. ''There's no one on you. You have my word.''

''Not exactly the same as a notarized statement, is it?''

''Don't be a fool.'' He was frightening her. His anger was spinning a web that could trap him. ''Where would you go? And how long would you last? You're too good a man to run from a fight.''

''Too smart to stand still and watch you people run over me, too. You tell Kolar those are my only words for him.''

''Don't you think that's a bit melodramatic?''

He grinned, and the tilt of it made it a mischievous admission of hands in the cookie jar. At that moment she cared that his phrase was, indeed, cheap melodrama. He said, ''I certainly hope so. I guess if someone was out to do me, they'd have done it that night I got thumped in my apartment. Has Kolar ever developed any ideas on that deal?'' His nearly instant change was a conjurer's swiftness, and she distrusted it accordingly. He was avoiding the issue, fending it off. There was no question of his right to do so, or the wisdom of it, but she wished it had been done forthrightly. There was an unfairness in the side-step.

She shook her head, then indicated the girls and their lecturer drifting closer. Draeger led her toward the windowed side of the building, stopping by a long, rectangular glass case. There was a skeleton in it, an ancient princess of this area, buried with her jewels and other possessions. A card identified the display as an exact replica, the original remains transported to Manila. For some reason it saddened Cindy.

''Something's got to break pretty soon,'' he went on. ''We can't suspend operations forever if Munson doesn't turn up. We've got to get back to work, and the first priority is to try to establish a link with Egg Roll. Kolar's got to realize that.''

''Why? Wouldn't that be more dangerous than simply waiting for Egg Roll to tell us what we can do to help?''

''No way. What he knows about exfiltration you know about space travel. He won't last ten minutes.'' He bent to her, holding her arm above the elbow, features stretched thin with insistence. ''You know damned well the hardest, nastiest part of this business is breaking and running. All he'll do is go like hell, and they'll be waiting for him, wherever he slows down. You don't know him, Cindy. Hell, I hardly know the poor bastard myself. But he's not like most of the people we deal with. He's a scared little man, afraid of everything but hope, and that makes him a lot braver than most. I feel responsible for him.''

''I'll tell Carl. He's been there, you know—he'll understand.''

''Yeah, sure. If I go anywhere else on the island, I'll be sure to leave an address or phone number where I can be reached, or a time when I'll be back if there's no phone. Good enough?''

She reached to touch his hand, and one of the uniformed girls caught the gesture. She smiled shyly at Cindy and their eyes held for a split second, and then she looked away. Cindy was still savoring the woman-to-woman understanding that had sparked between herself and the young girl when she lifted her face to answer Draeger.

''That's fine. I hope we won't be long.''

He nodded, and she resented his silent preoccupation. He continued to look directly at her, but it was as if his eyes were fastened on a point several yards behind her. When he left, he pulled his hand away slowly, so slowly his arm pulled away from his side, and he was already turned when the hand fell into its normal coordination with his stride.

Cindy remained in place, her eyes busy between watching Draeger to see if he was followed and insuring no one paid any attention to her efforts to do so. When he was out of sight, she continued to inspect the replicated bones and treasures of the long-dead heiress. A movement just beyond her range of vision made her turn her head. The girl who'd smiled at her was there, the smile back, a touch of apprehension about it.

"You are American?"

Cindy tried to make her own smile welcoming. "Yes, I am. How did you guess?"

The girl's shrug was an education. Half wriggling social embarrassment, the other half was the untrammeled grace of reeds in the wind. She spoke softly, her voice low in deference to the location and the fact that she was supposed to be paying attention to the lecture. "I don't know—the way you walk. The way you do things."

"Do I walk differently?"

"Oh, yes. It's not always possible to recognize an American lady, but some are very easy." She stood erect. "They walk prouder than the others. I think they are more free."

"We're working on it. What's your name?"

"Tina de la Rosa." She waited politely, accepting Cindy's hand gravely when it was offered.

"My name's Cindy Anderson. I'm pleased to meet you."

With the formalities out of the way, the girl returned to her questions. "Are you very rich?"

Cindy said, "I have a good job. I'm not rich at all."

"It costs much money for you to come here. Are you with that man who left?"

"We were just talking. Are you girls all from the same school?"

"Yes. We come here to learn about the past. They say it is important. I am more interested in the future. I would like to be a doctor, I think."

"There's no reason why you shouldn't be."

The girl made sure Cindy wasn't teasing her, then turned away to laugh. It was an honest sound, full of genuine amusement. "If you lived here, you would know there are reasons. If you lived here for a hundred years, maybe in that time you would hear all the reasons."

"Some people are born to prove there are better ways to do things. Maybe you're one of those people."

Tina looked at her again. Cindy's pulse quickened at the flare in the young eyes, but as quickly as it had come, it sank to a spark of nothing more than continuing curiosity. But there had been something. It wasn't as powerful as hope, perhaps, but surely speculation, the mother of hope?

"You asked me if I was rich." She tapped a finger on the glass top. The *tac-tac* of her fingernail carried to the lady lecturing, and she turned to stare mild disapproval. Cindy looked away hurriedly and continued. "This woman was a princess or a queen or something. You and I don't have jewels and gold like that. But she got married to whoever her father picked for her, and she could be bought or sold any time. She was a powerful person, but if her father or her husband fell from power, she could be a slave the next day. You live here, the same as she did. You can read, write, go to school, marry who you choose, have children—or not—if you choose. And if you work hard enough, any career can be yours. All because many women before you have demanded those things."

Tina continued to study the contents of the case long after Cindy was finished. Her voice was awed when she broke her silence. "Someone must have loved her very much, to put such nice things on her when she was buried. Maybe she married the man she wanted to marry and her children loved her and made her proud. There is accomplishment in that, the same as there is accomplishment in being a doctor. I think, if I am lucky, I will be a doctor and those other things. Maybe I am too romantic, but I would not want to be an old woman with nothing but money. I want to have a husband who loves me and children. Are you married?"

There was a sticky mass at the base of Cindy's tongue, a conglomerate of protests and rejected answers that tried to choke her. She swallowed with difficulty. "I haven't found the man I want to marry yet."

Tina nodded, understanding. The budding woman in the forming body momentarily achieved ascendancy, created a mind-shadow of the things that were coming to be. She measured Cindy. The sympathetic nod carried the feminine spices of scorn and wry empathy. Cindy was looking at the spirit she had seen in a thousand women's councils, and it always said the same thing. In that conclave, the only voices to be listened to were those of women who had borne a man on their stomachs, and the only ones to be heeded had born life from their wombs. The rest could be respected. They must be pitied.

The class lecturer called after Tina, favoring Cindy with a condescending smile. It was almost more than she could handle, although it had no connection with the hurt and anger burning through her system. When Tina smiled her good-bye, she half-curtsied, and the woman-in-waiting disappeared, overcome by the child of the present.

Cindy answered her smile briefly and let her gaze fall naturally back to the case. There was no great wisdom in it, she decided. The queen is dead and Cindy Anderson lives. So do Tina de la Rosa and what's-her-name—Ria. The only question was, how come they all seemed to exist in a different time zone? In a last attempt at communication, Cindy trailed her hand the length of the cool glass surface on her way out.

■　　**CHAPTER 25**　　■

Munson watched Pierce approach from the dock. Concern dusted the lean features, giving him the look of a troubled wolf. His lower lip drew back and strong white teeth worried at it, contributing to the image.

Pierce's jaunty step and happy waves for guests and employees made it obvious the trip had gone well, and it was that very insouciance that concerned Munson.

This was no time to relax, he told himself, and struck the window-sill with his fist as he turned away. He moved to a chair, stooped over, but the long legs carried him across the room with surprising speed. He settled in, both hands curled around the ends of the chair arms. His thoughts remained fixed on Pierce.

The man had to straighten up. Draeger would be alerted very soon, if he wasn't already, and he might prove more troublesome than they expected. Pierce would never learn to think in terms of the unexpected. He planned well to a certain point, then let everything slide and trusted to luck. That was one thing that never failed, Munson told himself grimly. If there was going to be any luck in an operation, it would invariably be bad.

There was more to it than that, though. Pierce wasn't behaving normally. The sloppiness in his operations had always been the result of carelessness, and the man had been at least subconsciously aware of his behavior and stayed afraid. He had always slid along the edge of panic under pressure, and now he was controlling himself. Shades of the old shamming surfaced occasionally, touch-ing off humor in Pierce's eye where there used to be nothing but attempted sincerity. Possibly he was amused at himself.

And that could be lethal. Munson interlaced his fingers and forced them outward from his body in a staccato of cracking knuckles. The plan depended on Pierce remaining Pierce. The entire operation was a matter of men, of personalities, and the predictability of their reactions. If Pierce broke that chain, God only knew what might fall out of place. He had no more nor less capability to destroy the plan than anyone else involved, but all of them could derail it. It wasn't a matter of manipulating them. That was always foolish, because people did what they meant to do. The trick was to eliminate their alternatives, put them in a position where they could only do one thing, and you knew what that thing would be. And if Pierce was changing his behavior pattern, he was threatening all the other delicate arrangements. It would be as if a surgeon reached for a scalpel and the nurse slapped a popsicle stick into his hand.

He grunted at the knock on the door, and Pierce swept in, still full of excitement.

"It went down like grease! Draeger was leaving town, going on some kind of a trip out of town, so he can't have any idea why Kolar's going to be coming down on him. The old man took the papers and started reading them, and that was it, man! He went for it!"

Munson fought back rage. Smirking moron, he thought, telling me Kolar himself is here, and making it secondary to his own insignificant part in the scheme. Such a fool. So many fools. If I don't do everything myself, it's a disaster. At least Benjamin's Swords accomplished their surveillance, gave me enough description to recognize Kolar. They spared me the shock of this imbecile's crude tale-bearing. But I knew Kolar would come. It had to be him.

Carefully, he prepared his words for Pierce, taking pride in his control. "I thought he'd take the bait. This unit means more to him than his life, Tony. Never forget that, because the obvious corollary is that it means more to him than ours, too. Tell me exactly what happened."

Pierce recounted his trip. At the end, Munson asked, "Who is the woman with Kolar? Did you learn anything?"

Pierce shrugged. "Kolar claims she's with him to doublecheck your company's business records. He says the budget can't afford that kind of loss anymore than a legitimate corporation. He wants to make sure everything works out right. He also thinks there may be a lead, something to give him an idea what happened to you."

"Good." Munson's anger washed away in a flood of satisfaction. "I knew that's what he'd do! What's he doing now? Wait!" An imperious hand stopped Pierce's answer. "I know what he's doing. The woman's been told to bring copies of the records, as complete as she can manage, to him. They're preparing to go back to the States, for further researching. Am I right?"

Pierce smiled and shook his head in a negative. Pressure expanded in Munson's head. He demanded hoarsely. "Don't lie to me! Tell me what they're doing!"

Still smiling, Pierce lifted his arm with the watch on it and turned it for Munson to look at. "They're not preparing; they're already on the way. At least Kolar is. The woman'll be taking off as soon as she gets back. You called it, but your timing was off a little bit."

Munson walked to the window to watch the sea, stalling until he could act amused. He was smiling easily when he turned back to Pierce. "You can't imagine how I feel right now. We've passed an acid test. Godalmighty, Tony, we're going to make it! We're going to alter history! And we'll be as rich as kings!"

"I'll settle for rich. What happens next?"

Munson laughed. "Kolar and his woman will find exactly what I want them to find—money diverted to unofficial activities, people hired illegally, supplies skimmed and lost to the system. He'll go out of his fucking mind, he'll be so angry."

"There's more to it than a little hanky-panky. What're you talking about?"

Munson slid back into his chair, poised forward, elbows on his knees. It was a coiled attitude, and Pierce leaned away from it, all the way to the back of his chair. Munson noted his discomfort. It added a fillip.

"I've been working toward something like this for years, Tony. Kolar'll never guess the details, but he'll get the picture I want him to see. He'll find evidence to make it look like Draeger was part of it. The papers you took to him are leads. When the whole illusion materializes, he'll be in a killing fury."

"You've said things like that before. Bilongon talks the same way. Look, if we've got to put Draeger in the shit, that's OK with me. Some education won't hurt him. There's no reason to kill him."

"If Kolar thinks Draeger's guilty of killing me and sabotaging his unit, what do you think he'll do?"

"He'll have him blown away."

"Wrong. Absolutely wrong. He'll have him questioned. Have you ever seen an intensive interrogation? Think what would happen to Draeger if Kolar chose the interrogator and told him he wanted answers at any cost."

A shiver ran through Pierce, and he shifted in the seat to disguise it. "Kolar'd never use torture."

Munson chuckled. "Believe that if you want. But you're the one who took him those papers. It's in your interest if he believes his only suspect is either dead or on the run."

The wind picked up, and Pierce faced the window to watch it comb the trees and shrubbery on the grounds. A mass of bougainvillea lifted and fell in erratic motion, compacted sprays of vibrant reds and oranges. The palms moved reluctantly, always struggling to retain their original position, complaining mightily in the hoarse rustling of the fronds.

Not yet Wagnerian, Pierce thought. The ocean's too calm and the sun's too bright. But it'll do. And if the wind shifts a little bit, we'll have our Wagner, sure as hell. Poor Draeger. Such a loyal schmuck. Just the fact that this is happening to him, much less the fact that I'm part of it, proves the system's no goddam good. We all get it sooner or later.

His stomach contracted into a dense mass.

Surely Munson doesn't think I'm able to kill Draeger? The question demanded out.

"Exactly what d'you have in mind for Draeger?"

Munson cherished the trepidation oozing from the voice, wished he could see it all, a balloon in a cartoon strip, words in italic, globules of fear bleeding from the letters.

"You're going to have to make the arrangements. We haven't got long. We could work with Boy Angel's people, but they're not very sophisticated. And if they're caught, they'll talk right away. We need someone with an awareness of the importance of what we're doing, someone with a cause."

"Bilongon's people?"

Munson said, "No. He's probably got someone smart enough and determined enough, but again, they're a pretty backward bunch. Draeger's no goddamned ribbon clerk. They'll get one try at him, if they're lucky. Miss him, and he'll disappear on us." He paused, the last word bitten off sharply, but he continued smoothly. "That's Draeger's responsibility. If he's good enough, he won't be hurt, and he's as good to us running as he is if he's eliminated."

"If it's not Bilongon or Boy Angel, who?"

"The Red Army people."

Pierce nearly flew from his chair. "Are you crazy? I don't know how to reach them, and if I did, I wouldn't. Those people are homicidal, for Christ's sake!"

"Bilongon knows. And if he doesn't you're going to find someone who does. Or do the job yourself, and I won't accept a miss from you. We've got to trust each other and all that, but let's face something right now. You're no finisher, Tony. I am. And I want an honest try where Draeger's concerned. I don't think you'd let him get away on purpose, but it's not in you to do this sort of thing.''

Pierce stared at Munson. The older man met it with a reptilian dispassion that rejected it. Pierce eventually looked away. "I don't know what to say to that," he said, murmuring. "I don't like the idea that you can't trust me, but I have to agree with you that I'm no murderer." He faced Munson. "And I'm not happy to learn that you are.''

"I'm not. You misunderstood. I'm only saying I could be."

"Shit. We're sitting here arranging to kill a man we called a friend once, and we're quibbling over the relative criminality of doing it or having it done. What have we gotten into?''

"History, Tony. We're into history.''

"You keep telling me that, and I keep telling you I don't give a shit. There's one thing you haven't addressed in all this, you know. You haven't mentioned the woman Draeger's with.''

The stolid expression fell back across Munson's face. "We've got a fortune coming to us. Are we going to throw it away on the chance some whore might be hurt?''

"I guess not.''

Munson sidled to Pierce and dropped a hand on his shoulder. "Get Bilongon. Tell him someone else bought the same information I did, and tell him where he's hiding. You don't even have to give the mark a name, Tony. Bilongon'll go to the terrorists and take it all off your hands.''

"OK. I guess I can do that. As long as there's no names. You were right about me. I couldn't put Draeger in the bag.''

"You won't have to, Tony. That's a promise.''

Pierce was outside when the last phrase penetrated his preoccupation. He thought about it and wished he'd gotten out sooner.

# ■ CHAPTER 26 ■

Luis Ramos leaned on the counter of the *sari-sari* store and watched his hand tremble in the light of the lowered kerosene lamp. It took all his will to keep his back to the road, a few feet away, knowing someone who recognized him and the devil, Cruz, could approach any time. Staring at labels and advertisements had calmed him a little, earlier, but he decided when they first called stores *sari-saris,* or general stores, they had larger ones in mind. There just wasn't enough stock to keep a man's mind occupied.

Luis sighed. The stock wasn't the problem. The flickering lamp was too dim for him to read the finer print, anyhow. The problem was Captain Cruz, the memory of his honeyed words a foul taste. "You've worked at the hotel a long time," he'd said. "You're trusted. All I want from you is news, the sort of gossip you exchange on the job all the time. Just keep your eyes open." And when he said it, his own eyes were as innocent as a child's.

If there had ever been a chance to hide anything, it was gone. Cruz always knew. What he didn't know, he guessed. He was frightening.

Irony wasn't a word in Luis's vocabulary, but he knew there was something remarkably wrong in the fact that he was afraid of Cruz. The men at the hotel—Pierce, and the seldom-seen, bearded foreigner that no one was to talk about, and the cruel-eyed Tondo man—anyone knew they were deadly. Yet it was the small man slouched on a stool beside him who truly frightened him.

Luis Ramos was experiencing his first professional interrogation. The ordeal had shattered men far more sophisticated. Cruz could have sought out the nervous vibrations plaguing his subject, if he'd needed them. It was enough to watch the eyes blink when the questions required hard answers. They made Cruz think of moths against the glass chimney of the lantern. Some of them cleansed themselves of the madness that drew them to the flame and dashed away in fitful, unsure bursts. Others succumbed completely and fell, battered and seared, to thrash out their lives on the packed earth floor. A smaller number whirled in ashen spirals upward to the roof where they were easy prey for the bulb-eyed *tok-tok* lizards.

There were no threats in Cruz's questions. He disliked threatening frightened men. It was poor technique, pushed them beyond their normal limits. Fright was necessary, but too much was counter productive. The man would say anything to get rid of his interrogator. It was important that the subject say only what was accurate. Bad information was worse than no information. Cruz asked questions carefully phrased to elicit conscious answers and equally important internal responses. The actual words were spoken softly. That was very good for security, of course, and had the added advantage of requiring the subject's undivided attention. Even the seating had been carefully planned before the subject arrived, with Cruz on the stool immediately adjacent to the display case full of sundries. It was a small thing, but it meant he was shadowed and the subject was in maximum illumination. The drops of sweat running from the subject's hairline, molten copper in the lamplight, were mute testimony to the wisdom of that minor detail.

When properly interrogated, the subject will provide his own fear. Perhaps twenty percent of an interrogation is audible and visible to a spectator. Perhaps three times that much is understood by the subject and the interrogator. The remainder, the untouched area remaining to each individual, is that person's mind-fortress, the genuine self. Breaching it is the goal of what is popularly called brainwashing, something Cruz understood and hated. The destruction of that refuge cannot leave the attacker unscathed.

Cruz asked, ''Are you sure the foreigner came at the same time as the Tondo man called Boy Angel?'' (*Never tell me anything but the truth because I will find out, regardless.*)

''I am certain.'' (*You probably checked with the airline. I won't lie to you. I want to help you.*)

"The foreigner never leaves his room?" (*I don't believe that.*)

(*Oh, God, why did you let me say that? I didn't mean never!*) "He goes to the beach, or to dinner, or something, but we have instructions to keep the other hotel guests away. I shouldn't have said 'never,' because sometimes he does."

"I see what you mean." (*See how understanding I am, how forgiving?*) "Who does the foreigner speak to?" (*I am forgiving, but I am not forgetful.*)

(*You want me to believe you are my friend, but you are not. Not really. You only want what I can tell you, and you do not pay enough for the risk I run*). "The foreigner speaks to Pierce and Boy Angel. That one speaks to them and to the waitresses. Sometimes to one of the women guests, but Mr. Pierce watches him too closely for him to do much of that." (*See, I could be your friend. I can be helpful. And I do keep my eyes open.*)

"Pierce cannot be everywhere all the time. Who watches Boy Angel when he must be somewhere else?"

There was no inclination for Cruz's mind to develop a complementary thought connected with the question. The subject exposed a vulnerable area, and it was attacked.

(*He doesn't know! He can't! How could he know! Who else talks to him?*) "We all watch."

(*Fool!*) "Pierce warned everyone. He depends on a few, the best he has. We both know that. How is Boy Angel watched?"

(*There is someone else! Lying bastard, which one are you? Look what you've done to me!*) "Ernesto, at the pool bar, Carlos, and of course, me. We are to call Mr. Pierce if he tries to talk to the guests. (*I hate you. And the dogshit that informs on us.*)

"Is Boy Angel a bodyguard?" (*Think about them. Consider your situation. You will fear them and you will fear me, and you must know that I am the one who will never let you escape if you run and always help you if you cooperate. Understand that.*)

(*You're fishing. You're asking me to tell you something I can't be sure of. You're not as much as you think you are!*) "I don't know if he's a bodyguard, or what. They don't talk around me that much."

(*You liked that one didn't you?*) "That's what puzzles me. You said the foreigner told you Mr. Pierce had a concussion, right?"

(*What's that got to do with Boy Angel? You're not being honest with me!)* "He was very tired. It was dark when they came in, you know, and he carried Mr. Pierce to the house with no one to help but the fisherman, then he stayed up the rest of the night with him, after he sent the fisherman away. When I came in the next morning, he told me to watch Mr. Pierce. He said something about a concussion. That's all."

"And Mr. Pierce remained the same until the next morning?"

"Yes. Ernesto was in the room when he woke up." *(Not me!)*

"Did you know a man can die from a concussion? It's a very dangerous thing. They must be doing something very secretive if they are willing to risk a life. If I was hurt that badly, you'd get a doctor, right? Foreigners aren't that different. They're not usually going to stand around and watch a friend die. I don't know what they're doing, and I don't know what I'd do if I couldn't depend on you to be my eyes and ears on that island. We won't forget, believe me. Don't take any chances with those people, right? There's no reason for that. You're a good citizen. We have undercover people who get paid to take chances. If we need them, we'll depend on them later. OK?"

"Sure. I understand. And I won't take chances. It would only make trouble for you, right?" *(I want to help. Believe me!)*

"Right. We've been here long enough. I'll stay until you're away." *(I know where you live.)*

The end of an interrogation is much like the end of any other emotional experience. The mind seeks rest. Cruz's drifted all the way back to the pedantic lecturer who taught interrogation, a man whose thoughts were steel blades that shredded other men's brains. His words rustled in memory, like the wind in the *sari-sari's* thatch. "It is important for the interrogator to leave the subject in a state of mind that causes emotional and psychological inner stimuli to create a satisfactory pattern for subsequent interrogation. A subject left without hope may resort to escape attempts. Equally, too great a release can create a euphoria. It is incumbent on the interrogator to maintain a strict balance between the extremes. Further, the subject is normally of perishable value and must be utilized with dispatch. Mishandling a subject may delay the acquisition of pertinent data and is to be avoided as diligently as the excessive zeal which leads to accusations of maltreatment and subsequent loss of intelligence-gathering effectiveness.''

Luis Ramos continued to tremble as he walked away. His knee joints were spongy. The back of his neck was greasy. He tried to evaluate the things they'd talked about. It was absolutely clear that Cruz wasn't going to push him into any dangerous situations. That thought helped stabilize his knees. And if Pierce and the others were as bad as Cruz hinted, it was a citizen's responsibility to let someone know about them. Still, his primary responsibility was to himself. Pierce might be rich and have his important friends, but Cruz had the government. Better yet, he had the government few men ever see and fewer yet can call friendly. A man who was important to someone like Cruz could walk through any number of accidents and never be touched.

Cruz continued to sit at the counter of the store until the owner's gray head popped up in a window of the house. He nodded, and the tiny old woman came out to join him. He gestured at the cooler behind him, and when she extracted a soft drink for him, he indicated she should get a second, for herself. The wrinkled face split in a wide grin, revealing incredibly white teeth. Cruz paid for the drinks with several bills, and the woman laughed at the amount. Unlike her teeth, the cackling amusement fitted her apparent age, as did the almost falsetto voice.

"You must come often, young man. I don't have any other customers like you."

He grinned at her. "If you ever do, you better tell me right away."

She continued to smile, and even made a feminine slapping gesture at him, but the good humor was off-shade. "Who else would pay me to close early and then open up later? And who would pay so much for a drink?"

"It could happen that another man might ask about it. You will tell them exactly what you saw, but do not ever describe the other man. And then tell me everything."

The old woman stepped back farther from the light, throwing the wrinkled face into even deeper relief, aging it magically. Her mouth bowed toward the pulled-in chin, twisting the surrounding flesh into a mass of descending sketch marks. Reedlike fingers fumbled at each other.

Cruz said, "Please, do not worry. There is no danger. That is why you must never lie about me coming here." He grinned again. "It would be a mistake to tell everyone, but you must tell anyone who threatens you. It is important to me that you are not hurt."

When she shrugged, the shoulder cresting under the dark blouse was a pencil-wide ridge. "I am an old woman, and poor. The money you pay is necessary. At my age it is a gamble to wake up in the morning. I will take care of myself, young man."

"Who could doubt it? And probably still give the men around here something to think about."

She cackled at him. "Young fool! When I was your age—agh!" She shooed him away, like chasing chickens. Her laughter followed him down the road a few steps, and then the light went out and it stopped. It made Cruz nervous. The two ending at once stuck in his thoughts. He told himself there was absolutely no significance to it. Nevertheless, more than a mile later, when he reached the restaurant where he'd left his car, the gaiety from the building clashed with the memory of the old woman's cracked amusement and the winking out of the puny lantern.

The island of Boracay lies off the northwest tip of Panay, an insignificant dollop of geography washed by the Sibuyan Sea. It is only eight kilometers long and, at the most, three kilometers wide. There is a midriff, a thing suggesting a Victorian's corset, a mere half-kilometer across. The people living on the island grow coconuts, corn, tobacco, and other crops, and they harvest the surrounding sea. In recent years many Filipinos have discovered Boracay, and its reputation as a languorous tourist location has grown. There are still no hotels, no restaurants, nor any nightclubs.

Boracay is stunningly beautiful. Its coastline is remarkably varied, featuring large stretches of white sand beach of a purity that is a splendor. So much dazzle would be unbearable without some relief, and the island affords that with more beauty. The fringe of coconut palms is reinforced inland by multiple greens of fields and wild plants. On the beach's other flank, restless as the wind-stirred plant life, the sea rolls multiples of silver-cresting blues, indigo in the distance, declining to colorless as the air itself in the tiny pools where the sand gives way to worn and pitted rock outcroppings.

It is very possibly as close to a South Seas paradise as anyone is likely to find.

Waterfront land has been purchased by people who can afford to visit the island frequently. A sort of cottage industry has grown up around them, catering to their needs. It should take little time for a tourist industry to debase this arrangement. For now, however, one usually arrives at Boracay and its simple beauty by chartering a plane to the town of Malay. From there, it is a short ride by pumpboat to the island. The pumpboat is, for non-Filipinos, an adventure in itself. They are, like the praus, narrow-hulled, stabilized by outriggers. They seat an indeterminant number. There is a figure prescribed by law. There is another one, prescribed by a finger's width of freeboard and only an occasional wave sloshing aboard. The latter is favored by most pumpboat captains. There is little conversation on pumpboat rides. Although there is only one engine, it is about the size of that in a small car. It sits on blocks in the single hull, sometimes shielded from the passengers by a sheet of removable plywood, sometimes not. Since a muffler would serve no purpose other than to protect the ears of the passengers and they have no choice but to ride the pumpboat, the engine is unmuffled. That fact alone would discourage most conversation. A little rough water threatening the tentative buoyancy massively emphasizes the superiority of meditation over idle chitchat.

Draeger loved it all. The small plane carrying them from Iloilo skimmed the mountains and swooped low over the coast, the pilot treating his passengers to far more than a routine run to Malay. The strait between Panay and Boracay was rough enough to be exciting, and the island waited for them in the sun, bright and inviting. Their cabin was the product of Ria's maneuvering, a simulated nipa hut—actually solidly constructed of plywood and lumber—raised a good five feet in the air on poles at each corner. It was decorated to look native and sat a few yards back among the coconut trees. Ria had arranged their use of it from a friend in Manila.

There were two rooms, an arrangement Draeger referred to as "a kitchen and everything else." The beds were mats that rolled up or hung out to air during the day. The floor was solid plywood, rather than the slats that are the style of many genuine nipa huts. There were no chairs, nor was there a television set, radio, stereo, or glass in the windows. There were some books. There was a kerosene lamp. The nearest neighbors were at least fifty yards away, invisible because of the growth. Fishing boats slid past out to sea, infrequent reminders of civilization. Ria had the shack's kitchen stocked with plenty of food and drink. At night they heard the stirring of unidentified things on the ground and under the place.

It occurred to Draeger once that, if the shack were on the ground instead of in the air, the creatures would have been that much closer to them and therefore more genuinely worrisome. At altitude, however, they were a mysterious presence, with the deliciousness of the unknown. It generated a visceral desire for human contact without the nerve-deadening touch of true fear.

The morning of their fifth day on Boracay marked the eighth day of their trip together. They had breakfast in bathing suits and, as on every morning, hurried down the steps and ran hand in hand to the waiting sea. They splashed and played until Ria tired, and then she returned to the hut. Draeger swam, stretching himself against the water in long, smooth strokes.

On this morning he stopped short and flipped over on his back, floating, staring into the unclouded sky. The sea rocked him softly, the meter exactly suited to his breathing, two complete rolls from right to left for each inhalation and exhalation. The water was cool, the sun hot on his chest and stomach, even penetrating to the slightly submerged surfaces of thighs and outstretched arms. The rays fought to keep his body dry where the infrequent wave swept across.

Ria said they could stay another four days, no more. Her work couldn't stand any more neglect. When she said it she looked at him expectantly, waiting for him to say something about his own job. When he hadn't, it embarrassed her. He'd had to explain that he wasn't fired, and that had led to more explanations about why he didn't have to go to work, all lies, and the trip had almost ended there.

Actually, it was Cindy's timely appearance in Iloilo that salvaged the whole thing. Taking off in the afternoon and leaving Ria to sit at the pool by herself had worked wonders. She had said nothing, but it was clear she realized she'd been supersensitive. Things had warmed up as soon as he returned from the meeting.

It certainly wouldn't do to thank Cindy for that. She was a broad-minded woman, but it didn't seem likely she'd take too well to being identified as a catalyst in someone's else's love life. There was a look about her that said she'd be a damned sight more interested in her own.

His determination to sort out some of his own problems crumbled, and he was thinking of her exclusively.

There was a curious fascination about her, he admitted to himself, a tremendous ambivalance in the way she talked to a man and the way she acted, or appeared to act, if you didn't know her. She was all ice, at a distance; crisp. Her vocal responses, and the minute movements and expressions were intensely feminine, implying there was a whole, different person waiting behind everything one ever saw. She defied definition, shielding desirability at one time, flaunting it at another, blatant in her air of accomplishment and almost surreptitious in her sexuality.

He decided it must be very difficult for her. If she was too much the woman, any of her accomplishments would be scorned as bought by her femininity. If she completely sublimated her physical identity, she stood in good chance of destroying herself internally.

He wondered if there was any man she could unwind around, a man she could lean on and support, share with. After a few moments' conjecture, he decided against it. There was an inference of aloneness in the way she handled herself. Not lonesomeness, an implied acceptance of the distance she'd created around herself. There was no one person with whom she was more at ease than anyone else. At the same time, he was sure there was no one who would make her so unsure of herself she would be unable to function.

The line of conjecture at once fascinated and depressed him. It was such a waste. She was more woman then any he'd ever known, in the sense of established capabilities and qualities. There was visible attractiveness. There was an ambient sensuality, a minor-keyed melody that wound itself through her movements and conversation, never overpowering the main theme she presented to the world, but there, nevertheless. It was too bad, really.

The current had pushed him down the beach, and he cocked his head to get his bearings, then moved a hand in a sculling motion until his feet were pointed toward the island. That accomplished, he paddled gently with both hands, propelling himself steadily shoreward.

He smiled to himself, considering that he'd intended to use this particular morning's exercise period to get some things ironed out in his mind. Instead, he'd spent the time daydreaming about Cindy. The smile broadened, became almost sardonic as he pictured Ria's response if she learned of that episode. There was a contrast for you, he told himself, Ria and Cindy. Talk about night and day! For all of Ria's independence, she didn't really trust herself on her own. And who could blame her? It wasn't a situation her society fostered just yet. Cindy's road was far easier in that respect, but she had to live up to the other side of the coin. No one argued with her right to be independent, but too many people expected women like her to be chairman of the board for eight hours and earth mother for sixteen.

Ria would be waiting for him. He flipped over on his stomach and swam for the beach.

Ria waited for him every morning, and that thought increased the pace of his swimming. The first morning here he had returned from his swim thoroughly tired out, or so he had thought until he stepped into the shack and found her waiting for him on the bed mat, arms upraised, the blackness of her long hair draped over her shoulders and down to the aurioles of nipples already swollen in anticipation. Since then their lovemaking had taken on an uninhibited pleasure unlike anything he'd ever known.

When he reached water shallow enough, he trotted ashore, continuing to jog toward the shack. He grinned at his own eagerness, sluicing water from his body with his hands as he went, wondering if anyone might possibly be watching him. He laughed aloud when he thought how they'd laugh if they knew why he was running. The steps were steep, and he scrambled up with hands and feet, monkeylike. Ria wasn't waiting.

"Ria?" She had been there every morning since the first one, at the door or waiting on the bed mat. It wasn't like her to be missing. He ran a hand through his hair and flipped the water through the door behind him. "Ria?" he repeated, concerned.

She stepped out of the kitchen, and her appearance sent a shock of raw lust boiling through his veins. She wore one of his flower-print shirts cleverly wrapped around her waist and hanging in loose folds. She held a section of palm leaf in her hands, extended to him, mounded with sliced fresh fruit. Above that her unrestrained breasts, upthrust, proud, held his eyes until she spoke.

"This is how I would have come to you, centuries ago. My skirt would not have been such fine material, but I would be as I am now. You would see yourself as conqueror. I would see myself as a tribute. I am glad it is not that way now. But if the world changed this minute, if we moved back to that time, I would not care. I would have you."

There were words in his throat, on his tongue. He ignored them. Eyes raising to hers, he took a piece of the fruit, ceremoniously. Sea brine diffused through heavy mango sweetness. He offered the slice to her and she bit it, barely parting her lips to make room, chewing in minute arcs. There was no sound in the shack but the wind in trees and leaves. His hand was clumsy as he tugged the swimming trunks. Free of them, he extended his hands, palms up, as if he had been through this many times before. She handed him the heaped leaf, still moving as slowly as dreams, then rid herself of the saronglike covering. He turned and put the fruit on the floor, and when he rose, she was reaching out to him.

They spent most of the morning on the bed mat. Draeger had no idea what time it was when he was wakened by the fly walking on his nose, nor did he care. He brushed it away, swatting at its persistence twice more before it droned out the window in search of a more complacent landing site.

Ria slept easily, head pillowed on his arm, effectively holding him in place. The arm was going to hurt like hell when she finally got off of it—it was numb already. He made a face and settled back down, letting the heat-induced lethargy combine with plain weariness and flow into his head. After such a completely satisfactory morning, he expected to find himself drifting in mental aimlessness. He hoped for it.

It refused to come, and he wanted to bang a fist on the floor. No matter what he did, no amount of exercise, no level of sexual satiety, no period of sleep absolved him of the feeling he was stealing. Ria wanted something he was not; she wanted a man who wanted her with the same singularity. He opened his eyes and looked at her, breathing so lightly, inches away from his face. The curve of her cheek was the softness of a bird's wing, an angle beyond computation. Without moving his head, he let his eyes travel the rest of her, the smooth, rolling terrain of the marvelous body.

That was what he had done wrong. The body came with a mind, and he hadn't cared enough about that. He'd enjoyed her conversation, admired her insights, been humbled by her artistic talent and knowledge. In the final balance, however, he'd pushed aside her view of herself. The passion she excited in him wanted only to incite an equal flame in her. And she wanted that, too.

But more. And why couldn't he want more, give more? What was wrong with a man who could lie next to a beautiful woman, a loving woman, and feel himself being twisted apart with the wanting of her and the wanting free? He wasn't the man she needed and she wasn't the woman he wanted to spend his life with. And he'd do anything to keep her by his side. There was nothing in the world like their lovemaking, and the depression that ate in his guts when he thought of leaving her was the blackness of hell itself.

He thought of leaving her. That was the maddening thing. Crude, blunt thoughts bellowed their message in the depths of his soul and told him that one day he would walk away from her. They laughed at him because they knew his mysteries better than he did, knew he'd never do it with integrity. Any excuse, reason, argument—he would never tell her he'd wanted her and didn't any more.

His world had grown to two problems, Ria, and the organization. Each was an infection in his thought patterns, had its own growth requirements. He could only face the reality of his relationship with Ria when he was replete, the burning desire for her temporarily stilled. Once he admitted his helplessness in that area, the other problem struck the way a reserve element is thrown into battle by a seasoned leader, not to create a breach, but to exploit it and send the enemy into undisciplined retreat. If he could find no legitimate answer to the liaison with Ria, he was even more obstructed in the other matter. He was patently unallowed to pursue it.

The feeling that he would have to pursue it himself grew stronger daily. No matter how he interpreted anything said by Munson or Kolar, a conviction was solidifying that, since it was his reputation on the line, he was the one who would eventually have to salvage it.

There was something else as well, a dark tug at his mind when he woke and slipped away from the sleeping Ria. Each night he woke with ice cold hands and sweat on his forehead. He was always in the same awkward attitude, and walk exercised the pain from his joints. More importantly, movement shook the fear from his bones and dispelled the ache in his lungs that was there each time he awoke because he came to inhaling with the strained gasp of a man trying not to suffocate.

# ■  CHAPTER 27  ■

The hesitant call interrupted them as they were finishing lunch. The sandwich lumped in Draeger's stomach, and he hitched his jeans nervously as he rose. Ria's quick pallor mocked the canary-yellow halter and shorts.

The man lounged against a tree at the foot of the steps. There was a familiarity about him that trembled on the edge of recognition. Boy Angel saw the flicker in the eyes, and his hand, hooked over his belt, tensed. The gun under it was a burning temptation.

Unknowing, Draeger took the offered piece of paper without another glance for him. He read the instructions, isolated by swirling thoughts and emotions. Time had come. This was a summons to prove himself. He welcomed it. There was also the fear of failure. His mind burned at the memory of Munson's injustice, the constant torment only occasionally overshadowed by the gaiety or passion springing from Ria.

And there was Ria herself, whose amusement was becoming over-bright and brittle, whose lovemaking grew just short of desperate, a clinging, draining coupling that left them both so exhausted they had come to the unspoken agreement that they invariably slept immediately afterward. Whoever woke first was obliged to let the other rest until ready to wake.

There was pleasure in what they were doing, almost to the point of pain, and there was increasing unease, which was pain enough in itself. There was addiction and destruction in what was happening. It was important that he get her back to the city, that they separate and search inside themselves for some understanding.

And he writhed inside at the thought of being away from her.

He went back inside and gave her the paper. "From my company," he said. She continued to read. He had to say something. "I have to go back. We have two days here and one for travel."

Three days was hours or eons.

She gave it back to him, and he said, "I'll get the man who brought this to make plane and room reservations, OK?"

"It's all taken care of, then."

He had been prepared for most reactions. This one was undefinable. There was too much, she had distilled a dictionary of emotions into six words.

"Do you want to give him any return message? For Arturo and Ruby, anything like that?"

"No. I don't want to think about Manila. Tell him to go away."

Draeger returned to where Boy Angel squatted on his heels. He got up to take the twenty pesos and agreed to make the necessary travel arrangements. Instead of leaving right away he remained in place, shifting from one foot to the other, and Draeger wondered what he was waiting for. He was about to tell him to get going when the man peered past him at the shack.

Ria was standing in the doorway when Draeger turned. She went inside immediately, and when he looked back at the man, he was leaving, so that only the corner of a brilliant smile registered on the eye. Again, there was a pull of remembrance. Sounds from the shack distracted Draeger. He walked up the steps into the building. Ria blinked rapidly, wiped at tears. He hurried to her and took her in his arms. She smiled up at him. "The sun's so bright on the sand, and it's so dark in here! It makes my eyes water to go outside."

He lifted a hand to her chin. "I thought you might be crying."

"I'm disappointed our vacation's ending. I wouldn't cry about it.

I'm a little stronger than that." She pinched the skin along his ribs, and he grunted, twisting away, still holding her.

"I know how strong you are. You've nearly killed me and that's for sure." He dropped the other hand to the roundness of the yellow-clad buttocks, pulled her against him.

She moved easily with the pressure and laughed. "You keep that up, and you may be too weak to get back to Manila."

"Don't tempt me."

She pushed him away. "No, you don't. I'm not being cheated out of my swim. I told you I wanted one this afternoon."

His suit was still on the floor, kicked off to the side. She stepped into the partitioned-off kitchen, a touch of modesty he thought both endearing and amusingly unnecessary in view of the activity of the past few days. When she came out in her white bikini he was already outside, waiting, tossing a frisbee. They jogged to the water's edge where the sand was cool and packed hard, backing away from each other there until the distance was right. He threw first, a soft rainbow that was a yard to her left, and she stepped into the water to sweep it out of the air. The joy of the exercise showed in her movements, rather than her face. Her features were steady, calm in concentration. It was her body that laughed in its strength and lithe expertise. Her return throw was a low, curving trace that kept the disc horizontal through its entire flight. Draeger made the catch without taking a step.

They played a while longer, tiring of simple toss-and-catch, and began deliberately making each throw a bit off target. They ranged up and down the beach, two alone, kicking up sand or spray in raw physical exuberance. The only sound to intrude on their laughing and shouting was the grumble of a deep-hulled luxury cruiser that pulled into view far down the beach. When it anchored and turned off its engine the natural silence of the place absorbed it so completely it might never have existed.

They perspired heavily, the sweat mixing with sea-spray to become gilt in the burnishing sun. They reached that state where the muscles have their own perceptions, are capable of enthusiasms, eager for commands. They splashed into the water and fell side by side, stroking out to deeper water without needing conversation. The pale shallows darkened steadily under them, and they veered to parallel the shore before reaching the forbidding hue of plunging depths. Shadows accompanied them, their own images painted on the sand. The light concentrated at the edge for some reason, outlining each with a rim of purer brilliance. Waves distorted the figures, as did any irregularity of the bottom. The shadows were disjointed, wobbling wraiths.

Ria watched them for a while, and when she turned to swim on her back Draeger didn't know if she was frowning or squinting at the sun's ferocity. She gave him a mischievous grin and before he had any idea what she was up to, she slipped a hand onto his chest and ducked him. When he surfaced, spitting and snorting, she was ten yards away. He yelled and gave chase.

He was startled to find how slowly he gained on her. Anything she lacked in schooled technique she made up with determination. He dug his stroke and set up a regular breathing pattern, resigned to overhauling her patiently. He used a long-reaching crawl, turning on his left to inhale, a move that kept his eyes toward the beach. Because of that, he heard the boat long before he saw it and only looked for it because the sound was so alien. It was well up the beach, heading the same direction they were.

The increased pitch of the sound pulled his head around again, and he lost ground to Ria's steady progress. He measured the distance to the beach and assured himself the boat was much farther out to sea than they were. He leaned more heavily into the race, giving in that much to a growing unease. When he'd recovered his lost distance he was more disturbed to see the boat was not only moving at considerable speed, it was on a course that would bring it directly behind himself and Ria. As he watched, it changed course again. It was coming at them. There was a man on the bow and although it was hard to be certain at such distance, Draeger had the impression he was staring at them.

He increased his speed, calling to Ria. He told himself he was a fool to be worried, but he set his mind against it. If he was going to make a fool of himself, so be it.

When he looked back the man was facing the cabin, alternately pointing at them and punching a fist in their direction. The bow of the cruiser rose perceptibly. Draeger swam as hard as he could. He shouted at Ria, gasping for the air to do it. She swam on, slower, but steadily as ever. He felt his strength ebb, believed if he could look at his shadow the corona around it would be weaker, failing. He tried to call and swallowed water, gagging.

He was gaining on her, but not as quickly as the boat was pulling up on them. He was almost close enough to touch her now. Her feet danced through the water in front of him in a sparkling welter that should have been beautiful. The white suit was gay in the sun. He cursed her idiotic obstinacy.

The engine was a metallic growl. It filled his head, clawed at his spine.

The man on the bow was erect. There was a submachine gun cradled in his arms.

Draeger lunged ahead, heaved himself onto Ria's back as the first rounds slapped the water beside them. Even as he prayed she had enough air in her lungs to sustain her until the cruiser's momentum drove it past, he wondered that he'd heard no shots. By then Ria was fighting, struggling for the surface in a burgeoning panic that endangered them a hundredfold.

The cruiser churned overhead, the screw no more than a yard above their heads. Draeger blessed the eager murderer steering. If he'd stayed to one side, the man with the gun could have fired directly down at them.

He thrust Ria upward. Her driving need for breath combined with his strength to lift her torso clear of the water. When she fell back she was pulling air in sobbing gulps. Draeger twisted her around to look at the boat. It was circling for another run, and they heard the man on the bow screaming at the cabin. He was shouting in Japanese. Draeger heard it, recognized it, and vagrant questions of madness dashed through his mind.

"Get ashore," he panted. "Don't look back. When it's time to duck, I'll hit your shoulder. Got it?" She nodded, mute, and he shoved her, hard. "Go goddamit, *go!*"

From somewhere she found the stamina, swam powerfully. He wished he could cheer. He wished he'd told her a great many things.

The island floated ahead of them, a dream of safety. Water peeled off his shoulders in rolling sheets. Hate fueled him. He welcomed it, reveled in it. He would beat them, survive. One day it would be his turn.

More bullets plowed into the water ahead of them. The weapon was silenced, Draeger realized, and that was a very bad sign. These were no crazed killers. They were professionals. He pushed Ria's shoulder, and she went under as the next burst crackled through the sound barrier overhead and drove into the water. Diving beside her, he forced her to cut a diagonal line toward shore. It was afternoon, with some surface glare from the declining sun, and he hoped the people on the boat wouldn't catch their maneuver until it was too late.

The cruiser passed to their left and the gunner missed again, thrown off by the light diffraction that makes spearing fish so difficult. He aimed where the bent light rays said his targets were. Draeger and Ria were a few feet away from that point. They heard the malevolent sizzle, saw the wild spiraling bubble path of the rounds dying in the water. Then the engine was whining stress and Draeger understood they were so close to the deep hull's minimum depth there might not be room for another pass.

The men on the boat came to the same conclusion, and they made one last try at their quarry. Bullets kicked up water around Draeger and Ria as soon as they broke the surface. He pushed her under again, and they swam until lungs demanded air. There was only a few feet of water under them. Draeger surfaced between Ria and the boat, facing seaward, the boat was creeping, obviously just far enough out to avoid grounding. The man with the gun shouted and squeezed off a short burst, more in anger than hope. The range was unreasonable for such a weapon. It was a last pitch of malice.

Ria stumbled ashore to the sound of the departing engine, dropping in exhaustion. Her arms and legs continued to move. Draeger stood, watching the boat, trying to think of a way to escape when they decided to come after them. The boat made no attempt to launch a dinghy, and only when Draeger tore his eyes from it did he see the large native fishing boat sailing up from the other end of the island. At that, he scanned the forested edge of the beach. No one waited there. The impact of their escape, now assured, drained the last strength from Draeger's shaking legs, and he dropped to his knees. He managed one last look at the disappearing boat before thudding onto his side, facing her.

Later, when their breathing slowed to regular patterns, he opened his eyes and was looking fully into hers, inches away. Tears tumbled from them, drops that swelled to overflow and course her face. No sobs moved her body, no sniffling grabbed at her. There was only the heartbeat pulse of the tears and a questing, agonized stare. The solemnity of it tore at him, and he tried to look away. He failed.

She said, "Everything's been a lie, hasn't it?"

"Not everything. There were things I couldn't tell you. I wanted to. I can't even tell you now."

"Who are you?"

He rolled onto his back, stared into the clouds.

Behind them in the trees, Boy Angel bit his lip and sneered at the last view of the cruiser. He scratched at his chest furiously all the way back to the motorcycle on its side next to the path. He started it with a vicious kick and sped away.

The sound came to Draeger as an intrusive buzz and ended his personal communion. He rolled back over to look at Ria. "That's not fair. You know I wouldn't lie to you about my name."

"I don't know that. Why wouldn't you? I don't care what your name is. Call yourself anything you want, but for God's sake, tell me who you are!" The tears were dry, replaced by anger and a touch of fright.

"If you don't care what my name is, it doesn't make any difference who I am, does it?"

She giggled and he tensed for hysterics. Instead, she was sardonic. "Now I know. You're a disguised Jesuit, researching sinners."

"Don't make it worse, please. I'm sorry I got you into this."

"Stop it." She closed her eyes, sighed gustily. "You stink of tension, Glen, and I wanted to know more about it. I wanted to know more about you. Wanted? Want? I don't know. I wanted to control the passion I saw in you. I wanted you to care for me. The whole woman. Ria Manong. I wanted that."

At her pause he put his hand on hers.

"I said stop it!" Each word cut. She jerked the hand away from his touch. "I have to think. I need some time with myself. I want to go home, Glen. Please, take me home."

A single tear slid from behind the eyelid, a sly thing, unannounced by the stolid, controlled face. It hurried down her cheek to hide among the remaining drops of sea water.

He said, "We'll leave now. If we can't find a place to stay in Maley, I'll find us a place to sleep tonight and we'll go from there." He rose carefully, testing his legs, brushing off sand.

She said, "Who were they, Glen? Why did they want to kill us?"

"I don't know who they were, Ria, I swear it. They weren't trying to kill you, I'm sure. It's me they were after."

Cynicism twisted her lips. "It didn't seem to make much difference, did it? Do many people die because they're too close to you?"

"I'll start packing," he said. He was very conscious of the words and committed them to memory. He found it hard to believe he'd managed to say anything. The sand whispered at his footsteps, but he closed his mind against it He'd heard everything he was interested in for one day.

■  **CHAPTER 28**  ■

Draeger was more convinced than ever that there were no coincidences in the intelligence business. He had been called to Munson's factory, and the factory had blown up. It was only Leonila's natural kindness that put her in the blast in his place. Munson was missing. It was obvious he was dead, probably had been since placing the call. Kolar's pretext for sending him out of town was transparent, in retrospect. Certainly something was wrong with the Egg Roll operation, and Kolar was having to dig like a cat to bury it before someone else found it. And how much easier it'd be to cover anything if there were no uncooperative witnesses around to contradict whatever you said. So you sent Draeger, the simple bastard who trusted everybody, out of town for a few days while you put an ocean between yourself and some thugs who did your killing for you. Pretty. Especially using Japanese for the job. Absolutely no connection with your own operation.

The more he thought about it, the more he admired the balls of the thing. It was masterful. Who'd suggest an honored spymaster could be rotten? Even the goddamned name was perfect. Kolar, for Christ's sake! A good, Slavic, no-nonsense name for a good, Slavic, no-nonsense KGB type. It was right out of "The Purloined Letter."

It was no wonder Munson came apart. Unless—That had to be it! He was *part* of the thing and Kolar cleaned him up! There were no coincidences.

Draeger blocked off the line of thought growing in his mind. The desire to simply strike out was overwhelming, and that was a mistake. Eliminating Kolar didn't explain where the leaks were, who'd been doubled, whose reports were being massaged to read incorrectly. The need was to prove Kolar's treachery, unmask the link with Munson, open the whole mess to the air. Hopefully, Kolar could be turned, used against his masters.

It was a much more appealing prospect. Kolar degraded, betraying his own people. That was a thing to work for, to be treasured in the heart. Draeger licked his lips, picturing Kolar living out his natural life in a small room under guard. Even as he told himself it was a degrading thought, potentially damaging to himself, he returned to the daydream.

The taxi driver's question pointed out the stupidity of that sort of laxity. "You said you wanted to get out here, sir. You sure?"

Draeger damned himself. He hadn't even noticed where they were or the taxi slowing. Draeger paid quickly. He leaned toward the man confidentially. "There's a lady picking me up. I won't be here long. You know how it is."

The driver grinned broadly. "Yes, sir. Good luck!"

Draeger had picked the street carefully. He was doing everything carefully, he told himself, except for the relapse in the taxi. That sort of thing had to be overcome. Objectivity. That was the answer. The goal mustn't be confused with the means, and anticipation must never be confused with accomplishment. Objectivity. Then execution.

He took stock of his location, the huge silent office buildings towering around him. He stood on a street that was the equivalent of one of the muscle fibers of a heart. This was a financial heart, the source of the money and management that ran the Philippines. Although he lived in Makati, and his cover office was in the middle of it, he was still awed by the incongruity of it. By day it was vital, bustling, supervising deals from the purchase of a water buffalo to the logging of an entire province. By night, as now, it was practically deserted, a point underlined by the suspicious scrutiny directed at Draeger from the closest door guard. In the fluorescent light from the lobby behind him his blue uniform took on an electric intensity. The shotgun in his right hand was a dull satin in comparison.

Draeger moved on at an even, assured pace he didn't feel. The walk to the apartment would be exquisite. The people hired to kill him knew he'd escaped. They'd try again. At least Ria was safe. The scene with Arturo at her house had been vitriolic, but the man had finally understood he could either exert his efforts to protect Ria or work some kind of vengeance on Draeger. Common sense carried the day.

That was a respite, not a pardon.

He moved slowly. The lapse in the taxi had its roots in the certainty no one had picked them up at the airport or waited for him to leave her place. It was what he'd expected. Professionals wouldn't bother to stay with him. They knew he was thinking of them all the time.

The safest thing he could do would be to get under cover and stay there. That was impossible, as things stood. He needed money, papers, clothes. He had to get back to his apartment. Thinking of the danger made him dizzy, and he concentrated on believing they wouldn't be waiting for him.

How many times he'd scoffed at himself for rat-holing money in the flexible plastic tube that fit so nicely above the electrical receptacle in his bedroom wall. He'd felt guilty when he'd seen the chance to keep the Canadian passport and hidden it away. Now all he needed was the opportunity to claim them. He promised himself he'd never get caught out like this again. In future, his getaway cache would be as distant from his living quarters as he could manage. On the other hand, he'd expected his friends to warn him of danger. It hadn't occurred to him they might be the danger.

A plan started to grow, a thread that doubled back on itself, twisted into something stronger, then doubled again. Kolar had made one mistake, miscounted the deck by one card. Egg Roll. If he was smart enough, and lucky enough, to make it across the border, he had a pickup signal that would work at any time. With the destruction of the copy of the op plan in Munson's safe, there was a chance no one would think of the flexibility built into the escape. And Egg Roll would come out knowing how he'd been uncovered, and he'd be champing at the bit. If he made it.

Pierce. An ambitious man. Not especially productive, if Munson's offhand remarks hadn't been mere sarcasm, and not much given to taking the chances ambition required. Another piece of the plan fell into place. He could go to Pierce. He had to hide somewhere, and Pierce could be manipulated. If that didn't work, he could be threatened. Pierce wouldn't stand by and let Kolar eliminate a man in his area, because he'd be involved. That was the answer, to involve him. He'd play then, because he'd have to.

Draeger was within a block of his apartment, and it was time to think of absolutely nothing but survival. He scouted the neighborhood, beating through it from all directions. The guard at the door greeted him with no apparent nervousness, but that meant nothing. A man who knows a poor performance can mean having his head blown off can be depended on for one hell of an acting try. Draeger imagined himself in the man's place. Wife, kids, bare nodding acquaintance with a foreigner. Would he risk his life, his family's future for such a man?

He didn't even bother to answer, too preoccupied with the elevator. As the doors hissed open, he stepped to the side, ready to duck into the stairwell. There was no one in it. He got in, pushed the button for his floor, and stepped out before the doors could close again. The guard looked at him strangely, and Draeger said, "Forgot to ask you to mail a letter for me." After a moment's fumbling, he turned a sheepish grin at the man. "I guess I don't even have it with me."

They were still chuckling about his absentmindedness when the empty elevator returned.

Safely on his own floor, Draeger mopped at the sweat on his face and approached the apartment door. The hair stuck across the juncture of door and jamb was still there, but that meant no more than the guard's smile. Any good professional would have found that and replaced it after setting up the room.

He considered the balcony, accessible from the one upstairs or downstairs, and decided he was damned if he'd dangle on a rope at this height even if he knew where to find one at this time of night. He swallowed and jammed the key in the lock, visualizing the wires waiting for it to provide the electrical connection that would send the door flying into his face in a bomb-blast of splinters. Nothing happened, and moving as quickly as he could, he flung the door open and dove inside rolling several times.

The room was silent. It appeared larger than normal to him as he got to his feet, as if holding itself aloof from such arrant foolishness. He went immediately to the bedroom and pulled out a suitcase, stuffing it with clothes and necessities, including his passport. When it was loaded, he slammed it shut and hurried to the wall receptacle. In moments, the plate was off, enabling him to move the electrical components and pull out the long, thin tube. When he uncapped it over the bed, a mass of tightly rolled bills spilled out. The Canadian passport was separate, wrapped in plastic film. He was slipping the last of the bills into his pocket when he heard the sound from the other room. Before he could do more than straighten up, he was staring at a tiny .25 caliber automatic.

Shock shivered his body in waves, bringing a fear that turned to nausea. It could only have been an instant from the time he saw the weapon to the time he recognized its owner.

Cindy said, "How did you get here? How did you know we were back?"

Mustering strength, he pointed at the gun. "You came prepared, didn't you?"

She lowered it quickly. "I didn't know it was you. We thought you were still out of town. I came over to—" She stopped abruptly, and Draeger noticed for the first time how very nervous she was. It was a good sign, and it gladdened him. If he was going to get the gun, he needed every advantage he could find.

"Kolar sent you?"

"Certainly." She stopped, then blurted, "We can't talk here."

"I won't go with you to him. You'll have to use that thing."

She looked at his pointing hand uncomprehendingly until she followed its direction to the weapon. Her eyes flew wide. "I forgot. I told you I didn't think it was you."

Their eyes locked, and he could see nothing in hers. Her move was over quickly. The handgun was in her shoulder bag. He prepared to spring at her. She said, "We have to talk. Look at you. You're within an inch of doing something really stupid. I think you believe you need my gun, and I'm going to make you a deal. Listen to what I have to tell you, and if you won't cooperate with us, you can have the damned thing."

She was good, whatever she was up to. There was concern in her manner. Nothing clouded the straightforward gaze. He said, "Give me the gun now. If we're going to have a conversation, I want to be sure I live long enough to speak my half."

It was her turn to consider. She took a half-step away from him. After fumbling in the bag, she extended the weapon. He slipped it into his trousers pocket and picked up his suitcase, indicating the door with his chin.

At the elevator he said, "How long before Kolar starts to wonder why you're not back?"

"We've got plenty of time. He told me to be extremely thorough."

Draeger nodded. A search. What was she looking for? When they were in his car and clear of the building, he asked her point-blank. She was equally frank.

"Those papers, the ones Pierce brought, prove your man Egg Roll was betrayed by someone inside. Munson had vouchers covering an operation we don't know anything about. It looks like he suspected your operation and was checking out Egg Roll's security. Quite a while ago, Glen."

"That's crazy. Why the hell would I want to burn my own man?"

When he glanced her way, she was staring out the window. A jeepney pulled alongside, and a child, no more than six, peeked at her over the top edge of the benchlike seat. The side of this particular jeepney lacked the fairly standard scenic view or swirling designs. Instead, it was peopled with Disney characters, Mickey, Donald, Goofy, and all the gang. The child's face was singularly appropriate. Draeger waited impatiently for her to answer, trying to ignore her wan smile for the youngster. It responded with an owlish solemnity that only emphasized the madness of the scene. The light changed and they moved. She continued to look where the small eyes had been, her voice distracted.

"Kolar can't put his finger on anything, but we have leads. There's apparently a lot of money involved."

"He really said I'd turn? For money?"

"He only says something or does something when he's sure. You know how his mind works."

"Now I do."

"What's that mean?" The question was a warning.

"He's a killer." He chanced looking away from the traffic for her reaction. There was a delay, a hitch in her features before the shock and anger. He pushed into that. "You're the only ones who knew I was going to Iloilo." In bitter sentences he described the attack, ending with a challenge. "I want to hear you tell me Kolar didn't check me out, didn't learn I'd left the hotel, didn't know I went to Boracay."

"He did, all of that." She spoke to the hands folded in her lap before swinging her chin up to face him. "But only because those damned papers frightened him, Glen, not because he wanted to send a team after you. Think how he feels! Whoever's doing this is tearing the heart out of the man! If you thought he was doing the same thing to you, wouldn't you try to protect yourself?"

The enormity of the clumsy phrasing hit them simultaneously. Her expression crumbled to a plea for understanding, but instead he grinned at her, feeling the skin draw hard across his cheekbones.

"That's what I'm trying to tell you," he said, and pulled the car into a squealing turn onto Roxas Boulevard, scattering other cars like a fox among chickens A descending cacophony of horns marked their departure.

He had been badly used, she conceded. A weaker man would already have broken, tried to run. The fact that he hadn't was at once a strength and a weakness. Strangely, that mix pleased her. She had thought of him only in surface terms. There had been no reason to try to see inside him. In fact, except for his devotion to his work and his interest in the Filipina, Ria, he'd given no glimpse of what was inside him. Until tonight. There had been anger before, in his conflict with Kolar, but that, too, was a purely surface attitude. It was predictable. But he'd stayed in the Philippines when he knew things were going against him.

She thought of the bulging suitcase in the seat behind them and dismissed it. After all, the man had been shot at. That was a bit different than being suspected of something. Only a fool wouldn't consider running in that case. Finding someone sent to search your room had to be shattering. Hell, it was no wonder he wanted to hide. She set her chin. It was clearly up to her to salvage this mess. He was in no mind to trust Kolar, and Kolar was more than half convinced Glen was in someone's pocket.

A smile worked at the corners of her mouth. No matter what happened, no matter how much progress women made, it seemed they were always the ones who had to pick up after the men. Here was a time when it was the whole man that needed picking up. There certainly wasn't anyone else to do it. The woman, Ria, was undoubtedly a wonderful person, but she had no idea of Draeger's occupation, nor could she conceive the ramifications of what was happening now, despite her own narrow escape. Her exposure to the killers might have been harrowing, but it was a matter of minutes, and that brought no knowledge, only fright. Whatever ability she had to even provide normal comfort to him was tenuous, now.

He pulled off the boulevard, slipping past a wheezing taxi onto the service street fronting the businesses.

A parking place opened in front of him, and he dashed for it. As soon as he turned off the engine, he said, "You wait here. I'll just be a minute."

Getting out, he pulled the suitcase with him. She watched him step inside the tiny lobby of a shabby hotel and speak to the clerk. A few bills changed hands, and the bag went across the counter and behind the desk. Returning to the car, he said, "Come on, we'll walk a bit. I want to know more about Kolar's thinking."

She fell into step beside him, ignoring the stares and murmured comments from some of the sidewalk loungers. One man said something in a foreign language, but the voice was international, crudely insinuating. She enjoyed feeling Draeger's arm tighten on her hand and a thrill of mingled apprehension and pride when he turned to stare at the man. It was a surprisingly impressive look. The eyes and features were flat calm, but there was an unmistakable message. She was shocked to feel danger in it, an attribute she'd never expected from him. It startled her so she turned to see the reaction of the other man. The smile had turned to a bravado mask, betrayed by troubled eyes. There would be no trouble from that one.

Walking loosened his attitude quietly, and the harshness of his expression eased to concentration. He was studying the situation now, and that was good. If he'd think, he'd be all right. She paused in her evaluation long enough to remind herself that he'd functioned for years with no trouble at all. Instead of soothing her, that touched off a flurry of concern that so many things coming all at once might disorient him, push him beyond his limits. The view of herself as mediator surfaced again. Whatever happened, there must be no injury to either Kolar or him.

Nothing had happened yet that couldn't be patched up. She must keep it that way.

When they crossed the street to the Luneta, he led her directly to a huge double-decker bus. It was old and battered, a weary relic, but it was splashed with bright advertising. Overall, it had a raffish look, a friendly old bum full of good stories. "The 'Matorco,' " he explained. "We'll head for the upper deck, out in the open. No one's following us, so it should be all right. It'll be relaxing, and I need that. I have to get some ideas straight." He paid the fare, and they climbed the stairs to the upper level. The increased breeze was a pleasant surprise. Cindy settled into her seat, regretting the conditions of the ride. What could have been an almost romantic experience would be no more than an opportunity to scheme and maneuver. Pleasure was a luxury she was growing used to postponing.

The bus grunted and lurched away from the curb with the antique machinery noises of old carnival rides. Draeger looked at her, and she essayed a small smile. He returned it, briefly, then looked to the front. She watched the couples strolling the Luneta, people too poor to afford much else. She wondered how many of them realized exactly how fortunate they were. Her own career flew past her inner vision in flickering glimpses. There were the years at the desk, cramming in night classes and working all day. Her husband said that's what killed her marriage. That was his excuse. The marriage died when her promotions started, when all the work and study began to pay off. When she had created herself. That's exactly what had happened, by God. The world said she was a clerk and a housewife and she said she was an executive and a manager, and she'd made them eat it.

And there was the clandestine factor. Nothing could touch the awareness that she was an unseen part of the highest-level decisions in the world. She admitted to herself it was more important than any amount of peer acclamation. She admitted it to herself, but to no one else.

Many nights she wondered about that. Heretofore, she'd steadfastly refused to think those thoughts in the presence of another person. They were of such privacy they demanded solitary thought. She recognized what was happening. There had never been such tension in the organization before.

Unlike a wound, the problem provided no focus for the danger and concomitant healing. This was a poisoning. The creature she served and which sustained her was ripping at its own guts.

The man who was the catalyst for everything that was happening was beside her, an unwilling factor trapped in a vortex of events.

Perversely, his animallike tension and preoccupation relaxed her. She felt enveloped in his protective awareness, ready to help if called on, but able to serve best now by keeping in the background. Questions came to crowd her mind, heavy as the breeze from the sea, and that was the direction that pulled her attention. From the bus she could see the ships anchored in the bay. Palms flanked the boulevard, and they screened the view so the red, white, and green night lights burst through the intervals, erratic and brief. So it was with her thoughts of herself.

Career patterns rarely go where one expects, she conceded easily, but her own had veered off with the violence of a ricochet. Kolar himself had brought her into the unit after hiring a legitimate executive placement agency to select a half-dozen possibilities. None of the others were women, and she'd been made aware of that from the start. Several times over the years that point had troubled her, because she was certain Kolar wasn't above goading someone with that kind of psychological ploy. A career with his unit offered nowhere near the salary her skills would have commanded in industry. She remembered the long talks with Kolar. Patriotism was wrapped around her need to feel she was influencing something, and she'd gone for it. Inside the unit she was admired and respected. And feared. Men who penetrated the hearts of opposing intelligence agencies or were themselves privy to the most jealously guarded state secrets looked over their shoulders when she made an appearance. Overlooked details killed in this business, sometimes only in terms of career, but sometimes very physically. Forgetting how to disguise payments or forgetting that you had to be able to explain the whereabouts of the deceptions was akin to asking a shark to doctor a cut finger. Amputation was the least danger.

Fear was something she understood. It came with the territory. Without wanting the power to create it, she was cloaked in it, simply because she had authority.

Doubt grew around the fear, a rank growth in a neat mental garden that wanted flowers and paths where everything was harmony. The hunted look in a man's eyes was a thing she dreaded. If she woke in the night, that was what was usually scorching her mind. She loathed it. The struggle to prove herself and rise to her authority never measured up to the pain of that look. The first time she saw it, she quit. Kolar talked her into staying by pointing out how dangerous to the unit the man had been. The second time she saw it, the man disappeared a few days later. No one mentioned him again and she went back to Los Angeles immediately.

The thought of quitting on that occasion died under the weight of precedent failure. Afterward, in other instances, it had tried of resurrection, never successfully. Not even strongly.

Thinking of those men cultivated the doubts. She argued with herself about it, telling herself it was the price of executive position. One made the hard decisions, one dealt with the things that needed doing. If a man was incompetent or went sour, she could hardly be blamed if her investigation unearthed the fact. One also expected to pay. There were no profits without debts. Isolation was a debt. Crawling the pyramid of success meant a smaller number of people around you. Life was becoming more and more introspective, because fewer people wanted to be close.

Draeger said, "I'm going to ask you to listen to what I have to say. Please don't interrupt. Make a mental note instead, O.K.? If I lose you, stop me and I'll cover the point again. But let me run until I'm done, will you? Just listen."

She nodded, unconsciously silent even in that detail. He started with his relationship with Munson, told of Leonila. Ria went unmentioned, except for the incident on Boracay. Cindy watched his hands clench and relax as he told of diving to escape the bullets, the rhythm quickening as he went. Oddly, the narrative was flat, dispassionate, delivered in a voice that never gave any indication of excitement. It made Cindy uncomfortable, like hearing a superb recording played at an incorrect speed, so that all the sounds are in correct relationship to each other, but the tonal quality is gratingly wrong. When he changed from specific to general, began talking of his feelings about the mission of the unit, sadness crept into his voice. Immediately, Cindy responded, an unexplained, unknowing sympathy filling her. She wanted to comfort him, to tell him she understood. In truth, she didn't. She only knew that his decline matched a feeling in herself.

The reason came to her in a shock that hurt. Out of all the training, the accomplishment, and now the debacle that had been visited on him, one thing had emerged. Alienation. He had cultivated individuality as a person, isolation as a member of a covert group, a solitary life committed to his work. When that broke down, all that remained was being alone.

He finished the narration. There was more coming, and from the way he turned to look directly into her eyes, she knew it was a literal moment of truth between matador and bull as a metaphysical coalescing, the ultimate blending of two disparate lives. One ends, victim to skill and grace it cannot understand in an environment it cannot comprehend, yet it dies with honor and integrity. The other life goes on, survives to test itself against superior strength and unreasoning fury yet again. That life, too, is honored. For the moment the lives, and the honor of the lives, is one. If the stroke is true, there is a savage beauty in the thing.

People strike with words.

"I've proved, circumstantially, that Kolar's working for the other side." When Cindy didn't move, didn't try to shout him down, he drove home. "I need you to help me to prove it."

They stared into each other's eyes. At last, Cindy could stand it no longer, and she pulled her head away, seeking refuge in the chaotic light-splintered night on the west side of the boulevard. In the bars there were other whispers of betrayal right that minute, none as evil as the one she'd heard, none any more understandable in its roots.

Draeger let her think. His hand sought the automatic, soaking strength out of it, but he said no more.

"You're wrong about Carl," she said.

He shook his head, and she marveled at the little-boy look of him, lower lip pendulous, eyes smoky in petulant refusal to meet hers. "It's the only logical explanation. If I don't get him now, he'll get all of us, eventually. It may already be too late. He had Munson killed and tried for me twice, simply because I'm close to the Egg Roll operation."

"What if Munson's alive?"

"If he was, he'd be after Kolar, not me. I didn't kill Leonila, and no one would know that better than Munson. And where the hell would he hide for this length of time? Look around you. Munson would stick out like a bonfire."

"And you think you can hide better? You're going to blend in while you hunt for Kolar?"

"If I have to, I can manage something. I'll get where I have to go."

Cindy looked away and back again, caught by an indefinable change. When she examined him again, what had been obstinacy was intent of a much different order. Separate gears were meshing, genuine alternatives were being considered and discarded. The eyes that had been full of muddled resentment were clear with determination. She felt the duality of her own fundamental nature, repulsion for the ferocity and attraction to the primal need for a woman's alliance with a man's capabilities. It was an ironic combination that had allowed her to relax beside him when he was tense. She feared it. It struck at the base of her self-possession.

"The only way I can genuinely help you is by convincing you you're wrong."

"If I am, I'll fail."

"Good God!" She reached up to sweep her hair back off her shoulder. The lights from a particularly garish bar caught it, turning it into a flowing coal. She said, "You're being medieval. We're not dealing with a trial by arms, God granting victory to the righteous.

We're talking about a man who respects and admires you. He'll help you prove you're innocent.''

"Why should I have to prove anything?"

"Oh, stop it! You know damned well we have to verify everything we do. Don't go all democratic on me. It's too late."

"Is it? You're asking me to accept Kolar's innocence! Do I prove he's rotten by getting killed? I *felt* those bullets, Cindy! And as long as he's free, I've got to expect it again."

"And if you're wrong, if Kolar's not the one trying to kill you?"

"He's in no danger from me if he'll stay away. I want to prove I didn't kill anyone, do anything wrong. I want to do my job. That's all. I want to do my job."

"Glen, can't you see? That's what Carl's trying to do! He never put a team on you, never!"

He shook his head, looking past her at the buildings. "You won't listen. You're as blind as I used to be."

They didn't talk on the way back to the Luneta. As they passed a multistoried apartment building, the top-floor rooms blazing with light, Cindy looked at them, wondering who lived there. Just then a slim figure appeared at one of the windows. It was too dark to distinguish sex, but the person was slight, either a woman or a boy. The right hand lifted a drink to the mouth, and the confident grace convinced Cindy it was a woman. She imagined her looking out over the sleepily stirring ships at their anchorages, watching the constant passage of traffic at her feet. Could the woman envision what was happening to two people on the bus passing her now? Would she care if she knew? Did she trust someone, perhaps too much?

"When this thing stops, I'll get you a cab," Draeger said. "For your own sake, go straight to Kolar and tell him everything I've told you. Don't try to help me. He won't forgive you for it."

She said, "What does our organization mean to you, Glen? Exactly how do you see it?"

He cut the air in front of him with a slashing gesture. "That's a cheap shot. I'm too wound up to be going on about patriotism and 'eyes for the nation.' Don't accuse me of destroying it. I'm trying to save it."

Softly, not much more than a clearly apprehended thought, her words lifted to him. "That's what I want, too."

"Yeah. Well, I appreciate you hearing me out anyhow. Remember, don't try to hold out on Kolar, whatever you do." He grinned, an immense inappropriateness. "I wouldn't be upset if you told the driver to take his time going back to Makati, though." He sobered as quickly as he'd smiled. "And tell Kolar I beat you out of the gun and that's why you came with me. It's what he'd do, only he'd keep you hostage."

"You believe keeping me hostage would stop him?"

Draeger answered slowly. "You might slow him down for a minute because he seems to like you. But I doubt it. Men like Kolar don't recognize hostages, and they don't take prisoners."

"And you?"

"When I have the proof I need, his ultimate value depends on his own behavior."

She stared at him, unable to keep her appearance under control, so her look of shocked horror spread in slow rearrangements, a slow-motion interior collapse recorded as an external event. " 'Ultimate value.' 'His own behavior.' What a pedantic bastard you can be when you want. You'll kill him if you have the chance."

"Only if he forces it."

"I won't let you."

He laughed.

"You can't stop me from exposing him, and that's what I want most. I hope he does live. I want to watch him."

"I don't believe you. All you can see is what's been done to you. I'm telling you he's not the kind of man you think he is, and I don't think you're behaving as the kind of man you are. I won't let you destroy each other. You'll carry the mission down with you!"

The bus was groaning the last few yards of its route. He offered her a hand up, the gentlemanly tourist enjoying the sights of Manila with his lady. Cindy took the hand and dropped it quickly, folding her arms against her breasts. He half-smiled, following her down the steps. From the sidewalk, he started to wave at a taxi, and she grabbed his arm.

"You can't kill him," she said, staring up into his face. The lights of the park that made the passing Filipinos olivaceous slurred

the paler tones of her skin, bled it almost stark white and emphasized the dark hollows of her eyes.

"It's not what I want. It's up to him. I do what he needs done."

She winced, hearing her thoughts from his mouth. "I'm going
with you. I'll help you clear yourself. I'll stop you from doing
anything else. The mission—our mission—is more important than
any man. If I help you, I keep the lid on. We can work together on
that."

He turned away from her. Pulling at his arm, she spun him back.
"Look around you, Glen. What happens if I start screaming? The
two soldiers guarding the monument over there—do you think they
won't come running? And all these people strolling around?"

He glared and she met it. Smells of hot, wet earth suddenly filled
her nose, and she wondered what was wrong with her before remembering the fountains farther along the park. The spray reached the
ground when the wind was right, and the change of direction had
brought the smell. She let it distract her, using it to keep his stare
from breaking hers, letting it carry her back to summer nights and
water fights on the front lawn. Winning wasn't even part of those
games. No one won, no one lost; everyone got deliciously wet and
cool and laughed until tears mixed with the hint of chlorine and the
selfsame smell of rich earth and grass. Now she must win, and the
cut of that realization severed her concentration.

Fortunately, he looked past her to answer. "I'll dump you the first
chance I get. Understand that."

"You do that. And remember that when you do, I'll be in the
nearest police station, calling for Kolar, as soon as I realize you've
done it."

On another occasion he'd smiled and surprised her. This time she
was amazed. There was no hint of duplicity in his manner, when he
took her arm above the elbow and said, "You're a tough one. And
crazy as hell. Maybe you'll be some help. We'll see."

Propelled along the sidewalk, bound for an unknown destination,
caught between obligations she could hardly articulate, Cindy couldn't
understand her own curious sensation of eager apprehension.

# ■ CHAPTER 29 ■

The atmosphere in the brightly decorated cottage was a mist of anger. Munson was in one chair, a ridge of flesh at the base of his spine his only contact with the edge of the seat. He suggested arrested motion rather than a sitting figure. Hands and feet twitching constantly added to the impression. Pierce paced a route that took him from the front door to the dining room and back again, a diagonal path that passed between the perching Munson and Boy Angel's glowering stolidity. Of the three, the latter saved his energy, or, rather, concentrated it in bottled-up fury. Silence ruled the room for a long time before Munson broke it.

"I can't believe the stupid bastards let them just sail away from the island and disappear in Manila. Goddamit, they had them for sure! It's bad enough they screwed up on the island. Why the hell didn't they stake out his goddamned apartment? What were they thinking of?"

Pierce turned the soulful eyes on Munson, the eyes that lied through softness. "How do I know? They're your pets, remember?"

"It was an easy thing." It was the first comment from Boy Angel, and the other two men turned on him.

Pierce said, "Maybe we should have let you do it. You're anxious enough."

Boy Angel smiled, and Pierce resumed pacing, rolling his shoulders as if working out a cramp. Munson continued to watch the Filipino from the corner of his eye.

There's something going on here, he decided. Boy was pretty rank about being pulled back here from Manila, and he damned near

begged to deliver the message to the pair on Boracay, the message
that was meant to insure they'd think they were enjoying their last
hours there and take advantage of the waiting sea. Munson swallowed a smile and resisted the urge to slap his forehead. It was so
clear! The sonofabitch wanted the woman! And it was as obvious as
daybreak. It just went to show you, the old ways always worked
best. Money, women, or both. No man stood up to temptation.

He amended that. No one ever tempted him while Leonila was
alive. With her gone, the memory was enough. All the rest were
nothing. There might come a time when he needed one, once all this
was over and done with, but there was no chance he'd ever want one
again. It was a sad prospect, but true. A combination of age and
fidelity, one leaning on the other for support.

The edge of the chair became painful, and he shifted back onto it,
nearly able to relax. The question was, how to use it? Any view of
another man's weakness should be used. After all, if you saw a
man's cards and ignored the information, you'd be too stupid to talk
about.

He held up a hand when he spoke, interrupting Pierce's steps.
"What'd Bilongon say about the Japs getting back in the game?"

Pierce shook his head. "They told him they'd plan something
else. I didn't believe it. They're too cautious. The days when they
just walked in and started blasting are all over. I think they've barely
got enough people to pull off the raid, and they're not going to risk
losing anyone. They missed their shot."

"That's crazy! If the operation's compromised, it's their ass
first!"

"And whoever's left of their organization will be after you."

Munson was unimpressed. "I've taken that into account."

"Swell. We planned on Draeger being dead by now, too." Pierce
threw out the remark lightly. He was completely unprepared for
Munson's reaction. The long frame, bonier now, levered upward in
a flair of arms, hands, and pumping knees. He was in front of
Pierce, their chests touching, before the younger man could do more
than drop his jaw. Munson's eyes burned.

"You're goddamned right he should be dead! More than dead!
Burned, like infection, scattered!" Pierce's goggling stare finally
checked him. Without a pause, he modulated the voice to cool

control. "I apologize for the outburst. When I think of that double-dealing bastard standing between us and what we stand to gain, it nearly unhinges me. I'll have to be careful."

Pierce swallowed, grudging even that small sound.

Munson smiled, sure the violence still seething in him could be seen in his eyes, and he moved agitatedly, trying to mask it. "We still need that diversion. We don't know where he is, what he's doing. Nothing from Kolar. It's like we were blind!"

Pierce said, "Kolar may already be holding him. Maybe Draeger's on the run and Kolar's chasing him."

Intrigued, Munson leaned back. "Yes, that's quite possible." He meshed his fingers and rested his chin on the hands.

Pierce told himself Munson was eroding. There was a red rim around each iris, a border that radiated a network of thinner blood vessels inward to the pupil. They reminded Pierce of the local aquaculture ponds. Once they were drained and the fish harvested, the sun raged at the exposed mud, searing it in a few short days to irregular plates, isolated from each other by similar erratic lines that lifted agonized, curled-up edges. Corresponding pain flickered in Munson's eyes. That alone was troubling, but there was more. His glasses were continually smudged. Fingerprints overlapped on them. It had to impair his vision, and he paid no attention to it. Unkempt tussocks of whiskers sprouted untidily from his beard. The ill-fitting clothes could be the result of more carelessness or of lost weight. Charitably, Pierce settled for lost weight.

Munson put an end to the inventory. He said, "Every military operation is studded with unexpected events. We're in the midst of something unanticipated by either side. What we must do is act."

He got to his feet and walked to the stoic Boy Angel. The smaller man remained seated, only the faintest dark line of a frown suggesting his concern. At the touch of Munson's hand on his shoulder, the corners of his mouth sagged a fraction of an inch.

"You've done good work for me," Munson said, "and I appreciate it. You know I've spoken to Benjamin about it. Now I have a special assignment for you. You heard me say we must act?"

Boy Angel nodded. The tentative frown disappeared.

Munson continued. "The Red Army failed miserably. If I'm to have the power to make the Swords the equal of Oxo or Sigue-Sigue or the other gangs, I need the money and power this operation will bring me. The man we're talking about, this Draeger, is the last obstacle. We have to be rid of him. Can you do it?''

Boy Angel nodded again, the bright, broad smile a sunrise of understanding. Munson smiled back at him, and Pierce turned to the distant sea.

"I knew we could count on you," Munson said. "But there's a problem." Boy Angel's face fell, and he leaned forward. Munson turned to shamble back to his chair, talking as he went. "There's the matter of the woman that was with Draeger on the island. We can't be sure how much she knows. She may even be working with the opposition, or with Kolar. I'm afraid she has to be eliminated.''

Pierce looked away from the sea, sought Munson's face. The spare features drew even tighter, willed him to silence. Boy Angel said, "She must die?"

Slowly, Munson faced him again and stood poised, heronlike, before answering. "She doesn't have to die right away, Boy Angel. If you want to take the time to—ask her some questions—it could be very helpful to us. Perhaps you could learn if she really is working for someone, you see? But, she is secondary. You *must* get rid of Draeger.''

Boy Angel's smile flowed back.

Pierce said, "Shit," and faced the sea again. Boy Angel looked hurt, an expression that gradually gave way to great thoughtfulness.

Munson winked at him. "Why don't you go get ready to leave? I've got some business to talk over with Tony." Munson watched him go and then whirled on the other man. Pierce continued to stare out the window, ignoring the weight of Munson's attention.

"We've got to get this thing about Draeger ironed out once and for all, Tony. Exactly what's your suggestion, if you find my ideas so distasteful?"

Small crests were forming on the swells. There might be rain by evening. Maybe that'd take the baked smell out of the air. Pierce wished he had time to check the clouds to the south. It was a bag of tricks, sure enough.

He said, "Draeger was to draw attention away from us. We should leave him alone. And you know what'll happen to the woman. The longer we fool with this thing, the bloodier it gets."

"I told you it's a war. The woman knows about Draeger. If anything he's told her gets back to Bilongon, you can imagine his next move."

Pierce continued to look out the window. "You don't have to tell me about Bilongon."

"Then you see where we're headed. If we lose control of events, we'll end up in that bamboo cage, or worse."

"Worse? Like that savage bastard'll treat that woman?"

"Will you quit harping on her? You want to save her? Do it! And remember you're pissing away a million dollars. Think how good you'll feel when they turn you over to the Philippine government as a spy!"

Pierce got a restraining hand on an arm and gestured at the window with the other. "Not so loud! You'll blow the whole thing right here." When Munson glared at him, he added, "It's not easy to think of Draeger going in the bag. It's not easy to think about Boy Angel and that woman." He maneuvered the unresisting Munson to a seat on the sofa, more disturbed by the decrepit feel of the stringy bicep under his hand than the unnaturally bright eyes. Seated, Munson stared straight ahead. He spoke at a pedantic pitch, lecturing.

"Once a person has seen war, once a person understands exactly what happens in a war, normal relationships pall. It's because that person has survived when he sent others into firestorms to die, you know, like little pieces of paper. I see them sometimes. *Abbott, F.P., serial number so-and-so, Corporal, United States Army; Appleton, J.J., serial number so-and-so, Private, United States Army.* Alphabetically. Pieces of paper. Records. Reports. Tumbling with the wind, into the flames—poof!—they're part of it, and there they go, up, up, burning, burnt, black. Gone. Gone away."

"Stop it, Roger." Too soft, the demand watered down to a plea. He corrected that. "Shape up, for Christ's sake! Are you quitting on me? You're the one who accused me of being too soft. What the fuck do you call this? Knock it off!" He slammed him back against the sofa. The eyes came back to life, outraged.

"That's not necessary! I'm all right. I'm all right! Jesus, can't you tell the difference between some personal reminiscences and hysteria?" He stood, stretching like a man waking. "We need information. The woman may have it. We do what we must to accomplish our objective. Do you have any questions?''

Pierce shook his head. ''We do what we have to do. Right?''

Munson cut his eyes at him, then away. ''I'm glad that's settled. Let's keep it that way.'' He strode out the door with a passable military bearing.

As soon as he was on the pathway back to the hotel proper, he slumped. I'm too tired, he told himself, just too tired to even pretend. Godalmighty, I have to hold everything together every minute. Pierce is such a fool. He's getting to be as bad as Draeger, prattling about responsibility to others and all that maudlin shit. When you make the choice to win, anything that doesn't contribute isn't excess baggage, it's dangerous. Draeger had his chance to be part of the operation, and he backed away. That made him a noncontributor, and that was tough shit. At least he's not whining and shiveling about the hard decisions. Not that Pierce had anything to whine about. He left the decisions up to me, didn't he? It's been that way from the start. The only one willing to get down in the dirt and fight the issues is me. Fuck 'em all. No more backbiting, no more watching someone's kiss-ass favorite get the meat while I have to smile and roll my eyes like a minstrel-show nigger for a spoonful of fucking gravy.

Harsh buzzing intruded, and he stopped, intrigued, searching the blossoming trees beside the path. After a few seconds, he spotted the source, a large bumblebee. It backed out of one of the pastel pink flowers with an irritable fizzing sound, as if unsatisfied with its findings. Undaunted, it moved to the next one, the bold black and yellow markings a vivid contrast to the dusty leaves and the pale blossoms. Munson watched its efforts, noting the tremendous speed with which the insect hurtled from point to point. Even the bumblebees were different here. Funny, he'd never noticed before. They looked like the ones at home, but they moved with an angry velocity totally unlike the carefree droning of the ones he remembered. The insect slashed through the air directly under his nose, sending him backward with a muffled grunt. It crawled into the depths of another blossom, complaining to itself. Munson considered swatting the flower, but the reemergence of his proposed victim, throbbing with pent-up energy, convinced him it would be a mistake. He lowered his hand and continued on the path.

Pierce watched him from the corner of his garden, half amused, half concerned, wondering if he was attaching too much significance to Munson's behavior. They were both under a lot of strain, and Munson was really suffering over his wife's death. By the time Munson's lank frame disappeared around the last bend before reaching the hotel, Pierce had convinced himself that Munson was still all right. He was also convinced that it was a situation that could collapse without warning. The conclusion brought a flush of the other excitement, the feel of danger's wings fanning behind him. Munson was shrewd. Protecting one's self against his potential failure would be extremely sensitive work. Necessary work, though, he told himself sternly. All the bullshit about how much money they stood to make was just that. Munson had his own goals, and the money was plain old bait to keep little Tony in line. He smiled. Munson would call the money a secondary objective, or some such military baloney. It wasn't. It was numero uno. Or maybe numero uno and-a-half. Tony was still the original numero uno. That was that, and all of Munson's gobbledegook would never change a bit of it. As long as the plan was working, Munson's foolishness was tolerable. But he was as expendable as Draeger or the girl, and if he, the expert on expendability, couldn't see the humor in that, then fuck him. He'd just have to learn to take a joke.

He walked back into the house, full of inner peace more satisfying than any he could remember. Trying to understand why was too easy. No matter how he examined the reason, it presented nothing more complex than a wholehearted commitment. The memory of his past was nothing but devotion to himself. In the depths of his soul there functioned enough integrity to grind out that grudging admission. The watchword had always been caution, regardless. Risks were avoided, and if unavoidable, every possible avenue of insurance was examined and utilized. This confession rested at a higher psychological level, one he would have felt free discussing with another person. He'd spent so much time covering his tracks he'd never taken a full look at where he was going. Life had been a series of steps freighted with fear, each step forward increasing the weight pressing from behind.

That was over now. He threw back his head and inhaled, letting it out with a grunt of distaste. The air conditioner embalmed the atmosphere. Moments like this demanded better.

Across the room, the sun broke from behind the coconut palms, sending its full force against the seaward wall of the house. The jalousied windows stopped most of it, but the light pressed itself through the interstices, golden warm blades slatting the floor and opposite wall. Pierce strode to the air conditioner and snapped it off, then to the window, where he flung the jalousies wide. Spread-eagled, he absorbed the sun, staring until forced to close tearing eyes against the implacable strength. Smells came to him, familiars, lifted from the furnishings by the heat. The grass-mat carpeting, the cloth of the upholstery, wood of furniture, his own body breaking into a sweat that made him think of himself as shining metal.

Minutes passed before he moved. Mental images formed, entertained, slipped away to be replaced by others. All dealt with his newfound commitment. Of all the pleasures in the new existence, the greatest was recognizing it for what it was. It was a physical, mental, emotional rearrangement. It was thesis and synthesis.

That was the secret beauty of it all. Everything was gained, nothing was lost. The memories were unclouded, the lessons of the past as sharp as ever. That was why he'd have to watch Munson. A tight smile pulled his face, dislodging a drop of sweat he had to wipe from his eye. It broke the mood, and he turned from the window, dropping to the sofa. A host of dust motes rose to dance in the sun in acclamation.

The conceit amused him, and his laughter echoed in the empty house. The possibility of instability came to him, and he dismissed it easily. If he could think of himself as crazy and laugh at the thought, there was little chance he was cracking up. Better yet, if the thought became oppressive, he could match his behavior against Munson's. There was madness, and plenty of it. The trick was going to be to string it out long enough for it to serve its purpose.

*There was a wasp that laid an egg on a living caterpillar. The egg hatched and burrowed into the host and fed on it. Marvelously, there was exactly enough caterpillar for the larva to grow to the pupa stage, so that the caterpillar died at precisely the right time for its desiccated hull to provide protection for the pupa while it slept its* way to adult wasp-hood. Or did the grubby little larva have the instinctive good sense to devour a vital organ when it felt itself ready to pupate?

What the hell difference did it make?

Christ, it was beautiful!

# ■ CHAPTER 30 ■

While Tony Pierce sat in the sunshine, Draeger was helping Cindy out of a small Cessna at the airport a few miles away. Since no planes were scheduled they had to wait for a taxi. It was the hardest time of the trip for Draeger. By the time the gleaming Datsun growled to a stop in front of the terminal, he would have ridden to town on a manure cart, anything to get away from there. Sweat literally dripped from his fingertips.

Cindy watched, worried, so unsure of the next move she vacillated between offering encouragement and trying to provide a diversionary concern by admitting her own unease.

She was unused to playing male-female games of that nature. In the end, she did nothing, and damned her ineffectuality.

He stepped in front of her at the taxi's side, but before she could snap her irritation, he was holding the door open for her, practically twitching in his impatience. Wordlessly, she twisted into the thing, doubled over, graceless.

They had traveled several hundred yards before it occurred to her to ask where they were going.

He said only, "A hotel in town. It's on the waterfront. You'll like it."

She looked at him with what she hoped was a proper degree of cold archness and sat back to observe her surroundings.

It was hot. The cab was non-air-conditioned and the wind from the open windows carried a fertile, exotic aroma that attracted even as it repelled. She closed her eyes against a boil of dust from a passing bus, and the act immersed her in the smell of the countryside. It was wildly unique, as unlike Manila as smoke is unlike fire. All the fundamentals of the earth she had ever experienced were there, and things she knew she would never identify. A thrill lifted bumps on her arms, sang through the vertebrae of her spine and neck. Not until that moment had she thought of herself as in tropical Asia. The knowledge was a huge thing. She felt alive with it, vital. And, as quickly, very much afraid.

There was nothing sinister in view. The distant mountains were serene, their jungled slopes no more than green and brown abstractions. Vehicles and pedestrians moved normally. An old man on a rickety cart swung out to avoid a playing child, and the taxi slowed dramatically, throwing her forward. A motorized tricycle passed in the opposite direction. It was actually a motorcycle with an attached side car, large enough to seat two. The vehicle was an artwork, featuring a black background covered with zodiac designs. Both driver and passengers were under a roof, protected by a common windshield that sported so many decals and saints' pictures visibility was restricted to a clear patch in front of the driver. Plastic antennae-like rods whipped violently along their eight-foot length as the gleaming machine jerked them from pothole to pothole. The tricycle driver watched the taxi, well aware of his machine's vulnerability in the pecking order. Two young men rode with him, and they peered through his windshield. They were intent on her, Cindy realized, and the fear was multiplied by an intense apprehension because she was simply different. There had been times in Europe she had felt that way, and there were sections of most American cities she avoided because she was abundantly out of place there. Now she was outside all law, and there would be eyes on her at all times. Privacy had become synonymous with imprisonment, with locking out the world and being locked away by it. She hadn't anticipated running would be like that, and the understanding of the situation married with the earlier, unidentified fear. She turned from the snarling tricycle and looked out the side window. They lurched forward, passing the cart. It was pulled by a lumbering water buffalo slathered with patches of dried gray mud. The course, black hair was dulled by dust, except for a bell-shaped pattern of smeared feces at the base of the tail, gleaming like wet leather. The tail pendulumed across the mess twice as they passed, slowly enough for Cindy to watch fat flies rise, hover, then drip back to their accustomed spot.

Revulsion swept her, and perversely, she was stricken with an overwhelming desire to giggle. Frightened, running from friends and enemies alike, alien among people and customs, she was riding to a hotel she'd never heard of with a man she hardly knew. And watching flies play jump-rope in buffalo shit.

She bit the inside of her lower lip. The warped laughter drained away, leaving an emptiness quickly discovered and filled by dread.

The taxi was moving easily again, paralleling a rice paddy, the plants vivid against dark earth and water. The stalks bent to the will of a breeze, an impeccable *corps de ballet* swaying in perfect unison. Still, even as she seized the beauty of the scene, Cindy understood that there was nothing in her experience to duplicate it, and the alienation theme trumpeted in her consciousness.

Draeger said, "We should be clean here. You heard me talking to the pilot?" He pitched his voice low and leaned toward her.

"I heard part of it. You've known him for a long time?"

"Yeah. He's flown me around on a lot of company business. He knows he's supposed to keep this trip quiet. He won't blow it around."

"I heard him say he could fix some records, or something."

Frowning, Draeger studied the back of his hand. "I told him not to do it. If somebody checks, I don't want him getting caught up in this mess. I told him it was a straight charter, nothing else, but I'd appreciate it if he kept his mouth shut. Why should he get crossways with the law?"

Cindy found the answer reassuring. He twisted his head and looked at her from the corner of his eye, trying to read her reaction. She smiled, and he returned it, speaking again. "I think we should just hole up for a day, get some rest, unwind. It's too late to catch the boat to Pierce's island. We'll catch it then."

"You think Pierce will help you?"

"Maybe not willingly. The odds are his operations are as badly compromised as mine. If I know Pierce, he's got something to hide. He'll help me to keep it from surfacing. I hope."

"If he's that kind, isn't there a chance he'll throw in with Kolar, turn on you?"

"No, I don't think so. I'll tell him Kolar's trying to eliminate us. That'll motivate him, believe me."

His confident tone failed to alter Cindy's view, nor did his certainty about Pierce's malleability reassure her. There was a lot of conjecture in what was being presented as objective analysis. Observations were forced through eyes that worked like prisms, broke circumstances into dazzling rainbows. The mind reassembled the colors to suit itself. The inherent flaw was not so much in the self-delusion as in the scramble to justify any actions based on it. Personality, pride, ego—the entire human lexicon became involved, and desperation was routine. She searched her memory and was appalled that she could remember so few instances where a person had failed to profit by good information and accepted the blame for subsequent failure. It looked as if it might be happening to Glen. If that was the case her situation was far nervier than she had anticipated.

Blaring horns shocked her out of her thoughts. They were involved in more wheel-to-wheel traffic, and the loss of the motion-breeze turned sweat to syrup instantly. The humidity added body to the thick exhaust of engines that never heard of emission controls. Coils of smoke roped into the air above vehicles in aimless eddies. What could have been a saving breeze from the sea was blocked by the two- and three-story buildings. More horns rose in protest, and the driver turned to smile and shrug his shoulders. Cindy looked at Draeger for his reaction and was pleased to see him calmly return the smile and settle back against the seat. She followed his lead, only to be shocked by Draeger's sudden vault forward. He shot his torso across the seat back, his head almost to the windshield.

Two policemen had a young man by the arms, each one cramping a limb behind the youngster's back. Slightly built, no more than fifteen, he looked far too frail to create such expressions on his captors' faces. They were more than grim, they were enraged. And frightened. Their agitated, jerk-and-push progress silenced the squalling hours. Tension squeezed the scene.

The boy himself looked physically ill, exhibiting the pallid shock that saps a man suddenly aware of mortality. He stumbled, and one of the cops lifted on the twisted arm. Cindy registered Draeger's muffled grunt of sympathetic pain and his hand tightening on the seat back. The boy's expression didn't change. That aspect of the incident lasted no more than a second, yet when the trio disappeared around the corner, her teeth were at the point of drawing blood from the knuckle of her index finger. She was surreptitiously massaging the insulted joint when Draeger settled back into the seat beside her. He looked at her helplessly.

The driver swiveled to them. "Not long ago," he said, pointing at the store front near the corner, "man set off a grenade in there. Hurt many people." He gestured with both hands, an explosion. "People very angry, frightened. Police watch now."

"God-damn," Draeger breathed. Then, "Did he have a grenade, or a bomb?"

The driver lifted one shoulder. "I will see." He hopped out of the taxi and moved smartly down the street to a previously unnoticed security guard in a doorway. He carried an ancient shotgun, and Draeger stared fixedly at the way he cradled it. Cindy put her hand on his arm, and he started violently. When he realized what she was doing, he continued to look at the hand, only belatedly raising his head. It was her turn to be surprised. There was a murkiness in his eyes, an evasiveness that cloaked whatever thoughts he might have. Worse, when he looked away, she was sure there had been a meaning he wanted her to know.

The driver was already trotting back to the taxi, and the jam was breaking up ahead of them. He was talking as he opened the door. "Foolishness," he pronounced easily. "Boy gets in argument with clerk, you know? He tells her somebody should throw a grenade at store again, maybe get her. Somebody else hears him say 'throw grenade.' They call police. They come, grab boy, take him outside. No trouble."

Draeger laughed. "I'll bet the boy's in trouble."

The driver shared the joke with him. "You be sure. I think maybe his father make him more trouble than any police." He shook his head.

Cindy caught herself repeating the gesture. It was another blow to her assurance. She looked at Draeger and marveled at the effect of the action on him. He was more relaxed than ever. The prospect of something actually happening was catharsis, evidently, much like the macho idiocy of insisting on remounting a horse. She turned to look out her window. They were passing some sort of public building, old, a crennelated heap of cut coral blocks. She knew she should be interested, but was unable to concentrate on her situation, other than to strain her mind in an attempt to understand the man she was trying to save.

How could he be so damned inconsistent? Considerate of the pilot one minute, and then able to enjoy a poor boy's fright and embarrassment. Worse, he was making emotional capital of a situation that smelled of physical danger and could, at the very least, have led to a police investigation of all people in proximity of the incident.

He turned to her. "The hotel's just a few blocks. Don't let the bumpy street trouble you. It's a nice hotel. Nothing luxurious, but comfortable. Good food, nice pool and bar."

Waving a hand at her clothes, she said, "Can I get you anything to wear? I've got to get out of these clothes."

There was a movement in his face and a glint danced across his eyes, but he answered with no vocal leer. "The barter market's right across the street, practically. You can get material there."

"Material?" She held him to the seat with her eyes, even though the cab was stopped. "What do you think I'm going to do, wrap some cheap cotton around myself and pretend I'm a South Seas native? I don't do comedy, Glen. I want some *clothes*."

He said, "I see. I'll check. There ought to be something." He threw the last line hurriedly, backing out of the cab. Cindy flounced onto the sidewalk. A little man with a case sidled up to her and opened it to display a collection of glittering stones and pearls. "See jewels?" he said. "Husband buy for you, eh?" He winked.

Cindy repressed a shudder. The man was dirty, smelled of sweat and stale tobacco. "He's not—No, I don't want any."

He pressed forward. "Very pretty. Very cheap. Make a deal."

Cindy whirled on the man. She was three inches taller, and she was hot, tired, and angry. There was a growing suspicion in her that she'd been a colossal fool. Strange men who pushed themselves at her were very low on her tolerance list. "Get away from me," she hissed. "Take your junk and get out of my sight before I lose my temper!"

Utter shock paralyzed him. He gaped, was still gaping when she bent forward and in a quiet voice that cracked like a distant shot said, *"Now!"*

He went without a backward look. Feeling quite pleased with herself, Cindy turned to see the taxi driver and Glen standing by the closed trunk, hastily averting their eyes, pretending they'd seen nothing. She brazened it out, chin up, trying to ignore the waves of heat rolling up her throat and into her cheeks. When the two of them were close, Glen said, "I was talking to the driver. His aunt owns a dress shop. If you'd like, they'll make up something for you this evening. Casual wear. We can catch the noon boat to the island tomorrow. There's a dress shop there, too. No problem, OK?"

She agreed quickly. Once more, he'd done a nice thing. It was very confusing. Draeger signed them in. Bits of conversation reached her, phrases dealing with lost baggage and mismanaged reservations. The pretty Filipina clerk was very sympathetic. The taxi driver stood with the blue-uniformed security guards and was terribly interested in the pattern of the tile floor. When he had his money he flashed Cindy a mischievous smile, a thing bursting with irresistible pleasure in life. He was gone before she could return it.

When they were alone in the room, Draeger dropped into one of the chairs.

"I'll make this as easy for you as I can," he said, indicating the square room. "We'll have to work at it if we're going to afford each other any privacy at all, and I figure the heavy responsibility's mine. I'll keep clear as best I can."

She nodded, simply said, "Thanks," and flopped on one of the double beds. Glen's chair gripped at a movement. The air-conditioner droned. The next thing she knew, he was tapping her shoulder. She demanded to know what he thought he was doing and half-way through the speech heard the total incoherence of it. He tried to keep a straight face and failed terribly, falling back into the chair. She swung her feet around and sat on the edge of the bed.

"I wasn't asleep," she said, and he howled.

"You should have heard yourself," he managed between guffaws.

You and your perfect diction—muggle, woof, blah!—it was unbelievable.''

She had to laugh with him. "I must have dropped like a stone."

"Plenty of time," he said. "Get your shower and we'll go get that batik."

The accommodations were below anything she'd been exposed to for years. Yet, with the shower refreshing her and the rest afforded by the short nap, she didn't mind. If things got no worse, as far as hotels went, it would all be fun. If the air-conditioner made noise, it also made the room cool. If the bed was less than the best, she'd certainly slept well enough on it for a first try.

The fear that plagued her on the ride in from the airport chose that moment to snake back into her thoughts. There was going to be a great more to worry about than mattresses. Perhaps Glen's reaction in the taxi was a good thing. Just since they'd met—God, only a couple of weeks ago—he'd begun to respond to situations with a greater physical emphasis. His gestures were sharper, his walk more controlled, the weight on the balls of his feet.

She paused in her scrubbing, a pensive expression marred by the shifting runnels of water across her face. It would be exactly like him to get back on a horse. It was logically unsound and extremely important to some men.

She resumed washing, thrashing up a lather. There was a lot of that macho stuff in the Filipino makeup—she'd read that. And he'd been here a long time. If there was any tendency in that direction, living among the people would obviously amplify it. Not that he was a Filipino. Far from it.

Except for Ria. She was to be expected. Some encouraged that kind of liaison, said it gave the men a clearer insight into the culture. Hogwash! No one ever suggested the women should find themselves a lover in the interest of greater acculturation. Goddam double-standard male chauvinist bullshit, that's what it all boiled down to. At least Draeger hadn't fallen into the "us and them" syndrome or some other Golden Ghetto stuff. He'd handled himself well. In the society, not of it. Aloof without being unavailable.

He'd shown some taste there where Ria was concerned. A bit what—voluptuous? The way she walks, the thighs are sure to be somewhat chubby. Beautiful face. Too expressive, though. No question about her feelings for him. The last time I saw a look like that it was on a sophomore cheerleader. Poor Ria! It must be like jumping in front of a train when it hits you like that. He probably treats her well. God knows he was upset about what happened on the island. Helluva way to end a week like that. Talk about your going native. Wow. Double wow. Grass shacks and the whole damned machine.

"I said we had time! We don't have forever!"

She smiled to herself as she dried off. The change in him was as pronounced through the door as it had been in his movements. New vitality rang in his voice.

Stepping out of the bathroom, she clutched the towel around herself, trying to cover a maximum of surface without pulling it so tight it was revealing and still not wanting to seem a complete prude. It was disturbing. It was even more disturbing to find him out of the room entirely. His voice filtered through the door.

"I'll be waiting on the patio. Come down whenever you're ready."

He was being extremely considerate, which made the vague irritation all the harder to understand.

# ■ CHAPTER 31 ■

From his vantage on the barstool, Cruz looked over his shoulder at the hotel behind him and reflected that life in the army wasn't all bad. Drinking coffee alone at the quiet bar, comfortable in civilian clothes, enjoying a completely free day—no, life was not bad, at all.

He watched the American stroll onto the patio and seat himself. There was no doubt he was American. The walk was there, the unselfconscious survey, the assured action in pulling the chair away from the wall, positioning it to his taste. When he sat, it was a declaration. The chair was now exactly where it should be. He had put it right and was ready to enjoy the fruits of his cleverness.

It was a hobby with Cruz, and not just the vocation of Captain Cruz, the security specialist. Foreigners were interesting. Trying to fathom Filipinos could drive a man crazy. Foreigners were all so much more direct. The Japanese could be pretty devious. Not in the same league as the Filipinos, of course, but adept bargainers. The Germans and Swiss were too easy, direct, demanding, and dumb. Their idea of striking a bargain was to offer an insulting price and scream until they ran out of patience. Then they paid far too much, a spite figure created by their own meanness, and went on their way howling about the cheating natives.

Of course, that wasn't universal, any more than all Americans were as full of confidence as the one by the wall. Not a bad-looking man. Not washed out, like so many of the whites. They came to the tropics ghostly and when they managed to get a tan looked as if they were wrapped in a kind of brown plastic. Made a man think of half-cooked sausage.

This one was brown. Not the clear *kayumangi* brown, but a rich sun-drawn color, nevertheless. And he had good features. Solid build, good jawline. Easy to describe to an artist. Again, a problem with foreigners. So many looked alike.

No doubt about him being American. They were the only ones who were interested in what everyone else was doing and still kept a distance. That wasn't the way they'd behaved when he was a youngster. Then, the so-called "old hands" couldn't wait to tell a Filipino exactly what was best for the Philippines. Or himself. Or his family. Or any other damned thing. After Independence they made a genuine effort to back away from being Big Brother. It must have delighted some of them to see the happy natives screw up a working democracy.

Ah, well, poor Americans. Damned if they did and damned if they didn't. Bowed to every politician who claimed to have some votes and never dared throw their weight behind anyone. If there was one thing a Filipino politician understood, it was who he could depend on, and that let the Americans out right off the top.

Maybe that was why the tourists were so much more cautious about what they did and what they said now. They used to be a pain

in the ass because they were big and loud, but they laughed with
people. You could get along well with a loud pain in the ass who
made it clear he liked you and wanted to be friends. It wasn't that
easy with these new ones, who kept to themselves, looked at everything from a distance. The best of them were like this one, a little bit
cautious, a bit withdrawn, but not forbidding. He might be a good
man to know.

Cruz looked back toward the sea. The boat people were lined up
along the hotel's seawall. The slim praus, six of them, rolled easily
with the swell, lifting their outriggers like wet, supplicating fingers.
The boats were rafted close together, bows pointed at the small oval
bar and the outside dining area between the old hotel and the new
wing. The boats were old, heavily used, their roughness rebuked by
the transparent sea that suspended them. Shadows played under
them, sharklike darknesses that slid from side to side in muddled
unison. The owners dozed, pinched in between displays of seashells
or matting or model praus or anything else they thought a tourist
might buy. Sometimes the children only had a few flowers. They
were actually more likely to find a customer than anyone. Two,
smallest of the lot, slept off to the right, separated from the raft
boats. Brother and older sister, Cruz surmised, asleep like two
kittens in a box. They waited for the American who threw them
coins.

Cruz smiled as the man walked across the patio at that moment.
He headed directly for the railing, as though he knew exactly where
the children should be, and the girl was immediately awake when
he appeared at the seawall's railing. There was an incredible rapport
between them. Without preamble the man scolded the girl for being
lazy, falling asleep, not offering to dive for coins for the tourists.
The child, no more than ten, was as saucy as he was large. He
loomed over the rail, long legs sticking out of shorts, almost blis-
tered red. His torso would have made six of the girl and perhaps the
small brother thrown in. Her voice slid through his deep mock
accusations like a whistle piercing thunder.

"Why you not here sooner? We hot. Thirsty. You don't come."

"You should be bothering the tourists. Make them throw pesos
for you." He waved a meaty hand across the crystal shallows. The
girl looked into the water, then back at the man, pitying.

"Can't you see got no tourist? Only got him, over at bar, and he not tourist. He don't give no money."

Cruz looked away quickly, affecting great interest in the blossoming orchids planted beside the dining area.

Draeger watched the scene with quiet amusement, careful not to smile. He rose quickly, dismissing them all when Cindy stepped out onto the patio. The liveliness of her step proved the shower had done her a world of good. He winced inwardly, thinking how long it had been since he'd showered, hoping they wouldn't be long at the market. He led her across the shining tiled lobby toward the drivers and peddlers massed on the sidewalk. They schooled like fish, milling in a tight ball, waiting for something to drop in their midst. At the sight of Draeger and Cindy they froze in position, finning, ready to strike.

Cruz appeared at Draeger's elbow, and the waiting faces fell, the bodies resumed their weaving passage of time. Cruz said, "You are new to Zamboanga?"

Draeger said, "Not exactly. I've been here before. The lady hasn't."

"Oh, I see. Are you going shopping?"

"We're on our way over to the Barter Market. We want to get some batik."

Cindy said, "Why do they call it Barter Market? Do we actually trade for stuff?"

Cruz grinned, holding out an arm to clear a path for her past the crowd on the sidewalk. Draeger was impressed by the way the men stood aside. Cruz was explaining, "There's no barter. There may be some, of course, but the fact is, it's a cash market. The local people import things from Malaysia and Sabah and so forth, and the government rents them stall space to sell whatever they bring back."

She looked puzzled. "Isn't that smuggling?"

Cruz's quick laugh was honest amusement. "It used to be smuggling. Now we rent stall space and call it free enterprise. You're beginning to peek at our secrets." He smiled at Draeger. "She is very quick. It must make life difficult for you."

Draeger glanced at her before answering. "She's usually too busy keeping me out of trouble to give me trouble."

"I understand. You are lucky. However, what she says is true.

But the government did the right thing. These are sea people. To tell them they cannot go here, cannot go there, cannot buy this, cannot sell that—you tell them that, they will fight you. Better to let them live as they always have.''

Draeger admired the way he talked with his hands, each gesture part of a phrase, the hands and head emphasizing words and shades of meaning. It was almost as communicative to watch him as to listen. And there had been a particularly revealing motion and sharp pat on his own chest when referring to the government as "we." It was unlike a Filipino to include himself in the government. Filipinos said "we" when comparing themselves to other people, other countries. All politicians were "they."

"You are with the government?" Draeger asked.

Cruz looked at him sharply. "How did you guess that?"

"Either you're with the government or very well aware of what your government's doing. What's your job?"

"I'm with the Military Command for this region." The right hand swept through a tight, controlled arc.

Swallowing, Draeger said, "You're with one of the troop units down in the southern islands?"

Cruz slowed, ostensibly to let a tricycle pass, using the opportunity to take a hard look at Draeger's bland innocence. Draeger looked back, knowing there was nothing for Cruz to see. Cindy's hand crept into his, and it was cold. Cruz resumed the walk toward the Barter Market. "Unfortunately, I'm a staff officer. You will hear about me from the people at the hotel soon enough. I am what is called the Intelligence Officer for this region. We have some trouble in the south. Insurgents. I try to get information that helps our government deal with the problem.''

Cindy leaned forward, looked around Draeger. "You find out where they're hiding and tell the General?" It was all very round-eyed innocent.

Cruz smiled. "Hopefully, no. We don't like to send in troops. We would rather send in school teachers and sanitation experts and small business instructors. The Moslem population in my country has been exploited since the time of the Spanish and at war for the same length of time. It is time to help, not fight. But some insist on rebellion." He shrugged. "Then we must fight."

"Are there many Moros around here?" Cindy asked. They were almost to the market.

Cruz's smile tightened. "Moro isn't what you Americans would call a 'fighting word,' but Moslem is much better. And, yes, we have a great many. Most of the people in this building will be Moslem."

He stopped across the street from an unimpressive cement structure hugging the ground behind a high woven-wire fence. Soldiers sat at a table by the entrance, checking randomly selected packages before letting the owners proceed inside. Other soldiers walked about through the crowd streaming through the gate. A loud buzz flowed across the street, reminding Draeger of the sound from a hydroelectric powerhouse he'd visited as a child. This building even looked similar, an unimaginative cement lump. He questioned the wisdom of entering, but Cruz was already on the way and Cindy was pressuring his hand, urging him to follow.

Passing the guards was a non-event. Stepping into the central aisle of the market was a wrench into the midst of another culture.

The market was built with a central alley and numerous right-angle, narrower alleys leading off from it. The light was good, bringing the colors tumbling from the material in the tiny stalls in acid-sharp flashes. The clothing of the packed customers swirled past, an elongated kaleidoscope, vibrant with every imaginable hue, full of curious faces turning at their passage. Piled on that were the other assaults. The sound heard outside was amplified by constriction. It burst from the booths and caromed off the walls. People shouted, babies cried, children ran screaming through the forest of legs and above it all, radios blasted from all quarters, the stridencies of rock stars tearing at each other and anyone unfortunate enough to be caught in the middle. Draeger thought longingly of the huge dynamo that howled its single, numbing note. Simultaneously, the smells fell on him, threads of a muzzy, hot tapestry. Unlike food market smells, these were the product of a new era. There were plastic and chemicalized cottons and man-made fibers. In keeping with the noise from the radios, there was the styrofoam stink of freshly unwrapped electronic components.

After a brief hesitation to recover from the shock of first entry, Cindy enjoyed herself hugely. So obvious was her excitement and pleasure the other customers and the stallkeepers were aware of it and pleased. By the time they reached the end of the first side alley, she was among friends. When she made her selections, ancient, buried instincts rose, and the merchants were delighted to find themselves confronted by a blond, blue-eyed demon haggler who enjoyed the game fully as much as they.

Draeger watched her with amusement and, he was surprised to discover, pride. The good will Cindy generated eddied in all directions, creating side currents that benefited him with smiles and nods from most of the faces in the crowd. The spirit of the moment was insufficient to make him forget exactly who and what he was, even so. He watched Cruz carefully. Most of the people accepted him easily. There were some frowns, a few more smiles, but most of the acknowledgments were the nods one exchanges with the man who lives down the street. If there was an antipathy for him and what he did, it was very well hidden.

Five hundred years was a long time to learn how to disguise one's feelings, a small voice reminded Draeger, and he closed his mind to further speculation on local political relationships.

Cruz helped them carry bundles back to the hotel, Cindy chattering happily about the batik bargains. Cruz was satisfied to let her carry on, exchanging occasional knowing smiles with Draeger. It was a relationship that suited the latter fine. The automatic in its makeshift holster tied to his ankle felt less like a howitzer when the small-boned Filipino waved them a cheerful good-bye in the lobby.

Once in the room, Cindy whirled on Draeger. At first he thought the walk up the single flight of stairs had winded her and was shocked. Then he realized it was the release of caged tension that burned in her cheeks and eyes. She held one fist in the other hand at breast level.

"Did I do anything wrong?" Her question pleaded. "I tried to keep him as distracted as I could. I didn't want to do a dumb blonde number on him, because he looks so damned *smart*. I could feel him looking inside my head, and I just knew he'd poke and poke and poke if we didn't convince him we're just ordinary tourists. You can see it in some people. You look like that when you find something you think is important, and when I saw him look at you like that I thought I'd—"

"For Christ's sake!" Draeger exploded in laughter. "Whoa, woman! Slow down! You were perfect." He dropped into a chair, propped his feet on the windowsill. "You couldn't have been better. We're home free, Cindy. You did everything just right."

A hand moved toward him. It dropped back to her side without making any contact, restored to proper order. She said, "I was so afraid. My God, the Intelligence Officer for this region! Do you suppose he knows Tony Pierce?"

"The way you know the price of batik. What's important is, what's he know about him?"

She cocked her head. "You really don't trust Tony at all, do you?"

Draeger dropped his gaze to his knees and thought before answering. "I won't believe Tony would deliberately do anything to hurt any of us. I'd like to think all those tests they make us take would eliminate that chance. Tony's slick, though. He's always got a deal. I'd never trust him with anything small."

He wished he hadn't told her. Concern dampened the amusement and sharing that had gone before. Tearing open packages, she pointedly concerned herself with her purchases. It was a short-lived charade. Dropping a bolt of cloth on the bed, she continued to stare at it as she spoke.

"You're a damned fool, Glen Draeger, and you embarrass me." The words strained to deny underlying stress. "Everything we do is lies. We're taught to lie to anyone and everyone all the time, but never to each other. And you believe that. Can't you get it through your head it doesn't always work?"

"You're helping me right now. I'm depending on you. Now." The last word was emphatic.

"Damn you!" She walked to the window, turned a straight back to him. "The first time I ever saw you I was Kolar's stooge. I was coached to break into the conversation, say exactly what I said."

"I was pretty sure of that. I didn't attach much significance to it."

"You knew I was acting?"

"I thought you might be. There's a difference. He wasn't."

She spun from the window, hair spanning in a golden auriole before floating across a shoulder. "He had a right to pressure you. I didn't have the right to do what I did. Now you won't trust him and you trust me, and I'm ashamed of myself.''

He got to his feet. "Everyone connected with this mess has reason to be ashamed. I intend to put it right.'' He raised a hand at her unformed protest. "Hear me out. I wanted to be as loyal to him as he taught us to be to this program. I've been a fool. Granted. OK, if I can't be that loyal to a specific man or group of men, I'll settle for a concept, and my country's the concept. I think Kolar's subverting it.''

She moved to the dresser, her legs working poorly. When she leaned back against it her upper body slumped forward and she spoke at the floor. "You're wrong. You watch. If we work together, I'll show you he's been on your side all along. Whatever's wrong, it's not Carl.''

Draeger nodded, letting the unborn argument die. Loyalty would demand she interfere if Kolar's situation became dangerous. On the other hand, once she saw for herself that he was behind everything that had gone wrong, she'd break with him. Her primary responsibility was to the unit. She would go to any length to insure its continuing function. After complimenting himself for that insight he surrendered to the contempt that swept in behind it. He would use the knowledge to manipulate her.

He said, "I'm glad you're helping me. I know you don't believe me about Kolar. You believe I didn't wreck the net or kill anyone. I hope you understand how important that is to me right now.''

She made light of it. "I'm along for the ride, Glen. Just protecting you from yourself.''

He laughed with her, an expression that failed to strike the seriousness from his eyes. "I'm going swimming. You have a good time with your clothing binge. I'll buy a suit at one of the local stores. See you in a while, OK?''

Nervously, she plucked at a sleeve hem. "I don't want to sound silly, but is it all right if I go into town? Those men from the island—'' The sentence drained away, the unspoken words eaten by the rumbling whisper of the air-conditioner. He moved away from the door, stepped toward her and stopped abruptly.

"I'm certain it's safe, Cindy. No one knows we're here." He shot her a quick, teasing grin, one side higher than the other. "Except the

Philippine security forces. Ain't that something? We outrun the best
collection people in the world and a bunch of terrorists, and the first
person we speak to is Mr. Counterintelligence for this whole damned
region. Can we pick 'em?''

She was only partially mollified. ''Am I wrong to be afraid? Is
field work always like this?''

''Field work is never like this, and you'd be crazy not to be
scared. For now, there's no real need. Go do what you want to do.
I'll be down by the pool when you get back, OK?''

She nodded and he left, hurrying, hoping she was more convinced
than he was that this place was safe. Coincidence. Cruz was a
coincidence. He couldn't possibly have a lead on them. Kolar
wouldn't go to the police.

Coming out the front door of the hotel, Draeger chose a tricycle
for the ride to town. He remembered the one on the ride in, how it
had obviously ranked near the bottom of the authority list. Big cars
made way for trucks, little cars made way for big cars, and so on.
Motor scooters and bicycles argued with tricycles. Keeping that
thought uppermost, he picked one with a large religious scene
painted on the passenger car and 'Nuestra Señora' emblazoned
across the top of the painting. The driver quoted a price slightly less
than the fare from the airport, and Draeger bargained dutifully,
going so far as to step outside the machine. With a price settled,
they growled off in a luminous cloud of blue exhaust.

Thirty minutes later he was back at poolside, lounging on a
comfortable chaise, face to the sun, cold San Miguel in his hand.
Beads of moisture ran down the dark bottle, forming a halting,
bucking stream along his finger and thumb to the wrist where they
married with sweat, rivering on down his forearm to the cloth of the
chaise. He watched the action intently, wanting to find a fundamental truth in the condensation and its subsequent flow. Warm moist air
condensed on a cold surface. Gravity pulled water downhill. It was
all very undeniable. It was hardly wisdom.

A girl splashed in the pool, squealing feigned fear. Water spurted
between his fingers he clenched the bottle so hard. Ria hadn't
crossed his mind since he looked into the pistol in Cindy's hand.
Now he thought of her. Closing his eyes, he saw her waiting for him
on the bed mat. Again, he remembered her offering him the leaf

laden with fruit and her eyes, the fire there reducing the symbolism of it to incidental trappings.

There was a hollowness in the memories. They stirred him, sent blood through veins that threatened to burst at the pressure. There was no similar desire to hear her voice, to watch her prepare a salad as she'd done at their first meeting. When he thought of that salad, he saw nothing but the luscious lips parting and the teeth gleaming.

In memory he saw the white bathing suit in front of him, heard the rounds overhead again. His throat ached with the memory of salt water choking his cries. The sun hammered at his eyelids, and when he moved his eyes behind them, a red dot pursued by dozens of things that looked like spermatozoa flickered into view. Tantalizing, the apparition refused to center and be identified.

He rolled on his side to watch the swimmers. The couple was about his age. The man was flabby. He bounced on the diving board, once, twice, flexed his legs and stopped the motion. Buttocks, breast-like pectorals, and stomach all wobbled to a stop. Draeger looked away.

Ria came back to his mind. And Cindy.

There had never been the need to communicate with Ria the way he'd had to speak to Cindy when he was leaving the room. It had been important that Cindy know he was glad for her help. Not for her sake. For his own. He *needed* her to know. What the hell was that supposed to mean?

The last swallow of beer was flat and warm. The stickiness caught at his throat and left a taste of stale bread. He rolled off the chaise and got a drink at the fountain and, impulsively, took off for the pool on a run, sailing over the surrounding cement walkway in a flat dive, cutting through the water so fast he had to double under to avoid hitting the far side.

The cool water cleared his head. Submerging, he pushed off from the wall, momentum carrying him in a lazy drift. When he rolled over he could see the sun on the surface, a thousand thousand suns, shifting and probing, hunting for him. When he needed air, the sun would be up there, completely organized in singular judgment, waiting. He turned his back on it, coming up facing the wall. Flattening his hands on the lip, he levered himself up and swung his legs onto the hot cement, then straightened and moved quickly back to his chaise.

He was glad he'd given in to the impulse to dive in. There had been just enough shock to stimulate some intelligent thought instead of sunbaked daydreaming. There was no point in comparing two women. Using Ria had been wrong, but she'd been a willing victim. There would be no more risk for her, in any case. Perhaps they'd get together again when this was over, perhaps not. He could relax in the knowledge he'd never endanger her again. Cindy was affecting him in an entirely different manner. Far more dangerous, really, because when he thought of trouble he thought of her as an ally. There was the masculine concept of protecting her, but there was the further concept that she could help. The whole thing was too complex. The clarity that filled him when his body struck the water was leaving him, sapped by the unending sun.

We're all pawns, he told himself, leaning back and closing his eyes. He draped a towel over them to frustrate the sun. No, not a chess game at all, he amended. It's a goddam clockworks, the world is a machine, and they put us where they want us and we turn and the whole issue does what someone else wants it to do. Well, goddammit, not this time. Draeger uses. I've earned it.

A motorcycle started in front of the building, a sudden batter of explosions. Even as his mind was correlating the sound, telling him it was an engine, a reflex was hearing a submachine gun and seizing muscles. His jerk rattled the chaise.

He took a deep breath, sighed, felt the acceleration in his heart subside.

I've earned my cup of ruthlessness, he told himself. I'm owed.

# ■ CHAPTER 32 ■

Boy Angel reluctantly tore his eyes away from the movie poster, forced to conclude the terrified starlet's ripped blouse was never going to be more revealing. For all eternity, or at least until her next role, she would display that much cleavage and not a millimeter more.

He turned and looked directly across the street at the blond American from Manila. He froze, afraid to breathe. She spoke to the taxi driver, and he reached inside the vehicle, pulling out packages. A plump woman bustled out of the dressmaker's shop. She greeted the American with smiles while the driver hurried to open the shop door. He followed them in, juggling his load, and Boy Angel exhaled in a gust.

He backed around a corner and leaned against the wall, trying to organize his thoughts. It was the American woman; there could be no doubt of that. Whites could be confusing, but she was the one who came to Manila with the big, silver-haired man. She was unmistakable, strutting around as if she had something special. The way she let the taxi driver and the idiot from the store bow and grin was terrible. It made them look like frightened dogs. Munson understood. He hated her, and he hated the lion-headed man even more. He feared him, too. Hate can live without fear, but they eat at the same table, Boy Angel thought. And usually from the same plate.

Deciding what to do with the information was a problem. He tapped the ticket envelope in his pocket and thought of Draeger's woman in Manila. He pictured her posed like the one in the movie poster, eyes frightened, legs spread, blouse torn down the front, held together by threads. Unaware of it, he was smiling.

Munson could look out for himself. If the big man and the blond wanted to learn something about him, let them.

The driver came out of the store and made his way a few doors down to a small open-front bar. Boy Angel waited until he was certain the man intended to stay awhile, then strolled past the dress shop. The blonde was looking at herself in a long mirror, a strip of material folded over her shoulder and hanging down in front. The cloth was black with orange and brown designs. The dressmaker spread it, emphasizing the slim waist and round hips. He stopped, looking, and the woman turned from the mirror, examining herself in profile, breasts jutting under the draped material. Her eyes changed their focus, her head lifted. She was looking at him in the mirror. He turned quickly, walking back the way he'd come, turning the first corner and continuing on.

He burned inside. Hard-eyed bitch, staring back at him! Any other time, any other place, he would give her something to look at. They were all like that, inside. So nice, promised so much, and what they really wanted was a slave, a dog. They couldn't understand that a man lives a man's life.

A clock in a window caught his eye and reminded him of his schedule.

The other woman would be in Manila.

He lifted a hand to flag a tricycle and dropped it, suddenly undecided. If the woman was here with the man, Munson would be very glad to know it. A few questions for the driver wouldn't take long, and a phone call to the island would make him very popular.

The debate lasted a full minute. No one knew he'd seen her. If he told them, they might cancel the trip to Manila. That wasn't going to happen. He knew what he wanted to do and how to arrange it. It was all planned out.

Arturo sat across a kitchen table from Ria. It was in a cousin's house, one where she could hide. The cousin stood in the doorway, agitated hands dry-washing, trying to force herself out of the scene and too fascinated to move. Children erupted in the background and a door slammed, solving her problem. With a look of exasperation tempered by relief, she spun and left, yelling names and admonitions. Arturo watched her go and addressed Ria. He was shaking with anger.

"I forbid you to go! What does it matter if he's with another woman? You said yourself you were through with him!"

Ria listened impatiently, chewing her lower lip. She leaned toward Arturo. "I cannot ask you to understand, but I love you too much to hurt you without an explanation. It is because I want to be done with him, and I must find out if the message is the truth. If he is with another woman I am free. I want to be free."

"Then do it! Don't chase after him! You are doing exactly what he wants! He probably had the message delivered himself. I bring it to you and you fly to Zamboanga, full of tears and making-up. You deserve more."

She reached to pat his hand, and he jerked it away. Her voice was gentle. "He does not hold me. He attracted me. No, he attracts me. It is something I cannot deny. What he does to me isn't half as important as what I do to myself, though. It is not enough for me to believe he's with another woman. I must *know*."

"You almost died because of him. Now we must keep you hidden like a prisoner. Your clients grow impatient." He stopped, blanched. He stared into the space over her shoulder, suddenly distant. When she touched him he started violently. Before she could speak, he said, "Please, Ria, hear what I have just thought and do not think I am only trying to win an argument. What if the people who tried to kill you sent this note? Perhaps they expect you to go to him so they can kill you both at once. Or perhaps they wish you to go on a plane and—" He shuddered and avoided her look.

Ria said, "I already thought of that," and she was so calm his head snapped up in disbelief. Her lips twitched in a hidden smile before she continued. "They would have to know which plane I was on. They can't watch all of them. And I believe Glen about one thing, at least. Those men were after him. I was just in the way." This time she allowed the smile through, and it was an open wound of self-deprecation. Arturo rubbed his temples at the sight of it. She went on, "Whoever brought this note probably knows the other woman, wants to break that up."

"I'll break someone's arms."

She squeezed his hand. "You are more than family, Arturo. You are a very special man. Please don't worry about me. This is something I must do."

He sighed and turned his square hand over to enfold hers. "You really mean to fly all the way to Zamboanga just to see if this worthless animal is cheating on you? Believe it! If he's doing it now, he will. He's no good. And what if he's there alone? What then?"

She closed her eyes and misery pulled at her cheeks, her lips, the corners of her eyes. It seared the youth from her features, transformed her into a crone full of bitter memories. Her hand in his tightened to a fist that stressed the knuckles to cold, white lumps. "Alone? If he's there alone? God help me, Arturo, that's the thing I fear the most."

He rose from the chair, clumsy because of anger-stiffened muscles. "I am not sure God spends much time in Zamboanga. If Glen Draeger is there, I suspect the city needs His full attention. I will go with you." When she attempted to protest he spoke through the effort. "No, I have decided. You are probably right it isn't dangerous, but we know Draeger is mixed up with some very bad people. At the first sign of trouble we go directly to the police. And from there back to Manila. Agreed?" The voice demanded affirmation. The eyes begged.

"Agreed." She came around the table and leaned against him, arms around the thick torso. He patted the back of her head, looking embarrassed. "I'll be happy you're with me, Arturo. Thank you."

He continued to pat her, pleased and still uncomfortable. Fixing a frown, he said gruffly, "The argument is over, Inez. You can stop listening outside the door and come in."

A sharp gasp revealed the accuracy of the verbal dart. Ria pinched him and hurried to soothe her wounded cousin. Arturo retained his expression for a moment, then turned away to let the smile break through. It was a sorry example, amusement smeared with concern. He wished he could enjoy the moment more. It took no great genius to understand there would be little to laugh at in the next few days.

The clerk at the hotel watched the mismatched couple hanging back from the rest of the early morning flight's arrivals with unwarranted apprehension. She noticed them when they came in, not like regular tourists, worried about baggage or looking to see everything at once. They stepped to the side, content to watch the others crowd the desk and register. Determination shone from the man's blunt features, and that was a puzzling thing in itself. Men who looked like that usually stormed the desk, demanding satisfaction. The woman was more disturbing. Trouble showed through her beauty. Well dressed in matching pale blue jacket and skirt, she observed the room deliberately, committing details to memory. The clerk was sure she knew exactly how many orchids were in the vases on the lobby tables. The woman was prepared for something she dreaded, set for a blow so completely anticipated it had lost its ability to frighten.

When everyone else was gone, the heavy man touched the woman's arm, and they moved to the desk. The clerk expected bombast and was grateful for the soft question.

"We are trying to locate a friend of ours, an American. His name is Draeger."

"We have no one here by that name, sir. We have several Americans, but no one named Draeger. We have not had, I'm sure."

The woman's swift facial reaction surprised the clerk, and she thought to herself that it would be difficult to describe. "Cautious" and "disappointed" suggested themselves, but that was nonsense. They didn't fit together. Could one be cautiously disappointed?

The man said, "He is traveling with his wife, an attractive blond woman." Arturo described them, as the message had described, and as he remembered, Draeger.

The clerk blushed. The man watched her and was very stern. Then, abruptly, he smiled. It was a good smile, one that put lights in his eyes and set deep lines like fishnet all over his face. He said, "You see more than you say, young lady. I understand it is the way of the world. I do not wish to embarrass you. The woman and the man were here, but not as Mr. and Mrs. Draeger. I see that." He paused, and she looked at the desk. Her ears burned. Gently, he continued. "If such a couple was here now you would not wish to say so, but perhaps if they were already gone you could tell me?"

Speaking in a voice full of secret urgency, the clerk told Arturo of

Draeger's departure with Cindy for Pierce's hotel. With a significant look for Ria, she added, "You should ask for Mr. Griffin. From Canada." With that out of her system, she turned away quickly, occupying herself with some mail. Arturo murmured hurried thanks, leaving in such a rush Ria was hard pressed to keep pace.

The cruiser came to the dock with a gentle thump, mashing only a minor complaint out of the white foam fenders. Small striped fish, looking like elongated bull's-eyes from above, dashed out of the shade of the dock at the vibration, frantic in their search for food. When they found nothing sinking to them they scattered back to cover, suddenly aware of their chances of becoming that which they sought so eagerly.

Ria and Arturo noticed none of it. They also failed to notice the muscular young man who loitered aboard until the rest of the passengers were off-loaded. One of the crew spoke to him as he left, and Boy Angel merely looked at him. The crewman found a line that required coiling. Boy Angel leaped lightly to the dock. Where the path inland forked he took the left branch, trotting to Pierce's cottage. Pierce was just finishing breakfast. He dismissed the waiter at Boy Angel's suggestion and listened with growing horror as Boy Angel's story unfolded.

"I was lucky to catch them leaving Manila," he said earnestly. "They know the man called Draeger is here. Someone who knows about him and the woman named Ria told her. They went to a hotel in town and asked some questions and before I could telephone, they were on the boat. I followed and ran here."

Pierce leaped from his chair and barked a number into the house phone. He pounded the wall with his fist until a voice crackled in the earpiece.

"Munson? Listen, we've got more trouble. The woman Draeger was running with in Manila is here, and she brought some cousin with her. They know he's here."

The instrument chattered, and Pierce held it away from his head to glare at it. Then, "Don't yell at me, goddamit! You're the big fucking General! I pumped Draeger pretty good; I got him tucked in and calmed down. I'm holding up my end. You're falling on your ass. He's supposed to be dead. Your tiger's the one who told me. You remember him, the wheel in your master-fucking-plan?''

Boy Angel forgot his own anger in the sinister silence that poured from the phone. When it came to life Pierce nodded curtly at the rattling phrases. Finally he hung up and turned away.

"You stay in this room," he ordered. "I expect to kick the Filipina and her cousin out of here in a few minutes. Watch the path to the boat, and when you see them leaving, go after them. This time they die, understand? Munson thinks you're some kind of expert, but all we've seen is bullshit. Don't fuck up this one."

The scar itched. It burned and throbbed, straining to rupture the shining welt. Boy Angel remembered to smile. Looking at Pierce, he could tell it wasn't working. It added to his fury.

Pierce said, "Don't make faces at me. Find some children to scare. Or a woman."

Boy Angel leaped for him. Quick as he was, Pierce was ready. Boy Angel had the terrible feeling Pierce not only anticipated the move but had arranged it. He banged into the coffee table. When he spun off it his shins hurt and he was unbalanced. Sparks erupted in his head, and he heard, rather than felt, the blow above his ear. Blurred colors swam in his vision. Nausea climbed halfway up his throat, stalled. Legs grown uncooperative buckled, and he slumped to a sitting position. He was embarrassed to find himself seated with his head slumped forward, legs spraddled in a V like an alley drunk. Looking up, he saw the long-barreled revolver in Pierce's hand and understood why one blow could be so effective. It was like being hit with a tire iron.

Pierce bent over him, the weapon carefully placed between thoroughly attentive eyes. He said, "Understand what I'm telling you. Munson thinks he's the brains in this operation, but I *know* I'm the balls. I want the woman and her cousin taken out. Mess it up, and I'll put a few of these Moros after you. They'll use you for fish bait. You got all that?"

Boy Angel nodded very slowly, gaze frozen to the black pistol.

Pierce straightened and walked to the door. "I'll leave this for you. Throw it in the sea when you're finished." The heavy piece thumped on the occasional table.

Scrambling across the floor, Boy Angel scooped it up and watched

Pierce amble off. The weapon sagged, defeated. Boy Angel accepted the loss stoically. It was unthinkable Pierce should live, but it was inopportune for him to die now. There were other matters to take care of. Then he would deal with Pierce. Slowly. When he saw what happened to the woman and her cousin, then he would understand what was waiting for him. Yes. Slowly.

Pierce approached the couple seated at the most discreet table in the outdoor dining area and made a mental note to compliment Luis on such good judgment. Off in a corner, partially shielded by a potted palm, they were easily overlooked. Once one noticed them, however, there was no chance of ignoring them. Pierce's first observation was that the woman was beautiful, and he sighed a compliment to Draeger's taste. And luck. It had been a long time since a woman played a part in his own life, and the thought of one as desirable as Ria stirred him more than he wanted to think about.

The chunky Filipino with her was a different number altogether, and Pierce found it easier to forget the woman when the wide-spaced eyes caught his own. There was a continuum in them, a solid fix on a purpose. It spread from there, led to the lips drawn back against the teeth, the squared chin tucked back against the neck. It made Pierce uneasy. Everything about the man disavowed compromise.

Sick envy grabbed him. This man would never dare death. He would grapple with it and exult in winning or cry in defeat, but there would be no wild excess. Whatever came of this search for Draeger, or anything else, he would end it in pride. He knew it. And because he knew it and wore the knowledge like a cloak, Pierce hated him at sight. His own sloughed fears loomed in his mind's eye as no different from a lust to seek death and torment it. This lump of a man looked into his eyes with a placid composure that made him ache.

He half-bowed and smiled at the couple. "Good morning, sir. You and the lady wished to see me?"

Arturo gestured at a chair and launched into his speech before Pierce was fully seated. "We are looking for a man. He is staying at this hotel. His real name is Draeger, and he is American. We believe he is claiming to be Canadian, calling himself Griffin. We want to speak to him."

Tenting his fingers, looking down his nose, Pierce stared, pretending to consider the situation. He let his eyes slip over the woman, favored her with a brief smile. She rejected it with a quick twitch, a movement suggesting trouble with insects. Pierce wanted to thank her for making things easier. He said, "I won't lie to you, sir. The gentleman you're looking for is here. As it happens, I was afraid of something like this. You see, he really is Canadian. He lives in Manila, and his wife stays in Canada. Toronto, I believe. The woman with him is not his wife."

Arturo half-rose, and Pierce spoke into the anger, quelling it before it could be verbalized. "Please, sir, try to understand our position. We can hardly insist on marriage licenses from our guests."

The woman asked, "You know he uses two names? How do you know that?"

He wanted to smile. Being prepared made it so simple, allowed him to face her with deep sadness. "He drinks when he's here, Miss. He becomes very confiding. There are things said best left unsaid."

Blood suffused Arturo's features. Ligaments strained in his throat, formed a sunken arrowhead at the junction of neck and chest. For one moment Pierce was certain he saw a fleck of mindless fury in the eyes. He wanted to examine it further, enjoy puncturing that annealed sense of purpose, but it was there and away. It angered him. "My concern is that we have no scene. If you have legal grounds to discuss, you should see the police or a lawyer."

Arturo said, "I would like to see him."

The woman touched his arm and looked into Pierce's eyes. "No, Arturo. We will leave now. I know what I needed to know. We can go home."

The gaze was disconcerting. It was necessary to eliminate them because they were complicating everything, and she had made it very easy with that brusque rebuff. Now she revealed a humanity, a warmth that twisted in his guts. Pierce concentrated on Arturo.

Jaws working silently, Arturo considered. Deferring to Ria, he turned in the chair to face her. "It's up to you."

She rose and both men hurriedly followed suit. "We're leaving, Arturo. May we use the hotel boat to return to Zamboanga?"

Pierce made another half bow. "Of course. Can we be of any other service?"

She shook her head, and a smile broke across her face. All Pierce could compare it to was the unexplained wave that flings itself onto a beach, taller, heavier, farther-reaching than anything to go before it or come after. He had seen it happen rarely, and it filled him with awe, an awareness of mystery beyond his understanding. The smile was like that. It spoke of new beginnings and unspoken memories. It made him wish he was defending her instead of sending a man to kill her.

Arturo said the good-byes for both of them. Pierce watched them leave and concentrated on the money he would have soon. When Boy Angel appeared on the path and moved toward the boat after them the thought crumbled.

"You are all right, Mr. Pierce?" It was one of the waiters, one of Bilongon's men. The ostensible concern merely glossed distrust.

Pierce said, "I'm fine," and the man nodded, then, "The special guest asks you to his room. He says it is important."

Pierce waved the man away, watching Boy Angel until he disappeared around a bend. With him out of sight, Pierce stretched as if waking, head thrown back, eyes closed. He left the patio briskly, hurrying to Munson's room.

The gangly figure sprawled on a chair, still dressed in his pajama bottoms. The top lay on the bed, wadded in a knot with twisted bedclothes. The sight irritated Pierce beyond its importance, and he stopped immediately inside the door and surveyed the room coldly. Munson watched with growing annoyance. "What d'you think you're doing, inspecting a barracks?"

"If this shithouse is any sign of what's happening to your mind, we're screwed."

Munson exploded upright. "Don't you dare criticize me! If I want to relax, by God, I will! I'm the one who's making you rich! Remember that!"

Moving into the room, Pierce tried to mollify him. "I'm not forgetting. I'm concerned about you. There's a lot of tension in this thing, and I don't want to see it get to you."

"Nothing's wrong with me." From fury Munson moved to truculence. "It's not strain that's bugging me; it's being stuck in this goddamned room, doing nothing.'' He bobbed his head at the window. ''I saw the two of them leaving, then Boy Angel. You're sure she won't recognize him?''

''He says she won't.''

''Good.'' Munson intertwined his fingers across his stomach, and Pierce's jaw dropped, shaken by the image of Scrooge. Laughter scratched at the roof of his mouth, and he tasted the hysteria in it. Munson's next comment startled him to sobriety. ''I want you to tell Draeger what's happened.''

''Do what?''

Munson grinned. ''Can't you see the symmetry of it? The inevitability? The woman comes looking for her lover, learns he's here with another woman. She leaves without making trouble. Why? Perhaps she means to blackmail him. Or inform a third party. The man doesn't know. He chases after her to force her to tell him, to make her agree to forget it all.''

Pierce curled a lip. ''Draeger? What the hell's wrong with you? His mind doesn't work that way.''

''We know that, but if he's dead and we say he was talking that way when he left, who can refute it? And if he interrupts Boy Angel, you can be sure he'll die for it.''

''What if Boy Angel just dumps them over the side? Draeger'll never know.''

''You should pay more attention to what's going on around you, Tony. Your man Luis told me Boy Angel asked if he knew a good place to take a woman for 'some fun,' as he put it. Luis told him of an abandoned logging camp, up in the hills. Now, you'll tell Draeger you saw the woman was being followed. Of course, you assumed he arranged it. He'll go after her. You'll supply a prau. It must be fast, but not fast enough to catch the cruiser before it reaches Zamboanga.''

''How's Draeger going to find them? Boy Angel'll kill them both and be back in town before he knows which way they went.''

Munson shook his head and chuckled, like a schoolmaster confronted by a willfully thick pupil. ''The man in the prau will ask Draeger why he's after your boat. He will help Draeger speak to the taxi drivers. After a proper interval, he will 'discover' one who knows something and report to Draeger exactly where Boy Angel and his victims have gone. You can be sure he'll rush after them like Lochinvar.''

Pierce sighed. ''Not telling Boy Angel about all this was crazy. We've got nothing to lose, I guess. Christ knows something has to work. I'm beginning to think fucking Draeger'll outlive everybody.''

''He won't.'' The venom in the words snapped Pierce's head up. Munson's eyes were empty, wide and staring.

Any other expression might very well have failed to send Pierce obediently to execute his instructions; this one convinced him Munson had drifted out of reality once more. The secrets to a million dollars were mired in that madness, and keeping Munson in working order until the money was in hand was imperative.

And Luis was the helper who suggested the logging camp to Boy Angel. Well, then, Luis could take Draeger. If there were going to be consciences raped along with the woman, Luis was entitled to a full partnership.

He paused on his way to the beach where the better praus were resting on the sand beside the curved trunks of the coconut palms, aware of a divergent train of thought, interruptions that demanded to be heard clearly.

Draeger had beaten the odds dramatically. Was it possible he was that much better than they'd imagined? Why did Munson hate him so? No matter what came up, he found a way to aim it at Draeger. There wasn't any sense in that. It lost track of the main objective.

He slapped his forehead, laughed out loud. He was even beginning to think like Munson. Main objective, shit. There was only one objective—make Pierce rich. If Draeger had to die for that, it was too bad. That went for the woman and the eager martyr following her around, too. And Boy Angel. No hard feelings there, for damned sure. And Bilongón could massacre all the Red Army troops he wanted.

That was a lot of bodies.

He shook his head and continued toward the praus.

# ■ CHAPTER 33 ■

"I want to go with you, Glen." Cindy pulled on his arm as if she'd keep him in the room by main force. He looked down at her, gratitude softening irritation.

"It's impossible, Cindy. If the man's part of the outfit that shot at us on Boracay, he's professional. You've never dealt with anyone like that."

"Neither have you."

He pulled his arm free, turned away. "It's time I did."

When he headed for the door she reached out again, the touch on his bicep so delicate they both ignored it easily. He stopped in the hall and looked back to wave. She hoped her smile was better than it felt. The dim hall hindered her view of his face, a view further complicated by the window farther behind him. Sunlight turned the prim rectangle into a distorted form, the edges obscured. It cheated her of any certain memory of his departure. From her window she watched him run to the beach where Pierce talked to a Filipino in shorts and T-shirt.

Pierce had been very helpful. Despite her own feelings about Glen taking off after the couple from Manila, it was gratifying to know Pierce was taking a personal hand in the selection of the man accompanying him. And it was important to protect the couple. It was only right, notwithstanding the fact that any furor they created would inevitably lead to Glen. Once that happened there was nothing left to do but run.

The man held the prau steady while Glen vaulted aboard. He settled into the hull with a minimum of fuss. She hoped the other men didn't notice him slip a hand down the inside of his left leg where they'd lashed the automatic. He'd insisted they tell no one he had it. It troubled her to exclude Tony when he was being so cooperative, but Glen insisted. At least he appeared embarrassed about keeping a secret from him. The strangest part of the whole thing, however, was her reaction to his insistence. Normally, a man who drove hard at having his own way antagonized her beyond natural stubbornness. That hadn't happened this time, and she didn't feel she'd lost anything by it. On the contrary, there was a feeling of involvement that was uniquely exciting and satisfying. Decision had come from him, but only after discussion, and now there was teamwork. There had been no transfer of power, no diminution of anyone.

The prau was a dot at the end of a whiteline on the ocean now, a finger pointing at a speck racing for the horizon. She flung herself on the bed, staring at the ceiling, and wondered if she could love him, wondered if she was falling in love with him. The more the question pecked at her mind the more it depressed her, the more hazardous his effort loomed.

She told herself she hated Ria Manong and closed her eyes and wished she could. Lower lip trembling, damning herself for it, she spoke into the self-generated darkness. "Glen Draeger, you're a nice man, a good man. If there's anything in you that knows how to be one mean son of a bitch, you better reach in and pull it out today, I'm afraid." Her fist flew to her mouth. "Oh, God, I don't want to hear that word. I am afraid, I really am."

She wasn't sure if that counted as praying or not.


Ria sat in a deck chair, unheedful of the sun, unaware of the wind ruffling skirt and blouse. Nothing penetrated her isolation from the time she'd turned her back on the hotel to walk to the boat. Arturo had tried conversation, remarking there was only one other passenger in so much space. Her response had been so lackluster it embarrassed her and offended him. That was when she decided to withdraw entirely, and he was relieved to see her go. When she chose a chair out in the full glare of the sun he made no attempt to reason with her. He moved his own into the shade of the overhanging cabin roof.

Her sole emotion wasn't melancholy. Relief was there too, an easing of emotional tension. Off in the distance she noticed a prau, sail ocher against the blue sky. The cloth was full, pulling easily. That was how she felt, she told herself, charged with energy but leveled out now, riding true. A smile lifted some of the hardness from her face as she hoped the energy moving her now wasn't as mindless as wind power. That had already happened, sent her careening through time and emotion out of control. Whatever moved her in the future would have to be better managed.

The best part of her feelings was the lack of a sense of loss. Already she thought of him as something in her past, a wild part of herself that she'd enjoyed and suffered. Nothing in her life would be measured to the same standards again. No matter what else he'd done, he'd released her from herself, and there could be no remorse in that.

Hate was another matter, and she turned her back on the cabin and the sulking Arturo, afraid some treacherous facial tick would expose the darkness of her thoughts.

White froth boiled in their wake, dazzling against the hard blue sea, and she stared into it, lost herself in the myriad forms.

The hatred was in her and she couldn't deny it, nor could she understand how it was possible to be grateful to the man for some of the things he did, to remember some of the time with him in yearning that sent fire through her veins, and have all that contaminated by the awareness that he'd used her and abandoned her. Logic consistently reminded her that he'd promised nothing. He'd pursued her with open intent. He'd been affectionate and considerate.

Another part of her mind snarled responses. He lied, cheated, exposed her to terrible danger. Whatever he'd appeared to be, truth wasn't part of it. All the good things that came from him were fruit from a poisonous tree. If he'd freed part of her, made her aware of herself in ways she'd never known, then equally he'd killed things that were no less important.

She got to her feet, thrusting the chair back hard enough to bang against the knee-high bulkhead behind her. Depression was the last thing she needed, she warned herself. The fantasies were all run out. The world was just another arena. Glen Draeger was no more than another participant, gone from her life.

A nagging worry wouldn't leave. She knew she would always wonder what he was, what he truly did. It was important enough to warrant people with silenced submachine guns. She racked her brain, trying to think of something illegal that would take him out of Manila on trips and be worth enough money to attract such a determined effort to kill him.

That was when Munson's laboratory came to her. Drugs needed processing. It was in the movies and on television all the time, making opium into heroin. She couldn't remember how it worked, but the police were always hunting for the laboratories on those shows, and the opium was always smuggled into the country in some rural place where there wasn't good police coverage. It all fell into place. Glen arranged the transportation, and Munson was the laboratory chief. He had an export business to ship things out, too. The theory explained a lot of things. Whoever killed Munson and Leonila wanted Glen out of the way, too. After all, it was Glen who was supposed to be at the warehouse when the explosion took place.

She could hardly wait to tell Arturo.

The man who came aboard after them was looking out the window of the cabin. He wore large sunglasses, so she couldn't be certain he was staring at her, but he was too casual in the way he swung away and disappeared. Arturo saw none of that because the man was behind him, but seeing Ria approach, he got up and moved to meet her.

He said, "I shouldn't have been upset. Not with you. It's just that I'm so very angry."

She patted his cheek. "I understand. I want to talk to you before we reach land. I'm going to the police."

Arturo's considerate look blew away, turned to a disappointed frown. "The police? What can they do? There's no law against what he did. Except moral law." He bit down hard on the last, too late to stop it. The pain in his next words ached in Ria's heart. "I'm sorry I said that."

She smiled, looped her arm through his, led him to the stern. He allowed himself to be guided, unwilling to look at her.

Inside the cabin, pressed against the door, Boy Angel tried to convince himself what he'd heard wasn't true. The police! That wasn't in anyone's thinking, not his, not the monkey-smart whites who knew everything. Scratching his chest with one hand, the other moved to his stomach where the revolver was hidden beneath his belt. He stroked the long barrel slowly, an intermingling of death and erotica untroubled by conscious thought.

Boy Angel cursed her with every word he knew, and when that provided neither solution or relief, he cursed Pierce. Pierce said the woman and her cousin died or Bilongon's men would be after him. There was no money for a ticket to Manila and escape. That meant the woman had to die now. He thought of some new things to call Pierce as he drew the pistol.

Kill the man first. There was time for the woman.

He braced the barrel against the jamb, holding it in both hands. The sights, the boat, the line of cropped hair at the back of the neck—all rocked in the same easy rhythm, bound together by his will.

The first joint of his index finger stressed against the trigger's resistance. His knees trembled at a completely unexpected pressure in his groin. He pushed at it with his left hand. She would scream when the man pitched onto his face.

Possibly over the rail, into the sea, unweighted.

Boy Angel stopped massaging his crotch, aimed at the center of the man's back, exactly where his spine was crossed by his belt. That would bend him backwards. He would hit the rail and fall properly.

When the man steering the boat hissed at him Boy Angel moved with blinding speed, one foot sliding the door shut to hide himself from the couple on the stern even as he turned and leveled the gun at the interruption. The pilot jumped away from the wheel, raising his hands until his fingers jammed against the overhead. At the look on Boy Angel's face the right hand dropped and executed a cross. When he survived for a space of several crashing heartbeats, he managed to speak. It took two tries for any sound to come out and a third before he produced recognizable words.

"Boat. There. Police patrol."

Boy Angel turned his head slowly, eyes fixed on the terrified mask. When the angle was right he flicked his eyes in the direction indicated and swore. Then, "Ignore them. Take us on as if nothing was wrong."

The man nodded violently and clutched the wheel. Boy Angel replaced the revolver and walked to the port side to watch the approach. The vessel was long and sleek. The dull gray paint gave it a particularly menacing look. Its only bright colors were the flag snapping at the stern and the grotesque shark's mouth, red maw and white fangs, painted on the bow. It would have been burlesque without the stark efficiency of the .50 caliber machine gun mounted on the deck above it. The comical shark had genuine teeth.

The boat angled toward them, closing slowly. The crew was obviously interested in Ria, standing at the stern with her hair streaming in the wind. They cruised beside the yacht until it fell off to make for the Zamboanga docks.

Boy Angel wished he could kill them all, wished they could taste his luck once in their lives.

The boat was still unsecured when he vaulted the rail and ran down the dock. Ria and Arturo watched with mild interest. The pilot crossed himself once more, yelled at the men handling the shore lines to hurry, and raced to the opposite side where he emptied his stomach. With his other two passengers ashore he was shouting at the line handlers again, backing off from the wharf immediately.

Ria and Arturo went directly to the end of the dock, ignoring the inter-island freighters and ferries loading around them. The dock was a major trans-shipping point for the constant flow of travelers throughout the Philippines. From Zamboanga one caught the smaller ferries that thumped wearily through the southern routes, plowing seas that still smelled of piracy's blood and suffering. To the south was a fabled place, Bilongon's fighting pit, a land where war was waged today with heat-seeking missiles and krises handed down from father to son for generations. Moslems and Christians of a dozen tribes mingled on the docks and tried to go about the business of making a living. The very air around the southbound vessels tasted of suspicion, fear, and hope.

Picking their way through the mass, Ria and Arturo made it out to the market area where they caught a tricycle. They never thought to look behind. From the wharf area they rode straight down Valerosa, past the castellated stonework mass of the City Hall building. Not far from the Barter Market they pulled in at the Police Headquarters building. A corporal listened uncertainly to Ria's story of an international drug ring and, to be on the safe side, called for Captain Cruz.

He ushered them into his office, produced coffee and hot water, and made her repeat her suspicions at length, probing frequently with questions. When he leaned back in his chair he held out placating hands. "I've kept you a very long time. I apologize. I'm sure you understand."

Arturo refused to match Ria's smile. He said, "I don't see why the Army's mixed up in this."

Cruz smiled at him, then turned the full force of his personality on Ria. "The Army and the police are essentially the same force now. I intend to look into this matter personally, for instance, because the drug problem undermines the country's ability to defend itself."

He carefully omitted his acquaintance with the man in Ria's story. If he was a drug smuggler, which seemed improbable, it would be horribly embarrassing if he wasn't questioned by one Captain Cruz. The thought of Colonel Arroyo's delight at the news his man Cruz had been guide and host to a big-time drug merchant knotted his stomach.

Ria asked, "We are done? We can leave?"

He skimmed his notes. "I see no reason why not. Will you be leaving in the morning?"

Arturo said, "What else? There's no plane until then."

Cruz continued to look at Ria. "The least I can do is offer a ride to your hotel. Where will you stay?"

Ria said, "We have no reservations."

"Why not stay at the one right on the water?" He lifted the phone. "That way you'll be close if any questions come up between now and the time your plane leaves."

Agreeing, she watched him make arrangements, avoiding the cold glances Arturo winged at her. She admitted her shamelessness, trying very hard not to laugh about it. The Captain's attention was worth far more to her than Arturo could ever comprehend, and in a way that would never cross his mind. The scars she carried would never show, but they were very real. This handsome man was helping her heal as no doctor or priest ever could, because they would know. It was the lack of knowing that made this man important. He looked at Ria Manong and saw no woman battered and humbled.

In his eyes she was a person pleasant to be near. The repetitive questions, the oft-reviewed answers hadn't escaped her. He liked being with her. He made her feel whole.

When they got to the jeep outside he gave them a sharp good-bye salute. Ria waved back, satisfied she'd done the right thing. Informing on Glen had come easy. For a while she'd wondered if it was too easy, if she wasn't actually dealing in revenge. The argument failed. If Glen was doing what she suspected, she would have had to go to the police regardless of any relationship. It was his own fault, and what could he expect, with two names, two identities.

None of her arguments would have impressed Boy Angel. He had squatted against the wall of the small grocery store down the street since they entered the Headquarters building. Watching a police station made his hands sweat. When they came out with the man named Cruz he muttered, "Snake," and quickly looked around to see if he'd been overheard.

He signaled a tricycle and was following the jeep before it rounded the first corner. Staying well back, he kept the driver on them with a shrewd guess, saying he wanted to go past the Barter Market. He watched until his quarry entered the hotel and the jeep left. Then he paid the fare and ostentatiously entered the market. A little while later he walked into the hotel lobby. The clerk peered up at him and returned to her paperback.

After a pause to wipe his hands on his flanks and tap the butt of the revolver, he sauntered to the counter. The girl arched her eyebrows in silent question. He said, "The couple that came in a few minutes ago, named Manong. They came here from Captain Cruz's office, and I have to give them a message. What's their room numbers?"

"We'll deliver it."

Boy Angel scratched his chest, and she watched his face change around the shielding dark glasses. His voice hardened. "He didn't want to write it down. I have to tell them." He half-turned, indicating the general direction of the headquarters building with a shoulder move. It gave him the opportunity to determine that the security guard was still outside. He continued, "You can call him, if you want, but he's going to be mad because he doesn't want the whole world to know who's working for him, understand?"

"Mr. Manong is in one-nineteen, the lady is in one-seventeen."

Boy Angel took the steps two at a time. There was a floor attendant's station at the head of the stairs, unmanned. Arturo opened at his knock and barely had time to be impressed by the full brilliance of the smile waiting for him. Then Boy Angel shoved the revolver into the soft flesh where neck and jaw join. Arturo gagged, motionless as if skewered.

Ria said, "What is it, Arturo?" and came through the connecting door. She cried out and prepared to leap back, but Boy Angel's command stopped her. She stumbled awkwardly and he gestured her into the room, pushing Arturo in front of him with the pistol. Kicking the door shut, he backed Arturo to the edge of the bed and shoved. The blocky body tumbled backwards. Ria muffled another cry with her fist.

Boy Angel said, "We are leaving. Do what I tell you, and you won't be hurt. I have no choice. If I don't bring you to him, he'll have me killed. He said he doesn't want to hurt you, either."

"Who doesn't want to hurt us?" Arturo sat up, keeping his eyes on the revolver.

Frowning, Boy Angel said, "You know. I already said too much. Come on, we don't have much time." He stepped away and tucked the gun under his belt, rearranged his shirt. Arturo tensed and Boy Angel smiled. "Don't even think about it. You can't reach me before I can shoot, I promise you. Help each other keep calm. Use your heads."

When he jerked his chin at the door they looked at each other, and he was immensely pleased with himself. It was no longer him against them. Now each of them would work to prevent any dangerous moves by the other. Their single best chance was to be bold together, and they gave that up in fear it might lead to harm for the other. They sold risk for hope. He knew they would.

Walking behind them, drifting from left to right and back again so Arturo couldn't know exactly where to leap if he contemplated something brave, he shepherded them through the lobby. Getting past the crowded steps was a few bad seconds, but, as he expected, they looked at each other with the same hesitant eyes, and he had them in a taxi before they could do anything. He put Arturo beside the driver, who sensed trouble and glanced at Arturo frequently, brisk, covert inspections. Arturo stared straight ahead. Boy Angel gave directions.

Uneventfully, they proceeded west. Fishing villages appeared, disappeared, nothing registering on Ria but a melange of boats, nets festooned from trees and racks, and crowds of children racing among stilt-legged houses.

She was unable to resist the temptation to look at Boy Angel. He'd removed the sunglasses, and she pictured him standing next to Glen on Boracay.

When the men shot at her in the sea she was certain she'd experienced terror. Now she realized her ignorance. Terror wasn't praying to stay alive, it was praying something would force death to touch sooner than it intended.

There was no point in running. Whoever was after Glen was always watching, the way hawks watch smaller birds panic before swooping. This man wanted her to believe Glen was waiting for her. If that was true, he was already a prisoner.

That was sad. There was so much life in him. Thinking of him was difficult. Before, she always saw herself in her images. Now he was alone, turned away, unaware of her attempt to contact him.

In her preoccupation she failed to notice where they turned off the coastal road. A bump in the new, more deeply rutted route threw her captor against her, and she recoiled. She saw the pistol slide from under his belt and searched wildly outside for help. They were on a twin-gouged dirt road leading uphill through second-growth forest. There was a bridge ahead. At Boy Angel's command to stop the driver slowed to look back at him, quizzical. The muzzle touched his cheek and he bent away, clown-faced in disbelief.

Boy Angel said, "Go to the middle of the bridge and stop."

The driver obeyed, and again when ordered to stop the engine and get out. He said. "I won't tell anyone, Mister. None of this is my business. Just don't wreck my taxi. It's all I have. It's how I live."

"Don't worry about it," Boy Angel said, and shot him in the head. Over the bellow of the heavy weapon the impact of the round carried like the sound of an ax driven into wet softwood. The driver's feet left the ground, and he hit the pipe railing of the bridge with enough force to somersault backwards. The soles of his tennis shoes were worn completely free of tread pattern.

Whirling, Boy Angel aimed at Arturo, who sat in stunned wonder. Boy Angel ran to the downstream side of the bridge, keeping the gun pointed at Arturo, not trusting the dazed immobility to last. Ripples in the thick brown water presaged the driver's appearance. The body floated into view face down. The rich red of the back of the ruined head was picked up by the earthen color of the water, encircling the body with a warmer tone than the rest of the river. An eddy caught him, an invisible trend in the current, and his extended arms wavered in flightlike up and down movement. It brought Boy Angel's weapon to bear instantly, and only when the face remained submerged did he relent.

Returning to the car, Boy Angel instructed Ria to drive, sliding into the seat she abandoned. Underway again, he was very nervous until they'd covered a good quarter of a mile. There were no houses, as Luis had promised, nor was there anyone else on the road.

He leaned back in the seat, angling to the side in order to see Ria's face in the rearview mirror. She was frowning, concentrating on her driving, fighting the ruts and potholes. Her hands were tight on the steering wheel. He had never noticed them before. They were surpisingly broad, more competent looking than delicately slender. He thought of her frowning like that, cute, while she did what he told her to do with those interesting hands.

Unwanted, unexpected, thoughts of Pierce and Munson crowded out his imaginings. Then Benjamin. And Bilongon.

What he was doing was crazy. They'd all be after him.

She crossed hands on the steering wheel, pulling hard to negotiate a turn. Muscles rolled under skin dappled by leaf-screened sunlight, honeyed cords under oiled silk.

All those others wanted to be rich, to tell other people what to do, order everyone around. The only thing he wanted was to be free to do what he wanted. No one would stop him this time. He was free of all of them.

# CHAPTER 34

The sight of the rapidly approaching dock cheered Draeger. Since intercepting the hotel cruiser on its return trip the man piloting the prau had maintained a brittle distance, squatting at the stern and looking apprehensive. Draeger was tired of sitting twisted in the narrow hull, one eye on the course and the other on him. He had long since surreptitiously moved the automatic to under his belt.

The captain of the hotel cruiser was clearly terrified. Neither he nor the prau man would explain why. They argued furiously in the Chavacano dialect. Draeger's rudimentary Spanish allowed him to catch one word in a hundred. After some fruitless translation he demanded to know where the passengers were. Now, as they approached the seawall near the docks and the engine's roar diminished, he spoke again to the man in the stern.

"What's your name?"

"Luis." He avoided Draeger's eyes.

"When we get ashore, you stay with me. I'm going to find the couple from the hotel."

Luis didn't answer immediately, looking toward the market at the landward end of the docks almost as if he hoped to see Ria and Arturo waiting. "I will help you, sir. Mr. Pierce already said."

As soon as the boat was secured to a bit in the wall, Draeger scrambled up to the street. The Filipinos watched with delighted curiosity. No white had come ashore that way in living memory, and they intended to cherish the image. Three small boys screeched happily and chased each other in circles.

Hurrying toward a crowded mass of parked jeepneys and tricycles,

Draeger sent Luis in one direction to ask questions and he moved in the other. Within minutes, each had half the information and was gesturing for the other. Luis was clearly relieved, a fact Draeger noted coldly. A fat taxi driver told of Boy Angel leaving the hotel in a different taxi with a beautiful woman and a short, heavy man. Luis's initial reaction impressed Draeger even more unfavorably when he saw dismay flood his face at the news of the earlier journey to the police station.

The tricycle driver said, "I only took them to the Headquarters building. The man who took them to the hotel said they came with the new Army man there. I forget his name."

"Cruz?" Draeger suggested, and the man smiled brightly. "That's him! Tough looking."

Luis was backing away when Draeger grabbed his arm and led him a few paces away. "There's something very bad coming down here." He looked over the shorter Filipino's head, intent on the mountains. "Ria and Arturo come from the island, go to the police, then leave with a man no one knows. You seem pretty goddamned worried about what we're hearing. I think I ought to explain something to you, Luis." His eyes fixed on Luis's, froze them in their sockets. "I'm worried too. I think you know what's going on. If I *think* that's true, and something happens to either of those people, I'll blow your fucking belly out, Luis, so you can watch your guts pile up in your lap."

A tremor settled on Luis's right eyelid. He looked as if he was fighting back a comradely wink. The rest of his face denied the possibility. He groaned and words broke through the sound with the surprise of figures emerging from mist.

"Mr. Pierce, he said I should help you find out where he is taking them. I had nothing to do with this! Nothing! I only want—"

"Shup up. You know where they went? Who is this man? How many are there?"

"There is just one that I know of, but he is bad, very bad. A gangster, from Manila." Luis gestured distractedly. Draeger grabbed his arm again. The drivers watched eagerly, strained to overhear.

"You're going to show me where. Can one of these tricycles make it?"

Luis nodded a frightened affirmative, and Draeger shoved him at the chosen machine. He'd spotted the driver earlier, and now he turned to him. The man was young, still capable of adventure. He wore a wedding ring, which meant he had expenses, as well. Draeger said, "I must find the people who left the hotel in the taxi. This man knows where they went. He'll give you directions."

The driver looked dubious, turned to the others uncertainly. Draeger said, "Five hundred pesos, if we leave in fifteen seconds."

The driver jerked as if burned, and Draeger's choice started his engine. "Hurry," he said, and laughed harshly. "If you pay that much, something is wrong, but I need the money. Let's go!"

Before they were around the corner the rest of the drivers were clustered around the ones involved in the matter. They listened to the fat one, enthralled, until he mentioned the fee. It was greeted by a low, worried buzz, no man making a direct comment. The excitement guttered, reappeared as apprehension. Two men simply turned and walked away, rejecting anything they'd heard or that was likely to happen. Another watched them, then turned to the ones remaining. He was older, unshaven whiskers grizzled. He coughed before he spoke, a small thing to give weight to the words.

"This is police business. They will learn eventually. When they find out you knew about it and said nothing—" He snapped his hand, as if flicking away something very hot.

The man involved was appalled. "Why would they be angry with me? I did nothing. I told one man I took another man and a woman to the police. No more than that."

"You listened to secrets. You didn't mean to, but you did. It wasn't your fault. The police will not care, however. They never care. They arrest people. You better go to them."

"What can I tell them?"

"Tell them what you told us. And now. This news is like a fish. If you take it to them and it is no longer fresh, they will blame you for the stink."

The man looked at the remaining listeners. Each met his eyes calmly, each look saying how unfortunate it was to have to call attention to one's self. He climbed into his taxi reluctantly.

A few kilometers west the bright green and yellow tricycle roared down the road. Potholes the driver couldn't avoid battered the machine mercilessly, throwing the passengers about like peas in a can. Luis winced continuously.

Draeger ignored everything but the route, regularly demanding of Luis the time and distance to their goal. Finally Luis could stand it no longer.

"I will tell you as soon as we get there! Please, leave me alone!" Draeger stared straight ahead.

"I meant no harm to her! I didn't know what he meant to do!"

Furious, Draeger turned on him, balling his fist. When he looked into Luis's misery, he saw himself reflected.

How many times had he told himself he meant no harm? He was more responsible for this situation than the frightened weak man.

Accepting that premise shook Draeger out of the instinctive pattern forced on him by the kidnapping. Until then, his single thought had been to rescue Ria. Now he asked himself how this could happen.

Kolar had guessed where he'd run. Telling Ria her lover was in a hotel with another woman would demand that she find out for herself. Pierce would never make a connection between the death of Ria, Arturo, and Glen Draeger and the gutted intelligence organization. He'd see only a murdered playboy and innocent victims. Draeger pushed forward to rest his palms on the curved forewall of the compartment. If Kolar meant for them all to die here, the plan had to explain all the deaths. And that had to include the driver and the poor damned fool beside him.

"Is there any other way to this place?" he asked Luis.

"Just one road, for the trucks and machinery. We turn off up there, by that *sari-sari* store." A soft-drink sign facing traffic announced "Celia's Sari-Sari," and the driver slowed to make the turn. Faces popped up in the windows of the weathered wooden store. In one of those tricks of the mind, Draeger remembered the small general stores of his rural childhood, so much alike and so terribly different.

Luis continued to explain. "This road turns to dirt in a little while. It's maybe ten, twelve kilometers to the old work place. They have buildings there, big ones for working on equipment, little ones for offices. I thought Boy Angel wanted a place for a whore, you know?"

He stopped at Draeger's look, subsiding to gestures. The driver looked at him scornfully.

Draeger said, "How close can we get before this Boy Angel can hear this thing?"

The driver answered. "Maybe within one kilometer. Closer than that, I don't think so. Pretty loud."

"That's it, then. Luis, you tell me when we come to a good place to stop. I'll get out. You two go like hell for a phone. Call Captain Cruz." Inspiration struck him and he grabbed Luis's arm, frightening him so badly he bit his lower lip and backed away against the wall of the compartment. "You said they worked machines up there. Is there a big cleared area, big enough for a helicopter to land?"

"Oh, yes, many times they do that."

"You tell Cruz that, you hear? Tell him to come by helicopter!"

Luis was happy. Then Draeger told the driver, "You see that he does it. I'll have a paper on me that says you don't get paid unless Captain Cruz was told. If I die, my friends will pay you, but not if Cruz isn't told to come up after us."

The driver slowed to stare at him. "I don't hold up lives for money, mister. You pay me for giving you a ride. You don't have to pay me for doing what is right. This Captain Cruz will hear you need him, don't worry."

"Thank you. I'm sorry." Wordlessly, he pulled a wad of notes from his wallet, started to count, then reached across Luis to stuff it all in the driver's shirt pocket. The man glanced down at the touch, then looked away.

Inadequacy, Draeger thought. Even in the matter of asking for help I'm coming up inadequate. God knows how many men Kolar's got on this team, and I'm trying to take them myself. I can't even ask for help without pissing off the only honest man on the goddamned operation.

The tricycle engine growled and snapped as they left the surfaced road and began to hammer across rutted dirt. Long ignored, the rough-cut road was already sprouting tough little shoots on its shoulders and even in the hard-packed center. Rainwater had carved ragged gaps in the red-brown soil, scars of black depth in the lowering sun. He looked away from them and was surprised at how high they'd climbed. The sea beckoned through the gaps in the roadside growth that also revealed awesome grades to tight valleys far below.

Luis sat up straight. "Stop!" he said. "This is as far as we dare to go!"

The driver cut the engine and looked suspicious, but Luis concentrated on Draeger. "Please, I will tell the Captain, but please, you must give me time to get away from here. If you live, you will please not tell Mr. Pierce I told you."

Draeger said, "Unless the woman is hurt. Then I may come looking for you. Now go tell Cruz." He reached past to shake hands with the driver. "Thank you very much." The man nodded, smiled tightly. "Good luck, mister. I will hurry."

Draeger swung off up the road. The sound of the machine dwindled rapidly, then died, only to return in a diminished rattle as it drove through areas where the foliage was thin enough to let the sound pass. The result was a lingering contact Draeger held to tenaciously. When it was gone his shoulders slumped. Then he moved out.

He covered only a few yards before he noticed the fresh tracks of a single car and cursed himself for not being aware of them sooner. His only thought had been to reach the end of the road as quickly as possible. That could be literally suicidal. He drew the automatic. From now on he'd be ready. He paced himself, stopping frequently to listen and survey the land ahead.

It was cooler here, and the shade of the towering trees was surprisingly dark. His sweaty shirt plastered itself to him with inescapable dankness. The forest showed the effect of man's brutality, but it was less ravaged than he'd expected. The logging had been done selectively, and, while what was left was a shadow of the marvelous growth that existed before, it was recovering. Already new aggressive saplings hurried toward the sun.

There was plenty of cover if someone fired at him.

Hugging a cut bank, he poked his head around a mound of earth collapsed from its surface and looked at a broad clearing, perhaps fifty yards on a side. The scraped surface baked in the sun, the cleared jungle gone like skin from raw tissue. A gap in the trees revealed the mountains in the distance, huge green waves of forest. There were two ramshackle buildings to the right of the break, a small one and, closer, a barnlike structure. Smells of oil, grease, and hot metal eddied from its depths. The windows were broken out, and there was no door at the large entry.

A taxi was parked under the roof of a lean-to on the nearest end of the large building, hidden from aerial observation. The kidnapper obviously felt safe from ground pursuit. There was no sign of anyone else. Draeger settled in behind the dirt bulwark and considered. Why would there be just the one man? Could he have picked up others outside town? If that was so, why wasn't there a guard?

He searched the area again. Then he heard the scream.

If there had been pain in it, everything might have gone much differently. This riveted him to the ground. It was Ria screaming utter despair. The mangled forest echoed it, understanding. Draeger was running for the car before he realized it, spurred by another scream, this one more like an extended sob. He came to a silent, chopping-stepped halt bent over beside the taxi. Up and running again, he slipped past it and out the back side of the lean-to. The building stretched off to his left and there was a loading ramp halfway down. The door hung open on one hinge. He raced for it, hugging the wall.

When he reached it he rushed inside, the automatic ready. Expecting shouts of surprise, possibly a slamming burst of gunfire, he stopped, crouched, searching for a target. Nothing happened. His heart thudded so heavily the extended pistol pulsed with it.

On three sides of him was a board wall about four feet tall. Woven wire fencing extended from that to the ceiling. The door to the main part of the building was directly in front of him, and a rusted lock dangled from the closed hasp. It had been fastened upside down, and the inverted U was a leering smile. Worse, there were boards nailed across the door frame. The room was a cell, opening only to the outside.

Ria's scream filled the building. He scuffled to the wall, peeked over it.

She was on her knees, slumped forward until her fists were on the ground, centered in the shaft of sun coming through the broken glass of one of the windows puncturing the long wall. The bright blue blouse was at some distance, crumpled on the floor like a dead bird. Her hair was disheveled, hung down along the plane of her arms, fanned across her back. She moved, and a wave of it slid off her shoulder. Only then did Draeger's eyes acquire enough vision adaptation to realize she was naked.

Boy Angel stood in front of her, outside the beam of light. There was enough illumination for Draeger to see he wore only shorts. He said, "Now you will be nice. We will try it again, and no more fighting." His right hand seemed to be massaging his chest. When Ria gave no sign she heard him, he stopped to grab a handful of the flowing hair. He looped it around his hand and yanked. Her head came up canted to the side, face warped with pain. Livid bruises distorted it further. There was a trickle of blood from her lip. Her mouth worked for a moment and, instead of speaking, she spat at him. His other hand swung across in instant reaction, cracking against her cheek hard enough to rock her off her knees. Boy Angel retained the grip on her hair, and she was suspended by it, looking away from him. Drager braced the automatic on the wire, knowing he was too far away and the light was too poor for any reasonable hope of hitting the man. The shot would distract him. With luck, there might be time to shoot the lock off the door and get out. Then he would worry about getting close enough to kill the man.

A muffled roar, a passion of impotent fury and hatred, grew from the darkness to the left of the front entry. It made Draeger think of a maddened beast and when he located Arturo in the gloom, he was shaken by the accuracy of the impression. The broad face, further disfigured by a gag stuffed in the mouth, almost defied human origins. The eyes bulged wildly; the jaw muscles were two ridged knots at the base of the cheekbones. Swollen veins throbbed under the flesh of his neck.

Suddenly his hands flew out from behind his back and he seemed to fly upward onto his feet. Frayed rope flopped at his wrists. One hand tore at the gag, and the other reached for Boy Angel as he roared and attacked.

The young man was a veteran of many street fights and moved to improve his odds first. He drove his knee into the back of Ria's head, and she dropped without a murmur. Only then did he sprint for his clothes. Draeger was pleased to see him whirl with a knife in his hand, rather than a gun. The sight renewed his hope. With Arturo providing the distraction, he could probably get close enough to make a first shot good. Grabbing the hasp, he yanked at it. It complained, but the nails gave. A quick look confirmed that neither Arturo nor Boy Angel suspected his presence yet. Even so, he worked with increasing desperation, cursing the small inaccurate pistol, fearing for Arturo.

At that point the heavier man took a cut across the chest, a thrust that would have been final if he hadn't pivoted at the last instant. Boy Angel was off balance, one arm extended. Arturo pivoted back the other way, lifting a knee, driving it at Boy Angel's crotch. The younger man was quick. He fell off to the side, and the knee caught his thigh. A huge knot swelled right away. Boy Angel staggered, limping, and Arturo swabbed at the blood running down his chest. Wary now, he backed away from Boy Angel, who was ready to let him do so while he got his own breath. Arturo snatched up Ria's blouse and whipped off his own shirt, wrapping both around his left arm. Shielded, he advanced again, the bloody forearm extended in front of him. Boy Angel looked anxiously toward his piled-up clothing, and Arturo shifted that way. The move triggered instant attack from Boy Angel, and Draeger knew there was another weapon in the clothes somewhere.

When Draeger tugged the first board the nails squealed outrage. Boy Angel stepped back, catlike, flicking his eyes in Draeger's direction. Arturo rushed him. They tumbled to the ground. Arturo gripping the wrist of the knife hand, Boy Angel feeling for his opponent's eyes with terrifying deliberation. The hand, in Arturo's grasp, spidered its way around his head like a live thing. Suddenly they broke apart, and Boy Angel was running for his clothes again. Arturo appeared to lumber in pursuit, but the gap remained about the same. Still, Boy Angel reached the clothes with time to rifle through them before Arturo closed on him. When Boy Angel turned, the long-barreled revolver glinted in his hand.

Arturo kicked at the arm just as the hammer fell. The noise in the building was immense. Both men stood transfixed by the spinning weapon, arcing through the air to drop among the litter on the floor.

Draeger pulled the last board free as Boy Angel reached for Arturo's shield arm. When Arturo jerked it away, Boy Angel struck with his knife. Arturo's gasp of pain carried a terrible disappointment.

He coughed and staggered across the bar of sunlight, and the racking bark from his lungs was visible, a mist of red and white.

The knife was a child of the light, curvetting in front of him. He held himself erect on the door jamb. He was blinking steadily, the eyes alert only for an instant after each pass of the lids. Boy Angel scooped a handful of dirt from the floor and moved closer. Timing his move, he threw it to catch Arturo's eyes just as they opened. When he was blinded, he drove the knife into him again. The blow was underhand and both men grunted at the force. Arturo fell back and to the side. The blade wrenched out of Boy Angel's bloody, slippery grasp.

Draeger was running toward them as Arturo curled up in a fetal ball, out of the sun, in the darkness of the building. Boy Angel looked at the knife once, conjectural, and raised his hands in surrender. The ridged scar down his chest, glowing angrily, heaved with his breathing. He said, "He kicked the gun out of my hand. I would have had you both." He was unconcerned by Draeger's mechanical raising of the pistol. "I'm unarmed."

Draeger stood with the pistol aimed at Boy Angel and looked at Ria. The hank of hair he'd twisted around his hand shrouded her face below the eyes, partially disguising ugly welts. Isolated strands swayed with her breathing. One of her breasts was exposed. It was bruised, the center of the discoloration darker, as though a small animal had bitten her. Behind Boy Angel, Arturo's chest rose and fell spasmodically, the lungs clutching at life. Blood welled at the base of the knife and streamed thickly to mingle with the flow of the first wound, the two of them charting the strength draining away.

The first round hit Boy Angel about two inches to the inside of his right nipple. The sharpness of the report startled Draeger and seemed to frighten Boy Angel, who said, "What?" and rocked back on his heels. Lacking weight and velocity, the small bullet had no chance to knock Boy Angel down, nor could that wound kill. Boy Angel was looking into the eyes of the man who fired it. The loud little gun bragged of death like some school-yard bully. The eyes promised.

Draeger shot him again, an inch lower and more nearly center, boring an immaculate hole in the confused tissue of the scar.

Erect, moving with infinite care, Boy Angel turned away and moved toward the door, sliding across the dirt surface as if the rigor of a full step might shake the remaining life from his shattered heart. Dust curled up around the sighing feet as he passed into the bright sunshine. When he fell it was a graceless collapse, a crude ending to such a staunch effort to find the light.

His lips moved and Draeger hurried to him, but all he could understand were the words "dark church" and something that sounded like "under stone sky." Draeger thought of the two people in the building and wished he could tell the man on the ground that wherever he died was satisfactory. Only the timing was in error.

Leaving him, he trotted back to where Arturo should have been lying on the ground. Blood puddled the place where he had been. Drag marks showed where he pulled himself away, back from the door. Ria was still in the same attitude. As Draeger looked, she stirred, lifted a hand as if to block a blow. He took a step in her direction. "Ria?" he called, hurrying, "Are you all right?" As an afterthought, he shouted, "Arturo! Where are you?"

The flash of the gun billowed from the darkness, a melon of fire, a blast that grew until it fell in on itself to expand again. He felt himself going over backward, too dazed to throw out his hands to break the fall. Impact with the floor created pain beyond anything he'd ever imagined. He didn't care. All that mattered was living. He forced himself to hands and knees.

Someone was crying.

It took all his strength to lift his head. Arturo was leaning against a pile of dilapidated tires, Boy Angel's pistol between his legs in pornographic parody. He strained to lift the weapon, lifted so hard bubbles formed against the bright steel of the blade where it entered his chest. Tears rolled down his checks as the gun slid from hands too weak to move it.

A roar started in Draeger's ears, overwhelming the ringing from the gunshot. It made him sleepy.

He was unconscious before his head reached the floor.

# ■ CHAPTER 35 ■

Consciousness came back with a jolt, a switch turned on. There were voices around him, not the debilitating roar in his ears. Still, he kept his eyes closed, fighting back the urge to open them and find out where he was. It was excruciating, but it was necessary. Figure out where you are, he told himself, and try to learn what's going on. Surprise may be your only weapon.

A vaguely familiar voice said, "His breathing is very good. His pulse is strong. The effect was more like a blow than a wound. There's hardly any blood at all."

Ria's voice. "Can you give him anything? We owe him our lives."

The temptation of medication for the headache was too great to resist, and he opened his eyes. Light stabbed through them, and he cramped them shut again. A soft hand settled on his brow. In its shade he was able to see, looked past Ria's concern to the objective stare of Captain Cruz. The latter changed as he watched. There was animosity there, a flame under control. It was a unique view for Draeger. He wondered how often another man had seen that same light from him.

Cruz said, "You have done all you can, Miss Manong. I must speak to him now."

Draeger said, "Wait, Ria? You OK?" The inanity was matched by the difficulty in articulating it. He hoped Ria would understand in both instances. Her physical damage was obvious. One eye was swelled shut, and an ugly lump extended from her cheekbone to a startling white bandage covering part of her upper lip. She wore an ill-fitting uniform, the trousers rolled up to accommodate shorter legs. The jacket draped beyond her shoulder line, hung like a tent.

She said, "I'll be all right."

When he reached for her hand, she moved it. He said, "I'm sorry. I came as fast as I could."

A darkness slid over her face, and she trembled inside the voluminous clothes, an almost invisible quickness like the flick of a wing. "I'm glad you got here when you did. I wish I'd never seen you before."

Cruz touched her shoulder. "The helicopter will be here in a few minutes, Miss Manong. Perhaps you should wait over where it will land. I must speak to this man, and your cousin will be worrying about you."

Draeger's surprise burst through. "Arturo's alive?"

Cruz said, "He's very tough. And very lucky."

"Damned popgun. If I had that big sonofabitch I'd have killed that creep from inside that room."

Examining a knuckle, Cruz said, "The little gun worked from close range."

Draeger closed his eyes, saw Boy Angel's image fracture into whirling pieces. He opened them again. "He came for me."

"No doubt. Or possibly you've got as many stories as you have identities?"

"I lied to you before." He checked, made sure Ria was out of earshot. "My name's Glen Draeger. The woman with me at the hotel is a business associate."

Cruz offered him a facial twitch that shouted disbelief and disinterest. "None of that matters. You've killed a man, a Filipino national. Between us, he's probably very overdue. Whoever you are, I've got you pinned."

Pursing his lips, Draeger thought for a moment before responding. Cruz had just shown a card. He wasn't anxious to take his captive directly to jail. If he meant to show the card was moot. The opportunity to capitalize on it wasn't.

"Where's my automatic now?"

Cruz cocked his head to the side and patted a jacket pocket.

"Is Arturo talking?"

"He's in isolation. The doctors and nurses know they're to hear nothing if he speaks.'' The half-smile showed perfect teeth. ''I usually ask my own questions.''

''When you get ready, I'll answer.'' Draeger's grimness clashed with Cruz's growing good humor. ''First I think you may want to listen.''

Draeger unfolded a tale of working undercover in the Philippines. He identified himself as a member of the CIA, hanging his head in shame at being caught. He was much heartened by the triumph that sparkled in Cruz's eyes. Describing a long-dead operation, he told how Kolar had used it to blackmail a government figure. When Cruz seemed to believe that lie, he told the big one, that Kolar was determined to kill him in order to preserve the secret. The Boracay attack was described, linked to the events just finished. Now, he finished, it was all up to Cruz.

The dapper Captain cocked his head again. ''Up to me? What is? What are we negotiating?''

That was another quick peek at a card, the concession that they were, in fact, negotiating. Draeger said, ''I want your help. I'll give you Kolar.''

''You are very kind. If you could catch him, what use do I have for him? Why would you be so generous?''

Forcing himself up on an elbow, Draeger said, ''For two reasons. First, to buy my way out of this spot. You've got me by the balls on the killing. But you sealed off the scene and isolated Arturo. You think you might have a use for me because you know goddamned well I'm not just a rubber tree inspector. The second reason is, I owe the bastard. And I'd rather see you catch him than my own people. In the States he'll plea bargain his ass out of it, I know he will.''

Cruz hardened. ''You would so freely betray your own intelligence effort?''

''It's already betrayed. And all you'll get from him is what's known about our work in your country.''

''Why would he say nothing more?''

''Because once you've picked him up he'll be told what the limits are. If he goes beyond them, he'll be eliminated.''

''So simple as that?'' Cruz was very skeptical.

''There are people who'd pay any amount to see him dead.''

The helicopter whacked in over the tops of the trees, and Cruz left

Draeger. A stretcher party carried Ria through the dust to the machine, and Draeger realized the tremendous effort she'd mounted to stay by his side. He waited for her to wave, afraid she wouldn't. She didn't, and he knew the picture of her being handed inside, ignoring him, would haunt more days and nights than he dared contemplate. Cruz stepped aboard to say goodbye, holding her hand in both of his for a moment. Draeger thought he saw her lift her head to say something. A twinge pulled at him, and for an instant he hoped it was jealousy. Integrity forced the admission it was guilt.

He reached to rub the side of his head opposite the wound, enjoying the soothing gentle pressure of the bandage. It calmed the headache temporarily. He didn't trouble to watch the helicopter leave.

Cruz returned brushing rust-colored dust from his starched field uniform. He said, "The Philippines lost nothing when you shot that creature over there." Draeger looked where Boy Angel still lay in the same position, arms slightly akimbo, one leg bent at the knee. Vertical, he would have been dancing. Flies explored the edges of the puckered holes in his chest. Cruz was saying, "It is degrading to think of one's country as a base for spies. Maybe we can help each other."

"I hope so."

Dryly, he said, "I'm sure you do. There are problems. I know you are not the man you claimed to be. Now you ask me to take your word you are this new man you describe."

"We both want the same man."

"And you want to leave the Philippines without passing through our prison system on the way." There was a taint of cruelty in the remark, a glimpse of the bared blade.

"Certainly."

Cruz stroked his chin with a forefinger. "If my government even suspected I knew of a foreign agent and didn't report him—" He left it to Draeger's imagination.

"I understand. I'd be in the same boat if my people ever heard I offered to cooperate with you."

"I think we are a couple of damned fools, you know? When Miss Manong told me how you happened to be here it was obvious you were very different. The most overstimulated market analyst in the world wouldn't rush up here to confront a Boy Angel alone. He might go to the police. He wouldn't arm himself. As soon as Miss Manong started talking, I kept everyone from her and Arturo. I think she has a good idea why.''

''You've been planning to use me.''

''Hoping would be a better word.''

Draeger shook his head, winced. ''You haven't checked me out. I could be a Russian. What're you setting up?''

Cruz threw back his head and laughed. ''A Russian? Have you ever met a Russian?'' Without pausing, he went on. ''No good Soviet man is going to get so mixed up with a Filipina he risks anything, Draeger. They're the worst bigots in the world! Oh, they play with the women, all right. Any man with a hard on is color blind, even a Russian. But one of their agents risk exposure to save a native girl from a little rough screwing? No way!''

''You don't like them much.'' Draeger laughed at his own understatement, but Cruz failed to smile.

''If I thought you were any breed of communist I'd have finished what Arturo started.''

It seemed like a good place to leave the subject, with Cruz speaking freely, a rapport growing. Draeger said, ''I can't figure why he shot at me. He must hate me more than I thought.''

''I don't think so. You've read of *amok* in our people. It's not restricted to men running through markets with knives, no matter what Hollywood says. It's a form of psychological explosion, a reaction to stresses out of control. He didn't know who you were, didn't care. Seeing her beaten, raped, his own life seemed destroyed. A man like that courts death by creating death around him, drawing killing attention you might say.''

''I think I understand.''

Cruz looked at him from the corner of his eye. ''I believe you do. But there's something else that must be clear between us. I don't trust you, and I never will. You risked everything to protect Miss Manong, and in the right circumstances you'd probably do the same thing for someone else. I know if this thing we're working on gets bad and you think your country's interests are in trouble, you'll screw me without blinking. Don't try to leave here without letting me know. You'll stay at Pierce's. I've got men on his staff, in town, at the airport. It's a good net and it gets better every day. I'll tell you plain, if you try to run you'll be stopped if it means killing you.''

"I may have to go to Manila. What if I have to go in a hurry?"

"Don't try it."

"Look, Kolar—"

"No. You look. He may be very big and we may get him. That'd be nice. But I have my own priorities, and you're working for me. Is Pierce part of your operation?"

Draeger's head swelled with the question. Cruz was probably guessing. There was another possibility, exciting. Why would Cruz think of Pierce in connection with intelligence collection? There had to be a link, one that Cruz knew about, or strongly suspected. Draeger's pain subsided. The goal was closer, not farther.

"Pierce works for Kolar. He won't know Kolar's after me, and Kolar knows I won't say anything to Pierce because I can't prove anything."

"You think Kolar sent Boy Angel here?"

"It has to be."

"Men like that." Cruz indicated Boy Angel with a careless flip of his hand. "Men like us. It will never end."

Draeger maneuvered himself to a sitting position, and Cruz helped him to his feet. Draeger said, "I want to thank you for showing up here. I'm glad it was you. We won't be blood brothers when it's over, but I think we'll be able to trust each other. A little bit."

Cruz laughed easily. "Honor among thieves, eh? Maybe." Then, businesslike, "Will Pierce tell Kolar you're at the hotel?"

"Kolar already knows."

"Perhaps." Draeger tried a clumsy step, and Cruz held onto his elbow. "Why don't we test Pierce? Tell him you don't want Kolar knowing where you are or what happened here. We'll see if he tries to make contact."

"Sounds good."

"You said the Anderson woman is a business associate. What business?"

Another barb. Part of the routine. Make the subject know he has no secrets. Draeger had done the same thing often, thought of it as a control technique. Now he knew it destroyed. He said, "She's with me. I'm responsible for her, and I won't have her interfered with. Leave her out of it."

Cruz glowered. "You're asking me to take too many risks."

"We're both taking chances." Draeger moved away, struggling to keep his balance.

Cruz kept pace. "We'll try it your way. I'll be watching."

When Draeger didn't respond, Cruz went on, "The chopper will be here in a little while. I'll see you at the hotel soon. Do as I said with Pierce. Also, learn what else he's involved with. I especially want to know about a rebel, a Moslem named Bilongon."

Draeger made him spell the name, his mind racing as it memorized the letters.

*I'm not going to prison. God Almighty. And I can still work on Kolar. Closer, closer.*

Cruz saw the intensity of Draeger's concentration and was gratified. It was underhanded to hold back the information on the second white man in the Pierce problem, the one who kept to himself so much. Draeger had to be tested. If he was honestly observant he'd learn of the other man and report him. If he didn't, both would be watched that much more closely. Draeger's job was to stir things around. Whatever fell out would benefit the Philippines. It was about time an American worked for them. For a change.

Draeger said, "I'm strong enough to give you a hand now, and I think we better get rid of the evidence." He indicated Boy Angel. Cruz looked uncomfortable. Draeger added, "You'd like to believe you've got this investigation squashed, but that's a chance I can't take. Help me drag him inside. We burn everything."

The demand put Cruz's confidence to the ultimate test. He would be an accessory, implicated in the destruction of practically all the physical evidence in a homicide. He reminded himself he had the pistol and the bullets might be salvageable. Every minute of his professional training and experience dictated against it. No instructor had considered the possibility of weighing an evil life against the national integrity.

He bent to lift an ankle, and they dragged Boy Angel. His head rolled from side to side while the arms reached back in dead appeal. Inside, they rolled the body on top of the tires. Cruz moved trash to the back wall and lit it while Draeger added other material to the pyre. The aged boards of the building burned as if anxious to be claimed.

The heaviness of the helicopter's blades was almost drowned by the roar of the flames when it arrived. The building was totally involved. Two young troopers hopped out of the machine as it settled, one carrying a body bag. He looked at the waiting men, the bag, the building, and, expressionless, jumped back aboard.

Cruz signalled for the plane to leave as soon as they were aboard. Amidst a storm of whirling refuse, they rose slowly, backing away from the inferno. The pilot lifted for a better look into the flames. Part of the roof was already collapsed, and Draeger looked directly into the area where Boy Angel's body was on its bed of blazing rubber.

Moving the body hadn't bothered him. The inspiration to assure its complete destruction came to him as a rational, reasonable thing to do. He murdered a man little more than an hour ago, and the body was being dispersed in off-white smoke cascading up a mountainside.

Because he wanted it so. Boy Angel died because Glen Draeger wanted him to die.

It was time to get on to other things.

# ■ CHAPTER 36 ■

Cindy watched Draeger sleep. Sprawled on a beach towel, he was in constant motion. Perspiration skidded across rounded muscles. The drops were absorbed instantly by the dark blue towel and outlined his body with a slurred black line. It never grew any larger. The moisture was offered back to the atmosphere almost as soon as it stopped moving, beaten out of the material by a sun so hot it made breathing difficult and turned the beach sand into a huge reflector. The turbanlike bandage had a sweaty discoloration as well, gray-white blending to purity where the thick black hair kept it elevated above the skin.

She envied his years of adapting to the climate, being able to sleep in the heat, using it to his advantage by letting it draw the stress from his body.

She looked at her tan. His was deep, the firm skin suggesting it had been steeped in the sun. Hers might have been sprayed on.

He stayed in one place long enough to adjust, long enough to blend, if not fit, in. He would never fit in. Not anywhere.

A perception? She decided it was, and backed further under her umbrella, wanting to pursue the thought but not willing to pay for preoccupation with a burned foot.

He was more than a loner, he was a singular person. As much as he appeared to want approval, as much as he apparently believed he wanted acceptance, he never mentioned anyone genuinely close. He spoke of Munson with a kind of nostalgia, almost melancholy. When he spoke of Kolar he was bitter and full of destruction, but an undercurrent eddied in his condemnation. There was a grudging respect in his references to Kolar, as though he mourned him. When he was tired, especially, and talked of either man, there was a feeling that he'd lost something irreplaceable, although not extremely expensive in itself. Sentimental value. That was the way he looked, the way people deflated when they said they'd lost something of sentimental value.

A strange man. She wondered what it would be like to live with someone who had the capacity to withdraw so completely into himself he seemed to evaporate.

His mouth moved in silent speech, and his face bent to a soft frown, entreating, arguing gently. It was an intriguing face, incredibly mobile when the guard was down. The defenses were very good, however. Not impenetrable. One of the few times she knew exactly what he was thinking was when he heard Ria was being followed. There was no question about that expression.

Would a man ever think of her in that "fair damsel" syndrome, could her rescue mean more than anything else? Sophomoric romanticism. She kicked at the sand. He had risked his life, the mission of the organization, everything, all in stupid derring-do. Then the clod refused to talk about it. "Had to have time to think." Typical male, she muttered out loud, then looked quickly to insure they were still alone on that stretch of beach. She was taken aback to see a couple had moved in only a few feet away. She'd seen them before, asked about them. Germans, they had no apparent interests beyond swimming, eating, drinking, and fondling each other. Cindy conceded it wasn't the worst program imaginable, watching them covertly. The girl was pretty, and the man genuinely handsome.

The girl said something and giggled, falling back on the beach towel, arms flung over her head. The hair matted under her arms was darker than that of her head, but where the latter was long and soft, the other was wound in tight spirals that looked like old-fashioned wooden excelsior leaking out a doll. Against her judgment, Cindy checked the legs. Hairy. Some of the individual spikes wore drops of sweat, crystal beads on their own fine pins.

Cindy looked away, trying to tell herself it was far more natural to go unshaved. The argument withered at birth and she admitted she was pleased with her own special mores. Shaving might be an artificial beauty standard, but so was keeping dentures in place and no one found that debatable.

Waking, Draeger opened his eyes too quickly, too wide. He looked around excitedly, finally recognizing time and place. He smiled at Cindy's concern. "I was dreaming. Couldn't figure out where the hell I was for a minute. Scary. How long was I out?"

"About a half-hour. You were restless. And if you're going to dream in public, the least you could do is talk out loud so a decent person could understand you."

"A decent person could never understand."

"Never mind. I want to know what happened up there today." She jerked a thumb toward the mountains. "We saw the smoke and heard the helicopters."

He nodded sharply at the couple, then got up and moved toward the water. "Out there," he said. Ineffectual protest sputtered on her lips as he unwrapped the bandage with sure, strong hands. When he was done and the ugly welt was revealed, Cindy felt her knees waver. Until that moment he'd merely been bandaged. Now he stood wounded. Lopsided smile to the contrary, the red blaze exposed his life as another fragile work. The skin was barely broken, more burned than battered, although purple bruising rippled outward into the heavy growth of hair. When he reached to trace it with his fingers she reflexively pulled his hand away. The feminine warning-sound and the shudder that accompanied her move came as twin surprises to her.

They walked through the hot sand to the water, and he broke through the moody quiet with a quick dash the last few yards, charging into the chopping waves until he was almost waist deep before diving. He was surfacing when she lowered herself into the shallows and stroked out to him. They settled at a point where the water came just to the base of her neck. He watched how the motion of the sea teased the ends of the hair, lifting it let it fall, gold tones shifting as air and water alternated influences.

She said, "Is Ria all right?" and he concentrated on what he had to tell her. He related the entire story, carefully expurgating the part concerning her, plunging ahead despite her horror at his exposure of the team. When he'd finished she was further away from him, her back to the land. The sun was almost behind him, and the glare carved the harsh frown of her disapproval ever deeper.

"You informed on us? All of us? The team? My God, Glen, can't you see what you've done? Cruz'll have everyone rolled up by morning! You've destroyed everything to stay out of jail! All your fine talk about mission and clearing yourself and—and—!" She broke into tears, words unequal to the task. At the touch of his hand on her arm she flung it off and stepped back. Sea movement staggered her, and her entire being warned him not to reach out to help. When she was secure in her balance she said, "I'm going to let Pierce know. He'll contact Kolar. You deserve whatever you get. When I think how many people you've endangered—" Again, she let the words remain unsaid.

Struggling to contain his own emotions, he said, "Cruz will live up to his word. He thinks he can use me to bust Pierce for smuggling or something. I gave away a blown net to keep from going to prison for murder. I bought some time, and I'm going to use it to prove Kolar's done us all. I'm not the one who burned us, he is."

"You're crazy." She backed toward the beach.

"Look, Kolar knows damned well we're here, or he couldn't have sent Ria and Arturo, couldn't have set me up. No one else knows who the hell we are or where we are except Pierce. If I try to leave, Cruz's people will step on me. That alone gives Kolar protection. You bring him around here, and Cruz'll have us all in the slammer."

She swam away. He followed, tightening his muscles more than necessary, welcoming physical strain. Pain etched a radiating web around his wound. He welcomed the hurt as an ally in the war against himself. To have pain, pain that drove away thoughts about Cindy, Ria, Pierce, or anything else—it was wonderful.

Cindy walked the last yards to land, waiting for him with the waves rushing around her ankles. Draeger approached slowly, positioned himself so she could look at him without squinting. She said, "I'm catching a plane out of here in the morning. Carl has to know. If he already knows where you are, I won't be hurting you. He'll be worried about me by now, too. He thinks I can't take care of myself." She turned away with a bitter smile she aimed at the sand. "It looks like I proved him right."

She moved away and he hurried after her. "Cindy, don't be foolish. This thing's only got a little further to run. Egg Roll's got to be posting his pick-up signal soon. Once I get that and get my hands on him, I'll have all the answers. You'll see I was right."

"I'm leaving. You made a fool of me."

He grabbed her arm, and she refused to stop or look up. She twisted in the grip, and his hand bit hard enough on the bicep to make the flesh bulge on either side of his fingers. She gasped and whirled on him. He let go.

"So you're strong enough to hurt me. Good for you. Are you going to add that to today's accomplishments, along with killing an unarmed man?"

Dazed, he couldn't speak. The words finally came, scraped from the back of his throat, machine like sounds. "I can't stop you. I'm concerned for your safety. When Kolar learns I've told you I suspect him and why, he'll have to silence you as well. Please, Cindy, don't do it."

Contemptuous, she said, "Why don't you give up? How's your man supposed to signal you, with a flashlight? And how do you get him away? You're a fool. I'm worse. I believed you."

"Pay attention. The original escape plan included a signal from him, once he was clear of his own government. Up to that point, none of us was directly involved. The escape transportation was contracted for. If Egg Roll's coming out his own way it's because he suspects, or knows, the plan is broken. But I'm his only hope. Without me he's got no papers, no money, no place to run. He'll get his signal to me. All he has to do is reach a telephone. The man he calls will telephone another cut-out, in Manila. He puts an ad in the classified section of the *Bulletin*. It'll say something like, 'Cook wanted. Must know Hong Kong specialties, speak American. Call 50-12-34, after 7.' "

She stepped back, rubbing the arm, still refusing to look at it. "He's coming out to Hong Kong?" Interest lifted her tone, and he heard it with an adrenalin surge of hope.

"That was the original idea. The point is, it'll work anywhere. He names any city and 'speak American' guarantees it's him."

"And how do you find him? He can't advertise his address."

"Yes he can. If you add each two-digit number in the telephone number you get a single digit- say a 5, a 3, and a 7. He's telling me on the third, fifth, and seventh day of the week he'll try for the meeting place. Subtract two from the time given you have the latest hour for the last day. In other words, on the seventh day he'll be there at five o'clock. On the fifth day, go back two more hours and he'll be there at three o'clock."

"And you have a meeting place for every city in Asia?"

"Most of them. He's got to set himself up in a city with an American embassy or consulate, so he can walk past it at the right time on the right days, and that's it."

"Even if it works, how're you going to get there?"

"I don't know." He looked away. "I'll find something. I have to."

She shook her head slowly. "I almost feel sorry for you. You've really put yourself outside, haven't you? I hope Carl can give you some kind of a break." Impulsively, her hand moved toward him, stopping inches from his chest, flattened out as if pressed to glass. She brought it back as a fist, pressed it between her breasts, then turned and hurried away.

He watched her without protesting. It was too late for that. There was only one avenue now, no options.

Above him, Munson watched from his window, smiling. It was an unpleasant smile, and Pierce watched it with his normally smooth features wrenched in disgust. Munson said, "I'm almost glad Boy Angel didn't kill the sonofabitch. Whatever she said, it tore his fucking guts out. And now she's left him. I'll give you any odds she checks out." He turned to Pierce, who hastily rearranged his expression. "You think he's queer? No, he couldn't be." He turned back to the window. "Impotent. I'll bet that's it. The Filipina gave up on him easy enough, didn't she? And now this one's dumping him. I'll bet he's impotent. I hope so."

Pierce said, "That's fine, but what do we do about him? Something bad's coming down. He killed Boy Angel, sure as hell, and Cruz is letting him run loose. Dropping that animal was no job for an amateur. He's a lot better than we thought, man."

"Don't tell me that!" Munson leaped away from the drapes as if they were trying to envelop him, arms flailing. "Don't tell me that worthless sonofabitch is good!"

"Keep your voice down! All we need is for someone to hear you!"

Munson rose to his toes, fists clenched and jammed into his waist at belt level. Color mottled his face and throat, alternate washes of white and red that scored the edges of the unkempt beard. The intensity couldn't last, and when it broke his breath raled as if he'd run a marathon. The agitated features subsided to a doughy mass. Pierce got to his feet and stepped away from his chair.

Munson mumbled, worked his way to clear speech. "He has to die. It's important." He moved back to the drapes, opened them a few inches and stared out at a sea gilded by the setting sun. Pierce thought he heard something about fire.

"We've had enough of Draeger," Pierce said. "It's time to shit or get off the pot. Let's get at the money."

Munson faced him, working to focus after the glare from the water. It gave him a querulous, antique expression. In contrast, his voice took on renewed firmness. "You really don't care about the effect we're going to have, do you? Literally millions of people's lives changed forever, and all you see is your money."

Pierce blew an exaggerated sigh. "You think one person in those

millions gives a damn if I live or die? You want a hero? Send for
Draeger. Pierce takes cash.''

Munson surrendered. "You don't know what you're asking. You
have no concept of the price I'm paying. Still, we have to get things
in motion. You'll have to go to Bilongon, get transportation to
Singapore, conduct some reconnaissance.''

"There's no way I'm leaving you here with Draeger around.
You'll come unglued, sooner or later. You go see Bilongon. He
likes you more than me, anyhow.''

Munson glared at the floor. "You're probably right. I'm far too
disciplined to do anything about Draeger, of course, but I have been
feeling the strain lately. I'll be much clearer, mentally, if I get out of
here.''

"I know I'm right. There's a prau ready to go.'' At Munson's
furious reaction, Pierce said, "You admitted it's best. I gambled
you'd agree and had a boat arranged. No harm done. Look, we're
moving, we're setting things up! The jackpot's waiting for us! Let's
do it!''

His enthusiasm failed to spur Munson to the same heights, but he
found a slice of a smile. He waggled a finger at Pierce, chiding.
Pierce slapped him on the shoulder. On his way out he promised to
drop in later for a good-bye drink.

Munson faced the sea again, admiring the single wisp of cloud
halfway up the bowl of sky. It was a jagged thing like a stylized
lightning bolt and the sinking sun burnished it to molten gold. Under
it, the sea was turning black, only a thin strip on the hoizon still in
the thrall of the day. He watched until that strip was gone and the
last thin edge of the sun itself sank. When he stepped away from the
drapes he carefully closed them, running his fingers along the seam
the way one seals an envelope.

He was smiling when he turned to the room again and looked
amazingly younger and stronger. He stood straight, and there was
precision in his movements. When he opened his closet the hangers
rattled, bare. The suitcase he lifted out was obviously heavy. Neatly
positioning it by the hall door, he sat on the bed, feet stretched out
in front of him, tented fingers rested on his stomach. Everything
about his manner spoke of great inner satisfaction.

Giving voice to that appearance, he said, "Ah, Tony. Ruthless and demanding and observant. Also very greedy and quite careless. I could have trained you out of those two sins, but you'd still be a loser. One move at a time. That's all you can project, one move at a time. You did try. I give you that. I expected to have to talk you into sending me to Bilongon. If you could only think, Tony, then perhaps you could produce a single reason why I'd let you go to Singapore or back to Bilongon. Maybe you'll survive long enough to see how this job is properly done. Frankly, I doubt it.''

# ■  CHAPTER 37  ■

Cruz waited for them on the dock the next morning. He stood apart from the arriving fishermen and farm-produce vendors, the jeepney and tricycle drivers. Unmoving, he made Draeger think of a rock in the middle of a boisterous stream, not so large as to cause a whirlpool but big enough and solid enough to create a clear space where even the force of that current checked, piled up on itself in a warning slick. He wore civilian clothes, a plain blue shirt and dark trousers. Draeger recognized it as a nicety, a thought-out courtesy, and he was unable to look at Cindy. He said, ''That's Cruz. I think I may be in trouble.''

She said, ''I told you not to come. There was no need. Will he believe you when you tell him you're just with me?''

''He won't have to. I'm not getting on the plane with him watching me, am I?''

''It's only going to make him more suspicious of you. You should have stayed at the hotel.''

Unexpectedly, he grinned. ''And miss the chance to excite my personal cop? It's worth getting up before daylight to shake him up a little bit. He won't be too concerned." Inwardly, he felt no humor at all. Cruz wouldn't meet the hotel cruiser unless he believed he had a good reason. Whatever was stuck in his throat probably concerned Cindy. She was the one with reservations. Cruz's presence was bad news. Appearing in polite mufti could only mean he intended to make trouble and wanted as little notice of it as possible.

Driving engines subsided to a slower pace, and the drum of the screws turned to a bubbling chuckle. Within seconds they were tying up to the wharf. Draeger handed Cindy down onto the cement surface, offering a half-salute with the free hand to the distant Cruz.

Walking toward him, Draeger grew more depressed with each step. How many hours he'd spent in his youth dreaming of walking on a dock exactly such as this! The sounds alone were romance. Wooden hulls rode up on wooden pilings, each squealing angrily at the abuse. A rooster crowed from somewhere, the key clashing with the timber friction noises. And the smells! Creosote: more than a smell on the mist of dawn, it slashed through the thicket of aromas hovering over the wharf. It scored the paint, the gas, and grease. A slight breeze, and it faded under the onslaught of copra and the sweetness of mangoes.

The last vessel they passed on their way to confront Cruz was a blunt-sterned relic, her last three colors of paint visible at one location or another, all scabrous. Tied up, she wallowed at the tiniest swell. Draeger shuddered to think of her in any sea at all. Yet, adjacent to her on the dock was a sign giving her name, her time of departure, and her destination as Jolo, a good sixty miles of open sea away. Her upper deck featured the bridge forward and stack aft, with a houselike structure running between the two. The lower deck was closed forward, the planks bent in a fat curve that formed a bow like the small end of an egg. The barnlike protected interior was full of row on row of plastic-sheeted cots. A man in shorts walked the aisles, hosing them down. A young man and a woman, not much more than teenagers, moved past the hose stream, the girl skipping lightly behind her man, tugging at her long black skirt. He moved with an almost strutting dignity, accepting his protector's role. His eyes fastened on Draeger, who nodded, a spare movement. When he smiled the young man's dignity fragmented on his answering grin, and at Draeger's inclusion of her the woman grabbed the man's arm and giggled behind his shoulder. One eye gleamed shyly at the stranger, and the visible round cheek was creased by the tag end of a continuing smile.

Draeger looked past them at the grubby old tub and longed to make the run to Jolo aboard her. He cursed himself for never having done it. The boy, the young man, all the people he started out to be would have found the time. The man he was made necessities of everything he did and carried them out by priority. He found a cause, a good cause, and pursued it with determination. He found friends and immersed himself in their companionship to the exclusion of others. Absorption with profession, divorcement from the world. Those were the sins, the perversions that leached his personality the way rain impoverishes soil it should bless with flourishing life. That was what was happening. Munson, Kolar. Even Cruz. They were ripping away the little bit of self he still owned.

Cruz said, "I hope my meeting you here will cause less embarrassment than if I waited for you at the airport, Miss Anderson. This way we can ride in my car and discuss our situation."

Draeger took her elbow. "There's no situation. She wants to go to Manila. You don't have any reason to interfere."

"You see, we do have something to discuss." Cruz smiled at both of them. "It's not a public matter, I think. My car is parked by the City Hall. One of the advantages of being a cop is you can park wherever you like." He extended his arm, a waiter's signal, and Cindy stepped ahead firmly.

She said, "I'm an American citizen, Captain. If you interrupt my departure, you can be damned sure the embassy's going to hear about it. Loud."

In the car, Draeger leaned forward from his seat in the back. He faced Cruz, closing off Cindy, who shared the front seat. "I told you before, she's out of this. You're going to blow the whole thing."

Cruz never had a chance to answer Draeger. Cindy said, "I'm going directly to our embassy when I get back, Captain. If I'm not on that plane to Manila, I'll—"

Cruz slammed on the brake, sending a following jeepney into hornblowing hysterics as it swerved around him. He turned to face her, and Draeger clenched his fists, reminding himself that Cruz held all the cards. They were at the curb, vehicles swarming past. For a heartbeat or two, no one spoke, the traffic noise pounding in the enclosed space. Then Cruz said, "Miss Anderson, I do not want to be impolite with you. I want you to understand that I am risking my career by not exposing Mr. Draeger. He should be in prison right now. If any of what he tells me is the truth, he is doing your country a favor. To protect myself, I have made some rules. To let you leave here puts me in more danger than I can stand." Cindy tried to respond, and he was brusque, determined to make himself clear. "And do not threaten me with your diplomats. They will do nothing. They want us to love them, Miss Anderson. They work to ensure their comfort and our satisfaction, and you are no more than an unavoidable nuisance. If you are an intelligence agent they will do anything to avoid being contaminated by you." He sent the car hurtling back into the early-morning rush, scattering lesser vehicles.

Cindy turned to Draeger. "You've really done it right. Now we're trapped until everything's completely torn apart around us. I'll see you in hell for it."

Ignoring Cruz's presence, he said, "You'll have to wait it out, won't you? I'll prove you're wrong."

"You've turned your coat, sold everyone and everything that depended on you. You know what happens to agents who get rolled up, don't you? Except the smart ones, the slimy ones that double. Like you, goddam you."

In any other situation, Draeger's smile would have cut like a weapon. Cindy took it with unaltered scorn. He addressed his words to Cruz, staring into her eyes as he said. "That's the kind of loyalty I had once. Before I was accused of compromising my own people, before my friends were killed, before I was shot at—"

Cindy cut him off. "We've heard about your hard times. Even Ria's cousin tried to blow you away."

Cruz answered. "Arturo doesn't even remember firing. He is very grateful to Mr. Draeger, actually. He sends his apologies." He laughed at himself. "I almost forgot."

Cindy taunted Draeger. "You've got one fan. Hooray."

Draeger wanted to ask her what else he could have done, wanted to point out that nothing was changed, the goals were the same as ever. Before, she'd been willing to believe he was wrong and work to help him find out what was right. He fought only to continue the original effort. Now she hated him.

The car continued on, the passengers silent. Half of Draeger's attention was taken by the kaleidoscope of activity passing the windows. They were on the same road he'd traveled the day before with Luis. Yesterday. He reached to the place where the bullet had clipped the hair down to the flesh. He wondered idly if he'd remain bald in that spot. Perhaps the hair would be a different texture, or color. A white streak? Had it been only one day since it all happened?

They passed the military barracks on the outskirts of town and the golf course, brittle in the sun, the grass fried down to roots that hid and waited for rain.

. A few minutes later Cruz pulled off, driving across the road to a patch of hardstand, still facing away from town. Ahead of them, large boats were under construction in the shade of coconut palms. They were large vessels, the fast cargo carriers called *kumpits*, each resting in its cradle, pointed at the sea. They looked eager, as if already afloat, the way gawky birds in a nest will thrash the air with unready wings and force themselves airborne for one exhilarating moment. Workers scrambled around and through them. Draeger had the feeling he was seeing something more than construction, that this was a symbiosis, the men serving her in return for the gift of her capabilities. She gave them reign of the sea, a sleek belly to carry dreams the way their women carried hope of the future.

He looked away. That was twice in the same morning he'd allowed himself to slip off daydreaming about the sea and ships. It took no psychiatrist to expose the escape syndrome in that. For him, the only hope was to fight clear. If a man eliminated his enemy, that was better than escape.

Cruz twisted behind the steering wheel, positioned himself to look at them. "I spoke to Miss Manong last night. A very strong young woman. I'm arranging transportation for her back to Manila tomorrow morning, with her cousin. I'm sorry you didn't come to me before chasing up the mountain after her." He flashed a smile. "She won't talk about you anymore."

Draeger said, "I don't think she left much unsaid when she talked to you before the trouble." Cindy made a harsh sound in her throat, and the men studiously ignored her.

Cruz continued. "It's hard for me to talk to you about this situation. it's very unusual. Some of my instructors were Americans, but I've never worked with one. Especially under these conditions. I'm not sure where to start."

Cindy repeated the earlier sound, and Cruz looked at her sadly. "I will try to explain once more. My country is like a bomb, ticking under all of us. We have the constant threat of the martial law that degrades us all. We have growing opposition who say they will return us to democracy through terror and assassination. To the south we have a small group of fanatics who want to secede from the Philippines and retreat to the twelfth century. In the middle of those problems, I have foreign agents using our country as a base. Mr. Draeger claims his life is in danger because of Mr. Kolar. Still, he comes out of hiding and commits the one act most certain to have him investigated. And he does it to save someone else. Tell me, does Mr. Kolar know where you are?"

Sensing the next question, Cindy thrust herself back from him, leaning heavily into the car door. "He knows Glen wouldn't harm me."

"Perhaps. Still, I wonder what he would do if you were in Miss Manong's place. Particularly since Miss Manong was in a good position to direct attention to the activities of your group. I think only a man like Mr. Draeger would act the way he did."

Refusing to answer, Cindy rejected both men, staring out the window. Her right hand wrapped around the fist of her left, and the ligaments stood ridged from knuckle to wrist.

Draeger said, "You have something on your mind, and it's not what we've been talking about. What's up?"

With a significant glance at Cindy, Cruz said, "It would be better if we stepped outside, I think."

Cindy's rush of color said more than any words. Still, when she reached for the door, Draeger put a hand on her shoulder. "You brought her in, Cruz. She stays. You don't trust me completely, and I've got some doubts about you. She's my back-up if anything goes wrong. And she can be a witness when this is over."

"You're goddamned right," she said through clenched teeth.

Cruz ignored her. "Some distrust between us is good, I think. It will keep us awake, right? And what I must tell you will make you dislike me as well as distrust me. I have spoken to you about a man named Bilongon and his dealings with Pierce. I have information that Bilongon is planning something big. I don't have any idea what or when."

"What do you expect me to do about it?"

"Listen. Ask. I have known for a while that some of the staff at the hotel are antigovernment. We have no reason to arrest them." He switched his attention to Cindy, and Draeger noticed that while he continued to speak perfectly naturally, his entire aspect changed. He pulled his chin down and back, slanting his face. He looked angry. "You see, Miss Anderson, we try to remain on the good side of your State Department. We cannot arrest dissidents on suspicion because we are a noncommunist tyranny. If we were a communist tyranny, it would be different. Wrong, but forgivable. When you tell them how nasty we are here, perhaps you'll mention that, as well."

She glared, disdainful. The look deepened, passed beyond the man until it was through him and fastened on a distant place. Draeger was proud of the performance. It left Cruz stranded.

The thud of a boatbuilder's maul drifted up to them, booming bass notes like a magnified pulse.

The wound on Draeger's head itched, and his fingers probed the edges without his conscious awareness, the caution of the contact resembling stealth.

Cruz saw only that Draeger was smiling and was very much offended. He said, "Pierce is as American as you, even though he's been here as long as you, I think, and lived here instead of up in the big city. He'll talk to you. I want to find out if he's having trouble with his Moslem workers not showing up for work or acting suspicious in any way."

"I'm surprised. You seem like a man who'd have good sources. Why do you need me?"

"I have excellent sources. They are afraid, every damned one. I've heard rumors, nothing I can use. There is talk of operations at sea, of men not being able to attend to fishing or farming because they must be available for something else. I suspect a large shipment of weapons and supplies."

"What can they do with a lot of weapons? I mean, they can hardly invade Mindanao or Luzon, can they?"

"I don't worry about that." Cruz permitted himself a smile that was more like a wink. "I wake in the night thinking of tons of plastic explosive instead of pounds, of long range rockets like the ones the VC used to fire into Saigon, of bombs in markets and cars, like they have in Belfast. We already have some small examples. You call it terrorism and blame it on politics. I call it murdering innocent people and blame it on murderers. You will help me put a stop to it. God willing, I will prove who is responsible in this area."

After a moment's thought, Draeger asked, "Do you think they're using Pierce's cruiser? Or using the hotel for a meeting place, a coordinating site? What do you think's happening?"

"Money is changing hands somewhere. I want those hands chopped." He gestured and convinced Draeger he was capable of the exact action. "I can't be sure that's all that's happening. If there is something else, like a raid, an attack, the planting of a bomb, I *must* know."

"I'll do what I can."

Cruz watched the boatbuilders for a bit before answering. "I know you will. You are not a dishonest man, I think. Oh, I know you will lie to me if you think you must, and you will never tell me everything. That is the business we are in. Maybe I am only doing all this because you are an American. I wouldn't do it if you were not. Part of our 'special relationship' stuff, eh? Anyhow, I know you won't do anything to compromise me. Not intentionally." He held up a warning finger. "I will not be destroyed to protect you."

"I understand. We can work together."

"Good. I'll come to the hotel. It's easier to talk there than in town. And I know where to find you." He grinned slyly at the dig, and Draeger acknowledged it with a grotesque smile.

He threw the car into reverse, the sudden rumble of the engine sending a small dog yelping for cover. For the first time Draeger noticed the phalanx of children advancing from the boatbuilder's village. They all smiled, some brash, most shy, pushing and shoving for vantage points that allowed quick escape. One, bolder than the rest, rushed a few paces ahead of the pack to strike a wild-eyed *kung fu* pose, chubby arms and legs clumsily imitating the stylized postures from the movies. Cruz raised a hand to his mouth in mock terror and whipped the car into a squealing turn onto the road. Behind them the children jumped and shouted and cheered. The miniature warrior beat his chest with one fist and shook the other at them as they rounded a bend out of sight.

# ■ CHAPTER 38 ■

They sat in the hotel room, she on the tan-and-brown sofa, he on the dark green upholstered chair. A modernistic lamp, globular copper shade on the end of a curved brass shaft, threw a quartering light across Draeger's features. Cindy was surprised at how it deepened his eyes, set them in the sockets. They waited, watching. The light had an opposite effect on his lips, highlighting them, making them fuller. They were down at the corners.

She was waiting for an answer, for him to tell her exactly how he intended to help Cruz. It took a long time for him to put the words together. "I'll talk to some people here. I'll poke Pierce a little bit." There was no enthusiasm in the voice, which pleased her.

"Well, after all, that's all you can do. I mean, he can hardly expect you to penetrate some rebel organization."

"That's not the point." He came out of the chair with smooth quickness, paced to the window and back. "He thinks Pierce is into the business of guns or something else very big. He's suggesting Pierce is using our organization to push it. And if that's true, then Pierce is protected from higher up the ladder. If Munson was the man, he'd have folded when Munson disappeared."

"Again? My God! Are you completely paranoid? A man asks you to ask a few questions, and you use that to indict a man who hasn't even heard of the problem!"

"You know I'm not crazy."

The muted complaint surprised her, disarmed the frustration that would have her continue to lash at him. Instead, she looked away. Her chin remained firm and her eyes clear, the decision-making expression in place. Slender fingers pulled at a seam, undisciplined. "No, you're not crazy. I wish you were. I could accept that more easily."

He thought about her answer. A word eluded him, the one that would summarize what it meant to hear her say she was concerned. The problems in his life formed a discordant mass of claims on his mind. Knowing she believed him wrong was merely another note. Knowing she wished it was not so created a single clear tone, and he worked with it until it was centered, forward of everything else, in stasis between the cacophony raging behind it and his conscious inability to properly define it. He felt if he could only name it he could make it expand, eliminate the other things. Nothing he considered worked, and the will to keep the single point in focus slipped away from him. He said, "I haven't really asked you to understand. It wasn't important. You said you'd help, but that was just so you could keep close, keep me from bushwhacking Kolar. Now, after what happened to Ria and Arturo, I think someone ought to know what's happening inside me."

"You've been hurt, Glen."

He dismissed that with a rasping noise, crude and effective. "I was prepared for the hurt. As long as I knew our people were with me, I think I'd have taken a lot. They left me, took my whole life with them. I never fired a bullet at a man in my life until yesterday. I enjoyed it. When the first one hit him and he only staggered, I was glad. I didn't want it to end that easy for him. It was a goddamned *gift* when I had to hit him again."

Fear frayed her words. "You blame Munson and Kolar?"

The earlier sadness swept him again. "I told you I'm not crazy. I blame them for the horror of the thing, that's all. A year ago I probably would've shot Boy Angel. A few days ago I'd have done it for sure. Yesterday it was a pleasure. Not like a good meal or a ball game, but I enjoyed it the way I'd enjoy collecting a debt long overdue. I've been taught to hate.''

The fingers at the dress seam were uncoordinated. "What Munson did to you was wrong. Unexplainable. I couldn't put together a clear picture of everything that was happening at his Control station, but I've some very serious questions and suspicions I didn't even mention to Carl.''

Draeger sat down, elbows on knees. It made Cindy think of an animal's crouch. She said, "I believe he had a China link close to Egg Roll, and Egg Roll discovered it. It would explain the courier. It would mean Munson moving to cut the lines.''

"You think he disappeared in a fit of remorse?" The sarcasm was harsh.

She continued unruffled. "I think he got caught in a squeeze. I can't guess if it was counterintelligence, blackmail, or what.''

He threw himself against the back of the chair. "When we left Cruz you were going to see me hung. Now you're working on the problem. And laying it on Munson. You wouldn't be running a con on me, would you?''

She colored, but the answer was controlled. "You've got me stuck here so I might as well think about why. And I'm a pushover for lost puppies.''

He smiled, briefly, got to his feet and paced some more. He stroked the point of his chin before reaching to scratch at the wound, baring his teeth. The expression lingered faintly as he spoke. "I've accepted that Munson was eliminated. There's no other explanation. But remember, whoever took out Munson expected to get me, too.''

"And you blame Carl. But what if it wasn't him? What if it's part of the effort to shut down your Egg Roll operation?''

The padding of his feet on the carpet stopped instantly. "God, I haven't thought about him all morning.''

"He's lasted quite a while, Glen. He's resourceful. Maybe the ad'll be in the paper today." She walked to him and put a hand on his shoulder from behind. "Don't be this hard on yourself.''

"People get close to me and get hurt. I don't want you to be the next one.''

She applied pressure to the shoulder, a signal of strength in reserve. "I'm different. I don't intend to be hurt, no matter where I take my stand. It's the world that better look out."

He smiled at her over his shoulder. She pulled the hand back and he started away, saying, "I wouldn't bet against you." He slowed, then turned. "I won't turn anyone for Cruz, I promise you. Everything I told him was either stuff he knew, was learning, or a damned lie. Maybe, before we wrap everything up, we really will be working together. Maybe next time, huh?" The muscles of his face moved imperceptibly, turned the expression sardonic.

He moved to the lobby quickly, the conversation about Egg Roll sharpening his anticipation for the Manila papers. Too disturbed to think of them before, now he fluctuated wildly between hope for the message and a cold fear that called itself rationality and said the man had no chance. Before he was fully settled on one of the lobby's heavy sofas, a green-jacketed waiter was asking if he'd care for coffee. He was sipping it when he saw the advertisement. He literally trembled, creating a tiny maelstrom of black concentric ripples in the cup. Using both hands, mantislike, he lowered it beside the vase on the table. Wisps of steam wound through lavender-blue orchids, fine tendrils that disappeared lazily among the flowers. The paper sighed as he spread it out flat.

*Cook wanted. Must know Singapore specialties, speak American. Call 30–22–07. After 7.*

Exactly as instructed. If the man had been in danger before, now he was worse off and had no way of knowing it. He considered himself free of pursuers, hidden, needing only to wait for rescue. By the time he discovered the man he depended on was a failure he'd be dying for his misplaced confidence.

Draeger lifted the coffee, sure-handed. He studied the ad, locking it into memory. Then, casually, he turned the page. Anyone would believe he was reading. He was not. His eyes were blank, their capability drawn inward. Increased blood flow made his head throb. He was only marginally aware of it or anything else physical.

It would be necessary to go to Singapore. That was a given. What was not so automatic was the manner of it. He weighed and counterbalanced and when the problem was dissected, its parts identified, gestured to the waiter for the check. The steadiness of the signing hand and the unconcerned scrawl pleased him. He allowed himself a moment's vanity before strolling onto the patio. The swimming pool was being churned by a Japanese family of father, mother, and four step-chair children in perfect boy-girl-boy-girl symmetry. Mother and father hung at the deep end, suspended by elbows in the splash trough while the children bounced and yelled in the shallows. Draeger proceeded to the path that led to Pierce's cottage.

He enjoyed the walk. The children's racket in the background was filtered, complementary to the gusting breeze that agitated the palms, set them complaining with irritable chuffing noises. The heat was still at bay on the path, and the forest smells had a temperate earthiness that lacked the fervid decomposition that would stain the air later. The dew was gone, but a lingering moisture glossed some better-hidden leaves, leaving a delicate film that made Draeger think of something vaguely secretive, a scented exhalation smudged on a woman's mirror.

By the time he knocked on Pierce's door the plan had been reviewed, altered, and approved. He greeted Pierce easily, feeling good. He fought the urge to let the good feeling show, knew he couldn't hide it completely. It surprised him to see Pierce's initial confusion begin to reflect some of his own well-being as they exchanged general conversation. It was Pierce who played the first card in the game.

"How's Cindy taking things? She's not used to being denied, is she?"

"She's OK. Handling it. Anything from the front office?"

"Since the shutdown order, nothing. Very low profile. Nothing in the papers about Munson, either. You think there's a connection between what happened in Cebu and the guy up in the mountains?"

"I don't know. Too much is going on. And that's why I'm here."

Pierce's expression of increased interest was admirable. A lift of the eyebrows, a slight turning of the head. Just the right amount of natural curiosity. What he wasn't aware of, and what Draeger had carefully positioned himself to see, was the sudden dilation of his pupils. There were no false starts with feet or hands, no perspiration. Drager watched the pupils and knew Pierce was more than interested. He was concerned.

Draeger continued. "Cruz is trying to squeeze me. He's got a mark on you, Tony. He knows I killed the man at the logging camp. He's staying off me because he thinks I'll tip you over as soon as I can catch you at something."

"I'm clean, Glen. He's seen me with some people around here, but, hell, they're business. If he had anything, he'd move. You don't know him."

"I don't have time to dance with you. You're dealing with some smugglers. You know it, I know it, and Cruz knows it. I've got to get out. I've got two choices, work for Cruz against one of my own people or run. If I stay here, how long can I stall him?"

Palms up, beseeching, Pierce said, "Glen, I don't know what to say. Sure, I know a couple of people who smuggle things, but I can't trust them to take you anywhere. They're bad news, man. And where would you go? Cruz'll be after you like a shot. Just sit. The longer he waits to do anything, the less case he's got. We'll outwait him."

"No chance. I'm not going inside. Not for you, not for the organization, not for anything." Draeger came forward in the chair, a convulsive movement that startled Pierce. "Look, you work with these Moros all the time. They've got to have some way of moving their men around, some sort of system. Get me in it. Once I get out of Zamboanga, I can get clear."

Disturbed by Draeger's proximity, Pierce got out of his chair, carefully avoiding contact. He moved to the kitchen, reappearing with coffee cups and the standard equipment. Draeger was enjoying the charade. Still, there was a disturbing confidence in Pierce. Possibly it was even more than a confidence. Whatever it was, it was overdeveloped, a meal too rich. In the past he'd acted confidence superbly. He had been a person pretending to be a confident Tony Pierce. This was Tony Pierce pretending to be someone else, and it was unsettling. An itching upper lip distracted Draeger, and he was shaken when the knuckle rubbed along its surface came away wet with sweat. Sipping his coffee, he stared at his foot, drove his mind to think only of breathing, heartbeat, composure. The heat from the cup bathed his nose and eyes, lulling.

Pierce's voice broke through his concentration, a rising hum like the sound of a car on the highway, growing and growing, demanding attention. Even as he let himself catch the words he wanted desperately to ignore them and linger in the shadowy mind-picture of a boy on a knoll looking down on a narrow, high-crowned blacktop ribbon of road.

"We've got to make it look like you took off on your own. If Cruz thinks I helped you, he'll be on my case even harder. I can't contribute anything to our organization if I'm spending all my time patching my cover."

Draeger gave him a noncommittal grunt.

Pierce went on, "We'll make it look like you took the hotel cruiser and met someone to take you further. You don't know the waters, so you'll have to 'kidnap' someone to run the thing. I'll set that up. I'll schedule an evening fishing run day after tomorrow. The crew'll dock late to clean up and refuel. They'll be working after dark. We'll have a power failure. While the lights are out you'll 'steal' the boat and be on your way."

"Your man knows how to make contact to get me further south?"

"I'll get that moving now. It's going to be very tight. And risky. I won't lie to you, Glen. It's dangerous as hell."

Draeger had to swallow to answer. An oily film clung to his tongue, obstinate. "I understand. At least this way I can make a fight of it."

The remark excited Pierce. He made a fist, poked in an abbreviated blow. "That's what we have to learn for ourselves, isn't it? They can't teach that in school, man, not even one like they sent us through. When push comes to shove, it's the ones who welcome a fight who'll win." His enthusiasm mounting, he bent to his coffee, drained it in a single tilt, then aimed the cup at Draeger, trigger finger through the handle.

"I'll tell you something I probably shouldn't. I never thought you'd come to that attitude. You're tough enough, but you were always so damned—" he struggled for the right word, waving the free hand, "—considerate. You can't be that way. Not in this business. If you're going to live, you've got to go balls to the wall, you know?"

Draeger said, "What do I do to get ready? I need money and paper. And a gun."

"Hold it." Pierce shook his head, admonishing. "Don't even think about it. You're dealing with people who'll kill you if they decide it's a fun idea. You give them any macho bullshit and they'll want to find out if you can die macho. Leave it alone. Either trust them or forget it."

"I just go, like a steer into a slaughterhouse?"

"It's dangerous, but what other choice do you have? And look at me. I've dealt with them for years, and I'm OK."

"Yeah." Draeger got to his feet, headed for the door. "Still, I want a piece. Can you help me?"

Pierce looked exasperated. "Sure, I can get you one. Just think about it, will you? Money's no problem. I've got a stash. We'll fix you up with a few thousand pesos and some green dollars. Bring me a pair of your trousers. I'll have some gold sewn in them."

"Gold?"

"Thin sheets, under the hem at the waist. Better than a money belt. Don't try to wear them through any metal detectors."

"I really appreciate it. I'll get it back to you."

Pierce waved the free hand, leaning over to replace the cup. "You'd do the same for me. Remember one thing. You and me, we do things for each other. The people out there, the world, they don't. Remember that when you leave."

"I will." He stepped out the door, onto the path. The sun had taken no respite while they talked, and its heat now permeated the earth. Leaves that had strained in vertical eagerness earlier maintained the same attitude, but there was a subtle difference. They hesitated, wanting the sunlight, needing it to live, and aware of its merciless capacity to burn them to death in minutes if they faced it directly. He saw the parallel in his own situation and felt fear settle on exposed nerve ends. It passed quickly. It would come again, he knew. It would have to be accepted and dismissed, ignored. Thinking about fear would be the ultimate mistake.

He strode the path, head up, arms pumping. So he was supposed to steal a boat and kidnap a crew, right? Right, giving Pierce corroboration for a story that he had no part of any escape. And Draeger would be wanted for another crime or two, in case the murder rap wouldn't stand. Not a bad fix, especially coming from a man who was clean one minute, knew some smugglers the next, and had dealt with them for years, in the end. Draeger complimented himself on deciding to tell Pierce about Cruz. The reaction seasoned the dish to perfection. Knowing Cruz was pressuring a friend to work against him, Pierce's instant decision was to eliminate the friend. No thought of striking at a mutual source of danger. No, Pierce would cut down the easy target.

Maybe that was the basis for his new-found appearance, that odd confidence thing. Draeger slowed in his walk. Could it be that a man who'd found the resolve to accomplish, even if the cost was murder, enjoyed a kind of superiority, a reach of knowledge beyond another man? Wasn't that what he was doing, himself? Killing Boy Angel, wasn't that part of the new Draeger? Was he the same as Pierce, under it all?

No, by God, he wasn't. He was no more like Pierce than the wolf is like the cattleman. Maybe they both killed cows to eat beef, but you couldn't make much of a case beyond that.

"Considerate." He muttered the word to himself, continuing on up the steps to the patio and the swimming pool. The family was gone. A red and black striped ball drifted on the broken blue-glass water, the toy and the waves the only reminders anyone had been there. The sun had already swept footprints and drippings from the edge.

He went directly to Cindy's room, and she fumbled at the door, opening it a crack to peer at him with a sleep-fuzzed eye. He said, "I've got to talk to you," and she stepped back, leading him inside. Rolling her head from side to side sent the long blond hair in waves across her back. She hugged herself before she turned, accentuating surprisingly broad shoulders and a narrow waist. Muscles in her buttocks bunched in the tight slacks. Draeger looked away, irritated by his vulnerability, trying to close the woman-smell of the room from his thinking. The rumpled bedspread, the disheveled pillows were an erotic map of suggestion.

He deliberately thought of Ria, of the things that happened to her because she became involved with him. It shamed him when he could only dimly perceive the scene in the logging camp. The naked body, the helplessness of her, the threat of Boy Angel standing in front of her—those things were clear. No image of her face would form. She looked out from his mind as from behind shifting pieces of cardboard, revealing random, disorganized features. It was she, and he could not see her. Shards, fragments were all he could identify.

One look at him woke Cindy completely. "Glen, what's wrong? You look terrible! What's happened?"

"Nothing, nothing." He avoided her reach, moving quickly to a chair and sitting down. She pulled the other chair close, looking at him with concern. He went on, "I've got some things to tell you, and none of it's going to be easy. First, I'm leaving here and you're staying."

She came bolt upright. He rushed ahead, told her of his conversation with Pierce, of his evaluation of the agreement. At that, she refused to be silent any longer.

"What can you hope to prove? You're asking to be killed!"

"You haven't let me tell you what I hope to prove. And I want you to know I'm depending on you to hold up one end of this. If you don't, I'm taking the chance for nothing."

"Hold up an end?" She was sputtering. "What do you mean, hold up an end? I won't be a part of this!"

He continued as if she hadn't spoken. "Cruz knows something's coming off, something so big it's shut off all his low-level sources. He thinks Pierce may be in on it. OK. So I suggest to Pierce he may be safer with me on the run, and he wants to *help*. Can you see it? He'd never take a chance on setting me up if he wasn't absolutely certain he can get away with it."

Her face fell, stricken, and her words were almost a moan. "The Kolar thing again."

He smiled. "I doubt it. I've done some thinking. It ain't easy for me, you know? It occurred to me that I may not be able to figure out what the hell's going on *not* because I'm stupid, but because somebody's playing it off the wall and nobody knows what's going on."

"Include me."

"Kolar's too good to let me run free this long. He'd have arranged something more definite than those guys in the boat. He's too businesslike to set a crazy after someone to smoke me out. No, I don't think it's him."

There was little change in her face, the wan hope that tried to assert itself washed away. "You've decided it might not be Kolar simply because you're still alive? What was the word? 'Businesslike?' That's disgusting.''

His composure cracked, and he snapped at her. "It's a disgusting business! Maybe you'd like to ask Ria how disgusting?'' At her wince he was immediately repentant. "That was a cheap shot. I'm sorry. Anyhow, I'm climbing inside Pierce's pipeline. It's the only way I know to find out who's at the other end. If I work it right, I'll use these people to get me all the way to Singapore and Egg Roll.''

"It could be weeks before you get there.''

"That's one of the things I want you to handle. Get to Kolar. If you don't hear from me, do whatever you think best. By then you should know if I was right or wrong.''

"*If* I can get out of here, I'll tell Carl. You have an idea along those lines?''

"I don't think Cruz'll hold you once I'm gone. If he tries it, tell him I mailed letters to several friends detailing everything that's gone down here, and if you get to Manila ahead of the letters, there won't be any problem. He'll have to go for it.''

"You're sure this is the only way to handle this? We could try to run, get to Carl.''

"No. I'm still not sure about him. If I was wrong, that's really all the more reason to nail whoever's done all this.''

"Who could it be?'' Her hand flew to her breast. "Munson? He's dead! His wife—!''

"I know. I was there. I've always believed she died because she was in my place. I wouldn't consider that Munson might be responsible. It's taken me a long time to deal with the unthinkable.''

"And Pierce?''

"In it up to his eyes. Watch him. And get away from here as fast as you can.''

The weight of the situation seemed to hit her all at once, and for a second Draeger was sure she was going to buckle. He moved to catch her, a hand on each shoulder, just as she stiffened. The will strengthening her was palpable under his touch, lifting the shoulders, straightening first the neck, then the back. He let his hands rest on her, ready, unneeded. She looked him in the eye, completely under control again. The blue of them, so suggestive of cold distance, was different. They were misty, intriguing. The forbidding glint was gone. They wavered, examining his face, memorizing.

When he stepped back he half-turned, and his hands fell to his sides with leaden clumsiness. She reached for the one closest, slowly, uncertainly. When he failed to object, she raised her other hand and clasped his between hers. He looked at that contact, then into her upturned face. She said, "This isn't like anything I've ever been involved with, Glen. I'm afraid. Not for me, not even when you're gone, but for you. This is more than I'm ready for. You're talking about leaving here in the middle of the night with people you're not sure of, and I can't even ask you to be careful without sounding like an utter, useless fool."

"That's not true. You've got a lot to do." At her expression, he freed his hand and cupped her chin. "I'm scared too, believe me. If I could think of another way out of this I'd grab it and run. The thing that scares me most is that it might be for nothing. I don't know if that's reasonable or not, but it's the way I feel. It scares hell out of me that no one may ever know I tried." He released her face, laughing softly. "Wow. Real mellerdrammer. Bet you haven't heard anything like that since your last TV late movie."

It took a visible effort for her to put on her own smile. "You may be right. That line gives me the right to ask you to be careful without being called a fool."

"Agreed!" He laughed again. "We've got two days. We'll enjoy them."

In the hallway, Draeger massaged the headache tearing at his temple. Excess pressure created a flash of pain from the wound, and he swore quietly, moving off.

The floor security man smiled to himself and made a mental note to tell his wife how the two strange Americans who pretended to be married managed a lover's quarrel before lunch. It would amuse her.

# CHAPTER 39

Illumination from tall pole lights fell on the white hull beside the dock in a benign grace for a favorite child. The pilings, the small praus tied nearby, the roughened dock timbers all merely existed in the glare. The larger vessel accepted its due. The darkness behind it massed heavier, the sea under it suggested deeper, more awesome mysteries.

Cindy looked at it from the safety of the trees, sleek in one of the batik costumes, scarlet on black, slacks and jacket. Until then it had made her feel exotic and alluring. The boat rendered her alien, temporary. The graceful shape filled her with loathing. A faint squeal of chafing plastic fenders reminded her of the dying cries of a mouse caught by her cat. It was a bad memory, buried in childhood, and it intensified her depression. She shifted from one foot to the other and Draeger sensed her disturbance, put an arm around her shoulder and drew her close.

"It's going to work out," he said. "Don't start worrying."

"If that's the level of your perception, you better not go. I've never stopped worrying."

"I'm glad."

Twisting in his grasp, she looked up at him. She knew what he meant and refused to pretend otherwise. Instead of feigned irritation or confusion, she merely said, "I'm not sure what's happening to me."

"It's been a good couple of days. I'm glad we had them. I mean for us to have more."

Sharp movement pulled her away, toward the dock. He asked, "What's wrong? If it's Ria—"

Checking him with a hand, she spoke without turning, walking as if concentrating on her footing, although the path was well lit by the outdoor lamps secreted in the shrubs. "It's not Ria and it is. It's her and this place and seeing you get ready to leave. It's things I can't even explain to myself."

Having said it, she wished she could have the words back. They resounded in her mind, obtuse and inexpressive. Of course Ria was an influence on her view of him and on her view of herself in relation to him. But she wasn't attracted to him because some other woman had been, nor was she disturbed because he'd been involved with another woman. That was idiotically romantic. The frightening thing was that she thought of him romantically and dreaded any hint that he'd thought of Ria in the same way. It was a devil in her, and there was no exorcism to drive it out.

Forcing her out of her introspection, he said, "I wish you hadn't come with Kolar. I wish we could've met in Los Angeles, a long time ago. But I'm glad you're here. Right now, this minute. Maybe that's what you're saying?"

"Maybe it is. I enjoyed our two days." She gestured, the hand sudden in the light, mothlike. "That's not the right word." Facing him for a moment, she smiled, and it wasn't until she spoke again that he realized the mockery in it was meant for herself. "You played a dirty trick on me, Glen Draeger. You made me think you needed me and then you made me wonder if maybe I don't need you. You made me think about liking you, far too much. Now there's this." They were at the landward end of the dock, and she pointed her chin at the waiting cruiser. "In an hour you'll be gone. I don't even know where you're going."

He found a laugh, said, "What the hell, neither do I," and she took it badly, refused to acknowledge him except for a slight forward pitch of her shoulders. He stroked her head, letting his hand trail the flow of her hair. "Not funny. Sorry. Look, it's not the end of the world. I won't be gone all that long."

"Don't you dare patronize me! You don't know how long you'll be gone, and you don't even know if you'll be back." She jerked away, stepped onto the dock and glared back at him. "You're off on an ego trip that may get you killed and you think you can stand there and hand me a lot of masculine 'Me Tarzan, you Jane' schlock, and I'm supposed to be reassured! You're behaving like a damned child, risking your life for nothing!''

The words had a life of their own, shot between her lips, flew at him. She pictured herself, contorted and ugly. He clenched his teeth. Muscles wadded his jaws. Waiting for him to answer sucked the life out of her knees. At last he relaxed, slid a startlingly pink tongue forward to wet lips still thin with anger.

"You said we have an hour.'' His voice was taut. "Let's not waste it, Cindy. We don't have any reason for teary good-byes and it's not necessary for us to hide the fact that we both wish we did. Too many things have happened, but the good things seem to have gotten away from us. For now, can't we just be two people? Do we have to make sociological declarations? Prove things?''

She turned away and damned the history and biology that said she had to cry at such a moment and screwed her eyes shut. Escaping drops on her cheeks embarrassed. A moment's fumbling produced a handkerchief, and she dabbed quickly. Action restored her control. When she opened her eyes again, he was watching with a sympathetic smile and a tilt of his head she hoped indicated some admiration. When he took her in his arms she responded with a whirlpool of emotions—desire and resistance, loss and discovery—a myriad of contradictory joys and pains. He held her close, enfolded, and she knew there was passion. A restraint that puzzled and hurt insulated him though, despite the contact of the embrace, and a dichotomy of yearning and resentment welled in her. Then the impossibility of their situation asserted itself. She took what comfort she could in holding to him tightly.

After a while, reluctantly, she moved back. His hands coursed upward from her waist, linked behind her head and refused to let her go further. Gently, they turned her face upward. The dark eyes sought her out, searched in hers, longing. Her thoughts branched out, uncontrolled. She spoke rapidly. "I'm going to believe you'll be all right. I'll worry, but I won't stop believing. That's the only declaration I want to make. I don't want to prove anything. I want you to prove I'm right.''

"I'll do my damnedest.'' The lopsided grin livened his face. He offered her his arm, and they walked the dock halfway to the boat, stopping directly under a lamp. Insects flittered in the cone of light, erratic pellets. Occasionally one damaged itself and spiraled downward to the water. Small fish shoaled nervously there in constant anticipation.

Cindy looked away as a fat beetle growled down from the bulb in an accelerating dive. It hit the water hard enough to make a tiny splash, the flailing wings abruptly silenced. The sound of the impact was immediately amplified by dozens of gobbling mouths. When she looked again, flecks of black carapace sank in leaflike fall for the hungrier fish to dart at and spit back out. Close by, a minute monster hovered, its shadow on the bottom a wavering projectile-figure. It was a small squid, motionless, huge eyes ridiculous in a body that rippled like jello. The eyes fascinated Cindy. In a moment she was convinced they were watching her, passing images and impressions inward to a brain that had no business being in such a primitive vessel. It unnerved her, tried to drag her back to her disoriented emotional state. Turning from it, she said, "I want to go back inside. Let's not look at this damned boat for another second, OK?"

"Sure."

They walked back slowly. She continually reached out with the hand away from him, touching, storing tactile memories to augment other senses. The palm trunks were rough, scored with ridges and welts, suggesting wearied fence posts in meadows. Then she knew that familiar world and this exotic place were juxtaposed in her mind. Other sights and smells would seize her someday, snatch her from a familiar place and send her mind arrowing to these islands. There was no way to predict what they might be or when they might come. Whenever she wanted to relive these few moments, though, they were indelible, waiting only for that rough, dry texture to recall each second. The thought was bittersweet.

Too quickly, they reached the outer dining area, the gaily lit bar now repellently garish. The laughter was worse, the signature of the lust for amusement that reduced the conversation to hoarse polysyllables and piercing shrieks. She searched the faces for a glimpse of sobriety, a sign of earnest discourse. There was none. They were all in a state of entertainment. Passing between the tables on the way to the lobby made her nervous, and she reached back for Draeger's hand. Once inside, past the gamut, she steadied herself before looking up at him with a smile she knew was as morally dishonest as it was physically perfect.

Pierce came to them. "Everything's set. Glen, you sit at the bar outside, with your back to the dock. The lights down there'll go out first. About five minutes later, the building lights'll go. That's when you take off. It'll take the boys a while to set out the lanterns and the candles, but they'll work as fast as they can because they're not in on this, of course. You're wearing the trousers?"

Draeger nodded and Pierce tapped his waist conspiratorially. "Your gear's aboard. There's a gun with it. Do yourself a favor and strap it to your ankle and leave it there. The less it's seen, the better, believe me."

Cindy said, "Gun?" and paled.

Pierce grabbed her elbow. "We've got to separate you two." She stirred, tried to protest, and he cut her off. "There's going to be one ballbuster of an investigation when Glen turns up missing, Cindy. I want no one to be able to say you were with him at the last minute. It's harsh, but Glen's out where we can't help, except to guarantee him running room. Come on, now." He pushed on the resisting arm.

Draeger said, "He's right. Go with him. I don't want to have to worry about Cruz bullying you. You knew nothing about me getting off the island, remember. Stonewall him." He bent forward suddenly, kissed her. It was gentle, an exchange. She looked in his eye as he straightened and saw no demand there, nothing but sharing. Words caught in her throat. Her attempted smile was skewed, ridiculous, and she turned readily at Pierce's insistence. Draeger waited at the door for her to look back and when she did, he winked. He looked confident and brave and unbearably vulnerable. It was all she could do to avoid rushing to him. Then he was outside.

Pierce led her behind the registration desk, opening the door to his office. He stepped aside for her to enter, and she said, "Why are we waiting in here?"

"I'm having some people join us. Important people. They'll be our witnesses."

A man entered immediately, carrying a tray with drinks. He

smiled for Cindy and looked to Pierce, who gestured to the far side of the room, closing the door. "Just put them on that table."

The man nodded again and moved away. As he passed behind Cindy he drew his right hand from under the tray, letting a narrow cloth bag slide off his wrist to dangle by a stout cord. He swung it in an arc and when it struck behind her ear it sounded as prosaic as someone irritably swatting a mosquito. She crumpled with dramatic totality.

Pierce leaped to her. "Holy Christ! Is she killed?"

The man pivoted, lowered the tray gently. He sounded hurt. "She is not dead at all. In a little while she will wake with a bad headache, not even the cut."

"Get her the hell out of here!" Pierce hurried to the desk and pulled out a hotel laundry bag, throwing it to the man. In a few seconds Cindy was gagged with the napkin from the tray, hands and feet bound with cord from inside the bag. The man grunted and heaved her onto his shoulder. Pierce opened the back exit for him. "Remember, the long way around! And wait until the dock's dark to take her aboard. Hurry!"

Minutes later Draeger watched the lights flicker and die at the dock. Casually, waiting until most of the crowd was looking in that direction, he turned on the bar stool. With his back to everyone, he closed his right eye, hoping that would help his night vision when the hotel blacked out. Two adventurous souls were actually starting past the bar, headed for the dock to investigate, when the rest of the lights finally went. There was no warning, and the result was pandemonium. Hilarity splintered into anger and pointless floundering. Tables and glasses crashed.

Draeger was off the stool and running, crouched. The protected eye was little help, and after he blundered off the path once he slowed drastically. Jerking, stumbling, he identified the dock, a dark protrusion against the star-reflecting sea. The crusier's whiteness beckoned, and he managed a trot. Hands reached out to hoist him aboard. His feet hit the deck simultaneously with the start of the engines. The cruiser was clear and headed to sea when the hotel came to life again, followed by the pole lights at the dock. Looking back, it seemed to him everyone must see them leaving, but they were apparently beyond the pool of illumination dancing on the empty surface. There were no cries of alarm.

The man at the wheel said, "My name is Juan. My partner is Jesus. He is in the main cabin, preparing it. We have plenty of food and things to drink. You want something, you tell us, OK?" Teeth gleamed eerily in the dim, green light from the instruments.

Draeger laughed, hoping it sounded relaxed. "It's a great way to run away. I'll say that much."

Juan laughed too, returning to his study of the sea, the instruments, and the constant circling stroke of the radar as it read the night.

Draeger found his way below and along the richly paneled corridor to the only open door. The room was spacious, the furnishings darkly opulent, the browns of the upholstery and bedding a blend of chocolate and coffee. The lamps were wood, lighter colored and spare in design, accents against the convoluted grain of the waxed bulkheads. It was an integrated whole, designed to accommodate in luxury. The man named Jesus straightened, putting a final pat on a pillow. "Good evening, sir." He pointed toward a corner. "There is your suitcase. Mr. Pierce said to remind you about strapping the gun to your ankle, sir. There is tape with it. He said I should tell you."

"Thanks, Jesus. Do you think the gun's a mistake, too?"

"No, sir. You go to the Moros, sir, and they are bad men, very bad. A gun is very important. It is the only thing they understand. A gun or a knife."

"I see." Draeger moved to the suitcase, and Jesus left. Alone, Draeger opened the bag and checked his belongings, examining both passports. The American one would sell for a decent piece of change, if necessary, and the Canadian paper was still clean. He riffled the money, smiling at the sight of the dollars. It'd been a long time since he handled them. They looked good.

Next he checked the pistol. It was in a cheap leather holster, slotted to fit a belt, but with no straps for shoulder wear. The metal was well-oiled and clean. He broke the weapon open and thumbed the ejector, letting the new-bright brass and copper bullets fall to the bedspread. They bounced and gleamed innocently. The barrel was worn but serviceable. He dry fired it twice, noting the trigger pull, watching the hammer drop on the empty chambers. Satisfied, he reloaded three rounds and suddenly hesitated with the fourth. He stared at it quizzically, tossing it up and down before examining all six under better light. Each bore minute sloping dents where the casing joined the bullet, invisible unless held at the correct angle. He gripped one round, twisting the slug with thumb and forefinger. Sweat stood on his face, and he was wiping his hands constantly by the time it came free and he was staring into the hollow brass cylinder.

Another round confirmed the first. Pierce had supplied him with a gun and six empty bullets.

Draeger stepped to the sink and washed his hands, swabbed his face with a wet washcloth. A grim expression stared back at him from the mirror. When he smiled at it the effort made him laugh. He preferred the grim man. There was some honesty in that face.

Treachery he'd expected. Now that he knew where some of it was located, he felt he'd won a round. The corollary to the pistol that wouldn't fire, of course, was the trip to nowhere. He considered that, holding back the fear that accompanied it, and discounted the notion. Cindy was back there and knew of the plan. Pierce wouldn't risk that sort of testimony. Beyond that, there was the chance Kolar was straight and had held off moving to pick up Cindy for fear she was genuinely hostage. In any case, the first order of the day was to improve the present situation.

When he entered the main salon from the passageway, Jesus was waiting. Draeger said he'd like something to eat, and the Filipino was pleased to show him the galley, down winding stairs to the compact stainless steel and enamel cubby. As soon as Draeger was certain they were out of Juan's sight he reached past his companion for one of the butcher knives in their slotted wooden holder. He watched Jesus's initial wonder blossom to concern and finally register as terror as the point of the blade pricked at the juncture of his jaw and throat. Jesus's hands sought purchase on the edge of the sink as he rose to tiptoe, anxiously obeying Draeger's finger-to-lip order to be silent.

"No lies, Jesus. One lie and you're dead."

Jesus crossed his eyes, looking for the knife. Draeger moved the point a hair and a red bead popped out of the taut brown skin, mingling with sweat to form a wine-colored rill. He babbled quietly.

"It was not our idea, sir. We had nothing to do with it. We meet a prau, and he takes both of you."

"Both?" The word hissed, and Jesus squealed fear.

"The woman, sir, the blond lady."

"She's here?"

"In the crew's area, sir. Unhurt, I swear! Still in the laundry bag, sir!"

Draeger chanced a look to the top of the stairs. Juan apparently suspected nothing. To Jesus, he said, "There are guns aboard. I want one. Now." Jesus managed to look even sicker. Rolling his eyes, he indicated a door forward. "The crew's area," he said.

Draeger let him lead the way. When they reached Cindy, he forced Jesus face down on the deck, kneeling on him while he checked her. After noting her breathing and taking her pulse, he examined her head, finding the lump behind her ear. Moving quickly, he slashed the cloth bag into strips and used them to bind and gag Jesus. After another assurance that Cindy was breathing easily and her pulse was strong, he rummaged through cabinets until he found a .45 automatic. Securing it under his belt, he hurried through the galley, composing himself at the steps, strolling up to the control bridge.

"Jesus is putting together something to eat," he said, leaning over to look at the radar scope. "Nothing out there tonight?"

"Very quiet tonight. Easy ride." Juan grinned, and Draeger was sure there was condescension in it.

"How many course changes? Is it a fairly straight trip?"

Juan looked at his watch. "No trouble. Next change in half hour. Easy, quiet. Good night to be out, huh?"

Draeger let him see the pistol and moved to the side. "Set this thing to automatic. Now!" He rapped one of the hands frozen to the wheel, snapping Juan out of his shock. Tougher than his partner, Juan silently clamped the hand in the opposite armpit. "Where is Jesus? You won't kill us. You shoot us, you lost out here."

"I'm supposed to die on this trip. You want to give me a reason to get rid of you?" He extended the weapon to Juan's head, pushed until he was forcing the other man off balance. Juan said, "OK, OK," and flipped a switch. "Where is Jesus?"

Gesturing, Draeger sent him down the steps and then into the crew's area. First he had Cindy hauled up to the open afterdeck and eased onto her side on one of the sunbathing chaises. Then they went back to bring up Jesus. After inspecting the cloth bonds, Draeger left him on the deck to roll with the cruiser's motion and gestured Juan back to his wheel. Then he pulled up a chair and sat down, some distance to the right rear.

It was over an hour before Cindy stirred, moaning. He sat up to look at her and caught Juan's sudden tensing. He gestured with the automatic and the man faced forward again. Draeger moved to her, chewing on his lip while returning consciousness exposed her to pain. She fought it, twisting and turning, ineffectual hands pushing at the air. Finally she opened her eyes. At the sight of him she stopped, and he saw the new struggle in them, the attempt to understand, to know. When it came, she gave a short cry. Before he could react she was sitting upright, her hands to her mouth heaving. He rushed her to the side where she emptied her stomach in long, racking spasms.

It seemed forever before she stopped and, clutching the rail, inhaled great draughts of air. He helped her back to the chaise and got her some water from the small bar. At the end of his summarized account of events, she said, "And now what?" He wanted to cheer.

"We make the meeting with the prau. You herd these two back to Zamboanga. If that doesn't convince Cruz you're on the side of the angels, nothing will."

She shook her head in argument and winced. "I don't think so. The way I see it, you've knocked a big hole in whatever plans Pierce had for us. That's a breakthrough. We have to exploit it."

He grinned appreciation. "You're right. Devious and nasty, but right. Let me think on it."

"Gladly. I'm going to wash up and find some aspirin or something."

"If you feel up to it, toss this tub. There has to be more than one gun aboard, and we need a search."

She returned almost an hour later, bubbling with enthusiasm. "Automatics! Three of them! And two rifles! Plenty of ammunition!"

"Great work. How're you feeling?"

"OK. Got a headache, but not bad. Found the aspirin. Do I dump the guns?"

"No, they'll come in handy." Her face fell, and he rushed to explain. "I'll use them to show good faith. Whoever I'm being handed off to can't trust Pierce any more than we do, so instead of coming in empty-handed, I bring the guns. After that it may be easier to convince them I'm the good guy and Pierce is setting them up for a sell-out."

"Just like that?"

"I'm going to need a lot of help, Cindy. You've got to convince Cruz he should leave Pierce out of jail, keep him under some sort of house arrest so he can be watched. He's got to make it look like Pierce is cooperating with the authorities. Get him to spread a rumor Pierce is going to Singapore. I'll convince these people I know where he's headed, that I know the contact. They'll get me there."

"What if they don't believe you?"

He threw up his hands. "We've been through it. Leave it alone. It's what I have to do."

She came to him, put her arms around him. "I don't care about any of it anymore, Glen. It's not worth it."

Over the top of her head he watched Juan consider his chances and give his attention back to the cruiser. Lowering his head, he spoke softly. "It's worth it to me, Cindy. And to you. Don't try to say otherwise. Quitting now would be worse than if we'd never started."

She shivered, and he took the opportunity to send her after extra clothes. While she was gone he took Juan's keys and found the one that unlocked the chain securing the dinghy to the stern. Dragging the clattering mass to the controls, he wrapped it around Juan attaching him to the steering wheel despite a sulfurous stream of Chavacano. When he was satisfied he snapped the lock shut and pitched the key over the side. The Filipino followed it with glittering eyes until it was gone, continuing to stare as if he could draw it back from the sea.

Gently, Draeger said, "Steer very carefully. If anything happens to this tub, you go with it. And you can forget about trying to surprise the lady on the run back to Zamboanga." Leaving him, Draeger retrieved the knife from the galley and cut some lengths from the nylon lifeline at the rail, doubling up on Jesus's lashings.

That done, he hauled him forward to lie in the corner of the control area, close to his partner, making it easier to watch them.

He waited for Cindy with his back to the rail, too keyed up to relax. Even the cold failed to trouble him. The breeze of the cruiser's passage pulled at his hair and his clothes, an incessant rumpling that sought every gap to pump in the predawn chill. He felt it work through flesh to bone and still there was no discomfort. Stiffened muscles would move a fraction slower in an emergency, a penalty offset by the cold air's invigoration. He felt good.

When Cindy came back on deck she sported an over-costume, a man's shirt and trousers. Bits of the batik jacket and slacks peeked out ludicrously, and graceful curves were transformed to a mass of lumps and bumps. She made a face at his unconcealed amusement, coming to his side to lean against him comfortably. The sight of the chain encircling Juan sent a stiffening wave through her, and he slipped an arm around her. "As a glamorous tropical experience, this has been a real loser," he apologized. She pulled the hand further around her shoulder, kissed it, said, "Take care of yourself. We'll make up for it."

They remained like that, moving infrequently, exchanging only brief words between long intervals of silence. Draeger watched the progression of stars, carefully purging the logic that wanted so desperately to come to grips with what was happening to him. In time, he was within a breath of surrendering himself to the raw atavism of enjoying the presence of a woman beside him and the prospect of outright adventure. The sea contributed, as it always has, stroking the hull, creating whispers that hinted of secrets unending. And, as the sea will do, it destroyed its own credibility. A course change brought them broadside to a hard chop that battered the cruiser, made it wallow and groan. Draeger became aware of scudding clouds cloaking the starlight. The deep-set cold bit fiercely at his vitals, no longer willing to be denied. He gripped Cindy in the curve of his arm and wished for the dawn that would eliminate this darkness that knew everything and understood it all.

A long time later the sunrise was a fiery slash on the horizon when Juan warned of the prau dead ahead.

# ■ CHAPTER 40 ■

The prau was large, with two men aboard. They worked well
together, infrequent vocal exchanges coming quietly in short bursts.
Making fast alongside, they made no effort to hide their surprise at
seeing Draeger accept their thrown lines. He doubted if they could
have ever hidden their surprise when they saw Cindy. A freshening
breeze came up as she reached the rail, and her hair streamed aft,
catching the first light of the burgeoning sun. The man at the rudder
made a pleased sound and his partner merely grinned and enjoyed.
Cindy smiled and waved. The man securing the two boats scrambled
from the prau onto the deck of the cruiser. Then it was his turn to
exclaim wordlessly, and natural curiosity fled, replaced by concerned wariness. He looked from Juan's chains to Jesus and stood
poised, hand on the knife at his hip while he turned his eyes to
Draeger.

Draeger said, "You speak English?" The man nodded. Draeger
worked up a faint smile. "These men think we will have trouble.
They want us to fight, me and you. Their boss, the man named
Pierce, wants me to be in trouble. He gave me a gun. I will show
you." Moving very slowly Draeger bent to the holster at his ankle
and pulled out the revolver. He watched the man by the rail improve
his grip on the hilt of his knife and subtly inch his weight forward
onto his left foot. When Draeger ejected the rounds he eased back.
There was no relaxation in his vigilance. At the sight of the hollow
catridges he released the knife and shook his head at Juan and the
recumbent Jesus. Then, pointing at the bullets, he asked simply,
"Why?"

"Because I know something he does not want me to tell your leader."

The man waited, unmoving, and Draeger shook his head, grinning. "I will tell him when I see him." That drew a smile at a bluff rejected. Draeger felt the calves of his legs ease. He needed a deep breath and thought he'd never tasted anything more welcome. Unless the man was a consummate actor, the tone was set for the next lap of his journey. There was to be some give-and-take. It was a thing such a man would never start if he simply intended to eliminate the other party at the first opportunity. Still, even as Draeger was thinking of that, the man gestured for him to surrender the automatic at his waist. Draeger pointed at the prau. "I keep the gun. You sit behind me. No problem. But I keep the gun."

For a moment it appeared the disagreement could grow to serious proportions. Cindy's calm voice defused the situation. "Glen, you forgot to tell him about the other guns."

The man hesitated, unsure of the words. Draeger said "Show him," and she hurried to the salon. The weight of the weapons had her staggering and banging the bulkheads when she returned. Juan frowned at that, and the inconsequence of scraped paint in the face of so much tension had Draeger burying fingernails in his palms to hold back laughter.

The man beamed at the loot. When he reached, Draeger put his hand on one of the automatics, indicating it was for Cindy to protect herself. The man stopped smiling long enough to nod complete agreement before lowering the rest to his partner, who accepted them with a quiet admonition, and a jerk of his chin toward the control bridge. Draeger interpreted the sound, rather than the words. He turned to Cindy.

"Be careful," he said, the inadequacy grating. "As soon as we're gone, Juan and Jesus'll be moaning about how uncomfortable they are, or misunderstood, or some damned thing. Leave them exactly as they are. Promise me."

Her glance their way frightened him, and he grabbed her arms. "Goddamit, listen to me!" She winced and he lowered his voice, loosed the grip slightly. "I don't know how any of this is going to work out, but the one thing I'm certain about is that I need to know you're all right, that there's something at the end of all this besides governments and bosses and lies and hate. I don't know what we mean to each other, but it's more than anything else we've got, isn't it?'' He was pleading, uncaring of the other men.

When she answered he knew she had dismissed them, too. He remembered her ability to cloak herself in her surroundings and make herself so individual she was practically unapproachable. She was like that now, contained, unique. She said, ''When you finish this, I'll be waiting.''

He kissed her, no more than a touch. It was the token men and women have exchanged as long as men have gone into danger and left the women to face the gentler terrors of loneliness, uncertainty, and predation from those who think them vulnerable. It is not a time for great passion so much as it is a time for communion. For Cindy it was revelation. As a woman who competed with men she had won and been reviled and lost and been scorned. She had been accepted as a working partner in her profession, and as a woman had known the burning darkness lovers share. Never before had anyone spoken to her of a commitment. Instinctively, speared by the genetic thrust of thousands of years, she knew his statement was conditional. The man must go, and he must survive. Worse, she looked in his eyes and knew he would always go. Like flames of different color, pride and dread spread through her breast. Practicality sneered at her, at all the idiocy that threatened the forthright matter of reproducing the species. A simple kiss, it told her more of herself than she had ever suspected and shook her soul.

When Draeger straightened from the same contact, there was no storm in him, no complex welter of thought and emotion. He only knew he had been released. What was to Cindy a statement that he must return told him that there was someone behind him who cared, and therefore there was both reason to go and to return. No man faces death so well as when he knows a woman will weep for him if he falls. Old men are no less susceptible than young ones, although they have the experience to know that when the woman stops crying, the man continues to be dead. For the young, it is refulgent hope. For the young who are experiencing it for the first time, they think they have discovered this thing, even if they cannot define it, and they go about their business with a great sense of invulnerability. Innumerable battles have been won on the dying efforts of men convinced of that truth. There will always be battles. Draeger kissed Cindy and was at last prepared for his.

Within seconds he was settling into the front of the prau. The rip of the unmuffled engine reached into Cindy's muscles, sapped them. Uninstructed, Juan started the cruiser's engines. The bass authority of the diesels immediately underfoot smothered the sharper pitch of the prau's departure. It broke the enervating spell, and she fixed the automatic on Juan's back and watched the narrow hull skim away until it was a needle in the distance trailing a cotton-floss wake. Juan altered course, the change in direction disconcerting her for a second, and when she looked back, she could find nothing but specks of foam pointing the way Draeger had gone.

For his part, he looked back only once. Taking his eyes from the dwindling hull, he caught the gaze of the man behind him and was surprised at the respect there. It was long into the trip before Draeger realized the man had been involved in similar good-byes himself. A warmth, a perception of kinship rushed across his thoughts, and he wished he knew this man better, understood his needs and wants, his aspirations. It occurred to him that the pursuit of some of those considerations might cause the man to blow his head off, and the incipient notion of brotherhood dwindled. He wriggled until his circle of vision included a clear view of the other man.

The sun was past meridian when they pressed directly for the small island. The vastness of the sea and sky held the scrap of land in a blue vacancy that balked his mind, made it seize on that solidity anxiously. Looking at it, he realized he merely used the sea.

The engine dropped steadily in pitch as they approached, letting the bow settle by degress until it was low enough to throw up bits of spray that blew back on Draeger. Until then, he hadn't appreciated how hot he'd become, excitement overriding the discomfort as it had the cold prior to dawn. He had to shake his head to convince himself that so few hours had passed. Then a canoe was slipping through the downed tree's branches. Within seconds he was transferred to it, along with the extra man from the motorized prau. A spider web in the leafy tangle avoided everything until he came, draped itself across his face. He struck out wildly, and his hand struck a small object that had a plump, fleshy texture. He jerked the hand away, lurched to the side of the canoe. The man behind him hissed angrily, and Draeger sat up, shuddering.

He looked back several times as they proceeded upstream, carefully checking the banks. A trail showed up on the left side from time to time, its course as tortuous as the stream's, almost parallel. Branches reached from the shore, and the memory of the spider web kept him in constant search to avoid any repetition.

The canoe stopped at a sharp bend. Several men stood around to watch him disembark, a group that could have been idlers, had they not all been carrying rifles and so quick to fall in behind him as he was guided toward the longhouses. Before they reached them he saw a man step from the central one. Draeger knew he was important. The man broadcast his status with stern features, stride that demanded way. He exuded a challenging arrogance. He wore native dress, the swirl of skirtlike dark material draped to his ankles and the jacketlike top in keeping with the primitive authority surrounding him.

On the spur of the moment, Draeger reached to touch the man who had ridden the prau with him and stopped short. The group halted, puzzled, and when he lifted the automatic from his belt, carefully using two fingers, a collective anticipation swept through them, the kinetic immobility of the pack savoring the smell of a strange wolf. Turning his back on the longhouses, he depressed the magazine release and let the rectangular box fall into his hand. Jacking the last round out of the chamber, he inspected the weapon and replaced it under his belt. He handed the ammunition to the man and turned to continue toward his meeting. A delicate sigh passed among the men, a rising and falling sound of approval and wonder. Draeger's confidence soared once more.

The man they approached stopped and waited for them to come to him. He had picked his spot well, a man who dealt in tactics emotionally as well as militarily. Feet spread across the narrow trail, flanked by a colonnade of tree trunks far more massive than any Roman stonework, his buildings floated on their pilings behind him, silent and mysterious as forest animals, thatched backs dappled with random sunbeams. There was no conversation, no greetings. Cloth rustled, weapons made embarrassed metallic clacks, feet scuffled. Draeger watched those he could see without turning. All eyes were on the man facing them. There was power there, and danger, and a vague sense of forces only marginally in check. Draeger walked to the man and put out his hand.

"My name is Glen Draeger. The man who arranged for me to come here has betrayed me and is no friend of yours. There are things we should talk about."

The man said nothing, gave no sign of hearing. His eyes took in Draeger with studied insolence, not intending to get an impression, but to give one. Initially, Draeger was infuriated, then decided it was to his benefit. Because he was aware of the other man's reasons, he had an advantage. He set his face, fastened his eyes on the incivility examining him and willed the ascetic face to look up, to meet his own, to let his eyes reveal themselves. When it happened he wanted to cheer. They matched stares until the man affected boredom, looked away. He called to one of his people and asked a question. The answer came with much head-bobbing and curtailed gesturing. At one point the man holding Draeger's ammunition held out a hand and displayed it. Draeger looked at it disinterestedly, noting the sweat greasing the older's palm. Satisfied he'd heard all the messenger could tell him, the man said, "My name is Bilongon. I have known Tony Pierce for a long time. I am not surprised he has betrayed you. It is his way. What interest is it to me?"

"Your man told you of the ammunition he gave me?"

Bilongon smiled. "That was very clever. I will remember it."

"He expected me to try to kill you or one of your men and to die for it. He injured a woman I care very much about."

Continuing to smile, Bilongon said, "But he knew you could not harm us. The ruined ammunition was for our protection."

"I disarmed myself. You saw."

"That could be an honest gesture or a very shrewd one. It is not an easy decision for me."

Draeger grinned slyly, indicated the armed men. "You think it was easy for me?"

Laughter exploded from Bilongon. Draeger was pleased to see relief and congratulation in many of the surrounding faces. It proved to him these were not mindless pirates who would kill a man to rifle his pockets free of disturbance.

"A man never knows what an American will say," Bilongon

said. "We will talk." He turned, then suddenly faced Draeger
again. "Tony gave me no instructions. No man does, especially no
foreigner, and most especially no one like Tony Pierce."

Draeger nodded, not even sure Bilongon saw, so quickly did the
Moro lead off. When they stopped they sat on a bench at the outdoor
theater.

"Why is Tony so anxious to see you dead? And at my hands?"

"He wanted to be sure the woman and I disappeared. I can't figure
why he wanted to mix you in it."

"You are such a menace?"

Draeger gestured. "He thinks so. I'm in a little trouble with the
government. I sell a few guns, a few pieces of hardware. I know
Tony can move people if he wants to, so I asked some friends some
questions, setting up some leverage, you know?"

Bilongon's features congealed. "So?"

"There's this guy I know who flies people around, people who
don't want to fool with customs and all—and who can afford him."
He looked sour, gauging Bilongon's reaction. What he saw encouraged him. "This pilot says Tony's arranging a very hush-hush run to
Singapore. When I ask Tony to take me and the woman, sort of
share expenses, he's all for it. Old partners. The next thing I know
the cops are on the way. Tony says our only chance is to take his
yacht and head here."

He looked away, composing himself, trying to appear hesitant.
What came next had to be perfect. "He said our best chance would
be to take you hostage and make you take us to Singapore. Lying
bastard said he'd hide me and the woman, because I know where
he'll be staying." As if an afterthought, he said, "He was making
damned sure he got one of us, wasn't he? I think you're in as much
danger from him as me."

Bilongon said, "I have always known he was capable of betrayal.
I cannot believe he is so foolish. He must know I have taken
precautions."

A slow chill moved through Draeger, starting at the extreme ends
of toes and fingertips, as if the night-cold had stalked him to this
steaming place and was fighting to claim what it failed to dominate
then. If Bilongon was truly covered, his hole card was worthless.
Trying to convince a man he was being double-crossed when he'd

already neutralized it would serve no purpose. There was one chance left, and there might not be another opportunity to take it. Bilongon had moved, almost imperceptibly, but he'd moved at the mention of Singapore. Draeger said, "Why would he be dumb enough to tell me I could get you to take me to Singapore, anyhow? What if I actually managed to make you a hostage? What the hell would he have done if we both showed up on his doorstep?"

Until he got a good look at Bilongon's eyes he was afraid the shot had missed. After seeing them, he was simply afraid. Totally dissociated, Bilongon's vision was centered on a point beyond Draeger, far beyond, and it bored through him to get there. Draeger stared into them, knowing they saw nothing of him. They were unblinking, alight with fury and calculation. Looking into that maelstrom revealed the mind behind the lenses, the messianic determination to fit the world to charismatic truths.

The faces of the men discreetly half-circled around them were as Draeger expected, enthralled, held as firmly as museum insects on their pins, individual spirits coalesced with Bilongon's into a fanatic whole.

Bilongon's next statement startled Draeger. "I am told the woman with you was ready to fight beside you, and that you let her take the two crewmen on Tony's cruiser back to Zamboanga as prisoners. That is true?"

The length of the statement saved Draeger from stammering. "Absolutely. She'll shoot them if she has to. Would have shot your men, too."

"Women are cruel and malicious, but I never knew one to show true courage." The soft voice rolled the language out easily. The earlier discussion might never have happened. "They are not like men. They are better than we are about pain. I have witnessed childbirth and that is a marvel of bravery, but they rarely have the strength to stand pressure for long periods. Your woman sounds different."

"She is."

"You are very fortunate. Perhaps." Bilongon leered. "She sounds formidable."

With another surprising change, he got to his feet, speaking with a greater lilt in his words. "Did Tony give you any details of his plans?"

When Draeger hesitated, he gestured him to his feet and applied gentle pressure to his elbow to start him walking. Draeger repressed a shudder at the touch and the unexplainable increase in interest from the men. A loathesome thing at the back of his mind giggled and whispered that this was a place that could take a man beyond dying.

Bilongon said, "You say Tony expected you to die here. You believe it. You could have escaped, but you came. You report the treachery. I know you want something, and I am growing impatient while you fish to see exactly what you can get in exchange for your own treachery. We are bargaining now. I think you are aware of the stakes. Tell me—what do you know of Tony's plans?" He indicated a turn at a fork in the path. There was a small hut along the branch to the right. A guard squatted in front of it, back against the wall.

A pair of armed men trailed Draeger and Bilongon. He glanced over his shoulder at them nervously before answering. "I want two things. I want out of here, and I want even with Pierce."

Bilongon stopped where the trail curved around a bend and lost itself in brush. He spread his arms. "Look at me. A poor man, a fighter for freedom. So many people try to use me. I must be very suspicious. It is all that keeps me alive. I distrust you, for instance. No, no—it must be said. However, you interest me. Unloading your own pistol as you did, delivering yourself to me with only this simpleminded tale—I confess my confusion. I must determine the facts of the matter. Either I will kill you or set you to kill Tony. We shall see."

He spoke sharply, and the two men hurried forward, weapons aimed at Draeger. Unspeaking, they jabbed at him, forced him around the bend. A man-sized cage waited there, and for an instant he refused to believe his eyes. A vile smell of decomposing feces wrenched his stomach. It wasn't until one of the men swung the door open that he reacted. The other, anticipating, clubbed his rifle across the back of Draeger's head. Dazed, he barely understood he was being searched, his pockets emptied. Material ripped, and the heavy weight of metal was gone from around his waist. A moment later Bilongen exclaimed aloud and laughed. Draeger offered meager

resistance before ending up bent over in the cage. There was insufficient room for him to fall to his knees, so that they jammed into the
poles in front while his buttocks wedged against the ones in back.
Pain tormented him out of blissful unconsciousness. He hung on the
bars and wiped a string of saliva off his chin with an unsteady hand.
The door was already closed and chained, locked.

Bilongon kicked the cage. "It would have amused my men to see
you in there with the blond woman. Pity. Maybe we can find other
ways for you to entertain us."

Draeger was alone in the cage with the stench and the multitudes
of flies for over an hour before he realized the black gummy mess
coming off the bars on his hands and clothes was dried blood,
reliquefied on contact with his sweat. He bit back a scream and
scrubbed and scrubbed his hands on his trousers, as far down as he
could reach in the cramping cage. By the time he was satisfied,
sweat was pouring from him, oozing through the seams of his shoes,
squelching nastily when he moved his feet. Jamming the tingling
hands in his pockets, he leaned back and rested, breathing steadily,
slowly, staring at the light-fringed leaf canopy until he was calm
again.

"Control," he said softly. "The secret is control." Gritting his
teeth, he began stalking the flies landing on the bars, flipping them
with a suddenly released finger, listening to their crippled buzzing
when they crashed in the forest litter. Falling darkness ended his
sport, and he spat quiet obscene curses into the night. The flies
would be back with daybreak, their numbers unaffected. He took
some consolation from the steady decline in the wirelike noises of
their dying.

# ■ CHAPTER 41 ■

Morning seeped into the forest warily, testing darkness's strength. Birds in the topmost branches knew of it first, their uncertain movements and tentative calls reminding the awkward shape in the cage of hospital sounds. It was a complaining, a cranky stirring, but it grew heartier as it grew louder. It was light enough for Draeger to see to the bend in the trail when the camp roosters put their raucous guarantee on day's arrival.

The man approaching him carried a kerosene lantern. There had been other movement off in the distance, infrequent sounds, bits of light flicking through the trees. Draeger saw the globular orange aura moving and knew it was someone coming to him. There was no reason to believe that, but he wanted it so desperately he made it a fact. The globe danced in the distance, the perfection of its shape constantly violated by intervening plant growth. For a freezing few seconds it disappeared entirely. When it reappeared Draeger stifled a laugh he knew would be an idiot giggle. The light had passed behind one of the larger trees, and that seemed unbearably funny, now that it was visible again.

The reaction passed quickly. He reached for the bars, forcing his fingers around them, pulling himself as erect as possible. The roof pushed his head down, put his chin almost on his chest. As a result, when the lantern-bearer rounded the bend his first view of Draeger was of a rearing beast, paws poised to grab, eyes burning out of a skull tucked back to protect the throat. It stopped the man in his tracks. He made a huffing noise deep in his chest, like a startled dog.

Draeger hadn't intended to create so dramatic an effect, but it delighted him. In the long, painful night he'd come to understand many things about character. Clearest of those revelations was the existence of weakness. Regardless of strength, weakness would triumph in the end. If they wanted to break him, given enough time they would do it. That had come to him while he considered exactly how he would resist. He knew he would be good at it. His self-argument started with the premise that he would be his own man each day, not let them turn him into some fawning fool, simply by forcing himself to anticipate rescue tomorrow. Then a small voice asked who would trouble, and the plan disintegrated. Of the people who knew he was missing, or who would learn, only Cindy would care.

He was alone.

When he tried to tell himself he was alone by profession, it was a flaccid lie that withered instantly. Aloneness had been a group condition, an outlaw association. One knew others. Working for an identifiable goal helped. His mind drifted to some of his more foolish attempts to be part of his homeland, the casual trips to and through Olongapo simply because there were Americans living on the base there. There were days when he went across the city to watch the flag atop the embassy. There was patriotism involved, but it was more than that. It was a personal reaffirmation that the country produced men who represented it, that his land waited. The inability to draw similar satisfaction from visiting with tourists or other expatriates puzzled and amused him. Part of his mind welcomed dealing with them, but a dim aversion drove him from their company. They were away from home of their own will, their mission was self-oriented, they were going back soon. His contact with them was fleeting and shallow. If any of that breed read of his disappearance they would cast even more covert looks at everyone not of their group and pull back further into their ghetto. The Filipino newspapers would drop the matter quickly, patting each other on the back for valiantly printing the news while wisely refusing to escalate the matter into something that might embarrass the regime.

*One morning I'll wake up, and I'll have to straighten my knees no matter what the cost. Pissing on myself, rotting my skin, and my*

*clothes will reach the point of intolerance. There'll be other things.*
*Worse. Then I'll do anything to get out of here. I'll make them work,*
*by God. I won't do it for them. They won't break me today. The*
*sun's already rising, the roosters are crowing. In a little while it'll*
*be noon, then night, and whatever happens today'll end and I'll be*
*through it. They won't get me today.*

And now he'd scored his first victory. He treasured the sight of
the jailer's sprung jaw, and widened eyes. Black shadows whirled
away from the lantern swinging in the arrested hand. A tremor jerked
the right eyelid in triple-beats, one-two-three, pause, one-two-three.

The entire episode lasted seconds. Draeger thought how long that
might have to sustain him and sagged. The man with the lantern
advanced and jammed a leaf through the bars. There was rice
wrapped in it, and some slivers of fish. Draeger lifted it to his mouth
with infinite care and scooped until the last grain was consumed.
Then he licked the leaf. That done, he considered eating it, but
decided there wasn't enough food value to take the chance on being
sick over it. Only after that did he think to look for the man who'd
brought it. He had no idea when he'd gone, hadn't even noticed the
disappearance of the lantern's glow. Music started off in the distance,
a surprising rock-and-roll radio broadcast. The music was welcome,
the babbling cheer of the disc jockey obscene.

Some time later, when the radio was silent and the camp murmured to itself, when the sun had risen high enough to make stained
glass of the forest roof, Bilongon appeared. There was no sound to
announce his coming. Today he wore more conventional clothes,
shorts and T-shirt. The inevitable knife in its polished sheath hung
from his belt. The shirt was old, but the green-lettered advertising
message for the United Coconut Planter's Bank was still clear.

Draeger worked his knees. One of them cracked, a confused
sound like fracturing bamboo, the destruction of multiple fibers
instead of one single stick.

Bilongon spoke quickly, and another man hurried around the bend
and busied himself with the door, then swung it open with a flourish.
Draeger stumbled forward, hanging onto the cleared door frame,
blocking it with his body even though he was unable to stand
without support. Unsure of the message in his eyes he looked at the
ground. Bilongon said, "Our radio in Zamboanga says your woman

arrived there safely. The two men are arrested. They will say only that you stole the boat and made them run it. Do you know Colonel Arroyo?''

Draeger shook his head. Bilongon continued. "He is an important man. He has gone on leave unexpectedly. To Manila. His dog, a Captain named Cruz, had Tony Pierce brought from his island and then returned. Several people report he is planning a trip to Singapore. It is said he is to meet a friend there.''

"Where is Cindy—the woman—staying?''

"Cruz has her where you stayed when you arrived with her. She is guarded.''

Draeger tested his legs, massaged the back of his neck. Bilongon made conversation. "You are the third American I have met in the past three or four years. What is happening to your people? Do you speak the truth to anyone?'' His laugh crackled like fire. "It would be well if one of you could be better at it than poor Tony.''

"He's a son of a bitch. He set me up.''

Bilongon dismissed Draeger's anger. "He does what he must, not what he chooses. He needs to feel superior. Information is his weapon. He thinks to make himself superior to me because he thinks he has the information to work behind my back. He will learn nothing is as he imagined, not even friendships. He is alone.''

The word lodged in Draeger's mind, an ice-particle of pain and memory from the night before. He forced himself a step away from the cage. The man who opened the door looked questioningly at Bilongon and was frowned back to immobility.

Draeger asked, "Pierce was working with this Arroyo and who else? I understand you've got a pretty good business going in logs and other stuff.''

"A pretty good business.'' Bilongon spat on the ground. "I am forced to damage the very land I am trying to save. That must change. There are people who will help us with arms, explosives. Soon we will take what we want from the government. Money from the bloodsucking banks, guns from the puppet troops. The people will rise with us.''

"Good for you. Exept Pierce is probably on his way to hijack your next load of guns or whatever right now.''

Bilongon widened his eyes in burlesqued surprise. "That is what you think? You are wrong. And the reason for Tony's proposed trip to Singapore is immaterial. The important fact is that he can no longer influence my intentions. Even his leaders are done with him.''

"Leaders?'' Draeger took another step away from the cage, held his balance. "What leaders? He doesn't have any leaders.'' The words almost ran away with him, he almost added *around here*.

"But he does. You should know that. You said you worked with him.''

"I worked with him. I don't know everything about him.''

"I wonder.'' Bilongon ran a hand through his hair, thinking. "Does the name Munson mean anything to you?''

Draeger tried to move too quickly, stumbled. The other man stepped forward in time to catch him. Draeger accepted it without a glance, eyes only for Bilongon, who stepped back.

"Munson? You saw him? When? Where?'' Draeger strained against the unyielding figure holding him upright. The man smiled at Bilongon, indicating his burden's weakness.

Bilongon said, "He arrived two days before you and left the same night.''

"Describe him.'' Draeger's voice cracked. He didn't care. He clenched his fists until the nails dug into his palms, dreading the truth, knowing what it must be.

"Very tall, very thin, blue eyes. No flesh on the face, all bones and skin. Beard. Glasses.'' He would have continued but Draeger stopped him, holding up a hand that suggested he was trying to stop a beating. Lamely, some of his rocklike assurance chipped away, Bilongon said, "You know him.''

"Jesus!'' Draeger slumped against the man holding him, sending them both staggering off the trail to lodge against a tree. Cursing, he pushed the man away and hauled himself fully erect. He steadied himself with a surreptitious hand planted almost naturally against the tree. "Do I know him? I thought I did. He killed his wife. He tried to kill me.''

"And you have no idea why he's going to Singapore?'' Another piece of Bilongon's composure fell away. Even in his self-recrimination, Draeger saw it. It gave him something to work with. There was a way out. He felt his thoughts resuming order.

"I don't know why exactly. I know they'll cheat you. I told you what Munson did to me. You're here and they're in Singapore? You don't have a chance."

Abruptly, Bilongon spun and stepped to the apex of the trail's curve, then faced Draeger again. "It would please me to kill you. You are cunning, a troublemaker. I do not know what you want. That gives you an advantage."

"I want to destroy Munson."

"I believe that. It is the only thing about you I do believe." He stopped, eyes penetrating, demanding. The colorless words smoked through the air. "You would not kill a man for causing you personal pain. You would punish. When you say that is the reason you want to kill Munson you lie. There is something else."

He spoke in dialect to the third man, then, "You will go with him. You will be given more food, and your clothes will be washed."

"What's going on?"

Bilongon turned again, belligerent warning in the thrust of his jaw. "I do not face uncertainty by standing still, so I must take a risk now. I do not like risks, and I do not like you. You will do what I tell you to do, or I will put you back in that cage and leave you there until we can lift the bones out between the bars."

After a few excruciating steps, Draeger's body responded to the new freedom. The pain retreated rapidly. He thought of men cooped like that for weeks, for months. Violent spasms rolled through his stomach at the thought. His guide led him to a different trail, one that led away from the camp to break out onto the slim, silver beach. From the forest to the water was a matter of steps, and Draeger took them almost gaily, throwing himself face down. Stripping off his clothes took only seconds, and he was gloriously naked, rid of the soiled mess. He pushed them to the bottom and danced on them in the shallows. He was still splashing when the guide popped out of the forest again, this time carrying a bar of soap, a mirror, and a knife with an eight-inch blade. Miming shaving with the weapon, Draeger sent the guide into fits of laughter, but he nodded that this was what was expected.

After scrubbing, Draeger sat in a foot of water with the mirror clamped between his knees and the blade in hand. There were a few unsatisfactory moments, but as long as he used plenty of soap it went well enough. He finished the job with only two small nicks. Plus a healthy respect for whoever sharpened the knife. He wondered if there was a shortage of razors in the camp or if the whole thing wasn't one more psychological nudge. When he hauled himself onto the beach the guide provided him with a pair of shorts, small but acceptable, and gestured for Draeger to hurry. Uncaring that his ward could only smile and nod, he talked constantly all the way back to the small hut Draeger had noted the night before.

It was dark inside, the only illumination coming from the open door and a shaded window. The cloth over the window was a print, dark blue and brown, admitting dim light and imparting a subtle wash to the interior. Standing just inside the threshold, Draeger felt immersed. The man escorting him snatched the wet clothes from his hand and sprinted down the trail.

Bilongon was seated at a table, the white T-shirt hovering in the gloom. The gesture with an arm was as much sensed as seen, and he said, "Sit down. I must ask you some questions."

Draeger positioned himself opposite Bilongon. Both men leaned forward in identical positions, forearms extended on the surface of the table, hands facing inward, fingers curled in loose fists. Bilongon smiled at the similarity. "We are alike in some ways, are we not? But we are very different, too. It would be interesting to know you better, although I don't think we could ever be friends."

"Not as long as you're able to stick me in that cage."

Bilongon's smile tightened. "That was necessary. Perhaps that is one of the things that separates us. I understand what is necessary."

"Right now it's necessary that I get out of here. I have things to do."

"And you've given me something to do. I want to be sure Munson and Pierce are not working against me."

Draeger favored him with a pitying smile. Bilongon shifted irritably. "You want them for your reasons. I must insure my plans are not compromised. I am taking you to Singapore with me." At Draeger's impulsive movement, Bilongon said, "You go as a prisoner. As long as I am satisfied Munson is doing what I wish him to do, he will never know of your existence. You are my hunting dog. You will get him for me if I choose it." Again, Draeger moved, and he correctly interpreted the visual cue. "You dislike being dependent on my choice. I understand. You see, a man in my position learns to use whatever weapons come to hand. That is why the strong call the weak untrustworthy and deceitful. Those are the weapons we use first.''

"And I'm another of your weapons?''

Bilongon lifted one shoulder in a delicate shrug.

Draeger continued, pressing. "Don't you think of yourself that way sometimes? As a weapon to free the people who follow you?''

"I do. I am.'' The sharp chin raised proudly.

"Don't you ever ask yourself, then, who is using you? If you can use me to catch Munson, who may be using you, and for what purpose?''

Camp noises swelled in the silence. A chicken clucked and scratched industriously. When Bilongon spoke, he rose to his feet to do so, leaning across the table at Draeger. "You are a very unpleasant companion. You twist people's words.''

Draeger said nothing, waited for Bilongon's next move. He went on, "We must move without delay. Munson is already in Singapore. We will leave here in a few hours and travel to a fishing village where there is a *kumpit* waiting. It will take us to Sabah, about fourteen hours away. There is a landing strip there, on the west coast. We fly from there to Kota Kinabalu and then to Singapore. Your passport will be taken care of. You will use which one?''

"The American.'' The answer was ready. Using the American passport might be helpful if he was being looked for. A small chance, better than none.

Bilongon left, speaking on the way. "You may want to sleep. Food will be brought in a few minutes. Stay here. I will send a man when it is time to go.''

And so it goes, Draeger thought, slouching in the chair. A step closer to Munson. Closer to Egg Roll. He's the one who can tell them. If he holds to his schedule, he'll be there.

While he delighted in Egg Roll's proximity to complete escape, he accepted the fact that it might be someone else to actually make contact with him.

He realized how much better the Chinese's position was than his own. He hadn't thought of it before. He wished he never had.

There was his own escape to engineer.

Maybe there was always one more.

■ CHAPTER 42 ■

They made a truly motley crew in the prau headed for the anchored *kumpit*. Each carried a suitcase, modern lightweight aircraft luggage, out of place as snowballs. All four passengers wore plain cotton khaki trousers and T-shirts. Draeger's featured a local rum. His other trousers nestled in the suitcase. They'd been returned with the lead foil Pierce had passed off as gold.

The two men Bilongon brought with him were young and had the poised, ready ease of soldiers who know their trade. The last man in the vessel was the owner, a sere, wrinkled ancient who looked at Draeger with unconcealed hatred.

The *kumpit* was dirty and she smelled of cow dung, fish, copra, and things too numerous and exotic to individualize. Once they were aboard, Bilongon sent Draeger below. There was no explanation, and he could only assume the measure was to avoid the possibility of being spotted by a helicopter. The discovery of a cot brought on the weariness he'd denied on the hike through the jungle. With nothing else to do, he stretched out on the slick plastic and enjoyed the syrupy relaxation of aching muscles. A huge cockroach perched on a packing case and wiggled curious antennae at him. The sight of it jerked him off the cot. It disappeared before he could reach it. He made some half-hearted sweeping efforts at his bed and lay back down.

The ship made little noise in her easy roll. Her timbers sighed, rather than groaned, sometimes raising a voice to emphasize a point. The odors faded to insignificance soon. He felt himself involved in the ambiance that struck him on the dock in Zamboanga. The spirit of the ship was in those quiet confidences she exchanged with her sea. Her flaws were cosmetic. There was a faithfulness in her. She would protect him. Not until that moment, enclosed in hot, humid darkness, slippery with sweat and surrounded by the murmuring soothing, did he ever understand the womanness of a vessel.

His thoughts fled the ship, went to Ria and Cindy. How would they react to his insight? Ria would be delighted. She loved moods, the emotional impacts of life. She would be involved in his feelings. Cindy would intellectualize the event, analyze why he would feel that way, understand the male function in him that would make him sensitive to such nuance. And she would be happy for him. She might never intuitively or even logically grasp his experience, but she would be glad for it, share its ramifications, if not its source. She would be part of a man the way a nut and bolt form a whole. Ria would want the elements welded. If a man failed to empathize that fully with Ria, she would feel rejected. Cindy would insist on her own emotional privacy from time to time, would demand occasions that no one should know exactly how she felt about anything.

Another thought came, and he struggled to keep it from his consciousness. It persisted and won. He saw Ria and Boy Angel, heard her screams, saw Cindy trussed in a bag, sent to whatever fate was waiting. He had drawn them into those circumstances. He searched inside himself for one excuse that didn't bring more guilt than it expiated.

Engines rumbled aft, and the ship shook off her lethargy, filled with impatient vigor.

*The dun mare frisked, gave a perfunctory crow-hop and settled into a stiff-legged trot. She wasn't really a pony. Mama said she was just a worthless runty horse, but Dad called her a pony and let him name her Buckshot. How many miles did they cover together, how many afternoons were they Roy Rogers and Trigger, how many coups had he counted when he was Flying Hawk and the iron-mounted jughead was the handsomest, fiercest warhorse of the whole Comanche tribe? Never enough time, always home for chores*

*or schoolwork. And the Fitzgerald dog, the mangy bitch that hid
behind the fence and rushed out to nip Buckshot's heels and set her
to bucking and rearing on the dangerous macadam. They'd fixed
her. Caught her almost a mile from home and chased her howling
ass all the way back. After that she ran under the house and barked
whenever they came by. Dad laughed at that. "Good work, boy.
Never get mad, just get even. Always remember that dog. Whoever
you go up against, win or lose, make damn sure they ache every
time they hear your name for ever after."*

The sea air flowed through the open hatch, cooling. Loose papers
on the packing cases fluttered softly. In moments Draeger was sound
asleep. He ground his teeth in rhythm with the movement of the
Celebese Sea.

Bilongon's people made the crossing of international borders a
joke. They made landfall on the west coast of Sabah before dawn.
Draeger had no idea where he was and asked only once. Bilongon
extended a limp hand and said, "Labuk Bay is that way," as if it
explained everything. In a sense, it did. It told Draeger he was mere
baggage.

After scrambling onto a rickety dock, they hurried ashore. The
welcoming party was small. Unable to see well enough to count,
Draeger estimated no more than five. Soft syllables tumbled in the
air among them, the long vowels predominant in Draeger's hearing,
altering the strange language to hushed songs. Rifles and at least one
submachine gun provided grim background percussion, clattering
into each other occasionally. The smell of oiled metal drowned sea,
ship, and people through sheer suggestion.

One of Bilongon's men brought up the rear, clearly watching
Draeger. The other hovered over his leader, and Draeger noticed he
stayed to the left. If Bilongon had reason to draw the knife, his right
hand was clear. Nor was there any delay in moving to the truck.
They went quickly, a fast walk, into the open shed where it waited
for them and onto the cargo bed. The suitcases went under a tarp,
and Draeger was presented with a soft hat, the kind used by the
military, so that his face was shielded when the brim was pulled
down. Bilongon moved close to inspect him better. He smiled his
satisfaction.

"You look enough like one of us to get by until the light gets too bright. There are no troops in this area, but it is best to eliminate gossip from the people who live here. Your lighter skin should be no problem." He chuckled, backing up as he did. "It must be strange for a white man to want to look like us. You should examine your feelings in this matter." He thought well enough of his joke to recount it for the two men with him. Draeger could barely make out their faces. Their laughter was like muffled brass.

The old truck delivered them to a rough field Draeger was glad he couldn't see well. Moving toward the plane, he stepped in a hole and nearly fell. Bilongon caught him by the shoulder. He chuckled. "The landing area is a little smoother, fortunately."

The aircraft was dark, an ominous blur against the night. The four of them crowded in, Bilongon taking the forward seat next to the pilot. There was enough light to make out individual trees as they swept by them on takeoff. The pilot hauled back on the yoke to avoid those at the end of the runway. Airborne, Draeger was able to attach some reality to the event. The forest and distant sea were gray-cloaked, waiting for the day.

They kept low on the flight. Draeger saw smoke pillars wavering up through the forest canopy and forgot his own problems in wondering what life must be like for the people down there.

Perhaps they prayed silently for the plane to sputter and fall. What a bonanza that would be, watches and guns and knives. Even the women would have something to cheer about, with all that wonderful aluminum for pots and utensils.

He smiled to himself. It was becoming routine to think of himself as part of a package, a commodity. What difference was there in a group of illiterate hunters and gatherers picking over his dead carcass and a group of scheming power-brokers pawing through his mind and skills for a particular asset to fit their wants? Maybe that said a great deal. At least the forest dwellers weren't actively trying to bring him down. They were willing to leave the matter to their gods. The power-brokers wanted to be gods.

Was that what he wanted? In the beginning, yes. The admission hurt. He wanted to control, to manipulate. In return, he'd been manipulated, seen the horrible results of others dictating movements. Still, he was in the intelligence business, and the soul of that was using people. There was no other way. Other troublesome thoughts loomed in his mind, like the distant clouds on the horizon.

"Kota Kinabalu." Bilongon's announcement interrupted him. The Filipino was pointing forward and down, indicating a sprawl of buildings, vivid against earth colors. Draeger wondered why towns always looked white and clean from the air and so scruffy when one was actually in them. They weren't even white, up close, but gray and brown, and violent primaries slapped against vitality-absorbing pastels. Now, however, the green roofs were crisp, to the right a dome of gold challenged the sun, and a bit farther away in the opposite direction something blue flashed, either a pool or tiles. Bilongon extended Draeger his passport.

"This is in order. Here is our story. We left Zamboanga this morning on our way to Singapore. The plane is needed back in Zamboanga. I am in the timber business. You are a forestry management expert. My men are my assistants. I have made many trips through here. The authorities are anxious to maintain a quiet relationship with the Philippines, so we will not embarrass them at all, you understand? Please be quiet if we are questioned. I will talk."

Draeger nodded, instinctively bracing as the pilot made a hard, sinking turn to line up the runway.

The officials were correct, precise, and suspicious. As with all law enforcement people, they had an awareness of things off-center. They looked at all papers and the dress of men ostensibly headed for a major metropolis. Bilongon's men casually opened the small cargo compartment and extracted the suitcases, stowing their knives as they did. Draeger could only be impressed by the smoothness of the thing. He'd seen border operations, but nothing so casually competent as these people. Even the officials afforded them professional respect.

They changed clothes in the washroom, consigning the old ones to the trash container. In his new costume, Bilongon was the mod-casual image of the alert Philippine entrepreneur. The others were his retinue. He led the way to the Malaysian Airlines counter and paid for four tickets. Breakfast passed in silence for Draeger while his three companions chatted in low tones in their own dialect. Their plane was announced, and they joined the boarding line, stepping out into the morning brightness, the red *kalantan*, the Malay kite that is the airline's logo, blazed on the silver body. This take-off was vastly different, the sleek Boeing sliding into the clear sky effortlessly. There would be much to do when the plan landed. Draeger slumped, saw inside his mind, watched his muscles ease and loosen. He willed himself to concentrate. One of the stewardesses caught him nodding and hurried to produce a pillow. Only as he was laying his head on it and she was leaving did the green and black of her batik dress register on him. He thought of his apartment, of the hanging on the wall. A long time ago he'd wanted to show that to Ria.

Even when the stewardess checked to see if his seat belt was fastened for landing, he continued to hide behind closed eyes. His thoughts had twisted, taken another course. He was stacking recalled injuries, misered coins to be spent extravagantly at the right time. The forces that held him in balance were testing strengths, anticipating acceptable compromises, moral limits, personal and extra-personal demands.

The thirty-minute taxi ride from the airport to the city was a welcome break. In its industry, its mass of population, Singapore is the Orient. It is polyglot, far more so than Hong Kong. Still, it is fundamentally Oriental and, at bedrock, Chinese. The entire environment reflects the Chinese penchant for hard, unceasing, do-it-better work. Buildings appeared to be leaping from the ground as they approached, newer crowding older, like trees in a forest.

The hotel chosen by Bilongon was antiseptically modern, touches of Southeast Asian influence strewn about to remind the tourists of their location, much as a manufacturer of antiques might leave a few square-headed nails showing. The place seemed a rather gaudy choice for a man representing people who might earn enough in a year to rent a room for a week. Bilongon rented two rooms, one for himself. They gathered in the other. He unfolded a map on the table. Draeger was curtly ordered away, out of visual range. The two men followed Bilongon's pointing finger, listening with growing concern. When he stopped they complained in cajoling tones. He spoke shortly and they subsided.

He turned to Draeger. "They are afraid something will happen to me, and they are sworn to protect me. I am going to question Munson. They are young and full of honesty. They can't understand that Munson needs me, can't imagine the confused coils we make of life."

"I envy them."

"I know you do. It is a failing that will elevate you to great position or destroy you in humble surroundings. I don't know which is most likely."

"Spoken like a fortune teller. You can't be wrong."

"I am saying this desire for integrity will drive you. Pierce has no idea what it is. Munson appears to have had it and renounced it. You have tried to throw it off and failed. Men like me use men like you. Power slips from us. You are there to catch it, but you don't want it. There is always one like me to relieve you of the burden. The game goes on."

"We're not in a game. Men have died. More will die."

"And while we live, we fight for power." He waited for Draeger's expression and laughed at it, pleased to have angered him. "Any goal that differentiates one man, one group, one nation from another view of that same goal creates a struggle for power. Man is destined to constant conflict."

Draeger rose, turned his back. Bilongon laughed again. Only when he spoke to his men did Draeger face him, and the smaller man looked at his prisoner as he got to his feet. "I am going. You will stay with these men. When I am satisfied I will return, and we will decide what to do about you. If I continue to suspect Munson I will send you and my men after him."

"You think he's going to tell you he's double-crossing you? You expect a confession?"

Bilongon posed. "I have been at this work too long. Munson will never fool me when we are face to face."

"You go to him alone and he'll kill you." Draeger saw his hope of vindication, his life, fading. He pleaded the case to the two men. "Don't let him go! Stop him!"

Bilongon frowned at them, and they dropped their gaze to the floor. He spoke to Draeger as he left. "Munson needs me, my people. I said I used men like you. It is true. I use you and respect you, and you are the only ones I fear. Men like Munson and Pierce are cowards. I use them, too, but only when I know I have something they must have."

Draeger could compare the departure to nothing but a thousand Saturday afternoon cowboy heroes, off to handle crooked sheriffs, venal land barons, and natural disasters. He didn't know if he should applaud, cry, or laugh.

# ■ CHAPTER 43 ■

A clean-shaven Munson watched the taxi roll to a stop with an expression of puzzled annoyance that snapped to furious disbelief when he recognized the passenger. An involuntary growl vibrated in his chest. Another man joined him at the window, a Filipino. His features were a series of minor disturbances on a plain. The eyes were too far apart and too small, the nose and mouth unsuited to the sweep of the cheekbones. The body was compact. An experienced eye would know it was in less than good muscular condition, but tough as bricks. He said, "Who is that? What does he want?"

"I don't know what he wants," Munson rasped. "He's not supposed to be here."

Bilongon paid the driver. Munson surveyed the room quickly. It was a large one, in a large house, a rich man's home, secluded on manicured grounds. Privacy alone was a testimonial to the success of at least one man's ability within Singapore's economy. The luxury of the place emphasized that success. The furniture was imperial in size, material, and workmanship. The art was eclectic and expensive.

Munson pointed at an easy chair near the sofa. "When he comes in, we'll sit over there. I want you in the blue chair so you can watch him. He can be very dangerous, Benjamin. Be ready to shoot." Suiting action to the warning, Munson hurried to the other chair and took a small automatic from his belt holster and shoved it down beside the cushion.

Letting the echoes of the door chimes dwindle, he silently gestured Benjamin to the proper chair. The mellow notes were sounding a second time when he swung the door open to act out pleased surprise at Bilongon's presence. "Bilongon, my friend! What are you doing here?" Suddenly concerned, then, "Is everything all right? No trouble?"

"I am here to see if everything is all right." Bilongon's smile was engineered to perfection. There was social grace, a hint of question, a touch of mystery. It lacked only a sign of gladness to make it genuine.

Munson ushered him inside, maneuvered him to the sofa. "I don't understand. Everything's exactly as it should be." He reacted as if seeing the man in the easy chair for the first time. "Oh, I forgot. This is Mr. Perez, Benjamin Perez. He's working with me here. Benjamin, this is Mr. Bilongon."

Benjamin was moving to shake hands until he heard the name. The gesture suddenly changed; the hand curved to land on Benjamin's throat where it scratched lazily. Munson tensed, even as he thought how wondrously feline of Benjamin to turn surprised rejection into a histrionic display of unconcerned intention.

Bilongon recognized the matter for what it was, refusal to come in contact with a Moslem. The silver bells spoke to him, shy, retiring, their music no more than a brushstroke across his hearing. When the music was like that, at its softest, his mind helped his ears by painting pictures that allowed him to see the sounds. If the bells grew louder, the pictures went away, but sometimes they left color behind.

He solemnly nodded to Benjamin and sat on the sofa.

Munson said, "Why did you come? It could be dangerous."

"Everything is fine. I will not be here long. I came because of some worrisome news. Arroyo left unexpectedly for Manila. I don't like it when he makes surprising moves. My people hear rumors that Tony Pierce is coming here. Both things at once convinced me I should speak to you."

The voice was properly concerned. It was the accent, the manner, that stung Munson. The words came as precise as guardsmen. It was privilege speaking to inferior, an assertion of superiority. He elected to ignore it for the present.

"I can understand your concern. The rumors are wrong about Tony. And Arroyo! Who knows why he'd go up there? Probably getting his ass chewed."

"Perhaps. Still, it is disturbing for someone as vulnerable as I am to see things happening and not know why."

Munson shifted in his chair. "All I can tell you is that everything here's number one, Bilongon. Tonight's the last night of the conference. By this time tomorrow it'll be all over."

"All over?" Bilongon exclaimed. "It will be starting for us."

"I didn't mean it that way. I meant the land operation would be over, that's all."

An old hand at tension and arguments, Benjamin slid his outstretched feet back across the carpet until they were against the base of the chair. While the other men stared at each other, he lifted his weight up on his elbows.

Without turning his head, Bilongon said, "I brought men to Singapore with me, Benjamin. They know where I am. If there is any trouble here, they will find you."

Munson said, "I think it'd be better if we talked alone, Benjamin. Wait outside, please." When the door closed behind him, he spun to Bilongon again. "You brought others? How many?"

"Three, actually. You would not know two of them."

"They know I'm here? That you came to see me?" Munson's voice rose steadily.

"As you said, by this time tomorrow it will be over."

"If they're caught they know too much!"

"The same is true of my men waiting to take the Japanese away. And it is even more true of the Japanese themselves. If one of them is captured we are all compromised."

Munson jackknifed upright so quickly Bilongon started. The tall man didn't notice, walked to the far wall of the living room and back again. "You force my hand. I have a confession to make."

The bells sang brightly, coming closer.

"I've altered the plan. Nothing serious. Safer. I've worried about our security right from the start. I've taken steps to protect us."

Bilongon said "And?" trusting himself no further than a single word. The bells sang blue, an acetylene flame. Exciting.

Munson sat down again. "We agreed to provide escape for the Japanese because the people who hired them want them rescued. They were supposed to be made to talk, though, admit who hired them. Right?"

Bilongon nodded, and the light-song jangled.

"As soon as the raid is over, I'll eliminate any of the Red Army people who survive. Benjamin has five men for that job. Once it's done, we leave for a ship. It takes Benjamin and his men to Manila and I continue on. At my destination I hold a press conference and the world learns who eliminated the terrorists and I reveal the people who hired them."

"You will confess to the counter-terror killing of Red Army personnel? You must be very sure of your hiding place. Where would that be, Roger? With the Chinese, after they lose people here? I think not. With the Soviets, where you identify them as anti-Moslem? No. In America? It would make them happy, certainly. They could cover themselves with soul-searching debate, have a huge trial for you. None of these things seem probable to me."

Munson sat straight, back rigid. His eyes had trouble staying in one place, strayed about Bilongon's features. The line of his vision caromed off, bulletlike, and he had to struggle to focus. "What are you saying? You accuse me of bad faith?"

"You are here with that pig Benjamin, and you tell me there are others like him. Yet you have only been here two days. You planned to eliminate the Japanese all along. You are protecting the people who use them. You are against Islam!"

"That's not true. I want to eliminate men like these terrorists, the ones who perpetuate power-bloc strife. I am part of an organization. We are a new face on the world! Look, as long as we have governments, we'll have wars. One day will come the big one. Who'll survive? You? Me? Hell, no. The ones who want power! So give it to them! How obvious it is! One government, controlling! No more arguments over pollution controls, land use, mining the sea! Stability!"

"This small group you mention, it will tell us how to manage our affairs, I'm sure. And you will, naturally, have an important position in that group.''

Munson was up and pacing again, long arms flailing. ''If I can destroy this conference I can show all the power-brokers that we can attack them any time, any place. Our group understands we need a world of order. I am a messenger.''

''And you are an example of this enlightenment?''

Unaware he was posed full in a pillar of sun pouring in a window, Munson halted. The light scribed the gaunt features, caricatured them. He gestured with an outflung hand, a cartooned blessing. ''Personal gain corrupts, personal sacrifice ennobles. I'm even turning my back on the government I've served all my life.''

''You turn your back on everyone.'' Bilongon rose from the sofa. ''If I had not come here and seen what I have seen, your man Pierce would have died as soon as my men returned with the news. You knew that. You would let him die.''

''He is a soldier. He had his function. It is over. Sacrifice is his duty.''

''But you will make money and survive. That is your duty?''

Munson flushed, closed his eyes. By the time he opened them his color was normal. ''The faction that provides me support is small. There is never enough money. For now, they need my experience and knowledge. The cause needs me alive, and I need money to live. Is that sinful?''

''In itself, no.'' Bilongon sighed. ''We find ways to make all our needs evil eventually, don't we?''

Munson produced a smile Bilongon had never seen before, a pursed-lip, squint-eyed thing of sugary piety. Through it, he said, ''The cause is good, and even if we must be harsh, we are not evil. There may be innocent victims, but we are steeled to accept that. Our enemies will not always allow us to choose targets with a proper discrimination. Eventually they will pay for that, as well.''

Bilongon moved toward the door, and Munson quickly sat in his chair again. ''You are leaving. You think we will fail. I even dared hope you'd join us. Your base of operations would be a wonderful haven for some of us.''

''Join you in your fight against the world?'' Bilongon's laugh razored chunks out of Munson's mask of brotherhood. ''I have enough trouble fighting the regime in the Philippines. Your schemes have too many spices for my taste, Roger. I am devious because I must be. For you, it is a goal, I think. I seek the truth. You wish to kill it. No, I will fight my own war my own way, thank you.''

Munson snaked the gun from its hiding place and leveled it at Bilongon. ''You know I can't let you walk away now. After the conference is eliminated, certainly, but not yet. You are worried about your Middle Eastern source of money, and you'd be tempted to interfere with my plan in order to protect it. I'm afraid you'll have to stay here.''

''That is foolish.''

Munson struggled to control his temper. ''It is not. The plan will not be disturbed. It is arranged.''

''There are many things you can't plan for in this world, Roger. You didn't plan that I should come here.'' He raised his voice, the triumphant mind-bells making it difficult for him to speak normally. ''The men with me know of this place. They know of you. If I am not back soon, the world will know. I will give you my word that I will not interfere, but if you try to keep me here you will destroy yourself.''

''But your men know nothing of our agreement. You are too careful for that. The plan will proceed. When the terrorists try to reach them for transportation, they will be eliminated, and your men will save themselves. It's going my way, Bilongon.''

''Glen Draeger,'' Bilongon said. He pronounced it very deliberately.

Munson's eyes glossed over with the satin luster that persists when the eyes themselves have no spark. Bilongon had seen it on many battlefields and after a few fire-lit knife fights, but never on a man who continued to breathe. Coughing, Munson kept the pistol pointed at him. When he was able, he said, ''Draeger? Where?''

''I said you would know one of the men with me.''

''Where is he?''

''I will take you to him on the promise you will let us return home. We will say nothing to the authorities. You may have Draeger.''

A bird scolded in the shrubbery, the grating screed of a spoiled child.

''If I let you leave I am too exposed. We must find an answer. There must be some way we can negotiate in faith.''

"If I do not leave soon, you will not find Draeger. In time, he will find you. He is persistent."

The gun drooped in Munson's hand. He watched it, bemused, finally raising his arm to the chair's, where the weapon rested on its side in his slack grip. He lifted his gaze to Bilongon, forced more words. "He killed my wife, Bilongon. Give him to me. I'll speak to my organization—we'll arrange support for you, military and political."

Bilongon smiled. "You have my terms. We can discuss these other things another time. I will welcome you."

Slowly, Munson rose. "You're an honorable man. I've dealt with too many of the other kind. I guarantee you'll be pleased with the final disposition of the Red Army personnel matter." He gestured. "You make me very humble, excusing the change in plans. We can make it up to you, eliminate that pig Arroyo. Or Cruz, if you'd prefer."

"I will fight alone, I think."

"As you will." Munson holstered the automatic. "Why did you bring Draeger here? He knows nothing about us."

"He came to me and said he had business here."

"Pierce!" Munson made the name a curse. "That sonofabitch told him I was coming here!" He spun away from Bilongon, pounding one of the huge chairs with a fist. "He told him! Why? Pierce can't know the conference is already on!"

Watching uneasily, Bilongon decided enough had been said. It would be handy to have this bit of misunderstanding to use in some future discussion with Pierce or Munson. If nothing else, it was helpful to create some hate between them. He remembered to thank the small bells for leaving him in silence to do his best planning.

Gradually, Munson calmed. He reached to shake Bilongon's hand. "You're the only one who's been scrupulously honest throughout this whole thing. And you're giving me the one man in the world I hate." He moved outside and called to Benjamin, telling him to bring the car around front. The scolding bird erupted again as they walked down the stone stairs, and Munson smiled in that direction. "He spends most of his time being upset. Carries on all day."

Bilongon tried to show polite interest. Munson chuckled at the response. "You must think I'm losing my grip, happy one minute, angry the next. Not really. I'm very excited. I think we're going to show some people the facts of life tonight, especially in my country. We've got to seize events, Bilongon, channel history before it gets away from us. You'll be one of us, in time. You'll see.''

The car rounded the corner of the house, the gravel drive hissing under the tires. Bilongon said, "I doubt it, Roger. We're too deeply involved in our customs and ways. We'd have to have absolute guarantees that we could pursue our religious consciences unquestioned.''

Munson clapped a hand on his shoulder. "We'll discuss it.''

Benjamin stopped in front of them, and Munson bent to open the door. Before Bilongon got in, he said, "Exactly how will I reach Draeger? You know how important it is to me, and I haven't much time.'' He reached to touch Bilongon's arm, dropped the hand self-consciously. The gangling body twitched.

"He is being watched by the two men who came with me. We will leave him bound in the hotel room when we leave." He glanced at his watch. "It will take me perhaps forty-five·minutes to get back there. You should drive into the city after me and wait in the lobby of the Hilton. I will call you there from my hotel and tell you where he is. In about one hour?''

"Excellent. I'll repay you some day.''

Bilongon said, "We are even, as you say. No debts.'' He bent into the back seat, and Munson drew the automatic and placed it within inches of the valley in the shirt that traced the course of the spine. Benjamin saw movement, and his eyes widened. Bilongon was looking at him. It was a small clue, but small clues were the keystone of his life. He flung himself forward as Munson squeezed the trigger. The noise frightened the ill-tempered bird, and it fled in a chorus of distance-muted cries.

The bullet paralyzed Bilongon's lower body, his momentum crashing him forward into the opposite door. He folded up on the floor, face down, humped over the driveshaft housing. The tiny hole in the flowered shirt formed a malevolent eye, black iris surrounded by an expanding red pupil. Bilongon clawed at the door panel, spidery hands whispering on the cheap plastic. Munson leaned forward, aimed carefully at the back of the gleaming head where freshets of sweat poured off the neck. When the round struck, one of the hands clutched at the door hard enough to tear off a fingernail. It imbedded, chalk-white at the fracture, half-mooned.

Straightening, Munson surveyed the scene for observers. There were none, and he was again grateful for the tranquil seclusion of the place. When he looked back at Bilongon the final electric tremors were fading and the framework was collapsing on itself, that peculiar puddling of tissue that differentiates unconsciousness and death. Munson had to stoop to see into the flat, dazed features of Benjamin.

"Don't just sit there," he snapped irritably. "Help me move this into the trunk. I've got to phone around to find out what hotel they're using, and I want any mess cleaned up by the time I finish. And for Christ's sake, don't forget that fingernail. It's like a god-damned lightbulb, sticking out that way."

# ■ CHAPTER 44 ■

The muscular young men assigned to watch Draeger sat together by the window looking out over the city, endlessly entertained by the urban activity. Originally, Draeger watched them avidly, convinced they would become so distracted he could attempt escape. It didn't happen. They made him sit on crossed legs in the middle of the room and never forgot him. If he moved there were four sharp brown eyes checking immediately, tight with anticipation. The two men might have been doctors and he a cell.

They grew troubled as Bilongon's absence lengthened. One spoke to the other, and there was a tinge of urgency in his voice. The second shook his head in a too-brisk negative. They turned as on a signal for a glance at Draeger.

Today was the fourth day of the week. Egg Roll would be passing the American Embassy at two o'clock, if he made it at all. If he didn't show today, it'd be the seventh day before he'd be scheduled for another try. Stress in those circumstances multiplied geometrically.

Ostentatiously, Draeger looked at his watch. The men at the window followed from the corners of their eyes and didn't look at each other. He was sure, then. If Bilongon hadn't stated a return time, he'd given them reason to expect him before now. They were disturbed. If Bilongon was much longer they'd get even more worried. If Bilongon returned, the odds worsened against him.

"Hey!" It was Draeger's first word since Bilongon's departure, and it came as a reedy croak. He indicated the bathroom. The men frowned and finally got up together. One helped him to his feet from behind. The other stood at a distance, poised. Pain twisted Draeger's face, and he bent to massage his legs. The man behind loosened his grip, let the hands lie flat on Draeger's back.

From his bent position, Draeger drove forward and up, gasping at the searing pain in his knees and calves. The crown of his head caught the man in front under the chin and lifted his feet clear off the floor. His teeth clacked, and he was limp before he landed. Draeger dropped to a crouch instantly, pivoting to his left as he did. The kick at his crotch from behind drove into his buttock, and the whole left leg went numb. When he slumped, catching the weight on his right leg, he fell off to that side, so that the follow-through kick was also partially dissipated. It caught him just below the heart, and for one agonized instant he thought it had been crushed. Staggering away, he inhaled. Flame sped through his rib cage, strained to join with the coals still glowing in his knees.

The man feinted another kick, drove the cutting edge of his hand at Draeger's neck. A raised arm took the shock, used the force to turn. Draeger drove his right fist at the man's stomach, legs and body behind the thrust, thinking of spears, thinking of driving completely through the point of impact. His hand registered the bite of metal from the belt buckle, complained as knuckles sacrificed skin that curled off like wood shavings. The man's lungs emptied in a rush. He caught Draeger behind the head and drove stiffened fingers at his eyes. Draeger was barely able to duck. The fingers drove into the skull already aching from the contact with the other man's chin, and Draeger grunted in pain. The man's fingers popped. The pain of their breaking drove the little dab of air remaining in his chest outward. The intended yell was a faint squeak. Draeger stepped forward, drove the right fist into the stomach again, this time coming up with it. The man staggered backward, hit his legs on the end of the bed, sprawled flat. He arched once, gasping, and was still.

The one with the bloodied mouth was on his side, groaning. Draeger checked the one on the bed, lifting him by the belt. A massive shudder racked him, and he sucked in air. His eyes remained closed, even as his breathing stabilized. Draeger moved toward the bathroom, cursing as the left leg wobbled awkwardly. Limping, he paused at the sink long enough to splash water on his face and sluice off his scraped knuckles.

A few minutes later he was getting into a taxi, blessing Bilongon's peculiar morality that would make a man a prisoner but leave his money intact in his wallet. The driver agreed to accept American dollars, but pointed out that the inconvenience of exchanging the bills forced him to insist on a better rate than official. When Draeger accepted a merciless gouging without demur, the man ripped away from the hotel into traffic that quickly forced them to a crawl. By the time they were a few blocks from the embassy and Draeger was asking to be let off, the driver was convinced he had asked for too little money and was in a foul mood. He practically snarled as he made change.

Draeger was oblivious to him. He was at work. Gritting his teeth, he denied the pain of the leg and refused to limp. He cruised the streets casually, stopping to admire buildings, vehicles, or anything that seemed likely to interest a tourist. From a distance, he determined which way he would bolt in an emergency, knowing the cracked ribs would cut him down in short order. Circling, he checked the street from the opposite direction. At ten minutes to two, he started his approach.

A van approached, slowed. The driver craned and searched. Draeger stopped, bent to pick up an imaginary coin, hoped his hands weren't shaking enough to attract attention. The van moved on. A motorbike came up from behind, hovered off his left shoulder, buzzing like all the mosquitoes in hell.

"What are you waiting for?" A male voice. *Young. Happy. Can't be part of this.* "I'm making a picture. Smile. You're in it." *A girl. Equally happy. Damn them both. Slow down. Take your time. Look. Think.*

The motorbike roared past. Another followed, echeloned right. The riders ignored him.

*Keep walking. Take. it easy. The phone number. Is this the right day? Add the numbers. Subtract—Stop it. It's the right day. It's the right time. Look for the surveillance. Look. Think.*

An old woman, blue-black skirt, white jacket, straw hat. *Saw her before! Where? Where? Idiot! Everywhere.* Police car. *Oh, God, no!*

The car was blocks away. It turned off. Draeger continued forward. *Would Munson remember Egg Roll's signal? Could he?* His head hurt, and he raised a hand to brush at it, tracing the roughened flesh under the stubbly hair. *There used to be headaches, but they went away when the real heat started. What the fuck is this, then? Forget it! Is anyone watching?*

It was five minutes to two. He slowed his pace, not wanting to hit the precise point until exactly two o'clock. He would examine the building and the area for one minute, cross the street, continue on slowly, be out of the area at two minutes after two.

*Four minutes.*

He shut down his mind, stopped every conscious thought. From now on he would respond to reflex. There were no options. All went well, or he went. Period. No more fight-or-flight, it was go-or-go, succeed or recede, a day in the sun or a life on the run—all the whiskey-funny phrases from more carefree times flashed past.

*On time. I'm here, goddamit, where are you?*

*Be natural. Look at the building. Observe. Look. Think. Oh, Jesus, help me remember, is there anyone I'm seeing I shouldn't be seeing? Goddamit, how can I keep track of so many of the fuckers? Be fair!*

*Thirty seconds.*

*Don't stare at the watch!*

*One minute. Been here a minute. Get away. Thank you, Jesus.*

*I'm sorry about Ria. I'm sorry about those men in the hotel room.
I'm not sorry about Boy Angel. Can't do it.*

He was twenty yards from the exact front of the building when the
taxi arrived. He heard it stop. A chill raced up his spine. Egg Roll
stepped out of the machine, shot the cuff of his jacket, and checked
the time.

*A maniac. The sonofabitch has flipped! Shit! Oh, shit! I'm stuck
with a fucking nut! I'll kill him!*

He hurried back to where Egg Roll now stood alone, studying the
passing traffic with unconcealed anticipation. Draeger appeared at
the edge of his vision, and he turned, expression hopeful until he
was sure. Then he beamed.

"I knew you be here! So very punctual! I remember, 'No more
than five minutes in vicinity for any reason.' Very important. I
remember."

He was taken aback by Draeger's hard clamp on his elbow and the
force that sent him hustling down the street. Biting off the words,
Draeger said, "Don't talk. Look natural. Pretend you're a tourist."

Egg Roll said, "I am a tourist. I am free. Free. What a wonderful
word. I knew you be there." He reached to put his hand atop
Draeger's grip on his elbow. "It almost not happen, you know.
Until this very morning, I certain I never get away."

"This morning?"

"The conference. The security. They have many guards, our own
government sends many people to watch. Very difficult for me be
included." Finally noting Draeger's attitude was less than as enthusiastic as his own, Egg Roll's accent thickened, the language pattern
stumbled. "There is a thing wrong? We are in some danger? You
hurry very much."

"Everything's OK. Just keep moving. We're all right." The scar
on his head itched, throbbed.

An engine clattered behind him, slowing. He turned to look. A
nondescript Oriental face smiled down at him from a van. Before
Draeger could react, the face said, "I'm looking for Mr. Kolar and
Miss Anderson. Can you help me? I'm a stranger here." The accent
rang in Draeger's ears. Pure New York.

"I could help you look," he said, prepared to spring. "Any idea
where they might be?"

The man shook his head. "Somewhat near here. I'm supposed to bring them an order of egg rolls, and things are getting very cool, you know?"

"I know." Draeger trotted to the passenger's side, pulled open the door and pushed Egg Roll aboard.

Fifteen minutes later they drove into a garage from a street full of horn-blasting traffic and bustling crowds. Signaling them to stay seated, the driver hopped out, trotted back and rolled down a flexible steel door. Then he motioned Draeger and Egg Roll to follow him, leading the way to a small office space. He knocked softly and walked away. The door flew open. Cindy stood there, half-smiling, half-afraid. Behind her, Kolar bulked larger than life, posed against the single lamp in the small office.

Draeger was too relieved to do more than stand and look at her. The drive that had kept him functional drained away. His legs screamed pain, his head threatened to crack. The broken ribs grated at every heartbeat. Unaware of the gesture, he reached for her and stopped, hands stranded in midair. She took a step and halted, unable to read the volatility of his changing expressions.

Kolar's voice boomed. "Why the hell are you standing there pretending to be British? Hug each other, for the love of God!"

They laughed simultaneously, rushing to embrace. Draeger made no effort to kiss her, anticipating the squeeze of his ribs, knowing it was going to hurt like hell and not caring, but knowing he couldn't kiss her and groan, either. With the groan out of the way, he did kiss her. They stepped apart, grinning like kids at a junior high party. Kolar applauded derisively. Egg Roll's face shuttled between confusion and puritanical disapproval.

Kolar broke the tableau, stepping forward, hand out. "Congratulations. We didn't know if you'd be in time to make the contact. It's good you trusted Cindy with the back-up to the exfiltration plan. I wish you'd confided in me."

It was a mild rebuke, but it brought a wince from Draeger. "I won't try to apologize, or bother with lectures about trust. It's too late. As for the plan, Munson must've altered it. I was to be eliminated, so who'd ever know? I'm glad he didn't think the details were important enough to memorize."

"Apparently he's still alive."

"An assumption? From you? Let's make it one of your facts. He's alive in Singapore."

Stonily, Kolar listened to Draeger's recitation of events. Despite that hard presence, Draeger's eyes flicked to Cindy.

He couldn't define the change in her. The radiance that had greeted his arrival was now crisp invulnerability. He recalled his first impression of her, an alloy of wits and determination that rejected contact. Something emanated from her, seized the atmosphere and neutered it. No sexual signals survived. The chill emptiness irritated Draeger. Physical pain merged with his emotional uncertainty to create a sense of being misjudged. He decided she would have to make her attitude clear at her own pace. The end of his report was directed entirely at Kolar.

Kolar looked to the Chinese, who now perched on the edge of a desk, looking quite ill. When he realized they were looking at him, he shook his head sadly. "I did not know," he apologized to Draeger. "All this time, in China, I tell myself, 'One day I will be finish with spying, with having fear.' I say it so many times I forget to be afraid when I leave today. No more people watch me. No more I watch people. When Cheng go to hospital early in morning, I know this is my day. Then I almost break everything."

"Don't worry about it." Draeger smiled easily. "Did you take this Cheng to the hospital?"

For a moment Egg Roll was startled, then he laughed out loud. "Me? I watch Cheng die any day. He is the man who suspected me in China. He tell security people watch me. That why I must escape, why I send last message, not send more."

"How do you know it was him?"

"A woman I know is friend of security man. He said I am suspect. I stop everything, send last message. They watch me every night. I do nothing. When I learn about secret conference to be here, I work hard, hard to come. Then I find out Cheng coming, too. He did not know about me until he ready to leave. He very—*was*—very angry."

Kolar said, "I don't know of any conference. What's it about?"

Egg Roll stood up, became animated. "Very secret, very good conference." Quickly he outlined the Chinese-Vietnamese meeting and its accomplishments. "You see? Safe, peaceful border in south.

Trade with Vietnamese. We have more strength to face white bears from north.''

Draeger turned to Kolar, shaken. "I told Cindy no one could uncover Egg Roll unless he was inside somewhere. If Cheng was on Munson's payroll—'' He left the sentence open for Kolar's own thoughts.

Cindy said, "That could explain some of the payments. I tried to tell you that.''

Draeger flushed, continued to talk to Kolar. "I'm ready to assume Cheng's Munson's man. Why would he leave this morning?''

Egg Roll interrupted. "Sick. He very sick. Vomit.''

Draeger said, "How much longer is this conference to last?''

"Over tomorrow. Celebrate agreements tonight. All go home tomorrow. Not me.''

"And not Cheng, I'll bet. There's something coming off. Munson and Bilongon weren't teamed up for another gunrunning operation. They're into this conference picture, somehow.''

"You know better than to assume something like that. Hell, you know better than to assume anything.''

"We're not dealing in anything. Our net's a shambles. We've got nothing, goddamit. I'm telling you Cheng's got the answers.''

Kolar said, "It's possible. You've been wrong before, though, haven't you?''

A particularly angry horn ranted wildly. Draeger caught himself counting the bleats, waiting for it to stop before speaking. "You've made a couple of mistakes yourself. When Cindy came with me, you didn't think it was voluntary, did you? And you didn't push to catch up to us because you thought I'd cut her throat, didn't you?''

Kolar turned the leonine head and fierce eyes directly on Egg Roll. The small Chinese involuntarily leaned away. "Where is Cheng?'' It was a growl.

"Hospital called Ross Memorial. Far from here, I think.''

Draeger interjected. "We'll go in the van. Does he speak English?''

"Not so good as me.''

Kolar muttered under his breath, then, "I must be crazy. They'll have security all over the place.''

"You don't have much choice.'' Draeger sat down in the desk chair, grunting pain. "This net's down the tubes. You're going to get eaten alive when the budget rolls around. Sure, you can show them Egg Roll, but what the hell is that? The ass end of a busted operation. What'll the money men say about Munson? Pierce?''

"So what's your point?"

"We go for broke. If there's a connection between the conference and Munson and Bilongon, we better be able to report on it. If one of our own people means to sabotage that meeting, and we don't even try to do anything about it, you may lose more than the Bat Team."

Crisply, Cindy interjected, "He's right. We need something spectacular."

The bulky man turned his back on all of them, standing with his face to the wall. At one point Egg Roll gestured that he had something to say, and Draeger's swift hand movement checked him. Cindy waited, tapping her fingers on a metal filing cabinet, the rhythm changing every few seconds. Finally Kolar turned. He concentrated on Egg Roll.

"What do you know about the security arrangements for Cheng?"

"Want to say earlier. Only one man. It was decided there not be so much attention. Why more? No one knows we are here." He flashed a smile, and Draeger knew he would wonder forever if it was sly or ingenuous.

Kolar said, "The arrangements are on to get Egg Roll out of here. I have no one to send with you, unless Cindy can help."

"It should be safe," Draeger said. "With no heavy security I should be able to get to him."

Cindy said, "If he's Munson's man, there's plenty of danger. There's reason to believe Munson eliminated Bilongon. Why should we think he intends to let Cheng live to talk about his operations if Cheng's his man? You'll need a lookout. I'm going with you."

Draeger looked to Kolar, who nodded. "She's right."

"OK." Draeger turned toward the door, putting his back to her. "I'm going to lean hard on him. Right now Cheng's wondering if he's going to get away with something. I'm going to put it in him and break it off."

Kolar frowned. "I thought you might. Whatever Cheng can tell us isn't as important as your avoiding capture. Don't worry about Munson. You can reach me here. Memorize the phone number."

Draeger shook his head. "I won't get caught. And Munson owes me. It's as simple as that."

Kolar watched him leave, irritably waving Cindy to follow. More to himself than his Chinese companion, he said, "Yes, I suppose it really seems as simple as that for you now, young man. You may get the chance to prove it."

# ■ CHAPTER 45 ■

Draeger stopped once on the way. He left the taxi with Cindy waiting and returned carrying a paper bag. When they were moving, he took a slim box out of it and removed a disposable hypodermic needle. Reaching into the bag again, he came up with a small bottle. Avoiding the driver's vision, he drew the colorless liquid into the needle's reservoir until he was satisfied. He replaced the needle in the box and handed it to Cindy. "Keep that in your handbag. If we need it, I'll let you know. I'll say something about—oh, what the hell, something about special medicine, OK? When you hear it, be ready."

Shock blanked her features, left her with no expression but rounded eyes. "Ready? For what?"

"I want Cheng. He knows Munson's operation. I'm going to talk him into leaving with us. The needle's for the guard."

"But Carl didn't say anything—"

"Nobody tried to kill Kolar. Nobody put him in a cage. He didn't have to see what happened to Ria."

Her face worked back to normal, but when she tried to argue with him, there were no words. They were outside the building, looking up at it, before she found the strength. "I won't do it," she said.

"It's dangerous, it's foolish. All you're doing is getting even, Glen. It's pointless and it's wrong."

"I haven't got time to argue. This man is as knowledgeable as Egg Roll. You're the one who convinced Kolar we need a spectacular to save the organization."

"If we're caught—"

"Give me the needle."

She handed him the box reluctantly. He jammed it in a pocket. "I'm sorry," she said. "You'll get the information Kolar wants. That's enough."

He walked away. "I'll get all anyone's ever going to get."

There was finality in it. She ran to catch his arm. "What d'you mean? What're you saying?"

Plodding ahead, he refused to look at her. "I mean I'm not letting him get away with it. Not him, not Munson, none of them. When I'm finished with him, that's that."

"You'll kill him?" When he didn't answer there was a mad instant when she wondered if her horror had robbed her of coherence.

"I don't have any choice. Not any more."

By hanging on and planting her feet, she stopped him. "You win. I can't let you kill him. You knew that. You knew it all along. What a bastard you are!"

"I'm doing what I know is right. It's not enough to prattle about good and bad. If you don't have the strength to eliminate the bad, you ought to shut up and quit agitating people. Either help or get out of the way."

Holding out her hand, she said, "Give me the needle, but take some out, first."

He shook his head. "That's not a lethal dose. That's why I kept the bottle. Just in case."

She was careful to avoid contact with his hand. When the box was in her handbag, she turned her face up to meet his gaze. They remained that way for a long moment before she said, "I'm trusting you. Promise me we'll shut down if everything breaks wrong. No killing. Promise that."

He looked away at a pack of bicycling children, smoothly working bodies, shining black hair like caps, eyes sparkling life. They were bright as flocking birds. Shots of chrome brilliance bolted from the machines, emphasizing, sensitizing for greater onslaught by red headbands, blue shoes, green shirts. Laughter boiled up from them like steam in the hot sun, billowing, falling off behind in rolls and trills and curlicues. They were gone before he nodded. He was looking after them as they walked the last yards and entered the building.

The hospital crawled into Draeger's body, permeated his soul.

It is an all-encompassing thing, a hospital, the closest our society comes to the ancient religious complexes. Its smells are unique, a melange of cleanliness and corruption, vigor and expiration. We have built a folklore around them and the activity inside their apertured walls.

*They won't treat you if you ain't got the money up front. Don't never go in the hospital, 'cause people go in live and come out dead.*

The sounds are endemic. Soft rubber shoes chirp uniquely on buffed wax floors. Discrete chimes of peculiar minor key interrupt muffled conversations. Nothing in the world rattles with the same timbre and pitch as a hospital pushcart, and, heard once, the sinister hush of gurney wheels rushing to destiny is an ember of recollection.

Draeger's hands shook, and he couldn't stop them. There was an itching sensation across his shoulders and down his spine, a branded T of irritation. His injuries throbbed.

Cindy said, "How do you expect to find him in here?"

Draeger clenched his fists. It stopped the tremors, at least. "I'm going to ask at the admissions desk. I don't know what else to do."

She looked dubious. "Would he use his right name?"

"Cheng? In Singapore? Why the hell not? The west wing proba-bly wouldn't hold all of them. I just hope I can bull through."

A crisp young woman greeted him at the desk. He explained he was looking for a Mr. Cheng, had a message for him. He stumbled badly over the pronunciation of the first name, confessed he couldn't spell it. Confessed again he didn't know the specific nature of Mr. Cheng's complaint. Admitted that morning, minor internal disorder.

The young woman let him see how she felt about slipshod messen-gers and dove into her files. She read a card and frowned. "Mr. Cheng is to have no visitors." Draeger was understanding. "It's important he get this message. Could I have a piece of paper? If one of the staff will see that it's delivered, I believe Mr. Cheng will make an exception."

Draeger wrote, "A well-wisher hopes you are all right and wants to talk to you. Our friend from Manila cannot greet you now in the same way because of large and unexpected business troubles." The young woman bustled off with it, trailing assurances.

Cindy said, "I hope he has the vocabulary to understand what you're saying."

"All we have to worry about is four little words—'friend from Manila' and 'trouble.' " He led her to the waiting area, helped her sit down. Adopting the speech methods of the other mendicants around them, he leaned toward her, breathed his words. "That's the ultimate horror of this business, you know? It's not seeing human nature at its worst or dealing with people you despise and smiling while you do it. It's the times when you wait, alone, wondering if anyone cares. Knowing someone's trying to nail you is better than sitting around being so goddamned alone. The guard's no help. For Cheng, he's an obstacle, another thing isolating him from what he wants. It's a helluva thing he's dealing with."

She stared at her knees, the forward thrust of her head and the continuing curve formed by tucking her feet back under her seat creating a defensive whole, an enclosure. Draeger was excluded, the hospital rejected, the matter of Cheng dismissed.

The efficient woman appeared in fromt of them. "You may see him," she said, not completely approving. She handed him a slip of paper with a room number and pointed at the elevators.

When he rose, Cindy watched, distracted. She stirred, said, "Now? Already?" and blushed in sudden awareness of her exposed apprehension. Draeger thought of her coming out of deep sleep. He said. "Don't worry. We'll be OK."

"It's not just us!" she said as loudly as she dared. He apparently didn't hear.

The guard was unmistakable, a man designed for his work. He stood in the hall, watching them come, loose cotton shirt and trousers unable to disguise blunt muscle and bone. He scrutinized Draeger and then Cindy with eyes that violated far more effectively than hands. When they passed he followed them, standing so close to Draeger he could feel the presence, smell an animal mustiness.

Cindy stood tensely off balance, trying not to lean away and only partially succeeding. Her hands on her bag were arched like talons.

The man on the bed twitched. Under the sheet, his entire body moved. He looked at Draeger with desperation. The eyes were large, the features full and symmetrical. Without the fear, it would be a pleasant face. He said nothing, and Draeger knew he was waiting for an exchange of *bona fides*. There was no choice but to brazen it out.

"You speak English?"

Lights intensified in Cheng's eyes, bits of pre-panic excitement. Draeger said, "There's no time for unimportant things. What of this man?" He gestured, the hand hidden from the guard by his body.

Cheng said, "English speak. He not speak."

"We know about the conference." Cheng jerked like he'd been slapped, and the guard inhaled sharply. Cheng spoke to him quickly, a drumbeat of Chinese. The man gave ground behind Draeger. In his thick English, Cheng said, "He not like Western peoples. You know my friend, Manila?"

"He is in trouble. We know he is your friend. We are looking for him. If you help us now, maybe we can help you."

"You no have him?" Cheng's smile almost broke through, gave him a look of hopeful cunning. "Maybe we not talk about same man. I think mistake."

"Roger Munson. Tall. Thin. Glasses, Philippines. Wife, Leonila. Business—"

Cheng pulled his hands from under the sheet and was gesturing furiously. "Enough! Same man." Despite the air conditioner, he was sweating. The cunning look remained. "You are not Singapore police."

"They know we are here. They want no excitement, everything very quiet. No trouble with China, no trouble with Vietnamese."

"I not talk you. I talk Singapore government."

"No. They can not speak about you until the Chinese government and the Vietnamese government announce the conference."

"I talk only government people. Not American. Singapore government."

Draeger bent to him, contorted face inches above the Chinese.

The guard started to move forward, and Draeger turned, held up an admonitory finger. A wordless growl of warning, and the look on

his face checked the advance. They matched stares until the guard
broke, folding his arms across his chest in a belligerent pose, saving
as much face as possible. Draeger looked to the figure on the bed.
Cheng was shaking again.

"You tell me everything or you go back to China, *now*. You and
your guard go back together."

Cheng's stomach rumbled. In the silence of the room it was
crudely revealing, as if a deep personal secret was involved. He
capitulated totally. Before he spoke, Draeger knew. The facial muscles relaxed, and age rushed in to dispose of the desperation, the
cunning, the hope. It left nothing but the wisdom of defeat. "Not
known plan. Munson, more people, attack conference people."

"When?"

"Not know time. Tell me not be there tonight. Say they come for
me tomorrow, go away."

Draeger smiled.

"Munson's escape plan is for tonight. We know that much."

"Ahhh." The ultimate unacceptability created no more than a soft
sigh. "Now I glad I never have time to tell him about Hsiu."

Draeger had to strain to remember Egg Roll's real name. "Why
was Hsiu important?"

"Work against us, work for Americans. Munson say."

"Where did Munson say you would escape to?"

"He go Mexico. I go Hong Kong."

"Not now. Now the Singapore police will hold you until your
government wants you."

Cheng's eyes narrowed. He measured Draeger, preparing to go on
the offensive. "I know many things you need. Much you want. You
help me?"

Draeger thought it over. "How sick are you?"

"Not sick. Make like sick, leave conference." He cut his eyes at
the guard. "He have gun. Very strong, too."

"We'll just have to give him some special medicine, I guess." He
smiled at Cindy. "When I head for the door, stop to speak to
Cheng. When I go for the guard, you stick him. Got it?"

She tried to smile, and he was afraid she'd give the whole thing
away. The guard sneered at them both and maintained his pose.
When Draeger moved for the door, he stepped back, insuring Cindy

had to walk in front of him to get out. Seeing that, Draeger turned and came back. He extended a hand to the guard, smiling. "Shake," he said. "Why can't we be buddies?" The guard curled a lip at the hand and stared at him.

With no attempt at science, Draeger leaped for him, wanting only to tie him up for Cindy's jab with the needle. The man was quick and even stronger than Draeger feared. He accepted the weight of the attack and wrapped Draeger in a bear hug that not only immobilized him but ground the ends of the cracked ribs against each other. Draeger stifled a scream by biting the man's shoulder as hard as he could and was rewarded by a lessening of the pressure on his chest and a grunt of enraged surprise.

Releasing Draeger with one hand, the guard swung the other in a broad arc behind him. Draeger could do nothing but hang on. From the corner of his eye he saw Cindy sprawling across the bed, white legs flashing in a backward somersault. Cheng ignored her totally, transfixed by Draeger's losing battle.

The free arm swung back, chopped at Draeger. He hurled himself against the guard, hoping to spoil the blow's timing and angle of delivery. It glanced off his shoulder, leaving a feeling behind that it had sliced meat off the bone. Draeger pushed with his left foot, forced the guard further off balance. When he felt the other man step to catch himself, he drove a knee into his crotch. The guard groaned, but hung on. Draeger drove up with the knee again, but the blow spent itself on air and Draeger was whirled around, released. He spun toward a wall, caught himself with flattened hands, ducked away.

The guard stood in the middle of the room, bent over, one hand at his battered testicles, the other reaching clumsily in Draeger's direction. His face was muddied, and he rocked like an exhausted bull. Slowly, he turned the reaching hand, felt his back. A tiny snap like a breaking pencil, and he pulled the hand around to stare at the empty hypodermic and the broken stub of a needle. A heavy frown gouged his forehead, and he looked at Draeger quizzically before crashing to his knees.

Cindy appeared from the other side of the bed, rubbing her upper arm. Draeger said, "Start undressing this ape! Cheng, get your goddamn clothes on! We've got to move!"

As soon as Cheng was out of the bed, Draeger moved to help Cindy. They had the guard prone, his head turned toward the wall and the sheet pulled up to the eyes by the time Cheng was dressed. Cindy held inspection, straightening clothes, brushing Draeger neat. She made Cheng throw his coat and tie back in the closet. When she was satisfied, she said, "OK. How do we handle this?"

Draeger steadied himself against the wall, aches and pains multiplying now that the adrenalin was stopped. "I'll call Kolar from the lobby. Let's go."

Downstairs, he watched Cindy position Cheng in a corner and shield him from view as best she could.

Briefly, allowing no opportunity for interruption, he told Kolar of the situation. When he finally stopped, the silence stretched to an almost unbearable length.

Kolar said, "You'll have to keep him now, of course." He rattled off instructions, telling Draeger to take a taxi to the Ocean building. "You'll be met. Look for a man in front wearing a blue shirt, khaki trousers, a red baseball-style cap. He'll have a newspaper under his left arm. He'll ask if you're the man from the loan office. You'll answer that you're not but you wish you were. The man will get in the taxi and take care of your passenger. You take another taxi, get out a couple of blocks away and walk in. Any questions?"

"No."

The phone clattered, and he was listening to the emptiness of the wires before he fully understood how abruptly Kolar had hung up.

Cheng moved in a stupor, snapping his head up infrequently as something caught his attention. The smell of fear palled the air around him, even when he was in his unseeing, castaway state. Draeger knew the feeling, found himself thinking of the ride to Bilongon's camp. He watched Cheng knit his fingers together and unwind them and hoped whoever ran his interrogation would have the wit to avoid hammering on the man. He'd taken a lot, he'd be taking even more. There was no point in brutalizing him.

They effected the exchange with no difficulty whatever, and Draeger could only marvel at Kolar's ability to produce personnel. The man meeting them went through his paces with the harassed half-smile of a conscientious clerk during the Christmas rush. Transferring a high-ranking Chinese government official was a chore.

Draeger helped Cindy into another taxi with the strange feeling the man in the red cap would have taken delivery of a loaf of bread or a live crocodile with the same smooth equanimity.

He started to say something about it to Cindy and stopped when he twisted to face her. The pride and determination were like rime ice on the fine features, covering and underlying dismay. The depth of her hurt was profound. Draeger was in pain with her, for her, and wanted terribly for her to understand.

He said, "Listen, when I was talking about not trusting people, I didn't mean you. If you hadn't gotten to Cruz, hadn't gone to Kolar, I don't know where I'd be."

Her quick head movement cut off his next line. The scent of her swirled in invisible imitation of the golden coil that tumbled across her shoulder. "What if I'd failed, Glen?" she demanded. They were speaking in tense whispers, flicking glances at the driver. "What if I'd backed out today? Would you trust me now?"

"Of course I would! Just because I'm bitter about some of the things that've happened doesn't mean I lump you in with them. We've got something very important started between us."

"That's accurate, 'started.' I mean, sharing a hotel room, walking under a tropic moon. And we had danger, too, didn't we? We got close. That's it. Close, no cigar."

He put an arm across her shoulders, pulled her closer. She offered no resistance, accepted him passively, still searching his eyes. She said, "I've seen you lie and deal until I'm sick. You're the one talking about trust, and it comes up one more word. I want to trust you. More than anything."

"I've never given you reason not to."

"Glen, stop it! I know you've lied to others, like that poor man back there in the hospital. You bullied him. You should've seen yourself!"

He pulled his arm away. "That creep? What's wrong with you? He tried to burn one of ours. He's betrayed his friends."

"He's a human being! A man! An enemy, no worse than that."

"Enemy's good enough."

"No less a man for being an enemy."

He drew away. Eyes locked to the back of the driver's head, he said, "The hell with that. That was before, when I thought there were rules."

They still hadn't spoken when they walked into the small warehouse. Kolar was seated at the desk, waiting, looking like a moderately successful middleman ready to negotiate. The man who drove the van was seated in the distance, having sought out the darkest corner. Draeger wondered if it was unconsciously professional behavior or simple instinct.

Turning his attention to Kolar, he said, "What's the program?"

Kolar said, "The locals are evacuating the estate now. The conferees are being moved to an air base for as long as it takes to get planes in to take them home. All very quiet. Since the terrorists expected to get away by sea, there's a massive sweep going on already. I doubt if they'll catch anyone, but it can't hurt."

Draeger gripped the edge of the desk. "That's it? No ambush? We don't even try to catch the bastards?"

"We?" Kolar was arch. "What would you have us do, dig foxholes and defend a beach? Our mission is to gather information. We aren't involved in any of this wild-west foolishness. Now we start rebuilding."

"And Munson?"

Kolar threw up his hands, exasperation breaking through. The heavy features reddened. "What the hell are you going to do about him? Call the police? Listen to me. Your disregard of facts and this crusade for justice or revenge or God-knows-what has strained our resources to breaking, threatened our security. The local government won't have a single answer when Cheng and Hsiu are discovered to have defected. They'll rip this city apart. If Munson's here, they'll find him. Do you think he'll take a vow of silence to protect us?"

"So after all this, you don't care. You're going to walk, let him get away with it."

Kolar stood up, moved to the side of the desk. "If it'll make you feel better, the word's out through every contact and agency I could think of. He's marked. It's the only deal we can make."

"It stinks."

"The world stinks, Draeger. Our job is to find out who's stirring in it. We take our beatings. This is one. Onward." He tried to make it light, loosen things up. In the face of Cindy's withdrawal and

Draeger's sullen hostility, it dropped flat. Unwilling to deal with Draeger, aware he'd ignored Cindy, he softened his manner, spoke to her. "I'm sorry, Cindy. I wish none of this had happened with you so deeply involved. All that's left is to police up some bookwork in Manila, and we can all go home. It's all over."

When she twisted away from him he saw the tear against the glare from the desk lamp, a moving diamond that trembled with compressed light until she brushed at it, turned it into a wet smear.

He was too distressed to hear the heaviness of his steps as he made his way out to the van. It didn't make sense, he told himself. It didn't seem like it used to be so hard to understand people. They didn't do what they were supposed to any more. They had so many different ideas, and they changed all the time.

Roger Munson wasn't a young man. God knew he'd changed. Maybe that was the style now. Reaching the side of the van entry, he hoisted himself aboard. While the others scrambled in behind him, he shook his head fiercely. Everything didn't have to change. You started with facts, you ended with facts. Even behavior was like that. Eternal verities, characteristics men lived up to, cultivated in themselves and taught those they were responsible for.

Munson's image swam in his memory. It made his ulcer burn like a tight blue flame.

# ■ CHAPTER 46 ■

Pierce approached the market cautiously despite the weariness that weighed his steps to a shuffle. He removed large sunglasses to wipe red-rimmed, sunken eyes. When he replaced them they combined with a stubble of beard to cloak the handsome features. A large floppy hat and cheap clothes further added to the disguise. Only close inspection would reveal he wasn't just another countryman. The heavy automatic under his shirt was intended to discourage anyone foolish enough to push the issue.

He had navigated a prau from Zamboanga north to Iloilo, and he was proud of it. Arroyo had promised a contact if he could escape Cruz, and he'd done it. It had been exhilarating. Two of Bilongon's men had pursued. The chase was magnificent, and he relished it as he advanced on the market, remembering the heart-seizing thrill of deliberately slowing, letting them close on him with their M-16 rounds spanging off the waves. The one in the bow died well when he fired back with his own rifle. The stern man quit, turned tail. Pierce spat, contempt overcoming the terrible dryness in his mouth.

The next leg of the escape would be easier. New papers, a jet flight. Arroyo had promised tickets. They would go unused. The new papers would let him get away to a place known only to himself, and then there would be still more new papers and a new life.

He entered the market through the side entrance, avoiding the main one. That was where the pass was to be made, but no papers were worth walking into an ambush. The possibility that Arroyo wasn't playing fair was a matter of course. It added to the excitement. He smiled at his own admission.

The crowd ignored him. He kept his head down, let himself be jostled along aimlessly. Suddenly he was assailed by the smell of roast pork and lanced by a vast hunger heretofore held in check by tension. Directly under his nose an entire pig's head lay on its side, grinning mouth open, the teeth baked to the color of the flesh, coated with rendered grease. Rays of sunlight speared through the lattice overhead and onto the head and the other cuts spread on the table, multiple beams like searchlights in a childhood sky. He turned away, seeing the market in a new, dazzling sense.

Nowhere could a man be more in the presence of life in death. Fish hung by their tails or gills, singly and in bunches like hammered metal grapes. Some had eyes that questioned from bodies rigored in amazement, others accused in permanent reproach. Catfish slithered in wide, shallow baskets, calling on primitive toughness to clutch one more minute of existence. In that, they were like the shrimp next to them whose frail insect bodies also harbored an unyielding desire to live. In another direction some chickens dangled by communally bound feet in an untidy mass, uncomprehendingly alert to everything around them.

While he was looking he felt a tug at his trousers leg and found a small boy offering him a pair of finches. The boy held them tightly, one in each hand and, to demonstrate their vigor, he thrust them at each other. The tiny beaks clashed like miniature broadswords as the trapped creatures parried to protect their eyes. Gently, Pierce forced the boy's hands apart. The large bird's coloring featured a cowl, black head and shoulders contrasting with a lustrous chestnut body. Its bill looked like ancient steel. The smaller bird was dingy brown. In another effort to display his stock's condition, the boy threw them in the air. They fled upward in an explosion of release to the limit of the string tied to their legs. Checked, they fluttered confusedly, quickly becoming entangled and falling to the ground. Neither struggled further.

The boy accepted four pesos with an alacrity that implied a deal too good to be missed. Pierce picked up the birds as carefully as his sapped strength would permit, marveling that such delicate structure had so far withstood such abuse. The black-hooded one—he decided it was a cock—stared at him with resigned defiance.

It took only a moment to cut the strings. This time they continued past the lattice and plastic-cloth arrangement that partially roofed the area. They circled, together, then struck off in the direction of the distant mountains. He'd been so sure they'd go that way that he faced that direction himself, even though the peaks were invisible from his location.

The smells of the place reasserted themselves then, and once more the dichotomy of its purpose came to him, the sharp tang of fresh-cut green mango mixing with the clotted stink of mounds of decaying refuse. When he looked for the mango stand he became aware of the amusement around him, and he smiled back at the people so entertained by his release of the birds. He wondered how many thought him mad and how many appreciated the magnitude of his sanity. He was still smiling when he saw the men approaching.

There were no papers. No airline held a reserved seat for Tony Pierce by any name.

The ambush was coming to him. Exhaustion fell away, leaving an inner hardness that scorned one more betrayal, expected it. He was glad to see they were Bilongon's men, wanted to shout to them, welcoming. It was gratifying they weren't the sort of scum Munson would hire.

The four of them separated. One drew a long blade from a primitive scabbard and, comically, Pierce caught himself thinking of the dangers of infection. A woman selling bunches of garlic looked at the blade and the man carrying it, followed his gaze to Pierce, and screamed like a reptured steam main. The pandemonium that followed exploded away from the confrontation like fragments from a bomb. Pierce drew the .45 and shot the man. The impact lifted him onto a table stacked with vegetables and fruit, sending a broken rainbow of colored produce in all directions. Another man shot at Pierce, the round hitting the roasted pig's head with a resounding thump. Pierce's return was better, catching the man's thigh. He spun with the impact, bouncing off a table, spraying blood. Trying to keep his balance, he danced awkwardly through the stuff on the ground, screaming above the shouts of the terrorized crowd. A pistol remained clutched in his hand, forgotten. Pierce fired at another man, saw him go down. He hardly felt the burst of M-16 fire that pounded into his back. His first awareness of the damage done came when he realized he was lying on his face in the filth of the market floor. Next he chided himself for not considering that someone else might use the side entrance.

He didn't think it necessary to be too harsh. After all, he was dying, and that was a very steep price. By working very hard, he was able to turn himself onto his side. There was something in an old song about that, he remembered. Feet appeared in his line of vision, dirty feet, with blood on them.

*It had been a poor life, a thing lacking merit or value. The death was a good one. Men would hear of it and remember.*

At the same time, Cruz sat at the desk in Draeger's dining room–office and read from a lengthy typed statement. He was in civilian clothes again, quality *barong tagalog* and knife-creased slacks. He spun the swivel chair and leaned back, looking satisfied but stern. Draeger and Ria sat in the living room, waiting attentively.

She no longer wore the bandage, but bruises loomed through her heavy makeup. Dark glasses in her hand would cover the discolored eyes.

"It's a good statement," Cruz pronounced. "I can close the books on Boy Angel. What we have done is illegal, but it is justice."

Draeger said, "I wish I could thank you properly."

"Leave the Philippines." Cruz was firm. "You have taken advantage of our laws, our hospitality. You are not welcome."

Ria protested and Draeger said, "It's OK. He's right."

She frowned. "I don't understand. I know what you're doing about the man who attacked me. There's more. Why are you so angry?" She directed the question at Cruz.

"It is impossible for you to ever know. Mr. Draeger knows, and that is sufficient."

Draeger said, "What about Pierce?"

Cruz smiled thinly. "He received a telephone call from Manila and disappeared from his island. We don't know where he is. Do you?"

Draeger shook his head. Cruz continued. "You know Bilongon is dead, killed in Singapore?"

"I heard a rumor."

"It is true. Murdered. Two of his men, also. His people are mad with grief and anger. They will blame the government."

"What'll his people do?"

"What they've always done. Fight. Why did Bilongon go to Singapore? And why take you?"

"I gave you my word it had nothing to do with you. Anyhow, he's dead. Everything that's happened that involved us is forgotten. We agreed." He pointed at the papers in Cruz's hand.

He broke into a bright smile. It shamed the earlier thin-lipped expression, made him handsome, likeable. "I lied. Someday I will see you on neutral ground and torment you until you tell me everything."

They were laughing when the knock on the door interrupted them. Draeger said, "That's funny. The intercom didn't announce any callers."

Cruz moved in the chair, and Draeger caught the quick shift of the right hand to check the location of the small automatic in the back holster on his belt. It was comforting to know about.

Draeger opened the door and stared at the stranger. He was short and gave the immediate impression of overweight. The eyes demanded attention, hard little buttons balanced on upswept cheekbones. The small mouth spread in a bold smile. "My name is Benjamin. I have something to sell you."

"How'd you get up here without the guard telling me?"

Benjamin continued to smile. "He knows me. I was here once before, looking for a book. A special book."

The impulse to look toward the kitchen door was almost irresistible. Draeger jerked a thumb at Cruz. "This man is with the Army. I could have you arrested."

"If you do, I can't sell you my information."

Cruz came to his feet with the menacing fluidity of a cat stretching. "Perhaps it would be easier for me to arrange for you to volunteer your something."

Before Draeger could speak, Benjamin said, "Your name is Captain Cruz. Colonel Arroyo called you to come see Mr. Draeger about some sort of statement. I waited for you. You are my protection. There have been men who did business with Mr. Draeger and died. You will not let that happen to me."

Draeger and Cruz exchanged looks. Benjamin's smile widened, opening the small mouth. He went on, "The man who asked me to come see you said you would pay to know where to find him. He wants to talk to Mr. Kolar. A deal."

"Where is he?" Draeger's intensity drew an audible gasp from Ria. Cruz tensed to grab him. The man called Benjamin slid back a step, continuing to smile. "First, the money."

"You know where he is? He can be taken?"

Benjamin's smile disappeared, leaving street-hardened blankness. "You will pay me, and I will tell you how to contact him. What any of you do after that is not my worry. I am only a messenger."

"I'll make a call."

Benjamin said, "Time is important. Bring the money to the Philippine Cultural Center in two hours. You know how much is offered. Be sure to bring it all in used bills. If there are any police, except Cruz, I will not make the contact."

Cruz said, "I want nothing to do with this."

Benjamin was unruffled. "You are my protection. Colonel Arroyo knows you will be present." At Draeger's quick move, Benjamin hurried to add, "He knows nothing else. He is being paid much money to have Cruz protect me, that is all."

"It's got Munson's smell on it," Draeger muttered, and Cruz asked, "Who?" and Benjamin snickered. Draeger grabbed him. "Cruz won't be able to protect you forever. Where's Munson?"

The laughter died, but Benjamin looked full into Draeger's anger without flinching. "Maybe you will see him later. You missed him in Zamboanga. He was sleeping in the same hotel, and you don't know who he is or where he is."

The muscles in Draeger's throat worked spasmodically as he very deliberately went to the phone. His free hand rubbed at his flank while he waited for an answer. He said, "This is Draeger. The man we want is in town. Yes, I'm sure. There's a messenger here. We're to meet him in two hours with the agreed package. He'll have something for us, but not the actual merchandise." He nodded twice, stiff-necked, and hung up without speaking again. To Benjamin he said, "It's a deal. Now get out."

Benjamin moved toward the door as ordered, his bearing blatant declaration of Draeger's incapability. There was an even stronger inference. Benjamin had arrived absolutely certain he would get everything he wanted. Confident as any cat with its crippled victim, he enjoyed each frustrated twitch. Draeger shared the knowledge with him and was shaken by it.

With Benjamin gone, he asked Cruz to excuse him, glancing significantly at Ria. He failed to notice the sudden tension in the other man, which was of no great matter, as it faded quickly. Moving with a diffident grace, almost courtly, Cruz escorted her to the window while Draeger busied himself with the telephone. She looked back at him worriedly for only a moment before giving her full attention to Cruz in a running commentary about the cityscape before them.

It took Kolar an unpleasant length of time to arrive. A flustered Cindy came with him, her composure further shaken at the sight of Ria. For a split second there was a look of vindictive pleasure on the Filipina's face. All the pain, the pleasure, the joy and fear that had been her relationship with Draeger was encapsulated in that one expression. Then she was acknowledging Kolar's greeting and motioning Cindy to join her on the sofa. The gesture and manner completely denied the first reaction. Draeger questioned his observation, but he knew what he'd seen. He wished Cindy had stayed in the hotel.

Kolar carried a briefcase. He held it at arm's length. "The money," he said simply. "I hope there's no question about the number. The grapevine tends to garble that sort of news."

Cruz said, "He'll probably try for more."

"Let him," Draeger said harshly, and Kolar frowned.

"We'd better go," he said, "We've got a long way to go and you know what traffic can be like." He turned to the women. "I want you to wait in the hotel. In the coffee shop, where there are plenty of people around." They rose without comment. Cindy went to the intercom to request a driver from the guard below. She looked puzzled at the strange obsequiousness of the tinny voice. Draeger's face convinced her this wasn't the time to pursue it.

With the women gone, Kolar said, "Captain, I'll be grateful if you'll leave us alone to conduct our business once we have Benjamin paid and out of the picture."

"You are on Philippine soil. I am sworn to uphold Philippine law."

Kolar smiled paternally. "Would you have me believe everything you do is within the law? Would you step over the line, perhaps just this much, to bring down Colonel Arroyo?" He held up thumb and forefinger, almost touching. Cruz grinned at him.

"You are a very bad man. You think Arroyo may be hurt by some part of this thing?"

Kolar was instantly serious. "No, I don't know that. I hope so, for your sake. We'll be discussing matters of great sensitivity, possibly, if Munson wants to barter. I'm asking for cooperation."

"You are leaving, all of you?"

"Every soul."

"You will not organize another net?"

"Of course we will. It'll take years, but we'll do it."

"You are honest about your crimes." Cruz's laugh was bitter, short.

"My interests are in protecting my country's interests, exactly as yours are. I don't want to see the Philippines colonized. I don't care what kind of government you have, as long as it doesn't actively work to frustrate my own. I'm asking you to allow me to retreat with dignity. We may cross paths in the future. Must we obstruct each other now?''

"I come from a long line of bargainers. You should know better than to try that on me. I can obstruct you. You cannot obstruct me.''

Kolar accepted the rebuff with pleasant good grace. He waited.

"Do what you must do,'' Cruz said. "There will be a price. There always is. One day I may need your help.'' He swept them with a challenging stare. "If I ever come to you, I want your word you'll help me.''

Draeger said, "National interest. I won't ignore it.''

"What I am doing has nothing to do with my national interest, but yours. Those are my terms.''

Kolar put a hand on Draeger's shoulder. "The real world, Glen. Believe me, I've made worse deals. I'll take my chances with the Captain.'' He faced Cruz. "You have my word. Glen?''

"And mine.''

"Good.'' Cruz indicated his watch. "It's late.''

Draeger stepped into his bedroom and returned carrying binoculars. In response to Kolar's raised eyebrows he said, "That peninsula's no place for a meet. Not for Munson. There's only one road off. That leaves the sea, and a moving boat, escaping, is too easy to spot. He's here from Singapore. Three ships are in from there. One's anchored close to the peninsula.'' He gestured with the glasses. "It's worth a try.''

Kolar pursed his lips and nodded gravely. "Good,'' he said. It was a judgment. "Very good. Always check. It gives life to the facts.'' He moved to the door with his rolling quickness.

They were in Draeger's car when he swore in exasperation. "Damn! I promised the back-up personnel I'd call!'' Looking to Cruz in the back seat, he said, "Nothing to concern you. I arranged a taxi and a man to wait across Roxas Boulevard, simply in case of emergency. They won't interfere.'' Overriding Draeger's protest, he went on, "I'll get a taxi and join you in front of the building. Here, take the money. Don't let him have it until I'm there.'' He was out of the car almost before it stopped moving, displaying an agility that belied bulk and years.

Cruz moved to the front seat, watching Kolar disappear back into the building. He smiled at Draeger. "I know you had a good operation based here, and I'm sure he's good. I think he's more embarrassed about forgetting his back-up people than anything else. Did you see his face?"

"Yeah. I guess forgetting a small thing is a fact a man can deal with. What's happened to us here—" The sentence broke on the sound of the car pulling away.

The two women made themselves comfortable in the booth. A clever decorator had utilized the ever-present Manila jeepney as his theme, and customers stepped up and into the snug enclosure as if embarking on a trip. The shape and designs were as authentic as anything on the busy streets outside, but the physical pressure of that world was at bay. The air in the hotel was clean, soft with muted music instead of clashing gears, chirruping warning signals, and blatting horns. Conversation out there was animated, thrown off with hand and arm gestures. In the restaurant it was the quiet meander of a stream, and only bits of sentences floated to the surface. While Ria ordered salads and coffee for them, Cindy overheard the man in the booth behind her.

"It's the way it's done," the heavy voice said. He was carefully confidential. "(Words lost) amnesty," he continued. "(Words lost) passport, (words lost) gross income over a hundred thousand, for Christ's sake, and (words lost). You have to pay it."

Ria interrupted the eavesdropping. "You are thinking very hard."

Cindy laughed. "Nothing important."

Unsure of that answer, Ria was defensive. "Is there something you wanted to say?"

Cindy reached across the table to touch her hand. "I didn't mean anything. I was thinking about something else. But, yes, I guess we have to talk, don't we?"

"Only to clear things up. I hated you when I first saw you, you know."

"You must have. And I had no idea why, at first. Now we have a problem, one we can identify, and we're able to talk about it. Is that a sign of wisdom, civilization, or what?"

Some of the tension left Ria's face. "I don't know. I don't think we even have a problem. We might as well get everything in the open. We're talking about Glen."

Cindy made no effort to hide her surprise. "The books say Filipino culture avoids direct statements. I think I'll let you educate me properly."

The waitress slid bowls of salad onto the table in the center of the jeepney body. A waiter followed immediately with coffee.

"Glen never adapted to our society. Roger Munson almost did. Still, I think Glen may understand us better. He's a watcher, Cindy. He holds himself out of society, and he watches it. He doesn't laugh at it and he doesn't cry about it. He watches. And yet I always had the feeling he was *doing* something to it."

" 'Something to it.' " Cindy savored the phrase, watching Ria. "That's an interesting way to put it."

"It's what I saw. Or think I saw. It's not important any more. He doesn't belong here. Poor Roger wanted to." She shook her head. "Glen could, you know. The thing is, I don't think he wants to belong anywhere. It's like you being surprised because I can be so frank with you. It's because you're not one of us. I can be different with you. I think women make adaptations more easily than men. We've had to. It may be genetic by now. Men never do it as well, and men like Glen are foolish to try. He's always over there somewhere," she indicated a point to the side and behind, "just where you can barely see him but he can see you clearly."

Cindy rummaged in her salad with a fork. "You know him well, don't you?"

There was sympathy and understanding in Ria's answer. "Not very well. I only know what he let me see, and there wasn't much of that. But I wasn't afraid, so maybe I could see better."

Cindy's head snapped up. Ria smiled, swallowed a bit of fruit. "He was a lot of things to me. For a while I thought he was the most important thing in my life. I never thought I was falling in love with him."

"And you think I am?" Cindy colored, dropped her hand to the table. The fork pointed at Ria in an unintended weaponlike attitude.

Ria said, "I think you're afraid, and I think that's part of falling in love. Everything Glen and I did was against what I've been taught about the way 'good' women behave. Still, my culture is full of 'good' women who watched their husbands spend most of their time with mistresses. Love and marriage create a lot of fear for us. You're afraid because Glen's mistress is his work. You are afraid she will take him from you, as from me.'' Her face twisted bitterly before the assured self took over again.

Cindy could eat no more. Suddenly the acid of pineapple, the silken sweetness of banana, the entire meal, all blended in a too-tropical mass that tossed in her stomach like a storm. "You're right. I'm afraid. Of falling in love with him and of you. I've never feared another woman in my life, and I've never been in love. It's not what they say. It's terrible.''

"I hope you are not too afraid, because there is nothing left for Glen and me.''

"But you still—care—about him." She stumbled over the word.

"I will remember him as a man who was important to me. I would like for him to be happy. He needs you, I think.''

Softly, more to herself, Cindy said, "I can do it. I know I can do it.''

Leaning forward, Ria heard and responded, laughing quietly. "It's a good thing he's normal. I think your only competition may be that one called Kolar.''

Cindy dropped the fork with a clangor that turned heads throughout the restaurant. Her eyes on Ria were like a hurt child's. "Oh, God, Ria,'' she breathed, a hand at her throat, "pray that's not true.''

# CHAPTER 47

The tableau in front of the Philippine Cultural Center trembled with hostility. Yards away, Benjamin pointedly ignored Draeger and Cruz, who stared at the sky as if the frothy clouds were the most interesting things in the world. A brilliant red and yellow taxi skidded to a stop in front of the pair, and Kolar got out. His hair was windblown, and individual strands swayed free, polished in the sun. Benjamin visibly relaxed but maintained his distance.

"We've been waiting," Draeger said, jerking a thumb at Benjamin. "He wouldn't even talk until you showed up." The three of them moved to the flat-featured man. He had a plastic shopping bag at his feet. He nudged it to the side at their approach. Kolar wasted no time on preamble. He took the briefcase, extended it. "It's all there. I don't have time for you to count it." He showed his watch. "We're exactly on time."

The small eyes refused to abandon the briefcase. "Munson said it would all be there. He said you'd be right on time, too." With a twist of his head he got his eyes to the plastic bag, reached in and pulled out a hand-held radio. Turning it on, he said, "This is the connection. Everything is OK. Got it?"

Metallically distorted, Munson's edged voice crackled. "Got it. That you, old friend?"

Kolar took the radio like something diseased. "It's me, Roger. What's your proposition?"

A dry chuckle cut across the hiss of static. "Not wasting time, are we? All right. First, instructions. Get Cruz and Benjamin out of there. You and Draeger leave there, too. I want you out in the open.

You understand. Get out on the peninsula beyond the Convention Center. Contact me again in ten minutes. Out.''

Cruz gestured Benjamin out of earshot. ''I can have a company of troops here in fifteen minutes.''

Kolar froze him with a look.

The Captain half-saluted and turned to Benjamin. ''If I'm going to keep you alive until you're gone, you better move fast, *putok sa buho*.'' He smiled over his shoulder at the Americans. ''A phrase you can take home with you. It says, 'exploded from bamboo,' and it means 'bastard.' '' He waved and was walking down the long, sweeping drive.

Kolar said, ''We're taking your car and my taxi. It may be important that we both have a way off this place. You follow me. I'll have the radio.''

Draeger fell in behind. They passed Cruz and Benjamin and then looped back onto the site. The real estate itself is a massive rectangle, surgically grafted onto the city, a lump extruding into Manila Bay. It is Marcos's Grand Pyramid, his memorial to his rule. Its impressiveness is undeniable. The buildings are huge, beautiful, of a scale that dwarfs the human figures at their bases. Draeger had little eye for their modernistic beauty, following Kolar.

In a while they were overlooking the flat waters of the bay and the tankers and freighters studding its surface. A long breakwater extended to the north, forming the city's South Harbor. Yachts nestled behind the protection, a few sailboats making sluggish headway in the still heat of the afternoon.

Kolar stopped and waved Draeger to a parked position between the taxi and the water, then settled back. Draeger got out to lean on the taxi's roof, looking out to sea. His hand drifted up to run through his hair, the fingers tracing the almost indiscernible mark.

Crackling abruptly into the quiet, the radio demanded their location. Kolar described it, and Munson said, ''I've got a man on one of the small boats by the breakwater. Stand out where he can see you.''

They moved closer to the water, leaving the vehicles. Munson came on again. ''He has you. Stay there. Now, here's my proposal. You set me up with a package—ID, location, job, the whole thing—in a place of my choosing, or I unload on everyone, Kolar. Names, places, and dates.''

"What if I'm not interested?" That message completed, he turned to Draeger. "Get in your car, the back seat. Get those glasses on him. Find him!"

Draeger hesitated, and Kolar spurred him with a guttural noise. The vehicle was close enough for him to still hear the radio.

"You have to be interested. I can burn damned near everyone in the organization, and I'll do it. You know I will."

"You can't mean that, Roger. So many years, so many good friends. It's unthinkable."

A tearing exhaustion distorted the answer to a pained drawl. "It's not my fault, Carl. I didn't want it to end this way. There are forces, immense powers we—" The radio hissed at the inarticulate failure, then, "It doesn't matter. I had everyone dancing for a while, didn't I? Made them believe there's an organization. I think you suspected all along. There's just me, trying to show them how wrong they are. Now I need protection."

"You knew it wouldn't work. And what did you hope to prove?" To Draeger, Kolar whispered, "Hurry up, Glen! Find him!"

Defensiveness crept into Munson's voice, a spurious liveliness. "It was a good plan, Carl. People have to understand the world can't go on this way, these power bloc confrontations, the nuclear build-ups, all of that."

"And you thought letting that conference be butchered would ease tensions?"

"Nothing will ease tensions! They have to be eliminated!" The shouting set off frantic buzzing in the speaker. "We have to have a stable world! This thing everyone calls terrorism is really the answer. We need a purge, a blood-letting, something to get the poisons out, something to force the powers to unite against a mutual enemy!"

Kolar lowered his radio, speaking out to sea. His voice barely reached Draeger. "We're seeing it every day. Terror only creates counter-terror. It's political genetics." A bit louder, he asked, "Do you have him?"

"Got him," Draeger said, embarrassed that the triumph was so abundant in the words. "That rust-bucket with the red and blue design on the stack, right where I expected him. The stupid bastard's wearing a white shirt and binoculars hanging around his neck. He's on the wing of the bridge, right out in plain view." Kolar half-turned, and the one-eyed profile glared, a cragged scar against the sky. Then it was turned back to sea. Munson was talking again.

"We'll have time to discuss it some other time. If you won't give me what I need, I'll have to sell what I can and take my chances."

"You'll have all of us hunting you."

Munson laughed. "Not the one with the best chance of finding me. The wolves from both sides will be at your throat as soon as I start talking."

"This whole thing is mad. Turn yourself in, while you have time."

"Prison? Not worth discussing. I have little enough left to lose, now that Leonila—" The transmission broke sharply, started again. "You'll have to do better than that."

"I can't. And what about Pierce? What do I do about him?"

"There's just me, Carl."

Kolar looked at the radio distantly, a trick of his eyes making it appear he was seeing through it and into the ground at his feet. When he spoke his voice droned. "Let me think, Roger. You've created considerable anger. Hatred wouldn't be too strong a word. I'll have to take many precautions."

Munson scoffed. "You're concerned about Draeger. You know, I think if I hadn't had to isolate him from his source in China, everything would have gone perfectly, but I couldn't be sure he wouldn't learn about the conference. That meant the courier had to go down. He'll get over things. That's the way we all start out, isn't it? Knights of the Game. The Draegers don't bother me. It's only the ones like us who do what we do. The rest of them get over things. I don't know what you want to talk to him about, but I'll give you fifteen minutes."

Before Kolar could open his mouth the radio blared into action again. "Where is he? Where's Draeger? What are you doing?"

Calmly, Kolar said, "He's right beside me, Roger, sitting in the car, where he's more comfortable."

"I've warned you! You better not be trying to tip me!"

"I know the stakes, Roger. Please, calm yourself."

In the car, certain the glare of the windshield protected him from Munson's observation, Draeger raised the glasses. Munson leaned forward, binoculars aimed directly at Draeger. The lenses shone black. Draeger thought how they reflected what was left of Roger Munson better than any eyes. Inanimate, they registered a world of unvarying hostility, of hiding and grinding pursuit. When the glasses lowered from the face, Draeger was sure he saw lonely pain in the distant paleness. He told himself it was absurd. It was a good eight hundred yards out there, and binoculars didn't reveal facial expression at that range.

Kolar was saying, "Let me know if he leaves the bridge," and Draeger was busy trying to watch Munson and Kolar at the same time. Munson continued to lean on the lifeline, staring unaided in their direction. Kolar moved to the taxi, speaking intently to the driver. Draeger couldn't make out the conversation, but the driver's reluctance to agree with Kolar was evident. When Kolar produced a sheaf of bills the man remained dubious, but his objections wore away. He nodded and walked off. Draeger lost sight of him but heard him stop behind his taxi and shout to Kolar, "Thirty minutes, mister, and I come back to the taxi. That's all, thirty minutes." From the corner of his eye Draeger watched Kolar hurry back to his original position. The bay breeze drifted the silver hair in soft waves as he jogged.

Draeger jerked a thumb at the retreating figure. "What's that about?"

"I don't want him around any longer. He hasn't heard anything yet, and I decided it'd be safer to send him along and keep it that way. He's walking back to the buildings for a half hour." As he spoke he watched Draeger. It made the younger man uncomfortable when the scrutiny continued past the words. He said something almost as a defensive measure.

"He's gotten clear, hasn't he? We deal on his terms, or he'll sell us all."

A wet sigh flowed out of Kolar as he joined Draeger, taking the front seat. He left his legs stretched outside the open door. He seemed to sag on his frame, the muscular tone of the body surrendering to the persistence of age, growing slack. "He won't get everyone, of course," he said. "I've already set up salvage moves, assuming he's exposed this entire operation. We'll protect most of our assets. Our own people will be evacuated as soon as possible. But to what purpose?" One of the heavy hands clubbed at the air. "We've existed for years on a basis of absolute trust. A hard-core knot of professional liars who trusted each other utterly. Munson is breaking our mirror. We'll never be able to look at ourselves or our contemporaries the same way again.''

Draeger protested. ''We'll survive it. Talk him in, give him what he wants. He's too smart to try to make a lifetime blackmail thing of it.''

Kolar leaned forward, elbows on knees, head in hands. He remained that way while a speedboat whined out of the pack of small boats. The tension in the stressed engine sawed the air. The boat rocketed into the bay, insolent against the hulking freighters.

From between his hands, holding the same attitude, Kolar said, ''You wanted to kill him, before.''

Draeger felt his face warm. ''I did. He was right about me. I thought I hated him. I guess I did. He's a pitiable man.'' He extended the glasses. ''Here, look for yourself.''

Kolar refused. A moment later he said, ''It has to be done,'' and Draeger closed his eyes against the words and the inner voice that told him he'd known it was inevitable. When he looked, Kolar was watching him with a grim patience that chilled the air in the car.

''We can't!'' Draeger wanted to slip along the seat, back away. He grabbed the edge, held himself in place. ''He's way the hell out in the bay! I can't do anything! I can't do anything!''

The silvered head turned to the ship again. The distant snarl of the speedboat honed the words. ''Do you honestly believe I'm so senile I'd forget about back-up personnel? There are none, just as Munson has no one to watch us. I went back to your apartment. Get out of the car on the other side and go to the back of the taxi.''

He joined Draeger and hoisted the trunk lid. He said, ''I hoped we wouldn't need this. And I hoped we would. I'm sorry.''

The batik wall-hanging lay there, folded, enclosing a long object. Draeger unwrapped the rifle. It came out of the last folds like some sentient thing unwilling to wake. Draeger held it, pivoting his head to inspect the entire length. He continued to Kolar. ''Munson was my friend. I know what he's done, better than anyone. Goddam, Kolar, he was my *friend*!''

''He tried to kill you, more than once. He set that animal on Ria. Forgive him that, if you wish. Can you forgive him for twenty men like Egg Roll? He'll condemn more than that, of course, but think of only twenty. Think of the men in the organization who'll wake up sweating tonight and for the first time when the questioning fear comes, an example will exist. An informer. You know what'll drive our people mad? He's getting away without being punished by his own."

Draeger sneered, and Kolar laughed shortly. "Haven't you admitted that to yourself yet, Glen? We're an *order*. Outlaw, we make our own laws. Loyalty is all we have. We work for the excitement and the knowledge we're unique. Not better. Harder, possibly. And we police ourselves."

He stepped away from the back of the taxi, looked toward the ship. "He'll be growing impatient, wondering what we're doing. Foolish, telling me he had us under observation."

Draeger had to try again. "So what if he gets out of here? We can outlast it."

Kolar continued to stare at the ship. "Be serious. He'll do exactly as he said. God only knows how much information he's stored away against just such an event as this." He rounded quickly. "It comes down to this, Glen—I'm asking you to stop him. I'm telling you you're the only person in the world who can. Think what he's done, what he'll do. Ask yourself if you want the responsibility for what will follow if he leaves with that ship."

Draeger looked past him, past the white blot that was Munson. Beyond them was the bay, flat and steel hard. At its limits mountains raised against a cloud veined sky like dark hands cupping the breast of the universe. He lifted the rifle absently, suspended it on the palms instead of gripping it. His stare intensified, and he shifted it to the bridge, the regular normal features stiff with hapless resolution. He said, "Is there anyone around who'll see if I break for the car?"

On Kolar's assurance, Draeger moved rapidly, slipping into the back seat. He managed a kneeling position that allowed him to rest the weapon on the back of the front seat. The diagonal arrangement kept the muzzle inside the car. He uncapped the telescopic sight and lowered all the windows. There was a round in the chamber, five more in the magazine. The wood of the stock was warm, smooth and fragrant with oil well-rubbed into the grain. It made the dead lumber alive, substantial and reassuring. The hard blue-steel barrel sought into the distance. An eye to the scope ripped Munson from his secure distance, brought him close. Draeger watched him raise the radio, wished in his heart he could thank him for not making him wait.

"Time's up," the metal rasped outside the car. "Let's hear it. I spent ten years of my life putting that operation together, Carl. My savings, everything. I expect some decent compensation."

"I can't help you, Roger. Too many things have happened. I can't get you out of this."

"Get me out? I was offering you a way out! I hold all the cards, can't you see that?" The radio paused noisily, then, "Of course you can't. You're a prisoner of the power that must be broken. Carl, we've been wrong all these years! There's no right and wrong! There's direction and stability! A society has to be in step, protected against itself. You can't turn your back on me! You'll be crushed! I'll piss on your grave, you hear me?"

Draeger blocked out the ranting. He was very precise, felt each move like metal gearing into place. He set the crosshairs. The twisted face under them spewed into the radio. The rifle was sighted in at five hundred yards. The cross slid up the face, onto the unkempt bulkhead. Draeger mentally registered marks on it to gauge a correct aim. He inhaled, let half of it trickle through his nostrils, listened to the unhurried regularity of his heart as he squeezed the trigger.

The explosion was awesome in the car, a physical blow that momentarily stunned him on its way to the sea and the echo-reflecting buildings. Munson bounded backward, and his arms flew wide when he hit the steel bulkhead. The dangling binoculars erupted in a spatter of glass and mental. The heavy bullet, distorted, and the jagged fragments of the binoculars ripped into his chest and the white shirt was instantly, magically red.

When he stumbled sideways, catching himself on the lifeline, there was blood on the paint behind him. He lifted the radio to a contorted mouth, a marionette jerking through a repertoire. He looked into the rifle's sight, his eyes minute, mysterious, strangely threatening. They were into Draeger's mind when he spoke, the words unbearably heavy. "Draeger," he said. "Hope—"

The radio dropped from his hand, glinted once on its way to the sea. Kolar's set reported its dying rattle. Two men ran out and dragged Munson through a hatch.

Kolar leaped behind the wheel and drove away, ignoring the half-frightened curious glances of the few people coming out of the buildings. The taxi driver waved cheerfully as they passed. Kolar maintained an easy pace until they were on Roxas Boulevard, then accelerated. They were nearly in Makati when he asked, "Are you all right?"

Draeger said, "I'm fine," and the ease of it amazed him. "I thought I'd be sick or want to cry or something. What I feel is empty. Nothing. I'm more worried about the police than anything else."

"Don't be. The people on that ship aren't going to get mixed up with the law. Roger Munson never happened." Kolar looked in the rearview mirror, and Draeger was waiting for him. Their eyes struck like flints. Kolar turned his attention back to his driving.

"You were right," Draeger said. "It doesn't change anything, but you were right. We can't exist unless everyone knows it's a total commitment."

Kolar nodded.

Draeger watched the traffic. Always he'd hated it, the stink, the noise, the pressure of it. Now he felt those things and didn't care. That created a vague unease and a perverse disappointment that he wasn't more emotionally torn. A calmer, rational view convinced him remorse or apprehension would be far more unsound. Uncalled-for, in fact. The choice had been correct, the action considered and unavoidable.

They were in Draeger's apartment when Cindy arrived in response to Kolar's call. Draeger let her in, handling the tension, greeted her easily. Kolar relaxed in a chair, legs stretched out and his arms hanging limp. "Too spent to rise, my dear," he apologized.

Her hands moved incessantly, and her eyes searched Draeger's face in fevered scans, erratic. "The radio said there was an explosion at the Cultural Center grounds. No one knows if it was a shot, or what, and there's no damage reported. What happened?"

Kolar said, "Glen'll be in the main office for a while, Cindy. I want to move him into admin, some sort of special operations slot."

At her sudden tired slump Draeger rebuked himself for not realizing how exhausted she must be. Her hand in his was freezing. Wires tightened at the backs of his knees, wound around his spine.

She said, "What's happened? Was it Munson? What have you done?"

The maelstrom threatened to tear his head apart. Scenes and visions screamed at him, and he fought them, fought the weakness undermining him. It seemed centuries, but when he looked she waited in front of him and Kolar continued to smile enigmatically from his chair. He found his voice.

"Nothing happened that didn't have to happen. It's the way things are."

He walked her across the room to the window, and she clung to his arm with the tremulous hope of a lost child, neither of them aware of Kolar's silent departure. When he pushed away the drapes she straightened and put her arm across his back and he crossed it with his own, pulling her to him. They looked out together. Night had fallen.

## PROOF

"Nice ears, Spock. Buy them at a convention?" At Charlie's look of puzzlement, Jane waved away the comment. "Never mind. Obviously, they don't have television on Lowth. I'll tell you about it sometime over a cappuccino. That explains the elf half of being a Whelphite. I suppose you have proof of the fairy half?"

He frowned. "You won't take my word for it?"

"The word of a drug-addicted white slaver who thinks he's an elf? Riiight." Jane snapped her fingers, feeling a twinge in her shoulder at the movement. "Cough it up, Keebler."

And that was when the clothes came off....

# What Do You Say to a Naked Elf?

## CHERYL STERLING

LOVE SPELL  NEW YORK CITY

A LOVE SPELL BOOK ®

January 2005

Published by

Dorchester Publishing Co., Inc.
200 Madison Avenue
New York, NY 10016

ISBN 0-505-52619-0

The name "Love Spell" and its logo are trademarks of Dorchester Publishing Co., Inc.

Printed in the United States of America.

Visit us on the web at www.dorchesterpub.com.

*To FNMS–the CommaKazi, POV Police, PETA, and all others. Without you, this would be a lesser work sitting comfortably in a drawer somewhere.*

*To Mom. She didn't live to see it in print, but she profoundly affected these words.*

*And finally, to the real Tivat. His sacrifice under my wheels started this adventure. R. I. P., bunny.*

# What Do You Say to a Naked Elf?

# Chapter One

*Kabloom!* The right front tire blew. The car's headlights illuminated the rabbit sitting in the middle of the lane. Barreling up the highway entrance ramp, Jane Drysdale didn't have time to react.

"Oh, damn," she swore. The animal disappeared between the front tires and the vehicle swung to the right. She heard a sickening *thunk, thunk* and tightened her grip on the steering wheel to wrest back control, but it was too late. Careening down the embankment, still going sixty miles per hour, she watched in horror as she headed for a stand of trees.

Jane stomped on the brakes. The car fishtailed, straightened and, for a few brief seconds, paralleled the road before a line of trees, smaller than the first, rose up before her. She jerked the steering wheel left and ground her foot into the brakes again.

The vehicle veered up the embankment, shuddered and died. Momentum threw Jane forward. The airbag exploded in her face.

Her last conscious thought was the memory of the rabbit shimmering into a more humanlike shape, then reforming just before it slid under her wheels.

An insistent pounding pulled her from the darkness. At first she thought it came from her right temple, where most of the pain in her head centered. It continued, and Jane recognized the sound of someone rapping on glass. With a groan, she twisted and peered out from one eye.

Less than a foot away, a man stared at her, mouthing words she couldn't understand and beating on the car window. He looked deranged. Automatically she reached to touch the buttons to lock the door and windows, only to remember she'd traded in her beloved Mercury the month before. This older Neon, with smaller payments, didn't have the luxury of power options.

Jane's left arm wasn't working too well, so she reached across with her right to lock the door. She noted that the button, inexplicably, was in the down position. Had Detroit changed how things worked? Still disoriented, she pulled up on the tab.

A moment later, the door jerked open from the outside. The man groped her middle with rough hands and fumbled to unsnap her seat belt. The catch gave, and he wrenched her free.

"Hey!" she yelled, not only from the harsh treatment but also a new set of aches that made themselves known.

"There is a fire!" an accented male voice said in her ear.

Jane twisted in her rescuer's hold. From the corner of her eye she saw a flicker of orange. She gasped and struggled against his grip.

"Let me go!" she shouted. She made her body go limp. Dead weight isn't easy to carry off to murder and rape.

Her rescuer released her, and Jane staggered to her feet. The scene before her was nightmarish.

She must have swerved the car too sharply: She'd plowed straight into the embankment, crumpling the car's front end. The hood had popped open, and under its steel canopy a fire the size of her microwave blazed.

Jane swore. *This will be nice explaining to the insurance company—oh my God, the toys!* At the thought of her merchandise, packed in Rubbermaid containers in her backseat and trunk, Jane lurched forward. She had a lot of money tied up in inventory, and it would definitely be impossible to explain to State Farm.

"Get back!" the man shouted. "Stay away!"

"Try and stop me!" she called over her shoulder, stumbling and slipping across the dew-drenched grass.

His hand closed over hers on the door handle. She yanked herself free, using the momentum to elbow him in the stomach. She had the satisfaction of hearing his *whumf* before she pulled open the door and tugged out one of six containers. By the time she had two free, he'd recovered and pushed her aside to get the third.

"Idiot mortal," he exclaimed under his breath.

"Mortal?" She crawled around him in the almost empty backseat. Smoke filled the interior, and she heard fire crackling. "What does that make you? Witch? Warlock?" She pulled down the split-rear back to expose the opening to the trunk. "Help me with this, will you?" Smoke billowed around them, making it difficult to see.

"Get out of here!" he ordered.

"Not until I get my stuff." The seat down, she grabbed the closest box and shoved it in his direction. She heard it slide away, accompanied by a string of what sounded like curses in a language she didn't recognize.

Smoke stung her eyes and burned her lungs, but it didn't stop her from crawling into the trunk and reaching for its release handle. Pulling it with her good hand, she kicked the lid open. Fresh air hit her. Someone helped her out.

"The boxes!" she cried.

"We have them," said a new voice, also accented.

Jane twisted around. A man regarded her, older than

the first, but with the same build—slight, wiry, an inch or two taller than her five-feet-six. She swiveled her head and saw four other men, similar in appearance, all wearing woolen hats or caps, jeans and lightweight jackets. Jockeys? Chimney sweeps? Circus performers?

"Who *are* you people?" she asked. She searched for the first guy, the one who'd pulled her from her car.

Backlit by the fire claiming her little Neon, he stood supervising the stacking of her boxes.

"Darrin," she cried. "Yoo-hoo, Darrin Stephens. Over here." Technically it wasn't accurate, Darrin being the mortal in *Bewitched*, but how many famous warlocks can one name? Jane couldn't name any. She nodded a thanks to the old guy, a move that made her head ache more, and tramped to her rescuer's side.

He caught her arm, his eyes bright with the reflection of the flames. "Get back. It will explode."

She shook her head. "You watch too many movies. It doesn't happen like that in real—"

A huge boom cut off her words. Her companion threw her to the ground, hurling himself on top of her. Jane cried out at the impact, her bruised body about to mutiny. They rolled several feet before coming to a stop. Shards of burning debris rained around them.

Pandemonium broke out. Shouts filled the air, again in a language she didn't know. Metal crashed to the ground, some of it very close to Jane and her rescuer. The roar of the fire intensified.

Jane lay for several moments under the stranger, adjusting to his weight, listening to the sound of his harsh breathing in her ear. After what seemed a reasonable time for him to move, she nudged him in the ribs with a pointed finger.

"Hey, Darrin, you mind getting off me?"

He muttered something and rolled away, taking her hand and rising with her in one fluid movement. "Are you hurt?" he asked.

She had a slight ringing in her ears and the beginning of a headache, plus various bumps and bruises. "From the crash? Yes. From the explosion? Not too much. How about you?"

He shrugged. "Nothing."

Jane looked around. Only the five other men seemed to have stopped at the accident scene. Of course, it was close to one o'clock in the morning. She verified the time on her Indiglo watch and realized Darrin still held her hand.

"Hey," she cried, pulling free. "Thanks for saving my life and all that, but I'm not giving out rewards. Not the kind you're thinking of anyway." She changed the subject. "Did you guys call nine-one-one?"

"Nine-one-one?" he repeated.

"Yeah, like maybe a fire truck or two." She watched in dismay as the husk of her car continued to burn. "Not that it will do me any good, but those hunky firemen like to practice. Keeps their hormones up."

"They will be here."

"Great." Jane shivered, aware that the temperature had dropped since she'd left Kendra's party. She'd made a lot of money tonight, and Darrin had helped save what she hadn't sold. Orders, checks and cash lay tucked in one of the boxes.

"Are you cold?" he asked.

"Yes, I am. Also bruised, battered, dirty, smoky and a dozen other things I'm too tired to think about."

"Come with me. I will give you something to cover you."

A sweater or a blanket sounded good. It was early April, and she hadn't thought that it might be cool after the party. Jane followed him a few steps, then stopped.

"I'm not leaving my boxes. As soon as the fire trucks show up, every gawker within a five-mile radius will rouse himself from in front of his television and hop in his pickup truck. I'm surprised there isn't anyone here yet, what with police scanners and CBs."

"You are worried about the boxes?"

Hadn't he heard what she said? "Yes."

He put two fingers in his mouth and emitted a multi-toned whistle. "My companions will bring them."

"Your companions? Er, I don't want to sound ungrateful or anything, but where are you fellows from?"

"Sylthia." He ducked his head and held a low branch out of her way as they continued their walk.

"Sylthia," she repeated. "And where is that, exactly?"

"Lowth."

"Uh-huh. Is that where you learned English? Because you really need to buy a contraction or two, Vanna."

"My name," he said, his voice firm, "is Charlie."

Charlie. Uh-huh. Just her luck to draw a Charlie for a rescuer. If this were a romance novel, his name would be Chase. He'd be six inches taller, forty pounds heavier, have buns to die for and reek of testosterone. Instead, she'd wound up with a reed of a rescuer who looked as if he didn't shave more than once a week. Without a sense of humor, too. Didn't he own a television? Of course, not everyone watched reruns night after lonely night as she did. Nevertheless, the guy didn't seem to have a clue.

At least he'd helped save her merchandise. Jane looked over her shoulder to check on it. The leader followed, one of the boxes in his arms. Good. She couldn't afford to lose any of her toys. Realm of Pleasures was the latest in her long string of get-rich-quick schemes. At various times she'd moonlighted from her ho-hum secretarial job. She'd tried various products with little success. Realm seemed to be the niche she'd been seeking: selling lotions, potions, massage oils and adult playthings to bored, rich women de-livered a slow but steady income.

Not that she had much use for anything that involved a partner, her love life being the way it was, but she could testify to the effectiveness of the vibrators. The Long, Tall Texan was her current favorite.

A gust of cold wind snapped Jane from her thoughts. She looked from the path they'd been following and realized they weren't anywhere near the highway. Furthermore, they'd been walking for some time.

"Hey," she called, stopping in her tracks. "Where are you fellows parked, anyway? Why aren't we up by the road so we can direct the firemen?" She turned, trying to make sense of the landscape. "Where are we?" Mist swirled around them, making it impossible to see more than a few feet. It muffled any noise. She felt as if she'd stepped into a white vacuum.

Charlie stopped, a look of impatience on his face. "We are almost there."

"How far away is it? Why are you guys out this late?"

Her rescuer touched her arm. "All will be answered."

Something didn't sound right about this. Jane tried to pull free from his grip, but he was stronger.

"Let go of me," she ordered. The mist swallowed her words. Not so much as an echo came back to her. "I don't like this. Where are your companions? Help!"

"They went ahead." He tugged on her to follow him. "We are almost there."

Jane resisted. She hadn't heard anyone pass them.

"You belong to some kind of cult, don't you? I could tell by the way you're dressed, like that Heaven's Gate guy. Ohmigod, you're white slavers. You're going to sell me into a prostitution ring." Her heart raced faster. She raised her free hand. "Watch out. I know karate."

"You are wrong." Charlie looked ready to do the Vulcan neck pinch on her.

"*You're* wrong. I'm not taking another step with you."

He sighed. "As you wish."

Before she knew what he'd done, she felt a sharp pain, like the bite of a ten-pound mosquito, on her bare arm. She looked down to see him withdraw a small syringe-like thorn from her flesh.

"Ohmigod," she said again. "You're into drugs, too." Then the mist changed to black and swallowed her.

Jane woke in an uncomfortable position. It took a moment for her to realize that the pressure on her stomach, the ground rushing at her and her body bouncing up and down meant that she lay across someone's shoulders. Charlie. She thumped his back, hard.

He dropped her. She fell in an ungraceful tangle of legs and arms into a bush, which practically devoured her.

"Hey," she yelled, trying to clamber from the foliage that was scraping her all over. "What'd you do that for?"

Charlie bent forward, his hands on his knees, wincing in pain. "Why did you hit me?"

"You?" she exclaimed. "I'm the injured party here. I banged up my car, then it caught on fire, and *then* I was kidnapped by white slavers with drug addictions. On top of everything else, I killed a bunny tonight."

Charlie straightened, wincing as if he'd pulled a muscle. "It was not a bunny."

She extracted herself from the woman-eating plant. "I ought to know one when I see one. He was definitely a Looney-Tunes-union-card-carrying bunny. I creamed him."

"It was not a bunny."

"Oh, yeah? What then?"

He looked her in the eye, as serious as an executioner. "An elf."

Jane burst out laughing. "Are you sure you didn't shoot up after me?" she asked, trying to catch her breath. "Or maybe I'm going nuts." She felt her forehead. No fever, but a low throb.

"You're quite sane."

"Then you're the one who's Looney Tunes. I thought you said I hit an elf."

"You did. His name was Tivat."

"Tivat the Elf, hmmm? What was his last name, Keebler?" Charlie shook his head. "I'm not familiar with that name."

"Of course not. Are you familiar with the term 'psychiatric treatment'? Because I think you've missed a few sessions, buddy."

"My name is not Buddy. It's—"

"Charlie. I know. Mine's Jane Drysdale. Get used to it. You'll be seeing it on quite a few legal documents after I figure out where I am and get to the nearest lawyer."

"I am the nearest lawyer," he said with a slight bow. "And you are in Lowth."

"Lowth? Your home planet? Go to Mapquest.com, buddy, because we're in Walker, Michigan. That road"—she pointed in the general vicinity of the way they'd come—"is I-96. There should be a house around here I can call from and get help."

"You have help, Jane Drysdale. Mine. I am your legal counsel."

Maybe the air bag hadn't inflated. Jane felt as if she'd suffered a serious head injury. "And why would I need legal counsel, Perry Mason?"

"For the murder of Tivat." He looked at her as if she'd forgotten that two plus two equal four.

"Tivat? The elf-turned-rabbit? Okaaay. And what is that called? Elficide? Vehicular Fairyslaughter? Reckless Endangerment of a Pixie?"

"It's called murder. I wouldn't joke about it, Jane Drysdale. The implications are serious."

Tenacious little fellow. "Riiight. Just call me Jane, okay? Hey, you used a contraction. What's up with that?"

He sighed. "You're on Lowth. The sap from the stitchtree thorn also works as a translator. We're speaking my language."

"Riiight. Very interesting, Charlie-defender-of-elves. Well, if you don't mind, I think I'll be going now. It's been a lovely evening. Let's try it again some time. Not."

Disgusted and tired, Jane spun and stalked off the way they'd come. Sooner or later she'd find a house and rouse someone from their toasty bed, then she'd get home and forget this crackpot.

She took a few steps before she noticed the difference in her surroundings. For one thing, it looked a lot lighter than the middle of the night. More pre-dawnish. For another, big trees, like sequoias, surrounded her. She'd lived in Michigan all her life and never seen anything like this. Least of all in Walker, with its industrial sprawl.

"Hey," she cried, whirling around. Charlie stood where she'd left him. "How long was I out, anyway? Did you and your buddies throw me in the back of a padded wagon and take me someplace different? Where am I?"

"You're on Lowth," he repeated, walking over to her. "As I said earlier. My world."

"Well, beam me back, Scotty, because I don't want to be here." She'd had enough of this train wreck. Either Charlie was crazy, or the stuff he'd injected had taken her on a trip to write up in *The Junkies' Home Journal*.

"Jane, there is no way back. The portal has closed." His eyes—brown, she noticed—filled with empathy.

"Portals don't close on their own. Turn the key or cast a spell or do whatever you elves do to open it back up." Jane blinked her eyes, hoping sanity would return.

No such luck. Giant trees still loomed over them. Too much green and too many leaves for the beginning of April told her she'd been transported to another season, as well.

Charlie watched her.

"Are you ready?" he asked with a touch of impatience.

She shook her pounding head. "Not until I get some answers. Who are you?"

"Charles of Sylthia."

"A lawyer?"

He nodded.

"An elf lawyer?"

"Technically, not an elf. I'm a Whelphite."

"And what," she asked slowly, "is a Whelphite?"

"Half elf, half fairy-sprite. Interspecies breeding is not uncommon on Lowth."

Jane took a step back. "Uh-huh. Don't get any ideas about breeding with this species, buddy. I'll show you a Klingon choke hold you won't forget for a while."

His brow wrinkled. "I'm not—"

"Familiar with that name," she finished for him, feeling exasperated. Jeez. Did the guy live in a time capsule or something? "I suppose you have some proof of this preposterous claim of yours?"

In answer, Charlie reached up and removed the wool cap he'd been wearing. She first noticed his hair, gold and long—like Legolas, from the *Lord of the Rings* movies. The next thing she saw went right along with the first: two pointed ears.

What kind of whacked-out Trekkie had picked her up? She hoped his ears were silicone, not the result of some sick mutilation surgery.

"Nice ears, Spock. Buy them at a convention?" At his look of puzzlement, she waved away the comment. "Never mind. Obviously, they don't have television on Lowth. I'll tell you about it sometime over a cappuccino. That explains the elf half of being a Whelphite. I suppose you have proof of the fairy half?"

He frowned. "You won't take my word for it?"

"The word of a drug-addicted white slaver who thinks he's an elf? Riiight." Jane snapped her fingers, feeling a twinge in her shoulder at the movement. "Cough up it, Keebler."

"You're not going to be satisfied until you've seen it all, are you?" he asked, arms crossed in front of him.

"Nope. I'm not budging another step. Don't even think about sprinkling any pixie dust on me, either."

Charlie glared at her, then softly swore. He unbuttoned his jacket and shirt. "I don't do this for everyone," he grumbled, shrugging them off. "And it's still cold out."

"I don't get to see a fairy strip every day, either. Too bad I don't have any dollar bills on me." She tried not to think of her purse, a charred piece of imitation leather somewhere in another world. Or, outside this hallucination.

Charlie's physique, however, wasn't an illusion. He wasn't thin and scrawny as she'd first thought, but simply of a slight build. It had been a long time since Jane had seen a man's chest, and he had a nice one: chiseled, with golden threads of hair sprinkled across it. Hoo-boy. She was about to let loose with a hoot when he turned his back to her. A pair of glimmering, almost transparent wings unfurled, catching in the morning breeze.

Jane fainted.

# Chapter Two

Jane woke to the smell of pine. It tickled her nostrils and made her want to sneeze. Intending to suppress it, she moved her hand in the general vicinity of her nose. On the way, her fingers brushed against something. Some*one*, she realized. Her eyes snapped open.

Charlie. Elf-man extraordinaire. His face wavered like the start of a cheesy dream sequence in a sitcom. Light filtered through leaves above him.

"Are we flying?" Jane asked.

"No," he said. A smile tugged at the corners of his mouth. Jane had a feeling he didn't smile too often and had to stop and read the instructions when he did. "You fainted."

"Fainted? Ridiculous. I never faint." She touched her head to explore for bumps and found a large one over her right eye. It throbbed like a bad rap song. "Must be from that drug you gave me."

"You fainted," he repeated, more firmly this time. "It's the third time you've been unconscious since I met you."

"And none of them my fault," Jane corrected. She

struggled to sit, noticing for the first time that she lay on the forest floor and Charlie knelt beside her. He extended a hand. She accepted his offer and swayed to regain her footing.

"Your friend Tivat threw himself in front of my car, then you shot me up with happy juice, then you surprised me with your wings. I'm the most unfaintiest person you'll ever meet."

Jane glanced around cautiously. Forest surrounded them, the trees as wide as her Neon, God rest its charred soul, and rising two hundred or more feet in the air. Fern-like plants crowded their bases and spilled into the path.

She swung her gaze in Charlie's direction. "These trees won't throw apples at me or anything, will they?"

He wrinkled his brow. "Why would they do that? Is that what the trees do in your world?"

"Only in the movies, Charlie, only in the movies." At his perplexed look, she added, "Remind me to tell you about it sometime."

Jane rolled up the sleeves of the jacket he must have put on her. She noticed as she did that he had his shirt on again, his wings no doubt folded underneath like a Japanese fan. Too bad. He had a nice body.

"Do you really have wings?" she asked, unsure she'd seen them now that she'd had time to think. So many strange things had happened to her tonight.

"Yes, I really do," he confirmed. His eyes, the color of coffee with two creams, filled with amusement.

*Kind of cute when he isn't being so serious.* Jane stuck her hands in the pockets of her slacks. "I don't suppose you'd let me see them again, would you?"

He looked baffled, as though women didn't ask him to undress every day. Which, come to think of it, they probably didn't.

She did her best Scarlett O'Hara impression, fluttering her Revlon-enhanced eyelashes at him. "Please, Charlie?"

"Certainly not." His voice huffy, he took a step back. "I only showed you the first time to prove my point."

*The prude returns.* "Oh, good grief. You act like I want you to audition for the Chippendales." At his usual look of puzzlement, she added, "I don't want to see you naked."

*Partial truths for one hundred, Alex.* She did want another peek at the chest she'd swooned over. Nicely sculpted, if she remembered correctly. As for his wings, she wondered what they felt like. Hoo-boy, did it always get this hot in Lowth, or had her part-time job affected her libido?

Charlie blushed. Charming, she decided. She didn't meet many men, and none of the ones she knew would be un-macho enough to blush.

"I didn't think you did, Jane Drysdale."

*Back to the full name.* She must have upset him more than she'd realized. Trying not to discomfort him again, she gestured ahead. "What's next?" she asked.

"We're almost to Sylthia," Charlie said, starting up the path, his relief obvious from his haste. He motioned for her to follow.

"Right. Sylthia. Elven city of mystery. Or is that elfish?" She followed alongside and attempted to keep up.

"Elven," he replied. "And the mystery we have does not concern the city. At least, not directly."

Her ears perked up. She slowed. "Mystery? What mystery?"

He glanced at her, adjusting his stride. "You must concentrate on your own problems."

She scratched her nose, which had begun to itch again. "Such as?"

"The murder trial."

"Oh, right. That." She'd killed a bunny. Correction, an elf. Tivat. She wondered what he'd been like and why he'd chosen that moment to dive under her tires.

"You hadn't forgotten it?"

"In one of my many moments of elf-induced coma?"

She sneezed and shook her head soberly. "Not hardly. But I have complete confidence in you, Charlie-defender-of-mortals. You've probably memorized every law volume in Elfdom—excuse me, Lowth. You do have books, don't you?"

"Of course we do." He looked at her, his gaze steady. She'd bet he never got in a fight with anyone. An odd profession he'd picked, then. A thought crossed her mind, chilling her.

"Charlie, what kind of lawyer are you?"

He looked uncomfortable and did not meet her eyes. After a moment he replied, "Trade agreements. Some family practice."

Shock ran through her. She stopped in her tracks, one hand on her hip. "You're not a criminal lawyer?"

Charlie shook his head. "We don't have much crime on Lowth. Petty burglaries, an occasional break-in."

Jane couldn't believe her ears. "Are you saying," she asked, trying to keep her panic in check, "that you've never defended anyone in a murder trial?"

He looked over her left shoulder, avoiding her eyes. "The last murder happened two years ago."

"Great, just great." She threw up her hands in exasperation and paced the trail. "You might as well lock me up in Elfcatraz now. I have no hope of getting free, let alone back to the real world. I knock over an elf in full view of six witnesses, the judicial system is rusted through with holes, and my defense attorney was in high school when they tried the last murderer."

"I was twenty-five," Charlie corrected. "I remember it well."

"I'm doomed," she said, finally buying into his story. A cool breeze ruffled her hair and continued downward to blast her heart. He meant what he said. Even scarier, she'd started to believe him. Murder? Her?

Jane took a step forward and caught her slacks on one of

the ferns that littered the path. As she jerked free, the pungent smell of pine hit her again and made her sneeze.

"What is this stuff?" she asked when she recovered. The delicate lace plant had taken on the characteristics of a Stephen King creation.

Charlie touched one of the leaves. "Bellefern. A rogue weed. It's taken over everywhere."

"Too bad you don't have Weed 'N Feed here." She brushed green dust off her slacks.

As usual, he looked confused.

Jane moved up the path. Action kept her from thinking too deeply about this mess. "What happens when we get to Sylthia?" They had been "almost there" for the last half hour. Of course, she'd delayed them with fainting and the drug coma thing. Inconsiderate of her, she knew. "Do I go on trial right away, or is breakfast my last meal?"

"You will have many meals," Charlie said with confidence.

"Yes? Why is that?"

"Because there is no body."

The human woman didn't say anything for a moment, which came as a welcome relief to Charlie. Growing up with three sisters, he knew how long and convoluted women's stories could be. But this one, this Jane Drysdale, hadn't stopped yapping since he met her. Half the time, he didn't understand what she said. She referred to things of which he had no knowledge. He'd be glad when he could hand her over to Eagar, steward of Sylthia castle, and go home.

Charlie glanced at her and noticed how much of a prisoner she looked already. Her green eyes sported purple bruises above them, the largest on her right temple. Bits of leaves stuck in her short brown curls, making her look like a demented Spriggan. Stains and a small rip in her clothes completed the disheveled effect. She smelled of smoke.

So did he, he imagined. Just his luck to be on community duty when Tivat, arrested for stealing sheep, had escaped and gone through the portal. Otherwise Charlie would be home now, instead of making the last leg to Sylthia with a crazy woman. And saddled with defending her! Maybe, if she kept her mouth shut—

"No body?" she asked: "Bunny body or elf body?"

Charlie didn't want to go into the intricacies of shapeshifting, or the effects of death on someone caught in another form.

"We didn't have much time to look. The fire would bring other mortals, and we couldn't risk discovery. We'd already taken a chance, coming so far. The portal is unstable at the best of times. It had started to weaken after the explosion. You had to be on the other side before that happened."

She moved in a circle around him. "They have no proof? Then you have to take me home. Case closed, problem solved, I'm free to go."

She didn't understand. "No, you have to go on trial."

"But you don't even know if the bunny was Tivat. There are thousands of rabbits in Walker."

"We tracked him from Lowth. We had him in sight when that machine of yours rushed from nowhere and hit him."

"Hit him, yes. Killed him? No one stayed around long enough to find out. Maybe I just grazed him." She pulled on Charlie's arm, tugging him the way they'd come. "Take me back. Even if I killed him—and you can't prove I did— you'd crossed the state line. It was outside your jurisdiction."

Charlie shook his head. "I know my duty. There will be a trial, I'll get you off, and we'll proceed from there." She didn't need to know now that the portal had a mind of its own and might refuse her entry.

Her brows knitted. "How can you be my lawyer if you saw it happen? Isn't that a conflict of interest?"

"At any other time—"

"I don't want to hear about another time. Let's talk about now." She tapped her foot on the dirt trail.

He sighed. She might as well hear everything. "I was last in line. I didn't see the murder. Jaspar, the one who helped you from your car, is the team leader. He declared me a nonwitness and your lawyer in the same breath."

She shook her head. "And they trust you to bring me in? Who's to say you can't look away for a minute, and I'll disappear?"

Charlie bristled. "Do you think me dishonest? That I would break the laws of the land I love?"

Her eyes flashed. "Excuse me, Mr. Rules, I thought you were on my side. You don't want this any more than I do."

His thought exactly. He'd never met anyone who made him feel awkward the way she did. Talking about wings and nakedness—the idea! The sooner she disappeared from his life, the sooner he could get back to his routine.

"I'm sorry," he said, placing their fates together. "I really don't have a choice. I'm bound to the law."

She regarded him for several moments before nodding. Some of the fire faded from her eyes. "All right," she acquiesced. "How long can it take? A day or two? I don't have any parties booked until Thursday. It will be like watching the Discovery Channel. 'The Secret Lives of Elves.'"

A few minutes later, they came to the edge of the great Malin Forest. The Sentinel, the largest tree in this part of the Malin, stood before them. One of the last of the old growth, it towered over everything. It had watched Charlie's ancestors build Sylthia thousands of years before. Only the Groke, in Malik Forest, stood taller.

"Wow," Jane said, craning her neck so far Charlie thought she'd topple over. "That is one whale of a tree."

He didn't know what a whale was, but it must be enormous in her world.

"Touch it." At her quizzical look, he took her hand and laid it on the well-worn bark. "It's good luck."

"I can understand luck." She rubbed the trunk. "Come on, seven. Momma needs a new pair of shoes."

Puzzled, Charlie looked at her footwear.

"Not literally," Jane admonished. She looped her arm through his, startling him with her familiarity. "I'll tell you about it sometime." She returned to the path to continue their journey, but stopped in her tracks.

"A castle," she whispered in awe.

"Sylthia," Charlie corrected. He followed her gaze to his favorite view in the world.

It lay on the other side of a vast plain of hardscrabble rock that had served as defense and battleground in the old times. Rising from the foundation of a hundred-foot plateau, it stretched another two hundred feet into the sky. Unseen from this angle, Charlie knew the other side plunged to the sea and boulders as big as houses. Impenetrable, it had been home to the Malin family of Elves for centuries.

"Walt Disney, eat your heart out," Jane said. "What a lucky man you are, Charlie, to have such a place to live."

He felt the warm glow that only Sylthia could give him. He'd come to it as a foundling. The city meant as much to him as his adopted family, maybe more. One of the reasons he'd chosen to be a lawyer was to protect it with the fair interpretation of its laws.

"It's your home now, Jane," he said, catching sight of Hugh, his adopted brother, driving a pony-pulled wagon. Eagar accompanied him. Neither looked worried about Charlie's delay in bringing the prisoner Jane to the place of her trial and possible execution.

Her home? Not by a long shot. As soon as this farce was over, she would head out. If she couldn't convince Charlie to take her, there ought to be an elf version of Han Solo she could hire to get her back through the portal.

Moving closer to Charlie, Jane eyed the two strangers who neared. So far, Charlie had been her only contact with Sylthia and Lowth, and she'd like to keep it that way. At least, until tomorrow morning when she woke up in intensive care, her head bandaged from her severe concussion.

"Who are they?" she asked her companion.

"The younger is my brother Hugh."

Hugh was the stereotype in every drawing Jane had ever seen of an elf. He had pointed ears, dark hair and skin, and a stockier build than his brother. They looked nothing alike.

"And the other?" A cold chill not caused by the weather made Jane hug the jacket around her. The smell of woods and smoke drifted from it.

"Eagar, the steward of Sylthia."

"Eager? What kind of name is Eager? Why is he eager?"

"Eagar," Charlie said, emphasizing the long *a* after the *g*. "A very wise man and one of our leaders."

The closer he came, the more uneasy Jane felt. The older man was dressed all in black, in linen trousers, leather boots and a tight shirt that emphasized his lean body. Not one hair grew on his head, making his ears seem more prominent and pointed. His eyes, as dark as his clothing, had three sets of bags under them. Jane's flesh crawled from the evil flowing from him. He looked like a pedophiliac priest or a satanic Uncle Fester.

She gulped and laid a hand on Charlie's arm. "Ummm, he's not involved in my trial, is he?"

Charlie looked at her, a surprised expression on his face. "Of course. The elders will hear your case and decide your future."

*This is not good news.* She didn't know why this elf should make a bad impression on her, but she'd learned long ago to trust her instincts, at least about people. Get-rich-quick schemes were another matter. Her people instincts never misled her. "A touch of the fey," her mother called it. Wouldn't it be more pronounced in the fairy world?

Her usual bravado deserted her. Jane took a deep breath and put on a wide smile. Eagar, partial holder of her fate, would not see her flinch.

Charlie stepped away from her to catch the bridle of the pony, stopping the wagon. He looked at his brother.

"Well met, Hugh. I did not look forward to the rest of the walk."

His brother took out a handkerchief and wiped his brow. "You passed safely?"

"Safely enough."

Jane caught the look that moved between them. Before she could comment, Charlie turned and drew her to his side.

"Jane, may I present my brother, Hugh Tanner, and Eagar Currge, elder of Sylthia. Gentlemen, this is Jane Drysdale, of whom you have no doubt heard."

Murderess of a shape-shifting elf, plower-downer of a body-sharing rabbit, car destroyer and hostage in Disney World. Or an unconscious victim of a violent accident? She preferred the latter; it seemed more real.

Hugh nodded, touching a finger to his brow as if lifting an invisible cap. Eagar stared at her, not a trace of friendliness showing. Jane gulped, despite her earlier promise to not show fear. She couldn't help her nerves. After all, she'd been accused of murder. Forgetting to ask Charlie the punishment for such a crime had been a mistake. To know the worst would curtail her wild imagination, which was wilder, seeing eager Eagar already condemning her with the look in his eyes.

Hugh leaned down and extended a hand to help her into the wagon. Jane took it. Already she felt shackles on her ankles and a noose around her neck. She settled behind Eagar, staring at his bald, malevolent head. She waited until Charlie sat down and Hugh turned the wagon.

The castle of Sylthia in front of her, Jane lifted her chin in defiance.

"Lay on, Macduff," she said.

# Chapter Three

"Shabby" best described Sylthia. "Derelict," maybe. A new coat of paint here, a planter spilling over with geraniums there, indicated some attempts at upkeep, but the place reminded Jane of an elderly neighbor she'd had while growing up. No matter how hard he'd tried, his efforts at taking care of his house and yard couldn't stop the gradual deterioration.

Jane didn't know castles outside of movies and the trip she'd made with her family to Disney World the summer she'd turned seven. Those buildings had been clean and well tended. Sylthia looked as if the king couldn't afford new curtains. Even the pennant at the top of the tallest tower, a blue cross on a white background, flapped in a half-hearted manner.

The wagon pulled through a second gate, then up a hill to the main building of the castle. The keep, Jane reminded herself from the picture book she'd read the week before to her brother Paul's children. Home of the royal family. Home of the royal dungeons. Jane gulped and tightened her hold on Charlie's arm. The thought of this being real and her never seeing her family again was sobering.

Hugh stopped the wagon. All three occupants turned to her.

"Is this when I'm clapped in irons and chained to the dungeon wall?" she asked, afraid she spoke the truth. She still couldn't believe her bad luck.

Eagar looked as if the treatment might be too gentle for her. Charlie squeezed her hand. Hugh, bless him, smiled, dispelling some of her fear.

"The dungeons have been closed for years. We generally put our prisoners in a storeroom while they wait," he said.

Storeroom? Great. Jane pictured rats gnawing her face while she slept. If she slept. She shivered.

"That's a relief," she muttered.

"Come, Jane," Charlie said. He helped her disembark, his hand on her arm. It did not reassure her.

Eagar followed, brushing dust off his impeccable clothes. Hugh remained in the wagon.

"See you later?" he asked his brother.

Charlie shook his head. "I'm too tired. I'll stay in my room here. Give my love to Mara." He stepped back.

Hugh chirruped to the pony and drove off down the hill.

*Mara?* Jane asked herself. *Who is Mara, and to whom does she belong?* Charlie's voice had sounded affectionate. A girlfriend? His wife?

She didn't have time for more speculation. They moved toward the entrance. She counted twenty steps before an iron-pinioned oak door swung open.

Threadbare tapestries and tarnish. Cobwebs and dimness. The rooms they paraded her through reinforced her first impression of the palace: It needed a massive spring-cleaning.

They walked down a hall wider than a four-lane highway to the far back and a carpeted stairway. Eagar hustled them around corners and along corridors to another stairway, inlaid with wood this time. Two flights down found them negotiating narrower halls and plain wooden steps. By the time they reached their destination, Jane felt lost and claustrophobic.

Eagar produced a key from a pocket she hadn't noticed and shoved it into the keyhole of a windowless door. It opened with a Boris Karloff rusty-hinges squeak. Jane expected bats to fly out, at least one of them a vampire in disguise, intent on sucking away her lifeblood.

"In you go," Eagar said, the first he'd spoken to her.

*You murderous tear-my-liver-out-and-serve-it-to-me-for-break-fast wench*, Jane knew he wanted to add.

It took a moment for her eyes to adjust to the dim interior of the room. Sacks of grain, no doubt rodent hors d'oeuvres, reached six feet up the back wall. Barrels sat in one corner. Dust covered everything. There were no signs of rats. Yet.

"Restful and homelike," Jane said, trying to be brave. Her insides had metamorphosed into enough Jell-O for a church picnic. She looked at Charlie imploringly.

"Leave her a light," he said to Eagar. "She can't do any damage, the room's made of stone."

Eagar hesitated. Jane bit her lip, knowing this wasn't the time to beg or plead. That would come later.

She watched the unspoken communication between the two elves and held her breath. At last, Eagar pushed past and walked into the room. From another pocket, he conjured a small torch. With a flick of his wrist, it flared to light. He stuck it into a hole in the wall and spun on his heel.

Panic tore at Jane. "Charlie?" she asked. Her voice wobbled. She clung to his arm, not wanting to let go.

His brown eyes filled with compassion. "It will be all right." He patted her hand. "Nothing will happen until to-morrow at the earliest."

*Don't go, don't go,* her mind begged. Maybe telepathy would work in this strange land.

Maybe not. He didn't seem to have received her signal.

"All is not lost," he reassured her. Bending closer, he whispered in her ear, "I still have a few ideas. I'll take care of you, Jane Drysdale."

He pulled away. "Try to get some sleep," he added. With obvious reluctance and a look she knew he meant to make her feel better, he backed into the hall.

Pure satisfaction on his face, Eagar shut the door. Although it was made of wood, it sounded to Jane like a 1940s movie, Jimmy-Cagney-on-death-row, prison-issued, you're-going-to-fry metal clang. She'd been abandoned to the sputtering of a weak torch and the imminent arrival of several dozen hungry rats.


A short time later, in his office next to the castle's receiving dock, Charlie was struggling to rid himself of Jane's image. He felt as if he'd abandoned her. She was alone in a strange land and afraid. Even though a prisoner, she deserved better treatment. A cot, some food—he'd make sure Eagar improved her spare conditions. For that matter, the castle had enough empty guest rooms to accommodate her.

Poor Sylthia. Poor Lowth. Charlie tried to get comfortable. Unable to concentrate on work, he'd been planning to take a nap on the cot he used when business kept him from returning home to the Malin village. *Which isn't often anymore*, he reflected. His side business, importing and exporting wool, like all businesses on Lowth, grew less each year.

*Because of the Dymynsh.* Faceless, an invisible entity, it spread its deadly tentacles to all corners of his world. Not exactly a disease, not exactly a blight, but both; no one could pinpoint when it had started. Old-timers said as long as twenty years before. Speculation on its cause yielded many theories. The current, most popular theory had to do with a spell cast by a wizard in the Malik forest. Charlie didn't care or wonder. He only knew that, in his ten years of working with the different trades, each harvest, each shearing, brought less to the market.

The Dymynsh didn't affect only wool, grain and cattle; Lowth's population had dwindled over the last few years as well. The elderly and infirm died more frequently. Rare illnesses swept the land, taking many victims. Charlie, the middle child in a family of five, belonged to the last generation of multiple-child families. Women couldn't conceive. A single offspring or, more alarmingly, none at all, seemed normal now.

Lowth was dying. The Dymynsh, insidious and persistent, hindered or prevented life. He'd seen how it had crippled his beautiful world. People, crops, livestock, food: all had suffered. Each brought more repercussions.

He stopped, postponing thoughts of Lowth's fate until later, after he brought about Jane's release.

Jane. Her green eyes haunted him. Outspoken, nonsense-speaking, annoying mortal she might be, but he'd never met anyone like her. Wanting to see his wings again—he groaned at the memory of her boldness. Her presence in his world upset his careful routine. He disliked that he had to represent her. But part of him liked being around her.

Charlie twisted on the cot, restless. Despite his reassurances, the lack of a corpse was her only defense. How strong would the prosecutor's case be? There were five witnesses.

Of course, if the elders found her guilty, her execution would contradict Charlie's people's fight against the Dymynsh. Her debt might be paid in another way. He closed his eyes, thinking about it. For the first time in hours, he relaxed. A punishment in Lowth made return to her world impossible. He chuckled. Maybe they'd found a cure for the Dymynsh after all.

He fell asleep to thoughts of Jane battling the scourge. It never had a chance.

"Move and ye die," a voice hissed in Jane's ear, startling her from sleep.

*Can't I ever wake to bluebirds twittering and coffee brewing?* she wondered. In the past twenty-four hours, she'd regained consciousness to a car wreck, after being drugged *and* seeing a man with wings, and now she rode The Disgruntled Pirates of the Caribbean ride, no doubt with Long John S'elf'er.

The cold touch of metal against her throat suppressed her snappy retort. Her heart hammering, she squeezed her eyes shut. *There's no place like home, there's no place like home.* She transmitted the plea in silence. *Glinda, hear me.*

"Name's Muttle, and ye ain't never goin' home," the stranger said.

Jane's eyes snapped open, despite the command not to move. *They change into animals and read minds. What next? Teleportation?*

"Death for ye, that's what," came the answer.

Jane stared at the little person in front of her. Not Little Person, like a midget, but a tiny, incredibly detailed miniature person. Or elf, or fairy, or whatever species he might be. Barely two feet tall, in tattered brown clothes, he stared back at her through multicolored eyes. Green and blue and hints of yellow swirled in their depths, like a fiery water opal. Thin brown hair covered his head. Slim, tapered fingers held a knife with a three-inch blade. She assumed its mate lay against her throat, ready to slice her to ribbons.

She'd never seen anything like him, and again the reality of her bizarre situation slammed into her. Last night hadn't been a dream. Those events had actually taken place—the accident, the murder, her imprisonment. George Lucas wasn't testing his newest animatronics on her. She'd left Earth. A new world had trapped her. Depression struck.

"You're real," she whispered.

"Of course I be real, daft mortal. Did ye expect else?" The creature moved back a step, releasing the pressure on her neck. He pirouetted for her inspection. "Like what ye see? It may be yer last sight."

Jane doubted he would hurt her. She had a feeling he was all talk and boasts. Slowly, she sat up from her lumpy mattress made of grain sacks. Aches and pains she'd forgotten reintroduced themselves. A car accident, being slung over someone's shoulder and a nap on a bushel or so of corn contributed to the stiffness of her body. With great care, so as not to alarm the halfling, she extended one hand.

"I won't hurt you," she reassured him.

"Hurt I? Humph." He twitched his little head. "I be not afraid of the likes of ye." He brandished twin knives in what should have been a menacing way. Instead, Jane smiled at his comedic attempt at fierceness.

"Who are you? What are you?" she asked.

He rolled his eyes in the same manner she had done to her parents countless times during her adolescence.

"Be ye deaf? I be Muttle, a Belwaith of Malin."

Belwaith? Was that some kind of fairy? A pixie? Or a half-breed? She wished she could ask Charlie.

"He sleeps," Muttle said.

How did he know?

"Lots of things I know."

"Hey," she said, rolling to her feet, heedless of any danger the creature posed. She towered over him. "Stop that. It's rude to dip into people's minds."

"I stop not." He thrust out a tiny chin.

"You stop, yes," Jane retorted, angry. When he flourished a knife in the air, she added, "What are you going to do, stab me in the kneecap? I can pick you up and fling you against the wall if I want. Stay out of my head, Muttle,

Belwaith of Malin. I am very, very dangerous." She emphasized the last sentence by stepping closer to the creature. She'd taken a lot of crap from the citizens of Lowth. If she had to fight back, a mini-Munchkin was as good a place to start as any.

Muttle regarded her through whirling, sea-colored eyes. After a moment, he grinned to reveal surprisingly white teeth.

"I like mortal," he said. "Mortal not afraid." The knives disappeared into the folds of his clothes.

"My name is Jane," she said, relieved the weapons were no longer an immediate threat. She tried to calm her heart. Her mother warned her often enough about the prudence of thinking first and speaking later. Maybe she should listen for once, especially with knives involved.

"Yes. Jane of the dryad's dale." He circled around her, no doubt as fascinated by her as she by him.

"Riiight. Dryad's dale." Why not? Maybe if she claimed kinship to them, she'd be exempt from the death penalty in a murder trial.

"How did you get in here? What do you want?" she asked.

Muttle crooked a finger and shuffled in bare feet to one of the barrels in the corner.

"Here." He pointed.

Jane fetched the torch and handed it to him. She took hold of the barrel and grappled it aside. A hole the size of a melon lay carved in the stone wall.

"Nice," she said. "Where does it lead?"

"Him."

"Him? Him who?" Charlie? God forbid, Eagar?

"No. *Him*." Awe filled Muttle's voice.

"Okaaay. Him. Are you going back now?" Maybe she could tie a message to the Belwaith. *Help. Save me. I'm being held captive by demented movie characters.*

Muttle took her hand, his skin cool and dry.

"Come, Jane of the dryads. Sent me to get ye."

"To get me? Who? Him?"

He nodded.

Jane disentangled herself from the creature. "Look, Muttle, as much as I'd like to escape from here and tick off Eagar, I can't do any of that shape-shifting, voodoo, hocus-pocus stuff." At his bewildered look, she said in a softer tone, "I don't fit."

"Yes." He nodded vigorously. "Sylthia like Jane. Sylthia move for Jane." He took her hand again. Tugging, he pulled her over to the opening.

Resigned to whatever he had in mind, Jane knelt down and let the Belwaith guide her. He put her hand on the stone.

"Pull," he commanded.

Jane sighed. It wouldn't do any good, but she gripped the rough edge and gave a halfhearted tug.

The stone blurred. She felt the hole expand to twice its previous size. Unable to believe she'd actually changed its shape, she threw all her weight into the next effort.

An opening the size of a refrigerator formed and stabilized.

Jane blinked in surprise. She looked over to Muttle. He smiled, delight dancing across his face.

"Well, bless my buttons," she exclaimed. "Come on, Scarecrow, we're off to see the Wizard." Taking her diminutive rescuer's hand, she walked through the gap.

# Chapter Four

"So, what's she like?"

Charlie looked up from his evening meal and over at his sister-in-law, Mara. She stood with one hand on an ample hip, regarding him through inquisitive hazel eyes.

"Who?" he asked, his mind on the work undone today. His nap short-lived, he'd tried to involve himself in his duties. Soon, that too had proved futile. Hoping to have better luck the next day, he'd left Sylthia to walk down the hill to the house in Malin Village that he shared with Hugh and Mara.

His sister-in-law blew out a breath in exasperation.

"The human. Jane. Hugh wouldn't tell me anything other than she has green eyes and shortish brown hair. You spent some time with her in the forest. What's she like?"

To tell the truth, he didn't want to think of Jane. Sure, after his nap, he'd tried unsuccessfully to hunt down Eagar to complain about her treatment. Past that, he didn't want to dwell on her bellefern-green eyes or her talent for irritating him. No, it seemed safer to wonder why the expected shipment of Randolph's wool hadn't been received.

He looked across at Mara. From her expression, she had dug in and wasn't about to be removed without hearing more.

"She talks a lot," he said. "She's very . . ." He searched for the right word. "Impulsive."

"Impulsive? How?"

Charlie shrugged. He'd be damned if he'd confess his partial nudity and the subsequent conversations regarding it. He didn't know what had possessed him to take off his shirt in the first place. Growing up in a family of elves—a whole town of them, in fact—made him self-conscious about his fairy wings. They, along with his light coloring, distinguished him from everyone he knew. He hated being different.

"She jumps to conclusions. She doesn't listen to anything I say. Her predicament is a joke to her, and she doesn't like Eagar." He didn't know why he'd added that last part.

Mara pursed her lips. "I can see where he might frighten someone who doesn't know him. Do you think she killed Tivat?"

Charlie sighed. "Mara, you know I can't talk about that."

She poked him in the arm so hard it caused a red mark. "Charlie Whelphite, since when did that stop you?"

"Murder is a lot different from how many hides you can trade for an acre of wheat." For some reason, he didn't like people speculating on Jane's guilt. Likely it was the main source of conversation in Malin Village and the castle tonight.

Mara nodded. "Yes, yes, it is. Poor thing, so far from home and accused of murder on top of it all."

Charlie chastised himself. The least he could have done was visit Jane and reassure her. He knew where Eagar kept the key. He could have moved down his own cot and arranged for a meal. Instead, he'd left the responsibility to others.

"I'm going back," he announced, surprising himself.

Mara looked shocked. "What? Tonight?"

"Yes, tonight." Charlie rose and kissed her cheek. "I should check on her. Don't wait up for me."

She removed her apron. "I'm going with you."

He loved his sister-in-law, but didn't want her involved in the trial, in what might be an ugly situation. To deter her, he said, "It will be full dark soon." Full dark to Mara meant goblins and sandobbles, two races not often seen in Malin, but a threat in her mind nonetheless.

She hesitated, then after a moment shook her head. "She'll need a friend. Goodness, she'll be tired of looking at your gloomy face all the time." She bustled about the kitchen, putting food into a basket. "When's the last time she ate? She must be starving. And what about clean clothes and a place to wash? Honestly, you men never think of these things. . . ."

Charlie, accepting his defeat, sighed and turned away. "I'll get the pony and wagon. It will save time."

Despite Jane's wishes, the opening in the storeroom wall was not another portal. It closed behind them, leaving her and Muttle in a very narrow hallway. No doors opened from it; no adornments hung inside. The walls looked unfinished. Rough boards were nailed in at angles; dust, the accumulation of centuries, lay thick on the floor. Cobwebs hung in profusion. Afraid of their burning, Jane took the torch from her companion.

"Where are we?" she asked, pushing aside a particularly thick swath of webs. How many times had she seen this played out in horror movies? The innocent visitor lost in the catacombs of the sinister castle, led to the villain by an accomplice? And they never suspected a thing.

*Beats the alternative of Eagar,* she thought.

"In the walls, Jane of the dryads," came the reply from her tattered little rescuer. "We be there soon."

Soon? Such as the all-night "soon" through the forest? She hoped not. Whoever "him" was, he'd better be worth a dark and scary journey. She still ached from the last one.

The longer they walked and the more staircases they climbed, the more certain biological needs made themselves known. Her stomach empty and her bladder full, Jane decided one or the other had better be attended to before she met the esteemed "him" and made a fool of herself.

"Muttle." She stopped on a landing, clutching her side where a stitch added to her miseries.

Whirling blue-green-yellow eyes regarded her with concern. "Jane of the dryads? Pain do ye have?"

For once she thanked his mind-reading abilities. As clearly as possible, she thought about her discomfort.

Muttle jumped back a step. "Why did ye not say?" he asked, irritation in his voice. "Daft mortal." He looked around their route. The yellow in his eyes increased.

"Come," he said after a moment. Taking her hand, he led her up another flight and halfway down the next corridor.

"Here." He pointed to a spot on the wall, indistinguishable from any other. "Open here."

Jane handed the torch to the creature and placed her fingers against the rough surface of the wall. "How?" she asked. "It's not as if I do this every day." The first time still overwhelmed her. She never expected to perform magic, let alone create openings through solid stone. Had she done it, or had the castle responded to her in some way?

"Put ye fingers in and pull," Muttle said, impatient.

Feeling like a participant on *Candid Camera,* Jane curled her fingers and pushed against the wall.

Immediately, her hands sank into the stone.

She felt each individual granule, rough against her flesh, ensnaring it. She felt, also, the thoughts of the workman, long dead, who had set this exact piece in place centuries earlier. She smelled his sweat, tasted it against her lips. Nenius was his name, thirty-two and already dying of kidney failure. Panic gripped her. *Trap!* she thought. With a cry, she jerked back, freeing herself.

"Oh, God. Oh, God. Oh, God." She shook her hands with fervor, trying to rid herself of all the emotions she'd experienced. Bile rose from her empty stomach. Her heart hammered into high gear. Sweat broke out on her brow.

"What kind of freaking world do you run here?" She spun around on the tiny landing, desperate to find a way out. No portals presented themselves. Nothing but cobwebs, dust, half-rotted timber and darkness surrounded her.

She wanted to scream. Who had signed her commitment papers to this Cracker Jack sanatorium? All she wanted to do was make a few extra dollars at a second job. Instead, she had to deal with elves that changed into woodland creatures, mind-reading creatures with rainbow-colored eyes, and now this: feelings reaching across millennia. It felt creepy, like being trapped in a pit full of beetles crawling on her flesh.

"Jane of the dryads?" Muttle asked, orange and red now twirling with the yellow in his eyes. The blue and green had disappeared.

Jane gasped, trying to catch her breath. "Why is this happening?" Why hadn't she felt it the first time? "What are you people doing to me?" Clasping her hands tightly to her chest, she fought for control.

"Sit ye down," Muttle said, pushing on her thigh.

She slid down the wall in an ungraceful heap. Fleetingly, she thought of the incongruity of taking orders from someone half her size.

"Look at I," Muttle ordered. Without thought, she obeyed.

For the first time, she was at the same level as the Belwaith. Up close, he looked more fragile, his bones delicate and fine. Concern showed on his face.

"Think not of the others," he counseled. "Ye must act quick to not feel. Power comes two-edged."

*With great power comes great responsibility.* Spider-Man? Why would she think of Spidey now?

"What do you mean, power?" she asked, wiping away tears.

"He explains."

Ah, he. That helped. Must be related to "him."

"Okaaay." Jane took a shuddering breath. For several moments she sat still, calming herself. She thought of Charlie, wishing he was with her, knowing he wouldn't panic. He'd find some placid, rational way to deal with the situation.

Taking comfort from the thought, she rose slowly, brushing the dust off her slacks. It was the same pair of slacks she'd worn for two days now, she reflected. A pair in serious danger of being wet if she didn't get to a bathroom soon.

"Okaaay," she said again, steeling herself for what she had to do. She gave Muttle the thumbs-up sign. With thoughts of Charlie to give her strength, she plunged her hands into the wall and ripped it apart.

They emerged into another corridor with banners, tapestries and sconces on the walls. Light filtered in from a window at one end. Evening, Jane observed. She'd lost all track of night and day in her imprisonment. She glanced at her watch. Seven-ten. Her stomach growled in response.

"Where to?" she asked, anxious to move again. The journey through the wall had been brief, the impressions of Nenius and his life fleeting. No doubt they'd revisit her dreams tonight.

"This way." Muttle moved to the left. They walked to the end of the hallway. With a wave of a delicate, four-fingered hand he gestured to a small room on the outside wall.

Jane cocked an eyebrow and handed the Belwaith the unneeded torch. The door opened with a light touch.

It was a bathroom, of sorts. A stone bench lay across one end, its edges smoothed by countless human— elven—bottoms over the years. A hole carved in its middle all too clearly proclaimed its purpose. Jane took a step closer and noticed another hole the size of a half-dollar in the wall above it. A cork, attached to a chain, was jammed into it. Curious, Jane pulled on it. A stream of water gushed out and flowed down the larger hole, presumably to an elven septic tank far below.

"It flushes," she exclaimed, delighted at the ingenuity of the device. She replaced the cork.

After taking advantage of the gadget, she washed her hands in a sink, similarly contrived, next to the elven toilet. A bar of sweet-smelling soap helped Jane feel better. She wished she could jump into a shower and wash away all the grime and the smell of smoke that permeated her clothes, skin and hair.

"I suppose it's too much to ask for a magic mirror?" she wondered. She leaned against the basin and stared at the stones behind it where one would traditionally hang a mirror. "Ah, well, all in good time."

She dried her hands on a convenient length of cotton and stepped out to greet Muttle.

"Humph," he observed, his eyes back to their normal blue-green color. "Better, are ye?"

"Nothing tactful about you, is there?" She wanted to pick him up and hug him. Now, if she only had some food.

They set off down the corridor again.

"How do they get water up this high?" Jane asked, curious. "We must be near the top of the castle."

Muttle raised two bony shoulders in a shrug.

"Wind." He made a circular motion with one hand. "Raises water from river below."

"A windmill?" Yes, that made sense. A pulley and ropes or chains, and buckets to lift the water into a reservoir. "There's a river below the castle?"

Muttle punched the air. "Through."

More ingenuity, to build a castle over a permanent water supply. She couldn't wait until she could explore. She might not be able to return to Earth right away, but no one could imprison her until then. She hoped.

"Cool." She looked around. They'd come to a more luxurious part of the castle, furnished in dark hardwoods. Intricate designs of colored stones patterned the floor.

"Are we almost there?" she asked, the question common since her arrival.

"We be here." Muttle stopped in front of a massive door.

"What is it?" Jane knelt in front of the Belwaith. "Muttle?" His eyes spun yellow—a sign of agitation, she was beginning to recognize.

"Him." He hesitated.

She waited patiently. "Yes?" She watched the struggle in the creature and realized that loyalty prevented him from voicing his usual direct opinion. "There's something wrong with 'him'?"

He looked at her with sad eyes.

Jane understood. Whoever "him" was, he needed to be treated with delicacy.

"Okay," she reassured Muttle. "I won't say anything or do anything to embarrass you. Pinky swear." She linked her pinky with the Belwaith's. At least she assumed it was his pinky. It was hard to tell when he had only four digits.

Muttle looked relieved. He swung away and rotated a small doorknob near the bottom of the door. It opened easily.

They entered a dark room. It took several moments for Jane's eyes to adjust. Heavy brocade draperies covered windows large enough to drive a bus through. A huge bed stood against one wall, shrouded by a dark canopy. Books were piled on several tables, the floor and numerous chairs. A fire burned in the fireplace. Women's dresses hung in the maw of an open wardrobe.

*Wait. Back up. Women's dresses? Muttle didn't say anything about a "her."*

"Welcome, my dear." The voice, very Vincent Price–ish, came from everywhere and nowhere.

Jane whirled, looking for its source.

"This way."

"This way? Which way?" She turned again. From the corner of her eye she saw movement.

Someone slumped in one of the chairs by the fireplace. Jane drew closer and recognized the form of a man. *Him.* He was old, bordering on ancient, with pure white hair that was long, thin, and wispy. Skin like parchment covered bones as delicate as Muttle's and folded onto itself in wrinkles, giving the old man the appearance of an albino shar-pei. Two onyx eyes gazed at her.

He was roly without being poly, a Weeble of a man she guessed to be taller than her own five-six. She counted six rings of various carats and gems on his fingers. His feet were encased in dark gray slippers, the kind old men wear. The rest of him was covered neck to ankle in a woman's dress.

*Holy transvestite, Batman!* Jane blinked hard. He still appeared before her in a green velvet dress, long-sleeved and ankle-length, with white lace at the neck and cuffs.

"Hello. Sir." She remembered her promise to Muttle and added the formality.

"Jane Drysdale." His voice shook. He motioned in the direction of the Belwaith. "Muttle, bring our young friend something on which to sit."

Envisioning the struggle the creature would have to move one of the big wing chairs, Jane grabbed the nearest one. She scooted it across from her host and sat down.

At eye level, she could see how much frailer he appeared than she'd first thought. A tremor continually shook his clasped hands as they rested on his little potbelly. His head tilted to one side, a look of permanence to the angle.

A trace of power clung to him. She could see it in the alertness of his dark eyes, the proud set of his mouth and the way he held himself, despite his attire and infirmities. Thirty or forty years earlier he must have been a man with whom to reckon. She wondered what would happen if she touched him. Would his memories flow to her the way Nenius's had?

"So, my dear, how is your stay with us?" he asked.

*Peachy keen. That Eagar, he's quite the host.* Jane erased the thought. "I haven't seen much of the castle. It appears to be magnificent." *Once upon a time.*

"Yes." He sighed. "Poor Sylthia. She has suffered lately. In my youth, she shone. People came from all over to be within her walls. The fairs we had, the tournaments . . ."

He drifted off. Jane wondered if he'd abandoned her for some internal, more comfortable world.

After a few minutes, he shook himself and looked at her, alert again. "My grandmother's name was Jane," he said.

"So was mine." She'd always hated her name, so old-fashioned. "Plain Jane" Drysdale. Her three brothers and her sister, Sheila Perfect, had teased her without mercy. However, they'd been her staunchest supporters if anyone else plagued her. She wondered when she'd see them again.

"So long ago," her host mused. "Would you like something to eat, my dear? Muttle tells me you're hungry."

"Yes, I—Muttle told you?" Possibilities whirled through her mind. How had they communicated? Could this man read minds as well? Had he heard every thought she'd had since entering?

"Sir? Do you and Muttle share thoughts?"

He chuckled, a dry sound, like leaves rustling in November. "Am I telepathic? I'm much better at receiving than transmitting. His thoughts are easy to read."

Jane twisted to see the Belwaith. She almost fell from her chair when she saw two Belwaiths. Another—a female, by the red bow in her hair—sat next to Muttle on a miniature love seat. They chittered together in a foreign, vowel-filled language.

"You haven't met Calme yet, have you? Let me introduce you." He squeaked out a command in their language. The two Belwaiths slid to their feet in unison and presented themselves.

"Jane, this is Calme, lifemate of Muttle. She looks after me most efficiently. Calme, this is the Lady Jane. You are to give her everything she needs."

Calme bowed her head. A duplicate of Muttle in appearance, dressed in the same brown tatters, only the red ribbon in her hair distinguished her from her mate.

Jane smiled. "I'm happy to meet you, Calme. If it wouldn't be too much trouble, I'd love something to eat."

"Fruit. Get her fruit," her host suggested. "Harvalins and tiances. See if there are any more maneuse seeds."

Calme scuttled off to fill the order, Muttle behind her.

"They're inseparable when they're together," the old man observed. "I shudder to think what would happen if one—"

Trying to make polite conversation until her meal, whatever it might be, arrived, Jane asked, "How long have they been together?"

After some consideration he announced, "Three hundred and ninety-two years."

Three hundred . . . ? How long did they live?

"Sometimes to eight hundred," came the answer, shocking her.

Jane looked up. "You read my mind?"

"Only when your thoughts are so loud." He paused. "Do

you watch the stars, Lady Jane Drysdale? There are some on Lowth who believe one's destiny is tied to the stars."

"Astrology." Jane struggled to keep up with the change in topic. "Where I come from, it's called astrology," she clarified.

"Oh, I know. I lived on Earth for a year."

*What?* "You did?"

"Certainly. St. Louis, in 1962. An interesting city. Help me up, will you?" He rocked back and forth in his chair.

Jane, bombarded with all these pronouncements, leapt up and offered a hand. As the man tottered to his feet, she realized the dress he wore was slit in the back like a hospital gown. She glimpsed elven versions of boxers and an undershirt, both red, clashing horribly with his green gown. Christmas colors.

*Dear God, is this where Santa sends his elves when they retire?*

The man shuffled toward the window and began to putter with a telescope. "Do you watch the stars?" he asked again. "It's almost dark enough out to see some."

Jane followed him.

"Sir?" He still hadn't introduced himself. "Do you know why I'm here?" A murder trial, she thought. Not stargazing. *Hi, I'm a Leo,* she considered saying.

He looked up from his adjustments. "Killing poor, unfortunate Tivat, wasn't it?"

Well, yes, that was it. So how much did this guy know? Jane touched the man gently on the shoulder. "Sir, who are you?"

He abandoned his tinkering and drew himself up to his full height. "I should have introduced myself earlier. I am Garmade, Malin the Sixty-sixth." Strength returned to his voice as he made the declaration.

Malin? The name sounded familiar. Of course, the Malin Forest. She remembered Charlie talking about it.

"You're connected to the forest and the castle, then?"

If possible, he stood taller.

"I am the forest and the castle." The sound reverberated in the room. "My name is Garmade, Lord of Sylthia, Ruler of Malin, and King of the Elves."

# Chapter Five

The drive from Malin Village up the long, sloped curve to the castle took too long, Charlie decided. The sun descended behind the imposing structure. Darkness fed the shadows in alleys, corners and shrubbery. He stayed alert for trouble. His remarks to Mara about goblins and sandobbles had been made in half-jest. Dealing with the different factions of the land as he did in his work, he'd heard rumors of unrest. A few outlying farms had been raided.

Goblins, being a nomadic race, had been the first to feel the pinch of hunger caused by the Dymynsh. Sandobbles, mobile splotches of quicksand, required little to survive, but Charlie had heard stories that they were on the move. They'd been contained in the Magwrosin Swamp for too long. Guarded by the dwarves, whose numbers stretched thin nowadays, the sandobbles could push through the barriers and escape.

Elves, dwarves, fairies and other races of Charlie's generation, though smaller in population than previous years, demanded more foodstuff than Lowth could currently supply. If they didn't have good harvests this year, they would be decimated when winter returned.

"This is an odd night," Mara declared. "All kinds of things can happen on a night such as this. I don't like it."

Charlie didn't either. He couldn't attribute it to Jane's influence, though she'd certainly upset his carefully crafted world. No, there was something different about the air: a change in the wind he would normally associate with a brewing storm. He glanced over his shoulder, expecting to see rain clouds marching across the night sky. Instead, the first of Lowth's two moons, Rest, crested the tops of trees.

Its appearance didn't reassure him. Something had changed.

Chirruping to the pony to hurry, Charlie pushed his uneasy thoughts to the back of his mind. He'd see to Jane's needs, then hasten home to the comfort of his bed.

The gates to Sylthia remained open. In times of peace they didn't close until the appearance of the second moon, Slumber, some two hours hence. There hadn't been a war in fifty years, but with rumors of unrest, perhaps the guard should be reinforced. Charlie made a mental note to mention it the next day to Jaspar, who was in charge of security.

Charlie headed to the docks, where the closest entry to the storerooms was. He and Mara would be able to slip in and out of the castle quietly. However, as they passed the main door, he heard someone hail him.

Recognizing the voice, he pulled on the reins. The pony and cart stopped. Charlie shifted on the seat.

"Hugh?" He searched the darkness. His brother was on community duty tonight, a task every able-bodied man shared after the disbanding of the army.

A man's form detached itself from the night and strode closer.

"Well met," Hugh said. "How did you hear so quickly?"

Confused, Charlie asked, "Hear? About what?" What could have gone wrong in such a short time?

Hugh stopped at the wagon's side and looked up at him. "The prisoner. The mortal has escaped."

Jane? Impossible. Charlie had seen her locked away.

"Someone must have let her out."

But who among the population would do so?

Charlie tossed the reins to Mara and disembarked from the wagon. "Go home, Mara. Get one of the boys to go with you."

"I'll do no such thing," she huffed, struggling to follow him down. "That girl is scared. She needs protection."

*Jane needs as much protection as a mother bear,* Charlie thought. He doubted she'd ever been scared, either. She didn't have enough sense to recognize danger.

His sister-in-law secured the pony to a post. Knowing from experience not to argue with her, Charlie turned and headed into the castle.

Almost at once, he encountered Eagar.

"Have you seen her?" the steward asked, looking upset.

"This morning, when you locked her in the storeroom. How did she escape?"

"That remains the question," the older man replied. "There is only one way in or out. A short time ago, I sent one of the women with some food. She raced back to say the prisoner was gone." He shook his head. "Impossible. That room is well constructed. Even mice and insects can't get in to ruin the stores." He leveled his gaze at Charlie. "Are you aware of any magic she has?"

Magic? Other than making one lose one's wits with her incessant chattering? He didn't think Jane capable of anything other than inflicting temporary dementia on someone. Besides, all students in their fourth primary year of education learned of other races: It was well known humans had no magic. It was a wonder they'd survived as long as they had.

"No," he replied. "None. How is the search organized?"

"Hmmm?" Eagar nodded to Mara, who'd joined them. "Jaspar took three others to the portal, thinking she might try to return to Earth. Ten others have spread out in the castle. You can start in the east wing."

"She's not there," Charlie said, astounding himself. "She's in the upper quarters."

The other man eyed him suspiciously. "How do you know that, unless you've aided her?"

Charlie held up a hand in protest. "Never. My job is to defend her, not help her escape." He shook off the feeling that had crept over him. Somehow, he knew the location of her whereabouts. He could feel it, a tingling on his skin, a vibration in his wings. *What's happening here?*

"You sense her, then?" Mara asked, laying a hand on his arm. "Charlie, you never told me of this."

He'd not been aware of it until now. Unlike most elves, he had no power, no sorcery born into him. Telepathy, the capacity to heal, the ability to move small objects without touching them; almost everyone he knew had something special that set them apart. Hugh was attuned to the weather and could predict a storm days in advance. Mara talked to animals, though that was a talent she rarely used as her husband was a tanner.

But not Charlie. He'd once pretended his ability was latent and would present itself upon his maturity; reality had forced him to lay aside that dream long ago. A half-breed, he only had wings to distinguish him from others. His classmates, who appreciated magical but not physical distinctions, had ridiculed him. Clumsy attempts as a teenager to fly had resulted in his shame about the abnormality of his wings. *And Jane has seen them!* He still couldn't believe he'd shown them to her.

"If you feel she is in the upper quarters, go there," Eagar said. "I was to search it myself." He looked at Charlie gravely, his eyes sending out a warning. "Remember to be discreet. King Garmade must not be upset."

Charlie nodded. All of the kingdom knew of their monarch's dwindling hold on reason. The past few years had seen his deterioration. Charlie wondered if the Dymynsh had affected their king, so closely tied as he was with the land.

Mara tugged on his arm. "Come on. If you can feel Jane's presence, we had best start. The poor thing must be scared, all alone and lost."

They moved toward the first of several staircases that led up to the royal suite.

"What if she meets the king?" his sister-in-law whispered.

Charlie shuddered to think of the possibility.

King of the Elves! What had she gotten herself into? All this time Jane had thought she dealt with a doddering old fool. Instead, she'd been patronizing a doddering old king. *You've put your foot into it now*, she thought. *A king can cause a lot of trouble, even if he does dress like Klinger on* M\*A\*S\*H.

Jane stepped back from Garmade. All the children's books she'd read and Disney movies she'd seen kicked in. She curtsied. A curtsy followed meeting a king, didn't it?

"Your Highness," she said. Twenty-four hours earlier she would have laughed at the phrase.

The old man leaned over and helped her to stand upright.

"No need of that, my dear. I have a feeling there will be no formality between us. Here comes Calme with your dinner."

Jane followed the monarch to a small, round table. He pulled out a chair for her and waited until she settled before sitting down opposite her.

Calme effortlessly carried in a tray too large for her. She

placed it on the table and began spooning fruit into a bowl.

Harvalins, Jane discovered, looked and tasted like pears. Peeled and sliced, they were cooked and covered with a warm vanilla sauce. Tiances proved to be unfamiliar in taste, texture and color. Red mottled with orange and the size of eggs, they reminded her of large grapes. The best were saved for last—red, juicy maneuse seeds. Similar to large raspberries, they melted in her mouth. She had two helpings.

Finally, her hunger sated, she sat back in her chair and looked across at the king.

"Thank you," she said. "I haven't eaten in a while." Not since the previous evening, snacking on what Kendra had stingily put out for her guests.

The thought led to those of the party and the stack of orders Jane had tucked into one of the Rubbermaid containers she'd pulled from her car. Where were her boxes? Had they gone through the portal, or been dumped alongside the path? Fat lot of good they would do her now, unless her jurors were sexually frustrated house elves with disposable incomes.

*Jurors!* Jane panicked. Charlie had said her trial would start soon. Try as he might, she knew he had no defense for her. She'd killed Tivat as sure as God made little green apples. She was going to fry. Then again, they hadn't discovered electricity yet. Probably boiling oil or being strung up on the rack would do as well. No doubt Eagar would invent something cruel and torturous with which to kill her.

"Are you well, Lady Jane?" the king asked. "You look pale. Perhaps you are too close to the fire. Is there aught I can get you?" His elderly face was etched with concern.

A pardon from the governor? A one-way ticket back to reality? A movie deal with Steven Spielberg? Jane had a sudden urge to scream in frustration. She'd been too bewildered and tired earlier to vent her anger at her situation. Her life, while boring at times, had been a good one. Mother, brothers, sister, lots of friends, a stifling full-time job—but a stimulating part-time one filled her days. No boyfriend, but only because Todd had run away with the copy-machine repair girl at Christmas. And now, because of circumstances she couldn't understand, she sat before the King of Elves, charged with murder, eating strange foods and ripping apart walls.

She felt ill. Maybe it was the maneuse seeds. They'd been rich, like honey and Bavarian desserts. Jane laid her hand against her stomach, but it still heaved and lurched. Dear heavens, she was going to ralph all over royalty!

By sheer determination, she kept everything down. The Belwaiths soothed her brow with delicate fingers and offered her a cold cloth. The king, frail and barely able to support his own weight, guided her to lie on the royal bed. He tucked warm, down-filled coverlets around her up to her chin. Jane tried not to move too much until her stomach settled.

"I'm so sorry," she said. "I'm normally very healthy."

King Garmade, sitting next to her, patted her hand. "It's perfectly all right, my dear. I'm sure you've had a notable turn of events." He looked at her with a paternal fondness. "You've certainly added some spice to my evening. It's been a long time since a woman visited these chambers. Once this room was filled with scores of bright, beautiful young women. They flitted around Elaine, loving her so."

Curious, Jane struggled to sit. "Who is Elaine?"

"My daughter," he replied. "The Princess Elaine."

That explained the dresses. They must belong to her.

"Where is she now?" she asked. She knew nothing of the occupants of the castle.

"Ah." The king sighed deeply. "Gone, alas, these thirty years. Taken by the goblins, never to be heard from again." He looked fragile, as if a slight puff would blow him away. His lower lip trembled. Tears welled in his dark eyes.

His sorrow touched Jane. She took his hand, mindful that he was a grieving father first, a ruler second.

"Tell me of her," she coaxed. "What was she like?"

"Hmmm?" King Garmade looked at her a moment before answering. He relaxed, as if glad of the opportunity to speak of his loved one. "Laughing and singing. She had a sweet, lovely voice and organized contests and performances for the people. I'll never forget . . ." He drifted off.

Jane yearned to know more. Fate had tossed her into this world; from what she'd seen so far, she had much to learn. Elves and goblins and fairies, a real king before her—Malin the Sixty-sixth. How far back did his family go? She'd ask Charlie, but knew the answers would be more interesting coming from the king. Not that Charlie would do a bad job, but he could be weary at times, as if he didn't want to talk to her.

"Sir? What did she look like? The princess Elaine?"

Garmade returned from wherever he'd mentally wandered. "Why, her mother, of course." He patted Jane's hand again. "You wouldn't remember her, you're much too young. Elaine and Helen were very much alike. Tall, with brown eyes and short, curly brown hair." He peered at Jane. "Similar to you, except your eyes are green. You're not an elf, are you?"

"No, sir, I'm not. I'm human. My name is Jane Drysdale, and I think I'm your prisoner."

He chewed over this information as if it were a piece of tough meat.

"Killed Tivat, correct?" he asked, a hopeful look in his eyes.

"Well, not on purpose. I'm sure it's a huge mistake and it will be changed soon. Er, you don't suppose you could make that happen, could you?" After all, he was the king.

Garmade dashed her hopes at once. "I'm sure Eagar has everything well in hand," he said, letting the matter rest.

Riiight. Old Eagar, the cat-kicker. He probably had

dozens of felines, one for every occasion. Jane bet he'd picked out the cutest, softest kitten around and named it in her honor.

"It's very confusing," she said, shaking her head. "Strange things have happened since I arrived. For instance, this evening I created a hole in a wall with my bare hands. I've never done anything like that before on Earth."

"Created a hole?" The monarch sat up, alert for the first time since she'd entered the room. "My, that is interesting. Do you know how you did it?"

"No, sir. Muttle said you'd be able to explain."

He pondered the problem. "This was here, in Sylthia?" When she nodded, he said, "The castle has ways we cannot fathom. She's inherited magic from her occupants in addition to her own. She's either taken a liking to you and allowed you this ability, or she's bestowed magic on you."

Taken a liking to her? His statement threw Jane off balance. The thought of the castle as a living entity blew her mind. She struggled with the concept. How many more surprises lay in wait for her?

"I can open walls from now on, or only when I'm within Sylthia?" she asked.

The king chewed on his lower lip. "It's hard to say." He shook his head. "Despite the proximity of our worlds, we have very little experience with mortals. The portal to Earth is temperamental. We can go out, but it doesn't often allow humans through. Few have passed into Lowth in the last hundred years. There was Stewart of Graham, and Lemieaux, and another, a woman, some years back. She returned home, the others stayed and eventually died here. I don't remember if they gained powers or not. It seems evident, however, that Sylthia has smiled on you. We'll have to keep an eye on you, my dear."

*Not if you execute me*, she thought.

"You say the portal doesn't allow humans through. Then how did I get here? Weren't Charlie and his friends taking a risk, hoping it would let them transport me?"

"It's only because you were with them that you could come. Charlie—he's the Whelphite, correct?—accompanied you. Only those with Lowth blood are allowed access. You wouldn't have been able to traverse it on your own. The portal would have refused entry."

Great. There went her plans of ripping open the gates and making a dash for it. Even if she managed to elude the guards, the portal might not open. She was stuck here until Charlie could prove her innocent.

Depression descended on her like a storm cloud. She was at the mercy of a senile king, a cold-blooded steward and Charlie, who only defended her out of a sense of duty.

*Stop being a coward,* she told herself. Normally upbeat, Jane didn't often allow thoughts of self-pity. Tonight was an exception. Torn from her family and facing a grisly death, she let everything get to her.

"It's not fair," she sniffled. "All I did was try to go home, and now I'm going to die." She snuffled and snorted, realizing she was making a terrible impression on the king.

He patted her hand, a gesture he was fond of, and muttered, "There, there."

"I'm terribly sorry," she apologized, her head resting on the green velvet bodice of his gown. "I don't know why I'm acting this way."

"Nonsense," he declared. "It's perfectly normal."

Jane, about to point out that it wasn't normal for her, was interrupted by the throat-clearing crescendo of Muttle.

"Visitors have ye," the Belwaith announced, disapproval clear in his voice.

Jane, still in the king's arms, looked to the doorway.

# Chapter Six

*By the first dawn, she's seduced the king!*

Charlie stared in horror at the scene in front of him. From the strange intuition he'd developed about Jane's location, he'd expected to find her with the king. But not in his embrace! What was she thinking? Did he need to watch her every minute? It was blasphemy to approach the king thus. If it had been Eagar who found her—

As King Garmade's hand slipped from Jane's back, Charlie felt a tightening in his gut. He hadn't thought of Jane sexually. Not really. Seeing her in another's arms started a disturbing awareness in him. It didn't matter if the one holding her was elderly and infirm. And his liege. Charlie fought against the sensation, refusing to name it as attraction to her.

A knot closed over his heart as he took in her appearance. She looked weary, rumpled. The purple bruise above her eye clashed with their bellefern irises, dewy with tears. Why had she cried? Were her tears real or for the king's benefit?

Charlie forgot his training until he heard a rustling behind him. Mara, panting from the long climb, sank into a curtsy. Aware that he stood in disrespect before his monarch, Charlie dropped to one knee.

"Your majesty," he said, his head bowed.

"Ah, Charles the Whelphite, is it?"

Charlie nodded, daring a glance.

The king gestured for him to rise. He indicated Jane. "It seems you've lost your charge."

Charlie rose to his feet. *Not mine. Eagar's,* he thought.

"Yes, sire," he agreed. Shock at his lord's appearance surged in him. They'd spoken on a score of occasions, usually on the subjects of trades, harvests, and the Dymynsh. He had not seen the king in months. The man's deterioration stunned him. There had been rumors that Garmade had taken to wearing women's clothing, but Charlie hadn't believed them. It saddened him that the end of his reign in Malin was at hand.

"She's been telling me some interesting stories," King Garmade continued. "It seems Sylthia has given her magic."

Charlie's head jerked up. His eyes narrowed on Jane, sitting so casually on the royal bed. *Magic? What is this about?* He wanted to ask her a thousand questions. Right after he shook her a few times. But at least she hadn't been seducing the king as he'd first thought.

Jane looked at him and shrugged. "I rip walls apart."

Walls? He didn't think he had the strength to ask. With Jane, a long, incomprehensible monologue followed any questions.

"Oh, my." The words came from Mara.

Jane smiled at her. "Hello. Who are you?"

To his astonishment, Mara dropped into a curtsy again. Why would she do that? And to a mortal?

"I am Mara Tanner, wife of Hugh."

A look of relief washed over Jane's face. "Mara? Mara? Wife of *Hugh?* You don't know how happy I am to hear that. Charlie didn't mention a sister-in-law." She shot a look of reproach in Charlie's direction.

What? What had he done? When had he had time to go into his family history?

"Are you feeling better, Lady Jane?" the king interrupted, his gaze kind upon her.

*Lady?* Charlie thought. What exactly had happened here? Jane was royalty now? His head spun in confusion.

"Lady Jane?" Mara inquired, echoing his thoughts.

"A small joke among ourselves," King Garmade explained.

Joke? Charlie felt as if he'd returned from a journey of many years and he didn't know anything anymore. When had he so lost control? For that matter, when had he had control with Jane? Only during her unconsciousness.

To his horror, she patted the monarch's arm in a disturbingly familiar gesture. Charlie didn't like it. She had no business touching anyone in such an intimate way. If anything— He closed his eyes a moment, imagining the silky feel of her skin, the flowery scent of her hair. . . .

*Stop*, he commanded himself, astonished at his reaction. *She murdered another. She is to be tried.*

Charlie pushed away his feelings with steel resolve. He addressed his lord, the words coming through clenched teeth. "Sire, I'll take charge of the prisoner now."

King Garmade's face crumpled, as if the reminder of Jane being a prisoner pained him. He looked at her. "I think you have more to tell me, my dear. But I see the wisdom of your counselor's words."

Jane nodded. "Yes, sir. We barely spoke of my newfound power. And I haven't said anything about Nenius yet."

Charlie shook his head. Power? What was she talking about? And who was Nenius? He couldn't wait to get her alone and find out the answers. Disturbing woman. Would she never be out of his life?

He directed his attention back to his lord, who was saying, "I feel there is much to learn from you, Lady Jane. But the night deepens, and you are tired. We will speak again in the morning." Garmade looked at his audience. "As our young charge has proven to be adept at escape, we cannot return her to where Eagar imprisoned her. She will stay the night in the keep, in a guest room. After that, she is free to stay where she sees fit. Muttle will accompany her."

What? Eagar would not like this. How would they keep an eye on her? Charlie saw his shock reflected on Jane's face.

"Sir, that's kind of you," she said, clearing her throat. "If you don't mind, and not to knock your hospitality, I would prefer to await trial someplace else. After our talk, I'm sure you'll understand how uneasy I feel here. Especially once I tell you of Nenius."

"Best not," interjected Muttle, entering the conversation for the first time.

King Garmade looked at his servant. After a moment, the monarch nodded. He turned to his guests.

"Mistress Tanner?"

Mara curtsied again. "Sire?"

"How is your household?"

"Sire?"

"Have you children?"

Mara shuffled her feet. "Alas, sire, none."

Charlie felt for her. He knew the pain it brought her and his brother that they had not been successful in conceiving a child. Another effect of the Dymynsh.

"You live with your husband?" the monarch continued.

"Aye, sire, and Charlie also lives with us, down in the village."

"Charlie?" Garmade eyed him. "Ah, that makes it better. You'll be able to communicate much more easily with your client."

Charlie had an uneasy feeling of where this conversation was headed. A slight vibration in his wings emphasized the warning.

"Sire?" he asked.

"Yes, it will work out well. Mistress Tanner, if you don't mind, I'd like you to host Lady Jane in your home. Might she be your guest during her stay with us?"

*What?* Charlie jerked at the suggestion. Living in the same house with Jane! She'd have the whole village of Malin in an uproar in no time. What had he done to deserve this?

Mara looked taken aback by the request. She fumbled with a response, then said, "Yes, sire, I would be honored."

King Garmade looked at Charlie. "Do you object, Whelphite?" The monarch's once-great power steeled his words.

Object to a royal command? Gritting his teeth, Charlie replied, "No, sire. She may live with us."

"Excellent." The king clapped his hands. "I'll see you all in the morning."

Before Charlie could think to act, Muttle had ushered them out.

"I want to talk with you." Jane heard Charlie say as she watched Muttle depart to take his position as guard outside the luxurious suite next to the king's.

"Ouch." She pulled away from his touch. He'd grabbed her left arm, which was still sore from the car accident. She could understand his anger at her escape, she supposed, but he was on her side, right?

"I want to talk to you, too," she hissed. "Why didn't you tell me about the king, and Princess Elaine, and the portal, and Sylthia being alive?" Her earlier happiness at seeing Charlie again had evaporated with his attitude.

"How much time did you spend with the king?"

"Long enough to learn there's a lot I don't know about this land. I'm getting a very Dorothyish feeling here, Charlie Whelphite, and I don't like it."

"When was I supposed to tell you about our three thousand years of history? When I pulled you out of your burning wagon? While carrying you in my arms through the Malin wood?"

"Maybe instead of drugging me . . ."

They glared at each other. Jane could fight dirty, too. She wanted to hit him with something, preferably something heavy and skull-crushing. Of all the pig-headed men she'd met . . .

Mara stepped between them, her hands raised. "Children, let's not fight. 'Tis grown late and we need our rest."

Jane felt a pang of regret. She'd taken an instant liking to the small, plump woman. She pitied her for living with Charlie on a daily basis. She tried to sweeten her voice to normal.

"I'm sorry, Mara, I shouldn't drag you into our argument." She'd rather have Charlie alone. It wouldn't do to have a witness to the abuse, both verbal and physical, that she wanted to heap on him.

Mara smiled. "I admit I am curious to hear your story."

Charlie, still visibly fuming, said, "No doubt it will differ from mine."

"And the truth lies somewhere in the middle," Mara guessed. "Forget it for now, Charlie Whelphite. The day has been long for you both. I will see Mistress Jane settled for the night, then we will go home." She turned to Jane. "I'll come again in the morning with fresh clothes. Charlie's sister, Tisha, lived with us until her marriage two months ago. She was around your size. I'm sure there is something you may borrow."

"It's very thoughtful of you, Mistress Tanner." Jane appreciated her kindness, some of the first shown to her since she'd arrived in Lowth.

"You must call me Mara."

Jane ignored Charlie's deprecating mutter. "All right, Mara. Call me Jane. I'm not a lady or a mistress. Go home to your husband. I'll see you in the morning."

"If you're sure you don't need anything else?" The woman looked upset, as if she hadn't fulfilled her duties as hostess yet.

Jane patted her hand. "I'm sure. Muttle will get me anything I need tonight. Besides, you're right. It's been a long day, and a long night before that. I'm so tired, I doubt if I have the energy to think about all the strange things that have happened." Which was true, she realized. Exhaustion had set in. Jane wanted everyone gone so she could crawl into what she hoped would be an angel-soft bed.

Mara studied her face. After a moment, she nodded, as if satisfied with what she saw.

"Good dreams, then," she said. She grabbed Jane and hustled her to a guestroom. She showed Jane inside, then took Charlie by the arm and manhandled him out the door.

Jane sighed after their departure. She felt guilty that she hadn't said good night to Charlie. Even though he was an irritating beast, he tried to be kind to her. Most of the time.

# Chapter Seven

The next morning, wearing a nightgown Calme had brought her, Jane woke to sunshine streaming in the windows. True to her prediction, she'd slept through the night.

She sat up and surveyed the room the king had gotten for her. Smaller than his, it was decorated in sage green, rose and ivory. She'd needed a stepstool to reach the canopied bed. A private bath lay in one corner, its amenities similar to the one Muttle had shown her the day before.

The day before! Had it only been that? Jane felt as if she'd been in Lowth for weeks. What would today bring? More secrets? A different cast of characters?

So far, when she thought about it, everyone with the exception of Eagar had treated her well. The steward's malevolence worried her; his membership on the council that would decide her fate gnawed her nerves. But Charlie had said it was a three-member council. Perhaps the other two wouldn't be fellow members of the Nazi relocation program like Eagar.

A knock on the door pulled her from her thoughts.

Mara entered the room, carrying a tray. "I thought you might be hungry," she said, a smile on her face, her tone cheery. She bustled over to the bed.

Jane returned her smile. "I am. The king gave me fruit last night, but it was all I had all day." *And it didn't settle as well as I hoped.* She prayed Mara's food would prove better than the king's.

"Then you will like what Cook has prepared. Eggs, bread, cheese, coffee." Mara lifted a metal cover, revealing a plate heaped with food.

Jane smiled at the mention of coffee. After the strange repast the night before, she'd wondered if all food on Lowth would be unfamiliar. She tucked into her breakfast with gusto.

"You slept well?" Mara inquired. At Jane's nod, she continued, "I'm honored to have you stay at my house. It's very humble. You're probably used to much nicer things—"

"It will be fine," Jane reassured her. "I'm not rich back on Earth." *Far from it.* "And I feel so uncomfortable staying in the keep." She didn't want to recount her wall-tearing adventures, it was too early in the morning, and she didn't care to remember it too closely. The experience unnerved her. She'd been lucky she hadn't had nightmares.

Inexplicably, she yearned to tell Charlie. He'd find a reason for its happening. When she wasn't upset with him for his logic, his I-love-my-rut stodginess, she admired him for it. Goodness knew she didn't have much stability in her own life. Her old life, she corrected. The one of the past thirty-six hours had even less.

"How is Charlie?" she blurted, then immediately wished the words back.

Mara didn't notice. "In a foul mood, let me tell you," she confided. "He's worried because he hasn't received a shipment of wool from Randolph. His business depends on it, and it's overdue by a week. He works too hard, and is taking on more all the time."

*Including me*, Jane noted. She would bet a murder trial in the middle of wool-gathering season really frosted his cake. She still hadn't explained her escape to him, or received satisfactory answers to the hundred questions floating in her head. She needed to see him again. *To see his sexy wings, too*, she added. If she could trick him out of his shirt . . .

"How is Hugh?" she asked in a rush, anxious to rid her mind of a half-naked Charlie.

"Hugh?" Mara looked up blankly.

Too late, Jane realized the other woman didn't often mention her husband. Was there trouble in elf paradise?

"Hugh is fine. I've not seen him this morning. He was on guard duty last night." Mara's tone was short.

Guard? Against what? Soldiers? Dragons? Jane felt frustrated by her lack of knowledge about this world. She needed a crash course in Lowth 101.

Mara said, "You know, you are lucky to be here at the castle. They have running hot water. At home, I'd have to heat it for you." She disappeared into the bathroom, and Jane realized the subject of Hugh had been dismissed.

Mara popped back. "Your bath will be ready soon."

Bath? Jane smiled at the thought. What a luxury. She'd not bathed in forty-eight hours. She scrambled out of bed and headed for the bathroom.

She would have preferred to loaf in the marble bath for hours, but she didn't know when she was to meet the king. She hurried through the process, shampooed her hair and wished for a hair dryer. She toweled off the best she could, wrapped another towel around her head and returned to the bedroom.

"Mara, do you have the clothes you talked about last night?" she asked, preoccupied with the thought of fresh underwear. She could do without a bra, lacking any size in that area, but panties . . .

"Here," Mara said. "King Garmade sent some with Muttle—" She stopped and stared.

Jane looked over her shoulder toward the bathroom. Had a ghost appeared? "What's wrong?"

"Mistress Jane, I didn't mean to stare—"

But she did, making Jane uncomfortable. Jane realized they might have different views on nudity on Lowth, but she wasn't exactly naked, for heaven's sake.

"What's upset you?" she asked.

Mara gulped. "The markings on your skin. There is nothing wrong with such—the dwarves favor them. I did not expect to see them on you, that's all."

Jane touched the rose tattoo above the towel line on her left breast. "It's called a tattoo on Earth. I have this one and another on my ankle." She lifted her right leg, where Bugs Bunny chewed on a carrot. "Then there's the design on my arm." She held out her left arm. A swirling design between two bands encircled it a handbreadth above her elbow.

"It says, 'Forever joined, heart upon heart, world upon world.'" Mara cocked her head, reading the words. "Very pretty. Did you write it?"

"*What?*" Jane jumped back. "It says something?" She looked at her arm, trying to see the upside-down lettering. Why hadn't she noticed it earlier? It looked the same as always, only now she realized she could read it.

"You are shocked."

*Lady, that's an understatement.* Fumbling around until she found a chair, Jane sank into it. She felt ill with the implications coursing through her head. This was unreal. *The Twilight Zone* had come to life and trapped her in a sickening rerun. She had tattooed Elven on her arm!

"Mistress Jane?" Mara knelt at her side. "Are you well? Should I call Muttle?"

"No." Jane all but shouted the word. Her fingers trembled as she traced the design, now legible. She fought a rising panic. "Until today, it was a design, nothing more. It had no meaning."

"I don't understand."

"That makes two of us. Look, is there anything I can use to write with?" Chalk? Blood? She couldn't think coherently.

Mara produced paper and a writing instrument similar to a pencil. Jane wrote down the words in English.

*Forever joined, heart upon heart, world upon world.*

What did it mean?

"See, can you read this?" She pointed to the script she'd written, hoping she was wrong, that this was a hellish nightmare. She had to be in a coma in a hospital back on Earth, right? Lewis Carroll would never do this to Alice.

The other woman peered at the words.

"No, 'tis squiggles."

Jane winced. *This doesn't make sense.* "Mara," she said, trying to keep her voice even, "until I entered Lowth, the tattoo was squiggles to me, too."

"Then how did it come to be written on your arm?"

Jane thought back to the first time she'd seen the design. She'd been five or six, learning to read and comprehend the alphabet. A thirst for knowledge had prodded her to copy letters in every free moment. Magazines, the newspaper, even her sister Sheila Perfect's diary—nothing was sacred.

"The design had fascinated me since I was a small girl," she explained. "I didn't know it was writing at first. It didn't matter when I found out. Its beautiful, flowing lines intrigued me. It was my first choice, years later, when I decided to get a tattoo." She remembered the anger spewed at her when she'd come home with the fresh markings etched on her arm. At the time she'd thought it was because of the deed, not the design.

The enormity of the words she was about to say caused them to catch in her throat.

"I copied it from something I found in my mother's journal."

# Chapter Eight

How in hell did her mother know the Elven language? *No, there must be some other explanation*, Jane reasoned. Marion Drysdale might be flighty at times, but who wouldn't be, raising five children? She had both feet firmly planted on the ground, and didn't believe in fairies, sprites, elves, ghosts or things that went bump in the night. She was a solid citizen, ex-PTA member, maker of a pot roast dinner every Sunday, and grandmother of five. How would she know Elven? She'd never been out of the United States!

"Your mother is an elf?" Mara asked, her eyes wide.

"She is not!" Jane exclaimed, jumping to her feet. "She's American as apple pie." At the puzzled look on her friend's face, she sought for a Lowth comparison. "It would be the same as saying you're as Elven as the Malin."

Agitated, Jane circled the room. "I don't understand this. There must be some mistake. Are you sure you read it right? You didn't make this up to trick me or make me go insane? Because, let me tell you, after all that's happened the last day or two, I'm about ready to wig out. It's bad enough I'm trapped in Lowth until the trial, but to think my mother might have been here . . ." She shuddered. "It totally creeps me out."

Mara sat in the chair Jane had vacated, twisting her hands. "I wouldn't trick you, Jane. I do not lie and I lack imagination to deceive. The marking on your arm says what I said it did. 'Forever joined, heart—'"

"'Upon heart, world upon world,'" Jane finished. "It sounds like a love letter. Why would she write a love letter in Elven? My father was the only man she ever loved. They were married for over thirty years until he died four years ago." Their marriage had been too Ozzie and Harriet for her mother to be unfaithful. Especially with an elf. And places on Earth to meet and fool around with pointy-eared men were scarce unless you belonged to the Vulcan Swinging Singles Club.

"Maybe she copied it from someplace, the same as you did," Mara offered.

"And where would that be? There isn't much communication between my world and yours." Precious little. In fact, none that she knew. You couldn't walk into Waldenbooks and pick up an English/Elven dictionary. Frommer's didn't publish *The Best Places to Stay in Lowth*. And as far as Jane knew, there'd never been any talk of her mother disappearing.

"Elves do go through the portal," Mara said. "King Garmade himself once lived on Earth. Perhaps he loved an Earthwoman and wrote a poem for her and somehow it came into your mother's possession—"

Jane blinked at her in surprise. "I thought you said you lacked imagination. No, there are too many coincidences for all those things to happen—and then I show up in the king's suite with his words tattooed on my arm? That's a stretch, don't you think?"

Mara pursed her lips, her forehead lined in concentration. "There must be an explanation."

Jane plowed her fingers through her damp hair. "I agree, but I'm fresh out."

"Perhaps Charlie can help. He has a logical mind."

*It's not logical, Captain Kirk.* Jane sighed. Handing the problem over to Charlie smacked of handing her Earth problems over to her brother Kevin: She didn't want to do it. Closest to her in age, he always complained she took advantage of being the youngest. Still, he helped her out of jams anyway. He'd been with her when she'd had the tattoo done. She wondered what he'd think if he knew it was written in Elven.

"Let's tell Charlie," she agreed. "After we see the king. Mara, this is our secret—mine, yours and Charlie's. If Eagar knew I had this on my arm, well . . . he might burn me at the stake."

She didn't try to hide her dislike of the steward. She'd gathered that the general population thought he walked on water. Of course, they hadn't accidentally killed one of his people, either. Such a blemish on an immaculate record *would* turn him to the dark side. Maybe he'd had a bad hair day yesterday. No, wait, he was bald. It must be too-tight shoes. It had to be the shoes. Like the Grinch.

Thinking of shoes made Jane realize she was still wrapped in a towel. She turned to Mara.

"Help me get ready, would you? What type of clothes did Muttle bring over from the king?" She hoped it wasn't something the monarch had worn himself. It was bad enough that she had to borrow clothes. To wear the king's second-hand dresses capped an already Marvin-the-Martian experience.

Mara held out a long, flowing, Kermit-green nightgown.

"Okaaay," Jane said, fighting not to make a face. She realized she lived in a different world, if, she hoped, only temporarily. It was necessary to take advantage of the resources offered, but this poofy dress wasted good fabric. "Is there more?" *A six-person tent, maybe?*

"Of course. There's the bodice." From underneath the yards of material, Mara unearthed a short, vest-type garment, low cut and laced in front. She handed it to Jane.

Jane touched it gingerly. *What a weird bustier.* "Is this for under or over?"

Mara looked affronted. "Over. Nothing is worn under."

"Nothing?" Jane gasped. "As in *nothing*? You're naked? No bra? Panties?" Her earlier worry about underclothes returned. She didn't need a bra, having little to lift and separate, but she wouldn't walk around with a bare bottom.

Mara stared, perplexed. Jane strode to the bathroom and returned with the clothes she'd worn earlier.

"This is what we wear on Earth," she said. "At least, some of us do." She didn't want to get into a discussion of the natural look or thong underwear. "The bra gives support," she explained. "Or, in my case, enhancement. The panties are for, well, modesty."

"Intriguing," Mara commented. She seemed especially enthralled by the hook-and-eye fasteners on the bra. "Jerrowes the blacksmith could make wire so fine."

"Of course he could," Jane said, taking back her clothes. "If you have someone who can sew, you could churn these out for all the women. You'd have a regular Sylthia's Secret." Jane thought of the naughty underwear packed in the boxes she'd pulled from her car. She didn't know if the elves were ready for such a leap of imagination.

"Sharezee is the royal seamstress," Mara said. "Perhaps she might make you others to wear during your stay."

The idea had potential. "Sure," Jane replied. "Knock yourself out. Have her make you some, too. I bequeath the pattern to the women of Lowth. No patent, no copyright, no trademark."

Tired of the subject of underwear, she gathered together the voluminous folds of the gown and departed to the bathroom.

Mara had failed to mention the Lowth equivalent of panties—knee length white bloomers with a drawstring waist. Jane rolled her eyes when she found them hidden in the folds of fabric. Grumbling, she put them on, followed by the chemise itself, yard after yard of green silk. Finally, she pulled on the bodice which, when laced in front, pushed her breasts up and forward, making her feel very serving-wench-ish.

As she entered the bedroom ten minutes later, her feet encased in soft leather slippers, she saw Charlie standing in the doorway to the outside corridor. Their gazes met. Her breath caught. Charlie, her protector, her own Clark Kent.

From his expression she knew he'd forgotten the previous night's harsh words. The look in his eyes told her everything would be okay. She didn't have to worry about residual anger from him. Or anything else.

"You look . . . pretty," he said.

Did she? Jane wished there'd been a mirror to check. There didn't seem to be any in the castle. She twirled, letting her skirts float around her ankles.

"I feel like a fraud. I'm not used to silk and lace." Or the open admiration in his eyes. Her cheeks warmed. "It's different from what I normally wear."

"The color suits you. It complements your eyes. I wondered how you would look in green."

He'd wondered? The warmth in her cheeks grew to a full-fledged bonfire. This new side to Charlie caught her off guard. She knew the I-like-my-rut Charlie; she liked to goad the what-have-you-done-now Charlie; but the I-wondered Charlie unsettled her. None of her previous boyfriends, though there hadn't been many, had ever treated her as if she were a cherished glass ornament at the top of the Christmas tree. The look in Charlie's eyes made her feel delicate and rare.

Jane glanced away in confusion. Across the room, Mara watched, obviously enjoying the encounter.

*Don't start matchmaking yet,* Jane thought. *We still have to weave an O.J. defense before we break out the bubbly.*

Her pleasure at Charlie's gaze spiraled back to reality. The trial. Eagar sitting in judgment. A presumed-dead elf. Hoo-boy. Yes, flirtation would have to wait.

"Right, then," she said. "Let's go see the king. Afterward, Charlie, Mara and I have a surprise for you that will rock your world."

Bemused, Charlie took her arm. Half the time he didn't know what she talked about, the other half he regretted asking. He didn't need another surprise, but with Jane it was like telling the wind not to blow.

He approved of her change in attire. The pants she'd worn earlier distracted him. Rarely did an Elven woman clothe herself in anything other than a dress. The gown suited Jane. Along with her coloring and the triangular shape of her face, she looked more Elven. It would be a slim advantage in proving her innocence, he decided.

Muttle met them at the door to King Garmade's suite.

"He be not well," he warned, his eyes whirling shades of yellow and green.

"Does he want to see us?" Charlie asked. He'd wondered if the previous night's excitement had been too much for the monarch, precipitating a breakdown of an already weak mind.

The Belwaith nodded. "Aye. But be quick." He stepped aside to let them enter.

Jane's sharp intake of breath prepared Charlie for the worst, but Garmade's deterioration still shocked him. The night before, the man had been semi-energetic and coherent. Now, lying with almost deathlike stillness on the royal bed, he was feeble and barely lucid.

"Come closer," the monarch said before the three could make obeisance to him. He gestured them forward, his shaking hand not rising from the mattress.

Charlie, Jane and Mara took positions at his side.

"Speak, my lady," King Garmade whispered, his gaze on Jane.

The compassion in her face bordered on tears. "Sir," she said, dropping into a curtsy. "Of what? So much has happened to me."

"Powers." A rattle shook the king's chest as he exhaled on the word.

She nodded and took a deep breath. "Twice yesterday the castle did what I wanted. The first time, when you sent Muttle to my cell, I reached into a small hole in the wall and stretched it large enough to pass through. The second time . . ." She hesitated, steadying herself. "The second time, when I made a hole, I could feel the thoughts of Nenius, the man who set the stone in place some three thousand years ago. Sir, it frightened me."

*Magic.* Charlie stared, looking for physical proof of a change in Jane. She remained the same, with tousled honey-brown hair and eyes moist with suppressed tears.

Magic bestowed itself unpredictably. Still, without checking Lowth's history books, Charlie knew not of a mortal with magic. What did it mean?

"A great gift," King Garmade wheezed. "More is to come. Guard it well. A strength returns to the land." He closed his eyes. His breathing continued laboriously.

"Enough," said Muttle, cutting off their chance to learn more. "He sleeps."

Calme appeared to stand at the king's side. Her mate all but pushed the others into the corridor.

"We go to the village." From his tone of voice, Charlie could tell Muttle's reluctance to abandon his king. Only the direct order from Garmade to watch over Jane would keep the Belwaith from his master's side.

The door shut behind them. Charlie looked at his sister-in-law and his charge, and saw both weeping copiously.

"Don't cry," he said, digging in his pocket to find a handkerchief for Jane. Mara had one of her own.

"Will he die?" Jane asked, scrubbing away the tears and blowing her nose in the white linen.

"I don't know," he answered truthfully. "He's been sick a long time." Charlie knew the king had become obsessed with ending the Dymynsh, but to see him weakened to such a state—

"What will happen to the monarchy without heirs?"

"I don't know that, either." He turned a corner and started down a staircase. The others trailed behind him. "Legend tells that there have been Malins at Sylthia since the time of your Nenius. Two brothers, Malin and Malik, fought over the land. Malik lost and moved north, to christen the Malik Forest and build the castle of Shallen. Malin stayed here, to become the first king and build Sylthia."

"Then there are heirs in Shallen?"

Charlie shook his head. "The two families have fought for centuries. The last battle was fifty years ago, in King Garmade's prime. He slew King Rodom, Malik the Sixty-third. No heirs exist." They descended more stairs.

"Who rules Shallen?" Jane asked, trying to keep up with him. Mara and Muttle followed farther back.

"Blacwin, a wizard. Rumor has it that he is the source of the Dymynsh."

"The Dymynsh? Charlie, what are you talking about?"

He didn't have time to answer. They rounded the last corner to the level where his office was located. Eagar stood outside his door. The steward looked angry.

Instinctively, Charlie placed himself in front of Jane,

protecting her. She'd had enough to upset her over the past two days. Eagar's wrath, while rare, was formidable.

"Why was I not informed of the new plans for the prisoner?" Eagar spat the last word as if it tasted bitter.

"It was late when the king changed them. You were not around this morning." Charlie knew Eagar lived by a precise schedule; he'd been at the stables for a routine inspection when Charlie arrived at the castle. Instead of taking time to inform the steward, Charlie's first thought had been to see Jane again. She needed more than Muttle's surveillance to keep out of trouble.

"Humph," Eagar commented. "It should have been brought to my attention. She is in my charge."

"No," Charlie said, annoyed. "She is in Muttle's. And mine." He didn't like the idea of Eagar claiming possession of Jane, any more than he'd liked seeing her in King Garmade's arms the previous night.

"Now wait a minute," Jane said, elbowing Charlie out of the way to push herself in front of Eagar. "I'm not some toy you boys can fight over. I'm a person, with thoughts and feelings." She punctuated her words by thumping the older man's chest with her finger. Charlie tried to catch her hand, but she slipped through his grasp.

"I have certain rights," she continued. "It's in the Geneva Convention. Okay, maybe you don't have the same rules here on Lowth, but I know you obey your king, and he says I'm free to go wherever I want. Muttle is to look after me." She touched the Belwaith gently on his shoulder.

"I think—"

She interrupted Eagar. "Don't. It will get you in more trouble. This whole thing is your fault, you know. If you'd run a decent prison, Colonel Klink, your prisoners wouldn't escape all the time and I wouldn't be in this mess."

Charlie smiled at her spirit in defying the most respected man in the kingdom. He admired her ability to defend herself, though he didn't need her bravery upsetting one of the men who would decide her fate.

"Jane," he said, laying a hand on her arm. "Let's go."

She snapped her head around to look at him. Fire blazed in her eyes. "But Charlie—"

"It's time to go," he said, treading the fine line between voicing a suggestion and telling her what to do, an action that would probably direct her temper at him.

Their gaze held for an intense moment. She looked away first, but her anger didn't stay dampened for long.

"Where are my boxes?" she demanded of Eagar.

"Boxes?" The steward looked confused.

"My boxes. I realize they might not mean anything to you, but I had a lot of money tied up in their contents. I'd like to get it back when I return to Earth."

"I've not touched your boxes or their contents," Eagar declared.

Jane looked him up and down. "No, you probably wouldn't know what to do with the stuff inside," she sniffed.

Charlie thought it best to intercede before another argument started. "I have your boxes. They're in one of the storerooms." Jaspar had placed them there after they all had returned from the portal.

Jane nodded. "Good. Let's get them and blow this popcorn stand. This place gives me the creeps." She looked directly at Eagar as she said the words.

Charlie slipped between the two and took her arm in a firm grip. Before she could say another word, he pulled her in the direction of the storeroom, leaving Eagar behind.

"Watch yourself, Jane Drysdale," he warned. "The king can be your friend to a point. Past that, others decide your fate."

\* \* \*

"What do you have to say to me?" Charlie asked an hour later, as Jane settled into Hugh and Mara's cottage.

Jane smiled at him, feeling more comfortable now that she'd left the castle. They'd collected her boxes and stored them in an unused corner of the barn behind the house. She'd successfully argued with Mara about not taking the main floor bedroom. Instead, she'd been shown the half of the loft recently vacated by Tisha, Hugh and Charlie's younger sister. A cot, a chair and a few pegs on the wall comprised the new quarters. And a curtain of fabric separated it from Charlie's similarly almost-bare half.

*Interesting*, Jane thought, sitting in a chair in the main room after descending the ladder. The firm set of his jaw confirmed that Charlie wasn't thrilled by the plan. Well, too bad. She was looking forward to it. Her attraction to him had only grown. Still waters ran deep, and all that. Fire and passion lay below his surface. She wanted to churn them into the open. The sleeping arrangements only made it easier.

"Do I have something to say to you?" she asked, all innocence and batting lashes.

"When we left to see the king, you mentioned you had a surprise that would change my world."

"*Rock* your world," she corrected. She exchanged glances with Mara, who stood at the stove cooking. Muttle kept guard outside the door, so Jane was free to talk. As free as she could be with a mind-reading Belwaith nearby.

"I do have a secret, but you have to promise not to freak out over it. This is as much a mystery to me as to you."

He pinched the bridge of his nose, as if battling a headache. "I'm almost afraid to ask," he muttered.

"Better to know now than later," Mara declared.

Jane began to unlace the front of her bodice.

"What are you doing?" Charlie asked, bolting from his chair.

Her fingers stilled. "You have seen a woman's body before, haven't you, Charlie?" She hoped he had; it would make things easier in the future. She wasn't promiscuous by any means, but the seduction of the strait-laced Charlie held more and more appeal. Those wings had been playing in her mind. . . .

"Of course I have," he stammered. He indicated the open room and Mara. "Only not yours, and not like this."

"I'm afraid it's necessary," she explained. Even her clients at her Realm of Pleasures parties had never been more flustered. She continued unlacing her bodice and slipped from it. "I promise to be discreet."

With exaggerated care, she loosened the neck of her chemise and drew out her left arm, exposing the tattoo. Charlie approached slowly, his forehead wrinkled in concentration. He knelt at her side and touched the writing with a delicacy that sent a tingle along Jane's skin. She almost jerked away at her body's reaction.

"How long have you had this?" he asked, his eyes solemn. He continued to trace the lettering with his fingers, sending major goosebumps down her spine.

Jane wet her lips before answering, her mouth suddenly dry. "About five years."

"Do you know what it says?" He gripped her arm just below the tattoo. His gaze, mocha-brown and steady, held hers.

The stillness in him frightened her. The room telescoped into itself, leaving her alone with him in a claustrophobic container. She fought to breathe.

"Not until today. Charlie, I copied it from something of my mother's."

"Does anyone else know of this?" he asked, looking from her to Mara and back again.

"No one," Jane answered.

He nodded. "Good. It must be kept secret."

"What does it mean? Why would my mother have an Elven verse in her possession?"

He shook his head. "I don't know. I can tell you two things about it, though. First, somewhere since I started working in Sylthia, I've seen this before. And second"— Charlie tapped the inscription—"it's not written in pure Elven. From its construction, I'm sure it's Malik."

# Chapter Nine

A sharp whistle from outside canceled any further talk.

"Muttle," Charlie explained. "Hugh returns." He stood quickly, placing himself between Jane and the cottage door. She scrambled to rearrange her clothing, tying the last lacing on her bodice as Hugh walked in.

Lunch followed. Talk of Tivat's death and the trial dominated the conversation, as did discussion of the delayed arrival of Wesant. The third member of the council to preside at Jane's trial, he was away on a hunting trip.

Jane tried to concentrate on the lunchtime discussion, but her mind returned to the words tattooed on her arm. The many conclusions whirling in her head finally narrowed to two. Either someone from Malik had contacted her mother on Earth or, scarier yet, Marion Drysdale had traveled to Lowth and back again. Neither explained why nothing had been said about the otherworld contact. Of course, on Earth, unless one wanted a lifetime of psychiatric treatment, it was best to stay quiet.

At the end of the meal, the men rose to return to work: Hugh to his tanning sheds and Charlie to the castle.

"Don't worry too much about this," Charlie advised as Jane walked him to the front gate. "I'll remember where I saw the inscription. It may give us more insight into this newest mystery of yours." He turned, casually waving good-bye.

Newest mystery. If she had any more mystery in her life, she'd need her own shelf at the library.

Jane returned and entered the cottage, intent on helping Mara with washing up. She stacked the dishes and watched with interest as the other woman added heated water from the stove to the cold water she'd pumped into the sink. The amenities here were clearly not the same as at Sylthia.

"Mara, what's the Dymynsh?"

"Ah, the Dymynsh." Mara plunged her hands into the dishwater. "An evil, Jane. A nasty evil come over the land." She explained the effect of the scourge—how everything was fading and dying—and the popular belief that Blacwin, the wizard of Malik, was behind it.

"You know this for a fact?" Jane asked.

"Well, no, it being so far away and all, but rumor has it the crops in Malik don't suffer. And I haven't heard of any Malik women losing babies," Mara added, her words sharp.

"I'm sorry." Jane touched her arm. "You and Hugh?"

"Nothing, after five years of trying." Mara twisted away, her expression bitter. "Not much of a marriage, either."

Jane suspected as much from observing the two, but she didn't want to get into a discussion of their marital woes.

"Tell me about Charlie," she said in an attempt to distract her friend. "It will be a long day before he opens up to me. Is he the only Whelphite in the family?"

"He's a quiet one, is Charlie," Mara agreed. "He needs to get out and enjoy life more."

"Oh, I think he'll soon have plenty of enjoyment," Jane predicted. Charlie intrigued her, what with his reserved manner, in contrast to her own get-out-of-my-way attitude. He had layers she wanted to uncover. Many layers. She glanced at Mara and grinned.

"Good, then." Mara returned to Jane's question. "Charlie's a foundling. In truth, Hugh's the one who found him. Named him, too. I would have picked different, but Hugh was eight at the time. Charlie's an odd name for an elf." She shook her head as if she didn't approve. "Anyway, Hugh was hunting with his father, heard a noise and investigated. It was Charlie, a few months old, lying next to the one they think was his real father."

"His real father?"

"They never knew for sure. A man of the fairy race. Dead, poor thing, from a bad heart. So far from Isleighah, the land of the fairies, it was thought he was on his way to the child's Elven relatives."

Poor Charlie. "The mother?"

Mara shook her head. "Unknown. Hugh's family took him in and raised him as an elf."

"But he isn't," Jane observed. "Though he pretends to be. He's more fairy than he wants. His wings"—she paused, stilled by her one and only, but she hoped not last, glimpse of them—"are magnificent."

Mara raised an eyebrow. "Seen them, have you? Charlie, there may be hope for you yet."

The woman dumped her dirty dishwater into a bucket and opened the back door. In the yard, she carefully poured the water into the window boxes hanging against the cottage. Sad-looking petunias and geraniums struggled to grow in them.

"The Dymynsh reaches even my poor flowers," Mara remarked, setting down the empty bucket.

Jane, remembering her mother's flourishing garden back on Earth, touched the leaves on a couple of the plants.

"I hope the water helps," she said, homesick for her family. When would she see them again?

As if sensing her mood, Mara linked her arm with Jane's. "Come on. It's time to meet the people in the village."

# Chapter Ten

A few days later, Charlie, bone weary, returned late to his family cottage. Lowth's second moon, Slumber, crested over the Malin forest to the east. Its companion, Rest, neared its zenith. An occasional dog bark or muffled voice disturbed the quiet of the village. A nocturnal breeze lifted the edges of his hair and tipped leaves from their anchors. A week had passed since Jane had turned his world upside down.

The delayed trial loomed closer. Wesant would return from his hunting trip the next day, and Charlie dreaded telling Jane the news.

His day had been hectic, starting with a confrontation with Eagar, an uncommon event. The steward's irritation at Jane's liberty manifested itself in paperwork that demanded Charlie's time. In addition, he'd been drawn into a protracted meeting with some of the village leaders, discussing the Dymynsh. Today, he'd talked them out of sending a small party to Shallen to speak with Blacwin the wizard and demand a reversal of the spell he'd cast.

Work lay on his desk, but Charlie didn't care anymore.

He was tired of not sleeping in his own bed. Twice, he'd set up his cot in his office. Fine for an occasional late night, it lost its appeal after a couple of uses.

He missed his family. Up early and returning late, he rarely saw Hugh or Mara. Or Jane. At the thought of her, his heart tripped. His wings, folded beneath his shirt, vibrated.

She hadn't caused any major catastrophes yet. From what Mara told him, Jane helped with the housework, fit in with the villagers and tried hard to adjust to a new world. *But she still sleeps in the next room*, he reminded himself. He heard her even breathing as he lay down each night, imagined the dreams that made her sigh, and wondered what she looked like in moonlight.

He didn't have to wait long for the last. As he approached the cottage from the rear, he saw Jane sitting on a bench near the back door.

"Well met, Charlie," she said in a soft voice. "You're out late tonight."

He stopped at her side, struck by her casual use of an Elven expression. "There's much work to be done at the castle," he admitted.

"Ah, yes, wool-gathering time. Literally." She patted the bench.

He hesitated. He'd not been close to her since the day she'd shown him her tattoo. Though preoccupied with its implications, he'd still been aware of her lightly tanned skin and the delicate scent of her tousled hair. A repeat of those distractions appeared inevitable, especially as she was dressed in something tighter and shorter than what he remembered women wearing to bed.

"I won't bite," she said, looking at him with wide eyes, her face luminescent in the moons' soft light.

Gingerly, he sat next to her.

"You have two moons," she remarked.

He glanced at the night sky. "Rest and Slumber. They follow each other, two hours apart, never to meet."

"Forgive the pun, but they sound like star-crossed lovers." She placed one ankle over the other, exposing enough bare leg to stop Charlie's heart for several seconds.

The word "lovers" conjured up myriad images in his mind, none decent or proper. He shook them away and cleared his throat.

"You have a moon on Earth," he said, remembering his fourth-year education on different races and worlds.

"With a dull, uninspired name of 'Moon.' Not as pretty or romantic as Lowth's."

Lovers. Pretty. Romantic. Was she trying to incite his emotions on purpose?

"I'm sure there are things on Earth that outweigh the attraction of our moons."

Jane sighed. "Walks on the beach always seem popular in the singles ads. But you have a beach, don't you? Tell me, Charlie, do lovers in Sylthia walk there in the moonlight? Make love in the sand?"

Charlie shifted uncomfortably on the bench. How had the conversation changed to sex? "I'm sure they do," he answered, wondering how to propel himself from the edge of the chasm where he teetered.

"You sound as if you don't know."

She turned. He swallowed hard. The front of her shift was cut low and hugged her body, leaving nothing to the imagination. Or leaving too much to it.

He struggled to remember what she'd said.

"I . . . I assume they do. Walk by the water, that is."

"Do *you*? Walk there with your sweetheart?"

She crossed her legs again. Charlie pivoted away, taking a sudden interest in the moons and stars. He willed his thoughts from breasts and legs and bare flesh and anything else that involved Jane and nakedness.

He cleared his throat again. "I'm not courting anyone." She must know this. Mara had probably told her his life history by now—his broken engagement three years before, the smattering of girls since then, his dismal love life lately. Though dating held a sudden appeal, he decided. He needed to find someone to take his mind off this troublesome Earthwoman. Someone he could hold and plow his—

Charlie stopped, stunned. He didn't mean it. It was the moons' light and a half-dressed woman and the change in weather that made the air thick and hard to breathe.

"What are you wearing?" he blurted, wishing the words back even as he spoke them. *Idiot!*

"This?" Jane glanced down at herself. "This is an Earth-style chemise. Sharezee, the seamstress, made it for me. She already has orders from some of the village women who've seen it. Sexy, isn't it?"

Sexy? Charlie wasn't about to comment on that. As for her other news, he closed his eyes and tried not to think of Elven women for miles around clothed in such attire. Or the effect it would have on their men. He'd been premature with his opinion that Jane hadn't yet caused a catastrophe.

"She's going to start making bras for them next week," she added, her tone proud.

He didn't know what a bra was and didn't have the courage to ask. With Jane, sometimes ignorance was best.

"The trial starts the day after tomorrow." The words escaped before he could stop them.

Her expression darkened. The spark in her eyes died. Charlie could have kicked himself for the callous way he'd presented the news. They had a slim hope of winning; he should have let her enjoy her freedom while she could.

She drew in a shuddering breath, and he thought her about to cry. He watched as she controlled her emotions and said, "Is it boiling oil, or does Eagar toss me from one of the towers?"

His heart squeezed in compassion. He felt an idiot, upsetting her and not being able to comfort her.

"Jane." He touched her arm, surprised by its coolness. "Jane, it won't come to that. I promise."

"How can you promise?" Her voice quavered. "You were there. I killed Tivat. It was an accident and I'm sorry, but the fact remains he's dead."

"We still have no body."

"But Eagar has five witnesses, including himself. How unbiased can his judgment be when he knows the truth?"

Charlie knew she was right, but only the king had the authority to remove Eagar from the deciding council. And the king was not in the best of health.

"I don't know," he said truthfully. "We can only hope the other two will listen to our reasoning and give you a fair trial. Jane—" He tilted her head up so he could see her eyes. "We still have a chance."

Her smile floated to him through layers of tears and worry. "If only I could bring him back to life, like the garden."

*The garden? What?* Okay, now he would have to ask.

"What are you talking about?"

"The garden," she sniffed, gesturing around her. "I thought I was done with my 'powers' when I left Sylthia, but they've only taken a new direction. I'm the anti-Dymynsh."

He closed his eyes a moment and willed the strength to understand. "What do you mean, the anti-Dymynsh?"

Her hand lay on his arm, insistent, disturbing, too warm.

"Just that. Everything I touch grows." The worry in her eyes deepened. "The day I came here, Mara commented on the ill health of her plants. I said something, I don't know, about how I wished they'd grow for her. When we returned from the market, the plants were in perfect health."

He didn't want to hear this. He did not want to know she was changing the planet.

"Perhaps it was something else," he ventured.

"No. I tried an experiment to see if it was me or not. I took two plants and told one to grow and one to die."

"And?" He dreaded the answer.

"The second died."

Shades! Couldn't the woman be like other females? He pinched the bridge of his nose where an ache spread upward.

"Does anyone know of this?" he asked in despair.

"How many secrets do you think I can keep? Without tearing Mara's garden apart, it's obvious something is happening here that isn't in the rest of the village. So far, I've used the others' ignorance of Earth to say I have special growing methods." Jane leaned closer to him, her face distraught. "But I'm starting to get requests for help. How can I say no?"

She couldn't, and he wouldn't want her to. Not with the way the Dymynsh reduced the food supplies.

"Can you control it?" he asked.

Jane shook her head. "I've tried. The plants act like puppies, overeager to please me. I can't turn them off."

She sagged against him, dispirited and exhausted. Somehow his arm slipped around her waist to support her. She felt incredible, right, fitting to his side like she belonged. Charlie's heart raced and his breathing came hard. A low vibration started in his wings, tingling and evocative.

He held her for long moments, wondering how to remove himself gracefully from the situation. It wasn't worth getting involved with her. She would be out of his life one way or another in a few days. Never mind that her breath warmed the side of his neck and stirred his senses. Forget the clean, apple scent of her hair, and her breasts almost exposed to his view. And her hand against the flat of his stomach, creeping upward. It wasn't going to happen. Not tonight. He thrust himself away from her and stood.

"We should talk about this in the morning," he said, pushing his fingers through his hair in agitation. "We'll ask Hugh and Mara's advice."

Jane looked disheartened. He hoped it was because he didn't have an answer for her, not because of her failed seduction.

She stood, brushing specks off her body-hugging shift. Charlie glanced away and thought of cold streams and winter nights and ugly women.

"Are you coming up to the loft?" she asked.

"No," he said quickly, his throat dry. The shirt on his back rippled from the movement of his wings. "I'll be there in a few minutes."

To his great relief, she nodded and moved away, disappearing into the cottage.

Charlie watched the light from her window come on, then fade. He waited until he felt sure she'd fallen asleep. He waited some more, until Slumber reached its zenith. Then, with the stealth of the best thief, he followed her.

At his bedside, he hesitated, listening. Hearing nothing, he took off his shoes and stockings. Then, in a nightly ritual he both dreaded and anticipated, he removed his shirt and spread his wings.

Oh, to not have the appendages. To be a normal elf, with the sameness of others. No one else he knew had both elven and fairy features. Countless times since his adolescence he'd wished his wings gone. But how good it felt to stretch them, to free them from concealment and release them from constraint.

A slight shuffling noise froze his movements.

"Charlie?"

He spun to see Jane standing by the curtain separating their rooms.

"Jane? Did I disturb you?"

"I couldn't sleep," she said softly.

Charlie flexed his back muscles. His wings started to fold.

"No, don't." She took a step into the room, releasing the curtain.

He feigned ignorance. "Don't what?"

"Don't hide your wings. They're nothing to be ashamed of."

He hesitated. It was rare to remain exposed like this. Only at night did he allow himself freedom.

"You say that only to make me feel more at ease," he said angrily, reaching for his shirt. Twice now she'd caught him off guard. He didn't like the loss of control he experienced around her. "And ease is—"

"No, don't," she cried, stepping farther into the room. She grabbed the bunched fabric from his hands. "I say it to make you feel *uneasy*." She inched closer. He felt the heat from her body. "Charlie, your wings turn me on."

Her phrasing might have been foreign, but not her intent. He couldn't look at her without his gaze straying to the fabric pulled tight against her breasts, outlining her nipples. The moons' light washed over her and illuminated her lithe figure, glinted on her lips, wet and dewy and ripe.

Charlie backed away.

"I don't know that expression." Safety in retreat, he decided.

"How do you feel at this moment?" she asked. "Hot? Bothered? Uncomfortable?" She closed in on him with the intensity of a predator.

"Insane," he admitted. He took another step back. "You shouldn't be here." It was insane what she was doing, the surge of emotions she caused in him.

" 'Pay no attention to that man behind the curtain'? Nope. Sorry. I don't think so. Can you deny your attraction to me?"

She'd backed him against the wall. He had no place to go.

"You said something once about interspecies breeding. Want to give it a try, Charlie?"

She bumped her hip against his. All the breath rushed from him in a whoosh. He'd never felt so many temperatures racing around in his body.

"I think at the time you mentioned a choke hold—"

"Klingon. They have some interesting mating rituals of

their own." She bumped him again and laughed as he jumped out of the way.

"Shhh," he said. "The others will hear you." All he needed was an audience to intensify his humiliation.

"I have it on good authority that they're sound sleepers." She tossed her head, exposing a long line of flesh from her jaw to the tips of her breasts.

"Jane," he warned. "This isn't a good idea."

Her fingers glided up the wall of his bare chest. He caught her hand, his grip stronger than his crumbling resolve.

"Jane, I mean it."

"So do I." She tilted her face upward, her lips open and inviting. "Kiss me, Charlie."

He laid a finger against her mouth, intending only to stop the next flow of words. As it rested against her firm, luscious lower lip, her hand snaked behind him. He felt the sensation a moment before she touched his wings, caressing the delicate, sensitive band that joined them to his back.

Explosions shook him, convulsing from the spot in divergent waves. His body trembled in her arms.

"Cool," she whispered, her tongue at the corner of his mouth, seeking entrance.

Cool? No, hot. Melting. Sizzling.

She moved her hand and rolled it across the rim of his left wing. His knees buckled at the force of his response.

It didn't matter what she'd done or where she'd come from, he decided. He wanted release—to hold her, to breathe her scent and watch her animated face while he made love to her.

He had only so much willpower. She'd shredded his restraint bit by bit over the past two hours. *I'll regret this, I know I will.*

With a groan of surrender, he lowered his mouth to hers.

# Chapter Eleven

"Oh, Charlie," Jane sighed. "You are a live wire, aren't you?" She moved against him, grateful his natural reserve wasn't from inexperience. She'd practically had to hit him, caveman style, to implement phase one of his seduction.

A *tough nut to crack*. She threw her head back and chuckled at the double entendre.

"What?" He looked up from the newly exposed distraction of her throat.

"Nothing. Don't let me stop you." Placing both hands on the sides of his head, she guided his kisses lower and lower. She gasped when he used his teeth to nudge aside her chemise and capture a nipple in his mouth.

"Don't tear the fabric," she warned, not caring whether he did or not. White spots danced in front of her, and her lungs must have collapsed because there wasn't room in them for air.

"I'll get you another," he growled.

*Riiight, like there's a Victoria's Secret around the—*

Jane stifled a cry of surprise as he swung her into his

arms. He strode to his bed and sank into it with her. It gave a traitorous squeak at their combined weight.

"We're going to have to take care of that in the morning," she observed. "A little WD-40—"

"Be quiet," he said and kissed her, his mouth hard and demanding, his hands moving across her.

"I can be very quiet," she whispered, assuring him that their lovemaking wouldn't be loud.

He grinned. "I wondered."

"Brat." She tugged gently on a lock of his hair.

In response, he flipped her onto her back and stretched himself on top of her. All the right body parts aligned with precision. She gasped as he ground his hardness against her. Two layers of fabric separated them, but she felt his heat and wanted to quench it with her moistness.

His wings haloed behind him in the moonlight, spread full in their grandeur, a host of contradictions. Transparent, but blue-green in color. Whole, yet segmented. Clear, but with whorls of watercolor design. Like liquid stained glass or a window made of seawater.

Remembering his earlier reaction, Jane stretched her hand toward their beauty. Charlie, intent on freeing her other breast, shuddered at her touch.

"Shades!" He labored for breath. "You don't know what that does to me."

Oh, she had a good idea. A new and unexplored erogenous zone. She smiled at the challenge and power she controlled.

"Do they get in the way when you sleep?" she asked, curious as to the logistics of making love to a man with wings.

"Does your leg get in the way? Or your breast?" He cupped the latter in his hand, a perfect fit. She moaned as his fingers played with her nipple.

"Make love to me, Charlie," she whispered, anxious, heated and needy.

His eyes darkened with full-blown elven lust. "With pleasure." He kissed her, a long, slow invasion. His fingers stopped tinkering with the fabric around her breast and descended to more explosive uses.

"Sweet heaven," she breathed against his mouth. "You are a wonder." Damn, she might not need the edible lotion she'd retrieved from her cartons. On the other hand—

*Be ye aware. Danger.*

*What the hell?* "Muttle, your timing is way off," Jane growled, angry with the Belwaith. For the past week, she'd seen little of him but was aware he patrolled the perimeter of the cottage. Now was not the time to renew acquaintances. *Three's a crowd*, she added emphatically. *Take care of it yourself. You're always flashing those knives of yours around.*

Charlie lifted his head from her breast. "What's wrong?" he murmured.

"Nothing." She pushed him back to his interrupted task. "Don't stop."

*I come. Danger. Now. Flee.*

Charlie stilled. "I heard that." He dragged her with him into a sitting position. In a split second, his manner had changed, become alert and intent.

"What is it?" she asked.

"I don't know. Get dressed."

Dressed? Not by a long shot. She hadn't spent all this time seducing him to let some demented Jiminy Cricket stop her.

Then she heard it. A shout from outside, angry and loud. Muttle's cry of pain. A whooshing sound.

"Get down," Charlie yelled.

Glass shattered. An explosion hurled Jane through the air. The roar of fire obliterated other noises. Charlie slammed into her as they hit the far wall. Intense heat spiked into the room. Screams filled the air.

"Charlie!" she cried.

What in the hell had happened? She reached for him, confused, afraid he'd been hurt. Orange flames licked across the ceiling, originating from her side of the loft. Acrid smoke burned her lungs and stung her eyes.

"Charlie!" she shouted again. "Are you okay?"

"Here." She felt his hand on her leg. They lay in a heap, but not the type of tangled limbs she'd planned earlier.

"What happened?" she asked, her throat raw.

"I don't know." He coughed. "Let's get out of here."

"You've got my vote, elf-man." She freed herself, rolling away, keeping low.

His hand at her back, he guided her toward the ladder. Smoke rolled over them, hot and reeking. Fire spurted from her room, the curtain aflame.

She found the ladder and blindly edged down, feeling Charlie's presence a step above. Six rungs from the top, strong hands grasped her waist and swung her to the floor.

She screeched and lashed out, connecting solidly with bone and muscle. The bomber—she was convinced it was a bomb thrown through her bedroom window—must have entered the house to finish them off. But why? And who?

"Hold, hold," Hugh said in her ear, his arms tight around her to keep her from flailing at him. " 'Tis Hugh. Follow me."

"Hugh." She relaxed. "Charlie's behind me." She felt disoriented. Smoke billowed from above, choking, burning her eyes and throat, her lungs tight, spastic. The corner of the house—her room—crackled in fiery anger.

"Come then." He released her.

Charlie dropped down. They fought through the smoke to the front door. Jane stumbled to the grass outside, overcome with the potency of the clear night air.

"Jane, are you well?" Charlie stood over her, his hand on her elbow, righting her.

Dazed, she nodded weakly.

"Stay well," he commanded. Cupping her face, he kissed her hard on the mouth, then stepped back.

Before she could say a word, he spun around, shouting orders to the emerging villagers, organizing a detail of men to put out the fire. His wings, not burnt from what she could see in the moonlight, did not fold tightly to his back. Neither did he have them fully extended. Instead, in a half-mast position, they proclaimed to her, and she hoped to others, that he was Fairy. Pride caught in her throat.

Standing in the darkness, watching Charlie work to save the house he shared with Hugh, tiny details sank into Jane's mind like coins into a slot machine. The crackle of flame as it pushed through the roof from the inside. The thatch catching as dry tinder, the fire racing across the top of the house. Villagers were pulled from their beds, reacting to the terror that this could spread to their own dwellings. Night air, warm and light, slid across her body, some of which shouldn't have been exposed to its touch. She'd forgotten her state of dress, or undress. She hastened to rearrange her clothes.

"Jane!"

She turned to see Mara rushing toward her, pulling a light blanket off her shoulders when she saw Jane's semi-nakedness.

"Are you all right?" the woman asked.

Jane dismissed the question. Time and a long bath would restore her to normal, but the cottage . . .

"Oh, your poor house," she said, laying a hand on Mara's arm. "What happened?"

Mara shook her head. "I don't know. I woke at the sound of the explosion. Hugh pushed me out the door and went back to help you and Charlie." Near tears, she watched the flames eat at her home.

Jane stood next to her, helpless. The men brought water

from neighboring cottages, passing it bucket brigade–style to others perched dangerously on ladders near the fire. To her eyes, it looked like a losing battle. The cottage would be ruined, and there wouldn't be any State Farm agent writing a check for its replacement.

A snuffling sound tore her attention from the destruction. Mara twisted away, her body shaking with tears.

"I can't look anymore," she sobbed.

Several of the women moved to comfort her.

Jane cursed under her breath. It wasn't fair. The whole planet, or world, or whatever one called Lowth, was not fair.

She scanned the night sky for a wisp of cloud. "If only it would rain," she said, hoping for a miracle.

"'Tis the wrong season," Mara sniffed. "Hugh says it won't rain for days—"

A flash of lightning cut off her words, followed immediately by a crack of thunder. The women around them looked at Jane. Two stepped back. In the next instant, a deluge poured from the sky.

*God in heaven, what is happening?* Jane stared in astonishment at the sudden change in the elements. A cold fear replaced her anger as she acknowledged that her remark had triggered the storm.

A storm without wind. Rain drove straight down without variance. Jane flexed her hand and tried to bend it with a flick of her fingers. No response. Mind control came next as she attempted to harness whatever force created the downpour. Again, no response.

Was she wrong in her assumption? She felt no different. Nothing magical coursed through her body. Her eyes didn't glow and sparks didn't shoot from her fingertips. She didn't own a mystical amulet that pulsed around her neck. None of the talismans common in the fantasy fiction she'd read applied. Yet she knew she'd caused the storm.

What was she supposed to do with this information? How could she control it? Worse yet, what affect would the knowledge have on her trial?

The flames sizzled and disappeared, replaced briefly by puffs of smoke. Still the rain came down, drenching the blanket she held around her, seeping through its thickness to the thin cotton of her chemise.

Jane lifted her face to the sky.

"Enough already," she said, at this point not caring who heard her. The damage had been done.

The torrent stopped almost immediately, sputtering out like the flame on a gas stove. The villagers, many shaking their heads, drifted off, no doubt to gossip about her. Mara stayed at her side, loyal to the last. Hugh and Charlie, after checking that the fire had been extinguished, joined them. All three turned to her as if she were the Sorceress of All Things Strange. Which, as far as she knew, she was.

She met their gaze, chin up, waiting for accusations and blame. Charlie approached her first.

"Are you all right?" he asked, his voice gentle. The light from the two moons, sinking toward the horizon, showed the concern in his eyes. Individual drops of rain, not yet evaporated, shimmered on his wings.

Jane's bravado faltered. She wasn't okay. She felt out of control. Things happened so fast in this strange place that she couldn't assimilate one before another took place. She shook her head.

Wordlessly, Charlie enfolded her in his arms. She slipped into his embrace, seeking comfort and understanding, leaning on his strength. He was her anchor. She needed his calm.

"What's wrong?" he asked after a moment.

She couldn't answer.

"Jane." He tilted her face up. "What is it?"

Hadn't he heard? Tears choked her throat at the thought of telling him something that would complicate his life more than she already had.

"Jane?"

She took a deep breath. If she had to hurt him, she'd make it quick and painless.

"I caused the rain."

He didn't rant and rave as she expected, but waited patiently for an explanation. His attitude helped her tell the story. When she finished, he looked over her head as if he expected to see a host of eavesdroppers taking notes.

"Who knows of this?" he asked.

"The whole village by now, I'm sure. You know how quickly word of this will spread."

Charlie closed his eyes for a moment, his fatigue visible. "This makes everything more complex." He took her hand. "Come, you'll have to return to the castle."

Jane pulled away, panic building. "Sylthia! No, Charlie, I can't go back." Memories of her wall-tearing incidents and Eagar's dislike fueled her fear.

"You don't understand," Charlie said, his voice fierce, almost scary. He forced her to look at him. "You're not safe here."

Hugh, standing quietly with Mara next to their damaged house, spoke out. "He's right. You can't remain here."

She looked between the two men, sensing an underlying tension. The marrow in her bones chilled.

"What happened here tonight?" she demanded.

"Jane." Charlie moved his hand to touch her cheek.

She knocked it aside.

"Don't 'Jane' me. I grew up with the six o'clock news. Tell me why someone threw a bomb into the house. Was it because of me?"

Their silence confirmed her suspicions. A cold hollow spread in her stomach.

"Why?" She turned to the one she trusted the most. "Charlie?" She watched his struggle, saw him sigh and accept defeat.

"It was one man," he said. "Capp'ear."

A sharp intake of breath came from Mara.

"He wasn't serious," Hugh said. "Don't take notice of his ramblings. He's ill in the head, has been since the death of his wife and child this past winter."

Jane felt like stamping her foot. What were they protecting her from?

"Why won't anyone tell me what happened?"

"Capp'ear heard about the incident in the castle, when you tore the walls apart," Charlie said in a rush. "I don't know how he found out. He also heard of your talent for growing things."

"I don't understand." This made no sense to her.

"He thinks you're a witch," Hugh said. "That you're out to kill us all, like you did Tivat."

"A witch! Ridiculous. Witches have warts and fly around on brooms. I'm the most unwitchiest person in the world." If she had any powers at all, she'd use them to go home. And her, kill other elves?

"Capp'ear was at the tavern tonight," Charlie explained. "He blamed you for his misfortunes and vowed retribution. Most there excused his ramblings as too much drink. Alfted even walked him home to make sure he stayed out of trouble."

"But he didn't," Jane said.

Charlie shook his head. "He came here and stood beneath your window, calling you a witch and waking the neighbors."

She'd been so focused on getting Charlie in bed that she hadn't heard. If it hadn't been for Muttle . . . She glanced around, looking for the Belwaith.

"Where's Muttle?"

"He's been watching you all night," Charlie said.

*A full-time job, with my knack for getting into trouble.*

Charlie pointed to her protector, sitting on the garden bench, his arm wrapped in a makeshift sling.

"He's hurt!" Jane cried. It was her fault. All of it was her fault.

*I be fine*, the creature answered with confidence.

"Before he could be stopped, Capp'ear tossed a bomb through your window," Charlie explained, drawing her attention.

If she'd been asleep in her own bed—Jane shuddered at the thought.

"You have bombs on Lowth?" she asked, suddenly surprised by the fact.

"They're simple enough to make," he replied. "An empty bottle, a rag, oil or whiskey or something else that burns. And anger at something one doesn't understand—"

Jane didn't understand it herself. She felt cold despite the warmth of the summer night.

*Someone tried to kill me.* Death as punishment for a crime she'd committed was one thing. That was logical, something she could understand. But this, it had the stamp of evil on it. To want to hurt her just because of who she was or what they thought her to be . . . ? She shivered.

Charlie broke through her musings. "We have to go to the castle, Jane. There is no other choice."

Numbly, she nodded. She looked to the other two. "Mara? Hugh?"

"We'll be fine. Friends will take us in," Hugh reassured her. "In the morning we can look at the damage and decide what needs to be done."

Jane wished she could drive him to Home Depot and order what he needed, charging the supplies on her maxed-out, lying-in-charred-ruins credit card. As long as she was asking for the impossible, she wished she lived in a world of tangibles.

Fate had a funny way of kicking you in the rear. Jane held out her hands to Charlie, as if expecting handcuffs to clamp down on them.

"Book me, Danno," she said.

# Chapter Twelve

Jane lay in bed at the top of the castle, in her room next to the king's chambers. Elaine must have been a morning person, she decided, noticing the dawn light cutting through the window and falling with precision across her pillows.

It was the morning of her trial. Over a day had passed since Charlie and Hugh had accompanied her to Sylthia's gates, causing an uproar. Only the brothers' familiarity with Jaspar and the others on community watch had won them entry as well.

Calme, who must have been alerted telepathically by Muttle, had met them at the front door. Hugh returned home. Charlie had taken up a guard position outside her room. Not *in* her room, or *in* her bed, she'd noted at the time. His behavior toward her didn't come from a tenderness in his heart, as she expected after their interrupted lovemaking. Instead, she felt as if she'd been diagnosed with a terminal disease, and he didn't know how to treat her.

She'd slept little since then. An early morning confrontation with Eagar, with Charlie hotly defending her, had upset her. Combined with the impact of the bombing, she couldn't rest. When she wasn't thinking about her powers, she worried about the trial.

Calme brought her breakfast, which Jane didn't touch. She dressed in one of Elaine's gowns, a slate-blue linen the wrong hue for her coloring. She felt dull, devoid of life and vitality.

Charlie knocked on her door midmorning. The concern in his eyes undermined her remaining confidence.

"Is it that bad?" Jane asked, her bottom lip trembling.

His smile didn't reach his eyes. "We have a chance."

"On Earth, it's called a snowball's chance in hell." She didn't have the strength to explain when she saw his puzzlement. It didn't matter, anyway. In a few hours she'd be dead, burned at a stake or boiled alive. She imagined Eagar had spent countless hours devising her torture.

Charlie squeezed her hand and repeated their defense. "They can't convict you of murder without a body." He started to walk down the corridor, toward the great hall where the trial would be held.

She wanted to believe him. However, she'd seen enough movies and late-night television to know that justice wasn't always just.

"Smile," he commanded. "You must present a positive appearance."

"Instead of being the homicidal witch that I am?" she asked, a bitter edge to her voice.

"Don't think that," he said harshly. "It was one man's ranting, that's all."

"Ranting? Or truth? Maybe I am a witch. I have powers I can't begin to understand or control in a world that is as foreign to me as Earth must be to you. Forget? Can you forget you have wings?"

She hadn't meant to be cruel; the words slipped out from frustration and fear. His jaw tightened, and he took the next staircase two steps at a time.

"Charlie," she called after him, skipping to keep up. "Charlie, I didn't mean it." She stopped him at the bottom of the stairwell, a hand on his arm. She searched his eyes and wanted to kick herself for hurting him. "I'm sorry. You're the closest thing I have to a friend in Lowth. You must know by now that I speak first and think later." A sound of exasperation left her. "Don't close up on me now. I need you."

He looked at her. She could almost see his thought process, but that was Charlie—deliberate, careful, and achingly endearing at times.

"Please," she added.

"Jane." He shook his head and smiled, as if he couldn't help himself. "I'll always be there for you." Gently, he touched her cheek.

She wanted to close her eyes and sink into his embrace, to feel safe. He'd make it right, whatever problems ensnared her.

A roar from a large number of people erupted around them. Jane turned her head, surprised that they stood outside the door to the great hall.

"What is it?" she asked, pulling away from him.

"Capp'ear's trial," Charlie answered. "The council put it before yours."

Capp'ear? The drunk who'd called her a witch? Not the opening act she would have chosen.

"A trial?" She shook her head in disbelief. "Why didn't they just pop him last night? They caught him red-handed."

"For the same reason they didn't 'pop' you," Charlie answered. "He's entitled to a fair trial."

A large crowd had gathered, only about half of them Elven.

"Where are *they* from?" she whispered, afraid to make noise and attract attention. As if she wouldn't soon enough.

"All over." Concern darkened Charlie's eyes. "Dwarves,

sprites, even a fairy or two. Your trial is of great interest to them."

Wonderful! Not only was she the headliner of this circus, but half the planet would see the show.

At the other end of the hall, far enough away that she recognized the council only by Eagar's all-black attire, her judges sat. Their attention was concentrated on a small ferret-like man with stringy hair and ill-fitting clothes. Capp'ear.

"It is the decision of the council—" said one of the judges, a florid, rotund man. Was it Wesant, returned from his hunting trip, or Tellise? "—that the willful destruction of property and the endangerment of lives deserve the strictest punishment available. If not for the timely appearance of the storm—" He paused. Jane felt as if everyone pivoted in accusation at her meddling with the weather. But the man only wet his lips and continued. "—the entire village might have been destroyed. Therefore, Capp'ear of Malin, you are sentenced to exile in the Magwrosin Swamp. May you die quickly."

A collective gasp rose from the crowd. Chatter began at once. Jane looked at Charlie.

"Is that bad?" she asked.

"It's certain death. It is the home of the sandobbles," he explained. "They are a race of mobile lumps of quicksand. Alone they are harmless, but when they group together, they form quagmires that will smother a man. They've been contained in the Swamp for the last hundred years by the Dwarves. Capp'ear will be escorted to the border and forced to enter. If he survives a day, he'll be free. If he doesn't—"

Jane shuddered. A cold chill rushed through her. If a drunken act of arson triggered such a horrid death, what hope did she have for her own life?

Others behind them jostled her, tilting her off balance.

As she straightened, grabbing Charlie for support, she heard Eagar speak.

"Will the accused, Jane Drysdale of Earth, come forward?"

Her throat closed as if a noose already tightened around it. Eagar's words echoed in her ears. The crowd rumbled in anticipation, some swiveling to look at her. She felt exposed, naked to their stares. Panic grabbed her, and she clutched Charlie harder, afraid he'd vaporize in this topsy-turvy world.

"Steady," he said. "Show courage, Jane." His warm brown gaze helped pull her together.

Okay, she decided, she could do this. For Charlie, she'd be brave. She'd show Eagar what Earthwomen were made of. She'd dredge up every late-night black-and-white prison movie ever made and be the unflinching convict headed to the chair. Jimmy Cagney, eat your heart out.

Jane straightened, twitching her long skirt into place. She loosened her grip on Charlie's arm and pushed forward.

The crowd parted before her as the Red Sea had for Moses. Curious stares watched her, hands covered mouths to hide whispered remarks. The sun shone through windows thirty feet up the stone walls, casting a spotlight on the council.

Jane refused to be intimidated. After all, she had powers. Okay, so she didn't understand them, but they grew stronger. Whoever or whatever gave them to her must have a master plan, right? If not, she'd wing it. If Eagar found her guilty, she'd drop a house on him. The same for Eagar-to-be numbers two and three.

The walk to the judges passed too quickly. She and Charlie stopped behind a dark wooden table and waited. Jane's chin tilted, she gazed at the three men before her.

Men? Two elves and one dwarf, that was. Eagar sat in the center, impeccable, his eyebrows drawn together. To his right sat the round flushed elf who had pronounced

Capp'ear's sentence. On the far left sat a Dwarf. He was short, maybe four feet tall standing, with bushy white eyebrows and a full beard. He was thin but with the jowls and neck wattle of someone who had lost a lot of weight. Disney's Doc does Jenny Craig.

Eagar spoke, his voice resonating through the hall.

"Jane Drysdale of Earth, you are brought before us to stand trial for the murder of John Tivat of Sylthia. I, Eagar Currge, along with Wesant the Hunter"—he nodded to the florid man—"and Tellise Rootshearer"—he gestured in the Dwarf's direction—"will hear evidence, your defending arguments, and then judge you. Are you prepared for trial?"

*And if I'm not?* Jane pushed away the thought. She squared her shoulders.

"I am, sir." She hoped her voice expressed confidence.

"Do you have adequate council?"

As if he didn't know. Was he irritatingly stupid on purpose? Or just plain irritating, trying to throw her off balance? *'Tis a game he plays.*

*Thank you, Muttle.* It heartened her to know the Belwaith was close by and shared her opinion. *You must be quiet now.*

Eagar looked at her expectantly.

"Charles Whelphite is my lawyer," she said with pride.

He marked something in front of him. What, a checklist? The top ten things to do before legally snuffing out an annoying Earthwoman's life? She badly wanted to take a peek. Only the seriousness of the situation and Charlie's disapproval kept her in place.

"Jane Drysdale of Earth," Eagar continued. "In the matter of the murder of Tivat of Sylthia, how do you plead?"

"Not guilty." She infused the words with as much strength as possible.

"Then we begin," he said, making another note on his

checklist. "Your prosecutor is Elowall, of the Malin Forest. You may be seated."

Jane stole a glance at her opponent as she settled into a tall, uncomfortable chair. Elowall was an Elf, lighter in complexion than those she'd seen in the village or castle. His hair was almost caramel in color, his eyebrows thin and sharply arched over amber eyes.

The first witness was Jaspar, the leader of Tivat's search party. "The old guy," she remembered calling him when he'd helped her from the Neon's trunk. She knew Charlie considered him a friend, but duty called for his testimony.

Jaspar sat in a chair apart from but next to the judges. "Tell the truth, the whole truth and nothing but the truth" didn't apply on Lowth. Nor did they swear on a Bible, their mothers' graves or any other icon. Elowall plunged in with questions, leading his witness from the discovery of Tivat's escape to the last sight of him under Jane's wheels.

He skillfully played up the drama of the pursuit—the decision to enter the portal, despite its lack of stability, the bravery of those who bridged the two worlds, knowing they might be trapped, the shape-shifting abilities of Tivat and the almost immediate change in footprints from Elf to rabbit. By the time the court adjourned for lunch, he'd made Jane sound as if she'd been waiting on the road, gunning her motor for the opportunity to mow down a poor, defenseless bunny.

Mara and Hugh joined them for a meal no one seemed able to eat. They waited until a harried castle worker had served them before speaking.

"Don't mind Elowall," Mara reassured Jane. "He owed Eagar a favor. Taking on the task of prosecutor cancels his debt. He no more wants to be here than you."

Jane glanced at the man in question, sitting at an adjacent table. "For someone who doesn't care whether he wins or loses, he's showing a remarkable killer instinct. I'd hate to take him on when he's passionate about something."

"We still have to cross-examine his witnesses," Charlie said. He'd already told her that he would not present his own witnesses, as she'd been so shortly in Lowth.

"Charlie is very good in the courtroom," Hugh added.

Jane wanted to believe in her Whelphite. She hoped his expertise in the bedroom carried over into court. *Too bad I have to wait for his legal mind to triumph before I take advantage of his physical body.*

Court resumed as soon as the staff cleared the lunch remains. The crowd, many of whom had eaten in the courtyard, abandoned their wagering on the trial outcome and returned to the hall. Without air conditioning, the temperature soon rose from a combination of the slant of the sun and the output of several hundred bodies—some unwashed, Jane noticed, trying not wrinkle her nose in disgust. *Not everyone has running hot water,* she reminded herself, thinking of the work involved in the baths she'd taken every other day at the cottage.

Charlie cross-examined. With deceptive craft, he tore apart Elowall's earlier work. He made Tivat's flight sound like the result of an inept prison system, the same system that had later allowed Jane to escape. The late-night pursuit became a comedy of errors as the tracking team argued, adding time to a ticking clock. He questioned Tivat's "certain" transformation from Elf to animal. The last sighting of the prisoner's footprints coincided with the appearance of a small stream able to obscure the direction of flight.

No proof. Charlie honed in on his angle. No proof. No body. No murder.

*Wow. My lawyer's like Columbo,* Jane thought, her eyes opened to another of Charlie's layers. So many of his techniques mirrored the TV detective's: the casual phrase that made the crowd pause and think, his cunning allusion to

Jane's magic—a gift? A threat? The lack of a body when, according to earlier testimony, death had been instantaneous. The time elapsed from escape to the rabbit sighting, and more importantly, the time available to look for a corpse before the fluctuation in the portal had prompted the group's return.

Jane felt the crowd's mood shift perceptibly in her favor. By the time the story had been retold by the others on duty that night, Tivat's skill at trickery had grown wildly in proportion to his pursuers' ineptitude. Of course, the crowd didn't decide her fate, but she saw enough doubt on Wesant and Tellise's faces to think they'd vote in her favor.

The day wore on. The staff silently provided illumination which they placed in holders around the hall. Backlit in such a way, everything took on a more sinister cast, tightening Jane's throat.

*Nonsense. It's nerves, that's all.* She couldn't stop a shiver from sliding down her spine, a gesture she attributed to the evening air.

They broke for supper, a meal Jane picked at with half-hearted interest. Her companions chatted optimistically. Several times someone detached him or herself from the crowd and gave her words of encouragement or congratulated Charlie for a job well done. Almost all their comments ended with, "It can't be certain without a body, can it?"

*It ain't over 'til the fat lady sings.* Her napkin worried into a crumpled ball, the hem nervously picked apart, Jane waited for the next stage of her ordeal.

Elowall and Charlie made their closing statements, both powerful and able to persuade anyone still sitting on the fence. A restless quiet descended on the crowd as the three judges rose and retired to another room.

"Let's get some fresh air," Charlie suggested. He helped Jane from her chair. Her knees creaked in protest.

"How long does this usually take?" Jane asked, thinking of Earth verdicts, sometimes days in the making.

Charlie looked at her, his eyes a dark brown reassurance. "It will be soon," he said. "Eagar will not have the castle house and feed this crowd overnight."

Rather cheap of him. Expediency in justice to save serving a few more chicken dinners?

They walked the short distance to the courtyard, already thronged with what seemed half the population of Lowth. The sun had set, but the apricot-hued Rest was not yet out. Soft lights from the castle suffused the darkness. Small clusters of people gathered, first by species, then by gender. Jane and Charlie stood near a group of Elven women, some of whom she recognized from the night the cottage had burned.

No one approached as they had at supper. With the verdict imminent, Jane figured they didn't want any death cooties on them in case she was found guilty. Not that she could blame them. She wouldn't snuggle up to a soon-to-be-convicted killer, either.

Stone benches littered the courtyard, placed strategically to view the central gardens. She and Charlie found an unoccupied one in a far corner, tucked against a wall. She sat on it and leaned back, tentative at first because she feared another Nenius episode. *No more séances with dead masons, thank you very much.*

The golden-rose brick, warmed earlier by the sun, felt good through her gown. In contrast, the cool evening air slipped across her cheeks and ruffled her hair. She lifted her hair off her nape, wishing for a cold, wet cloth for her neck.

*I don't know how these women do it,* she thought, imagining shorts and halter tops, wispy dresses and two-piece swimsuits. She looked at some of the women moving in and around the courtyard and imagined them in scantier clothing. They'd taken to the idea of chemises and bras; perhaps she could talk them into shorter skirts. . . .

*If I have time. I might not get it. By tomorrow . . .* She sighed.

Charlie, sitting quietly next to her, asked, "What troubles you? Anything more than the trial?"

"How much time do you have?" she asked, keeping her tone light. "To tell the truth, I was thinking how different our worlds are. I don't fit in here, do I?"

"You've adapted well," he said.

"Yeah, right. Touching dead people's lives, inciting a bombing and becoming the trial of the century. Not exactly a stellar beginning, or a quiet one. It's harder when you look different, when you don't know how to do the most basic chores because machines have always done them for you." She paused. "How do you do it, Charlie?"

"What?" He looked genuinely perplexed.

"Fit in." They'd never talked of it. "How hard is it to be a Whelphite in an Elf world?"

He looked away, watching the crowd so long she thought she'd bungled their friendship. Someone near the hall played a stringed instrument: a guitar, she thought. Its music, slow and melodic, drifted to them.

"When I was younger," he said slowly, "it bothered me that others could predict the weather a week in advance, levitate small objects or overhear a conversation a mile away. I . . . I couldn't fly, so I couldn't awe them. After a while, it became less important. I adapted, found my strengths and concentrated on making those better. Now I can't imagine another life."

He sounded forlorn. Jane squeezed his hand. "I heard about the other day when you stopped a posse of men from going after that wizard. Hugh told me you changed their minds. People look up to you, respect you. Have pride in that."

Charlie smiled ruefully, returning the pressure of her hand squeezes. "I doubt my advice will stay with them.

They'll think of Blacwin the next time the Dymynsh causes another hardship."

"But you stopped them this time and probably saved their lives in the process." She warmed to the theme. "Imagine taking on a wizard! Are they crazy?"

He chuckled. "I suppose I did them a favor."

"There you go." For a few minutes, they slipped into a more companionable silence. Jane felt compelled to ask, as long as he was so open about his Whelphite origins, "Did you ever want to find the truth about your birth? Who your parents were?"

"My parents are Owen and Claire Tanner," he said evenly.

*Careful now*, she told herself, but pressed anyway. "Your father was on his way to Malin. You might have blood relatives here, people you see every day. Wouldn't it be nice to claim them as a family?"

"I have a family, Jane." Anger colored his voice.

*See past the trees, into the forest*, she wanted to shout.

"What of your father?" she persisted. "Surely, Charlie, if you went to his homeland and inquired, someone would remember a baby born to a Fairy father and an Elf mother. You could get in touch with your roots."

"My roots? No." He rose, agitated. He raked his hand through his hair and paced back and forth. "My family is here. Just as yours is on Earth. Would you trade for another?"

No, but her situation was different. "Your true kin—"

"These people are my true kin." He gestured wildly at the others in the courtyard. "Do I feel alienated at times because we're different? Yes. Does it matter anymore? Not a bit. I am what I am."

*And that's all that I yam.* Popeye aside, Jane disagreed with Charlie's decision.

"Then why don't you show your wings?" She jumped up. "You'll flaunt them to me, an outsider, but no one else."

"Flaunt?" His nostrils flared. "You overestimate your importance in my life. Would you like things sprouting from your back? I keep them hidden because it makes others uncomfortable."

"Yeah, right. I'm so uncomfortable." She wiggled her fingers in front of her face, as if mocking him. "Does my being the youngest child make *you* uncomfortable?"

"What does that have to do with anything?"

"They're both accidents of birth."

"Mine's physical," Charlie bit out. He turned his back on her and strode away a few steps.

She'd never win this argument. He wouldn't acknowledge his true self. If only he would see himself as she did. Influential. Important. A leader. Able to be who he really was, all the time.

"Okay." Unwilling to argue anymore, she crossed to his side. "I was curious, that's all. I'm sorry. Let's not fight."

Charlie tipped up his head, as if looking for answers in the sky. He sighed and turned. "I don't want to fight, either. Time is too precious."

He took her hand and led her back to their seats.

Jane leaned against the wall and thought of families and the profound effect they had on one's character. She'd been lucky, growing up. Three annoying brothers, even her sister, Sheila Perfect—oh, how she missed them. She fought tears, trying not to think about it. She'd see them soon. They wouldn't believe her story—except her mother. Jane had unfinished business with her mother, to the tune of an Elven love poem.

Sounds of the night washed over her. The guitar music, soft laughs and Charlie's presence calmed her. She tried to concentrate on them instead of things she couldn't change.

The breeze, fragrant with late roses, teased her, playing with her hair. She relaxed, controlling her breathing, inhaling the good and releasing the bad. Magic and love and the cosmic universe filtered in through an invisible beam at the top of her head, pulling it in, filling her lungs, and shooting it through her arteries. Her veins collected all the bad, the uncertainty and tension, pushing it through an equally invisible pipeline down her leg, to absorb into and be healed by the earth.

Jane practiced the relaxing technique her brother Kevin had taught her. She drifted on the edge of consciousness. Not asleep. Relaxed. On the verge of twilight between two states. Still aware of this world—the muffled voices, the music, a dog's bark—but pulled to another. Quieter. Calmer.

The wind in her hair. This world or that? A moon in the sky. The soft rustle of grain, the lap of waves. Leaves talking to the heavens. A voice, the merest wisp, the smallest presence, like a bean blossom three fields over.

*Anjinaine.*

Hmmm? Too far away to pull it toward her and mingle with the other good.

It came again, a sigh on the breeze. Lethargic, she tried to grasp it. Elusive, it slipped away.

*Anjinaine.*

A caress against her cheek, the barest brush. Warmth suffused her. Acceptance. Love. Understanding. Exquisite tenderness.

*Welcome, Anjinaine.*

Then it was gone.

Jerked from the other world, snapped as quickly as a camera shutter, traveling back at an incredible rate of speed, she was dumped into her body on the bench. She heard a cry in the air and recognized it as her own. A tremor rolled over her.

"Jane." Charlie shook her. "What is it?"

She looked at him with fear and awe. "Someone called my name."

*  *  *

Charlie scanned the area, but he and Jane sat in a remote spot with few others around.

"It could be anyone," he said.

Jane shook her head as if to clear it. "Forget about it. I must have fallen asleep." She felt him tense. "What?"

He stood, his gaze scanning the crowd. In the darkness she couldn't see his expression.

"The crowd gathers," he said a moment later. "The judges must have made a decision."

*Oh, God. Oh, God.* Her palms sweated; her heart raced. She looked at him in panic. "Charlie?" Her voice wavered.

He took her hand in his, rubbing the back with his thumbs. "It will be all right. We can always appeal to the king."

Garmade? Jane remembered her last meeting with him when he'd been too weak and infirm to speak for more than a few minutes. "Where is he?"

Charlie looked up at the balconies surrounding the courtyard, though little could be seen in the darkness. "You can be sure he's aware of everything that happens."

*Strength returns to the land,* the king had told her. *More is to come,* he'd said about her power. She hoped she would have a chance to prove him right.

They followed the tired crowd into the hall and took their seats, Mara, Hugh and Muttle close by. The judges sat at their table, lined up like penguins, black and white and serious.

*Muttle?* Jane reached out to the Belwaith.

He refused to tell her the decision. *Best to know on your own.*

*Bad news then.* She gulped and tried to keep down what little supper she'd eaten.

"Jane Drysdale of Earth." Eagar's voice startled her.

She stood, Charlie rising with her. "Sir?"

"In the allegation of the murder of John Tivat of

Sylthia . . ." He paused. The crowd held its breath. Hell, she held her breath.

*Get it over with.*

"We find you guilty as charged."

She sagged against Charlie. His arms came around her to take her weight. A murmur of disbelief rose from the crowd. Mara touched her, tears flowing down her cheeks.

Jane closed her eyes and clung to Charlie, burying her face in his shirt. She tried hard not to cry out. Her family—she'd never see them again.

"—unaware of the laws of Lowth," Eagar was saying. She tried to focus on his words, but they sounded so distant. "If a majority vote had been reached, the sentence would have been carried out at once. Because there was a dissension, you will not be punished to the full extent of the law."

More murmurs filled the room, intensifying as those assembled absorbed his words. Eagar banged repeatedly with his gavel to restore order.

What did he mean, dissension? Who had voted for her? Jane scanned the judges' faces, looking for a telltale sign, a wink, or the thumbs-up gesture. Nothing.

Eagar continued. "Due to your unusual abilities, sentencing will be delayed until an appropriate answer is found. The court will reconvene at a later date." He struck his gavel with a fierceness that made her jump again.

Confused, she looked at Charlie.

"What does it mean? I don't understand."

He grinned at her, his eyes dancing. "A reprieve. And don't you see? They can't sentence you. If they tried to burn you, you could call the rain again. If they 'tossed you out the castle window,' you'd bring the wind to lift you to safety. If they imprison you, you can make holes in walls. Jane, they're afraid of you."

"They don't know how to kill me?" Truth and irony started to sink in.

"Exactly. They don't know of a way that will work."

"They can't do it in my sleep?" *What am I doing, giving them ideas?*

"You must be aware of the punishment before they can carry it out. That's justice." Charlie nudged her toward the door. "You're free to go."

"Home? Earth?" Hope sprang in her chest, radiating outward.

His expression darkened. "No. Not there."

She felt as if she'd found a treasure map, only to have it snatched away. Her heart cracked in disappointment.

"Jeesh. What kind of—"

"Freaking world do we run here?" Charlie finished. "Come. Let's celebrate."

Riiight. Champagne laced with arsenic, compliments of Eagar's wine cellars.

Oh, what the heck. A reprieve was a reprieve. At least she'd have time to make another stab at seducing Charlie. . . .

# Chapter Thirteen

"I have to get out of here," Jane whined from inside the doorway of Charlie's office.

He didn't look up, but concentrated on the papers in front of him. He'd heard her litany over the past two days, since the end of the trial. "I'm bored." "I hate this place." "Why can't I visit Mara?" She repeated them at every opportunity. He wondered if she ever returned to her room. She seemed forever underfoot. The day before, she'd followed him to the gates of Sylthia, where she'd had a tantrum because he wouldn't let her go farther.

The verdict and lack of sentencing had put the burden of responsibility for Jane back on Charlie's shoulders. While grateful she'd been spared, the situation didn't make his life easier. Her constant presence aggravated him in more than one way—he, who prided himself on his calm, logical approach to life. Every one of her sighs, every toss of her apple-scented hair reminded him of the night in the cottage.

What madness! How had he lost control so quickly? Yes, she'd seduced him with her scant attire, big doe eyes and brazenness, but he'd allowed it to happen. If it hadn't been for the fire . . . He pushed away the thought. He didn't want to repeat either event, especially that of holding her in his arms. He'd survived without Jane Drysdale for twenty-seven years; he could do so for a few more days until Eagar and the others decided what to do with her.

"Charlie, are you listening to me?"

"No, I'm not," he replied, amazed at how easy it was to be rude to her. He continued with his work, avoiding looking at her. "You want to visit Mara. I'm sorry, it's not possible until Hugh or I can escort you. You're still in danger, more so as the trial exposed your 'powers' to a broader audience."

He sighed and reached for a tablet on the corner of the desk. He needed the latest currency rate for Dwarf pelfins against Sylthian indrans. He hadn't told Jane yet, but his experience with the back trails on Lowth was needed. He'd been asked to accompany the group of men who would escort Capp'ear to the Magwrosin Swamp.

"You're bored," he continued, finding the figures he needed and writing them down. "I can't help that, either. I have a job to do, and it becomes more complicated every day. Why don't you visit Sharezee and check the progress on the undergarments she's making?" He said it with sarcasm, wishing for about the thousandth time in the past two and a half weeks that he'd never been on duty the night of Tivat's escape.

"I did," she replied. "She had some things done for me."

He nodded, intent on completing his work so he could go home. It had been a long day.

"Charlie, look at me. Charlie?"

"What?" he asked, slamming the tablet down, angry at her constant interruptions. He glanced up, about to add more of his wrath.

And stopped, mouth agape, blood draining to a pool at his feet then slamming back with force to his groin.

"Wha-what . . ." He struggled to find words. "What do you have on?" Or, to be more precise, what did she *almost* have on?

The top . . . the bodice . . . *shades*, he didn't know what to call it. A triangle of fabric, bright blue, exposed her midriff, bare arms, the throb of her pulse at her neck. And below her waist! Bloomers, stopping above her knees, but tighter, obscenely tight. Charlie pulled the neck of his shirt open with two fingers. This defied logic. What was she thinking?

"You like?" She pirouetted for him.

*Shades*, the top had no back, just a tie at the neck and above her waist. More bare skin gleamed at him. His anger building, he noticed her shoulder blades, a mole above her waist, the tattoo on her arm—

"I don't like," he barked, jumping to his feet. "Are you mad? Haven't you caused enough trouble without inciting a riot? Can you—will you—" Taking firm control of himself, he said through gritted teeth, "You are *not* wearing that."

"But, Dad, all the girls are wearing halters and shorts. Don't you want me to have a date for the prom?" She batted her eyelashes.

He couldn't concentrate with so much flesh showing.

"I. Don't. Care. Take. It. Off."

Expecting an argument, he was unprepared for her next move. Jane shrugged, reached up and untied the fabric.

"No!" Charlie yelled, leaping the short distance to her. He caught a glimpse of her breasts, small and pale and perfect, before he grabbed the top and savagely retied it.

Jane made a gurgling noise, her hands at her throat. "You're choking me."

"If only I could," he muttered. He pulled his shirt off and shoved it over her head. Spinning her around, he all but threw her into his chair.

A muscle twitched over his left eye. His head pounded,

and he could not erase the vision of her breasts from his mind.

"Charlie." She leaned forward.

"Quiet." Pacing the floor, he forced himself to breathe deeply. He avoided looking directly at her.

Several minutes passed while she fidgeted in the chair, but she stayed uncharacteristically silent. When he felt calm enough to speak, Charlie perched on the edge of the desk.

"Jane," he said, trying logic first. "People dress a certain way here for a reason. Protection, modesty, practicality, tradition. To change that invites ridicule and gossip. I know you feel trapped. It's understandable that you want to be more comfortable by surrounding yourself with familiar things. But, Jane, your Earth wardrobe can't be one of them. It's unacceptable behavior."

"Charlie," she said, her tone mocking his. "I'll dress however I damn well please. You people need to be brought out of the Middle Ages. I don't know how long you've had your present wardrobe, but it's hot and uncomfortable. It's impossible to do chores with skirts wrapped around your legs, let alone keep them clean after dragging them in the dust. If others are offended by what I wear, it's too damn bad."

He felt his temper rising. "You will present yourself to this world by wearing appropriate attire. You forget that you are a guest of the king."

"And you forget that I'm going to die. Or be imprisoned. Maybe today. I don't care what I should or should not do, king or not. What has he done for me lately? I don't hear the phone ringing off the hook with a royal pardon."

"Treason!"

"Ignorant, backward people! Stay out of my way, Charlie Whelphite. You don't want to see me mad."

"Nor do you want to see my temper."

"As if." She laughed. "You don't scare me."

"No," he said, determined to have the last word. "But I can issue an order to keep you in the castle, locked in your room until it's time for your death."

"Mary, Queen of Scots." She shot to her feet.

"Whomever. Jane, Queen of Earth, prisoner of Lowth, you will obey me."

"Make me!"

Something snapped in him—sanity, temper, desire, he didn't know which. He did the only thing he could. He kissed her. Hard, demanding, tasting her blood and not caring. He leaned back against the desk, pulling her with him. Her shirt rubbed against his bare chest, making him aware of her breasts underneath. At their memory, he groaned, moving his hand to cup one, thumbing the tip to arousal.

Jane responded with a low moan.

"Oh, Fly Boy," she whispered, taking his bottom lip between her teeth and tugging. "You need to do this more often." She slid one arm behind him and touched his forewing, tracing the raised pattern on the membrane.

Charlie shuddered in reaction. A sharpness, two-edged, a tormenting ecstasy, bisected him like a sword blade. Generated by her fingertips, it convulsed his body, slamming back and forth, looping and knotting before it refocused and shot to his sex.

With a swipe of his hand, he cleared his perfectly organized desk. He lowered her onto its surface, his mouth on hers again, fumbling with the tie at the back of her waist, eager to free it and gain access to her breasts.

"You drive me mad," he growled between kisses. "You tempt me, invade my thoughts, distract me beyond reason. I wonder how you survived on Earth, the way you act with men."

She smiled and traced his ear with one hand, the other wrapped around his neck. "I didn't act this way with Earth men. Just you, Charlie." She licked her lips, a long, slow movement calculated, he was sure, to ensnare him.

He shifted one knee between her legs, uncaring of the time or place. He *would* have her. Perhaps then he would have release from the torment she put him through.

A sound of pleasure escaped her. She closed her eyes, her beautiful, bellefern-green eyes, long-lashed and honeyed. Charlie traced an eyelid with one finger, across her cheekbone and down to her lips, swollen from his kisses. He brushed them lightly, knowing she wanted his touch, teasing her in return, and moved across her cheek again. His fingers tangled in her hair, found the shell of her ear and outlined it upward from the lobe to the bud of a point at the top . . .

Point? It took a moment to sink in, for the implication to rise through the fog of desire and make sense. Sprawled on top of her, moments from taking advantage of her open invitation, he knew he should deal with this abnormality later, after sating his hunger. But it didn't make sense.

Curiosity won over lust. Shaking, Charlie parted the curls around one ear and stared at the developing point. An Elven point.

"By the first dawn," he swore. He didn't bother looking at the other ear; it would be the same. And what in the two moons was he to do?

Jane, unaware of the discovery, chuckled at his outburst. "Too much for you, elf-man?" When he didn't respond, she opened her eyes.

To Charlie, they blazed at him. For an instant, for the tiniest part of an instant, an act of his imagination and not reality, a spark of green lit and extinguished.

He jumped back—away from her, off of her, his desire gone.

"Witch," he grunted, scrubbing at her kisses with the back of his hand. "Capp'ear was right. You mean to enslave me."

Jane sat up on his desk and smiled, amused. "Don't go weird on me, Charlie. I'm no more a witch than you are. If you don't want to have sex with me, then say so, but I don't believe that's the case. I think you like your stuffy little rut, and you're afraid to lose control and let go."

Afraid? Yes, he was afraid. He was involved in something he couldn't handle. Not just lust for her. He couldn't deny that anymore. He'd been pulled into something deeper. It lay at a higher level, perhaps beyond magic, or the beginning of a magic of unparalleled strength in Lowth.

"Fine," he said, drawing a hand over his eyes to block out the picture of her half-dressed. "Believe what you will. I cannot help you with your needs, Jane."

"I can help you with yours, Charlie," she said softly.

His eyes flew open, and he half expected to see her stripping again. Relief flooded him. She sat demurely atop his desk.

"What's it going to be, cowboy?" she asked.

"A respite," he said. "A little time to breathe." And sort out, maybe, what all this meant—ears, eyes, tattoos, and rainstorms. And his feelings. He couldn't shake the conviction that her tattoo held the key. Its familiarity haunted him, but he'd been unsuccessful in remembering where he'd seen it before.

"Okay." Jane scooted off the desk. "I can't give you too long because I don't know how long I have. Tonight, however, you're safe from attack." Her smile promised another story for tomorrow.

"Now," she said, brushing her hands together. "When am I going to see Mara again?"

Charlie groaned. He didn't have the strength to deal with this argument again. "I'll take you there in the morning. But only if you don't wear those ridiculous clothes."

"Deal," she said quickly, too quickly. She walked to the door and reached for a package she must have placed there earlier. Unwrapping it on the open surface of the desk, she pulled out a skirt and blouse.

"How about these?" she asked, holding them up. "I call it the modified Dale Evans look."

The skirt was full, midcalf in length. The blouse had short sleeves, long enough to cover her tattoo, but shorter than what most women wore. With a sinking realization, Charlie knew he'd been tricked. If she'd originally asked to wear these, he would have refused. But in comparison to what she wore under his shirt, they looked almost matronly.

"Jane," he warned, taking a step toward her.

"I knew you'd see reason," she said, moving backward to the door. "See you tomorrow. By the way—nice wings." She blew him a kiss and disappeared.

"It looks like rain," she said the next morning, peering through the cottage window at the clouded western sky. She and Mara sat in the main room after a squealing, joyous reunion.

Charlie had abandoned her. He'd driven Jane and Muttle to the village. Still miffed by her antics of the previous day, he'd hardly spoken to her. Soon after dropping her off, he declared he had business in town. He rationalized her need for extra safety by declaring Muttle more than capable for the job. If danger came too close, the Belwaith would call him.

So much for guarding her. *Riiight. I'll just flash the Bat Signal over Gotham City and you can fire up the old Batmobile and come to the rescue.*

"Hugh says the rain will clear by tonight," Mara said.

"Oh, yes?" Jane shoved Charlie to the back of her mind. Let him pout. At least it showed he thought about her.

"He predicts the weather," the other woman continued. "Except for the night of the fire."

"That was all my doing." Well, not exactly; Jane felt sure she hadn't been alone in drenching the blaze.

"He says it will be clear for tonight's festivities."

Festivities? Jane snapped to attention. Whoa, Nelly. She *had* to leave the castle more often.

Mara looked at her oddly. "Charlie didn't say anything about them?" She paused. "No, he wouldn't, would he?"

"What do you mean? Why would he keep it secret?"

"It's Midsummer's Eve."

"And?" Jane fished for more details.

Mara looked up, down, and in every direction but Jane's. After hesitating for as long as she could, she said vaguely, "A time of renewal. Both moons will be full . . ."

Jane leaned forward. Sómething was definitely strange. "Not getting your drift here, Mara."

The woman cleared her throat. In a rush she said, "In the olden days it was a fertility rite, to ensure a good harvest in the fall."

Fertility? Ah, yes, and all its accompaniments. No wonder Charlie hadn't mentioned it. Jane's interest escalated, her mind revving to high gear. Full moons, parties, Charlie. Charlie's wings. Hoo-boy.

"They serve mead," Mara added.

Mead? Oh, beer. Yes, that would help speed the process.

"Is it still a fertility rite?" Jane tried to remember what pagan festivals entailed—drinking, bonfires, nudity, and wanton lovemaking.

Mara blushed, obviously thinking the same.

"Say no more, say no more." A sudden thought occurred to Jane. "Not to sound nosy or anything, but are there other women in the village trying to conceive?"

Her friend's face darkened, as if she didn't like thinking about this aspect of her marriage and the Dymynsh. "Several," she said tersely.

"And are there some who might need help, beside the full moons and the mead and the general toga party ambiance?" Jane's mind was going *click, click, click*. She had no use for her merchandise now that her could-have-been-lucrative part-time job had crashed to a halt. What better way to dispose of it than to the benefit of the local women?

She looked around as if expecting Charlie to return. He'd probably be gone for hours, which would give her more than enough time. Two could play this game. She'd attack the Dymynsh in her own way.

"How many women can you get here in the next few minutes?" she asked, trying to remember what remained in her boxes after Kendra's party.

"I don't understand."

Jane rose and threw her arm around the other woman's shoulders. "Let me introduce you to the double-A battery."

It was the best party she'd ever hosted. The women of Malin, after their initial shock at the premise of the impromptu Realm of Pleasures party, dove in with enthusiasm. About thirty in all crowded Mara's cottage, stuffed and wedged in every available spot. More trickled in as word spread that the Earthwoman, famous for making gardens grow and rain appear, was selling devices to improve relations. In their minds it meant one thing—conception, especially on the prophetic day of Midsummer's Eve.

Jane, feeling generous, cleared out her merchandise at rock-bottom prices. Lowth prices, that was, consisting of the currency of indrans and using the bartering skills of Mara. Clothes, jewelry, favors and even a chicken or two were traded for the contents of her Rubbermaid containers that the Elven men had unwittingly transported through the portal.

Foregoing her usual practice of privately filling orders, Jane opened all the boxes and let the women go at it. Soon they argued over body glitter, massage oils, edible undies, fantasy candles and lubricants. They fought and traded them as actively as they would eggs on market day.

The vibrators sold the most quickly, the partygoers comparing them to their husbands' sizes and abilities. Jane passed around samples of her products, gave out door prizes and explained some of the more obscure items, such as nipple chains and love beads.

Two hours of bawdy remarks later, the room finally cleared. All that remained were a couple of novelty ice cube trays and some board games, unintelligible in English.

"Charlie won't like this," Mara said, picking up discarded paper, boxes and plastic. "Hugh probably won't, either."

"Charlie doesn't like a lot of what I do," Jane replied. "But I can guarantee he'll like what I'm going to do tonight." She'd kept a few items for herself. She planned on getting him semisnookered with mead and retreating to the castle for Charlie's Seduction, Phase Three.

The women exchanged glances, grinning in the Cheshire Cat–grassy knoll type of conspirators' way.

"We'll leave you and Hugh to yourselves," Jane added, trying not to laugh at Mara's embarrassment. "If it's a girl, I want you to name her after me."

Mara blushed. "If anyone can help with our problem, it's you, Jane. After what you did to my garden . . ."

"Well, a geranium and a baby are two different things, but I'll cast my spell on you." She proceeded to make a hocus-pocus sign with two fingers in the general vicinity of her friend's womb.

"It will have to be magical, because after tonight, Hugh is gone." Mara picked the last scrap of paper up off the floor.

Jane grabbed her arm, not liking her tone. Had her sentence been determined? "What do you mean?"

Mara blinked, as if she might have said something out of turn. "He and Charlie and three others are taking Capp'ear to the Magwrosin Swamp."

Anger flooded Jane. "What!? Charlie never said anything."

"Charlie is too quiet. You should have been told."

"Damn straight! He's traipsing off to some swamp for another prisoner's punishment while I'm left alone to meet mine? Oh, that crisps my fries. Where is he?"

*Tavern*, Muttle interjected quietly, the first she'd heard from him in hours.

"Hanging out at the bar? Muttle, you're the only one I can trust anymore." She pulled on Mara's arm. "Come on, we're going downtown."

"Charlie?"

It sounded sweet, but he knew the tone too well. He'd done something wrong in her eyes and was about to pay the price.

"Jane?" He turned to look at her. Uh-oh. He recognized trouble in the sparks flying in all directions. "I thought you were at the cottage."

She came to a stop in front of him, her revolutionary attire garnering more than a few glances. "And I thought I could trust you."

"You can." He took a sip of mead, fortifying himself. What had he done?

A hand on one hip, the other pointed at him, she said, "Why are you leaving me alone with Eagar?"

Charlie didn't understand. The raw talk in the tavern had been about tonight's couplings. He couldn't imagine her and Eagar together. Truth be told, he couldn't imagine Eagar with anyone, and Jane with no one but himself. The thought of her hands moving over his naked body—

"I heard what you're up to," she continued, growing more heated by the second. "How dare you desert me? I need you here, not throwing the Unabomber in a swamp."

"Oh, that." He'd not planned on telling her until the last minute, knowing they'd have this scene.

"Yes, that. Why can't they burn him at the stake here instead of transporting him so far?"

"Now, Jane," he said, taking her arm and hustling her out of the tavern. The street might have as many spectators but they'd sensibly keep their distance, unlike the louts inside. "The laws may seem complicated at times—"

"Don't patronize me, Charlie," she said, pulling herself free. She blinked several times, adjusting to the bright midday sun. "When, exactly, were you going to tell me?"

"Never" seemed the incorrect answer. Instead he fumbled, wishing for inspiration, determined to keep his temper.

Activity at the end of the street saved him from answering. He heard shouts, and people appeared from different buildings, drawn toward the commotion. A few from the tavern stepped out, shading their eyes.

"What's going on?" Jane asked, clearly upset that her tantrum had been interrupted.

"I don't know." Whatever it was, it was timely. "I'm sure I need to find out."

Jane followed behind him. Charlie tried to ignore her, hoping that whatever had caused the halt in activity was trade-related, requiring his immediate attention. He pushed through the crowd that surrounded a bulky shape in the middle of the road. It took him a moment to fathom that the shape was two full-grown sheep harnessed together, with a man tied to their backs. A man with an arrow in his back.

"'Tis Randolph," Patrance, the local cartwright, said. He knelt by the man's head, laying it back where he'd lifted it for identification.

Randolph! A coldness pierced Charlie. The man had been due at the castle three weeks earlier with his shipment of wool. He was not three weeks dead, but he was certainly dead.

"What type of arrow killed him?" Charlie asked. He knew the answer, recognized the design on the shaft, the length of the fletching. The type was rare in this part of Lowth, but he knew where it had been made.

"Not Malin."

"Nor Goblin."

"Dwarvish neither."

The guesses from the crowd didn't come close. None but perhaps Wesant the Hunter traveled as much as Charlie and would know it came from Malik. To make sure he was correct, Charlie leaned forward to inspect it. Shock hit him when he realized a piece of paper was wound tightly around the shaft.

"Give me a knife," he said, holding out his hand. He knelt by the body, trying to ignore the stench. Carefully, he cut the strings that held the paper, pulling it free. He stood and unrolled it.

Shock hit him a third time, this one the most terrifying. Shaking, he looked over at Jane. He held the page out so she could read:

*Return the mortal to me.*
*—Blacwin*

# Chapter Fourteen

"I can't believe I'm here again," Jane said under her breath. "I can't believe an arrow and a freakin' wizard are incentive enough to get the Supreme Court to reconvene."

She stretched her neck to see the crowd filter into Sylthia's great hall and sit on benches. They numbered fewer than at the trial. Oh, God, had it only been three days ago? After all the talk of her "powers," Jane expected the council to take a long time to find the correct punishment for her. Maybe fifty or sixty years. Instead, the appearance of two smelly sheep and an even smellier dead guy spurred them to action.

Within an hour after the commotion in the village, word had reached her and Charlie to report to Sylthia. Once there, they'd had to wait more. It was three o'clock on a blistering afternoon, and she hadn't eaten yet, a fact proclaimed by her grumbling stomach.

"Hush," she warned at its latest protest. "You're still entitled to your last meal." She asked Charlie for the twentieth time, "How much longer do you think they'll take?"

"I do not know," he replied for the twentieth time. He

**NAME:** _____

**ADDRESS:** _____

_____

_____

**TELEPHONE:** _____

**E-MAIL:** _____

_____ I want to pay by credit card.

__ Visa          __ MasterCard          __ Discover

Account Number: _____

Expiration date: _____

**SIGNATURE:** _____

*Send this form, along with $2.00 shipping and handling for your FREE books, to:*

Love Spell Romance Book Club
20 Academy Street
Norwalk, CT 06850-4032

*Or fax (must include credit card information!) to: 610.995.9274.
You can also sign up on the Web at www.dorchesterpub.com.*

Offer open to residents of the U.S. and Canada only. Canadian residents, please call 1.800.481.9191 for pricing information.

didn't look up from the paperwork he'd grabbed from his desk on the way in. No doubt it was some important schedule that needed to be completed before his journey. The castle couldn't function without his schedules.

"Don't get in a snit, Charlie," Jane said, pulling a piece of paper from the pile and holding it close to read. It made no sense whatsoever. "I know you're mad at me."

"I am not mad at you." He snatched the document back and returned it to its proper position. "I am busy." His tone suggested she'd never been busy.

"Hey, I work, too, you know. At least I did." She couldn't count the number of boring insurance forms she'd filled out during the day for her boss, Bernie Toulouse, owner of the Toulouse Insurance Agency. What a stupid name. What a stupid job. Who named their kid Bernie when he'd have a hard enough time with Toulouse-Lautrec jokes all his life?

Charlie glanced at her.

"I drew a paycheck," she protested. Two paychecks, if she included her income from Realm of Pleasures. Too bad she wouldn't get any commissions for this morning's party. That would have been a fun check to cash.

"I know you're mad at me," she repeated, goading him. He could be so stick-in-the-muddish sometimes. "You drop your contractions when you're upset. That's something I've noticed about you." One of the few non-wing-related things, such as that he wrote left-handed, and his eyes were the same color as the way he liked his coffee—black with cream. A nice latte brown.

"So, what do you think Eagar is going to do with me?"

Charlie stopped writing and stared at her. She didn't understand how someone could make it look as if they rolled their eyes without actually doing so, but he had it down to an art.

"Whaaat?" she asked, all innocence.

"You talk too much."

"It's nerves. You should know that about me by now. I get nervous, I talk. They're a pair, like coffee and cream, bread and butter—"

"Gags and mouths?" he suggested.

"Yeah." She smiled. "Kinky, but yeah. You into that kind of thing?" Jane tried to remember if she'd kept a pair of handcuffs.

He acted as if he hadn't heard. Oh, well, tonight she'd find out his level of kinkiness. Tonight. Her insides warmed at the thought.

"If they ever get this circus on the road," she muttered. "What possible connection can an arrow and a wizard have to do with me? What did the note mean? 'Return the mortal to me.' I've never been to Malik. How can I return?"

Charlie did the non-rolling eye roll again. "I do not know."

"Take a guess. What do Eagar and Company have planned for me? Are they going to chain me to a goat until I suffocate from the smell? Trade me to the wiz—" Jane stopped, appalled by the thought that popped into her head. "That's it!"

"What's what?" He looked annoyed, his usual expression when she went on a tangent.

"They're trading me to the wizard. They can't kill me, so they'll let him do it for them."

"Jane, what are you talking about?"

"I figured it out. The wizard wants me bad enough to kill Randolph, the messenger. And what does Sylthia need in exchange? What do we need that he has?"

She had his full attention now. She could see the gears working in his mind.

"The means to stop the Dymynsh," he said slowly.

"Bingo. Give the man a prize. Charlie, they're going to use me as a bargaining chip. My life for the end of the Dymynsh."

She watched his disbelief war with the possibility. He shook his head. "No, they wouldn't—"

"Give me a good reason. This is a win-win-win situation. The wizard gets what he wants, Eagar is rid of me, and he looks good by doing something about the Dymynsh. Who loses?"

His eyes darkened. "You do, Jane."

She'd already thought of that. She smiled. "That's why I have you, Charlie. To negotiate better terms with Blacwin."

"Negotiate? With a wiz—," he blustered.

Jane patted his hand. "I trust you. I have from the start. Who knows where I'd be if you hadn't argued so well in court? Did you ever find out who voted in my favor?" Her money was on Tellise, the Dwarf, with his double chins and blue eyes. Wesant the Hunter had a hardened look to him, and Eagar had expressed his opinion on more than one occasion.

"No," Charlie answered. "They're not required to tell. We may never—"

A murmur rose from the crowd. Jane swung toward the room where the judges had retreated. They came through the door and walked to a raised platform.

Charlie slipped his arm through hers as they stood.

"Jane Drysdale of Earth," Eagar spoke. She wished he'd drop the Earth part. She'd never see it again, and his use of the term rubbed salt in that wound.

"Sir." Her backbone couldn't be any straighter. *Ha. Take that, you old goat. I know your plan. I'm going to win.*

"Your imprisonment and trial have cost the Kingdom of Malin considerable expense." He paused, as if expecting an apology.

Expenses? What, some wall spackle for the storeroom and a few hundred chicken salad sandwiches during the trial? Hang the expense. She knew his words were for the audience. *The witch Earthwoman takes precious gold from the royal treasure, gold that can save us from starvation. Ergo, send her somewhere else so she can use their gold.*

"Your presence in Malin continues to drain our resources." Again, then came a pause to let the words sink in with the crowd.

Jane stood rigid. Damned if she'd let him see his effect. She ate no more than he did. The hypocrite.

"Considerable time has been spent devising your punishment."

Spent, drain, cost . . . did she sense a theme here?

"Unfortunately, we have been unable to find an appropriate penalty for your crime. Until today."

*Drum roll, please.*

"In a unanimous vote, we have decided to comply with the wishes of Blacwin, guardian of Malik. Negotiations will be made to turn you over to his custody."

Reaction swept over the crowd, building in intensity as they mulled over Eagar's words. A communal light bulb went off in the hall. Comments started again; stares focused her way.

Eagar spoke again. "We depart tomorrow. This case is closed."

Wait! We? We, as in Eagar and Co.?

"I object!"

Oh, God, had that come from her?

Charlie's hand tightened on hers with such force she almost cried out, which would have defeated his purpose.

"Sirs? If I may?" He waited for a nod from Eagar before continuing. "If there is a plan regarding my client, I would like knowledge of it."

Eagar stared at him, his eyes sharp, black stones. Charlie, who had worked with him for ten years, wondered for the first time if he really knew the steward.

"There is always a plan," he answered. "A party of twelve leaves tomorrow, including the prisoners Capp'ear and Jane Drysdale. Capp'ear will be escorted east to the Magwrosin Swamp. From there we will proceed to Gaelen, home of the Dwarves. Then north and west to Malik, to begin negotiations with the wizard Blacwin."

A party of twelve. Twice the number six, supposedly a lucky symbol in Malin. But tomorrow? And Jane's entourage tacked onto Capp'ear's, the man who had tried to kill her?

"You are to join us?" Charlie asked.

Eagar nodded. "Wesant remains at Sylthia. Tellise will join us until we enter Gaelen."

Wesant was sound, solid, a good defender of the castle, a friend of King Garmade. A wise choice.

Charlie directed his attention to Jane. Under her calm exterior he saw the grip she had on her fear. She held tight control on her shock at making the voyage in Eagar's company. He needed to get her out of here before she said or did something to jeopardize her trip.

He turned back to the elders, who waited for him to say more. Instead, he nodded to them, took Jane's arm and hustled her from the hall.

He led her up a flight of stairs to a small room with tapestries on the walls and an informal arrangement of chairs. She sat in one of them, and he knelt in front of her. She hunched over, her hands covering her face, shoulders shaking.

"Jane," he said. "Jane, calm down. It isn't that bad. It's but a few days' journey to the swamp, and two weeks at the most from there to Malik. You won't be in Eagar's company long. I'll keep him from you." In truth, he'd never been to Malik, but he knew a good guide. They could travel swiftly, but to what end? He did not want her death. As much as he hated to admit it, her vibrancy and courage brightened his days. She twisted his life upside down, and he couldn't imagine it without a new daily calamity.

"Jane, don't cry." The light fragrance of flowers drifted

from her hair. He lifted a curl between his fingers and let its softness slip through them.

"I'm not crying," she said, tilting her head. Tears glistened in her bright green eyes. "I'm laughing."

"Laughing?" He couldn't keep up with her mood changes. "Why?"

"I've beaten the bastard," she crowed. "He doesn't know what to do with me, so he's turned me loose on a wizard. A wizard! As if that would stop me."

"A wizard is a serious thing—"

"You're a serious thing." She poked him hard in the chest. "Have you ever known me to be beaten? I'm going to win at this. Watch me."

There had been the time when she'd cried in King Garmade's arms, but Charlie thought it best not to mention it. "Never," he lied.

"Oh, Charlie." She launched herself at him, knocking him off balance. They fell in a heap on the floor, Jane laughing.

His body reacted immediately to her nearness. Desire drove into him with a startling intensity. He wanted no entanglements, and he would have none with her. Soon, she'd be gone, either destroyed by Blacwin or, if she won, sent back through the portal to Earth. He couldn't imagine her fate but knew he was tied to it in some cataclysmic, almost horrific way. He had been from the start and would be, it seemed, to the end. He might as well get some enjoyment from it. Why struggle with himself? They both wanted a physical relationship. Why deny it?

"Jane," he whispered, touching her cheek gently.

"Isn't this the best?" she asked, her face alight. "To win? I can stand Eagar's presence because I know I've bested him."

Charlie cleared his throat. "Let's not talk of Eagar."

"No, let's not." To his amazement, she scooted off him

and sat up, crossing her legs under her sheared-off dress. "Let's talk about tonight."

Tonight? He had plans with her for tonight. But he had plans for right now. Couldn't she see his desire?

Apparently not. She reached over and, with a tug and him scrambling to hide his erection, she got him into a seated position opposite her.

"Is it romantic?" she asked. "The full moons and the dancing and the summer heat?"

He wanted to show her romance. Now, not hours away. But Jane had an agenda of her own, and with Jane it was wise to stick with her wishes. To do otherwise opened up only possibilities for disaster.

"Yes," he said, pushing away thoughts of her naked body beneath his, and concentrating instead on the intricacies of pagan fertility rites. It was a shift that brought the same results. "It's romantic. It will rock your world."

He'd bet on it.

Eight hours later, Charlie's desire nearly overcame him. He stood with Jane in a meadow above Malin Village, on the banks of the river that rushed from the heights of the forest to join the Tarradine Sea. The young and elderly had been taken home. As midnight loomed, those remaining hastened to lose their inhibitions. Mead and wine overflowed all cups. Music pulsated, wild and frenzied, the crowd thinning as couples paired off.

Charlie fought his throbbing need. His palms sweated and his heart banged in his chest. The memory of Jane's perfect, creamy breasts engulfed him. The intricate cross-weaving of her silk dress covered them. He could only think of the fastest way to rip the garment from her body.

A bonfire burned in the center of the meadow, the flames scratching the black sky. Kindled with ferns and pine needles, it crackled from the fuel of nine different woods. Dancers gyrated around it in an urgent rhythm, spinning faster as the night grew. From experience, he knew that many of the women tonight wore nothing under their gowns, bringing them closer to the earth and sky. He wondered if Jane followed the tradition. Waiting to find out nearly killed him.

"It's beautiful," Jane whispered. She craned her neck to look at the twin full moons. Rest, larger and closer, hung like an apricot-and-coral engorged globe. Slumber came after, a marbled lavender. They'd cleared the trees and cast a glow on lust-filled features and guided lovers to hidden trysts and wild couplings.

Charlie's loins twitched at the thought of his planned rendezvous with Jane. How could he get her back to the castle? She seemed intent on staying the night, to join in the ceremony of watching Lowth's highest spire pierce the moons, the way a man would take a woman.

"Is it like this every Midsummer's Eve?" she asked, her gaze on the whirling dancers.

"No." He could barely speak. His throat felt raw with desire. "There's a frantic energy tonight, as if this will be the last time, as if the Dymynsh will claim us all by next year."

"Live for tonight, for tomorrow we die?" she asked.

"Yes," he ground out. "Who knows what will happen?"

The thrumming of the drums matched that in his body. He needed her. Now. He wanted her hot and shameless and under him.

"Can we go back to the castle?" Impatience drove the question.

She looked at him, startled.

He watched her. *Yes, this is Charlie, who usually runs from you. You don't know him at all.*

"Yes," she whispered, her voice husky.

Charlie knocked back the last of his wine and threw the empty cup on the ground. The path to town dipped and rose again to the castle. He knew a quicker way, across the hill, through short grasses and hard rock. His footsteps were hurried as they crossed it, the moons lighting their way.

On some level he was aware of Muttle trailing them. The Belwaith, as the king's servant, was trained to be discreet. He would say nothing.

Charlie's wings hummed in anticipation. His hand on Jane's bare back burned at the touch. If he didn't get into her bed, into *her* soon, he'd burst into flames. Damn her for making him feel this way.

They reached Sylthia's gates, and long minutes later the keep. In darkness, he led her up the many staircases. Hunger gnawed at him. His heart pounded like the distant drums.

He picked her up and swung through the archway, kicking the door closed behind them. Her windows faced the wrong way to catch the moonlight. A fraction of Slumber's lavender blush glossed the room. It would have to do; he had no time to light candles.

"You strive to tease me," he growled, his control breaking. His hands tugged at the intricate lacing of her gown. "You think you're safe, that boring old Charlie will remain unmoved." He trembled, shaken by the violence of the emotions beating in him. Frustration. Desperation. Need. "You're not safe with me, Jane Drysdale. There is only so much I can take, and I have reached that point."

The fabric of her dress ripped, splitting at the seams as he jerked on it. With a grunt of satisfaction, he peeled it over her head to expose her pale skin, dusted with a glimmer of gold. Her breasts, the perfect size to cup in his hand, budded in welcome. He lowered his head and sampled them, the taste of her honeyed skin lingering on his lips.

Jane whimpered and pulled him nearer, her arms reaching around him.

"Wings," he whispered harshly. "You like them, don't you, Jane? Touch them. Feel them." He pulled off his shirt, stepped from his pants. His wings unfurled, encircling her, undulating over the skin on her back.

His breath died in his lungs. He'd never felt anything so erotic in his life.

Charlie pushed her against the door, pinning her against his erection. Through the roar in his head he was dimly aware she wore no other clothing. It made him want her more. Her smooth skin, the look on her face—

Pale moonlight bathed her features. Her eyes, glazed with passion, watched him, unafraid. The beginnings of a smile curved her lips.

"Not Charlie mild and meek," she breathed. With deliberate slowness, she stretched to touch his left forewing.

An explosion rocked him. If he couldn't have her soon—

She laughed softly. He stopped it with a kiss, taking her mouth by force, seeking, wanting, grasping for her sweetness. She kissed him fiercely, her tongue invading him. Her low, desperate cries escaped into the shadows.

Yes, that's what he wanted. Her surrender. She intruded into his life. He resented her, was fascinated by her, desired her. *Needed* her.

She touched him again, sending a shudder to the core of his being.

So close. He shoved her against the door, his hand reaching for her slickness, parting her to make an opening.

"Charlie," she gasped in response. She turned her head, her lips hot on his throat, kissing his jaw, seeking his mouth.

He plunged his hardness into her, taking her against the door, gaining entry at last.

It was more than he dreamed, wild and wet, a raging storm. His whole body vibrated in rhythm with hers. Jane moved against him, her nipples pebbled against his chest, her hands in his hair, scratching his back, tracing the edge of his forewing.

Charlie thrust harder, fighting for control, aching for release. He wanted to fly with her, to soar on the drafts of the night wind, coupled in flight.

"Yes, yes," she breathed, curling one leg around him, granting him better access. She gasped as he plunged deeper.

Her cries incited him. He picked her up, molding contours, opening, delving to inmost folds. Buckling, sure he would break before he climaxed, trembling at this madness. He wanted more—softness, roughness, ecstasy, wetness, her touch. This was what he wanted, needed—to be with her.

She called his name. Charlie felt her convulse around him.

"I can't wait," he gasped. He tried to hold on longer, to give her release. Her intense pleasure broke his control. He exploded, hot, wild, and violent.

"Anjinaine," he cried, and fell into darkness.

# Chapter Fifteen

*Oh my God, I've killed him!*

Charlie lay motionless on her bedroom floor. Moments earlier, he'd slumped against Jane, pulling out of her right when things had started to get interesting. Blind luck, dexterity and one foot almost on the ground had saved her from tumbling down with him.

"Charlie, don't die on me," she cried, tears in her eyes. She dropped to her knees at his side, trying to remember the CPR her brother Kevin had taught her. Lowth didn't have an equivalent of 911, and anyone with medical experience was probably passed out from too much midsummer partying.

She shook him, and when he didn't respond she clamped her ear to his naked chest. *Wha-thump.* Yes, a definite heartbeat. Thank God!

Muttle had probably heard their violent lovemaking through the door, thick as it was, but Jane hesitated to call him. If Charlie had simply fainted, he'd be embarrassed by the attention.

Speaking of bare asses, he was completely exposed to

her. At any other time she'd have enjoyed the sight, but it would be voyeuristic, not to mention sick, to ogle an unconscious man. She wrestled him back into his pants and snatched a blanket off the bed, grabbing her robe at the same time.

"Don't die on me," she sobbed, covering him. "I need you, Charlie Whelphite. That crack about Klingon lovemaking was a joke. How was I to know I'm too much woman for you? No wonder you fled from me." She slipped her arms into the robe and belted it. "I promise to be gentle next time. I love you, Charlie."

And there it was, as simple as that. She'd fallen in love with an Elf. An I-love-my-rut-don't-mess-up-my-day Elf who happened to be half fairy. And a lawyer. And a dozen other important things to a small kingdom in a parallel universe. Who said love was easy?

*You really know how to pick 'em.* Tears rolled down Jane's cheeks, and she halted a sniffle before it could escape. It was hopeless. She'd finally found a man to love and instead of celebrating, she was headed into a battle with a wizard.

Well, she wasn't going to lose that fight, and she wasn't going to lose this man, either. Not for a wizard, the Dymynsh or any other curveballs Lowth threw at her. Jane shook herself, ashamed of giving in to weakness.

"Charlie, wake up." She patted his cheek gently.

He groaned and moved his head.

"Jane?" he asked, his voice thin and distant.

"How are you?" She bunched a corner of the blanket into a pillow under his head.

Charlie opened his eyes, blinking several times, as if trying to focus. "Confused. What happened?"

She winced. "I'm not sure, but I think I knocked you out. We were making love and you fainted. I'm sorry. I didn't realize I was so potent." Jane brushed his hair from his face. It fell through her fingers like fine threads.

He struggled to sit, looking sheepish. "That's the first time I've fainted during sex."

"I'm sorry." She helped him stand, catching him under the arm when he wobbled.

"Don't apologize. Unless you used your 'powers' on me," he said in a half-joking manner.

Jane bit her lip to keep from replying. She'd have to be more careful next time, at least until he built up some tolerance to her vigorous lovemaking. There went her plan for using her vibrator for mutual satisfaction. He'd probably go into cardiac arrest.

Charlie lurched, throwing her off balance.

"Dizzy," he murmured. With one hand he reached for the edge of the bed.

Jane steered him toward it. "Maybe you should lie down for a while."

"Maybe I should."

Carefully she helped him, then retrieved the blanket. Fascinated, she watched him fold his wings so they didn't take up much room. Jane scrunched in bed next to him, her back to his front, spoon-fashion.

"This isn't so bad, is it?" she asked when they'd settled, the blanket covering them.

"No, it's nice."

His breath ruffled her hair, the sprinkling of hairs on his chest rubbing through the thin fabric of her robe. Knowing he couldn't see her, she smiled, her heart doubling in size with her love. Who would have imagined she'd fall for a levelheaded, brown-eyed Elf? Her mother had worried about her taking off with a biker or a circus performer, and instead she'd tumbled for a lawyer. A rock of the community: he'd done so much for the kingdom. If only he realized it.

"Why did you call me Anjinaine?" she asked, entwining her fingers with his.

"Did I? I don't remember." His voice sounded tired.

"It's the second time this week I've been called by that name. Someone's trying to tell me something important. Did you grab it out of the air, or what?"

"I think it was in a dream," he murmured. He shifted her in his arms, pulling her closer.

A warm purr escaped from Jane. *I could get used to this.* She knew when she'd dressed for the festivities that she'd end in bed with him. It was a matter of time and patience. It sure helped when he took matters into his own hands. And what capable hands! Stick-in-the-mud Charlie had depths she'd never dreamed about. *It's always the quiet ones.*

She rolled over, intent on interesting him in an encore. He slept.

Jane stirred softly, a weight pressing against her back, side and stomach. She opened her eyes; the gray predawn light outlined an arm across her. Charlie. *Oh, this is interesting. Morning sex?*

Her head hurt from too much wine the night before, but she knew of an effective hangover treatment. Endorphins. The best way to get the little chemicals—she thought of them as mini Pac-Men—shooting through her blood involved some heavy breathing. An adrenaline rush. Definitely some arm wrestling. Toe, foot, and tongue wrestling while they were at it. Oh, and fingers. Wings, too. A tingle started in her middle and spread outward.

"I'm awake, you know," Charlie said from behind her.

"Oh," she squeaked, half-turning to look at him. Guilty thoughts made her blush. "You scared me."

"You scared me last night." His eyes looked incredibly brown and sexy and dangerous. "What was that about?"

She shook her head. "I don't know. I think . . . it's outside the both of us."

"Lowth playing more tricks on you?"

"Yeah." Jane found it difficult to lie in his arms and not shout out that she loved him. Restraint came hard to her. "I wish I knew what it all meant."

He moved his hand so that his fingers played in her hair and touched her face. "I think we'll find out soon. We leave today."

Reality. Such a cruel intrusion. She wanted nothing more than to stay here in his arms for a long, long time. "I know." She rubbed her cheek against his palm. "How soon?"

Charlie glanced at the sun's location.

"Oh, I think there's time," he said, smiling.

"Time for what?"

"For what was interrupted last night." In a quick movement, he flipped her onto her back, the sheet falling away to expose his naked form. Jane gulped at the sight of his erection. When had he shed his pants?

"My, my," she said, reaching to cup him. "Mrs. Claus needs to say hello to Santa's *big* helper."

*Gentle, gentle* . . . Jane tried to convince herself to go easy, but in reality, she wanted to savor loving him. His caresses, his nakedness, the brush of his long hair against her nipples—every movement created new sensations.

She closed her eyes as he rained sweet kisses from her mouth to the inside arch of her foot. She cried in passion as he raised her to him, bare thigh against bare thigh, his fingers massaging her throbbing need. They twisted in the bed, limbs entangled, heated mouths against even hotter skin. Pulses raced in unison. He slid into her as if he'd been there a hundred times. But she'd never felt this way before—whole, bursting, fused with another into one being. Charlie. Her love. Her reason for living. How strange the way she had found him.

As the sun broke into the room, Jane crested in a series

of increasingly larger waves. She took Charlie with her on the last, their combined cries splintering the dawn.

They drifted into day, satisfied aftershocks rippling through them. Jane sighed and fell asleep, one arm wrapped around the man she loved.

# Chapter Sixteen

"A little more," she said, raising her arms to let the cooler air flow over them. "Ah, that's perfect. I love it. Don't stop." She wanted to purr in satisfaction.

"Jane?"

Charlie's voice snapped her from her contentment. She spun, her eyes seeking to distinguish his form from the other half-shadowed objects around her.

It was after dusk, almost fourteen hours since they'd departed that morning from Sylthia's gates. Fourteen hours of unrelenting heat. She couldn't remember being so hot, even during Michigan summers, when the temperature and the humidity battled to reach the nineties.

The sun blazed in the sky. The air, vibrating from the heat, shimmered with hallucinogenic irradiation. Even during the short time they traveled under the canopy of the Malin Forest, they saw the lack of vegetation, the effect of the Dymynsh. Whirlpools of dust kicked up from the path, and all the shadows had a tawny cast to them.

Eagar drove them relentlessly. Breaks were short and infrequent. They hiked until Hugh protested they would not have light enough to strike camp.

God, she'd hated camping since she was little. Cooking over an open fire and sleeping under the stars sounded romantic until the first time you needed to go the bathroom or take a shower. It sucked then, and it sucked now.

"Jane?" Charlie called again. She heard the dry undergrowth crack as he made his way through the small stand of trees Hugh had selected as their campsite.

"Over here," she directed. Darkness hid him so well he seemed to spring from nowhere. The moons' light had not found its way into the valley.

"What are you doing so far from the others?" he asked, taking her hand.

Her heart zinged at his touch. Last night and this morning had been wonderful, but she doubted they'd have any opportunity to make love on this trip. Not with ten pairs of eyes watching.

"You shouldn't stray," Charlie said, his other hand cradling her head, drawing her against him. "It's dangerous."

She bit her lip to keep from crying out. *Like a moth to a flame.* She had such an obsession with him now. She ached to feel his touch. His mouth, hand, anything, it didn't matter.

"It's more dangerous at camp," she confessed, tossing her head back so she could see him in the dying light. "I thought Eagar was going to skin me for dinner. Capp'ear's not much different. They hate me."

Charlie's fingers made slow circles against the base of her neck. She leaned into him.

"I don't understand Eagar. He's acted strangely since you came to Lowth." He chuckled. "I've acted strangely."

"Charlie . . ." She stopped herself from confessing her feelings. Bad timing. He might act tender to her, he definitely wanted her, but he'd freak if she said she loved him.

It hurt to keep the secret. He was her anchor, the eye of the hurricane raging around her.

"Shhh." His thumb rolled across her bottom lip. "We're alone, and I don't want to spend the time talking about Eagar." He lowered his head and kissed her.

A low, desperate sound escaped Jane. It felt so right to be in Charlie's arms. They might come from different worlds, but nothing would separate them. She'd find a way to make it work.

"Do we have to go to the swamp?" she asked later, snuggled in his arms. He leaned against a tree, and they waited for the appearance of the first moon before going back to the others. The camp wasn't far, but they'd agreed on the moon's rising as their measure for returning.

"We don't have to," he stressed. "Though I suppose, formally, we should be there for Capp'ear's punishment. Eagar likes things tied up neatly."

"Can't we skip going to the swamp? And Malik?" Jane watched him as she drove her point home. "Can't we run to the portal, Charlie, and slip away to Earth? I've probably lost my job by now, but we can start over, find a new living for you."

He shook his head. "We can't do that. We have to see this through, good or bad. And it will be good, Jane."

"Can you promise?" His words had dashed away any hopes of escape, but she didn't expect less of him. He'd always do the honest thing. It was another thing she loved about him.

"All I know is that there is something better planned for you than death at a wizard's hands," he said firmly, an intensity to his voice that almost convinced her. "Why else would you have these strange powers?"

Why indeed? But Jane had spent too many sleepless nights thinking about them to believe they might be for the best.

"Maybe King Garmade does want me to overpower

Blacwin and end the Dymynsh," she confessed. "But if I don't, I'm condemned to die anyway. Tossing me at the wizard loses nothing. Except my life," she ended softly.

"Oh, Jane." Charlie drew her closer, kissing the top of the head. "There's more to it than that."

She laughed harshly and stepped away, overwhelmed and depressed by her out-of-control circumstances. "Yeah? I'll show you what good it is, what I was doing when you came. It's so damn hot that I was using my 'powers' to cool down."

She raised her arms with a flourish. "Lowth, do you hear me? Step up the wind a notch. No, make that six notches. I want to see Charlie's hair blow."

A gust of air tore around the trees, whipping small branches and rustling leaves. It hit them full force. Jane, who'd had time to brace herself, tilted slightly at the impact. It pushed Charlie back a step, against the tree he'd been leaning on earlier. To her satisfaction, his long blond hair streamed out behind him.

"What are you doing?" he shouted, reaching for her. "Are you insane?"

"This whole freakin' world is insane," she yelled over the roar of the wind. She looked up at the night sky and said one word. "Enough." The gale died to the gentle, cooling breeze she'd ordered earlier.

"If I wished for the sun to come out right now, would it?"

He grabbed her arm. "Don't."

The fear in his voice sobered her. "You don't seriously believe I could do it?"

"Do you want to try?" he countered.

No, she didn't. That would be too weird.

Jane shook her head. "Some things are better not known."

"I agree. Please don't do that trick again. If you want to make a small breeze to stay cooler during the day, fine. Bringing a high wind is not a good idea. You'll draw attention to yourself with such antics."

"It's a little late for that," she muttered, her mind on her past "antics," namely the party she'd hosted yesterday morning. She had no doubt that the past night's boisterous celebrating was due in part to her toys and the women of Malin's enjoyment of them.

"Jane," Charlie said in that tone of voice she dreaded. She felt as if she were seven and caught with her hand in the cookie jar.

"Ummm, yeah?" She wanted to scrunch to the size of a bug and hide under a leaf.

"What have you been doing? Have you already been drawing attention to yourself?" The moon had edged over the hilltop, and she read the annoyance on his face.

"Confession time?" she asked in a small voice.

"Definitely confession time."

"Hugh didn't say anything about last night?" She knew the brothers were close but hoped it didn't include boasting about their sex lives. Eww. How humiliating if it did.

"Should he have?" Charlie narrowed his eyes. "I assume you don't mean our last night, but last night in general?"

Jane nodded.

"Something to do with the celebrations?" he guessed.

"I kind of enhanced them," she admitted, ducking her head.

"And how," he asked evenly, "did you do that?"

She took a deep breath. "Do you know what I did on Earth? To make a living?"

He furrowed his brow. "You were some kind of scribe?"

A scribe. An unusual way to explain being a secretary-clerk-gopher to an idiot insurance agent.

"Yes, you could say so. That's what I did during the day. It didn't pay well, and to make extra, I hosted Realm of Pleasures parties."

"I'm afraid to ask," he said under his breath. "What is Realm of Pleasures, and why do I not want to know?"

Selling the products involved some explicit explanations. Holding the toys occasionally made her blush and stumble over the words, but she'd always plunged ahead. Jane had given over a dozen parties, sometimes in mixed company, but she'd never had a more difficult time than now. When she'd finished telling Charlie what she did during her free evenings, and how her merchandise just happened to be in Lowth, she could barely talk. Her throat had closed from a major case of humiliation.

Halfway through her story, Charlie found a log and sank onto it. During the last few minutes he watched her, mouth open. Disbelief and outrage joined the shock on his face.

"Is this a common habit on Earth, to boast of sexual inadequacies and buy aids for them?" he asked when she'd finished.

Jane wished to take back the last three months of her life. Had the little bit of money been worth his disgust?

"We're a liberal society, Charlie. I admit I was reluctant at first, but everyone has a good time—"

"I bet they do." He rose to his feet. "Gossiping about such matters. You're no better than the village women when they get together . . ." He paused at her sharp intake of breath.

"Jane," he said in a dangerous tone. "Please don't tell me you had one of your parties here."

She held one hand in front of her face and peeked at him through her fingers. "Sort of."

"Sort of?" He was calm, too calm. She liked him better when he acted all prudish.

"Yesterday," she admitted, taking a backward step. "While you were down at the tavern, before Blacwin's message was found. I kind of had a Midsummer's Eve clearance sale."

"A sale," he repeated. "You had a sale." He shook his head, as if trying to understand a foreign language. "I suppose all of the village women were there?"

"I don't know," she confessed, taking another step back. He was ready to erupt, and she wanted a running start. She'd rather face Eagar than have Charlie upset with her. "We probably had thirty or forty. How big is the village?"

"Thirty?" he sputtered. He groaned and held his head. "I'm ruined. Utterly. Completely. Forever."

"Sorry," she said in a small voice.

He looked up. "You're sorry? No, I think you have that wrong. I'm the one who's sorry. I didn't want to defend you, but I did, and probably saved your life in the process. What do I get in return?"

He was building to a climax of epic proportions. In a sick way, Jane admired his technique. If she had been the one ranting, it would have been her best performance. For Charlie, who didn't let go often enough, this was a major breakthrough.

"I get," he continued, ticking off the items on his fingers, "a woman who opens stone walls with her bare hands, is found in the king's bed the first night she's here—"

"I never touched him!" she blurted.

His gaze drilled into her. Jane shut up.

"A woman with Elven tattooed on her arm. My brother's house almost burns down within two weeks of her arriving. She starts rainstorms, controls the wind and seduces gullible lawyers. Did I mention that she gave away sex toys to most of our female population?"

"I didn't give them away," Jane protested. "Mara traded for them."

"Wonderful. You've corrupted her as well. It makes it easier to bear, knowing my brother is away from her side, escorting you and the man who tried to kill you to your deaths. At least she'll have new curtains and fresh meat in exchange."

Jane's anger burst forth, rivaling his. She'd never seen him in this sarcastic mood, and she didn't like it.

"Listen, buddy," she said, closing the distance between them and poking him in the chest. "This is who I am. Half the stuff you've listed I had no control over. I was kidnapped into this sorry little kingdom, and it's been doing everything it can to crawl into my flesh and possess me. Not a nice feeling, let me tell you. I've had better times."

"So have I. Most of them involved not risking my life."

She let out a sound of exasperation. "When? Now? There's no one around for miles."

"Except a swamp full of sandobbles. And goblins on the loose between here and the nearest wizard. But no, I was referring to three weeks ago."

Three weeks? She could barely remember three days ago.

"When I and five others went through the portal into Earth," he said harshly.

"Old news," she spat. "Tried and sentenced for that crime. Get on a new kick."

"You and your 'toys' risked our lives, Jane." Fury enveloped him. "We were in a strange land and had tenuous contact with the portal. After the explosion, we needed to get you through as fast as possible. You burdened us with six boxes of rubbish. We could have easily been trapped."

"Okay, you have a point, but how was I to know I'd be forced to come to this freakin' world?"

"You're the freak," he said, echoing her gesture by prodding her on the shoulder. She had to step back from the pressure he applied. "You're so different from everything I hold dear that it scares me."

"Everything you hold dear is going to go *poof!* if I don't do my freakish voodoo and get rid of the Dymynsh." Tears stung her eyes. "How do you know I wasn't sent here for a purpose?" she continued. "Maybe the Dymynsh isn't caused by a wizard, but because you guys aren't having enough sex or having it the right way. Maybe my 'toys' are the spark needed to jolt you people into a sexual revolution. I'm your answer. Did you ever think of that? Huh?" She punched his shoulder.

He caught her wrist. "That's the stupidest thing I've ever heard."

"Use it or lose it." She felt suddenly drained. A spirited discussion with Charlie was one thing. This hurt.

"We no more need creativity than—"

"What? Than you need to fly? Why not fly with me, Superman? Birds and bees do it in the air. Why can't a Whelphite and a mortal?" It was a last attempt to find and recapture what they'd shared.

"Ridiculous," he said, spinning away from her, solidifying her opinion of his pigheadedness. "Last night and this morning were mistakes. Blame the effects of Midsummer's Eve. Blame too many hours spent in each other's company. I don't know or care. We're forced to spend the next few days together. Stay away from me, Jane. I want nothing more to do with you."

# Chapter Seventeen

Two miserable days later, Jane stood on the banks of the East Malin River, surveying the desolation of Magwrosin Swamp. Its appearance fit her mood exactly. A low-lying fog, burnt orange and slate gray in color, writhed at the feet of spiked ferns. Bronze, copper and metallic green, ten feet in length, they shouldered their way above the mist, as if anxious to pull free. Branchless, misshapen trees poked overhead, battling for sunlight. A wet *plonk-plonk* sound, mixed with a Hitchcockian bird screech, assailed her ears. It looked like the perfect place for the Four Horsemen of the Apocalypse to hang out between jobs.

"This has to be the most dismal place on Lowth. Strip mining would only improve it," Jane commented. *Perhaps a wizard isn't such a bad punishment after all.* Feeling hot and sticky despite Lowth's attempts to keep her cool, she looked at Hugh. The merciless sun burned down on them as they'd followed the river over the dry scrabble rock where little grew.

"It's been a prison for fifty years," Hugh replied. "Since King Garmade and the Dwarves defeated King Rodom of

Malik and the sandobbles. He split the river, one arm on each side of the swamp, and increased the depth and breadth until it reached the ocean, leaving no way out."

The mud had a greenish-gray cast, and the consistency of brownie batter. Jane imagined it rising up to form a creature that would swallow her whole.

"Why don't the sandobbles escape?" The river didn't look deep or dangerous.

"If they try to enter the water, it thins them out. They wash away with the current."

*I'd find a way to get out*, Jane thought.

"How will Eagar get Capp'ear to the other side?"

"I think we're about to find out." Hugh indicated the steward, who beckoned the group together. Jane, Hugh and Muttle joined the others.

Charlie stood to one side, watching her. He'd silently trailed behind her the past two days, at a distance but close enough that she could see his glowering stares.

Jane felt as if she'd betrayed her best friend in the fire-and-brimstone-plagues-of-locusts kind of way. It hurt doubly now that she knew she cared so much for him. Before, she'd baited him, egged him out of his stodginess in an amusing game with no consequences. Looking back, she saw things through his eyes and realized how her actions had damaged his trust.

She should have told him about the contents of the boxes. But how could she have explained such intimate objects when she slid dangerously closer to him every day? The appearance of Randolph's body and her sentencing had precluded a "hey, by the way" confession afterward.

Circumstances fortified her excuse of reluctance. She'd have to find another way to apologize.

"Fellow citizens," Eagar called, snapping her attention back to the present. "A judgment has been made against one of our own, Capp'ear of Malin." He turned to the weasely man who'd been heavily guarded during the three-day journey. "For the crime of attempted murder against Jane Drysdale of Earth, you have been sentenced to the Magwrosin Swamp. If you survive a full day, you will be freed. If you do not—may your death be swift and painless."

Eagar looked at Jane, his gaze piercing. The triple layer of bags beneath his black eyes contrasted with the leanness of his body. Dressed in his habitual dark wardrobe, he looked more demonic than ever. He conceded to the sun by wearing a scarf on his bald head. He only lacked a mask and a cape to enter the Zorro look-alike contest.

"Do you have anything to say to the prisoner?" he asked.

She panicked. What was death row etiquette? "Good luck"? "See you on the other side"? She looked at Charlie, who stared back, his expression blank.

"No," she told Eagar, directing her words to Charlie. "There is nothing I can say to change things."

The steward nodded. "Very well, then." He looked at the prisoner and raised his hands in the air with a flourish. "Your sentence commences now."

Capp'ear levitated off the ground.

Several people gasped in surprise. Jane grabbed Hugh's arm, her mind whirling in fright. What other powers did Eagar have? She'd been so flippant with him at times. . . .

The prisoner leveled off at a height of about ten feet. The group watched his progress as he moved across the river and into the swamp. He hovered several moments over the swaying leaves of a fern, then the mist swallowed him.

Jane felt cold. Of all the things that had happened to her since her arrival, this had to be the worst. Because of her, a life was about to be snuffed out.

She turned her head, afraid she'd cry or be sick. Hugh put his arm around her in comfort.

"Don't think of it," he said. "The man's not been right since his wife and child died last winter. If not you, he would have tried to hurt someone else."

Jane hiccupped. Her voice wavered. "But he picked me. You all must think I'm terrible, turning your world upside down the way I have. Murder trials and rainstorms, your house almost burning to the ground. I'm sorry, Hugh."

He patted her arm. "It was upside down before you came. The Dymynsh has ruined our lives, robbing any normalcy from them. Perhaps you're here for that purpose."

Jane lifted her head. "Do you really think I'll be able to stop it?" Until now, she'd been consumed with getting through each day and, somehow, going home. Others' opinions of her effect on Lowth and its scourge hadn't much entered her thoughts.

"Some do. We've gone so long without hope." He glanced around. "Of course, some, such as Eagar, think you're worse than the Dymynsh. You'll have to do more to prove yourself to them."

She stepped back. "I'm not your savior. I don't want to die to make your world right again." As always, when she allowed herself to wonder about the possible negative outcome of this journey, she shivered.

"Charlie won't let anything happen to you."

"Even though we're off to see the wizard?" The unknown specter of Blacwin haunted her dreams.

"Many people of Sylthia trust my brother. I trust him. Maybe you should as well."

Would Charlie's feelings be strong enough to bind them together? Except for the one night they'd shared, which Jane highly suspected he felt ashamed of, he acted more as if she were a nuisance than anything he cared about.

Hugh turned her away from the swamp. "Let's help make camp. It will ease your mind, having something to do."

"Is it safe here?" She looked at the sight, high on the banks, a copse of wood to one side.

"Safe enough," he replied.

She touched the knife strapped to her leg to reassure herself. She'd protested when he'd given it to her at the start of the journey, insisting she wear it and not tell Eagar. The blade might not cut through a sandobble, but other creatures roamed Lowth.

Later, around the campfire, Jane spoke to Muttle. By accident, she'd found out that the Belwaith regularly communicated with his mate, Calme, and could give accounts of what went on in Sylthia. Several times a day he zoned out, his eyes whirling a deep purple.

Jane ached to ask if there'd been any repercussions from Midsummer's Eve, but figured it best to keep that topic off-limits. Instead, she inquired, "How is King Garmade?"

"He sleeps. He sad." The Belwaith answered so quickly that Jane had the feeling he'd tuned into the monarch directly.

The news disheartened her. The king had made a rare public appearance the morning they exited Sylthia. Dressed in a faded blue dress, he leaned heavily on Wesant's arm. He spoke only to Eagar, giving his blessing and then retiring to his chambers. He said nothing to Jane. She expected at least a glance from him, some indication that they'd spent time together, but perhaps he didn't remember. Dementia acted in strange ways.

"Give him my best," she said, her voice thick. She hoped she'd have the chance to say good-bye to him after she defeated Blacwin. With the mission half completed, the days grew closer to her trip home. She hoped.

*What do I do about Charlie?* Instinctively, she sought him out from the others near the campfire. If she could get him to talk, if they made up, what then? Would he accompany her to Earth? If he refused? Could she stay here, away from everyone she loved, in a land of elves and sprites and wizards?

He looked up from speaking with the dwarf, Tellise. Their gazes locked over the length of the clearing. Jane half rose, intending to cross to him and apologize. A hand on her knee stopped her.

"Stay," Muttle said.

"But . . ." She wanted Charlie, and she wanted him now. Muttle had a curious sense of timing.

"Many eyes watch."

Jane felt them staring, condemning her, convicting her as a murderess despite Hugh's assurance that some supported her. Midsummer's Eve had been an aberration, a temporary insanity affecting all. They could understand the moons' pull and the seasonal lustfulness of the night. They might not accept an upright citizen of Sylthia such as Charlie becoming permanently involved with a killer.

Jane backed away, blending into the shadows. She'd already damaged his reputation with her behavior and the party. Their talk would have to wait until another time.

*Where is she going?* Charlie watched, perplexed, as Jane slipped into the darkness. She looked as though she wanted to approach him. He didn't know what he'd do if she did.

He'd always prided himself on his diplomacy and tact, two traits that drew people to him and made his life as a Whelphite easier. Patience, kindness, understanding— these attributes could always be relied upon. Until three weeks ago. Until Jane burst into his life with all the finesse of a wild boar. Upsetting his life, tempting him with her flagrant clothes, seducing him . . .

Seducing him! Thankful that the campfire hid his blush, Charlie sank to the ground. He'd been drunk on Midsummer's Eve, but not enough to lose reason. Lust controlled him, born of frustration and two perfect, cream-colored breasts. How could he not give in? Why shouldn't he again?

He curled his hands into fists, resisting the urge to follow her. He was due to take his turn on night watch. Since they were so close to the swamp, Eagar had increased the patrol. Tomorrow would be soon enough to speak with Jane.

Unfortunately, he fell asleep after his stint, waking mid-morning. Duties around the camp kept him busy until after the noon meal. All the time, his gaze sought Jane, but she remained elusive. She acted subdued, no doubt affected by her part in the mess with Capp'ear.

No unusual sounds issued from the swamp. The prisoner had probably met his fate silently, but they all waited until the appointed hour nonetheless. Others had managed to escape during the fifty years the Magwrosin had existed as a prison. Either way, an hour before sundown, they'd strike camp.

Jane, all rose and tawny, emerged from her tent. Charlie stopped what he was doing and watched her, his heart and lungs functioning improperly. *It has to be the heat.*

She looked to the sky and, for a moment, he thought she would call the wind. Instead, she walked toward him.

"Charlie," she said, chin tilted. Clad in a pair of trousers that looked suspiciously like Hugh's and a loose blouse, her breasts taunted him from beneath the white fabric, the curve of one visible through the open neck. Not that he looked. He should say something about her attire, and if she dressed provocatively she should expect comments—

"Jane," he said, trying to sound harsh. Too bad she'd caught him empty-handed. He had nothing to inspect, to pull apart or put back together, to make it look as if she came second in his attentions. He crossed his arms in front of him.

"Charlie, let's not argue. We've been friends since I came to Lowth. I should have told you about the party. Forgive me?" She laid a hand on his arm.

Couldn't the woman stand still? The swaying of her hips prevented him from thinking. They hypnotized him. An itch started in the center of his palm. He wanted to clasp her on each side to stop the movement, then pull her to him and rock her in a different, more primitive way.

"I don't like it when you lie," he said, hanging on to his anger. It still hurt that she'd deceived him. The toys, ripping walls apart, regrowing the garden—what shocking thing would she hit him with next? "I'm not some village idiot with whom you can amuse yourself."

She jerked back as if struck. Her nostrils flared. "Is that what you think I'm doing? You rate yourself wrongly, Charlie Whelphite. You're the least amusing person I know. Try boring. And stuffy. And pompous. Just a minute, let me look in my thesaurus for some juicier adjectives. Oh, that's right, you don't have one on this backward planet of yours."

Damn, he hadn't meant to sound so harsh, just to get his point across that they had to have total honesty between them. How had it spiraled downward from there?

"You're making a spectacle of yourself." He grabbed her arm and tried pulling her from the camp.

"God forbid that you should have that happen. Charlie-don't-make-waves. Charlie-leave-me-alone. I'll leave you alone, all right. I'm sorry I ever took up with you. Wings! Ha!" She pulled free and stormed away.

"Where are you going?" he asked, conscious of the curious stares they'd invited.

Jane popped into her tent and emerged a moment later with a small bundle.

"To have a bath," she said over her shoulder, tramping upstream from the campsite.

A bath? Was she crazy? There were eight men in the area, and who knew what else loose in the swamp.

"It's been three days," she said, pushing aside branches. "A cloth dipped in the river isn't going to cut it anymore. I want a full immersion, soap-lathered bath. Muttle says there's a clear pool nearby. I'm going to use it."

Charlie ducked, avoiding a faceful of pine needles. "You're making a mistake. It's not safe around here."

"Then I guess you'll have to stand guard. It's not as if you haven't seen me naked before."

His mind filled with memories of three nights earlier. She'd been magnificent. Perhaps, if he apologized and she stayed still long enough to see reason, and all the stars aligned perfectly, they might repeat the performance.

The land sloped to a clear turquoise pool with overhanging branches of willow and silver maple. Sunlight mottled the leaves of a small copse and dusted the grasses underneath.

Jane slipped off her shoes and tossed them on the bank. She waded into the water, making girlish, squealing noises. In a moment, she stepped out of her trousers, revealing undergarments of a new breed.

Charlie's throat clogged. He sputtered for words. "What? Jane! You're trying to kill me." His hand slid to his chest.

"Do you like it?" she called, the water obviously diluting her bad humor. "It's called a thong."

Sucking in air like a blowfish, he thought his heart had stopped. First, he fainted, and now this. Did the woman have to affect him so much?

She bent down and unstrapped the knife sheath from her calf and threw it in the general direction of her clothes. The movement gave him an awe-inspiring view of her rear.

It was his undoing. His emotions overwrought, he strode down the slope and into the river, mindless of the water seeping into his boots. Mindless altogether.

"Wench." He pulled her to him, her nakedness smooth on his skin. "You tempt a man past reason."

She leaned full-length against him. "Why, Charlie—"

"Why? Because of clothes like these—always teasing me, seducing me in my office, bewitching me on Midsummer's Eve. You invade my thoughts. Wanton, troublesome mortal."

"Stuffy old Whelphite."

"Elf," he corrected, nibbling on her ear.

"Riiight. An elf with wings. Let's fly together."

"Jane, don't start that again." He had no room for anger.

"But it would be so much fun, soaring through the air . . ." She batted her lashes, her eyes full of mischief.

"Let's try it on the ground first," he promised.

With a groan, he kissed her, a flame kindled anew. He stripped the rest of her clothes from her, not surprised that she wore nothing under her blouse. His mouth seared kisses on her every surface, and he picked her up, grunting with satisfaction when she wrapped her legs around his waist.

He marched up the bank, his mind focused on the shade of the linden trees, sheltered from curious eyes. Releasing her long enough to smooth out her towel for them to lie on, he lowered her to the ground.

She reached for him, her eyes clouded with passion. "Love me," she whispered and pulled him down.

The fire ignited, his lust wakened from a forced solitude. Frustration tore at him. He wanted her now, wanted to feel her spasm around him. Once more, before she left him forever.

"Take it easy, Fly Boy. We have all afternoon." Jane chuckled, caressing his face with her fingertips, along his jaw and the rims of his ears.

He wanted and feared her touch on his wings. Tugging off his clothes, he forced himself to slow down, to linger over and reexplore her body.

Leisurely, he watched her eyes change, listened to her soft moans. He loved to see her face, the sun dappling it, as she yielded to him. Feelings knotted in him—tenderness, solace, joy, rapture, a jumble of emotions. Loving her this way was familiar and necessary.

She twisted and bent her head, nipping the flesh of his inner thigh, snatching little bites of kisses down his length. He gasped and released her, breathless. She rolled away and he pursued her, finally pinning her against a tree. Jane laughed softly, her hand outstretched to his wings. The air snapped and crackled like an approaching thunderstorm when she touched them.

Their lovemaking intensified into a tangle of legs with lips pressed together and hot, slick bodies. He moaned when she trapped his hardness in her hands, stroking, heightening his sensations.

Lying on his back, he plucked her into the air, the muscles in his arms bunching as they lifted her above him. His need throbbing, he brought her down, swift and hard, unerringly accurate, mounting her on him.

Jane threw back her head, a long line of neck exposed, eyes glazed. Sweat glistened on her body.

He rolled his fingers over her nipples. He ached to close his mouth over them, but she rode him, her body bent backward.

Gasping, he felt her pulsating around him. She cried out as the spasms shook within and without. Charlie held on, wanting to prolong her pleasure, delaying his own release. He slipped his hand between her leg and touched her mound, rubbing its swelling as she came again, shouting his name.

Suspended in time, holding on to the edge, he let her ride, sustaining her climax for as long as he could. Then the sunlight and their glade blurred into a whirling vortex. The intensity increased. He couldn't endure another moment without letting go. With a cry of joy, he erupted in her, his seed spurting to fill every sweet, dark inch.

Charlie gasped as the aftershocks gripped him. Realization hit. *What have I done?*

Bliss. Sweet, sweet heaven. Jane sighed with contentment as she snuggled against him. The man was a magician. She rolled to her side. With nice pecs. She traced hard male angles and golden sprinkles of hair on his chest. Looking up at him, she saw concern on his face.

"What's wrong?" She tried to smooth out his wrinkles with one fingertip.

"A moment ago—" He hesitated. "When I came in you—"

"And very nicely, too, I might add." She grinned.

He stilled her hand. "I'm serious."

"What?" What had she done wrong? They'd been perfect together.

His eyes darkened. "Jane, if you should conceive a child."

"No." She laid a finger against his mouth to stop the dreaded words. *We should have thought of that a few nights ago.* She knew where she was in her cycle, and it wasn't a pretty place. Birth control had stopped being a part of her life after her last relationship ended at Christmastime. How ironic that the sex toy lady had been caught without a condom.

"No," she said again, aching at lying to him so soon after he'd ranted about not telling the truth. "The timing's not right." But she'd worry about the possibility after her meeting with Blacwin. If she survived. One Lowth-shattering problem at a time.

"You're sure?" Emotion clouded his voice.

Expectation? Regret? She wouldn't be sure for a couple of weeks. It wasn't as if she could run down to the corner drugstore and buy an EPT test.

She settled against his bare chest, determined to forget about his inquiry.

"But, Jane—"

She laid her hand on his lips. "Later. Don't ruin the afternoon." She might be home by then. Foisting an unwanted child on him would be an unfair way to win his love.

Insects buzzed overhead in a soothing drone. Late afternoon sun poked through a canopy of leaves and warmed their bodies. Soon she drifted to sleep.

Less than an hour passed before she woke. Three days on the trail and she'd become a human sundial, telling time from its position.

Charlie slept sprawled on his stomach, naked as the day he was born. A smile quirked the corners of her mouth at the memory of their lovemaking. Delicious.

Not wanting to wake him, Jane slipped from the glade. The cool pond beckoned a few steps away. Grabbing a bar of soap, she padded to the edge and walked in.

The water was plentiful if not deep. She ducked repeatedly beneath the surface, lathering and rinsing with abandon until she'd washed away all the sweat, dirt and grime of the last three days. Humming softly, she emerged from her bath.

She gathered her thong and blouse from the bush where Charlie had dropped them. The pants she'd borrowed from Hugh and her shoes lay at the water's edge. Crushing them into a bundle, thoughts filling her mind of a reverse striptease for Charlie's pleasure, she searched for her knife.

The sheath lay upside down in the mud. Jane flipped it over, her heart going cold at its lack of weight.

*Trouble*, her mind screamed.

A twig snapped. Someone grabbed her from behind, an arm crossed over her bare breasts, a hand clamped on her mouth.

Jane felt sun-warmed steel against her neck.

"Looking for this?" Capp'ear whispered.

# Chapter Eighteen

*I'm going to die.* Jane had no doubt in her mind.

"Witch," Capp'ear hissed, his breath foul. He smelled like a mixture of locker room and garbage dump.

He jerked her backward against him. She felt a thick layer of slime ooze between them as they made contact.

*Charlie, help me.*

"I can't let you talk," he sneered, as if reading her thoughts, "because you can bring the rain to stop me. Or something else. Rip that shirt you're carrying."

Jane thought about whipping it over her head to catch him from behind. A quick twist, and she could strangle him. But additional pressure of the knife on her throat stopped her.

*Don't do anything stupid. You'll have no chance.* She fumbled with the hem, but couldn't tear it.

Capp'ear let out a sound of exasperation. Jane heard the fabric rend as he severed the hem with the knife.

"Finish it," he said savagely.

She tugged the two halves apart. He grabbed one and

tied it around her mouth. The other half manacled her hands.

Hope of running away died when he hit her in the back. She dropped to her knees in the mud, tears of pain coming to her eyes.

"I survived, despite your evil plan," he gloated above her. "Want to know how?" When she didn't respond, he yanked on a lock of her hair. "Do you?"

Stalling for time, Jane nodded, the pain in her scalp replacing that in her back. The longer she could keep him ranting, the sooner Charlie would rescue her.

*Muttle*, she added, *send out reinforcements.*

She tipped her head back and caught the first glimpse of her assailant. Above and behind her, she saw only his face. It was enough to chill her bones.

His eyes scared her the most. Anguished, as if he'd seen things no one should. Haunted. Filled with pain. And hatred of her. They only needed to glow red to complete the picture.

His demonic smile twisted his face into ghoulish lines. *Nightmare on Elf Street.*

"Pretty witch," he said, freezing her heart.

*Oh, no, let's not go there. Keep your thoughts on revenge, buddy, not my naked body.*

"Everyone takes Capp'ear for granted," he continued. "The only Elf around without talent. But they're wrong, because he has one, kept it secret for years. Want to know, pretty witch?"

Jane nodded, meeting his gaze.

*Hurry, Charlie. The wacko's referring to himself in the third person. I think he wants to rape me.* She knew her Whelphite lay out of sight, fifty yards up the bank. Asleep.

Capp'ear dropped in front of her, the knife held tightly in one hand, her hair in the other. She willed herself still.

"He mimics the talents of others," he said, shifting

closer. "Watched them and later went home and imitated what they'd done. Never worked well. Never lasted long and couldn't duplicate it more than once, but it saved his life."

This "he" business creeped her out. She flinched when his hand trailed across her cheek, leaving behind the feel of wet, viscous swamp mire. Jane's mind raced with all the self-defense moves she could adapt from what she knew. Her legs behind her, hands tied, the options looked limited.

"Thought he was dead," Capp'ear continued. "Then Eagar lifted him into the Magwrosin." He leaned toward Jane. She swallowed back nausea and fear.

"Mimicked his levitation. Sandobbles couldn't reach him. Effort almost killed him. Could have escaped, but kept his end of the bargain. Twenty-four hours, then fell and ran. Fell and ran 'til he saw a witch swimming and found a knife." He raised it in the air. Jane saw the glint of sun on the blade.

"I'll take my reward now," Capp'ear said calmly and brought his hand down.

*Charlie!*

The word screamed in his mind, jerking him from sleep. He was on his feet in an instant as his gaze swept the copse for Jane. Not seeing her, he pulled on his pants and reached for his knife when he heard another voice in his head.

*We come.*

*Muttle? What's wrong? Where's Jane?*

It seemed as if an eternity passed before the Belwaith answered. Charlie stood coiled for action, ready to spring.

*Capp'ear escaped.*

*Capp'ear! By the first dawn!*

"Where?" He spoke out loud.

*At the pond's edge. We come.*

She must have gone down for her bath and surprised him. Or got the surprising. Would she never learn of danger?

Charlie unsheathed his knife and raced toward the water.

Instinct took over. Jane dropped to her side and swiveled on her hip, bringing around both feet to kick Capp'ear in the gut. He fell with a *whumph* and she rolled away. It wasn't until she stumbled to her feet that she felt the pain in her shoulder.

Looking down, she saw a gash above her left breast, bisecting the rose tattoo. Blood flowed from it, smeared with mud. It felt like the mother of all paper cuts.

*This can't be good*, she thought grimly. *Think of it later—but damn, it hurts.* She spun in the direction of the glade, desperate to escape. Capp'ear grabbed her ankles and pulled them from under her.

She hit the ground hard, no soft mud to cushion the blow. The jar to her injury made her cry out, despite the gag. He gripped her arms and flipped her over, eliciting another muffled gasp when her weight landed on her bound hands.

His weight too, as he straddled her almost immediately. "Pretty witch," he gurgled, leaning closer.

*Oh, God, not like this. Please, not like this.*

His long, stringy hair brushed against her nakedness, and it was all she could do to keep the bile from rising. The thought of asphyxiating in her own vomit kept it at bay.

He brought out the knife. Jane's heart stopped cold in her chest. She closed her eyes, not wanting to see the fatal blow.

They snapped open as a biting pain tore into her shoulder. Capp'ear flicked at the edges of her wound with the knife, enlarging it slowly, methodically, humming to himself.

*I can't take this. I'm going to faint.*

"Let her go."

*Charlie!* She twisted in the direction of his voice, but she lay at the wrong angle to see him.

Capp'ear hesitated a moment then continued carving.

"I said, let her go." Charlie's voice, full of menace, sounded closer, twenty or thirty feet away.

Her assailant didn't look up. Jane squirmed under him, trying to get a foothold to throw him off. The burn of the wound increased with every movement. He brought his hand down hard, using his fingers to claw into her flesh. Jane screamed into the cloth stuffed in her mouth.

"Get away from her!" Charlie roared.

She heard a sickening thunk and Capp'ear toppled off her. She scrambled to sit up, to dart away, and stopped in a crouched position. He lay face up, half in and half out of the water, a knife hilt protruding from his shoulder.

Then Charlie was there, retrieving her knife from Capp'ear's outstretched hand, pulling his own free. He wiped the blood on the other man's tunic and strode to Jane. He knelt at her side, cutting her bonds and gag free.

"Are you all right?"

Her heart went zing. He'd never looked so un-lawyerish, so entirely delectable as he did at that moment. Solid and strong, half-naked and better than any movie hero she'd ever seen. The setting sun at his back outlined the extension of his wings and hid his expression from her. She didn't care. She didn't need to see his face to know how much she loved him.

"What took you so long, Superman? Perry keep you at the *Daily Planet?*" she asked, her heart twisting around in a wild, love-induced, grateful Möbius strip.

He touched her face gently with long, tanned fingers. "Sometimes I don't know half of what you say, but I'm damn glad I get to hear it."

"I bet you say that to all the mortals," she joked, then winced as pain shot through her again.

"You've been hurt," he said, as if noticing for the first time all the blood and gore and exposed body goo.

"Yeah, but it only hurts when I laugh."

"Then don't laugh," he murmured, finishing the old routine as if he'd been born into vaudeville. His hands gently probed the edges of the gash.

A shout hailed them.

"Muttle," Charlie said. "And Hugh, Eagar and the rest."

"About time the cavalry showed up." She tried to stand. *Naked*, her mind shouted. Then *whoops!* when the ground tilted. She saw Eagar's shocked face in the periphery of her vision, and the ground lurched again and rushed at her.

Charlie caught Jane and eased her down. Hugh rushed over.

"How bad is it?" he asked, concern in his eyes.

"It's not deep." Charlie tried to sound positive. "But it's ugly. Give me your shirt. The last thing she'd want is for everyone to see her without clothes."

Hugh shrugged it off and handed it to his brother. Charlie laid it over Jane, leaving the wound exposed.

"I'll need water, cloths, some soap and salve." He rattled off the list, fighting panic. They were miles from the nearest healer in Gaelen, and field medicine wouldn't help.

The brothers looked at each other over her prone form. Both had seen how easily a minor wound could cost a man his life.

Hugh broke the gaze and directed his attention to Jane. "He sure carved her up, didn't he?" he asked.

Charlie nodded grimly. "I don't think I killed him."

"You didn't," the other man said in such a way that Charlie's head jerked up.

"What do you mean?"

Hugh gestured to the pond. "He's gone."

"Gone?" Charlie stood, looking to the spot where he'd

last seen Capp'ear. It was empty, the churned mud the only evidence he'd been there.

"Where?"

"Into the woods," Eagar said behind him. "He was fleeing when we crested the hill. The archers drew on him, but he was out of range. I've sent a couple of men after him, but there's not much daylight remaining." He looked down at Jane, his lips pursed in disapproval. "How is she?"

"She needs a healer," Charlie answered, angered by the steward's lack of compassion.

"Right." Eagar nodded. "Let's move, then." He began shouting orders.

They carried her farther up the bank onto dry grass. Dirt and grit embedded in her wound made it difficult to clean. Charlie rejected the idea of stitching the ragged edges together. Instead, he and Hugh packed the opening with clean cloths soaked in salve and bound her arm to her side. They'd have to wait several hours to be sure infection didn't set in.

Jane woke with a whimper as they finished the dressing. She looked strong but pale, distress scoring her eyes. Charlie's heart tugged to see her hurting so much. He smoothed her hair from her forehead.

"Did you get the number of the truck that hit me?" she asked, her voice weaker than he liked, the corners of her mouth upturned in an attempted smile.

"You're going to be all right," he said, fervently hoping so. He decided to wait to tell her about Capp'ear's escape.

"He levitated while he was in the swamp," she said. "Something about a latent talent." She stopped to gather a breath. "Does that make sense? He rambled a lot."

Charlie glanced at Hugh. Neither knew this about Capp'ear. They didn't socialize with his friends, men who cared more for the contents of a bottle than their homes.

"Shhh," Charlie said. "I'm going to give you an injection, similar to the one you received when we first met. It will help with the pain." *And knock you out for several hours.*

Eyes closed, she nodded weakly. He slid the stitchtree thorn into her good arm.

Darkness had fallen by the time they'd settled her into the makeshift litter Tellise made. Tied between two of the pack animals, she swung above ground level, like a tightly wrapped cocoon. The archers sent after Capp'ear returned empty-handed. Eagar declared the hunt over. Grimly, the party started the long trek to the Dwarf capital of Gaelen.

They traveled through the night, their path lit by the waning full moons. Thrice, they had to ford branches of the East Malin River, untying the litter and holding it overhead.

By morning, Charlie knew Jane was in trouble. Her skin felt hot, and several times he'd had to stop the procession to change blood-soaked bandages. The last time, he'd seen a yellowish discharge from the wound.

She thrashed around, her words incoherent. He injected her again, using his last thorn. The effects lasted about six hours. By afternoon she'd be crying in pain. They'd be nowhere near Gaelen.

*Damn!* he thought as he walked at her side. Damnation to Capp'ear for hurting her, to Eagar for punishing her, and to Jane for making him love her.

The last took him by surprise. He stumbled over a tree root, catching the litter for support. Jane cried out at the movement. He soothed her back to fitful rest, watching how shallow her breaths had become. If he lost her . . .

And he would. Inevitably, she'd disappear, either at Blacwin's hand or by returning to Earth. Impossible, unmanageable, exciting, provocative woman! She'd entered his world with fire and spunk, turning everything upside down, the same direction she'd spun his heart. It hurt to love her. It hurt not to.

He'd bet she'd depart with the same flair, but she would depart. He couldn't ask her to stay in Lowth, and even his love couldn't break through her yearning for her home. Following her, living on Earth, as she'd once asked him, wasn't a viable answer, either. How could he live in a world of mortals with wings sprouting from his back?

By the time they reached the gates of the Dwarvish capital, Charlie had decided to say nothing to her about his feelings. He'd love her while he had her, but he'd convince her it was nothing but a physical attraction. To do anything else would lead to false hopes and ultimate heartache.


It took over a week for Jane to recover. She lost the first three days, obscured by a dark cloud of heat and a burning pain that engulfed her entire body. Vaguely, she remembered sun streaming through treetops, an unquenchable thirst and Charlie's presence, always at her side, soothing away the hurt.

Since she'd awakened on the fourth day, feeling as weak as a newborn kitten, Charlie's absence had been almost palpable. Muttle never left her, the healers kept her comfortable, Hugh visited, but the one she ached to see the most avoided her.

She heard him when he thought she slept. The moment she stirred, he'd exit. Sometimes he wouldn't enter her room, but stand in the hallway and speak to the healers, then leave without seeing her. Those times hurt the most.

How often had she angered him since coming to Lowth? More than she could count. Bathing unescorted, then being attacked must have been the veritable last straw. Maybe distancing himself helped him get his life in order. He still had to go with her to Malik, but she could see how he'd want to keep as far from her as possible.

*It's been fun, Charlie, but two can play this game,* she thought on the tenth day of her forced convalescence. *I'm *not going to let you hurt me.* Even as she repeated the words out loud to reinforce them, she knew they rang false.

Charlie, standing in the doorway, heard her and backed away. His heart pinched as if in a vise. He'd never meant to hurt her, never even wanted to be involved, but fate had another opinion. Or, following her convoluted reasoning, Lowth itself had a hand in their lives. How else could he explain her powers, or calling her "Anjinaine" when they'd made love?

He coughed, paused, and came through the door, averting his gaze so she could compose herself. She'd almost done it when he stopped at her bedside. Streaks from tears marked her cheeks.

"How are you?" he asked, her misery so obvious he wanted to fold her into his arms and kiss away the pain. *I love you.*

"Better." She tried and failed to look past his chest.

"Good." Then, because she needed to know and he'd been delegated to tell her, he said, "We depart again in two days."

She gasped sharply. "To Malik?"

"Eventually, yes. We have to stop on the way and pick up a guide, Bryant of Malik. He knows the area better than I." The hunter's cabin, on the edge of Isleighah, was as far north as Charlie had ever ventured. The trails were but lines on a map after that point.

"How is your shoulder?" he asked. *How is your heart? Why can't you stay here with me when this is over?*

"They tell me it will be as good as new. I have some exercises I need to do to make it stronger."

Gingerly, she held up her left arm, rotating it to show her progress. The loose sleeve fell away, exposing her tattoo. Charlie read the inscription again and, with a start, he realized where he'd seen it before. Bryant! On one of his trips to visit the hunter, he'd seen the same words stitched in wool and mounted on the cabin wall.

His mind racing, Charlie made an excuse to exit. He couldn't risk her sharp mind figuring out his distress. Bryant! How was the man connected to Jane? With a sinking clarity, he knew. And in four days, Jane would, too.

# Chapter Nineteen

The party came to the clearing in the early morning. A tawny fog lay low over brittle, dry grasses. The trees thinned, the leaves stripped off. In the parts of Lowth she'd traveled, Jane thought this particular corner best defined the Dymynsh's twenty-year grip. She'd never seen such a sad, austere land.

The cabin rose from the mist before she realized it was there. Neat, trim, and made of felled logs, it looked solid.

Hugh had barely dismounted before the door swung open and a man stepped out as if expecting them. Jane watched as greetings were made and negotiations began.

The stranger, Bryant of Malik, was an Elf. He stood taller than Hugh. His weatherworn skin was lighter, a golden, creamy brown, a Nordic tan or a mocha light with a splash of butterscotch. His hair reminded Jane of caramel apples.

She sat back on Pasha, her little pony, enjoying the respite and the cooler morning. Eagar drove everyone hard in his quest to lay her at Blacwin's feet. He showed no compassion for her injury or recovery. The week delay in Gaelen must have stuck in his craw something fierce.

The bargaining complete, some of the party began to dismount. Jane moved Pasha closer to the cabin to join the others. They'd take a short break while Bryant got ready.

Except he didn't move from the doorway. He stared at Jane, mouth open, pain in his eyes. He clutched at his chest.

*He's having a heart attack,* Jane thought, alarmed. She slid from her pony's back, careful not to jar her sore arm.

"Bryant?" she said, moving toward him. She tried to catch Charlie's attention.

The guide continued to stare at her. "You came back," he said, grabbing the doorframe for support.

"I never went anywhere to come back from," she said softly, looking up at him, concerned by his sudden pallor. "Are you all right? Maybe you should sit down."

"No, I'm fine." He passed a shaking hand over his eyes. He made a pitiful attempt to chuckle and gazed down at her. "Just long-dead memories returning to haunt me. An old man's wistful thinking."

Old? He couldn't have been more than fifty. Gray touched his temples and creases lined the corners of his green eyes.

"Who did you think I was?" Curiosity drove the question.

"It doesn't matter," he said. "She wasn't Elf; you are."

Perhaps he was getting old. "No," she said, "you have your words mixed up. I'm not Elf."

Charlie came up beside the older man, his face a grim mask. The hairs on the back of Jane's neck sprang to attention. She knew him well enough by now to recognize that he was upset. And hiding something from her.

"Charlie?" Her voice cracked. He didn't meet her eyes.

"Of course you're Elf," Bryant continued. "There's no other way to explain your ears."

"Ears?" Her good hand shot to her ears, probing, outlining. She groaned when her fingers came to the definite points. Why hadn't she noticed them before? *Because there are no mirrors in Sylthia, and how often does anyone touch their ears?*

"Charlie?" she asked again, anger surging. "How long have you known? Why didn't you tell me?"

He hesitated, as if searching for the right words. Well, he could look to hell and back because none existed. Typical, cautious Charlie.

"Since the day in my office when you tried to seduce me," he answered. "I didn't tell you because you had enough to worry about—"

"Enough to worry about," she sputtered, enraged. "You never thought to mention it in the two weeks since? Knowing about the tattoo and where I copied it from?" Oh, God, she had Elf blood in her, at least the part that went to her ears. And that meant—

Jane's knees gave out. Vaguely, she realized that Bryant caught her and picked her up, taking her into his cabin. She sat in a chair, tornadoes and hurricanes and locomotives rushing in her head. Her breath came too shallow, and she thought she'd throw up. Suspicions filled her mind, clues clicking into place like the last five minutes of a detective story. Part Elf, the tattoo, and this man who thought he'd seen her before.

The room spun and she took joy in it, letting the g-forces press her against the walls. Maybe, if her luck held, it would spin her into outer space and she'd wake up in her own bed, like Dorothy in *The Wizard of Oz.*

Crouched in front of her, Bryant held out a glass of water. Silently, Jane drained its contents, laced heavily with brandy. She coughed and hiccupped and wiped the resulting tears from her eyes so she could look at the man before her.

"Does the name 'Anjinaine' mean anything to you?" she asked, watching his face closely.

Bryant paled significantly. "She is my foster sister. My parents died shortly after my birth, and her family took me in. She lives in Shallen."

Jane nodded. Yes, it made sense to be named after someone he loved dearly. She shuddered, preparing herself for the next question, going for broke, all the cards and marbles and chips on the table.

"How about Marion Drysdale?"

A strangled sound came from deep within him. The last vestige of color washed from his face, and he sat down heavily on the floor, a devastated heap. The pale morning sun threading through the windows dimmed.

"Yes," he said in a whisper. "A long time ago."

He didn't elaborate. Jane didn't need to ask. With care, because it still hurt to do so, she moved her left arm, pulling up the loose sleeve to expose the tattoo emblazoned at the top.

"And this? Have you seen this before?"

The words leapt out. Neon colors, strobe lights, and phosphorescent glow in the dark paint couldn't have made them more obvious.

Bryant stared at it, stock-still. Finally, he wet his lips and turned his gaze to hers, torture in his eyes.

" 'Forever joined, heart upon heart, world upon world,' " he quoted. "Yes. I wrote that for her."

"Her?" Charlie asked, miles from their intricate world.

"Marion," Bryant said, a caress in his voice, never looking from Jane.

She felt her heart tighten. Knowing his next words, she tried to brace herself.

His voice quavered as he said, "I think I'm your father."

# Chapter Twenty

Jane felt as if she'd been stabbed again. Her heart twisted in pain.

"No," she protested, holding out her hand, trying to keep the truth at bay. "My father was Ray Drysdale. He died from a heart attack four years ago. My parents were married for thirty years. They had a happy marriage!" She shouted the last words, jumping from her chair. Moving to the other side of the room, far from Bryant, she asked, "How dare you say otherwise?"

Fear choked her. She didn't want to believe him, even against all the mounting evidence. How could her mother abandon her family to come here and have an affair?

Sitting on the floor, leaning back against the chair, Bryant stared at her. Tears filled his eyes. He held a shaking hand to his face.

"I never knew," he murmured. "I wouldn't have let her go if I'd known. Believe me, Anjinaine—"

"Don't call me that," she cried. "My name is Jane Drysdale. Not Anjinaine. Not Ann Jane. Just plain Jane. No middle name. Capital J, small a, small n, small e. Jane."

Her heart raced feverishly. She wanted to throw something at him in retaliation for all the hurt he'd inflicted on her. Her gaze swept the room, looking for a heavy object, and came to rest on a cross-stitched sampler hanging on the wall. Staring back at her, in shades of blue wool, were the same words she'd tattooed on her arm.

With a cry of anguish, she slumped to the floor. Charlie rushed to her side. Weakly, she batted at him, still angry with him for lying to her, but he ignored her. Lifting her, he carried her to the bed in the corner and sat down. From the relative safety of his arms, she decided to delay her anger at him. She could only fight one battle at a time.

Sniffling into his shirt, Jane looked up at the sound of a knock on the door. Hugh stuck his head through the doorway.

"What's the delay—" He stopped and stared at Bryant. "Trouble?" he asked after a moment.

"Trouble," Charlie replied. "We're going to be a while. Can you make sure we're not disturbed?"

Hugh nodded and left, quietly closing the door.

Charlie moved her head so she had to face him. "It's time for answers to some of your questions," he said softly. He touched her hair, tucking a strand behind her ear, his fingers outlining the tip.

*As if I need reminding.* Jane met his gaze and found a strength in their brown depths. She'd leaned on him in the past for much worse than this. *This will be a piece of cake. Only it's awfully hard to swallow.*

"Yes," she agreed, wanting to burst into tears.

Charlie wiped her cheeks with the ball of his thumb. Taking her hand, he led her to a rocking chair. He and Bryant sat opposite.

"Now," he said, addressing their guide. "Let's start at the beginning. We need to hear this tale."

Bryant nodded and brushed at the tearstains on his cheek with the back of his hand.

"First," he said, looking at Jane. "I must know. Marion—your mother—is she well?"

"She's fine," Jane replied, the resentment she felt against this man replaced with warmth as she thought of her mother. It had been almost six weeks since she'd last seen her.

"Good." The older man nodded. He looked ready to say more, but stopped, a great pain darkening his features.

Charlie stirred at her side. "Bryant," he prompted.

"Yes, yes." Bryant nodded again and took a deep breath, picking his words with care. "Twenty-seven years ago, I was a raw young man of twenty-three. I'd traveled all of Lowth and decided it wasn't big enough. I went to Earth." He chuckled ruefully, a slight smile on his lips at the memory. "It didn't last long, two days perhaps. Marion inadvertently came back with me."

"How?" Jane asked, her mind clicking. "I mean, the portal opens along I-96. I'm not even sure the road was there at that time. Why would she be alongside the road, following a stranger?"

Of course, that's what she'd done. At his look of puzzlement, Jane glanced toward Charlie.

"You know the portal is unstable," he said. "Not only does the timing fluctuate, but also its location."

His words hit her like an ax. "You mean, if I went back today, I might not come out by my car?" Where would she end up and how would she get home without her purse, which contained cash and her ID? Not that it would do any good, melted by the heat, lying in her car in the graveyard for extra crispy Neons.

Charlie nodded. "It's possible."

"Then the night you followed Tivat—"

"We might not have returned near the Sentinel."

Another thought crossed her mind. She looked at Bryant. "What do you mean, twenty-seven years ago? I'm twenty-four."

He hesitated before answering. "She was part of my life for three years."

"No." A cold pit opened in her stomach. "Kevin is two years older than me. He's not Elf . . . is he?" Oh, God, her mother cheated not once but twice.

Charlie reached over and touched her arm. She swung back to him, seeking logic and reason.

"We don't know much about it," he said. "But we think time fluctuates as well."

"Time," she murmured. "The space-time continuum thing." She'd watched enough *Quantum Leap* episodes to know how that worked. It also explained how no one had ever said anything about her mother disappearing.

Swallowing too much information hurt her brain. She'd assimilate all the facts later, when she could sort it out.

"Go on," she told Bryant.

"Marion followed me by accident when I returned. The portal closed and stayed that way for three years."

He looked from Charlie to Jane. "She was distraught. She'd left behind a husband and children. It killed her to think of not seeing them again."

Jane tried to imagine her mother at that time. She'd have been twenty-five, married seven years, a mother for five. Of course she'd have been upset. *And I've repeated the pattern*, she thought, her mouth dry.

"I took her to Shallen to stay with my family," Bryant continued. "At that time, the portal emptied near Malik. I checked it almost every day; nothing was more important to me than making her happy by returning her home. But it remained closed." He leaned back, stretching his legs.

"Eventually, she climbed out of her depression and accepted that she'd be in Lowth the rest of her life."

Charlie moved his chair closer to Jane and squeezed her hand. The coldness in her stomach spread. What if she couldn't get back? Lowth seemed to have plans for her. . . .

She shook her head, focusing on this unknown chapter in her mother's life.

*Poor Mom. Every day that passed took her farther away from Daddy, Sheila and the boys.*

Except *her* Daddy hadn't been Ray Drysdale. And her mother hadn't been gone long enough—Earth time—for him to realize his wife carried another man's child. With a start, Jane knew she would have done exactly as her mother had: forget about Lowth and go on as if nothing had happened. No wonder she'd been so upset when Jane tattooed the Elven verse on her arm.

"Did you love her?" she asked Bryant, noting for the first time that his green eyes were her own.

A softness infused his face. "With all my heart. Two years after her arrival, I married her."

"And?" she asked, entranced by his narration. It was if she were listening to a bedtime story, not the tale of her parents.

Sadness darkened his eyes. "We'd almost given up visiting the portal. I don't know why we went to the meadow that day, except the weather was perfect. We packed a lunch—"

"And made love," Jane finished, thinking of her last time with Charlie.

Bryant nodded.

*How I spent my summer vacation. Conceived in a meadow, the union of a human woman and an Elf.* Unbidden, Jane's gaze strayed to Charlie. It had been two weeks since Midsummer's Eve. She'd know soon if she carried his baby.

"We talked of having children," Bryant said, following her train of thought. "To take the place of the ones she'd lost. We agreed it would be named after me if it was a boy, and Anjinaine, my sister, if it was a girl. Ironic, isn't it, that her replacement child ended up being raised with them?"

Jane wanted to cry at this tale of bittersweet love. "What of when she left?"

Pain flashed across Bryant's face. "We had so little time. The portal started to close. She had to make a decision in seconds—stay with me, or return to her family." He shifted uncomfortably in his chair.

"She made the right choice. I'll never fault her for that, but it hurt unbearably. It still does. I don't know if I could have survived if I'd known she carried my child."

Conflicting emotions assailed Jane—compassion, shock, desire to believe him, and an equally strong abhorrence of the whole subject. She looked to Charlie for guidance. She could count on him to give her a fair assessment.

"Nothing else explains what's happened since you've been here. It seems incredible, but I think he tells the truth."

"What of Lowth?" she asked. "I still feel as if it has a hand in this, that we're being led down a path of its choosing. Maybe my ears and what I do with the wind and the rain are because Lowth wants me to be something else, some unknown factor in this puzzle."

Bryant held up a finger to make a point. "I can control the wind and rain," he said, sealing the deal on her paternity. "As I said, my parents died when I was an infant, but I've been told they had strong powers."

Jane slumped in her chair, finally accepting the truth. "Where do we go from here?"

"To Malik," Bryant replied. "To Blacwin. I sent your mother home to Earth. I'll do the same for my daughter."

Daughter. Jane swallowed the word. It sounded foreign.

"I think," Charlie said, "this needs to be kept a secret, with only the three of us knowing the truth. We've had complications enough on this trip."

Jane nodded, though seeing Eagar's face when he learned of this tempted her.

"Deal," she said, her gaze on Bryant. "Forgive me if I can't call you Dad."

"Perhaps not yet," he agreed, smiling sadly.

*  *  *

Within half an hour, they were on the road again. Jane took the blame for the delay, telling an impatient Eagar that she'd felt ill and had to lie down.

After the midday meal, Charlie rode to Jane's side. Since leaving the cabin, she'd been quiet. Too quiet; a dangerous situation in his experience.

"Care to talk about it?" he asked. His pony stumbled, and he pulled on the reins to bring it back onto the path. They'd passed from Bryant's valley and ridden the steep inclines of the lower Andair Mountains. Tomorrow they'd reach the swift-moving Fendi River and more dangerous trails.

Jane shot Charlie a glance meant to melt steel. "I'm not talking to you," she said, turning her head away.

The flush of anger in her cheeks warmed his blood. He was glad she was getting spunky again.

"It's not like you to pout," he said.

"It's not like you to lie." She kicked her pony, which trotted forward several steps before resuming its sedate pace.

He realized what was bothering her. "Aren't you upset, hearing about Bryant and your mother?"

"Don't change the subject. You've known about my ears for two weeks, and you've said nothing. And, yes, I am upset about Bryant. How would you feel if your world was spun upside down? My father isn't who I thought he was, my mother lied to me, and, on top of everything, I'm half Elf."

"I'm half Elf, too," he said, angry that she thought so little of her newfound heritage. "But I know who my father is. It isn't the man Hugh found in the woods, it's the man who raised me—Owen Tanner. Your father is the man who took care of you when you were sick. He's the man who came to your rescue—and I can bet you had to be rescued frequently. It's not someone you met a few hours ago." The fervor with which he spoke was surprising. Jane moved him, made him want to do wild things, to be spontaneous. *Crazy Charlie of Malin.*

"We're still connected, Bryant and I," she argued, bent on proving her point.

"No more than I am to Isleighah," he said. He regretted the words the moment he said them.

She pounced like a starving man onto a banquet. "That's another thing. Hugh told me we're close to the path to Isleighah. Why won't you go there and ask if they knew your parents?"

Old memories returned—childhood ridicule for being different, the grim determination to fit in. Jane brought it all to the surface. Unconsciously, he looked to the northeast, remembering the woodland kingdom from the only time he'd been within its borders. Cool, green forests, barely touched by the Dymynsh, cascading waterfalls, a softness of magic.

Angry for allowing himself to be seduced by the thought, he shook it off. "My job is to guard you," he grunted.

"It will only be a few hours out of our way—"

"No. I don't want to talk about it." He couldn't have been more adamant in his refusal to go. Didn't she understand how little he cared about that part of his life?

"Stubborn man."

"Smart man," he corrected. "It doesn't interest me."

"Liar."

"I learned a long time ago to pick my battles." *And you won't win this one.*

Jane switched topics with a speed that made him dizzy. "Is that why you lied to me about my ears?"

He leaned forward in his saddle, allowing a slight breeze to stir under his tunic and around his wings. "You've had a lot to think about the last few weeks, Jane. The changes in your appearance didn't strike me as important."

Her green eyes darkened with hurt. "Do you know how hard it's going to be, returning to Earth with these things? The Spock jokes will be unending."

"What?" She still baffled him.

"Never mind. I can't function in society with these ears."

She could in his society. Had she thought about staying here? She talked about going back, or him joining her. There was a third option. It hurt that she hadn't thought of it.

"You yelled at me about lying to you, but you haven't been straight either. What else have you lied to me about?" She continued listing his shortcomings.

"Capp'ear's not dead," he blurted. Damn, he hadn't wanted to say it so baldly.

"What?" She almost fell off her pony.

He shrugged. "You wanted the truth."

Sarcasm dripped from her words. "Your truths come about two weeks after the fact. I thought you killed him."

"Well . . . I probably did. He couldn't have lived long with that wound. He fled while I tended to you, and we were too concerned about your injury to look for him." Concerned? He'd been scared to death she'd die on him. Even now, she should have been resting instead of traipsing over mountains.

"You think he died?" Jane asked, looking over her shoulder.

"How could he survive?" The knife had gone into Capp'ear's shoulder to the hilt. He'd had no medical attention. . . .

Hardness edged Jane's words. "How did he survive the swamp? Nothing he does is normal."

"Forget about him."

"Yeah, I have other problems, don't I? A father returned from . . . well, wherever; an upcoming meeting with a crazed wizard; and a boyfriend who can't tell the truth." Angry, she kicked her pony, and this time, it trotted away.

*Boyfriend?*

# Chapter Twenty-One

*I'm still mad at him,* Jane tried to convince herself two days later. Watching Charlie ride at the front of the line, his wings folded under his loose shirt, the way he clenched the pony's side with his thighs—the man made her hot. It seemed like forever since they'd been together.

And there was no hope of being together. At least, not until she'd defeated Blacwin, a showdown that loomed closer. Hugh estimated less than a week before they'd be at Shallen's gates.

This morning they'd passed the turnoff to Isleighah. Charlie again refused to listen to her pleas to get in touch with the fairies. They were so close, and if the stubborn, mule-headed man would listen to her, he might find some answers to his past.

If Lowth was manipulating her, and her elf heritage meant something important, could Charlie's fairy blood be as significant? She couldn't shake the feeling that they needed to have a better understanding of his roots.

Not that she'd been happier finding any answers to her past. It still hurt to look at Bryant and know his true identity. She didn't doubt him, but her mother's defection from her family, however unwilling, hurt Jane. The assault to her self-image confused her. *Shouldn't that be 'elf-image?* she thought wryly.

Pasha stumbled, and Jane snapped her attention back to the trail. They'd passed the highest elevation of their journey and now followed the Fendi River downstream. Unfortunately, this was the most dangerous part. Strung out like lumpy beads on a necklace, they descended a path along the canyon walls. The river twisted below them. Sheer rock rose above. *One misstep and it's curtains, Jane.*

An explosion ripped through the air, spewing rock and gravel in angry missiles. The sound cracked off the walls, howling down their length. Men and ponies screamed. The trail collapsed, cutting the band of travelers in half.

Jane grabbed her saddle tightly as Pasha reared up. The pony tried to rush back the way they'd come. It skidded in the dirt and gravel. Jane pulled on the reins, fighting for control, trying not to think of the fifty-foot plunge to her left.

"Get down," Eagar shouted at her. Suddenly, he was at her side, one hand on the pony's bridle. "Do you want to die?" he asked, his black eyes snapping. With his free hand, he reached up and jerked her from the saddle. She fell in an ungraceful heap on the path and scrambled to get out of the way of her mount's hooves.

Muttle pulled her back against the rock face.

"What happened?" she asked, grabbing his shoulder for balance. She swiveled in the direction of all the noise and disturbance, forgetting about Eagar.

The man ahead of her in line, a guard called Nare, lay dead ten feet away, his pony nowhere in sight. In front of him, a muffled shout carried to her.

"Charlie!" she screamed, panicking. He'd been four ahead of her, Bryant and Hugh in the lead. She started forward, determined to find a way to him if she had to scale the cliffs to do so.

Eagar pulled her back. "Don't be a fool," he hissed.

"I don't care. I have to get to Charlie." Jane glanced at the steward. Behind him she saw Warren, the tracker, trying to quiet the horses. "Let go of me."

The pressure on her arm increased. "The explosion was set on purpose," Eagar said, pulling her back to reality. "You're in more danger than you realize."

She shook her head. "No. Who'd want to hurt—" She screamed as she saw the one responsible on the path behind them. "Capp'ear!"

The sound of steel leaving a scabbard rang in the air. Eagar thrust Jane behind him, his sword drawn. Muttle joined him. Warren released the horses and took up a defensive position.

Capp'ear dodged the animals as they swept past him. Jane saw dried blood on his tunic where he'd been stabbed by Charlie's knife two weeks earlier. He was dressed in rags; dirt and mud clung to him from head to foot. She wouldn't have known him except for the madness of his eyes.

"Pretty lady," he said, bowing to her.

"Ye won't have her," Muttle yelled, launching himself into the air, his two knives brandished in a whirl of metal.

All hell broke loose after that. Capp'ear and Muttle fenced up and down the narrow confines of the path, going at each other like a couple of demented Errol Flynns. Where had he gotten a sword? He'd been defenseless when he escaped.

In the meantime, Eagar and Warren hacked at several creatures who'd slipped onto the path from the sheer ninety-degree-straight-down-to-the-river side of the cliff. Jane had seven-tenths of a second to realize they were sandobbles before two grabbed her from behind.

"Charlie!" she screamed before they picked her up and

handed her down the cliffside to another pair. Within a couple of minutes, she'd been bodysurfed to the river's edge. They dumped her into a crude boat tied to an outcropping of rock. Clinging to the ledge like overgrown leeches, they snapped at her when she tried to disembark.

Above, things looked grim for her rescuers. Warren was down, a host of sandobbles swarming over him. In moments, they covered him, cohering into a fluid unit, suffocating him.

Muttle was nowhere in sight. Eagar had retreated, giving up the fight, allowing Capp'ear to be carried down to the boat by the sandobbles. Her nemesis freed the boat from its anchor and clambered aboard. The swift current pulled them away from the rocks.

"Pretty lady," he said, moving forward to touch her.

# Chapter Twenty-Two

Charlie watched in horror as the nightmare unfolded before him. In the first confusing moments after the explosion, he fought through the debris and dust to make his way up the trail to Jane. But it wasn't there. It was blown away, a ten-foot gap separating them. One man lay dead on the other side, two wounded on this side, a pony was missing and others were crying in pain.

He heard Jane shout, then the sound of metal on metal. Fools! They'd strung themselves out too far, making such an attack possible. With their forces divided, she'd be easy prey.

The dust cleared enough to show the sandobbles carrying Jane down the cliff. In moments, the fight had ended. With a dawning fear, Charlie knew he'd lost her. The little boat flowed into the current of the Fendi.

He almost turned away, ready to meet with the others and plan her rescue, when he heard a victorious yell. Muttle, in a feat of remarkable acrobatics, threw himself across the distance to the boat, landing on Capp'ear's back. Moments later, Eagar dove off the cliff. His timing was perfect, and he splashed into the water within reach of the others. He pulled himself aboard, and then he and Muttle fought Capp'ear. Jane threw herself into the fray as the boat rounded a bend and disappeared.

"Hugh!" Charlie roared in the direction he'd last seen his brother. "Gather everyone together. We're going after her."

"Oh, no you don't!"

Jane crouched lower in the boat and fumbled for the knife strapped to her leg. Capp'ear loomed over her, all but smacking his lips. She felt like a piece of French silk pie in the presence of a chocoholic.

"Get back!" she yelled as she tried to figure out whether to continue struggling to free her knife or to try and knock him into the river. *I should have cut the rope when I had the chance. But that would have taken me away from Charlie.*

Capp'ear squatted next to her, removing her advantage of leverage to tip him over the side. Jane scooted to the bow, ready to kick him where it would do the most harm.

A shout from above caused her to look up. Muttle flew through the air and came down with a loud thump on Capp'ear's back. He twisted in an effort to remove the Belwaith, but Muttle held on, lambasting the elf with a string of curses.

Jane caught sight of another movement and heard a nearby splash. Eagar bobbed to the surface, emerging from the river's depths. He swam over and grabbed the side of the flimsy boat. Boarding without looking at her, he joined the fight.

*Why should they have all the fun?* Jane lunged at Capp'ear, whacking him on the head with the elbow of her good arm.

The boat tilted, and they all shifted, losing their balance. The combatants collapsed like a house of cards, Jane landing on the bottom. Pain shot through her back and down her right leg. The struggle continued on top of her. Capp'ear's clothes smashed against her nose, the stench making her ill.

"Get him off me!" she yelled to her companions.

A couple of sharp movements ground her farther into the boat, then a sudden stillness descended. Limbs untangled, and Capp'ear was rolled off her. Jane stared up at the black crispness of Eagar's eyes.

"Are you hurt?" he asked, slightly breathless.

*Since when do you care?* She pushed away the ungrateful thought. After all, he'd jumped in after her.

"Ask me again in an hour," she said.

He held out his hand to her. Gingerly, she took it, aware of his touch. Contrary to her expectations, her flesh didn't shrivel, and nothing burst into flames. He felt cool and slightly damp from his dunking.

Jane sat up and released his hand. She flexed her arms and legs, checking for injuries. Her shoulder twinged and her back ached, but it didn't feel like anything serious.

"Thank you," she said, her gratitude to this man making her uncomfortable.

He nodded, then glanced at the prone form of Capp'ear, slumped in an unconscious heap next to Muttle.

"Give me your belt," Eagar said to her.

"It's the only thing holding my pants up." She'd abandoned her skirts in the first days of their journey.

Jane fumbled with the pack around her waist, untying the strings. "Take my fanny pack," she said, and held it out to him. She'd fashioned it out of a cloth pouch and strong cord.

"Fanny pack?"

Jane shook the bag in front of him.

He took it and wrapped the cording tightly around Capp'ear's wrists. Eagar moved to the bow of the small vessel. She scooted out of his way. He grabbed the rope that had anchored the boat to the cliff wall and held out his hand to Jane.

"Give me your knife. I know you have one."

She hesitated. Relinquishing her weapon was tantamount to surrender. Eagar might have saved her, but he was hardly her friend. With Charlie lost, Muttle became her sole defender, and she didn't think he was a match for the steward.

"Don't be a fool," Eagar sneered. "It's the only weapon we have. You'll get it back."

*Buried in my back or dragged across my throat?* Jane pulled up her pant leg and drew the knife from its sheath. Reluctantly, she handed it over, alert to Eagar's every movement.

He cut the rope where it was attached to the bow and used it to bind the prisoner's legs. Next, he tore a length from Capp'ear's tunic and started to tie it around his mouth.

"At least wash it first," Jane exclaimed, revulsion filling her at the memory of its smell.

Surprised, Eagar looked at her, one demonic eyebrow raised. He tossed the strip of cloth to her and waited while she dipped it into the river and rinsed away most of its filth.

With Capp'ear safely trussed at her feet like a Thanksgiving turkey, Jane breathed her first sigh of relief.

"What now?" she asked, looking from Muttle to Eagar. "Toss him in the river?"

Eagar's nostrils twitched. "He remains our prisoner until we join the others. Then he faces trial again."

*A real stickler for protocol, aren't you?* "And throw him back in the Magwrosin?" Jane shook her head. "I don't think so. I say we get rid of him now, before he calls his new friends, the sandobbles, and we're all dead."

"He deserves a fair trial—"

"And Nare and Warren deserved to live," she shot back, angry. "Let's not forget them." She tried to push away the memory of their deaths, especially Warren's, swallowed alive by the sandobbles. Who knew how Capp'ear communicated with them, or had enlisted their aid? Waking up, he might send out a telepathic distress call.

"We'll talk of this later," Eagar said, his jaw firm.

Jane bit her tongue. She'd save the argument for when she had more ammunition.

"How do we land this thing and get back to the others?" She scanned the boat for a sail or oars. Neither was evident.

Eagar looked at the sheer walls rising above. The Fendi poured between them like a water in a tube.

"I doubt if there'll be a beach anytime soon. We'll have to wait until we see one and hope the current slows enough that we can paddle over to it." He squinted into the sky.

Jane followed his gaze. The sun had already passed over the thin opening above the canyon. Shadows crept down the striated rock, signaling how close darkness lay.

"Through the night?" Jane panicked. For the first time, she realized she was alone with a man who'd treated her almost as badly as Capp'ear. And her knife hadn't been returned.

Eagar shrugged and settled back against the side of the boat. "We have little choice. Make yourself comfortable. It's going to be a long night."

"I don't think so." Jane spoke her thoughts out loud, hearing a sudden roaring. Her gaze swept the river ahead. "Eagar," she said, wetting her suddenly dry lips. "There's trouble ahead."

They survived the first waterfall. By sheer, dumb luck, they bobbed like a cork between rocks, scraping the hull in several places. White water foamed around them, pushing the small craft inexorably faster, hurrying it from one drop to the next. The chasm narrowed, pushing the crippled vessel around jagged boulders and plunging them six feet at a time to the next level. Finally, the river dumped them into a dark blue pool. The boat spun around before it resumed its journey downstream.

Jane peeled her fingers off the wooden side. "That," she said, trying to regain her breath, "was better than any ride at Cedar Point." She'd never before considered a head-over-heels tumble along a river a good way to get down a mountain.

Distaste marred Eagar's features. Muttle, decidedly green around the gills, slumped against her. Capp'ear stared at her, his eyes wide with fear.

"We could have been killed," Eagar said, reproach in his voice. He made her feel like a muddy child.

*I bet you alphabetize the socks in your drawer.* She'd never met a more Felix-Ungerish, rigid, anal man in her life. Charlie was regimented, but with a wild side just waiting to pop out. Unlike the steward. *He probably schedules sex.* The thought of Eagar in the throes of passion with anyone made her feel queasy. She shoved it away.

"I laugh in the face of danger," she scoffed. How long had she waited to use that corny phrase?

"You'll think different if we crash."

Jane shook her head. "Not going to happen. And if it does, I'll survive. I've made it through fire and swamp, a stabbing and white water rapids. A little swim won't be any problem."

"You think you're invincible?" he asked with scorn.

She nudged Capp'ear with her foot. He growled at her through his gag. "Our friend proved I'm not. But I'm destined for important things."

Eagar barked in laughter. "Conceited mortal. Do you think a great plan unfolds with you at the center?"

Put that way, it did sound egotistical. "I think there is more to Lowth than meets the eye." *Understatement of the year, puffball.*

He swelled in anger. "I've given fifty years of service to this land. Do not speak lightly of it, Earthwoman."

Jane bristled. "Listen, Bluto, stop calling me that. My name is Jane." It seemed as if she'd had this conversation once before. At least he didn't call her Anjinaine. What would he say if he knew the truth?

Muttle tugged on her arm, drawing her attention from the verbal sparring with Eagar.

"What is it?" she asked.

"Trouble." He pointed to the bottom of the boat. A hole the size of a dime burbled, letting in a steady stream of water.

Panic seized her. "Great, just great. I had to open my big mouth." She turned to Eagar. "Cut off some more of Capp'ear's shirt. I'm going to try to plug it. In the meantime, Muttle, start bailing."

"We don't have anything to bail with," Eagar said, unsteadiness in his voice.

*The man operates a castle, but he can't handle an emergency.*

"Use your hands," Jane yelled, scooping as fast as she could. She spotted another hole and swore. As she moved to the bow to plug it, her gaze caught an irregularity in the river ahead. She straightened and shielded her eyes from the contrast of the last light of the day and the darkened shadows.

"Crap," she said with vehemence. "Double, triple crap."

Eagar looked up. "Now what's wrong?"

She stared at the rise of rock rapidly bearing down on them. It neatly split the Fendi. "The proverbial fork in the road. Which way do we go?"

Eagar sized up the situation. "To the right," he said without hesitation. "Away from Malik."

"Away from Malik?" His decision shocked her.

He returned to bailing. "Unless you want to float into a goblin camp. The right fork loops back toward Isleighah."

*Goblins or fairies? Not a tough choice.* Leaving the other two to keep them afloat, Jane paddled.

They swung around the curve, bumping against rock,

grating the wood hull. Their vessel looked less a boat and more like Tom Hanks's raft at the end of *Castaway*. Bouncing and bobbing in the swift current, Jane paddled and bailed and kept her eyes peeled for an opening in the canyon walls.

"There. Head that way," she shouted twenty minutes later, pointing to a small grove of trees in the distance. It offered the possibility of a landing.

They abandoned their hopeless task of saving the boat and concentrated on heading it toward shore. The current pulled them to the river's center. As they came within a hundred yards of their goal, Jane knew why. The sound of rushing water changed to a telltale roar. Looking ahead, she saw the river fall away into . . . nothing.

"Another waterfall," she cried in alarm. They wouldn't survive this one; Niagara looked like a wave pool in comparison. "Get out!" She grabbed Muttle and threw herself overboard.

Charlie swore. They'd made terrible progress since the explosion. Two of the guards, Enwl and Dimus, had been hurt, but were well enough to ride. Leaving them behind never entered Charlie's thoughts, though worry about Jane's safety ate at him.

The men could do little to help the injured ponies. Bryant ordered their destruction. He and Hugh disposed of them as humanely as possible. Charlie shook his head at the waste of life Capp'ear and the sandobbles had caused.

A saddened party of six continued the journey downstream, four horses between them. Bryant and Hugh were in the lead, then the two injured guards, Alfted from the village, and Charlie in the rear. They moved at a slow pace due to the dangerous narrowness of the trail and for the benefit of those who walked.

Bryant called a halt as the shadows grew longer.

"We're endangering ourselves," he said. "We must stop."

"No," Charlie argued. "As long as there's light out—"

Hugh stepped in front of his brother. "He speaks the truth, Charlie. We can't be stumbling around in the dark on these narrow ledges. Stopping is the sensible thing to do."

Charlie didn't want to be sensible. He should have been the one to jump in the river after Jane. He should have rescued her from Capp'ear, as he'd done at the swamp.

Bryant touched his arm, drawing his attention. Charlie saw pain and sorrow in his eyes.

"I lost her mother. I'm not about to lose my daughter. Another trail splits off from this one a mile farther. It leads to the top of those other cliffs. We can camp there for the night."

Charlie looked at the swift current of the Fendi, willing it to dry up, stopping Jane's progress. *She must be miles downstream by now.* Knowing he did the right thing, but not liking it, he nodded in acceptance.

They set up camp, easing the injured men from their mounts and making them as comfortable as possible. Dinner was dried rations. As exposed as they were, they couldn't afford a fire.

Charlie took third watch. Rest's new moon rose in the blackest part of the night. He remembered other moons, full and glowing, a lifetime ago on Midsummer's Eve. That night he'd first made love to Jane.

*And only once since then.* Would he have another chance? She'd been so sick, then so prickly. And angry, and now vanished. How could he not have told her how he felt? She was the moons to him, and the stars, and all the other worlds to which Lowth connected. He couldn't deny he wanted her to stay when this ended. He'd chased after her for weeks now, though it seemed as if he'd fled her most of that time. No more. Once he had her safe again, he'd tell her he loved her. This journey had taught him that delays and postponements were mistakes when it came to reality. *Tomorrow isn't always a possibility.*

Hugh clamped his hand on Charlie's shoulder, making him jump. "My watch," he said, and sat down next to him. "Go rest. You'll need your strength for when we find her."

Charlie nodded but did not move. "I love her," he said into the darkness.

"And no one knows this? Ah, perhaps the lady herself. You spar too much and love too little."

"I follow my older brother in that habit," Charlie said, trying to see Hugh in Rest's feeble light.

"Mara and I are happy now, and you and Jane will be as well."

"As soon as I find her, set her on course for Malik, help her overcome Blacwin, end the Dymynsh, and send her home?" Charlie shook his head. "I don't see happiness here."

Hugh chuckled. "Something will happen. It always does."

"That's what frightens me. Too much has happened already."

Silence held between the brothers, broken only as Slumber appeared on the horizon.

"Do you still feel her?" Hugh asked.

The vibration in Charlie's wings lessened with each passing hour. He feared it might disappear before he found her.

"Yes," he said to allay Hugh's doubt. "I feel her. I'll always feel her."

Jane gasped and pushed the remaining few inches up the riverbank. Mud sucked at her legs. With her last ounce of strength, she pulled free and collapsed, her breathing hard and irregular.

She moaned as every ache and pain introduced itself. *Like a wedding reception line—hi, I'm elbow, all scraped up. Hello, I'm knee, I used to work with femur.*

Muttle, glued to her since they'd jumped from the boat,

disentangled himself. He made a squishy sound as he sat down.

"Lady Jane?"

"Hmmm?" Rolling to her back, she stared into the inky sky, hoping the unfamiliar stars would swallow her whole.

"Ye be well?" Concern filled his voice.

"Ducky, Muttle. Nothing a Valium and a fifth of whiskey couldn't fix."

"Where be Eagar?" he asked, twisting his head to look out to the river.

*Over the edge?* Jane pictured the steward flailing wildly as he tumbled into oblivion. A smile curved her lips. "Don't know, don't care," she said. Her heart still pumped frantically from her exertions. It had been all she could do to save herself and Muttle. Capp'ear and Eagar ranked last in her worries. She wanted nothing more than to lie in the mud.

Muttle straightened, his thin body alert. "He be alive." He stood, shivering.

Jane moaned and hauled herself into a sitting position. "Where?"

The Belwaith pointed into the night. "There."

She saw exactly . . . nothing. With great effort, she rose to her feet and took a couple of stumbling steps. "Eagar?"

"Jane? Help me." The man's weakened voice came from her left.

*Those are three words I never expected to hear. 'Jane,' not 'Jane Drysdale of Earth,' and 'help me.' Self-sufficient, always-in-control Eagar needs a hand.*

Her body protested, but she slogged through the water until she saw him. He swayed against the current, his arms barely holding the still-bound Capp'ear.

"Is he alive?" she asked, rushing to the steward's aide. Between the two of them, they moved Capp'ear onto the bank.

"I don't know." Eagar's hand trembled as he passed it

over his bald head. "I grabbed him before he could go over. He was unconscious then."

Unconscious or dead? Jane clamped her ear down on his chest. She couldn't tell over the sound of the rapids, but his heart had either stopped or was too weak to hear. He definitely was not breathing.

"Right," she said, grim determination taking over. "Untie him." When Eagar did not move, she lashed out at him. "For God's sake, he's no threat the way he is now. At least take his gag off."

The older man produced the knife—her knife—and sliced through the gag and ropes.

Jane bent over and stifled the revulsion welling in her. *Ya gotta do what ya gotta do.* Trying to think only of the mechanics involved, she started CPR.

It seemed forever before Capp'ear jerked spasmodically and coughed up a good share of the river. Jane sat on her heels and watched in sick fascination as he came back to life.

*Auntie Em, some of it was horrid, and parts of it were beautiful, but the whole time I kept thinking, I want to go home.*

She closed her eyes, determined to sit all night, like some kind of mud-encrusted gargoyle. She didn't have the strength to lie down.

"Jane?" Eagar said softly. His hand touched her shoulder. She wanted to jerk away but couldn't make herself move.

"We must seek shelter."

Her head lolled back, tilting farther and farther as gravity took over. Her vision swept past his face until she looked at the stars again.

"Must we?" The words dragged past her lips.

"We're in unfamiliar territory with little defense. Come, you can rest soon." He helped her to her feet. Half-supporting her, with Muttle and a weakened Capp'ear following, he started back the way they'd come.

With Muttle's infrared-like vision guiding them, they

found a cave. It was above flood level and a thick bush covered the opening. Jane collapsed on the cool floor, not moving once she was down.

"There's food in my fanny pack," she whispered, hunger the last thing on her mind. Closing her eyes, she fell asleep.

Morning brought the promise of a new beginning. Muttle caught some fish and Eagar smoked them in wet leaves over a small fire. Well-fed and rested, they started the steep climb to the top of the next cliff. From there, they could watch the river and keep an eye out for Charlie and the others. If all went well, they'd meet up before the day ended. She couldn't wait to see him again. He deserved an apology for her surly mood. So what if he hadn't told her about her ears?

Capp'ear, unfettered, followed behind them. His demeanor had changed since they'd pulled him from the water. He said little and watched Jane constantly, but in a more puppy-dog than fringe-lunatic kind of way.

They'd almost reached the summit when Muttle, ahead of Jane, stopped, his body at attention.

*Someone comes.*

*Who?* Her mind filled with images of Charlie, sandobbles and goblins. She thought to warn Eagar, but he and Capp'ear had fallen behind, around a bend in the trail.

*Two. One is elf. The other . . .* Muttle broke off and stared at her, his eyes whirling green and orange.

Jane glanced around, but there was no place to hide. Rock and gravel and an occasional straggly bush lay everywhere she looked. Except down. Down offered an eighty-foot drop.

A voice boomed above them. "Hello! We mean no harm."

*Isn't that what the evil aliens always say?* Jane took a step back, ready to flee. She looked up at the man who approached them. And saw an Adonis. A hunka-hunka burnin' Elf. Tall and tanned. Buff. Long, flowing dark hair and emerald green eyes.

*Good grief,* she thought. *It's a good thing I'm in love with Charlie.*

She held out her hand and stopped, a memory teasing her. The morning mist shimmered behind him. It shimmered again. For some reason, Jane thought of a rabbit. Her mouth went dry.

"Tivat?"

He smiled, his teeth dazzling white.

The sound of loose gravel on the trail drew her eye upward. Her heart lurched at the sight of the woman scrambling down the trail.

"Mom?"

# Chapter Twenty-Three

Jane moaned and opened her eyes to bright daylight. She turned her head and realized she lay on the ground. Her mother knelt nearby, hands fluttering.

Jane stared, believing her to be part of a horrifying dream. Or maybe Tivat's presence had made her hallucinate—if this was Tivat. An unlikely event, as she'd killed him and had a murder conviction to prove it. She groaned and looked away, trying to make sense of this new wrinkle.

"You'll be fine, dear. You've had too much excitement," Marion Drysdale said, smoothing her daughter's brow.

*You don't know the half of it.* Jane propped herself on her elbows. She had to break this habit of passing out; it ruined her self-image of being the most unfaintiest person around.

"Mom? What are you doing in Lowth?" She slowly sat up.

"I could ask the same of you, but John and I figured you must have fallen into the portal after you hit him."

"John?"

"John Tivat. I'm sure you've heard his name mentioned since you came to Lowth—"

"Yeah, it's come up once or twice," Jane replied, her voice bitter. If she hadn't killed him, why had it taken a month and a half for him to return?

"Such a nice boy," Marion said.

Jane's gaze strayed to where he stood in the near distance, arguing with Eagar in low, heated tones. Interesting. She tried to tune in her new ears to their conversation, but the pair spoke in a dialect she didn't understand.

Speaking of dialect, she realized she and her mother had been talking in English. "Where did you learn Elven?" she asked, yanking her sleeve up to display her tattoo.

Marion blanched. She sat down hard, her face twisted with myriad emotions. "Oh, dear," she said after a few moments.

"Yeah, oh dear," Jane lashed out. All of her hurt and betrayal rose to the surface. "Care to explain either of your trips to Lowth?"

Marion's eyes filled with sadness. She looked away from Jane, then back again. But instead of starting at the beginning, she took the coward's way out.

"When they told me of your accident," she said, "I nearly went berserk. The next day, I drove to the spot where your car had been abandoned. Things didn't feel right, and I started to look around for clues. Instead, I found John. Oh, not the way he is today, but in the form of a rabbit. A rabbit with green eyes. It's a mighty strange sight on Earth, let me tell you. I knew right away it had to be connected to your disappearance, so I brought him home with me. He kept shapeshifting between bunny and man. Two weeks ago, he stabilized and told me his story. We started making plans to return to Lowth. I wasn't going to leave my baby alone."

Jane narrowed her eyes. "You blackmailed him," she said, knowing full well that her mother couldn't pass through the portal without Tivat's Elven companionship. She wondered why he hadn't continued his flight.

"I think I did mention gratitude and a mother's concern, duty, honor and a few other choice synonyms," Marion admitted, a sly grin on her face. "In the end, I persuaded him to come back and throw himself on the mercy of the court."

Jane glanced at the "court," namely, Eagar. He was in a definite snit. His communication with Tivat had broken down. The two glared at each other, their looks and body language hostile. She'd give a million indrans to know what they'd said.

"A pretty story, Mom, but it doesn't explain why you've lied to me all my life." She pushed back the curls from around her ears. "Or why I have Elf blood."

She couldn't have planned better to get a reaction from Marion. Her mother's hand fluttered to her heart, and a pinched look tightened her white face.

"Oh, dear," she said, her voice high. "When did this happen?"

"About twenty-four years ago. It's been latent until two or three weeks ago, when Charlie first noticed it—"

"Charlie?" her mother asked, interrupting her tirade.

"My lover," Jane shot back, not caring to be polite or sweet or politically correct. "You should know about Elf lovers, Mom, as you took one while still married to Daddy."

Marion changed from white to gray. "How . . . how do you know this?"

Jane flicked her right ear. "It's evident, don't you think? Besides, I heard it from Bryant's own mouth."

"He's alive?" The other woman pounced on her words. "Bryant's alive? You've seen him?"

"I talked to him yesterday." Had it only been the day before? "We should meet him again today." She didn't want to go into the long story of the past six weeks.

"I loved Bryant," Marion said, her eyes alight. "It's nothing I planned. When it looked as if I'd never return home, I made the best of the situation. An opportunity came to return home, and I did, however much it hurt. As for telling lies, Jane, would you have believed me? Can you believe it now that you're here?"

"We'll talk about this later," Jane said. It still chafed to know she'd been deceived. "It's too much right now." Despite her earlier feud with Charlie, she wanted to get back to him, to his common sense and logic. She wanted to crawl into his strong arms, warm herself in his embrace, and forget goblins and wizards and elves. Oh, my!

The ramifications of Tivat's return hit her like a freight train. Why would she continue on her trek to Malik if the reason for her punishment lived?

Charlie spotted them as the sun reached its zenith. The sum of four ponies for six men and the worsening condition of the wounded slowed his progress. They had to walk the animals around fissures and cracks in the ground. The heat continued to rise, while the cool depths of the Fendi glided by far below.

At noon, he caught sight of a clump of shadows bobbing in the distance. He looked to Hugh, who had better eyesight.

His brother took his time answering, a frown on his face.

"I think it is them," he said. "But something is amiss. They are with two others, or it is a separate party of six."

*Two others? What has she done now?* Regardless, Charlie needed to see her.

"Take my horse," Hugh said, slipping from the animal. He handed over the reins. "I know you are anxious."

Charlie shot him a look of gratitude and mounted the beast. With a kick to its side, he galloped off.

A shout rose from the other party as they spotted him. He was within a half mile when he saw movement to his left, on the edge of the cliff.

*Sandobbles!*

His heart in his throat, he watched them swarm up the side and close the short distance to the unsuspecting group.

"Hey!" he called, knowing they couldn't make out his words. He waved his hands over his head, his knees pushing the pony faster. "Danger! Attack!"

*Muttle!* He tried to warn the Belwaith.

A quarter mile separated them. He heard screams and saw Eagar shift to stand between Jane and the creatures.

*Charlie!* Her cry echoed in his head.

It was a reenactment of the debacle from yesterday. The quicksand beings surged over everyone standing and pulled them down. She and Capp'ear rode above them, mud hands holding them aloft. Charlie spurred his mount on, conscious of Bryant close behind.

*Capp'ear, no, don't hurt my friends,* Jane pleaded.

The attacking sandobbles disengaged from their victims. Congealing into one liquid mass, they joined with those transporting Jane and Capp'ear. They flowed away with deceptive quickness, rolling across the landscape, already a quarter mile distant by the time Charlie passed the others. He goaded his poor pony forward, but his quarry had disappeared in the distance.

"Halt! Charlie, stop!" Bryant shouted, grabbing his bridle and forcing his mount to a standstill.

"No!" Charlie roared. "She won't be taken away from me again." Rage filled every inch of his being.

"She already has," the hunter pointed out. "Let us regroup, then we can follow." He indicated an obvious trail: finger-sized lumps of mud dropped from the departed creatures.

"We have to find her," Charlie yelled, trying to regain control of his pony. He would not let Jane vanish from his life, not to rivers or crazed madmen or sandobbles.

Bryant held the animal in check. His voice pounded like a hammer in Charlie's head. "You'll kill your mount, and yourself, galloping over this uneven ground. Listen to what I say! We have injured, weapons that won't hurt the sandobbles, and Capp'ear is traveling too fast. We can't fight this battle by ourselves."

"I can fight," Charlie declared.

"Not alone. Not for long. You saw what they did to Warren. Do you want to suffer the same fate?"

"But Jane—"

"Is my daughter. I'm not about to give her up."

Charlie hated listening to reason. Not pursuing Jane went against every instinct he possessed. But he had to acknowledge the other man's wisdom. Again. They were in no condition to follow.

"What do you propose we do?" he asked, angered at the decision to stay.

"We get help," Bryant said with confidence.

"Where?"

"From the closest source. From Isleighah."

*No!* Charlie's mind screamed. "Impossible."

Bryant looked at him, his gaze steady, his green eyes so much like Jane's. "It's her only hope."

*What goes around, comes around.* How often had Jane told him this? With a sigh, Charlie acquiesced. He would go to Isleighah and beg for help. He knew, without a doubt, that she'd get her wish, and he'd learn of his heritage.

Two things struck Charlie as he returned to the others. Neither shocked him, each seeming a rightful inclusion to this adventure. The first: He recognized Tivat as one of the four figures lying prone on the ground. Second, at Bryant's shout of, "Marion," he realized another had to be Jane's mother.

Charlie's mind clicked through the possible answers to

where and when they'd met. Their gear, new and foreign-made—probably on Earth—told him Tivat had escaped Lowth, and escaped Jane's vehicle as well. Fresh scars on the man's arm and leg pointed to recent injury. Struck then, and hurt, to be found and nursed by a curious mother, a woman who desired to return to Lowth in search of her daughter?

Bryant cradled the woman, soothing words flowing from him. Charlie watched a moment, then dismounted and walked to Hugh. His brother knelt at Eagar's side.

"Does he live?" Charlie asked.

"His lungs are injured, as well as the others'. A few more moments . . ." He shook his head. "They need medical attention."

"We ride to Isleighah," Charlie announced, his voice grim, the decision still rankling.

"And Jane?"

Charlie moved away. "Jane will probably talk Capp'ear to death. He shall end up paying us to take her back."

*She is vindicated now,* he thought, glancing at the unconscious Tivat. *Or will be when we find her.*

An hour later, the crippled group headed back the way they'd come, upstream to the headwaters of the Fendi. Of the ten, six were injured. A small stand of timber was cut down, young trees made into litters. The worst hurt, Marion and Muttle, lay in these, pulled by the ponies. The others rode the animals, guided by the healthy.

Afternoon slipped into evening, then into darkness. A crescent moon lit the way, and at midnight, another slipped into the sky. Eagar woke, shaking, and threw up a weak curtain of magical light around them—no more than a lantern would give out.

The murmur of the river to their right accompanied them during the long night. At dawn, they curved away from it, to the northeast, and entered the path to Isleighah. They descended into wide valleys, crossed shallow streams and climbed long, low hills. Here, so far from home, the grasses grew with a depth of color that hurt the eye. By midmorning, they'd entered the cool, green forest of Isleighah, the last of the ancient forest that begot the Malin. The injured, restless on their mounts and pallets, calmed, as if soothed by old magic.

A fairy appeared on the path, barely discernible from the trees. Charlie had a feeling they'd been under surveillance for some time. But what threat did their disabled group pose?

The stranger waited for them. As they drew to a halt in front of him, Charlie saw others farther back in the woods.

"Who are you, that come to our land?" the fairy asked, his voice the murmur of wind in trees, of water on pebbles.

Bryant stepped forward. He'd aged in the past day, his concern for Marion and his daughter drawing dark circles under his eyes. "We are poor travelers, many wounded, and seek assistance from the people of Isleighah and their king. I am Bryant, long of Malik and these, my companions, dwell in the south at Malin. We also carry an Earthwoman."

The last caused a stir, like the wind whispering secrets to the topmost leaves.

Bryant continued, "You know of me. I have hunted with your king, the great Tuniesin. Come, we have no quarrel. These injured have suffered from the sandobbles, scourge of Lowth. Even as we speak, they hold captive another, my daughter."

The fairy considered his words, then nodded and extended a hand in greeting.

"Well met, Bryant, long of Malik. I am called Rasleigh. The sandobbles are enemy to all, and elves and fairies have forged bonds in the past." He glanced at Charlie, as if he could see his wings under his loose shirt. "We will guide you to Kerreleigh, the king's residence. You will be aided there."

Others of his kind joined him until six escorted the

band of travelers. They continued for another hour. At last, they came to a break in the trees and Kerreleigh stood before them.

Shaped of trunks and limbs millennia ago, the light of oak, the burnish of maple, the dark of walnut and isel-wood, a complex design wove through the home of the king of fairies. Of the forest but separate, it housed scores and generations. Time and history merged in its walls.

They entered a great hall. With care, the injured were taken to the healing rooms, Alfted and Bryant at their sides. Rasleigh showed Charlie and Hugh to rooms to freshen and rest.

An hour after their arrival, Rasleigh returned and escorted them to the heart of Kerreleigh, the throne room. Comfortable settees lay scattered around its perimeter. Rich, vivid tapestries lined its walls, with scenes depicting hunts, the stages of the moons, butterflies so real as to be captured in midflight. Great circles with eight-pointed stars, for the eight holidays, patterned the ceiling twenty feet above a floor made of one plank. Light streamed in windows without glass. Charlie's eyes adjusted to the radiance, and he saw a man seated in a chair off-center in the room. King Tuniesin.

Tuniesin looked to be in his early forties, but who could tell with fairies? The monarch was tall and slender, his face unlined, his hair sable brown, his eyes linden green. He smiled at Charlie's interest and beckoned him forward.

"A Whelphite," the king said, his voice surprisingly deep. "They are rare nowadays. And a Isleighah-Malin combination. The Malinese will now only take a Wing-back for a mate, our cousins to their south, if they choose to crossbreed."

Charlie felt something tighten in his stomach at the mention of his fairy characteristics. He bowed to King Tuniesin, whose wings rose from his back in golden splendor.

"Forgive me," the monarch apologized. "It is rude to

comment on such. I can see you are uncomfortable with your fairyness. Why else would you hide your wings?"

"Sire?" The conversation wasn't going the way Charlie had planned. The king's directness caught him off guard.

"Why do you wait until you are in such distress before you claim aid from your people?" the other man asked.

Switching tactics, Charlie decided to be direct as well. He bowed his head to the king. "I have known none but elves all my life. What you say is true. Most fairies who visit Malin come from the south. Because of the way I was raised, I do not consider myself one of them."

"You should not, as you are not. You are Isleighahan. Take off your shirt." The king snapped his fingers in command.

Charlie looked at Hugh. His brother gave him a do-as-royalty-tells-you look. Reluctantly, Charlie lifted his shirt and drew it over his head.

"Open your wings," the king said with a gesture.

*What is this? How will this help Jane?*

Feeling he had no choice, Charlie spread his wings to their full extent. Except for Jane, it had been a long time since he'd let anyone see his appendages. He watched Hugh's eyes grow wide in amazement.

"Magnificent," Tuniesin said, rising from his chair to inspect Charlie's wings. "The color is true, the pattern is Largare's."

*Largare? Of whom did he speak?*

The king sat down and addressed Charlie. "Did your father not teach you of his heritage?"

Charlie knew he did not speak of Owen Tanner. The sinking feeling spread in his gut. The truth lay around the corner. "My father . . . my elf father . . ." The strangeness of the words tangled his tongue. "Died in the Malin Forest when I was an infant."

"But surely your mother's family—"

Charlie interrupted him. "Unknown, sire."

"This is not right." Annoyance darkened Tuniesin's

voice. He looked at Rasleigh on his left. "Has no one known all this time? Are we so isolated?"

"Sire," Rasleigh said, "it was thought the babe arrived."

"Does he not live and work in Sylthia, for Garmade?"

Charlie felt a shortness of breath. They inched closer to the truth he didn't want to hear. A vision of Jane came to him, riding on the backs of sandobbles, in the clutches of a madman. Helpless. Well, as helpless as Jane could be. The time had come to stop this and get the aid he needed. His temper rose.

"Your majesty," he said, breaking into the conversation. "How many Whelphites of my age and gender are there in Malin? Of Malinese and Isleighahan mix? Only I. If confirming I am the babe of whom you speak aids in the search for the woman I love . . ." He paused to take a deep breath. "You must tell me."

Tuniesin studied him, looking for something in his face. He nodded. "Very well. It is confirmed. I tell you so you will know of whom you are descended. Your father was Largare, from a well-respected family of long lineage. Thirty years ago, he rescued your mother, an Elf, from a goblin prison. He brought her here, ill and frail. Later, they married and you were born. She did not survive the birth."

Charlie felt his mouth go dry. Twenty-seven years of denial, and if not for Jane he'd still be in ignorance. He took the last step necessary.

"Name her."

"Elaine, daughter of Garmade of Malin."

# Chapter Twenty-Four

*The trouble with bringing the rain,* Jane thought, *is that you're perpetually wet.* She glanced at the thundercloud glowering above her. So far, she'd failed in her experiment to wash away the sandobbles. The same with commanding the wind to blow them into oblivion. Whatever power she'd held over the elements had almost disappeared since she'd extinguished Hugh's house fire and cooled herself on the trip to the Magwrosin almost three weeks before. Her brilliant idea of diluting her captors resulted in perpetual mist that trickled down from an ugly storm cloud.

Her efforts hadn't done much harm to the sandobbles, but she had slowed their progress. After her abduction, she and Capp'ear had been carried down the north escarpment of the Andair Mountains. Her captors converged into a liquid vehicle, rolling like a fluid Sherman tank over everything in their path. They followed the north branch of the Fendi, called the Ilian, past the waterfalls where her boat had crashed.

At first, she'd ridden on the malleable shoulders of the sandobbles. When she tried to roll away to freedom, they pushed her to their center. Only after she'd had time to get over the shock of her capture did she think to bring the rain and wind down on them. With less than favorable results.

The sandobbles dropped her and retreated to a safe distance. Their pace slowed. She splashed forward, wet clothes and sopping shoes, in the middle of a one-woman, pitiful, not-quite-a-thunderstorm.

*What I do for you, Charlie*, she thought. *You and this cursed land of yours.*

She endured throughout the day as they hugged the eastern shore of the Ilian, walking miles out of their way. Jane knew they didn't cross it because Capp'ear wanted to protect his minions from dilution. Even the small streams that fed into it delayed them as they looked for the shallowest crossing.

Her basic knowledge of Lowth's geography came from going over Hugh's maps with him each night, tracing the route he'd plotted, asking questions. It had given her a sense of the scope of the land. North of the river, except for a green area blocked out as Isleighah, the land was uninhabited.

With little wonder, she thought. Elves and dwarves preferred high ground next to the sea, with tall trees at their backs. The Andair Plains offered none of that, only low hills and troughs of undulating grass as far as the eye could see.

Capp'ear called a halt as dusk approached. Mumbling to himself, he didn't seem to notice their lack of progress or the odd storm cloud that followed their journey.

"That's enough," Jane said to Lowth, certain they'd stopped for the night. The drizzle extinguished itself.

Jane stood in the middle of her captors, water dripping off her hair and back. She took a step forward, her feet wet, foot rot no doubt moments away. In answer, the sandobbles shifted perceptibly as they adjusted to new parameters. If she hadn't felt so exhausted, it would have been funny.

The smell of freshly washed grasses drifted to her. Clean and pungent, it rose from waist-high spears that surged forward to the horizon. It reminded her of the sharp scent of the geraniums on her mother's front porch.

*Mom! Did you survive the attack?* Jane wondered for the hundredth time that day. What of Muttle and Tivat? Her heart sank into her chest. She'd traveled slowly, but many miles had passed from where she'd last seen them, lying unconscious on the ground. Had the sandobbles killed them?

*Muttle*, she cried, sending out a distress signal. Only the post-dusk wind answered.

A contingent from the rear of the pack came forward and dumped a pile of firewood at Capp'ear's feet. He snatched the driest pieces and arranged them in a pyramid on the flat ground. One of the creatures covered it, not smothering, but puffing up like a mud-encrusted parachute to shield it from the wind. Capp'ear reached into a pocket and pulled out a flint rock. In moments, the kindling sparked.

*Holy Boy Scouts, Batman!* Jane watched as the blaze grew. The flint rock looked suspiciously like the one Eagar used. Had it been stolen from him as the creatures withdrew from his body?

"Are you hungry?" Capp'ear asked.

"Hmmm? What?" Breakfast had been smoked fish, lunch a freeze-dried culinary delight Tivat had mixed together. "I could do with dinner." Though what it might be, she had no idea. As far as she knew, they had no weapons or tools.

Capp'ear whistled. One of the sandobbles approached. In mud appendages that resembled arms, it carried Tivat's backpack. Her captor ripped it open and pulled out an assortment of prepackaged dinners. He handed one to Jane.

Freeze-Dried Chicken Stew. She flipped it over to look at the ingredients. Potatoes, cooked chicken (chicken meat, mechanically separated chicken), carrots, peas— Wait! Mechanically separated chicken? Visions of a Rube Goldberg, Wile E. Coyote contraption sprang to mind. She shuddered at the mental illness of the engineer who had designed *that* device.

"You mix it with hot water," she said, reading the directions in the dim light. As much as she'd have liked Capp'ear to choke on dehydrated food, the packet served two, and she wanted hers hot and nonlethal.

He dug around in the bag and pulled out a saucepan and passed it to his minions. In bucket brigade fashion, it traveled down to the Ilian, returning filled with water. A few minutes on top of the fire and Jane took the container and mixed a portion of the hot liquid with the food. Squishing the bag, she set it before her to wait the required ten minutes.

"When did you take this?" she asked.

He shrugged. "My friends have many talents."

"That's something I've been meaning to ask," she said, and sat down. "The last time I knew, you'd escaped a sure death in the Magwrosin. Then you show up on the cliff with an army in tow, all under your command. What's up with that?"

He joined her on the ground, a safe distance away but still creepy in appearance. His clothes remained shredded, dirty, and bloodied, and he smelled of a mixture of rotting garbage and dead animals. Jane scooted around the campfire to sit upwind. She didn't know where she stood with him. He'd tried to kill her three times. She'd pressed her luck once too often.

"They admire me," he said. "Few have survived the swamp. I'm their hero."

*Hero. Uh-huh. You're as much a hero as Mr. Magoo.* "That's

nice," she said, trying not to sound too patronizing. "Where are we headed?" *In case Muttle isn't dead, and I can send him a message.* Or Charlie. She hadn't been able to contact him, either. Did distance dilute their telepathy? Had he been hurt in the attack?

"To their homeland." Capp'ear nodded to the nearest group of sandobbles. "On the shores of the Tahmdee. They've been separated from it for over fifty years. They were brought to the Magwrosin against their will and imprisoned. As I was. They only want to go home."

"I understand, Toto. Don't we all?" She fingered the food pouch, then opened it. Using a utensil from the camping paraphernalia, she scooped half of it into the saucepan. Handing it to Capp'ear, Jane sat back and tried to eat her meal.

"How come they kill people, then, if they're peaceful?"

Capp'ear swallowed a bite of the concoction. "They will be peaceful once they return home. Wouldn't you fight to get back to where you belong?"

Jane leaned forward, her interest in her dinner lessened. "I've been fighting for six weeks, but I don't go around smothering people."

"Add fifty more years to your quest," he said softly. "You did agree to go to Malik in order to win your freedom."

She put her food down. "I had little choice in that decision, though I still think it holds the key." Tivat's reappearance meant a change in her role, but without Eagar's ruling she was stuck in limbo. "I'm not going to Malik, am I? Why did you take me hostage? Are you going to kill me?"

*Smart, Jane. Bring up the subject you've been dancing around all day,* she thought, regretting her words.

"Kill you? No, no, you misunderstand. I mean you no harm. We only wish for you to go with us to the Tahmdee."

Jane took a deep breath. "I'll regret asking. Why?"

He glanced at her. "You are to rule as their queen."

*Ew.* She tried not to show revulsion on her face or lose what little bit of supper she'd swallowed. "And you?" *Please don't say king. Please, please don't say king.*

"I am your subject as well."

"What?" Of all the answers she'd expected, this one shocked her the most. "Wanna run that by me again?"

He dipped his head in acquiescence. "You saved my life yesterday. For that I am in your debt."

Jane held out her hand to keep him at bay, then snatched it back, afraid he'd try to kiss it or something. "That . . . that's okay. You're welcome and all that. Why don't we call it even and go our separate ways?"

He looked crestfallen. "But I did great harm to you," he said, moving closer to her. "Three times I tried to take your life, yet you had the compassion to save mine."

Jane stood up, angered. "You'd drowned, for God's sake. I had to do something."

"Eagar said you gave me your own breath."

*Ew, again.* What goody-two-shoes motive had prompted her to do *that?*

"I erred," Capp'ear said, scrambling on his knees to bow before her. His voice was solemn. "The magic in you was hidden from me. I see now that you arrived for a purpose."

"I don't want to be a queen!" Jane scuttled away from him. The sandobbles moved in.

"My lady, you have no choice," he said firmly.

They stared at each other, a test of wills.

*We'll see. If I can change a stubborn lawyer, I can change you.* She'd have him thinking differently in no time.

Later, settled in a bed of fragrant grass, she faced south. By the shadows against the sky from the waxing moons, she saw where the Andair Mountains lay. It comforted her to know that Charlie might be looking at the same sky. This was the longest she'd been separated from him since coming to Lowth. She ached to feel his arms around her again.

*Soon*, she thought. *I'm here, my love. Second star to the right, straight on 'til morning.*

At breakfast, she passed on the freeze dried precooked eggs with bacon, the thought of ingesting them turning her stomach. Instead, she grabbed a couple of granola bars. The coffee boiled over, but it was hot and strong, waking her up to prepare her for the day's activity—stalling.

Except that Lowth finally decided to get into the act and put a damper on Capp'ear's plans. The rumble of thunder from the mountains reached her as she woke. Dark clouds gathered over their far-off peaks, and she saw flashes of lightning.

They packed their meager possessions and Capp'ear extinguished the fire. Jane noticed with interest that the sandobbles stood back from the flames. *Pottery in the making?* She stored the information away for later.

By midmorning, they reached the next stream to spill into the Ilian. It surged forward, swollen with rainwater, overflowing its banks. The sandobbles minced around it, retreating from the swift current.

Jane stood with her hands on her hips, her gaze on the stationary storm over the mountains. Had she caused it, some latent backwash from yesterday? But no, Lowth had answered when she called, albeit weakly. Her still-damp shoes could testify to that. It must be operating on its own, delaying their passage north. Its actions verified her theory that Lowth was a living entity and knew of her presence. And had plans.

*I'll play along.* It felt creepy but comforting that she'd escaped serious injury so far because she had a benevolent planet watching out for her.

"Are we crossing here?" she asked Capp'ear.

He shook his head. "No, we must go upstream." He looked resigned to the delay.

They turned east. Within an hour, they met a smaller

creek joining the first. They couldn't ford it either and curved south. So lay their journey the rest of the day, spiraling east and south, as if Lowth had chosen this place to make a stand.

Jane fell asleep the second night of her captivity within sight of the borders of Isleighah.


"No!" Charlie cried, all other words stuck in his throat. He stumbled backward until his knees hit a bench. He sank onto it and looked from King Tuniesin to Rasleigh. "There must be some mistake. She couldn't be my mother!"

"The Elf in you is pure, descended from generations of Malinese royalty," the king clarified.

"No," Charlie said again, shaking his head. "I do not accept it."

Rasleigh stood, his posture defensive, his hand on his knife hilt. "You question your monarch?"

"No, no, I did not mean— My monarch?" Events moved too quickly to assimilate.

"You are descended from generations of the Leander family." Tuniesin said, an edge to his voice. "As such, you owe allegiance to me—though, in truth, we are equals." He smiled to soften his words. When Charlie did not respond, he added, "One day, you will be king as well."

King! He hadn't had time to think of the possibility.

"If we had known that you remained unaware," the king said, "we would have made contact earlier. As it was, we respected Largare's wish to explain your existence. We did not know of his death until much later, after you had started to work for King Garmade and lived under his protection."

Charlie took a deep breath. "Parts of your story puzzle me." He waited for the other man to nod before he continued. He did not want any more miscommunications. "Why didn't King Garmade"—*Grandfather,* he thought in shock—"know of his daughter's—my mother's-presence here?"

Tuniesin hesitated. He and Rasleigh exchanged a meaningful glance. The monarch nodded his head and turned back to Charlie.

"When Largare rescued Elaine from the goblin prisons, she'd suffered much. They . . . broke her. She knew little but her first name. We did not connect her with the king's daughter. We did not know of the princess Elaine's disappearance. We are a reclusive community. Sometimes too reclusive.

"Her health remained delicate. Largare stayed at her side constantly and, after a time, they married. It was as she expected you that her memory strengthened even as her physical health weakened. She made Largare promise to take you to Malin, to have you introduced to the court and officially named. I think she knew she would not survive your birth."

Charlie sighed. All his life he, as most Malinese, had heard stories of princess Elaine. He'd never connected her with his unknown mother. In some dusty corner of his mind he'd occasionally wondered if he'd ever meet the woman who'd given birth to him. Not to disrespect Claire Tanner, whom he loved, but a niggle of curiosity remained.

"What of the servants?" he asked. "Largare did not travel all the way to Malin without at least a nurse."

"He had a nurse, and two other servants as well. They did not return after the journey ended. It was thought they stayed in Sylthia. We did not know their fate until later, when the nurse returned for a visit.

"It seems a love triangle developed between the servants. One of the men killed the other and ran away with the nurse. Largare journeyed alone with you.

"I apologize," King Tuniesin said. "We do not travel often. The care of Isleighah and Kerreleigh take up our time and resources. The Dymynsh has crippled the planet. It's all we can do to hold it back. However, that is no excuse. We should have paid more attention to our own. For that, we owe you much."

He rose, and to Charlie's astonishment, closed the few steps between them and knelt at his feet. "Welcome home, Charles, Prince of Sylthia, Earl of Leander, heir to Malin, future ruler of the Elves."

"Do not call me so," Charlie said. "I don't feel comfortable with the titles. Or the honor." He helped the other man to his feet. They stood face-to-face.

"It will take some getting used to," Tuniesin said, a smile on his lips. "I imagine you will want to tell your grandfather before it becomes common knowledge." He glanced around at the others in the room. "I will swear to the discretion of those here. Because of the markings and color of your wings, you will be known only as a kinsman of the Leander family."

"Then, as a kinsman, I ask for your assistance." Charlie hadn't forgotten Jane and her plight.

"Ah, yes. Bryant's daughter and your . . . ?" Tuniesin sat back in his chair.

Charlie was not offended by his inquiry. "My love," he answered. "I have never loved a woman thus, even though she causes trouble wherever she goes."

The king laughed, his teeth white and even. "The queen is much the same. If your Jane is anything like Wellonna, we will be needed to pick up the pieces of the sandobbles and this Capp'ear person."

Charlie nodded. "You hit closer to the mark than you might think, sire. I have a plan that will do almost exactly that."

Later, alone with Hugh, Charlie paced the floor of his room. After a promise of help from the king and an early morning start, the brothers had retired for the night.

"Well, sire." Hugh chuckled. "I did not expect such a story when I picked you out of the brambles so many years ago."

"Perhaps you would have picked a better name if you had," Charlie scoffed. "King Charlie! Ha! A very unnoble name."

Hugh cocked his head. "It suits you. You will make a fine king. And what of me? Am I now your squire? How may I serve Your Majesty?" He lowered himself in an exaggerated bow.

Charlie threw a pillow at him. "I did not ask for this and can hardly believe it is true. How would you react if you were told such news?"

Hugh arrayed himself over a plush chair. "I would order up pretty girls by the dozen and ride fast horses." He waggled his eyebrows. "Or perhaps the other way around."

A second pillow joined the first. "You are happily married now, and would not be unfaithful to Mara."

His brother nodded. "You know me well, Charles, future king of Malin. You will not change, either. Jane will love you in spite of your title."

Charlie spun around, anger in his voice. "Do not jest. I am worried for her. If she survives . . ." He stopped and drew a breath, pushing away the ugly images his mind had created in the past two days. He hadn't had a chance to apologize to her after their fight. Guilt ate at him. "This will change what I have with Jane. I had little to offer her before. Now? A kingdom. She will run from the responsibility. *I* want to run from the responsibility." He thrust his hand through his hair in agitation. "With Tivat alive, her sentence is void. She will want to return to Earth as soon as we can find the portal." The news of Tivat and Marion arriving in Lowth at a spot other than near the Sentinel shocked him. "I cannot follow her and live on Earth."

Hugh rose and clapped a hand on his brother's shoulder. "That is a discussion you will need to have with her, isn't it? I do not see either of you shirking your duties. As for the portal, we elves can sense its fluctuations. We will find it for her to use, if she still wishes, which I doubt. In regard to her well-being, you still feel her, do you not?"

Charlie bent his head. The admission came hard. "It grows weaker." The vibrations in his wings that acted as a compass toward Jane lessened with each hour. What would he do without her? How could he let her go?

"Ah, then let me tell you what I know," Hugh began.

A tap on the door interrupted him. Charlie crossed and opened it, letting in Bryant. Putting aside his problems, he asked, "How are the others?"

"Fair," the older man replied. He looked around the suite.

Charlie remembered his manners. If either mother could see him, they'd have boxed his ears for rudeness. "Will you have a drink?" At the other's nod, he crossed to the small bar and poured three glasses of vestale. They sat.

"Tivat is the healthiest," Bryant replied, swallowing the liquid as if a man parched. "He waits in self-imposed isolation until Eagar can convene a trial for his crimes. Eagar is weak, but awake. The doctors say he will recover with bed rest."

"And Muttle?" Charlie asked. The Belwaith's injuries had shocked him the most.

"Muttle drifts in and out of consciousness. When I visited, he said, 'Sixth stream.' I don't know what it means."

Hugh shifted in his chair. "I might."

"Marion," Bryant continued, then broke down, unable to hide his worry. "She is the worst. The doctors—"

"Will do their best. Isleighah has magic. This is the best place for her," Charlie reassured him. He placed a comforting hand on the hunter's shoulder. He could see the man still cared deeply for the mortal.

After a few moments, Bryant composed himself. "Yes, I know this is true. If we had stayed on the cliffs—"

"You forced me to make the decision to come here." Good or bad, Charlie knew he'd been unable to avoid his heritage.

"We must hope for the best," Bryant said. "However, I come tonight to offer my help in the morning. I've heard you ride out to save my daughter. I would like to accompany you."

Charlie hadn't known how to ask the hunter to leave with them. He played a part in the plan, yet tearing him from Marion's side might be difficult.

"Good. We've great need of you." Charlie turned to Hugh. "What did you mean, a few moments ago? What do you know?"

"There is unusual weather to the west," his brother replied. Briefly, he explained to Bryant his talent for forecasting the weather. "A storm rages in the mountains, but it doesn't move. It's associated with Jane. Either she controls it, or it's done for her benefit. Muttle's words of the sixth stream give more clues. The sixth stream that flows into the Ilian has many inlets. I believe she is near its banks. The storm is centered in an area that feeds its streams. It has flooded and the sandobbles cannot cross without washing away." He sat back, his wide grin evidence of his satisfaction.

Charlie stared at him in astonishment. He'd always taken Hugh's predictions as truth but had never looked into their intricacies. "You can feel all this?" he asked.

Hugh nodded. "Just as you will feel Jane's presence as we draw nearer. Between the two of us, we'll find her, wherever she's hidden."

Charlie's heart soared. He allowed hope to ignite in his breast. Tomorrow he would see her again.

He spent another hour explaining the plan to Bryant and refining it. It neared midnight when the three men separated. Charlie was about to extinguish his light and try to sleep when another knock on his door announced King Tuniesin.

"Only a moment of your time," the monarch said, waving away the other's bow. "I bring you a gift from the lady Wellonna. She is your kinswoman, by the way. She does not rise early, but wanted you to have this before we ride out." He presented Charlie with a white box.

Charlie took it to a nearby table and opened it. Inside, wrapped in muslin, lay a vestlike garment, lightweight, soft green in color. He lifted it by one corner.

"My gratitude," he said. "But what is it?"

Tuniesin grinned. "It is the Leander crest and colors. She felt pleased to find it at such short notice."

Looking closer, Charlie noticed fine, darker lines that resembled the markings in his wings. The color matched as well.

"What is this?" he asked again, noticing the two slits in the back. Trepidation made his voice deep.

"It is called a jouroke, traditional garb for you to wear when you fly into battle tomorrow."

*Fly?*

# Chapter Twenty-Five

Clear-eyed, his jaw firm with determination, Charlie sat astride his mount the next morning. Sleep had eluded him. The dark hours magnified the sudden complexity of his life. Twin responsibilities jockeyed for prominence and decisions.

In some ways, the alien concept of flying seemed the easiest choice. All he had to do was fall flat on his face, and no more pressure would be applied to try again. Running a kingdom, however, posed multiple problems, the least of which would be the reaction of Eagar and King Garmade.

Charlie struggled with the questions in the blackest part of the night—of the king's frail health and Eagar's ambition. Dare he present himself to them, claiming to be a long-lost heir? Dare he not, and deny his heritage, however unwelcome?

And Jane? *I've not told her of my feelings. How can I ask her to take on the responsibility of a kingdom? Yet I must. It would not feel right to delay telling her.*

He could no longer wish for days gone by, of routine and

sameness. They'd disappeared weeks ago. A new path was being forged, and he had a role as a leader. How many times had Jane said she felt like a player in a game controlled by others, even by Lowth itself? The same fate carried him as well.

Charlie rose from his bed that morning, all illusions and childish wishes swept away. He donned the gift of the jouroke, the lightness of its weave a heavy burden to wear.

The sky changed from gray to pearl to rose. The men and women of Isleighah gathered in Kerreleigh's outer courtyard. All wore jourokes of various colors indicating their family lines. Charlie watched with a new interest. A similar group waited in Malin for his eventual rule. Could he do it?

*It depends on Jane. Everything depends on Jane.* Without her at his side, he didn't want to exist, let alone rule a kingdom. Even as the thought formed, he knew he had no choice.

A murmur washed over the crowd. They parted to clear a path for King Tuniesin, Lord Rasleigh and the small group of royalty accompanying the rescue party.

King Tuniesin smiled as he approached, his green eyes snapping like the banners that hung from the boughs of Kerreleigh.

"Well met, Charles Whelphite, kinsman of Queen Wellonna," he said, his voice raised for the crowd's benefit. He looked over them, satisfaction playing on his lips. "It is a good day to hunt sandobbles."

A roar of appreciation rose in the soft air. Even the leaves of Isleighah nodded in agreement.

"Are you ready, kinsman?" Tuniesin asked.

"I am, sire," Charlie replied. "A great debt is owed to the citizens of Isleighah for the aid you give us this day." Charlie turned in his seat and indicated his companions, travelers on a long road with him. "I bring my brother, Hugh Tanner of Malin, Alfted, a marksman of Sylthia, and the hunter Bryant of Malik, father to the captive." A feeling of pride swelled in him. Their number might be small, but they'd survived many adventures together.

"And I, Eagar Currge of Sylthia," said a weak voice.

Charlie swiveled on his mount. He gazed at the steward, who stood in an archway to the courtyard. One hand gripped the stone for support, the other dangled a cane, as if he disdained relying on it. Dressed in his habitual black, Eagar struggled to hold himself erect. He took a tentative step forward.

"Good King Tuniesin," he said, bowing to the monarch. "I beg your forgiveness for my sorry appearance. As you must be aware, I have been in my sickbed. I arise to accompany you, if it is your wish. The Earthwoman remains my responsibility."

Charlie bristled at his words. *King Garmade gave her to Muttle and me to watch. Anyway, with Tivat alive, she is no longer a prisoner.* He ached to shout his newfound identity, to lay claim to the power that would free Jane.

King Tuniesin bowed to Eagar. "Join us, Eagar Currge of Sylthia," he said, holding out his hand. "You are most welcome in this historic hunt. Today we not only free the Earthwoman, but also our world of the dreadful scourge of the sandobbles. Residents of Lowth will rejoice."

Someone in the crowd shouted. Soon others joined, an excited buzz swelling through their ranks.

Eagar shuffled to the monarch's side and stiffly bowed. A page ran to fetch a new mount, delaying the hunt. A groomsman brought a pony and assisted the steward into its saddle.

A half hour after sunrise, a party of one hundred and sixty Isleighahans, a Malik hunter, and four determined Malinese set out to find Jane.

They headed due west on trails that did not show before they reached them and blended into the forest once they passed. A blushing gray tinted the sky and shaded darker as they drew nearer to the storm. The wind stirred the previous autumn's leaves, twirling them in patterns among those who flew. All around him, Charlie could feel the magic of the old woods.

Enchantment lay everywhere, but the music enthralled him the most. Rhythmic tinkles and splashes as the Isleighahans forded streams, melodies coaxed from the trees—the trill of the willows, the rumbling bass of the oaks. The fairies harmonized. Those on the ground and in the air sang.

They set out to win a victory, and the songs echoed their hope. Ancient words filled the air, words of triumph and pride, of valiant deeds and honor, of death hard-won. He joined them, a clear tenor woven among the other voices, the verses and their meanings, once unknown, coming from him as if he'd read them only this morning.

Charlie recalled the tales of Princess Elaine, of how she'd loved to sing. He wondered if her spirit lived on in the woods. Or in him.

After a time, they reached the edge of the Isleighah Forest, and the songs faded. How much time he could not tell, for the magic pulsed strong.

By unspoken agreement, they broke for a midday meal and to lay the last pieces of their strategy. King Tuniesin approached Charlie, who leaned against a tree eating bread and cheese.

"You did not fly," he chastised, waving away the other's attempt to stand.

"Sire, you store great confidence in my abilities. As I said last night, I am sadly out of practice. Even if I could support myself, I would tire in minutes."

The monarch gestured to the trees, where many of his subjects had landed to eat and rest. "You will have noticed that we do not stay aloft for long. Flying is tiring. Endurance is for the young and for warriors."

"We *are* warriors today," Charlie reminded him. He did

not like to think of the consequences if his plan did not work.

"You proudly wear the jouroke." Tuniesin nodded toward the garment. "I am surprised, after your protests."

"No more than I. But it is tradition, and though I have denied it for many years, I am of fairy blood. My kinswoman gave it as a gift. Perhaps she knows it may be needed before the day ends." He gazed past the forest edge, to the rolling plain and the gathered storm clouds. Somewhere close by, Jane waited for him. He itched to end this delay and run into the flowing grasses to see her again. Fly if he must. Nothing would separate them. *Except her decision to return to Earth.*

The king clapped him on the shoulder, startling him from his thoughts. "Do not let fear of others' ridicule sway you," he said. "We have flown since infancy and have more experience. Besides, if you choose to join us, it is an effortless thing to ride the air currents. Have you never flown?"

Charlie thought of his disastrous attempts with the Malin Village boys mocking him. "Fifteen years ago," he admitted.

"Ah, you were a lad then," the king said. "You are now a man and a future king. Though you are not to rule the fey, your participation will be the thing of which songs are made. Come, we must talk of your plan and put it into action."

They gathered, Tuniesin and Rasleigh, Bryant and others.

"The storm moves north," Hugh said, tracing an invisible path in the air from the mountains to the Andair Plains. "An unusual direction. Jane does not control it. I believe the land acts on its own." He paused and looked at the others, as if daring them to dispute his claim. "Her power is weaker than before. I cannot tell if she is hurt or hindered in some way." His gaze held his brother's. A silent communication passed between them. Charlie knew Hugh did not hold back any news.

"An isolated storm brews north of the main one," Hugh said. "It's small, unnatural. I'm certain Jane makes it." He swept his hand and pointed to a spot on the horizon about a mile distant. "There. That darker smudge. If you look close, you'll see it rains in fits and starts. She uses it to keep the sandobbles at bay."

Hope grew in Charlie's heart. Jane's dark smudge signified the first good thing of the day. Turning, he asked the king, "What do your scouts say?"

"Much the same," Tuniesin replied, stroking his chin. "A ring of sandobbles and an unusual cloud of rain. They cannot tell what lies inside."

*My Jane,* Charlie thought, pleased at her resourcefulness. "Are your warriors ready?" he asked Rasleigh, who nodded. At last they'd start. "Then we split, half to fly in from the south, using Lowth's storm as cover. Half from the east. Stay low. Bryant, can you direct the wind from here?"

The hunter gestured to the plains. "I'll pass on the king's offer to be flown to the scene. I can conjure a windstorm to take all the sandobbles to the Tahmdee."

Charlie grinned at his fervor. "Make sure you do not create so much that our friends are blown away as well. We need their wing power to dry out the creatures." His plan, from the moment they'd carried Jane away, had been to dehydrate the sandobbles. He'd noticed the trail they left—dried lumps that had fallen off the main group. With Bryant and the fairies working together, they would reduce the enemy to sand and rescue Jane.

Hugh raised his finger. "Perhaps," he said, "you might tell the lady in question to stop her storm. Otherwise, we will dry them out only to have her bring them back to life."

*That would be like her. Mayhem. The woman is nothing but mayhem.* Charlie wouldn't have had her any other way.

"It would be easier if Muttle were here," he said, missing the easy communication of the Belwaith.

"You can't talk to her?" Hugh asked.

Eagar, until then a quiet observer, spoke. "What's this?"

"They sometimes talk with their minds, as Muttle and Calme do," Hugh clarified.

Charlie shot him a look that should have spliced him open. He regretted he'd shared that information with him. Eagar didn't need to know everything.

"Is this true?" the steward asked, his eyes narrowed.

"Yes. Sometimes," Charlie hedged.

"Then you must use this talent," King Tuniesin ordered, "if it is to help in her rescue."

Charlie didn't want an audience when he had his first words with Jane. They'd not been speaking when Capp'ear tore her away. She might be mad and, as a woman, probably blamed him for the kidnapping. But better to incur her wrath than have the plan fail.

He nodded and stepped away. His gaze centered on the cloud in the distance. Closing his eyes, he cleared his mind of outside distractions, of the wind and the murmur of voices. Only Jane. Her green eyes and soft skin. Her talent for finding mischief. The way she felt against him.

As if on cue, a slow vibration hummed through his wings. He turned a fraction to the north and sent his message.

*Jane.* In his mind's eye, he watched the word pierce the air, reaching her as surely as an arrow.

*Charlie?* She hesitated with her answer. She sounded different, weaker. Discouraged. *Where are you?*

*Near.*

*My mother?*

*She recovers.* He did not want to delve into the details of Marion's illness. *Love, we come for you. Stop the storm.*

*Love?*

He broke off the communication, afraid to say more.

Time for that later. Impatient, he whirled back to the others.

"Let's go," he said.

The fairies divided into two groups, Tuniesin leading one, Rasleigh the other. Charlie's wings thrummed in anticipation, an excitement filling him. Overpowering, insistent, he couldn't control the primitive urge. And suddenly he didn't want to. With a shout, he vaulted into the air. The ground rushed away at an alarming speed, but he paid little attention to it. He focused on the vanishing cloud over Jane's location.

He maneuvered as easily as if walking, but stayed in formation with the others, resisting the temptation to swoop and circle. The muscles on his back stretched, a good, tight feeling. His wings beat down and up, making minute corrections in flight.

They arrived, and he faltered in his effort to backwing. Tuniesin caught him by the elbow and steadied his position. Charlie shot him a look of gratitude and stabilized himself.

Glancing down, he saw a dark ring of earth surge and roil toward two figures—sandobbles revolving around Jane and Capp'ear. A wet, sucking noise, a menacing burble, rumbled from its midst.

*We are here.* Charlie cast his thoughts down to her.

At a signal from the king, the Isleighahans stroked the air harder. A great wave of wind swirled, eddied and grew. Another force joined in, a natural current, strengthened by Bryant's talent. It intensified. With a shock, Charlie recognized Jane's touch, though it was weaker than he expected. *Good work.*

The fury continued, the combined efforts of the elves and fairies entwining to create a tempest of unusual proportions. The sandobbles clung together, but the gale hurled bits and pieces from the outer edges into the plain. Their dark color fluctuated, lightening as they evaporated.

In a frenzy, some of the beings flung themselves into a nearby stream, acting as a wick to carry moisture to the others.

Rasleigh's group wedged the sandobbles away from their water supply. The fairies stroked on. A heat rose from Lowth. Capp'ear, shrieking like a madman in the teeth of the storm, threw himself between the creatures. Then, as they shriveled in size, detaching from each other, he spun toward Jane.

The glint of metal spurred Charlie. Memories of the man's previous attack propelled him from Tuniesin's faction. He dove.

Jane stood in the midst of the destruction, her hand shading her sight, gazing upward. The forces Bryant and the Isleighahans made twisted around her, but she stayed unmoved, in the eye of the storm. Adjusting for shifts in air pressure, Charlie plunged through the turmoil and snatched her up in his arms.

They broke through the fury into the relative calm of the surrounding plain. His wings beating rhythmically, Charlie tacked toward the forest. Selecting a spot at a distance from Hugh and the others, he backwinged and landed.

Jane, whole and healthy and gloriously in his arms again, threw back her head and grinned at him.

"Look, up in the sky. Is it a bird? Is it a plane? No, it's Charlie Whelphite," she cried. Her laughter edged toward hysteria.

"Are you well? Did they hurt you?" Charlie did not want to release her, even to let her stand.

"No, nothing like that. They made me their queen," she hiccupped. Panic scurried through her voice.

"Their queen?" Only Jane could be kidnapped by sandobbles and end up their leader. "I'll make you a queen," he said, promising her his heritage.

"Will you? With a big, fat tiara and a velvet robe—"

"Jane," he warned. "Have I ever told you that you talk too much?"

She looked at him, a little sobered. "Yes, Charlie."

He shifted her closer. "Then shut up and kiss me."

Charlie kissed her long and sweet, unable to let go, but unwilling to tell her his true feelings. He murmured her name over again and breathed in her scent.

"You smell like rain," he whispered.

Jane tilted her head and traced the side of his jaw. "You would, too, if you'd spent three days in a storm."

"It slowed them. Hugh was able to spot you because of the weather you and Lowth created." He'd never felt so proud of her as he did at that moment.

"Me? And Lowth?"

"So he says." He nibbled on her ear, noticing its points' infinitesimal growth since last he'd nuzzled it.

Jane pulled away slightly, leaving her hand on his chest. "Ah, Charlie, there's a fairy guy staring at us."

He shifted her to the side. Over her shoulder, he saw Tuniesin grinning at them.

"Not just any fairy. This is their king." He made the introductions.

"All is well?" Charlie asked, remembering the battle.

"The prisoner Capp'ear escaped, carried away by the last of the sandobbles," Tuniesin said. "Most perished, sacrificing themselves to jump the stream with him on their backs. They headed north. Eagar said to let them go."

Shock ran through Charlie. "Eagar said?"

The monarch shrugged. "Capp'ear was the steward's prisoner. I have no authority beyond our forest."

Anger flooded Charlie. Letting Capp'ear escape opened the opportunity for him to hurt Jane again. "Yet you stepped beyond the forest today," he said to the fairy king.

Tuniesin's eyes narrowed. Charlie guessed he rarely had his decisions challenged.

Jane placed herself between them. "The sandobbles will take him to the Tahmdee. It's their home."

"How do you know this?" Tuniesin asked.

"They told Capp'ear. They've been imprisoned in the Magwrosin against their will. I think if they're allowed to return to their river, they'll leave everyone alone."

Charlie cocked an eyebrow at Tuniesin, challenging him.

The other returned the stare. "We'll speak of it at Council later."

Jane sagged against Charlie. He could see the fatigue in her eyes. "Charlie, are we near the castle? I'd like to see my mother."

He put aside his anger. She needed to rest and recover. Everything else could wait. Picking her up in his arms, he joined the Isleighahans in flight back to Kerreleigh.

As soon as she entered the forest stronghold, Jane disappeared into the healing rooms. Charlie did not seek her out, but spent the next few hours in meetings. King Tuniesin, with a weakened Eagar seconding the suggestion, recommended that a guard observe what remained of the sandobbles. If they rehydrated and headed toward the Tahmdee, they should be left alone. However, if they posed any further threat, they would have to be dried again and scattered in a remote corner of Lowth.

Eagar, on the verge of collapse, retired to his suite. Charlie and Hugh joined Bryant and Alfted in the healing rooms.

"How are they?" Charlie asked, indicating the two guards hurt in the explosion.

Alfted answered. The men had been under his command. "Broken bones and bruises, mostly. The fairies have offered to let us stay until they recover."

Charlie nodded. He expected to remain in Kerreleigh for some time and convince Jane to become his queen.

"Muttle has improved since yesterday," Hugh reported.

The Belwaith looked healthier, his eyes whirling blue and green, only a hint of yellow in their depths. "Death for damn sandobbles," he said, grinning.

Charlie knelt at his side. "Sorry you couldn't be there, friend. You would have enjoyed the hunt."

"Carve them up." He made a twisting motion with his hand.

"I'm glad you're feeling better."

Muttle nodded. "Speak with Calme. Many messages. One for ye." He pointed to Hugh.

The brothers parted, and Charlie slipped into Marion's room, looking for Jane. Bryant sat next to the bed.

"I took her to her room," he said, answering Charlie's unspoken question. "She's more exhausted than she let on."

"I know. She's gone through much the past few days."

"More like the past few weeks," the hunter said. "Kidnapping and almost being drowned. She still hasn't recovered from the stabbing. She's going to push herself to take care of Marion." He indicated the woman in the bed.

"How is she?" Charlie asked, pulling up another chair. Jane's mother looked less sallow than when he'd last seen her.

"The fairies tell me she'll recover. I'm going to make sure she does." Bryant stroked Marion's arm. "I love her, and I lost her once. It's not about to happen again. I'm going to ask her to marry me when she's better."

His confession didn't shock Charlie. He'd seen how the hunter looked at Marion, knew his devotion to her since her illness. Still, he needed to voice caution. "You haven't had a chance to talk since she's been back."

"Who needs words, when your heart speaks for you?" the other whispered, his gaze not straying.

Charlie decided to be candid with Bryant. "I need to speak with Jane." He hesitated. "I don't know what her heart says."

"I can guess her answer, but she has a difficult decision to make. She gives up many things to stay here."

"It will be more difficult when I tell her my news," Charlie muttered.

Bryant looked up. "News?"

"I'm sorry, I cannot say more. Just that, because of this journey, I'm no longer a mere lawyer." Or a mere Elf.

"Because you have fairy blood?" the other asked.

Charlie didn't want tell him the truth yet. It belonged to Jane first. "Yes, I have a heritage here from a powerful family. I don't know what her thoughts will be on it, or what she thinks of my loving her." Her path was open now. Would she take the simplest way out and return to Earth?

"Give her a day or two to rest and assure herself of her mother's better health," Bryant advised. "Then ask. I know I've been absent from her life, but for what it's worth, you have my blessing."

Though it killed him, Charlie stayed away from Jane the next day, and the one following, until he heard that Marion had regained consciousness and rested well.

Hugh brought other news, relayed from Calme to Muttle. Mara and many women in the village were pregnant, having conceived on Midsummer's Eve. A thought struck Charlie, squashed in with other realities—his waiting kingdom, the crush of his feelings, the force and power of their lovemaking that night. Could Jane be pregnant as well? He left in search of her.

# Chapter Twenty-Six

*Jane.*

Charlie's voice resonated through her mind. He hadn't spoken to her telepathically since her rescue.

*Charlie?* she asked, tentative in her response. *I'm in the solarium.*

Temporarily banished from her mother's side—for her own good, Bryant said—Jane explored Kerreleigh's halls. That morning she'd found the solarium, jutting out from the fourth level on the south side. One flawless pane of glass enclosed it from the elements. The floor consisted of colored stones laid in an intricate knotted pattern. Comfortable benches huddled under vast sprays of foliage. Butterflies flitted past.

Jane sat on one of the benches and waited for Charlie. In truth, she'd avoided him the past three days. Fatigue and worry for her mother took most of her time. She'd used those excuses to delay making any decisions about the future.

*And here it is, staring you in the face.* She closed her eyes, her hand drifting to lie in a protective gesture over her womb. She could no longer deny the truth. Her loss of appetite, the queasiness she experienced that couldn't be attributed to the smell of Capp'ear's unwashed body or a vacuum-packed meal: it all pointed to an unexpected pregnancy.

She carried a child. Not from the time she and Charlie made love in the glade, but from Midsummer's Eve, when he'd taken her against the door. And fainted. Jane was convinced that his fainting had not been an accident. Most likely, he'd spent all his energy on releasing the winning sperm.

A child of destiny, contrived by Lowth to exist. How else could she explain all that had happened? The whispered call of "Anjinaine" in the courtyard during her trial? The coincidence of Tivat in front of her car, with Charlie and the others close behind to whisk her away? A planet's strategy to return her to the land of her conception? She lay at the heart of a master plan. She'd survive whatever trials came in the future, because, she now knew, you didn't mess around with Lowth.

*How do I tell you, Charlie? You are part of this, too, though I don't know how.*

She felt his presence before he spoke, and she opened her eyes.

"Hi," he said, his voice unsteady. Fatigue showed in the lines around his latte-colored eyes.

"Hi, yourself." Jane moved her hand from its traitorous position and patted the bench next to her. "Sit down."

He remained standing, keeping a distance from her. She sensed his awkwardness. Obviously, he had something on his mind. The end of their relationship now that she was no longer accused of murder? The thought stabbed at her more painfully than Capp'ear's knife had.

"Mom is better," she said, filling the silence. "The doctors expect her to make a full recovery. She should be able to travel within a week." *There's your opening.*

Ignoring it, he walked to the window. His hand pressed against its smoothness, his back to her, he said, "There are things we need to discuss, Jane."

Coming up behind him, she stopped a foot away, aching to reach out and touch the corded muscles in his neck, bunched from tension. His exposed wings lay against his back, tightly closed. The entrance of two fairies into the room prompted her to ask, "Should we go for a walk?"

He turned and nodded, agony on the planes of his face. He led her down stairs and through opulent rooms until they reached a door leading to the outside. Silently, they walked along a trail crisscrossed by patches of sunlight. Birch, rowan and pine mingled with the larger iselwood trees. After a mile or so, Jane heard the sound of water to her left. They abandoned the path and descended into a small ravine. A shallow pool lay before them; graduated waterfalls poured through fissures and tumbled over outcroppings of rock to fill it.

"Charlie, it's beautiful," Jane cried in awe.

"Bryant told me of it. He's visited here before and thought you might enjoy it." A sliver of tension fell from him.

"I do." She looked around, gauging the distance between trees, at the lack of undergrowth. Memories of another pond in another glade returned. "Are we safe?" she asked.

Charlie touched her arm in reassurance. "The forest watches over us. At last report, the danger was far to the west. Capp'ear can't hurt you anymore."

The heat from his hand traveled up her arm, suffusing her with warmth and longing. Slowly, they leaned toward each other. Jane parted her lips to speak. Charlie watched her, his expression softer. He raised his hand to outline her mouth with his fingertips. Jane sensed a change in the forest, a gentleness in the air. They heard the music of a distant song.

*Somebody needs to draw this guy a road map*, she thought at the delay. Their gazes met. "Charlie," she whispered.

"Shhh. Listen. The land sang to us when we came to rescue you." He drew intricate designs on her forearm with his fingers. "I always hear music around you." He bent his head and kissed her, his lips brushing hers at first, as if afraid to break the tentative peace. Then he groaned and pulled her nearer, one hand in the small of her back.

"I've missed you." His breath mingled with hers. "I'm sorry I made you angry."

Total body meltdown threatened. She whispered. "It doesn't matter anymore."

"Nothing matters except you and how I feel."

He kissed her again. Jane felt her toes curl in response. All coherent thought vanished, a wash of sensations threatening to drown her. When she came up for air, she laid her head against his shoulder and smiled into his dusky brown eyes.

He brushed a curl off her forehead. "I love you, Jane Drysdale," he said, his voice breaking.

Her heart *ka-chunk*ed in her chest. "Oh, Charlie."

"When this is over—"

"No, let's not talk of the future."

"Jane," he protested.

She placed a hand over his mouth. "It's not ours to command." Other forces interfered. "Who knows what tomorrow will bring? Love me for today."

Dark emotions shadowed his eyes. With a sigh of resignation, he nodded. His fingers traced along her arms, sending shivers cascading through her body. Heat crackled in her nerve endings. Charlie slid his palms across her breasts. The depth of sensuality she felt staggered her.

"Perfect," he breathed. He rolled her nipple between his thumb and forefinger.

"Too small," she said in an incoherent gurgle.

He looked her in the eyes, and a smile tugged at the corners of his mouth. "They're perfect," he breathed.

Jane wanted to lose herself in him. He nuzzled her earlobe, the throb of her pulse at the base of her throat. She reached behind him, fingers grazing the edge of his wing. Charlie groaned. She did it again, stroking this time. A shudder ran over him. He swung her into his arms, then lowered her into the sweet-smelling grasses at the edge of the pool.

He tasted of clean air and cinnamon. His tongue invaded her mouth, eager, insatiable. They kissed frantically. His fingers tugged her blouse free. The buzz of a nearby insect joined the murmur of rushing water. Jane expected the bees to send out scouts and report on their lovemaking. She imagined them coming back later to glean nectar from the flowers crushed under her and Charlie's bodies.

Charlie removed her blouse with a startling finesse. Giving a cry, he lowered his head to her breasts, laving first one tip, then another. She whimpered with wanting and frustration. His lips trailed down the center of her body, scorching wild kisses on a path from her mouth to her waistband. His fingers dipped below the fabric, then untied the knots and lacing. With a growl, he pulled off her skirt.

His hand rubbed through the thin fabric of her thong, the one piece of Earth clothing she still retained. He pushed it aside, his fingers seeking her swollen need. Jane cried out at the sheer ecstasy, afraid he'd push her over the edge.

*Two can play this game*, she thought, her head light from lack of air. She raised a hand and laid it against his chest, shoving his tunic out of her way, the sprinkle of chest hair rough against her skin. She gripped the frame of his wings with her other hand and traced the raised pattern.

"By the two moons," he exclaimed with a shudder.

"You like?"

"I'll show you how much." Barely touching her, he ran a finger across her bare stomach. Her muscles convulsed. Invisible flames combusted along the path he made.

"Don't," Jane cried, though she wanted more. She pushed away, the cool transparency of the waterfall calling to quench her fire. She slipped the remaining distance to the pond's edge, but Charlie caught her in a fierce embrace.

"I love you," he whispered.

"Oh, Charlie, I love you." She wanted to tell him about the baby, but couldn't bring herself to spoil the moment. Time for truths later, when rationality returned.

Jane leaned into him until they lost their balance. They fell into the water, performing an aquatic ballet, losing the rest of their clothing between snatched kisses. Charlie lifted her and strode halfway up the waterfalls. He laid her on a stone shelf behind a curtain of water in a hidden cave. The mist felt soft against her skin.

"Vixen." He covered her with his body, his erection teasing her with its nearness. His knee nudged her legs apart. She opened for him, eager for them to join.

Jane smiled in the muted light. "I bet you say that to all the Earthlings."

His mouth descended on hers. "Only one. You."

All thoughts of home, the baby, and her future flew away under his assault.

Jane gasped as he entered her. She arched her body and rocked her hips, changing the angle of his thrust. The tune from the waterfall changed, no longer bubbling but beating. Water fell in sheets, the force changing to match their rhythm.

Charlie drew his length out of her, then plunged in again. She thought she'd die from the sensation. A cry escaped her. Water ebbed and crested around them, a *From Here to Eternity* wave crash miles from the nearest sea.

Isleighah joined in their lovemaking, adding an accompaniment to sensation. Music and rhythms surrounded them and swept them away, each wave greater than the last. The light changed. Charlie bent over Jane, his gaze on her face, his eyes dusky, half closed. He feathered a hand across her jaw, and she turned toward him, nibbling at the flesh of his thumb.

Their bodies surged together, slipping in and out. The water around them rose and fell, the tide synchronized with their movements. A joyous noise engulfed them. Jane cried at the pleasure, her tears mingling to join the stream. Cymbals and drums beat in time, building, stretching toward a crescendo. A simultaneous release broke over them.

Farewell notes withdrew. The sounds in the cavern returned to the everyday rush of the waterfall. Light diffused to normal. The tide receded from the ledge.

Charlie lay at her side, his breathing hard and sharp.

"Did I imagine that?" she asked, her limbs weak. The faintest trace of enchantment shimmered in the air of the cave, like the afterglow of fireworks.

"It's the magic of Isleighah," Charlie said.

"Wow." She shook her head, unable to grasp the concept. "Wow. It's almost as much fun as flying with you."

He smiled and touched her face gently. "Maybe next time we can do both."

*What?* Startled, she sat up. "Superman? Do you really mean it? Flying sex?" The logistics boggled her mind. Charlie even *considering* it boggled her mind.

"I have fantasies," he said, pulling her into the crook of his arm. "I'm not any different than any other man."

"Yes, you are." She snuggled deeper. "You're better."

Sated, she drifted toward sleep. Music tinkled far off in the distance.

"Jane?" Charlie said after long minutes passed.

"Hmmm?" She wanted to lie quietly, undisturbed.

"Jane? We need to talk."

She rolled onto her back, unmindful of her naked form. "I hate those four words."

Once started, he hesitated.

"Charlie, what is it?" Alarm ran down her spine. She sat up, tucking her legs beneath her.

"Something happened while you were gone." He pulled the words out, as if reluctant to relive his experience.

"What?" She couldn't imagine anything to upset him so.

He sighed and looked away, through the sheen of water pouring over the ledge. "I learned of my heritage."

She leaned forward and touched his arm in excitement. "Charlie, that's wonderful. . . ." Only, by his behavior, he didn't seem to think so. "What's wrong?"

Jane listened while he told her of his first meeting with King Tuniesin. A cold, hard knot formed in her stomach. Now she knew his part in Lowth's plan, and that it wasn't over.

"I never dreamed any of this," she said when he'd finished. "What happens now?"

He shook his head, utter desolation on his face. "I don't know. Tell King Garmade? I couldn't ask you to share in any future without letting you know. Do you see?"

Jane nodded, her thoughts grim. She needed to change her plans again. Her head whirled with what had to be done.

"There's one more thing," he said, his tone solemn.

"What?" She could think of one hundred and seventy-two things.

"Muttle relayed news to Hugh that might affect our plans."

Cold chills crept up the insides of her arms. She forced herself to ask, "What?"

"Mara is pregnant, as well as most of the village women. Due to your influence, they say."

She felt the blood drain from her face. Dread at what he might ask overpowered her joy at the news. "Charlie, I didn't have anything to do with it. Maybe the Dymynsh is over."

"Broken by you?" His gaze pierced her to the core. "Jane, are you pregnant?"

She had no recourse but to lie. She looked him in the eyes and gathered all the deceit in her body. "No, I'm not."

How could she tell him the truth when she didn't have all the answers yet? Suspicions raced through her, a half-formed belief that Bryant had more importance to Malik that anyone thought. If her child bore the royal blood of Malin, why not that of Malik as well? The machinations of Lowth astounded her, plotting to unite two of its houses.

She had no proof. Not until she could get to Malik's capital of Shallen and question those who might have been present at Bryant's birth. All while dodging Blacwin.

Jane watched Charlie struggle to believe her.

"If there are heirs of my body, it is more significant now," he said, searching her face.

"Wouldn't I tell you?" She crossed her fingers.

"Would you?" he asked, angry. "What are your plans now that Tivat is alive?"

She couldn't tell him. So much depended on slipping away from Isleighah and finding her way to Malik. Without him, Muttle, or the entire flying population of Kerreleigh finding her. "To get my mother well," she bluffed.

"Then?"

She tilted her chin and met his gaze. "Have Eagar lift my sentence."

"Then? By the light, Jane, I want to have a future with you." He punched his hand into a puddle of water for emphasis.

"As Queen of Malin?" Her future role, and that of her unborn child, magnified. All the more reason to know the truth before telling him. He'd only stop her.

"I don't care about that aspect," he said.

"You should." He presented a perfect opportunity to pick a fight. She needed to divert his attention from speculation on her pregnancy. "Eagar and King Garmade need to know."

"It can wait."

"Damn if it can. For once in your life, don't be the mediator, the one who smoothes ruffled feathers. Fight for what's yours."

"It's mine only if I'm recognized as heir."

"You have King Tuniesin's word on that. He knew both your parents. Is Eagar going to call him a liar?"

"We both know what he will and won't do. He controls a lot of what happens in Malin." A vein throbbed in Charlie's temple.

"All the more reason to take a stand now, and show him who's boss." Jane pushed the subject, hoping to tick Charlie off enough to keep from inquiring about her plans again.

"He's boss now," Charlie said through clenched teeth.

"You're king," she pointed out.

"I'm a half-breed." Bitterness edged his voice. "Lawyer, trade negotiator, and anything else Sylthia needs of me. I live in my brother's house and have nothing to show for my life."

*No, that's not true. You have me. And our baby.* Jane bit her tongue to keep from blurting that out. She desperately wanted to reassure him, but fate changed that. The first order of business had to be unraveling Lowth's plans. It wouldn't let her do anything else.

"You're heir to Malin," she cried. "Be a man and grab what's yours."

He pulled her to him roughly. *"You're mine,"* he growled. "Are you willing to make a commitment to me?"

Jane stared at him, seeking a way out of this dilemma. His face remained hard. Her heart breaking, she turned away, answering his question with the movement.

"Fair enough," he said. "Until you tell me where you stand, I remain silent on my background."

*Unfair,* she thought. She didn't like his passive-aggressive response. The future of Malin shouldn't rest on her shoulders. *But it does. Until I go to Malik, we stay in limbo.*

Feeling the weight of her decision, she pushed past him to dress and silently make her way back to Kerreleigh.

# Chapter Twenty-Seven

Five days later, Jane tried to appear calm while lying through her teeth to the man sitting opposite her. He made her nerves zing like electrical wires. The favor she'd asked of him didn't ease her turmoil, either.

"So you see," she said, finishing her long, convoluted story of the Dymynsh, pregnant women and rainstorms on demand. "You're the only one who can help me."

She met John Tivat's intense emerald gaze. It pierced her through to her core, and she felt as if he'd exposed every flaw in her plan. She suspected he knew more than he showed.

Leaning forward, Tivat asked, "What of the Whelphite? Why can't he accompany you to Malik?"

His question shot holes in her theory of an all-knowing Tivat. Though in self-imposed exile, he must have heard rumors of her estrangement from Charlie earlier in the week. Kerreleigh was a small world; the news had swept through the tree community, instigating strange looks in her direction.

Jane fell against the blue velvet cushions of her chair,

her gaze drifting to the subtle opulence of his suite. *Why does a prisoner have such nice rooms? And why does he stay?* With his shape-shifting talent, he could escape at any time. *There's more here than meets the eye.*

Idly playing with the silky fringe of a pillow, her senses alert to any changes in her companion, she said, "Charlie and I aren't talking. Even if we were, he'd stop me. He'd chain me down if he had to." Her eyes misted, and her voice trembled with emotion. "I've been a handful at times. I don't think he'd like me careening to Malik to save the world."

"But you feel you have to?" Tivat watched her, his manner deceptively calm. She saw his caged power and wondered how he'd landed in Sylthia's prison the night before he'd escaped to Earth. He didn't seem the type to lose control of his life.

She smiled wanly. "Other than the fact that I obviously didn't kill you and was being sent there for my punishment? No, I'm meant to go to Malik and end the Dymynsh. It's kind of a destiny thing."

Lowth had made her a big believer in destiny. How else could she explain Tivat literally running into her? Or that Charlie had been in the pursuit party? Or his royal background, and possibly the royalty of Bryant and herself?

"Why not ask Bryant?" Tivat said, as if reading her mind. "He grew up in Malik and should know it well."

"He's taking care of my mother." Jane averted her eyes. She wondered if he knew the history of the hunter and her mother. The devotion between the two had set tongues wagging. It wouldn't take a rocket scientist to make the leap from their relationship to Jane's pointed ears.

She was grateful that Eagar had had a relapse from his sandobble injuries and was staying in his rooms. It delayed overturning her sentence for murder, but it also kept them from returning to Sylthia. It would also put her, unexpectedly, right where Eagar wanted her the most—through Shallen's gates.

"Muttle told me you've traveled all over Lowth and know Shallen." She picked at the pillow fringe, glancing at Tivat to see his reaction.

He took the object from her and tossed it in a corner of the room. "Before my life of crime?" he asked, nodding. "Yes, I can get you into the castle undetected. But what makes you think I'll jeopardize my freedom?"

She knew he'd ask. So far, he'd been exemplary in his conduct, returning from Earth, locking himself in these rooms to await trial. Again, she had to ask herself why. What was in it for him? Helping out your future queen wasn't an answer she could give him, not unless it became absolutely necessary.

"Look," she said, warping bits of truth and logic to suit her purpose. "If I get to Blacwin and negotiate the end of the Dymynsh—which everyone wants—then I'm a hero. You're a hero for getting me there. No one's going to punish you." She batted her eyelashes in a feeble attempt to influence him. "Are you with me?"

She held her breath as he took a long time to answer. "There are many obstacles," he finally said in protest.

*I've got him.* Cocky with triumph, she said, "Yeah, I know. Such as a couple of full moons, an army of flying fairies, goblins, a rogue sandobble or two, not to mention Capp'ear still on the loose. You've got your work cut out for you." She smiled, trying to dazzle him with charm.

"If I say no?"

"Then I go it alone. Are you in or out?" She watched him stretch his long legs, his attitude too casual. With sudden clarity, she wondered who had tricked whom into going.

Tivat smiled at her, his demeanor changing to a sharper focus. "I'm in," he said, leaning forward. "Now here's what you have to do before tomorrow night."

\* \* \*

*Jane!*

Charlie woke from a dead sleep, his heart pounding. His wings throbbed in warning. He swung his legs over the side of the bed and fumbled in the dark to light a candle. It cast strange and menacing shadows against the wall.

He bent forward to catch his breath, his wings spread, alert to danger. Every nerve cried of impending trouble.

*Nothing can get into Kerreleigh to harm her.* He tried logic to calm himself. *But what of getting out?* Hard on the heels of this thought came the one thing that had bothered him since earlier in the day.

She was wearing pants.

He'd seen her that evening, dressed in Hugh's trousers, cleaned and pressed after their adventure from Gaelen.

Other clues hit him, seemingly insignificant at the time. News traveled fast in Kerreleigh. He'd heard of her visits with Bryant and Muttle, of hours spent talking to them outside the range of normal sickroom conversations. That morning, she'd made her way to the dispensary and kitchens. All indications pointed to one of Jane's grand plans. Charlie intended to put an end to it before she hurt herself.

Alarmed, he called to her.

*Jane!*

She'd refused to listen to him telepathically since their fight at the waterfalls, and she'd virtually slammed the door shut in the last day. He couldn't get any response from her.

His breath still uneven, he dressed quickly. Taking the candle, he left his room to journey down the hall to hers.

A tentative knock on the door brought no response. Opening it, he wasn't surprised to find the chamber empty. His wings felt her presence in another direction, farther away.

*Jane, where are you?* Charlie let his anger show in the

question. She'd caused enough trouble in Lowth. He
didn't need her making more, especially in the middle of
the night.

If she wouldn't answer him, maybe she'd listen to Muttle. Silently, Charlie traveled through the quiet hallways
of Kerreleigh. He extinguished the light as he stepped into
the healing hall. Candles flickered in sconces set in the
walls, illuminating the rooms for those who worked
nights.

His hand raised to knock on Muttle's door, Charlie drew
back, startled to hear Eagar's voice. His senses heightened.
As far as he'd been told, Eagar had suffered a relapse and
hadn't left his bed since Jane's rescue the previous week.

"Tell him the plan goes better than expected," the steward said. "She should be at Shallen's gate in three days."

*Shallen's gate?* A cold fear dropped onto Charlie, immo-
bilizing him. "She" could only be Jane. Why would Jane
head for Shallen?

*Blacwin! By the first light, she's going there anyway.*

He moved to push open the door, but Muttle's next
words stopped him.

"He be pleased. Tivat will get her there safely."

Charlie reeled from the statement. The Belwaith's in-
flection on "he" could only refer to King Garmade.

He felt a sudden anger at the king. His grandfather!
Why would Garmade need Tivat's help to lead Jane to
Malik?

"The escape will look natural," Eagar said. "Just as it did
the night we brought her to Lowth. We have no control
over Tivat's shape-shifting abilities. Him taking the Earthwoman hostage will be incentive for us to continue to Malik, the Whelphite included. Then all the pieces will fit
into place."

Charlie dragged his hand through his hair, trying to
make sense of all this new information. How long had he
been blind to the plans made around him? When had Ea-

gar and Garmade started them? *The night we brought her to Lowth? It hadn't been an accident?*

He took a deep breath, clinging to sensibility. His mind raced. If Tivat was an implement to bring Jane to Lowth . . . If the murder trial and its consequences had been manipulated into being . . . Jane was headed into great danger. An unwilling pawn? Charlie didn't think so. He'd bet Jane had the idea to go to Malik first, some altruistic deed to end the Dymynsh, or another reason of her own. Eagar had found out about it and twisted the situation to fit his plans.

Charlie resisted the urge to barge into Muttle's room and demand the truth. Much better to back away and let them think him ignorant.

*I'll use their knowledge against them.*

Five minutes later, he pulled the jouroke over his wings. Five minutes after that, he took to the night sky.

# Chapter Twenty-Eight

"You're kidding, right?"

From the light of the twin full moons, Jane stared at Tivat. It neared midnight. They'd been on the trail for an hour now, leaving Kerreleigh without detection. It had been almost too easy.

Tivat coiled a length of rope and fastened the end securely.

"How did you think we'd make it to Shallen?" he asked, his features clear.

Jane shook her head. "I don't know. On foot, the same way you traveled with my mother."

"Time wasn't of the essence then, but we'll follow the same path for a while." He glanced at the sky. "There're six hours of night left. We'll be past the borders of Isleighah by daybreak, but I don't think the edge of the forest will stop a fairy pursuit. They'll be on wing and will rapidly catch us."

"But changing into a horse?" His earlier suggestion repulsed her. To watch him change, then sit on his back and feel him move between her thighs—she didn't like the thought of him in that position. Could she forget he was a man? It sounded highly erotic. Riding Tivat smacked of unfaithfulness to Charlie.

Tivat placed the rope on the ground with the other supplies she'd brought—provisions stolen from Kerreleigh and, upon reflection, inadequate for two people for half a week.

"It's what I do," he said, shrugging. "Shape-shift."

"But doesn't it hurt?" Visions of *Star Trek* and the transporter room came to mind. Rearranging his body into another form might smart a bit.

He smiled. "That's the beauty of the plan. I don't feel it. However, switching back and forth takes energy. Once I'm in horse form, I'll only change back at night, when we rest."

"Or if there's danger," she added.

"I might be able to defend you better as a stallion."

A stallion? Jane gulped. She did not want to think of mares and stallions, full moons and hot summer nights. Better to consider him Mr. Ed or John Wayne's horse in the Western of your choice, or a painted pony on a carousel.

Jane reminded herself that she carried Charlie's baby. Once she established its heritage, a task that could only be carried out in Shallen, she'd tell Charlie. Then she could write the happily-ever-after part of her story.

After she defeated Blacwin. The last hurdle. She sighed and looked at Tivat. "Do what you need to. You're the guide."

Tivat nodded. To her astonishment, he pulled off his shirt.

"Hey, wait a minute, elf-man. What the heck do you think you're doing?" Jane backed away, alarmed.

He stopped, his hands at his waistband. "My clothes don't change with my body," he said matter-of-factly, as if they might be discussing the weather.

"Riiight. The Incredible Hulk effect. I hope you don't mind if I turn my back." *I only want to see one elf naked. Charlie.*

Tivat shrugged. "As you wish." He tugged at his pants.

Jane swiveled around and kept her gaze fixed on a distant tree. A few moments later she felt a change in the air pressure. She tentatively turned her head. A magnificent roan stallion stared back at her.

She blew out a breath. "Okaaay." Gathering her common sense, she loaded the bags that contained their supplies onto Tivat's back. She mounted the animal and grabbed a handful of mane, adjusting to the sensation of him under her. With the feeling that this was a major mistake, she nudged him in the ribs. They took off through the Isleighah Forest.

Charlie spotted her late the next evening as the western clouds turned lavender and shadows dug deeper into the woods. Finding her had been easy: the sensation in his wings followed her in the forest, mountains and plains. He'd have caught up with her sooner—by his reckoning, he'd left Kerreleigh three hours after her escape—but flying took unexpected energy. His short adventure the week before hadn't prepared him for an extended flight, and he'd stopped several times to rest.

He landed in a clearing several yards in front of her, the waning sun at his back casting a long shadow. Emphasizing the effect, he spread his wings to their full length. He hoped it made him appear large, looming and angry.

Jane's horse halted of its own accord a few feet from him. She shaded her eyes before speaking.

"Charlie. I wondered when you'd show up." She sounded slightly out of breath.

He strode to her. The horse sidestepped away. "I thought I'd drop in and see what trouble you're causing." He wanted to throttle her.

"I'm on my way to Malik." Defiance thickened her voice.

"You have no idea the danger you're in." He grabbed at her horse's mane to keep it from moving. It tossed its head, glaring at him through green eyes. *Green eyes?* "What's going on here?" He indicated the animal.

"I asked John to be my guide."

"John? John Tivat?" He almost choked on the words. He figured Eagar had been wrong, that Tivat would have left her at the first opportunity.

He pulled her off the horse's back and hauled her, kicking and spitting, to the edge of the clearing.

"You don't know what's been happening in the background, what Eagar's been up to—," he rasped.

Her hands immobilized, she kicked him in the knee. "I'm trying to find out. No doubt Eagar is in the thick of things."

Charlie ignored the pain and tightened his grip. "Tivat is in this as well."

"You don't think I know? We're using each other."

He followed her glance to Tivat, who'd shifted back and stood nude in the dim light.

"Put some clothes on," Charlie snapped at the naked elf. The other man rummaged in a knapsack for clothing. Charlie garnered slight satisfaction in the fact that Jane only glanced briefly at Tivat.

"I'm going to Malik," she repeated. "I don't care if Eagar, Tivat or Bozo the Clown is involved. Everything will be solved at Shallen."

Where had he heard those words before? Oh, right, from Eagar's mouth. Did she know the steward's part in this?

"Jane—"

She jerked free and stood rubbing her wrists. "Don't try to stop me," she warned. She strode to Tivat and snatched the knapsack from his feet. Glaring at Charlie, she took off.

He let her go. She'd be easy enough to find again. But first he had to deal with Tivat.

"Wait," Tivat said as Charlie reached him. "Something's wrong."

"You bet there is," Charlie replied, enraged.

"No." Tivat stopped him with a hand to his shoulder. "Can't you feel it?" He stood still, as if sensing a shift in the wind.

*Coward*, Charlie thought. But as he cocked his fist back to hit the other elf, a warning pain shot from one wing to another. A familiar rush of air pressure made him turn his head toward the path. Then Jane screamed.

*The portal!*

"Damn you," he cried, and swung at Tivat. His fist connected with the elf's jaw, and Tivat reeled back. "Did you bring her here on purpose? To let her go back to Earth?"

Tivat put out a restraining hand. "No, I swear."

Anger and fear pummeled Charlie. "I'm not going to let her go." Already he felt it too late to stop her. "Give me your shirt." He wore the jouroke and his wings needed to be covered on Earth.

Tivat whipped off his shirt and tossed it to him. Charlie jerked it on, swimming in the extra fabric.

"It's not the portal to Earth," Tivat said.

"What?" Charlie stopped, an icy dread possessing him.

"The portal I used with Marion is over twenty miles from here. Can't you feel the difference?"

Yes, it had an unfamiliar resonance to it. But random portals? There'd been rumors of them for years. It didn't matter to Charlie. He'd go wherever he needed to find Jane.

"We're wasting time," he shouted. He ran and stepped into the portal.

White mist curled around Jane, disorienting her. She'd taken one last look at Charlie, then unintentionally run smack dab into it. Three steps in and she didn't know east from west, night from day.

*This isn't right.* She stopped, stretching her hand before her. The fog hid her fingers from view. Snatching them closer, she swung around, her heart hammering. *Which way is out?*

*Charlie!* All her bravado at making the journey alone deserted her. The milky air undulated around her, like amorphous tentacles, waving, stretching closer. She took another step and felt something against her cheek, like a cold caress. A scream left her, instantly swallowed by the night.

Groping for a tree or bush, anything to anchor her to Lowth, she felt nothing but the ground beneath her feet. Then the tips of her ears tingled. Without being told, she recognized it as a sign of danger. And knew its source.

*The portal!*

*No!* her mind screamed. *I don't want to go back!*

She swiveled, unsure which way would return her to Lowth. It all looked the same. Then, in the distance, she saw the bobbing of a pale yellow light. Not a white, artificial light that Earth would host, but a warm glow. A fire?

Thinking Charlie had lit a torch, Jane hurried toward it.

And fell right into the middle of a goblin camp.

The goblins surrounded Charlie before he had a chance to escape. They leapt on him when he burst through the portal, tackling him to the ground. Within moments, a rough rope bound his hands and feet, and a gag cut off his words.

Light from the full moons and the goblins' torches illuminated pale green faces. Hauling him upright, slight frames belying their strength, they carried him into the center of the camp. Without ceremony, he was dumped on the ground near a large fire.

Charlie twisted, seeking the leader. Though they'd never met, he knew of Wo'mmarph's reputation. Fearless,

Wo'mmarph had taken control of the nomadic goblins when the Dymynsh began decimating their numbers. By sheer guts and determination, he'd kept them alive. Even if it meant theft, raiding parties, and, more recently, the death of innocents.

After several minutes, Wo'mmarph made his appearance. Bright feathers tied to long braids distinguished him as leader. His clothes, simple homespun and tanned animal skins, mirrored those of the others. He circled the fire once before he stopped in front of Charlie.

"Welcome, Whelphite," the chief said in a low, guttural voice, his words thickly accented.

Charlie growled in the back of his throat. He'd been stupid to run through the portal without thought of what lay on the other side. Earthlings or goblins, he should have prepared better, but his thoughts had centered only on Jane. They still did. Nothing he'd seen or heard indicated her whereabouts. He had no idea what had happened to her. His telepathic inquiries were not returned.

"You arrive before expected," Wo'mmarph continued. His eyes, typical of his race, bulged like a frog's. "We did not know if the portal found you or not."

Found him? The portal had looked for him? Charlie reeled at this new information. Did it think on its own, or did others control it? The goblins? Blacwin? After learning of Eagar's schemes, Charlie didn't think he could be surprised anymore. He'd miscalculated.

"You save us time," the goblin leader said. He waved expansively. "Shallen lies close. Tomorrow you go there."

*Wonderful*, Charlie thought. Wo'mmarph's comment worried him. It proved an alliance with Blacwin—news Charlie did not want to hear. He'd expected to meet the wizard, but on more equal terms, not as a prisoner.

The goblin threw a blanket in Charlie's direction.

"Sleep, Whelphite," he said. "Much happens soon."

* * *

"Get up," a rough voice ordered.

Jane groaned and turned over, her body protesting the movement. Why did she ever agree to horseback riding with Tivat? Certain parts of her anatomy ached more than she'd thought possible. Her head as well, she realized. What had they put in her drink before she fell asleep?

At the thought of alcohol and her pregnancy, Jane struggled to sit up, a difficult task as ropes bound her wrists and ankles. Coarse hands grabbed her and spun her around.

She looked at a goblin much like the dozens that had swarmed around her the night before. Bug-eyed and long-limbed, they had skin that reminded her of a dirty McDonald's St. Patrick's Day shake. Minty green mud. Except this particular goblin had Irish green eyes.

"Tivat?" she said with hesitation.

"Shhh." He held an elongated finger against thin lips.

"Wow, you morphed into a goblin," she said in amazement.

"Except the eyes—I can never get them right." He crouched next to her. "I'm going to get you out of here."

"Charlie?" Her voice broke. "What about Charlie?" She hadn't heard from him, and it worried her.

Tivat shook his head. "I don't know. I spent most of the night searching for you."

Jane looked around. Predawn light showed scores of tents reaching into the distance. Purple mountains hunched over the camp. The faintest smell of the sea hung in the still air.

"We lie an hour from Shallen." Tivat answered her unspoken question. "I fear we underestimated our enemy."

Jane drew in a sharp breath. "Blacwin?"

Tivat nodded. "I heard talk. He's in league with these goblins."

She tugged against her bonds. "You have to get me out of here. I need to find Charlie."

His expression of grim negativity frightened her. "Dawn comes," he said. "Too many eyes will see. We must wait until tonight."

Panic crawled under her skin. More time spent with her captors wasn't on the top of her list. She'd been lucky yesterday. Several times she'd heard them call her "elf." What if they learned of their mistake and found out she came from Earth? Had Blacwin put a price on her head?

"They'll see us tonight, with the full moons," she protested. "Why not go now?"

He placed a hand on her arm. "It's too risky."

"Tivat—"

"Do you want to meet Blacwin as a prisoner?" he rasped.

"No, of course not."

"Then you must wait." He rose.

Jane clutched at his leg with her tied hands. "No, you can't go."

He looked her in the eyes. Conflicting emotions clouded his own. "I can't stay. I'm goblin now and must blend in."

"You'll come back?" Her voice cracked. She wanted to spill her guts about being the future queen of Malin, to throw a royal command his way, but first she had to prove her claim.

Tivat nodded. "At full dark." Abruptly, he moved away.

Jane noticed two other goblins walking toward them.

"How will I know you?" she croaked. "I haven't been too friendly with these guys. I don't want to punch you by mistake." At his hesitation she added, "You all look and sound alike in the dark."

"You'll know me," he said, his gaze on the two who had stopped. They were engaged in a heated debate.

*Probably about me*, she decided. To see who gets the first round. She didn't want to think about what the activity would be.

"Wait, Tivat." She wanted to delay his departure as long as possible. "Let me give you a password to use."

"Password?"

"You have them at Sylthia. Charlie told me."

"Yes, yes." He glanced at the two goblins, anxiousness in his body language. "What do you want me to say?"

What did she want him to say? She thought furtively. Tivat took a step.

"The crow flies at midnight," she blurted.

"The crow . . ." Amusement tugged at his mouth.

"Flies at midnight," she finished. The two goblins had finished their argument and continued their journey toward her. "Remember," she cried to Tivat.

Charlie realized they'd drugged him. After Wo'mmarph had left, someone had given him charred meat and bitter ale—heavily laced with dalc cone, his pounding head testified. The drug was most effective if injected, but stirred into a drink it could lead to unconsciousness.

The angle of the sun and the blue skies overhead told Charlie he'd slept through most of the morning. A gentle rocking motion indicated a journey by boat. Probably across Lake Shallen, a large inland body of water that surrounded the city.

*It's come to this.* Trussed up like a bird, his wings useless beneath Tivat's shirt, he had no means of escape.

*Jane is lost to me*, he thought in despair.

One of the goblins rowing the boat noticed Charlie's wakefulness. He muttered something in his own language. The others laughed, glancing at him in cruel amusement. He felt a sharp prick on his arm, and the sun exploded in his head.

"The crow flies at midnight."

The amused whisper roused Jane from a light doze. On

hyperalert all day against possible trouble from the goblins, she'd lain down after supper. She fully intended to stay awake, but exhaustion claimed her.

"The deer run in the meadow," Tivat improvised, his breath in her ear. She felt his hands at her bonds. "The midsummer moons come but once a year, and the babies are born in the spring."

For a moment, Jane thought he referred to her baby. Then she remembered Charlie telling her that most of the village women conceived during midsummer festivities.

"Very funny," she said. "How did you get past the guards?" Those two had hung around her all day.

"This." Tivat held up something. A knife. It glinted in the moonlight that escaped into her tent.

Jane felt the pressure on her wrists lessen. The rope slipped away. She rubbed the circulation back while he took care of the binding around her ankles.

Two dark lumps lay in the corner of the tent. Definitely goblin-sized. Definitely dead. Her guards, Mork and Dork. She'd seen nasty things on this journey, even death. Reality slammed into her.

"Tivat?" she said, her voice shaking.

He held her gaze, the hard flint in his eyes underlining the necessity of his actions and her continued peril. Slowly, she nodded. She'd asked him to be her guide, right? That role included protector and whatever it took to keep her alive.

"Are you hungry?" he asked, breaking eye contact. He pulled a small bundle out of the backpack that had been taken from her the previous day.

Hunger shoved aside all other emotions. Jane snatched it from his hands. It smelled of roast beef. The dried-out leather she'd been fed earlier wasn't fit to be made into shoes.

"A Double Whammy burger," she cried at the sight of meat wrapped in soft bread. She bit into it eagerly.

Tivat sat back on his haunches and watched her devour the sandwich. "I like a woman with a healthy appetite."

She shot him a killing glance. He apparently could be a chauvinist pig at times. Unfortunately, she needed him to get to Shallen.

"Did you find Charlie?" she asked between bites.

He hesitated long enough for her to grow suspicious.

"What?" she asked.

"Jane, they took him to Shallen earlier today."

"He's still alive?"

Tivat nodded.

"Good. We'll get him back. I wonder why I can't hear him." She'd told Tivat of her psychic abilities the day they'd started this journey.

"That, I don't know. Something must interfere."

"Or someone. Does Blacwin have that kind of power?"

Tivat's hand closed around her wrist. "An in-depth discussion we can have another time. Right now we have to leave." He tossed her a bundle of clothes. "Put these on."

Jane recognized the homespun cloth the goblins wore. "You're kidding, right?"

Tivat released her. "The watch doesn't change for two hours. Eyebrows will not be raised if your guards disappear into your tent until then."

The implication was clear. Jane swallowed hard.

"Despite the moons' light," Tivat continued, "it's still dark out. If we're very lucky, I can get you out of camp."

"You don't have a cloak of invisibility on you?"

His gaze bored into her. "This is no time for jokes. Change."

"Turn your back," she said sullenly. She'd glimpsed him naked and didn't want the favor returned. As quickly as possible, she donned the coarse garments, rolling up her own and stuffing them into the knapsack.

"I'm ready," she said.

Tivat did not move.

"What?" she asked, alarmed. His hesitation seemed out of character. "John, what's wrong?"

He glanced away. "I have bad news."

Jane's heart froze. "Charlie?" she gasped.

Tivat shook his head. "Something we didn't anticipate."

"Tell me."

"The portal," he began.

"Which one? Door number one or door number two?" His hesitation exasperated her.

"The one to Earth."

Earth. She tried to think of a threat that might come from there, but it had been so long since she'd been home. Sharks? Killer bees? *The Sopranos?*

"Tell me." Portals, wormholes, parallel worlds. Carl Sagan had told her there'd be days like this.

"Jane, someone followed your mother and me. He's here, being held prisoner in another area of the camp."

She grabbed at his fur vest. "John, you're making me angry. I'm not pretty when I'm mad." She gave him a slight shake. "I killed you once, I can do it again. Who's here?"

"Your brother Kevin."

# Chapter Twenty-Nine

Charlie lay on a plain cot, his hands bound, his head aching from the aftereffects of the dalc cone injection. He couldn't tell the time or how long he'd been unconscious. A candle stuck in a wall sconce flickered in the windowless room.

Something creaked to his left. He turned his head. The door swung open, admitting two figures. Not goblins, he noticed from their silhouettes. One was tall, erect. The other was small, warped and gnarled.

Blacwin and his henchman.

*They can do what they want with me, as long as Jane is safe.*

"Whelphite," Blacwin said, his voice deceptively soft. "You come too early. We did not expect you until tomorrow."

"I took a shortcut," Charlie replied.

"Ah, yes, the portal. It catches all types of strays." He flicked at his dark cloak. "Too bad it has a mind of its own and we cannot control it. It would save time if we could have all the players in place."

His words heartened Charlie. If they didn't have everyone yet, then hope remained for Jane.

Blacwin circled, and Charlie got his first glimpse of the wizard's face. A long-healed scar ran from jaw to forehead. A black patch covered his left eye.

"We must wait for the Earthling," Blacwin continued, his thick eyebrows wagging. "Do not fear, Tivat will bring her."

*That's what you think.* How had Jane escaped capture? She'd run straight into the goblin camp, and her luck wasn't that good. Unless Tivat had found her. Jealousy grated at Charlie's nerves. He hated relying on the elf for Jane's safety, especially when the result would be the same. She'd stand in front of Blacwin and receive her fate.

"Leave her alone." Anger spurred Charlie. He launched himself at the wizard, but a heavy blow to the stomach knocked him onto the cot. For the first time, he got a good look at the henchman who'd hit him.

The dwarf stood no more than four feet tall, but was built as solidly as a stump. Powerful arms hung at his side, great hams of fists curled at the ready. A cruel pleasure warped his darkened features.

"My assistant, Dave," the wizard said in introduction.

Charlie and the Dave the Dwarf glared at each other.

"We have quite the reception ready for the Earth-woman," Blacwin continued. "She is the center of a long, complicated plan. As are you."

"Why here?" Charlie snarled between clenched teeth. "Why bring us to Shallen? We were more vulnerable on the trail." He thought of several times during the journey when they'd been easy prey.

The wizard looked shocked. "Obviously they do not teach half-breeds the history of Lowth. Shallen is the ancient seat of power. If we are to change the world, it is most effective if it's done here."

Half-breed. The term rankled Charlie.

"Whelphite," he corrected, proud of his heritage for the first time in his life. He came from admirable stock on both sides. "The elves of Sylthia taught me well." Without preamble, he threw himself again at the wizard.

Blacwin sidestepped the attack and snapped his fingers. "Dave, take care of him. Keep him sedated until we're ready."

The henchman's muscular arms bent Charlie to the ground. He felt the now-familiar prick of dalc cone. Blacwin's face swirled before him, and then there was nothing.

A thousand questions assailed Jane. *Kevin here? Why?*

"Is he okay?" she blurted. Her mind filled with demonic tortures the goblins might perform on him.

"He's fine. Confused, but in good health," Tivat assured her.

"Confused?" She felt the same way. How had Kevin got onto Lowth?

"He doesn't understand where he is or what's happened."

"You've talked to him?" Jane tightened her hold on Tivat's vest. "You knew he was here and you didn't tell me?"

Tivat shook his head. "I found out this afternoon, patrolling the camp borders. We didn't talk."

"Then how do you know?" The two dead guards on the ground, the hundreds outside and a brother that needed rescuing frayed Jane's nerves. She longed to flee.

"Ashara," Tivat said, his mouth lined in disapproval.

"Who?"

"Ashara Visance. An old comrade of mine."

The way he said the name led Jane to believe they'd been more than comrades. But were no longer on the best terms.

"She found him in the Andair Forest, close to where your mother and I appeared from Earth. He must have followed us."

"Then we have to get him out." Jane stood and flung on her backpack. A glance at Tivat showed his dislike of the idea.

"Don't even think about refusing," she warned, shaking a finger in his face. "We're not leaving my brother to these creatures." She gestured to the dead guards, expecting their replacements to burst in at any moment.

"Jane . . . ," Tivat warned.

"No is not an option, John." She pointed toward the tent opening. "See if the coast is clear."

As they moved around, she saw the vastness of the camp. From her view earlier in the day, she'd counted eighty-seven tents. For a people exterminated by the Dymynsh, they had a heck of a remaining population. Upward of a thousand goblins must have survived. Fortunately, most of them slept. Only a few patrolled the perimeter.

Tivat produced a scarf and Jane settled it over her hair. She supposed, to someone with very bad eyesight or on their way to a hangover, she might look like a goblin.

"Why are you skulking around?" Tivat asked as they negotiated between tents.

Jane skipped to keep up with his long strides. She looked furtively to each side. "Skulking? Am I? Why aren't we hiding behind things?"

He chuckled. "The best place to hide is in the open. We're just a couple out for a stroll." To emphasize his point, he put an arm around her and drew her close. "Don't struggle," he said under his breath as she instinctively pulled away. "Your life depends on this."

Right, sure. At any other time, she'd cuddle with a green goblin and play smoochy-face. Tonight didn't fit the bill, especially with Tivat as a goblin and Charlie's jealousy being a mile wide. Even if he had been taken to Shallen. To lie in a dank, dark dungeon. Chained to a wall. Eating weevil-filled gruel and stale water. Open sores on his back. His wings shredded and useless.

"Stop," she cried, afraid of where her thoughts drifted.

The goblin at her side did so. "What's wrong?" he asked.

Jane shook her head. "Nothing, nothing to do with you, Tivat. I'm being a paranoid, freaked-out idiot."

He took her hand in his, a comforting gesture. "We're almost there." He pulled out a folded piece of paper and scrutinized it in the moonlight.

"What is it?" she asked.

He smiled. "Blacwin's orders to bring the prisoners to Shallen. It seems there's been a mistake. All this time, the goblins should have been looking for an Earthman, not an Earthwoman."

Smart. She liked Tivat more and more.

"Clever," she said. "What do you want me to do?"

He moved a step away. "Stay here." At her protest, he said in hushed tones, "I mean it, Jane. I can't have this reunion with your brother attract attention. You'll have time later to squeal over each other and trade stories."

Not fair. She wanted to pout. But Tivat had been a criminal far longer than she; he knew the way to deceive the enemy. Maybe she could learn from him.

"Okay," she acquiesced. "Don't take too long."

He held up his hand and mouthed, "Five minutes." A moment later, he turned to a small fire burning in front of a tent separated from the rest.

The negotiations took longer than he'd said. Jane hopped from one foot to another impatiently while trying to look unconcerned to any onlookers. None took notice.

Finally, Tivat left the three guards and headed her way. He carried a rope tied to two figures. Kevin and the woman, Ashara. They stumbled as they walked.

"Drugged," Tivat whispered. He looked around, senses on alert. The guards still watched them. "Don't say anything," he warned.

Jane pulled back the hand outstretched to Kevin, words of welcome dying on her lips. Instead, she tugged the scarf farther down and shuffled behind Tivat.

They made slow but steady progress. After ten minutes

or so, Jane heard the lapping of water—the nearby Lake Shallen. Tivat had briefed her that they'd use a boat to leave.

A breeze blew off the water as they descended to the beach. It whipped the scarf off Jane's head. At the same time, Rest, the brighter of the two moons, leapt from behind a cloud. A spotlight couldn't have been more damaging.

Jane chased after her scarf, the wind playing cat and mouse. She tripped over a root and sprawled in the dewy grass. As Tivat helped her up, she heard a voice from someone she'd long thought dead.

"My queen, my queen!" he shouted.

*Capp'ear!*

Stunned, Jane clutched Tivat, panic and revulsion battling to empty her stomach.

"He's dead," she cried.

"Apparently not." Tivat hefted her to her feet. Together, they swung toward the incessant bleating of her former captor.

"My queen."

Capp'ear stood at the top of the hill, waving bound hands, his shackled legs moving six inches at a time toward her.

"Could he be any more obvious?" Jane asked.

"We'll discuss it later." Tivat propelled her forward until they reached the lakeshore. "Damn," he swore. "The boat's anchored west of here. We won't make it in time."

Events accelerated. Curious about the noise, goblins poked their heads up. Capp'ear's guards chased after him. Kevin, in the worst timing of his life, emerged from his drug-induced stupor and recognized Jane. Ashara did the same with Tivat, a dozen profanities spewing from her mouth. The moons blazed.

"Get out of here!" Tivat shouted. He pushed Jane away while trying to wrangle the other two in the direction of escape.

She dug her heels into the soft mud of the lakeshore. "I'm not leaving without Kevin."

"He won't be any worse off than before. The plan depends on you, Jane, no one else." The appeal in his green eyes almost changed her mind.

God, why did he have to be so right? The plan. Always the plan. Leave her brother or save the world? Who made up these sucky rules, anyway?

*Lowth doesn't make mistakes. Neither does the portal.* If Kevin was here, it was for a reason.

She shook her head. "No dice," she told Tivat. "It's all for one and one for all."

"Stubborn Earthwoman," he said, reminiscent of Charlie. He sliced through the bonds holding her brother and Ashara.

A nearby shriek stopped further argument. A goblin had Capp'ear in a choke hold. Another pushed past him, his liver-brown gaze locked on Jane.

A blade gleamed in the moonlight.

*Always a knife,* she thought.

"My queen," Capp'ear cried. He escaped from the first guard and pulled down the second.

He never had a chance. A brief struggle ensued. Both goblins attacked Capp'ear. The knife plunged into him twice, in the soft tissue of his stomach. He screamed and collapsed.

The guards, breathing heavily, stood over him. Then, wiping the blood from the knife, they looked at her.

Tivat broke the tableau. He grabbed her arm and shoved her into the water.

"Can you swim?" he asked.

As if it mattered at this point. Shock at Capp'ear's death ran through her. "Why?"

"Because goblins can't."

Jane plunged into the lake, a dazed Kevin close behind. She blessed all the trips her family had made to Lake

Michigan in the summertime. She and Kevin could both swim like fish.

"Where the hell are we?" her brother asked, more alert.

"Lowth," she said with affection. Disgruntled goblins gathered on the shore, watching them swim away. "Remind me to tell you about it sometime."

They found the boat and boarded. She had a small sail, miraculously dark against the night sky. The moons popped behind convenient clouds, and the small group sailed to the other side of the lake. The goblins, in their bulkier rowboats, couldn't catch them.

It took three hours to reach their destination. The city of Shallen, the heart of Malik, rose from the lake's center, dimly outlined.

Against Jane's protests, Tivat shifted back into his elf form, naked again. The goblin clothes being too tight, he wrapped the scarf she'd worn around his middle, loincloth-fashion.

Her opinion of his resourcefulness had grown. They'd be dead if he hadn't taken charge.

Ashara didn't share Jane's opinion. Instead of being thankful she'd been rescued, she spent most of the trip alternately arguing with or ignoring Tivat.

Definite history between them, Jane thought. She turned her attention to Kevin, overwhelmed to have him back.

"You don't know how good it is to talk to someone," he said. "It's been gobbledygook since I landed in this place. Where are we?"

Summarizing her adventures as best she could, Jane told him the events of the past seven weeks. Aware of the other two in the boat, she gave him an edited version of why she needed to go to Shallen, leaving out the royal heritage, I'm-going-to-have-a-baby stuff.

Kevin shook his head. "Unbelievable. Or at least it was

at one time. Since I've been here, I've seen things I thought impossible."

"How did you get here? And when?" She'd been dying to ask him since she'd heard of his arrival in Lowth.

"Through the magical portal of Oz, how else? I thought he"—Kevin indicated Tivat—"was after Mom's money. She acted so strange after you disappeared. Not grieving-strange. Weird-strange. Then I found out John Tivat was living with her. A man twenty years younger, who made trips with her to Galyans and Gander Mountain." He leaned against the side of the boat. "I followed them one night. They carried enough camping gear to make L. L. Bean proud. The next thing I knew, I was in a forest. And captive of Her Highness."

"Her Highness?" Jane looked at Ashara. The elf woman intimidated her. She stood over six feet tall, with long, flowing red hair and violet eyes, and dressed as a woodland goddess. The clothes she wore would have scandalized someone on Earth, let alone here on the more prudent Lowth. A fawn-colored top exposed one shoulder and her midriff and complemented a leather miniskirt in the same hue. Her legs stretched forever.

"She's strong enough to whip your ass," Kevin said. "A definite Bowflex woman. I didn't understand a word she said when we met. We communicated with sign language. As soon as she found I'd come after Tivat, she had me hog-tied and helpless. Seems she's not too fond of him."

"Yeah, no kidding. When did the goblins get you?" The wind, a nice steady breeze against their sail, tangled Jane's hair. She pushed it from her eyes.

Kevin looked at the sky. Dawn crept closer. Rest hovered near the western horizon. "Four days ago. Boy, was she pissed. I think she killed six or seven of them before they threw a rope around her. They brought us to the camp yesterday. I got the impression we'd be moving out soon. Probably to this Shallen place—" He stopped and stared at her. "Hey, you've got pointy ears."

Jane sighed. She laid a hand on her brother's arm. "Yeah, there's a story that goes with that."

She told it to him later, after they'd landed the boat and taken refuge in a series of caves on the northern shore of the lake. Tivat and Kevin pulled the vessel into a heavy stand of trees and obliterated any trace of its passage up the sands.

"You've been busy," Kevin exclaimed, settling on the cool floor of one of the caves. "I can't believe Mom married an elf and lived here for three years." He shook his head.

"If things work out, I'll marry Charlie and live here," Jane said, keeping her voice low. Tivat kept watch outside; Ashara slept in an adjoining cavern. They wouldn't move again until evening, at storm-the-castle o'clock.

"How are you doing?" she asked, distracting herself from thoughts of Charlie and why she hadn't heard from him.

Kevin took her hand, as if sensing her turmoil. They'd always been close; at times it seemed as if they read each other's mind.

"I'm hanging in there," he said. "It would be better if I understood what everyone said."

Jane pulled away, a small "oh" escaping. "I can help," she said, smiling. She felt inordinately pleased.

Crossing to her backpack, she rummaged in its depths. She'd seen something earlier when she'd pulled out her regular clothes and changed from the goblin disguise.

"Here," she cried in triumph. She held up a stitchtree thorn she'd stolen from Isleighah's dispensary. "Charlie gave me an injection of this when I first arrived. It's an anesthetic and will knock you out," she warned. "But when you wake, you'll understand Elven."

Kevin turned it over. "How does it work?"

She shrugged. "I don't know. Magic. It's made by elves."

"Baked by little 'uns in a hollow tree?" Kevin joked.

Jane hugged him. "I'm so glad you're here."

He looked embarrassed by her affection. "You need someone to keep you laughing." He held out his arm. "Shoot me up, elf-maiden."

"So what's the plan?" Jane asked Tivat as they left the caves later. She didn't feel adventuresome. The hot weather had made sleeping difficult. A storm brewed in the west, kicking up a breeze, stirring dust in miniature whirlwinds.

"We head south," he replied. Lines of fatigue darkened his eyes. Jane and Ashara had taken second and third watch, sparing Kevin, but Tivat had rested little.

"For how long? You know I have to see Anjinaine before Blacwin." She worried about the time crunch—find a way into the castle, locate Bryant's older sister and establish if he had royal blood from Rodom, the last ruler of Malik. Plus they had to free Charlie and confront the wizard. All while avoiding detection from goblins and any other goons.

"I'm aware of your schedule." He sounded testy. "We'll be there in an hour, provided the wind holds steady." So far, luck had been with them; a stiff breeze blew at their backs.

Jane hadn't given much thought to his feelings. "What will you do when we're through?" she asked, curious as to his plans.

"It depends on how this works out."

"If it doesn't?" She had serious doubts. The closer they got to Shallen, the more nervous she became. Her constant fear for Charlie hung over everything. Their telepathic communication sometimes misfired, but she'd never gone this long without hearing from him. Especially as they both faced danger.

Tivat shrugged at her question. "Then I go home."

Home? "But aren't you still a criminal? Stealing sheep or something?" He'd fled to Earth to avoid trial.

He looked uncomfortable. "Yes, well, I'd sneak in, of course. Visit my family, then take off. Maybe travel to Mystgalen, to the east. Ashara's originally from there."

Jane didn't answer. Something was rotten in Denmark. He'd been too anxious to accept her offer to leave Isleighah. A man with his capabilities didn't need help. Before she could investigate more, Kevin piped up from the back of the boat.

"What exactly is the plan?" he asked, looking slightly green from the motion of the small vessel.

The wind raised whitecaps on the lake. The sky, a pinkish blue, outlined the city of Shallen rising from the water. Instead of a traditional castle like Sylthia, it consisted of hundreds of individual structures, similar in appearance—thin, rectangular buildings, three to six stories tall. Each had a light on top, giving the impression of a miniature city. It reminded Jane so much of Earth that she wanted to cry.

"All the buildings connect under the lake," Tivat replied. "What you see is but a small portion of the city. We'll enter through the north windmill and take an abandoned tunnel."

"Won't it be occupied?" Jane asked, remembering the importance of the mills at Sylthia.

"No." Tivat shook his head. "A couple of years ago, Blacwin cast a charm on the natural springs that feed the lake. They all flow in the same direction, powering a central waterwheel beneath the surface. Gears and shaft were built from it, giving power to everyone. The windmills were awarded to their keepers. The owner of the one to the north died two months ago. It hasn't been lived in since then."

Jane narrowed her eyes and glared at him. "You seem to know a lot for a common thief."

He smiled at her, a high voltage, Tom Cruise–Mel Gibson, I'm-so-cute-look-at-me smile. "I get around."

She didn't say any more, but stewed over the conversation. Something Charlie said came back to her. *"Tivat is in this as well."* Was he more than a common thief?

They reached the windmill as the last light faded from the sky. Kevin and Tivat unmasted the boat and pulled the vessel into the living quarters. A few minutes later, Tivat opened a trap door that led to the tunnel.

The four exchanged glances.

"Well?" Jane asked at their hesitation. "Are we in this to win, or to not lose?"

"I, for one, signed on to win," Ashara said, her red hair blowing around her.

Kevin nodded.

Jane looked at the last holdout.

Tivat smiled. "Let's go."

# Chapter Thirty

Through chance or Tivat's design, the stone tunnel emptied near a storeroom. Ashara popped the lock with little trouble and the group helped themselves to the clothing they found.

"It's old," Tivat said, holding up a pair of trousers to his waist. "At least it's not moth-eaten."

They all changed, a hat plopped on Kevin's head to hide his nonpointed ears. The cloth felt coarse against Jane's skin, quite unlike the finer weave she'd received from the fairies.

"We separate now," Tivat said when they'd finished.

"What?" Shock ran through Jane. "No, we're in this together. We don't break up."

"Jane," he said in an all too condescending way. "Think of what we have to do tonight. Provided we find Bryant's sister, we have to free Charlie and confront Blacwin. And still not get caught. The odds are better if we split up."

"He's right." Kevin came to defense of the elf. "Didn't you say we're a three-day journey from Isleighah? From your description, I'm sure this Eagar fellow left as soon as he discovered your escape. He'll be here sometime tomorrow. Do you want to risk the chance of him turning up early?"

Eagar. Jane had forgotten about him. How many things could she keep in her head? She hated to cave to the logic of Kevin's argument, but she had to look at the big picture.

"All right," she conceded. "We'd better get started." The enthusiasm she felt when they'd entered the tunnel faded.

"Good." Tivat nodded. "Ashara and Kevin will look for Charlie—"

Jane's head snapped up. "Now wait a minute. They don't even know what he looks—"

"How many Whelphites are being held prisoner?" Ashara asked. "If he's here, I'll find him." Grabbing Kevin's hand, she pulled him along the corridor.

Jane turned to Tivat. He shrugged and said, "Now is the time to practice your skulking skills."

If she didn't know any better, Jane could have sworn that the elf knew exactly where he was going. He didn't hesitate over which passageway to take, but zigged and zagged for miles. Finally Jane smelled fresh air ahead.

"Quiet now," Tivat warned, as if she hadn't been silent the entire time.

He pushed open a wooden door and cautiously peered out. Satisfied the coast was clear, he motioned for her to join him on a stone walkway. Buildings rose on both sides, bridges connecting several of them. Lights hung from poles softly illuminated the night.

She glanced around. No one was in sight.

"How do you know where she lives?" she whispered.

"I get around," he repeated.

She swallowed her nervousness. "John, who are you?"

He continued his surveillance. "Why do you ask?""

"Lots of reasons."

He cocked his head as if hearing something. After a moment, he turned to her. "Jane, greater forces than you or I control things. You'll have to wait for the answers."

"Yes, but will I be alive to hear them?"

He ignored her. "This way," he said, taking her hand.

The supposed dwelling of her namesake, Anjinaine, lay a block down the lane. They skulked in and out of doorways until they reached one that met Tivat's satisfaction. With a nod to Jane, he rapped on the wood.

An eternity passed in which they stood, risking exposure. Finally a woman's voice called from the other side, "Who's there?"

Tivat whispered, "We bring a message from Bryant of Malik."

A lock unlatched. A woman peered at Tivat, her mouth grim. Then she swung her gaze to Jane. And gasped.

"Marion." The name squeaked from her.

"No, her daughter. And Bryant's," Jane added for good measure, revealing the secret she'd kept from Tivat. She'd never told him the reason she needed to see Anjinaine, only that it was imperative before meeting Blacwin.

"By the two moons," the older elfwoman whispered. She swung open the door. Jane and Tivat scurried through.

They entered a cozy room, wood-paneled, with overstuffed chairs and comfortable clutter. A fireplace burned brightly.

"Sit down, sit down." Anjinaine gestured to the chairs. "Can I get you anything?" She fluttered about.

"Tea would be nice." Jane felt she needed to give the woman something to do in order to calm her nerves.

Jane and Tivat sat. She took a good look at her aunt as she made their tea. Anjinaine was plump, unlike her lean brother. Gray hair escaped from a bun, and her blue eyes crinkled.

"Why are you in Shallen?" she asked as she poured tea

and handed out sugar and milk. "I can't believe this is a social call. Not that I don't appreciate the visit, but this one"—she nodded at Tivat—"usually brings trouble with him."

Jane turned to Tivat. He looked as innocent as a puppy. *In a pig's eye*, she thought. As briefly as possible, she told her aunt how she'd landed in Lowth and of her recent adventures.

"Marion's here?" Anjinaine interrupted. "Then something's definitely afoot. The portal doesn't normally act this way."

"No, it doesn't," Jane agreed. She still had trouble thinking of the portal as a living entity, moving on its own, deciding who passed through it and when. "I don't think Lowth is acting normal, either. In fact, I'm beginning to believe they're in this together."

"In what?" Tivat asked, leaning forward.

"In whatever cosmic decisions were made to be sure I came to Shallen." All of them mind-bogglingly complicated.

"But you were stabbed and almost drowned," Tivat protested.

"And I probably should have died in both cases. Instead, I kept being shoved in this direction."

"To meet Blacwin."

"I'm not so sure. Maybe it's enough I'm in Shallen." Jane didn't mention Charlie's part in this.

"For what reason?" Anjinaine asked.

"You tell me."

The woman looked flustered. "How do I fit into this?"

"You're familiar with Tivat." Jane shot a glance at him. "Your presence on Earth wasn't a coincidence, John. Things have been orchestrated behind both our backs."

"Now, Jane—"

"I'm not a fool," she lashed out, "or paranoid. Too much

has happened." She turned to the older woman. "I have one question for you, then all the pieces fall into place. Who was Bryant's family?"

Anjinaine set her cup in its saucer, rattling the china. She spread her hands across her lap and licked her lips. Glancing from one to the other, she said with resignation, "I knew this day would come."

"And what day is that?" Jane asked gently.

"When the truth about Malik is finally known."

"Did you think it would be silenced forever?" Jane took the other woman's hand in hers. "It's time, Anjinaine. The portal and Lowth and fate say it's time."

Her aunt looked her in the eyes, worry crossing her brow. She sighed and nodded. "Yes, you're right. Where do I begin?"

"How about with how Bryant came to your family?"

"You know, don't you?"

"I've guessed. Tell me, Aunt Anjinaine."

The "aunt" part did the trick. The woman smiled, her eyes looking away to memories. "My father was a servant of King Rodom's. During the last great battle with King Garmade, Shallen was under siege. In desperation, Queen Lannami, with my father's help, smuggled the infant heir out of the city. They took him to our family's ancient home of Traun." She paused and drew a shuddering breath. "King Rodom died shortly afterward in battle. Queen Lannami was ambushed on her way back to Shallen. The baby remained with us."

"Bryant," Jane breathed, her guess correct.

"Dyonn," Anjinaine said. "We renamed him."

"Why not return him to the crown?"

Sadness edged the woman's eyes. "He was too young. My parents decided to wait until he reached his majority before telling him the truth."

"But they didn't."

"They died when he was in his teens. I'd married by

then and lived in the city. By that time, Blacwin had taken over and we were prosperous again. What acceptance would a mere boy receive compared to a wizard?"

"So you said nothing."

"Bryant grew older and more restless. He started roaming Lowth, then he made his trip to Earth and brought your mother back. After she left, he was bitter. He wanted nothing more to do with life. I thought it best to keep quiet."

"Why tell me now? You could have lied."

"I don't like what Blacwin's doing. This talk of an alliance with the goblins is upsetting."

Jane sighed. "Yes, well, I don't know how all that fits in yet, but I'm sure I'll find out. Soon." She stood and brushed her hands across the rough cloth of her pants. "Thank you for your honesty. I'm sorry we can't stay, but I've got a wizard to see and a world to save." She nudged Tivat, who'd quietly listened to their conversation. "Wake up, John, we're leaving."

"Ar! Awake, yon elf."

Charlie groaned and turned over on the hard pallet, every movement a struggle. His body ached as if he'd been beaten by waves against jagged rocks. His head pounded and his tongue felt twice its normal size. Peering from one eye, he saw Dave the Dwarf standing before him, hands on wide hips.

"What do you want?" Charlie croaked.

"Something you can give me." The dwarf scratched his nose.

"You're not getting anything from me." Gingerly, Charlie sat up. He'd been twisted more than once by the dwarf. Every time he surfaced from the effects of the drugs, Dave injected him again, sending him into unconsciousness.

"Where's your master?" he taunted, trying to keep the conversation going long enough to clear his head. "I thought you didn't move or think on your own without the powerful Blacwin to pull your strings."

"Ar! I'm no man's puppet." Dave circled the cot.

"Tell me another story." Could he take him?

Dave pulled a knife. "I've no time for stories."

"Are you sure we're supposed to meet them here?" Jane asked Tivat. She poked her head inside the abandoned tavern where they were to rendezvous with Kevin and Ashara. "It looks awfully cloak-and-daggerish." She sat on one of the nonbroken bar stools and looked around. Dust, cobwebs and neglect lay in every corner.

"Olly, olly, oxen free," she called, cupping her hands.

Tivat clamped his fingers around her arm and jerked her upright. "Fool. Do you want to be heard? We're not that far from others."

Jane gulped. "Sorry. I talk too much when I get nervous."

He glared at her. "Try to control it. We don't need to get caught at this stage of the game."

She sat back, afraid to move. Her mind spun with what she'd learned tonight—the confirmation of Bryant's heritage. Long-lost heir to Malik! Just as Charlie was the heir to Malin. And the child she carried? The culmination of a plot by the land to reunite the two kingdoms. But Lowth could only manipulate events so much. Who was the human factor?

"John, who do you work for?" she asked, chewing on her fingernail.

He turned from his supersleuth surveillance game. "Why do you ask?"

Jane blew out a breath. "Oh, puh-leeze. There have been too many coincidences to deny it. Escape on a night when Charlie was on duty? Stopping in the middle of the road in front of my car? Despite facing criminal charges, you bring my mother back here, and we manage to find each other, out of all the places in Lowth? And when I suggested escaping from Isleighah, you couldn't wait to leave. Is it life on the lam or paying a debt to society, John? There's a saying on Earth: 'You can't have your cake and eat it, too.' Why not 'fess up and tell the truth?"

He studied her for a long moment. "You're not just fluff and nerves."

She tilted her head. "And you're not just a tracker in bunny fur."

"Obviously. I'm sorry, Jane. I can neither confirm nor deny your suspicions." He cracked a twig into thirds and arranged them on the bar.

"Oaths and sacred trusts and things like that," he added, a twinkle in his eyes. He switched gears before she could react. "We can't wait all night for Ashara. I'll leave a note."

"Leave a note? Are you nuts? Someone else might read it." Jane rose and dusted off her pants. This bar was different from any she'd been in—a wide plank floor, dirt and grime. Three empty kegs sat in the corner. How bad did a society have to get before the people stopped coming to the bars?

"Not all messages are written in Elven," Tivat said. "Or in words. Where do we go next: Charlie or Blacwin?"

"Charlie," she said without hesitation. His continued silence gnawed at her.

Tivat nudged one of the wood pieces into a different position. "Okay, message sent. Let's go."

Jane gaped at the three pieces on the table. "That's it? That's the message?"

"Ashara will know what it says."

"If she's still alive," Jane muttered. She had complete confidence in the Elven warrior, but Kevin was another matter.

"She's alive," Tivat said with conviction.

They continued their espionage game, weaving in and out of alleys and doorways. Several times they hid when

Tivat heard someone coming. Twice, they returned to the underwater tunnels.

"Do you know where they're holding him?" Jane asked after they'd traveled for some time. She'd lost all sense of direction.

"I have my suspicions," Tivat said. He turned the knob on a filthy-looking door in one of the lower channels.

Jane punched him in the arm, her anger burning. "You've known all this time where Charlie is? Did you tell Ashara?"

"I don't do Ashara favors," he said grimly, resentment bubbling to the surface. "And it's a suspicion only. Blacwin keeps his prisoners in different locations. We might have to look in all of them." After checking the other side of the door, he drew Jane into a dimly lit corridor. "We can start here."

They saw blood in the hallway before they reached the cell. Lots of it. It looked like a true-crime TV show. Jane felt her own blood rush from her head and pool in her gut. She swayed and grabbed at Tivat's arm.

"I can't look," she gasped. Did Charlie lie dead inside?

Tivat propped her against the stone wall. Her legs made of rubber, she slid down and immediately put her head between her knees. *I will not faint. I will not faint.*

Tivat left and returned a moment later. He knelt at her side.

Jane forced her head up. "Tell me the truth," she whispered. "I can take it."

"He's gone. No, not dead," he amended, catching her as she tilted. "Not here."

"What?" The seeds of hope burrowed into her soul, ready to take root.

"He's not here, Jane," Tivat enunciated. "But you should probably see this." He helped her up.

With his support, she wobbled into the prison cell. A badly wounded dwarf lay crumpled on the floor.

"Ar!" he said, not lifting his head. Blood bubbled at the corner of his mouth.

"Where's Charlie?" Jane asked, holding her hand to her nose. The place reeked of death.

"Gone." A rasping breath shook the dwarf. He touched the wound on his chest, where a red stain rapidly spread, and gestured to the blood-splattered cell. "No more."

*Dead?*

Everything turned gray. Jane's head buzzed and sweat beaded on her forehead. A tight cramping centered in her stomach. It pulled feeling from the rest of her body.

"I'm going to be sick," she cried, hand outstretched, grasping for support.

"Steady," Tivat said from somewhere in the vicinity of Jupiter. For the second time in minutes, he lowered her to the floor. He joined her, holding her in his arms for comfort.

Jane fought to keep control, tears springing to her eyes. Charlie! The reality of his loss was too much to comprehend. He couldn't be dead. They hadn't come this far for Lowth to blindside them now. The dwarf must be wrong.

Drawing a shaky breath, she said, "Where is he? Where's his body?" There'd been a struggle, but what had happened to Charlie?

"Took him away," the dwarf wheezed. His eyes glazed over.

Took him away? Numbness settled on Jane as a blanket of winter snow. So many people had died since she'd come to Lowth—Warren and Nare from the village, Randolph the shepherd, not to mention goblins and sandobbles. Poor Capp'ear, who'd changed from trying to kill her to giving his life. And now her wonderful, stick-in-the-mud Charlie, who never wanted his world upset.

"Jane?" Tivat asked, his voice gentle.

She lifted her head, not realizing until that moment that she sobbed against his chest. She swiped the tears away and tried to smile, failing miserably.

He handed her a poor excuse for a handkerchief.

"What do you want to do?" he asked.

Only one thing remained. Maybe, this was her destiny after all, to meet Charlie, conceive an heir, and carry on alone.

*Crappy plan, Lowth.*

"Go home," she said, her voice sounding watery and far-away. She looked at him, knowing how important eye contact was in telling a lie. "Take me out, John."

They left the dwarf in the prison cell. Jane laid a hand on Tivat's arm and turned to face him.

"We separate here," she said.

"Jane . . . ," he protested.

"No, John. You need to find Kevin and Ashara. I don't know the city as well."

"Come with me."

"I can't." She stopped, unable to speak for a moment. The enormity of what had happened and what she must do overwhelmed her. "I need to be alone for awhile. Find someplace safe for me and come back with the others."

He looked as if he'd argue, then decided against it. Sighing, he took her arm and led her through a maze of hallways.

They stopped at another abandoned building, a storefront judging by the shelves and broken boxes.

"Stay here," Tivat warned. "No matter how long it takes, even if daylight comes." He pulled something from his pocket and handed it to her. It looked like beef jerky.

"I'll be back, Jane." He hesitated, then leaned forward and kissed her lightly on the forehead. "Take care."

He slipped away. Jane counted to one hundred and followed.

It took less than fifteen minutes to be caught by Blacwin's guards. She flagged them down as she walked into a more populated area. Holding up her arms to show she had no weapons, Jane stepped forward.

"My name is Jane Drysdale of Earth. Take me to your leader."

They shoved Jane into a too-small, hot room. One guard posted himself outside the locked door. Another stood watch, his fingers curled around a knife blade in its sheath. Heckle and Jeckle, Jane decided to call them. They wore black uniforms with hats as shiny as a crow's eye.

She perched on the edge of an uncomfortably hard chair, waiting for Blacwin's promised arrival. The size and furnishings of the room suggested an official office of some obscure bureaucrat—the liaison to the assistant to the undersecretary of civil and goon affairs. Not a cheery place.

Blacwin took his time. Evidently, even a Prince of Darkness and Ruler of Hell needed his beauty sleep.

Jane sat for at least half an hour, wilting from the heat, feeling the sleeplessness of the past two days. Charlie's disappearance and likely death crushed her. Had she dragged him to his fate, or had it been preordained? What did it mean? All along, she'd thought she and Charlie were to reunite the two kingdoms and rule them as one. Their child, or children, would inherit the titles and everyone would live happily ever after. But something had gone wrong. The dwarf had murdered Charlie and shattered her life.

With Jeckle watching every movement, Jane vowed not to show her devastation. Time enough for grief later.

She jumped as the door snicked open. Jeckle drew his knife, daring her to make another move. Instead, she turned her head toward Blacwin the Wizard.

He looked as unlike Merlin as possible. In his midseventies, with sparse hair except for thick eyebrows, he glided into the room. A patch covered his left eye and a scar split his face. He dressed in black from head to foot, a long cape settling around his ankles as he stopped before her.

"The Earthling," he said, his tone haughty.

"Lord Vader," Jane replied, raking her gaze over him. "I wondered when you would show." She stood, removing his advantage. His height equaled her five-six.

"You've led us on a merry chase. Where is your companion?"

"I ditched him. He's unnecessary. We can handle this between ourselves, *mano y mano*." She hoped her voice didn't sound as shaky as she felt. Only her obligation to Charlie's child kept her from collapsing.

Blacwin unclasped his cape and threw it over a table. He flicked dust off his sleeves before raising a darkened gaze.

"I agree," he said. "Would you like a refreshment?"

*Yeah, how about some nice papaya juice?* "Let's finish this."

He inclined his head. "Very well. If you'll follow me."

Heckle and Jeckle trailed behind them as they wound up and down stairs. The rooms grew larger and more opulent, showing the capital's wealth and history.

They stopped in a grand hall. A gallery ran around two walls, overlooking a massive table, chairs, and a fireplace big enough to burn sequoias. The ceiling lay high above, far from hundreds of candles illuminating the room. Magnificent windows showcased Lake Shallen, which glittered in the moonlight.

"Grayson Hall," Blacwin said. He moved toward one corner, where a fountain bubbled. "Owen's Pool, one of the few places on Lowth where its power lies close to the surface."

What would happen when she stepped into it? Visions of a special-effects, *Raiders of the Lost Ark* melting-flesh horror assailed her. The elf blood in Jane ran faster; the tips of her ears tingled. She could feel Lowth's power drawing her like a magnet. It scared her.

"The reason I'm here," she said, controlling her fear.

"You're an astute woman."

Astute? No. More like the wrong Earth elf in the wrong place. She took a shuddering breath. *Maybe not. Lowth's kept me alive so far.*

"What do we do now?" she asked. "Is there a big ceremony with days of preparation? Cakes to bake and floats to decorate?"

"No." Blacwin shook his head. "It's fairly simple, but there are some who need to be here."

"Anybody I know?" Her heart pounded, and she fought to keep from running. The seconds counted down to an end she didn't want to see.

"As a matter of fact, yes." Blacwin turned to a figure she hadn't noticed, standing in the shadows. "My younger brother."

"Hello, Jane," the man said, stepping into the light.

*Eagar!*

"Traitor!" she screamed in fury, and threw herself at the steward. She'd kill him quickly, before anyone could stop her. Forget torture and suffering; she'd cut his body into pieces and feed it to the rats. Right now he had to die!

She gouged out a chunk of his face with her fingernails. Heckle and Jeckle pulled her off and threw her to the floor, holding her down.

"Bastard," she yelled, spitting and fighting to rise. "You knew all along. Damn spider, manipulating people into your web. I hate you!"

"You're so young," Eagar said, wiping the blood from his cheek onto a handkerchief. "I admire your fire and passion, but you don't know the complete facts." He signaled the guards to haul Jane to her feet.

"I know more than you think. You've been working with Blacwin the whole time."

"Of course. Loyalty runs strong in our family." He turned to his brother. "Where's the Whelphite?"

"The dwarf was to take care of him," Blacwin replied.

Eagar nodded. "Good. We'll need him here. One they touch the essence of Owen's Pool, Lowth will give us the answers."

"I'll go," Heckle said. At a nod from the wizard, he left.

*Your dwarf is dead,* Jane thought, getting no satisfaction from it. Heckle's departure didn't cheer her, either. Her anger, burning hot a moment ago, fizzled with the reality of how few defenses she had against the wizard and steward. She couldn't make it rain inside and doubted she had the strength to whip up a good whirlwind. Charlie's death and Eagar's appearance had hit her like a one-two punch.

*Oh, Charlie, how long can I be brave?* Despair filled her.

"Let's get started," Eagar said, curling his fingers around her arm.

# Chapter Thirty-One

Above Jane, deep in the shadows of the gallery, Charlie watched, his heart crushed by her obvious agony. Every nerve he possessed screamed at him to act, to swoop down and carry her to safety. But he had others to think of: the warrior woman Ashara and Jane's brother Kevin. They weren't in place yet to be effective in their planned coup.

They'd burst into his cell as Dave the Dwarf attacked. Ashara engaged him in combat. A short, bloody skirmish followed, the elven warrior clearly at an advantage. Dave had been mortally wounded.

Sweat from the aftereffects of the dalc cone beaded on Charlie's brow. He wiped it away and scanned the hall, alert for his companions. They'd known each other for two hours, and already he trusted them with his life. Their appearance in Shallen surprised him. Kevin's identity shocked him. Of all the rescuers he could imagine, Jane's brother ranked at the bottom of his list.

*Where are they? One more minute and I'm going without them.* They'd had plenty of time to get into position.

Ashara moved like a cat; she'd be hard to spot. Kevin would be easier, as he didn't seem the type for stealth.

A slight movement gave away the man's location. Charlie stood, anxious to get to Jane. Resolve flooded his veins like molten steel. Any weakness left from the drugs vanished at the challenge of battle.

His wings fully outstretched, he stood on the gallery railing and signaled the others.

*Jane*, he whispered, *I'm on my way.*

*Charlie?* Jane's knees buckled from shock. She grabbed Eagar's arm for support as he yanked her toward Owen's Pool. Her mind spun with hope and the awful realization that she'd finally lost it. Fear and hopelessness made her delusional.

"Hold on a sec," she told Eagar, her breath and heart rate uneven. She took a step away. Human sacrifice would have to wait.

*Damn it, Charlie, where are you?*

Eagar reached to grab her, but Jane pulled back.

"Can you wait a minute?" she snapped. "Can you wait one freaking minute while I pull myself together? Jeez, you two." Her gaze swept the room to her right. "You've got Jeckle to stop me if I try to run. What's the big hurry?"

*Charlie, please come out and play.*

She heard him chuckle. *Patience, my darling.*

Her heart lurched. It hadn't been a hallucination. Charlie was alive! And he'd called her "darling."

Everything happened at once. Jane heard a *twang* and Jeckle dropped at her feet, a shaft in his throat. She turned to see Ashara in front of Blacwin, another arrow nocked. Then Kevin scooted into view, winking at her in passing. The least athletic, least macho of her brothers, he pointed a crossbow at Eagar.

*Want to fly?* Charlie asked.

The flap of his wings filled the hall. Jane looked up and saw him hovering above her, grinning widely.

"Charlie!" she cried, reaching a hand in his direction.

He landed and she ran to him, jumping into his arms. He kissed her, a Superman-should-have-kissed-Lois-this-way kiss. Jane felt it down to her toes.

"Oh, Charlie, I thought you were dead." A flood of emotions deluged her, fear and happiness, relief and an overwhelming urge to cry.

"Dead?" He laughed, pushing her hair behind her ear with one finger. "Not a chance. I had to save you, didn't I?"

"Most magnificently. I love you, Charlie Whelphite."

"What a nice coincidence, because I love you, too, Jane." He kissed her again, the rasp of his beard scratching her skin. He felt solid and warm, his wings enveloping them.

Ashara cleared her throat, pulling them back to the drama in the room. "Want me to kill him now?" the warrior asked, placing the tip of the arrow against the wizard's throat. Blacwin flinched, his dark eyes murderous.

"Enough killing for one day," Charlie directed. He looked at Blacwin. "We've some negotiating to do." To Eagar he said, "Why am I not surprised you're in the middle of this?"

The steward sniffed. He looked as unruffled as always. "You constantly misunderstand. What I do—"

"I do for Lowth," Charlie finished for him, disgust shading his face. "A warped sense of duty for the land you profess to love so much." He pointed to the pool and Jane. "This isn't right, it should never have happened."

He turned to Jane. "I'm going to get you away from here, then I'll come back and clean up this mess."

Jane rebelled at the idea. Leaving him for one minute went against her better judgment. She'd just found him again. "I'm not going."

"Jane."

"Don't 'Jane' me. I've been through hell the last few days. I'm not about to go away and open the possibility—"

A loud clattering cut off her words. Kevin had dropped the crossbow, and he and Eagar scrambled on the floor for it. Charlie leapt into the fray. Suddenly, Heckle was there, returned from his errand. Damn! They should have watched for him. Jane screamed and jumped on his back, pounding on him, fighting for Charlie. From the corner of her eye, in the direction of Blacwin, Jane saw blue, wizard-like sparks fly.

A fist hit her in the shoulder. She spun to the ground, one hand instinctively protecting her child. She landed hard.

The scuffle lasted less than a minute. The dust cleared. Eagar, looking uncharacteristically rumpled, straightened and pulled a knife from his leg sheath. He pressed it to Kevin's throat.

"Kevin!" Jane screamed and lunged forward. Charlie stopped her, his grip fierce on her arm.

"Know this young man?" Eagar asked, out of breath. Kevin had lost his hat, and his nonpointed ears clearly told of his race. "Another Earthling. Relative? Brother?"

Jane's heart climbed into her throat. Fear for her brother stopped its beating. Bravery died; she'd seen too much killing and wouldn't risk Kevin's life. She nodded.

Eagar backed up a step, dragging Kevin with him. He gestured to Owen's Pool. "Then I suggest if you want to stay related, you and Charlie get into the water."

So they'd be sacrificed after all. She glanced at Charlie. She could see his mind working, planning his next move, but with Ashara captive, Heckle plopped none too daintily on her, they had no choice.

Jane gave a tiny shrug of her shoulders. What could happen? A little dip in the pool, a piranha attack, acid eating at their bones? Just another day in paradise.

She looked at the water, bubbling with an Old Faithful innocence. She reached out and took Charlie's hand, squeezing it in encouragement. "Here goes nothing."

"Stop!" A commanding voice bellowed from behind her. She froze. *Don't ask me twice.*

"Enough!" the voice continued. It sounded strong, imperial, used to giving commands and having them obeyed.

"By the two moons," Charlie whispered in awe. He released her hand and sank to the floor. Eagar followed suit as well as Blacwin.

*What the heck?*

Jane turned—and stared into the intelligent black eyes of King Garmade of Malin.

"Sir, sire, your grace," Jane stammered. Oh, Lordy, she was making a mess of this. She gave up and sank into a curtsy so quickly she lost balance and landed on her rump.

"Perhaps, it's unnecessary for them to get wet, Eagar," the monarch said. "It is enough they are here, where Lowth's power is strongest."

Garmade leaned over her, his face kind and so different from the befuddled monarch she remembered.

"Rise, young one," he said, extending his hand. "No need to worry. You've had a long and tiring journey, and now is the time for your reward." He pulled her to her feet without effort, his grip strong. When had he stopped shaking?

Beyond awe, Jane allowed him to help her stand. The change in his appearance and demeanor shocked her. Not only did he act Sean-Connery-I'm-in-controlish, but he didn't have on women's clothes. In fact, he looked every inch the king, dressed in blue-and-white silk. He even wore a crown of diamonds.

Jane, openmouthed, gaped at him, and Garmade motioned for the others to stand. As they did, she realized the room had filled with his entourage. She saw—bless him!— Muttle at the king's elbow. King Tuniesin grinned at her, a dozen fairies surrounding him. Farther back, she spotted Hugh and the rest of their fellowship from Sylthia. John Tivat, the cheeky so-and-so, winked at her. Bryant and her mother smiled, so obviously in love, Marion a trifle pale, but looking well.

"Pinch me." Jane's knees felt weak. "I need to sit down or I'm going to faint." Where the heck had everyone come from, and how had they gotten here in the middle of the night? *Muttle?* She turned to the Belwaith, so pleased to see him healthy again.

*We fly,* he said, astonished. *The king comes by portal from Sylthia. He met us in the goblin camp. They are our friends!* The Belwaith sounded shocked.

Someone brought a chair and she sank into it. Her face hurt from smiling so much. She grinned at Garmade, who watched her like a benevolent, rich, very powerful, central-casting uncle. *How about grandfather-in-law?*

Whoops! She'd almost forgotten that aspect. Wait until he found out. Jane searched for Charlie and took his hand in hers.

"Okay," she said, twisting her head to look at them. "Miss Marple's assembled all the usual suspects in the drawing room. I'm guessing it was Colonel Mustard in the library with the red herring. Who wants to tell me what's happening and why I feel I'm the last to know?" She directed her gaze to King Garmade.

He sat next to her and indicated for the others to sit. Chairs scraped on the floor as the assemblage took their seats.

"Because you *are* the last to know," the monarch explained. "You and Charlie. We couldn't have it any other way. Lowth's tests had to be completed, and we needed confirmation of our choice. So much rested on your independent decisions."

"Independent?" Jane scoffed. "I don't think so. We've been nudged toward this spot for weeks."

"Even before," he said simply.

Jane gasped. "Then you did send John to bring me here." She searched and found Tivat. He shrugged, holding up his hands in a helpless motion.

Garmade looked at Eagar, who stood next to him. *God forbid he should sit.* The steward surprised her by smiling. Yeesh, maybe the man did have a heart.

"A wise choice, sire," Eagar said. "Lowth is well served."

"Indeed." Garmade stroked his chin. He lifted his gaze to Jane. "Yes, my dear, I sent John to Earth with the express purpose of discovering if Marion Drysdale, wife of Bryant of Malik, had borne a child. Bringing that child back here was important."

"You could have done it a little less violently," Jane exclaimed, remembering the *thunk, thunk* Tivat had made when, à la bunny, he'd gone under her tires.

"An unfortunate circumstance we used to our advantage."

"Yeah, by arresting me for murder and putting me on trial. You almost put me to death." She wanted to brain the guy. Except he looked so regal, so much the ruler who'd defeated countless enemies in the past. His subjects had died following him into battle and, for the first time, Jane understood why.

"It never came to that. We made certain of it." Garmade included Eagar in his statement.

"Hmmm. Very convenient for you."

"Very clever, too." He all but clapped his hands in delight.

Honestly, he was worse than a little kid. A toy soldier general, moving lives around on his own private battlefield.

"What about Charlie?" Jane asked. "What's his part in this?" *Other than being your grandson. That'll take the wind out of your sails.*

"Charlie is the other half of the key," the king said.

Some of this was starting to make sense. "Why not tell me all of it? From the beginning."

Garmade tented his fingers. "As Lowth became weaker under the Dymynsh, I sought answers. One was 'The Quaven,' an ancient poem, a riddle. The more I investigated—obsessed about it—the more convinced I became it was the only answer."

"Wait a minute," Jane interrupted. "How old is this poem?"

Garmade looked at Eagar. "Over a hundred years, I'd say. Yes, at least that."

"And you want me to believe something written that long ago prophesied me and Charlie?"

He shrugged. "This is a land of magic, Jane."

"How long have you unraveled this mystery?" she asked.

"At least ten years."

Astonishing, the amount of work that had gone into this. "Unbelievable," she whispered.

"Freaking unbelievable," Charlie said in her ear.

Her heart sang at his use of her verbiage. She loved this man, Elf, Whelphite, whatever, so much. Wait until she had him alone.

"The most difficult part was finding 'one on Earth,' as the poem prophesied." Garmade continued. "Then I found a reference to your mother's visit to Lowth. The search became easier, tracking her and her offspring."

"Me." Jane shook her head. "Back up a minute. When, exactly, did the Dymynsh start?" She wanted to visualize it on a timeline.

The king and steward looked at each other. "As the records tell us, the harvests began decreasing twenty-five years ago," Garmade answered.

*Twenty-five?* A dozen pieces fell into place, completing the puzzle. Jane threw her head back and laughed.

The others looked at her as if she'd gone hysterical.

"Don't you see?" she hiccuped when she could draw a breath. "While you were manipulating us, Lowth was manipulating you."

"I don't understand," the monarch said.

"Neither did I, until a moment ago. Your majesty, does anyone know why the Dymynsh started?"

He shook his head.

Jane glanced at Bryant and her mother. "It's because I wasn't here. I'm the cause of the Dymynsh."

A murmur rose from the crowd.

"Jane, what are you saying?" Marion asked.

"I know," said Blacwin, who'd been silent. They turned to the wizard. "Lowth and the portals have a complicated relationship. Each tries to control the other. I believe they let you in; then, three years later, they had a disagreement, and the portal allowed you return to Earth."

Jane snapped her fingers. "Lowth didn't know Mom was pregnant with me at the time. That's why the Dymynsh started. Lowth was grieving for me."

Silence followed her words. Everyone in the room digested what she'd said. Jane glanced at Charlie. He seemed as shocked as the others.

"If what you say is true," Garmade said, taking a deep breath, "then much is explained." He still looked puzzled, but she could see logic taking over.

"What I say *is* true. The Dymynsh ended the moment I came to Lowth. How tall are the crops this year? How many babies have been conceived?" She looked across the crowd to Hugh and smiled. She didn't want to say anything about her own child, not yet. "This dog and pony show of getting me and Charlie to Shallen wasn't necessary. All I had to do was come back."

"And are you going to stay?" Charlie asked.

She met his gaze. More than curiosity for Lowth's future lay in his eyes.

"Are you asking?" Jane's mouth felt dry and her heart skipped a beat. The world suspended for several moments.

He brought her hand to his mouth and kissed each fingertip. "Yes. *I* ask you to stay, Jane."

Oh, wow. Holy Scarlett and Rhett, Tracy and Hepburn, Blondie and Dagwood.

"Then I'll stay," she whispered, touching his cheek.

They could have stared at each other a millennium or two, but King Garmade tactfully cleared his throat.

"Excellent news," he pronounced. "Most excellent. I have several questions, of course—"

Jane reluctantly turned from Charlie. "So do I, sire. It's hard enough to believe there's no bad guy in this story." She shot a glance at Eagar and Blacwin, brothers in no crime, tools of their monarch. She imagined they'd gone into royal service at the same time, Eagar in Sylthia and Blacwin in Shallen. "But why the charade? Why pretend to be senile and incapable of running your kingdom— rather, kingdoms?"

Garmade slumped in his chair. He shook his head. "It accelerated events. Perhaps Lowth manipulated me that way. I found the most important clues when I was ill. Eagar noticed. We experimented and discovered that if I stayed under the influence of dalc cone, we made more progress. We made it look like I'd lost my sanity to hide our actions."

Jane wanted to cry at the sacrifices he'd made—they'd both made—as Eagar helped his king slide into a drug-induced world.

Garmade smiled, falsely bright. "And now we have our two halves of the key," he said, his voice unsteady.

Jane laid a hand on his arm. "Perhaps there is another reason Charlie and I were got together. Something that you didn't know of, nor did I when this started." She took a breath and dropped the bomb on him. "We are two halves of a *royal* key."

As concisely as possible, she relayed the tale of Elaine and Largare, of Bryant's relationship to King Rodom. She looked around the room as she talked, noticing the shock on Bryant's face, the confirmation from King Tuniesin.

Gray hair caught her attention, and she saw Anjinaine watching, nodding her head. When had Tivat found the time to fetch her?

King Garmade wept when she finished. He stood and reached for Charlie, enveloping him in a hug. Charlie looked embarrassed by the whole ordeal.

"My grandson," the king sniffed, his hand shaking as he wiped away tears. "Under my nose the entire time. I did not know, Charlie, I did not know."

Charlie patted his arm. "I'm still unused to the idea."

"Much to discuss," Garmade muttered, suddenly looking his age. "The two kingdoms united in love! I never thought to see the day." He leaned on Eagar.

"Rest, sire," his steward said, his tone gentle. "There are beds here. Tomorrow is soon enough to talk of the future."

The crowd made way as the two elderly men left the room. Blacwin, with a nod to Jane and Charlie, followed. Some of the others departed, until only a handful of key players remained.

"Jane?" Kevin asked, approaching her with reluctance. "Are you really a princess?"

She hugged him. "Always your sister first." Tears welled in her eyes. "Are you staying?" It broke her heart to ask.

He shrugged. "I don't know. Lowth is so different." His gaze wandered to Ashara. "Though there are compensations."

*Good luck*, Jane thought. Ashara seemed too wrapped up in her history with Tivat.

She turned to her mother. "Mom?"

"Oh, I'm staying," Marion replied. She tightened her grip on Bryant. "I had to abandon Bryant once. I won't do it again. Once the portals stabilize, I can return to Earth to visit. I'm sure the family wonders where the three of us have disappeared to. I'll try to make them understand."

"I hope so." Jane watched as her mother and Bryant

drifted off. After a few minutes, their questions answered, the others departed. She and Charlie were left alone.

It must have been close to why-am-I-still-up o'clock. Rest had set, and only Slumber illuminated the night. The quiet lapping of water against the building echoed in the hall. Jane felt as if she'd stepped from a bad dream.

"Well," Charlie said, breaking the silence. "I finally have you to myself." The look in his eyes melted her heart. She could look into their brown depths forever. Caramel mocha. Oh, yummy.

"Did you mean what you said?" she asked, wanting to jump his bones and have hot, wild sex. There might not be a waterfall handy, but a lake beckoned outside.

He slid her into his arms. "About staying? Yes. Did you mean what you said?"

She snuggled in tighter. "Home. This is where I belong." Not just Lowth, but in his embrace.

Charlie tipped her head up. "Are you sure? We're a simple people. No automobiles or fancy gadgets."

"Simple?" She chuckled. "Ha! Worlds that think and kings that plot? Sandobbles and goblins, portals and two moons? You are sadly mistaken. Besides," she said, tracing the edge of his forewing with the tip of her finger. He shuddered against her. "There's magic here."

He kissed her, his lips promising a fabulous rest of the night. And morning. And their lives.

"There's magic here," he said, nibbling on her ear. A shock hit her, running right to her core. Hoo-boy. No wonder he got so turned on when she touched his wings.

"And here," he continued, pressing his lips to her eyelids. "And especially here." He found her mouth again.

A moment later, when she could barely stand and the thought of a bed triumphed over waves and a shoreline, Jane took his hand in hers.

"There is one more chapter in this story," she said. "The real reason Lowth brought us together." She guided his hand until it rested below her belly. When he attempted to move it lower, she stopped him.

Jane looked at him, her gaze steady. She wanted him to know the importance of the secret she'd kept.

"The full moon wanes," she murmured. "Do you remember the last full moon, Charlie?"

He'd grown serious, watching her. "You're not talking about Isleighah, are you?"

She shook her head. "No."

"Then Midsummer's Eve?"

She touched his cheek with her free hand. "We've been through a lot together. Not too long ago, you asked a question, and I told a small lie." She pressed his hand against her womb. "A very, very small lie."

Realization hit him like a sledgehammer. His face darkened. Then it lit, and he swung her in his arms. Laughter escaped him.

"You're sure?" he asked, raining kisses on her. "Absolutely sure?"

"Oh, Charlie, would Lowth make a mistake?" She gave herself to his embrace, loving him more than ever.

"You'll have to marry me now," he said, kissing her.

She stopped him. "Are you asking?"

Charlie looked at her, his face inches from her own. His eyes glittered from the few candles that still burned. "I ask."

Jane rasped her hand against his scruffy jaw. "Then I say yes."

He whooped and swung her around some more. "Do you suppose Blacwin has a room for us?"

Jane laughed. "You can ask Muttle. He's by the door, discreetly waiting for us to leave."

"Is he? Bless the Belwaith." Charlie kissed her, long and hard and not nearly satisfying enough.

Still carrying her, he walked toward Muttle.

"I love you, Jane," her Whelphite said. "I don't care

about kingdoms united, or portals or anything else. Just you. And now our child. I'm glad you're not going back to Earth."

"Charlie, I love you, too." She snuggled into his arms, content and happy. "I'm glad I'm not on Earth, either. You know why?"

Guided by Muttle, they'd reached a staircase. Charlie took the steps two at a time.

"No, why?" he asked.

Jane laughed. "They don't do it anymore, but they used to test for pregnancy by making a rabbit die. Charlie, I could never kill a bunny. Look at what happened the last time I did."

# STILL LIFE
# MELANIE JACKSON

Snippets of a forgotten past are returning to Nyssa Laszlo, along with the power to project her mind. Each projection thrusts her into a glowing still life of color and time, and her every step leads deeper into undiscovered country. Things are changing, and dangerously so. She is learning who she is—whether she wants to or not. She is also learning dark things are on the rise. From the Unseelie faerie court to Abrial, the dauntless dreamwalker who pursues her, the curtain is going up on a stage Nyssa has never seen and a cast she can't imagine—and it's the final act of a play for her heart and soul.

--------------------------------------------